Praise for Thief of Slaves

"The author has a way of drawing you in, to the point where you truly believe the characters exist. I know them all personally: Pavo, Taru, Tred, Landros, Nagaro; I care about each of them. I love how pure of heart Nagaro is.

As always, I'll wait with great anticipation for the next book in this series, and it would be fine by this reader if the series never ended. I hope some day to be able to purchase a full set in hard cover. These characters, this world, is as beloved to me as Lord of the Rings was when I was young.

Give it a read. You'll be hooked."

*— G. M. Barlean, Nebraska author of eleven books. Best known for her cozy mystery triology, **The Rosewood Series**.*

Other Books by Carol Louise Wilde

Books of the Nagaro Chronicle

1. *Gift of Chance*

2. *Covenant of the Sword*

3. *Return to Lankura*

The  Nagaro Chronicle 4

Thief of Slaves

Carol Louise Wilde

Dedication

*To my father who understood the grand tale of history,
but loved even more the making of it.*

Acknowledgments

I am ever grateful to my fans, who keep me going. And of course I must thank those who gave me input on the manuscript including especially my test readers for the final version, Suzanne Coulter and Aubrey Lyons. As usual, there are the members of ScHoFan, a critique group under the auspices of the Greater Los Angeles Writers Society (GLAWS), who gave me feedback on versions of the early chapters. In alphabetical order, they are Carol Ann Alves, John Gwinner, Ken Hughes, Scott Kilburn, Katy Mann, Carmen Mendivil, Robin Reed, Taguhi Tavitian, and Garrett Weinstein.

I continue to be grateful for the support of my husband and the other members of my family, who by now have gotten used to this. I'm also grateful for the continuing support of my dear friend Suzanne Coulter who has been at my back from the beginning. My deepest thanks go to my editor, Kristie McCue, who has given so much to this project despite her own travail. And, last but not least, I am grateful to Anne Bannon who stepped into the breach to help me get this work published.

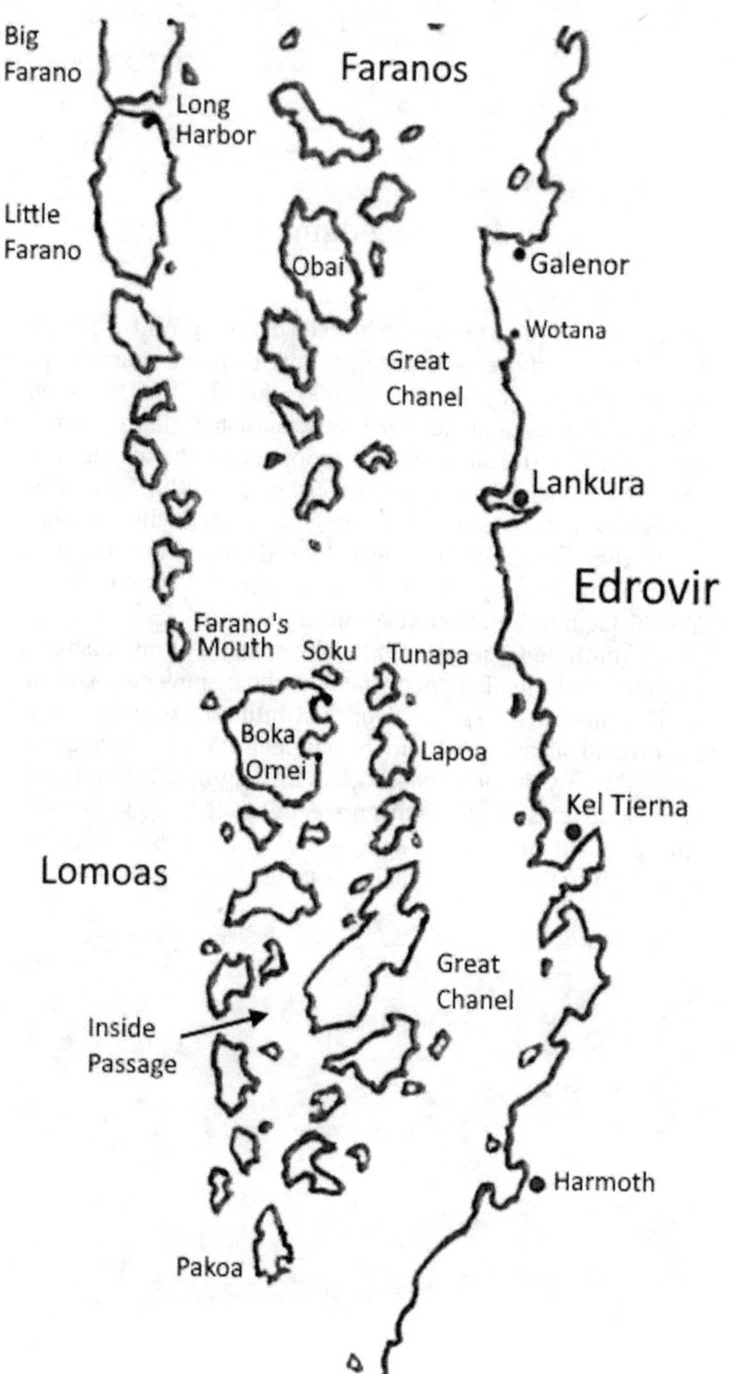

Big
Farano
Faranos
Long
Harbor
Little
Farano
Obai
Galenor
Wotana
Great
Chanel
Lankura
Edrovir
Farano's
Mouth
Soku
Tunapa
Boka
Omei
Lapoa
Kel Tierna
Lomoas
Inside
Passage
Great
Chanel
Harmoth
Pakoa

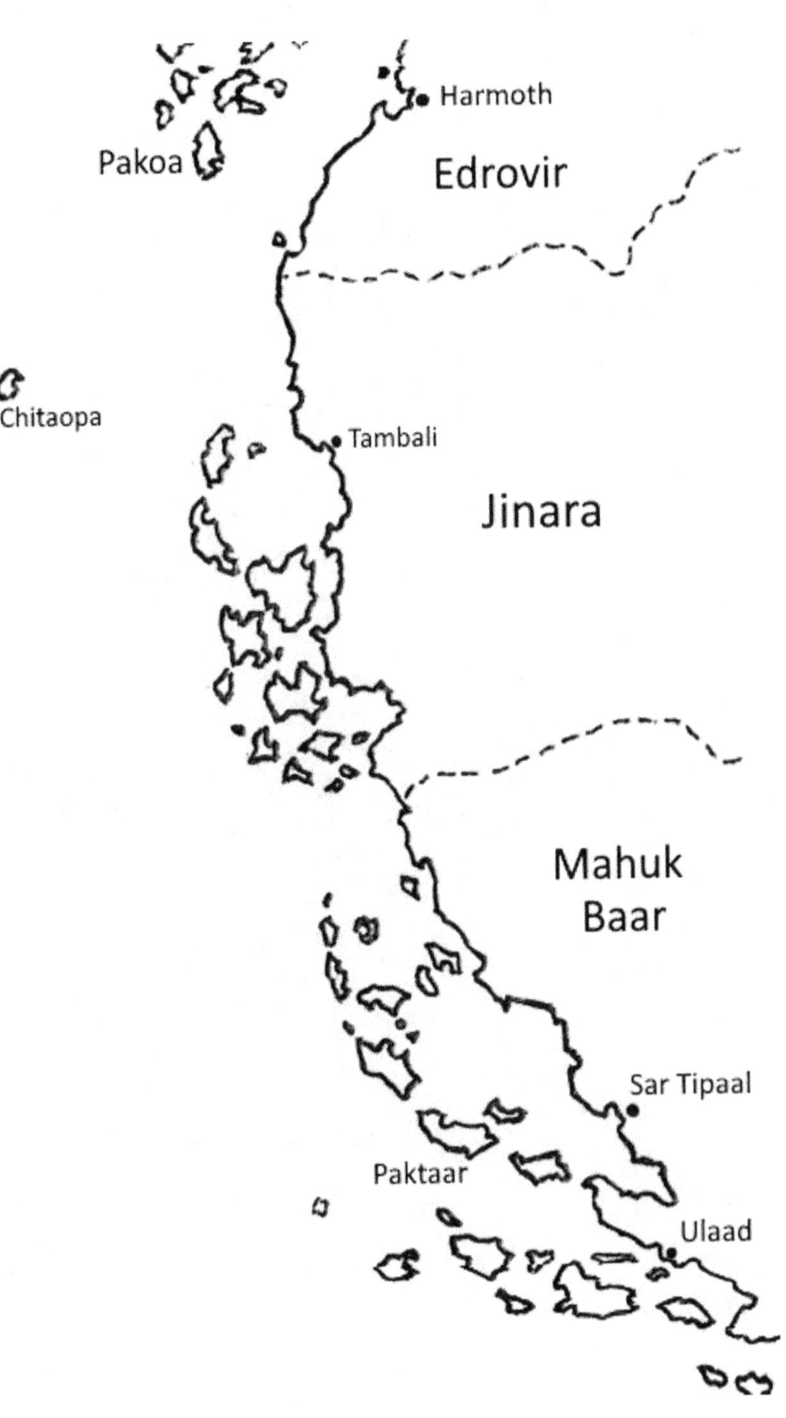

Harmoth
Edrovir
Pakoa
Chitaopa
Tambali
Jinara
Mahuk
Baar
Sar Tipaal
Paktaar
Ulaad

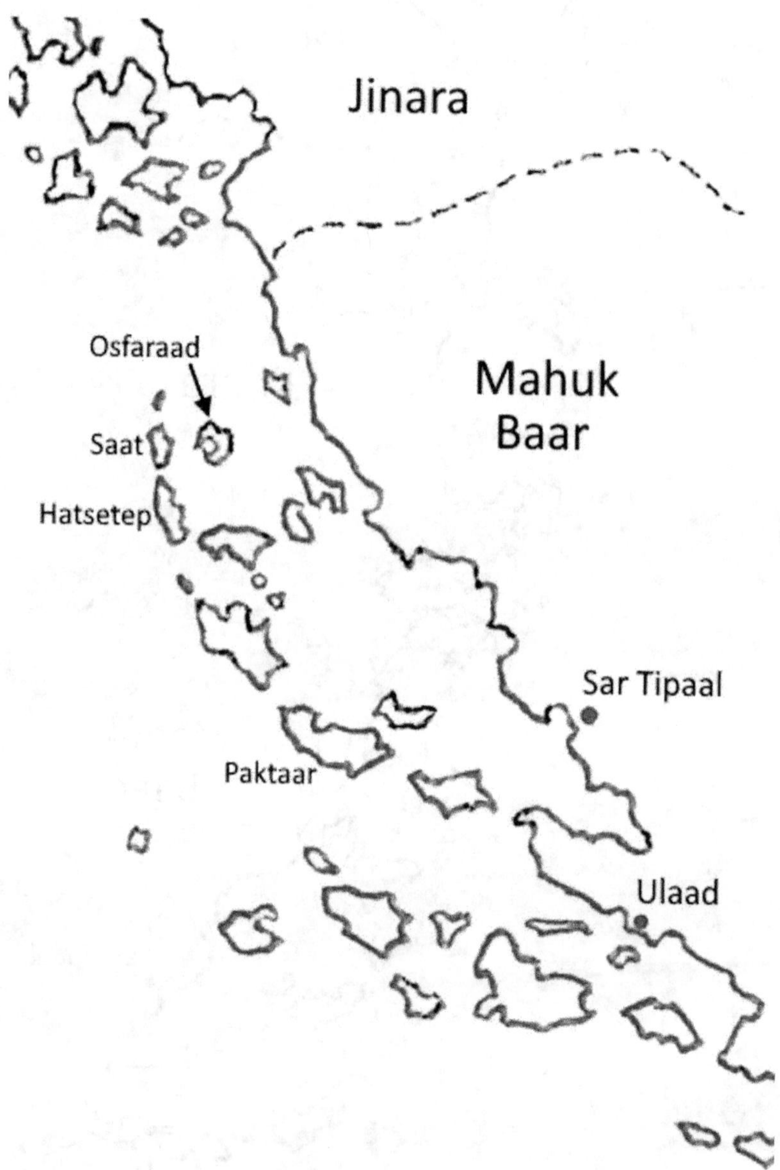

Jinara
Mahuk
Baar
Osfaraad
Saat
Hatsetep
Paktaar
Sar Tipaal
Ulaad

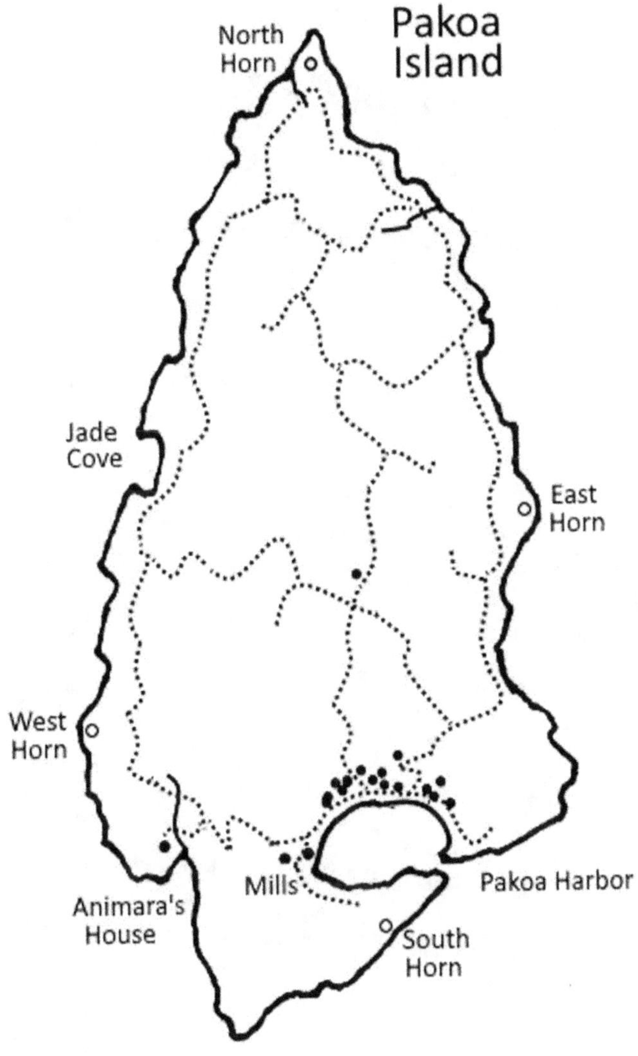

Pakoa Island
North Horn
Jade Cove
East Horn
West Horn
Animara's House
Mills
South Horn
Pakoa Harbor

CONTENTS

1: New Recruits

Nagaro stood stiffly to attention under the eyes of the three men in the reviewing stand. Behind him stood the ranks of his men, all equally stiff. It was a clear autumn morning, bright with watery sunlight that slanted across the hard-packed earth of the parade ground inside the encircling wall of the compound housing the Royal Fleet of Edrovir. Back on the island of Pakoa, Nagaro would have been out riding on such a morning, enjoying the clement weather. Instead he was here, on the mainland in Edrovir's capital city of Lankura, enduring the scrutiny of Kuran Kel and two of his senior officers. The Lord of the Fleet sat in the middle of the front row of the small reviewing stand, flanked by the two officers. None of them looked particularly pleased and Nagaro was beginning to wonder whether he and his men should have stayed on Pakoa.

They had responded the previous spring to Lord Kuran's request to "mind his back garden" by patrolling among the islands of the Lomoan archipelago, watching for Mautep—enemy sea raiders from the Mahuk Baar. The task had taken them farther afield than Kuran had intended and had culminated with their arriving in the nick of time to help drive a marauding Mautep force from the royal palace and the city of Lankura. The nation of Edrovir had been grateful, and Kuran had seemed to be favorably impressed. So impressed, in fact, that he had offered Nagaro a captain's commission in the Royal Fleet and had promised places to any men who chose to come with him. That had been last spring, however, and there had been four months for the Lord of the Fleet to change his mind. Based on Nagaro's conversations with Kuran that past spring, he'd felt comfortable enough to communicate his acceptance in a letter, rather than face to face. *Had he presumed too much?* He'd arrived in the month of Sedrin, instead of in mid summer as Kuran had originally proposed, and had brought more men than he'd expected. *He'd explained the uncertainties in his letter, but...*

He tried not to wince as Kuran's eyes raked him again.

Those jet black eyes and the Fleet Lord's bronze complection bespoke the man's Turowan blood, while his narrow high-bridged nose and sharp jaw were evidence of the Kelorin half of his mixed ancestry.

His black hair and beard were lightly peppered with gray. Both of his officers sat taller in their seats, by virtue of being taller men, but their movements conveyed their deference to him. They were both pale-skinned, one being a dark-haired Kelorin, the other a blond Leithian with a haughty gaze.

All three men had been engaged in a close conversation since taking their seats, accompanied by pointed glances at the presumptive new recruits and interspersed with frowning consultations with the clerk who was standing dutifully at the foot of the reviewing stand. The clerk, a spare, middle-aged Kelorin, carried a small note board bearing the list of names Nagaro had supplied in response to a request delivered to his ship the previous evening. As Nagaro watched, the blond officer made yet another gesture at the note board and seemed to ask a question. The Kelorin officer nodded and laughed. Kuran smiled fleetingly, then sobered and gave an instruction to the clerk who promptly turned and began to walk towards Nagaro.

Nagaro waited with some trepidation as the man approached.

The clerk made him an abbreviated bow and said, "My Lord Kuran wishes to speak to you, Zirda."

Nagaro swallowed and inclined his head to the man in polite acknowledgment. Then he squared his shoulders and advanced with a firm step, taking comfort in the familiar swing of the elegant Mahuk sword in its black leather scabbard at his hip. Halting directly in front of Lord Kuran, he bowed with practiced grace, grateful for the instruction he had received from his guardian, the Lady Maramine, dead now more than seven years. Straightening, he noted that the three men before him were all in the full Fleet uniform of matching dark blue pants and smartly tailored sleeveless tirkas. The latter, bearing the insignia of their ranks, were worn over crisp white shirts. All three men wore their hair clipped short about their ears. The two lesser officers were clean-shaven, however, unlike Kuran with his precisely razor-trimmed beard.

Nagaro was conscious of the contrast presented by his motley crew. The pirates wore their hair any way they liked, and were presently dressed in whatever each man owned that he thought would make the best impression. The result was distinctly miscellaneous. He himself was dressed as he preferred to be in a plain white shirt with black pants and boots. He wore his dark hair in the traditional Turowan fashion, shoulder length and bound at the nape of the neck. His black beard and mustache were un-shaped by a razor, but clipped as close to the skin as a scissors would allow. Kuma stain darkened his skin to a shade that matched that of his Turowan friend Taru, standing behind him. The hair, beard, and kuma stain were all elements of his disguise and had so far served him well. No one he had encountered during his earlier appearance in Lankura had recognized him as the so-called idiot prince, Leyel Virden.

Ignoring the curious stares of the two flanking men, he spoke directly to Kuran, saying, "My Lord?"

Kuran cleared his throat. "Captain Nagaro," he said formally. "Allow me to introduce two of my commanders. This is Strad Olbern, recently elevated to the rank." Kuran indicated the man on his left. "You might remember him from the victory banquet last spring."

Nagaro quickly measured the Leithian, a heavily built man in his early thirties with white-blond hair and pale blue eyes. He vaguely recalled the man being seated at the farther end of the banquet table, but they had exchanged no conversation. Nagaro executed a carefully correct bow and said, "I give you greeting, Commander."

Commander Strad returned him a stiff nod, a cool glance, and a single word of acknowledgment. "Zirda."

"And this is Geldoran Finrad," Kuran continued, "whom I don't believe you've met."

Nagaro turned his attention to the Kelorin seated at Kuran's right hand. This, then, was Lord Kuran's presumed successor. Geldoran looked to be about forty. Loose-limbed and gaunt, he was far from handsome. His cheeks were too hollow, his chin too sharp, his nose a bit crooked. But his gray eyes were almost luminous. Those eyes were at present studying Nagaro with considerable interest.

Nagaro bowed to him in turn. "Well met, Commander."

"Well met indeed, Captain." Geldoran's voice was unexpectedly low-pitched and resonant. "And while we haven't met face to face, I believe we've encountered each other in our ships at sea."

Nagaro nodded. "I believe so, Commander. Last spring, off of Obai in the Faranos after the attack on Long Harbor. You ran us off as I recall."

Geldoran smiled somberly. "For which I beg your pardon, Zirda. I didn't know you came as friends, and I was in no mood to stop and ask your intentions."

Nagaro bowed in acknowledgment of this gracious apology from Lord Kuran's second in command. "That is certainly understandable, Commander."

Kuran cleared his throat again. "It's the seventeenth day of Sedrin, Captain," he observed, and though his face bore no trace of a smile, there was the hint of a twinkle in his dark eyes. "Your letter said I should expect you by mid Sedrin. You are one day late."

Nagaro had read the man's eyes with relief, for it seemed that he hadn't completely fallen from Kuran's good graces. He spoke to the twinkle in those eyes. "Not so, My Lord. We arrived late yesterday, but your harbor master told us to tie up our ships and present ourselves to you this morning." He saw Strad's frown sharpen at this and realized that the Leithian had missed the levity. Judging by the smile playing about Geldoran's lips, the Kelorin had not. "Yet I beg your pardon, My Lord," Nagaro added quickly. "We were delayed by bad weather in the channel. I should have allowed more time in view of the season."

Kuran managed to conceal his mirth as he said, "See that it doesn't happen again." Then the twinkle receded from his eyes and he leaned forward. "You seem to have brought nearly half your force. I count eighty-five men, including yourself."

"That is correct, My Lord."

Not a muscle of Kuran's face so much as twitched. "Yet in your letter you expressed concern that you might not be able to join us until spring for want of enough men to sail a single ship."

Nagaro swallowed. "I wasn't sure what to expect when I wrote that, My Lord. And the final number frankly surprised me. But you said you would take any who wished to come, and your concern seemed to be with having enough ships. So I brought two ships to accommodate the number of men." He paused, but Kuran continued to regard him sternly and the other two men's expressions offered no help. He swallowed again. "I was under the impression the ships would be welcome," he added.

Kuran raised a hand to massage the bridge of his nose. "They are," he said dryly. "And, as you say, the number of men *is* appropriate to the number of ships. Unfortunately, however, I was only anticipating one ship, and no more than half the number of men, and this presents a problem. We lack space in the barracks to house so many. Estevad—" here Kuran indicated the clerk—"informs me that we may just manage if we bring in extra beds and if your men share quarters until we can get the builders in, which could take some time..." Kuran let his words trail as he regarded Nagaro with a probing gaze.

So that was it. Nagaro felt sick at the thought of having to tell some of the men that they'd come all the way to Lankura for nothing. "My men are accustomed to sharing quarters," he said quickly, "and sleeping on the floor, if it comes to that. I doubt they'll complain, however long it takes to house them better."

Geldoran raised an eyebrow at this.

Strad smirked. "Wouldn't it be easier to just pick out the best of them, as I've suggested, My Lord?" he began. "I know you expected there might be *some* Turowans among them—because of... ah... where they come from. But, frankly, all of *these*—" His gesture swept the ranks of Nagaro's followers, nearly half of whom were Turowan.

"—are most gratifying to see." Kuran cut in before the Leithian could finish his sentence, even as he gave Strad a sharp look. "We don't ordinarily get nearly enough applicants from among my mother's people, and here we have at least thirty who are not only keen to apply but already trained in seamanship and swordsmanship." His glance came back to Nagaro. "They *are* all trained to the sword and have served under you for at least a season?"

Commander Strad had frozen, his face a mask.

Nagaro's opinion of the Leithian had gone down several notches. "All but eight of them, My Lord," he replied, "who only became free men this summer and have no training except as slaves at the oars. They wanted to come, although I told them I could promise nothing."

Kuran raised an eyebrow. "Which ones are they?"

"At that end, My Lord." Nagaro gestured. "Their names are at the bottom of the list."

Kuran surveyed the men in question. The group numbered three Leithians, four Kelorin, and a single Turo. "I suppose we *could* let them go, in the spirit of keeping only the best," he drawled. "What do you think, gentlemen?" The last was apparently directed at the two commanders.

Strad sat tight-lipped, his dilemma obvious.

Geldoran shrugged. "They stand as tall as any," he observed.

"They're eager to impress, Commander," Nagaro volunteered. "And they've had a few weeks to observe the other men. On Pakoa I would give them a chance. Some men take to it. Others show little aptitude or find the work not to their liking."

Kuran smiled tightly. "So it always is with new recruits," he said. "These at least know how to row. And the two ships would be short-handed without them. If they are indeed willing to sleep on the floor, I see no reason to deny them." He turned to his clerk. "I want those last eight men housed with the new recruits, Estevad—two or three to a room. And tell them they'll have to work harder at swordsmanship to make up for lost time."

The clerk nodded. "Yes, My Lord."

Kuran rubbed his hands together. "And having taken *those* to fill the ships, we must clearly take all the rest." He spoke with rather more relish than resignation. "They'll have to share quarters too, of course, but do the best you can to find them places in the barracks."

"I shall do so, My Lord."

The Lord of the Fleet returned his attention to Nagaro. "Now, Captain, which of these men have served as officers, and in what capacity?"

Nagaro let out a breath of relief at this acceptance of all of his followers. "There are five officers besides myself, My Lord," he explained. "Their names are at the top of the list. There's Taru Nareyo, my first mate, whom you've met. And my second mate, Pavo Maat. The other three are all former Fleet men who wish to return to your service. Landros Torenin has been serving as a captain. Tredhold Ferth is a ship's doctor. Both of them you know. The last man is Rubo Ataya, who was a cook, but has been serving as a first mate."

Kuran nodded. "Good enough." He turned once again to the clerk. "Please call off the officers' names and have them stand over there, Estevad." He indicated a place a short distance from where he and his officers were seated. "They should be housed according to their rank, but feel free to double them up when you make the assignments. Once the officers have been separated, you may line up the other men and take their oaths as soon as I send you a witness. The officers' oaths I will take, myself."

Estevad bowed. "Very good, My Lord," he said crisply and stepped away to carry out his task.

Watching as the officers moved to their appointed place, Kuran abruptly frowned. "The Hashtep, there," he said, addressing Nagaro. "What exactly is his history?"

Nagaro had known this moment would come, and was encouraged that Kuran at least used the correct ethnic term *Hashtep*, rather than the ill-informed *Mahuk*. "Pavo Maat and I were slaves together, My Lord," he replied. "At times chained at the same oar. He's been my second mate for more than three years."

Kuran rubbed his chin, frowning. "I'm... *surprised*... to see him here."

Commander Strad looked more than surprised. He was staring darkly at Pavo, and even Geldoran was frowning.

Nagaro kept his own expression neutral. "Pavo seems determined to follow me wherever I go. I told him I would see that he isn't treated badly because of his heritage."

Kuran gave him a sharp glance. "Did you, now? Let's hope there's no trouble."

Geldoran stirred. "How well does he speak the Common Speech?"

"Better than I speak Hashti, Commander."

"But he's not one of *us!*" Strad blurted. "He's a foreigner! We've never taken a man who wasn't Edroviran-born."

Kuran sighed. "There is that." He turned to Nagaro. "I wish to ask him some questions. Please call him over."

Pavo came immediately to the summons, striding across the intervening space to halt smartly in front of the Lord of the Fleet. "Greeting, Lord Kuran," he said, and ducked his head in what for him passed as a bow.

Nagaro stepped a bit to one side to allow Pavo to speak for himself.

Kuran studied Pavo narrowly. "Where exactly were you born, Pavo Maat?"

Pavo's face remained impassive. "Small way north of city of Sar Tipaal, Lord Kuran."

"So, you're a citizen of the Mahuk Baar?"

There was a shadow of uncertainty in Pavo's narrow dark eyes. "I do not know what is *citizen*, Lord Kuran," he said.

"Ah, your pardon." Kuran gave a slight inclination of his head. "To be a citizen of a country means to dwell there by right of law."

"Oh." Pavo dropped his eyes, but raised them after a moment's pause. "I do not know if I am citizen of any country," he said seriously. "I have escape from being slave of Lord Baalkir, and some Mautep have call me traitor to Mahuk Baar because I follow Nagaro. I have live for five year on Pakoa, that is part of Edrovir, but I do not know if that means I am citizen of Edrovir."

Strad and Geldoran silently exchanged glances past Kuran's head.

Kuran rubbed his chin, considering. "How did you come to be a slave?"

Pavo didn't hesitate this time. "It was judgement," he said, and the two commanders exchanged another glance, both frowning. "Because I have kill two rabbit that belong to Lord Baalkir."

"Two *rabbits*?" Kuran sounded skeptical.

Pavo remained impassive. "Yes, Lord Kuran. My two brother and I were very hungry because it was end of winter and we had no more fish. But rabbit belong to Lord Baalkir, and his man catch me. So I have to go to galley to be slave, until I die."

Geldoran reacted to this with shock, murmuring, "That's a harsh punishment."

Shock also flickered in Kuran's eyes, and even Strad looked a bit dismayed. The Lord of the Fleet cleared his throat. "How long had you served before you escaped?"

"Almost two and one half year."

Significant looks passed among all three officers this time, and they bent their heads together to engage in a muttered discussion, their expressions and gestures suggesting disagreement.

The debate ended with Kuran and Geldoran looking satisfied while Strad appeared resigned. Kuran turned back to the young Hashtep. "Pavo Maat," he said. "I judge that you have more than paid for your crime. What would happen to you if you returned to the Mahuk Baar?"

Pavo considered this. "For having made escape, I would go back to galley and be slave again," he said. "But I also have sailed with Captain Nagaro and have help to steal many slave. And I have killed Mautep, that are high-born man, in battle with sword. I think Emperor Baalkir maybe would take my life for these thing."

"So you have no desire to return to the Mahuk Baar?"

"That is true, Lord Kuran."

Nagaro finally spoke. "He has a wife on Pakoa, My Lord. She will bear their first child in the spring. And his two brothers have recently come to Pakoa. It was no longer safe for them in the Mahuk Baar because of Pavo's service with me."

Kuran's black eyes flickered. "I see." He returned his gaze to Pavo. "Are you prepared to take an oath of allegiance and service to the Royal Fleet and the nation of Edrovir?"

Pavo nodded. "I will swear in name of Sheptuum, that is god of my people."

Strad's face clouded at the mention of the Hashtep deity, though it elicited no obvious reaction from Kuran or Geldoran.

Kuran turned to Nagaro. "Do you bear witness, Captain, to the truth of this man's words?"

Nagaro nodded. "I do, My Lord. I have direct knowledge of some of what he says, and for the rest of it, I trust Pavo's honesty. I've never found him false."

Kuran inclined his head. "Then I will put it to King Elgurn that the Hashtep Pavo Maat should be declared a citizen of Edrovir."

"What of the other Hashtep who have sought haven on Pakoa, My Lord?" Nagaro asked. "Will the same status be extended to them?"

Kuran pursed his lips. "A fair question. I'll put that to the king as well." He turned back to Pavo. "I must say, Zirda, I'm curious to know why you left the Hashtep community on Pakoa to follow your captain to this place where there are no others of your folk."

Pavo calmly considered the Lord of the Fleet. "Nagaro is my friend," he responded. "Also I want to see how his story end."

"His... *story?*" Kuran frowned in puzzlement.

"Yes." Pavo spoke earnestly. "Surely Sheptuum does not make such good man as Nagaro except if he have some purpose."

Nagaro ducked his head in embarrassment.

Kuran's expression was opaque. "I see. Thank you for your answers, Pavo Maat. You may return to the other officers."

Pavo made his little half bow, and retreated to join his comrades.

The young Hashtep was scarcely gone when Strad exclaimed, "How can the man think his god has some plan for a mere pirate?"

Nagaro felt the blood in his face, under the kuma stain. "His people believe their god shapes the lives of men into stories to teach moral lessons, Commander," he explained. "I don't credit it any more than you do."

Kuran frowned. "Sheptuum will have to wait his turn, in any case," he muttered. "I have my own purposes." Then he pinned Nagaro with his obsidian gaze. "I understand you train your own men in swordsmanship,

Captain."

Nagaro drew a breath, wondering where this was leading. "Yes, I do take charge of it, My Lord. Though I have help from others, such as Landros, who've had formal instruction."

Kuran nodded as if this were the answer he'd expected. "As it happens," he said, "we just lost our Fleet swordmaster— quite unexpectedly and on very short notice. I must therefore press you into service to fill the need until I can hire a new one. If Landros or any others wish to assist you, so much the better."

Nagaro caught startled movements from Strad and Geldoran at this announcement, suggesting it was news to them. He felt rather shocked, himself. It wasn't the work he'd come to do. Still, he remembered that Kuran had asked him in the spring whether he could take orders, and he didn't wish to question the first assignment he was given. He did have four years of experience, after all, even if it was outside of the Fleet. "If you wish it, My Lord," he managed.

"I do," Kuran replied curtly. "Thank you, Captain. You may now join the other officers. I'll come down shortly to hear your oaths."

Grateful to be released, Nagaro executed a bow, straightened, and strode away to join his friends. He found Landros, the grizzled Fleet veteran, in the process of teaching Taru and Pavo how to perform a proper Fleet salute.

Taru shot him an eager grin. "So Kuran's going t' take the lot of us?"

"So it appears."

Landros crooked an eyebrow. "Did ye have to do some sweet talking?"

Nagaro shook his head. "I just told him we'd be willing to share rooms if necessary. I think Kuran wanted to take everyone, but needed to justify it. Geldoran was amenable, but the other man— Strad Olbern— wasn't happy to see so many Turo. I have to say I wasn't very impressed with him. I can't help wondering why Kuran has made him a commander."

Landros gave a short laugh. "Politics, lad. Kuran has to balance the number o' Leithians and Kelorin among his senior officers."

Nagaro frowned. "I thought the king gave him fairly free rein."

"The king does, but the factions don't. I'll wager the Leithian Faction put forward this man Strad. He'll be a high-born Leithian. They're the worst sort for prejudice."

Tredhold ran a hand through his sandy hair. "They may be the worst, as ye say, Landros, but they've plenty o' company," he said in measured defense of his own people.

"I'll grant ye that." Landros nodded ruefully. "But in the Fleet it's mostly the officers ye have t' worry about. The common seamen are used to having a few Turowans in the ranks. They don't care as long as a man does his work."

Standing beside Landros, the leather-faced old Turowan named Rubo flashed a tight smile. "They'll have t' get used to a few more of us now," he said. "I'm guessing our lads'll more than double the number o' Turo in th' Fleet."

Landros and Tredhold nodded in sober agreement.

Nagaro shot a glance at Pavo who was listening with his usual impassive silence, but wary eyes. To turn the subject, he said, "Kuran says they just lost their swordmaster and he wants me to take on the duty until he finds a new one. I'd be grateful if you all will help me."

"I'll be happy to, lad," Landros assured him.

Tred and Rubo echoed the sentiment.

Pavo was looking past Nagaro's shoulder. "I will help, too," he said. "But here come Lord Kuran and other man."

*

The three men in the reviewing stand had watched Nagaro go.

"I must say he took that well," Geldoran observed. "Some men would be insulted to be handed a civilian's task."

Strad started to laugh, then caught Kuran's look and stifled it.

"I meant him no insult," the Fleet Lord said sharply. "It's skilled work, and we're lucky to have a man who can do it."

"You believe he's up to the task?" Strad asked cautiously.

"I've every reason to. His men performed well this past spring by all accounts. Besides, the assignment will give everyone an oportunity to become acquainted."

Geldoran nodded sagely. "It's a good thought, My Lord, since the captain and his officers didn't come up through the ranks." He paused, frowning. "Although I must say that his men work so well together that I think you should keep them so. When we met them off Obai, the fog lifted quite suddenly and we found ourselves bearing down on them, head to head and at close quarters. Those four pirate ships made as sharp and swift a turn as I've ever witnessed. And then they outran us, besides."

"So they're good at *running away?*" Strad was frankly contemptuous.

Geldoran regarded the Leithian coolly. "Sometimes running away is called for," he observed. "In which case you'd better do it as well as you do everything else."

Strad had the grace to look abashed at this rebuke from the more experienced man.

Kuran had noted the exchange without comment. Now he stood up, gesturing his intention to leave the reviewing stand. "I'll consider your advice about keeping them together, Geldoran," he said, making for the steps. "But they must also learn Fleet ways. From what their captain has told me, he has a looser approach to command than we expect."

Geldoran moved to follow his commander. "They'll learn much from daily drill," he ventured. "And if you let Captain Nagaro form crews for his two ships, and let me sail with each one on maneuvers, I'll soon get a sense of them. Perhaps I'll choose one for my new flagship since we've spoken of letting Strad take the *Valor*."

"Mmm... yes..." Kuran stepped down onto the packed earth of the parade ground, the other two men following. "Landros Torenin has a temperament well-suited to being a flagship captain..." His gaze swept the array of men before him and his thought shifted. "I see that Estevad is waiting for us. Strad, please go stand witness so he can get started with the oaths of the rank and file. Geldoran will join you when we've finished with the officers."

"Aye, Zirda!" Strad saluted and strode off.

Kuran approached the newly recruited officers at an unhurried pace, noting that the six men were talking among themselves in apparently comfortable camaraderie.

Geldoran, at his elbow, must have made the same observation, for he said, "Do you think the captain might favor his own men on the training field?"

Kuran shook his head. "I think not. His Vothrin upbringing won't let him be anything but even-handed."

"A strict Vothrin?" Geldoran gray eyes glowed with satisfaction. "I suppose we needn't worry, then, that he won't live up to Fleet standards?"

"Indeed." Kuran's dark eyes hardened. "I'm much more concerned that *we* won't live up to *his*. And more than a little worried about what he might do in that event. I could wish that the words of the Fleet oath were a trifle more... *specific*... about some things."

Geldoran raised an eyebrow, but had no time to comment since he and Kuran had reached the group of men, who were all plainly aware of their coming. He did, however, pay particular attention when, a minute later, the young Captain Nagaro touched his hand to his brow and earnestly recited the oath that officially made him a Fleet warrior, prefaced as was customary by his personal choice of binding words:

"Upon my honor and in Vothra's name, I hereby pledge my service to the Royal Fleet, and swear to uphold the honor, laws, and interests of the people and nation of Edrovir."

2: The New Swordmaster

Six weeks later, Nagaro sat in the bottom row of one of the tiered wooden stands that flanked the north and south sides of the Fleet's practice field, watching the final match of the informal sword tourney that was a part of the regular weekly practice. He shivered as a cold gust of wind swept the field and adjacent parade ground. It was late in the month of Todrin, the day was waning, and the sky promised rain. Still, the seats in the stands were packed with sea warriors. Although huddled in their cloaks against the chill, they raised full-throated choruses of cheers or groans in response to the actions of the two fighters on the field.

Nagaro was aware that Lord Kuran, together with a wiry gray-haired Kelorin, was watching from a place at the low fence that separated the practice field from the parade ground, but he took no particular notice. Kuran had given no evidence that he was in a great hurry to find a new swordmaster. The Lord of the Fleet asked for regular progress reports, and often observed the men's training—even fighting an occasional demonstration bout. Although he sometimes brought other men with him, these others came and went without being introduced and Nagaro had ceased to take heed of them.

Altogether, things were going well for the former pirates. Nagaro had found it easier than he expected to settle into the routines of the Fleet Compound. With autumn deepening into winter, there was limited opportunity for rowing practice and ship-maneuvers, and the men's training was focused mainly on daily sword-instruction. He'd found it quite easy to step into the role of swordmaster. Sword practice was sword practice and his experience stood him in good stead. The initial skepticism of the veteran sea warriors had evaporated as they'd found that Nagaro clearly knew what he was doing.

He had quickly realized that his fame up and down the coast of Edrovir would make it difficult for him to be "just another Fleet warrior," but being the swordmaster brought him attention that had a purpose beyond mere curiosity. The fear of being recognized as the "idiot prince", which had wracked him on his final night in Pakoa, seemed remote when facing the mundane reality of the practice field. He felt secure, here, in his physical disguise, knowing that his behavior now was completely unlike that of the apparently simple-minded Leyel Virden, who had been paraded through the streets of Lankura seven years ago to the echo of taunts and jeers.

The other former pirates had settled in with similar ease. They had come in such numbers that they wouldn't have been isolated even if the other men had tried to ignore them, and they also had Landros, Tredhold, and Rubo, all former Fleet men, to ease their introductions. Whatever prejudice Taru and the other Turowans encountered among the high-born Leithian and Kelorin sea warriors was largely mitigated by their association with Nagaro, as well as by their own accomplishments. Even Pavo was finding acceptance. Kuran's men had naturally looked askance at first at a man they considered a "Mahuk", but Nagaro's authority as swordmaster had allowed him to ensure fair treatment for his friend. Tensions had eased as the men saw what Pavo could do with a sword, and Pavo's honest good humor had made him difficult to dislike, besides.

Lord Kuran, standing at his place by the fence, pulled his cloak about him as the wind tugged at it. The man beside him hunched his shoulders against the gust. Both men were focused on the two Fleet warriors who circled each other with swords drawn, the older one blond, the younger man dark-haired.

The combatants came at each other, their blades ringing together, then leapt apart again.

One of the two judges, standing at the foot of the stands, cried, "Second hit for Rastian!"

"Aye. Second hit," confirmed the other.

The gray-haired man at the fence spoke over the wind. "I'm grateful, My Lord, for this chance to see what your men can do before ye make the announcement."

"Mmm." Kuran nodded fractionally. "You came on a good day for it. Every Sixth Day we have this competition for any who wish to participate. The men choose off two teams and go against each other. These two men are among our best swordsmen, so the contest has come down to them. I'd like to hear what you think. The Leithian is Brodig Fane. The Kelorin is Rastian Korven."

The gray-haired Kelorin watched in focused silence as the two combatants moved together and apart again in several rapid exchanges. "They're both fine swordsmen, and well-matched," he said. "But I saw the Leithian drop his guard just before trying a feint, and the young Kelorin sometimes overextends himself when he lunges."

Kuran grunted in affirmation.

"Three hits for Brodig!" came the cry. "That's the match!"

"Aye, match it is!" The other judge's words were almost blown away as he echoed the call.

Brodig raised his practice sword in a triumphant gesture. Rastian bowed graciously in defeat.

Nagaro rose from his seat and raised his voice. "Well fought, Brodig and Rastian! That decides our contest in favor of the south team." He shrugged his cloak closer and glanced warily at the lowering sky. "Let's have all the new men on the field for a melee—before the rain starts."

"Aye, Captain!" Came the excited chorus as Brodig and Rastian retired and the new recruits came bounding down from the stands to arm themselves with practice blades and take their places.

At the fence, the gray-haired man turned to Kuran. "Is that the man ye have serving as swordmaster, My Lord?"

Kuran nodded. "Yes. Captain Nagaro."

"So that's Captain Nagaro! He does look a bit of a pirate wi' the beard and the hair tied like that."

Kuran gave the other man a sidelong glance. "What he looks like is a Turo who keeps the traditional ways," he observed mildly.

"Ah." The gray-haired man seemed not to mark the mild rebuke. "How has he served ye?"

Kuran turned back to watch the new recruits, who were quickly forming up lines. "Quite well," he observed coolly. "If it weren't that I have uses for his other talents, I'd be pleased to keep him in this capacity. In which case I wouldn't need your services."

"That's so, My Lord," the gray-haired man conceded. "I should be grateful he's got those other talents. Not too full of himself, then, is he?"

Kuran shook his head. "The man is modest to a fault. There was some private grumbling when I made him swordmaster. Some of the men let me know they expected the worst. But the veterans have come around in the short time he's been here, and the new recruits can't do enough to please him."

"Does he coddle 'em, perhaps?"

Kuran's mouth twitched. "I would say not. But see for yourself."

The melee was about to start. Nagaro stepped up to one end of the imaginary line that divided the two forces. He held up his arm, then brought it down in a chopping motion and cried, "Forward!"

The two lines swept together and the clatter of their swords rang in the air. The mock battle moved first one way and then the other. Nagaro moved slowly along behind one line, observing carefully, then around the end and up the other side. When he'd covered the entire line, he put up both hands and cried, "Halt!" Then he moved forward among the men, pausing to speak to first one and then another, sometimes taking one of the swords in his hand to demonstrate something.

The gray-haired man at the fence had been watching with avid interest. Now he muttered under his breath, "I can guess what he's saying t' *that* one. Yes! He's showing him how he could ha' turned that stroke t' the thigh—" He broke off and turned to Kuran. "It seems the man knows what he's about, My Lord."

Kuran smiled faintly. "What I find remarkable is that I've never heard Nagaro shout at a man. All the previous swordmaster seemed to *do* was shout. But Nagaro tells me his two best tools are praise and patience. If a man does well, he gets praise. If he does badly, it's patience. And he *does* work them hard, Zirda."

The gray-haired Kelorin looked thoughtful. "It sounds a bit like my own approach."

"All I can say is, there's been good progress since he started. Before, we had a dozen men we thought we were going to have to let go. Now the number is down to four. The rest have all turned themselves around."

"And these are the shoes I'm to fill?" The gray-haired man gave Kuran a wry glance. Then he frowned. "But, what's this?"

Competing chants had begun to rise from the stands of, "Geldoran! Geldoran!" and "Nagaro! Nagaro!"

Kuran smiled broadly. "Ah, they're calling for a demonstration bout. They never seem to tire of this match. And there's Geldoran, coming down. It seems he's game. He never turns it down, though he's been beaten every time. And Nagaro has put his cloak aside and is choosing a sword. *Now* you will see something, Zirda!"

The field was suddenly empty of all but the two new combatants, and there was no sound but the whistling of the wind. The two men stepped up to one another, bowed, and saluted with matching formality. Geldoran was the taller of the two, by perhaps two inches. He had moved with a deceptively awkward loose-limbed gait as he crossed the field, but it was replaced by a tautly controlled grace when he bowed. He stepped out of his salute and came on his guard in a fluid motion. Captain Nagaro moved with the same lithe, easy grace whether walking, bowing, or dropping as he now did into a fighting stance.

It was impossible to say which man moved first. Their swords flashed and rang, as they came together and moved apart, circled, and came together again. Geldoran seemed to be looking for a way around Nagaro's guard, first to the left and then the right. The commander's movements gave the impression that he was concentrating everything he had on the fight. In contrast, Nagaro seemed to move lightly, with little effort.

Now the lanky Kelorin made one of his quick darting lunges. Nagaro turned it aside with a flick of motion, and Geldoran was back out again, but not before one of the judges cried, "First hit for Nagaro!"

The other judge spread his hands in a gesture of uncertainty.

Geldoran spoke with resignation. "It was a hit."

Even as Nagaro was nodding an acknowledgment, Geldoran moved again, apparently trying to catch his opponent off guard. Nagaro's response, however, was instantaneous. The initial gambit was foiled, and there followed a rapid series of attack and counter-attack, during which the men's swords rang repeatedly.

When the two men broke apart, Nagaro spoke first: "I felt a hit."

"And I," came Geldoran's rueful rejoinder.

"One hit for Geldoran. Now two for Nagaro."

Once more the two men began to circle.

Standing at the fence, the gray-haired man muttered, "It's quite remarkable: Geldoran is very fast, but Captain Nagaro is a trace faster. And he doesn't waste *anything*. Every move he makes is just exactly what it needs t' be."

Kuran nodded appreciatively. "He's something of a mystery, though. He won't even tell me where he learned his swordsmanship. I thought perhaps you might shed some light on it."

The other man frowned. "Well, his style is somewhat unusual. I'd guess he's picked up things in all the places he's been. Still, if I had t' make a wager, I'd say he was trained by a master o' the Northern School. I could perhaps tell ye more if I faced him myself—"

The man broke off as the scene before them suddenly erupted in ferocious action.

Geldoran had thrown himself into another frenzied series of assaults, the effort beyond anything he had so far displayed. Still Nagaro turned every stroke, moving with swift and flawless precision. And somehow in the midst of this lightning-fast defense, he managed to slip through a third hit, and the match was suddenly over. Both men stepped back, to salute one another amid a roar of cheers and applause.

At the fence, the gray-haired Kelorin shook his head in disbelief. "*Astonishing*," he murmured. "*Remarkable*."

"Of course," Kuran drawled, "as the newly hired Fleet Swordmaster, I expect you to go a bout with the victor."

The man cast Kuran a rueful look and gave his head a shake. "Only if ye promise I'll still have th' position if I'm beaten, My Lord. That man is beyond good, and I'm not as quick as I once was."

Kuran chuckled. "Of course you will," he said. "Didn't I say I have other uses for the man's talents?"

On the field, the cheers subsided. Nagaro was standing where the match had ended, catching his breath and relishing the exhilaration of the bout. He wiped his brow with the back of his hand. "You nearly got through that time, Geldoran," he said earnestly. "If you keep this up, you'll beat me yet."

Geldoran, two paces away, shook his head. "No fear!" he gasped. "But I like going a bout with you. Keeps me on my form."

Abruptly Lord Kuran's voice rang across the field, drawing everyone's attention.

"Gentlemen and warriors!" he cried, "I wish to present the man I've just hired to take over as Swordmaster. Please give welcome to Master Fendar!"

Nagaro froze. Fendar! *Oh, no! Vothra, no!*

He scarcely heard the men's welcoming cheer over the roar of blood in his ears. *This couldn't be happening. Here he'd begun to think he was safe, and now this!* It was a calamity he hadn't even thought of when he'd reviewed the dangers all those weeks ago on Pakoa. Master Fendar was one of only a handful of people left among the living who had known him from the days *before* he'd been drugged with heskial and brought to Lankura, where everyone else had known him only as the idiot prince.

For a moment his limbs seemed locked in immobility. But he knew he couldn't just stand there... He drew a breath and forced himself to move... to turn... to look at the man who had taught him to use a sword.

And it was unquestionably Fendar. The man was older, and grayer, but he came vaulting over the fence with the same grasshopper spryness that Nagaro remembered so well. Now he'd flung his cloak away... He was calling for a sword... Saying something about a match with the winner...

No... oh, no...! Nagaro drew a long shuddering breath. *Why him, of all men? Why now?* Lokundas was unspeakably cruel to play him such a turn!

Had he felt a tiny drop, just then? Nagaro glanced at the sky. If only it would rain! But he knew that would only delay the inevitable. If Fendar was to be the new Fleet Swordmaster, there was no way on earth that Nagaro could avoid facing him... speaking to him... crossing swords with him. He glanced around at the stands. He caught a glimpse of Taru's horrified face, but Taru couldn't help him. And everyone else was waiting, watching. There was no way out.

Mechanically, Nagaro stepped toward the center of the field where Fendar was also taking up position.

Once again the crowd fell silent and there was no sound but the moaning of the wind.

Fendar saluted with his sword. "Well met, Captain Nagaro," he said calmly.

There was nothing in the man's face or voice—at least not yet—to indicate that he recognized his opponent, and Nagaro dared to hope.

"Master Fendar." Nagaro kept his expression as neutral as he could and his response as short as he could without being rude. He wished he knew a way to change the sound of his voice. The handgrip of his sword felt slick in his hand as he returned Fendar's salute. Still, he read nothing more than keen interest in the swordmaster's eyes.

A gust of wind swept over them, with a few scattered raindrops. One of the judges cried, "Begin!"

Fendar immediately took the offensive, moving through a series of quick but relatively standard attacks that Nagaro parried with ease in spite of his distraction. His gaze kept returning to the swordmaster's eyes, however, looking for evidence of the recognition he dreaded to see there.

All of a sudden, the other man moved with lightning speed in a maneuver Nagaro had never seen before. Nagaro's response was almost quick enough, but not quite. He felt Fendar's blade glance off his shoulder and heard the judges cry, "First hit for Fendar!" He heard the shocked gasps of the onlookers.

Bishka! He swore inwardly, knowing he should have turned that thrust. Allowing himself to be distracted was a mistake. In the past, he'd both beaten this man, and been beaten by him. Which one happened today didn't really matter as long as he didn't lose so clumsily as to raise questions. And there *would* be awkward questions if he lost badly, even if Fendar failed to recognize him.

Forget who the man is. Just fight the bout and let Lokundas do as he will...

With an effort, Nagaro forced his attention back where it belonged: on every aspect of his opponent's actions. The eyes weren't unimportant, but he'd been watching them too much, and for the wrong reason. He realized now that he should have been more wary. Fendar's early moves had been too easy, too ordinary—not approaching the cleverness of which the man was capable. If Nagaro hadn't already known that, the last attack had proved it.

Nagaro decided it was time to make his own offensive. Fendar had stepped back after his successful attack, almost as if surprised by the result. Nagaro stepped in, moving fast and low. As he saw Fendar begin to move to block his stroke, he saw another opening, a different target. Changing direction in the blink of an eye, he drove straight for the other man's chest, striking just left of center, slowing his thrust at the last instant to avoid striking the man too hard with the blunted blade tip.

There was another shocked gasp from the crowd, and Fendar sprang back with a look of dismay.

One of the judges cried, "A hit for Nagaro!" The judge sounded as if he were choking on the words, and for good reason. In a demonstration bout, Nagaro's hit counted no more than any other, but everyone present knew that in a fight for blood, Fendar would have just been slain.

The fight took on a different character after that. If either man had underestimated the other, it was so no longer. Each now called upon every move in his repertoire. Nagaro was fighting with focused intensity, trying to recall everything he could about this man who had been his instructor. But Fendar was showing him things he'd never seen before. Either the man had learned some tricks in the past eight years or he'd kept some of his knowledge from his pupil.

With his mind now firmly where it ought to be, and facing a skilled opponent who was fighting at his best, Nagaro found the match both challenging and instructive. After perhaps a minute, he managed to score a second hit with a blow to Fendar's right thigh, accomplishing it in the same manner as the first, by beginning with one move and ending with another.

"Second hit for Nagaro," came the cry, and there was a satisfied murmur from the onlookers. The hit had put their favored man ahead.

Almost immediately, however, the new swordmaster executed a maneuver entirely outside Nagaro's experience, succeeding in slipping under his guard to strike him on his left side at the base of the ribs.

"Second hit for Fendar! Two for each!"

There came a collective groan intermixed with cries of grudging approval. This was a good match!

For a moment, the two men circled, trying to catch their breath, both aware that the next man to score a hit would win the bout. A gust of wind buffeted them, this time bringing an unmistakable spatter of rain. In the calm after it passed, the drops continued to fall. The afternoon was darkening. Even without the rain, the fight would soon be hampered by failing light.

Nagaro looked across at the swordmaster, gestured skyward with his left hand, and said, "We should try to finish this before everyone gets wet."

Fendar met his eyes with a penetrating look. "Agreed," he said, and made a sudden lunge.

There followed a furious exchange of blows that drew gasps from the crowd. It ended when Nagaro saw an unexpected opportunity and took it. Engaging the guard of Fendar's sword with the tip of his blade, he twisted the other man's weapon from his hand and sent it spinning off across the beaten earth of the practice field—earth that was rapidly turning into mud.

There was a brief stunned silence before one of the judges cried, "Master Fendar is disarmed! The match goes to Captain Nagaro!"

The announcement rang loud in the silence. It was rare to see a man disarmed in a demonstration bout. Difficult to achieve with a skilled opponent in any case, disarming was forbidden except in place of a third hit, since a disarming traditionally ended any match and no one liked to see a demonstration bout end too soon.

The silence was broken by a wild cheer from the men in the stands, un-dampened by the rain that was falling now with a quickening rhythm. The crowd began to break up, then, and scatter as the men sought shelter.

Fendar bowed, without bothering to recover his sword, and said, "Well fought... Captain."

Nagaro felt a little chill at the pause that had preceded the word "captain." *Had the hesitation meant something?* He hastily returned the gesture, murmuring, "Well fought, as well, Zirda." He couldn't quite read Fendar's expression, though the man was staring at him rather hard.

When the swordmaster turned and dashed for the fence where he'd left his cloak, Nagaro breathed a sigh of relief. He hoped he hadn't been recognized. After all, it *had* been eight years since the man had seen him last, and he'd changed his appearance considerably.

Gratefully Nagaro turned and made a dash for his own cloak, which he'd left on the bottom tier of one of the stands. As he was donning it, one of the judges appeared at his elbow to collect his practice sword. The man took the thing with a hasty bow and hurried away again, head down against the rain. Nagaro settled his cloak about his shoulders. Reaching up to raise the hood, he turned around—and found himself confronted by a similarly cloaked and hooded figure. It took him exactly one terrible second to register that it was Fendar.

In the dimming light, Nagaro couldn't make out the man's expression under the shadow of his hood, but he caught a gleam of the swordmaster's eyes and his heart misgave him.

"That was indeed a good match, Captain," Fendar observed in a casual tone. "It's been a long time since anyone has disarmed me. Ye've learned a few things... from studying all those Mahuk warriors ye've been fighting, I fancy."

Again that little pause...

Nagaro shrugged. "I study every man I fight," he said, keeping his voice deliberately flat. "Usually I learn something."

"A wise practice." The swordmaster nodded. "But ye gave away that first hit."

Nagaro turned his face away and began to walk briskly towards the opening in the fence that gave passage to the parade ground, following the crowd and trying to spot Taru or Pavo.

Fendar fell in beside him, obviously expecting a response.

Nagaro kept his eyes straight ahead. "I was distracted. I shouldn't have let it happen." He was inclined to be honest in any case, but this time he found himself answering honestly almost reflexively, evaluating his performance for his former master. With another part of his mind he was desperately trying to think of how he might disengage from this uncomfortable conversation.

"Ah." Fendar nodded again, as if approving, very much as he had always done when his pupil had accurately assessed himself. "And ye've mastered the feint well. I never guessed either time what ye were planning."

They had passed through the opening in the fence. The nearest of the other men were still some way ahead, making for the dining hall. The rain shrouded the world like a curtain.

Nagaro frowned. The swordmaster's familiar way of talking to him worried him, although everything the man had said so far could be innocent. "I never plan a feint," he said, because he felt he had to keep talking. He'd thought for a moment that he'd seen Taru and Pavo dimly in the crowd but had lost sight of them again. "Sometimes I change my mind in the midst of a move. It works just as well." *Should he try to get in among the crowd, to see if he could lose the man and find his friends? Or hang back where no one would overhear?*

"*Ah.*"

There was something subtly different about the way Fendar said the word that reclaimed Nagaro's full attention.

"Yes," Fendar continued. "Ye told me that once, years ago. And I've never met another man who could make that claim... *Leyel.*"

Nagaro's feet stopped dead, even as his heart seemed to stop in his chest. It felt as though an icy hand had gripped and squeezed it. After a pause that seemed far too long, though it might have only lasted a second, he forced himself to take another step. But he moved slowly, now, for he definitely didn't want anyone to hear. "My name is Nagaro," he said tightly, and added, hoping the swordmaster might not be certain, "If that was intended as a jest, Zirda, I don't think much of it."

Fendar shook his head. "I meant no jest," he said seriously. "I never forget the lads I train. And I *know* ye, Leyel—though I'll admit I didn't at first. Ye've changed your looks, but ye can't change the way ye *move*... the way ye handle a blade." The older man paused, and there was a hint of reproach in his voice when he added, "Will ye say ye've forgotten your old swordmaster?"

Nagaro's already chilled heart had been sinking steadily. Now his shoulders sagged and his feet again came to a halt. For several heartbeats he made no answer. Then, "No," he said bitterly. "Vothra knows you deserve better than that, Fendar. After all, it's what you taught me, as much as anything, that's kept me alive these past few years." *There was nothing he could do now but try to persuade the man to keep silent...*

"I'm glad t' hear ye say that, Leyel." Fendar sounded quite sincere.

"I always hoped ye were alive somewhere, in spite of everything they said... that ye'd managed to get away somehow. I saw ye once, at that sword tourney—at the palace—looking like something carved out o' wood. What did they *do* to ye, lad?"

"*I don't want to talk about it!*" The words were jerked from him. Nagaro forced down a flood of emotion. He was not going to talk about his ordeal under the will-enslaving drug. He still couldn't make out the swordmaster's face in the gloom, and he was grateful that his own must be equally unreadable. "I don't wish to be known, Fendar," he said desperately. "Please don't use—*that name*—again. And promise me you won't reveal my secret!"

"Well... all right, then." Fendar sounded taken aback. "Ye have my word, in Vothra's name. I'll keep it close. I guess I can see why ye'd want it that way—"

"Don't even say you know me. It... could be dangerous."

Fendar nodded. "I... think I understand," he said carefully. "But it's a hard thing, not being able to claim the best pupil I ever had."

At that, Nagaro forced a bitter laugh. "You never called me *that* before."

Fendar laughed then as well. "It doesn't do for a man t' think too much of himself—" He broke off, then lowered his voice and muttered, "Here comes Lord Kuran, lookin' for me."

Abruptly Fendar stuck out his hand, and Nagaro had just enough presence of mind to take it.

The swordmaster pumped Nagaro's hand vigorously. "Ye've done a fine job with the new recruits," he declared in a loud, jovial voice. "I'll be wanting ye t' work with me some, at the beginning, of course—'til I've got a feel for them." He slapped Nagaro on the back then, and said, "Good luck t' ye, lad!" Then he turned and strode off to meet the approaching hooded figure, whose stature and manner of movement identified him as the Lord of the Fleet.

Nagaro made his escape in the opposite direction, stumbling a little because his legs were shaking.

*

Kuran wasted no time after intercepting his new employee. "There you are, Master Fendar," he said crisply. "Let's get out of this rain. I've a few matters to discuss and my study will do nicely."

Fendar shrugged. "As ye wish, My Lord."

Kuran promptly set off, leading the way, but as he walked, he turned to the other man and said in a low voice, "Well, you said you wished to cross blades with him, and I'm anxious to hear what you've learned."

Fendar coughed. "I'm sorry t' disappoint ye, My Lord," he began uncomfortably. "The man clearly was trained by a master of the Northern

School. He answered the routine moves as ye'd expect for one with that training. But I'm afraid I can't tell ye more than that."

Kuran glanced sharply at the swordmaster's hooded face. "Can't? *Or won't?*"

"My Lord, I don't understand—" Fendar began, innocently.

They had reached the covered porch at the door of Kuran's quarters, and the light of an oil lamp hanging there illuminated both men's faces. Kuran paused, his black eyes boring into Fendar. "*You* are a master of the Northern School, if I recall."

"Ah... yes... there are a fair number of us..."

"Oh come on, man! '*Good luck t' ye, lad!*'" Kuran quite accurately mimicked the swordmaster's parting remark to Nagaro. "You can't say you don't know him!"

"*My Lord, I*—" Fendar writhed.

"Asked you to keep mum, did he?"

"*I*—" Fendar hesitated, then abruptly hung his head. "My Lord, I gave him my word."

Kuran studied the swordmaster for several seconds, then sighed. "Well then," he said, "I won't ask you to break it. But there's one thing I'd like an honest answer to: Can you swear you know nothing against the man? No misdeeds he's trying to hide?"

"No, no, My Lord, nothing like that! By Vothra's Eyes and Ears, I swear it!" Fendar's relief was palpable.

"Ah. *Good.*" Kuran turned the handle and opened the door. With a gesture, he ushered the other man inside. "And if the circumstances were to *change* in the future—with respect to you having given your word—I trust you'd feel you could confide in me?"

"Well, aye," Fendar said quickly. "Of *course*, My Lord."

3: Vell Sobring

Nagaro blundered ahead, his head down against the rain. He felt sick, and his thoughts spun wildly. He started violently when Taru and Pavo suddenly materialized directly in front of him out of the gloom.

Taru put out a hand to stop his friend. "Nagaro! Where are ye going?"

"I don't know... to my quarters—"

"No!" Taru gripped his arm. "Come t' the dining hall—"

"He *recognized* me, Taru! I had to beg him not to tell!"

"Did he promise not to?"

"Well, *ye-es*... He gave me his word, but—"

Pavo spoke. "Then it is go to be all right." The young Hashteip sounded calm and steady, though Nagaro couldn't see his face in the gathering dark and pelting rain. "Taru have told me this is man who taught you to fight with sword," Pavo added. "But if he have promised not to tell, it is go to be all right."

"*He said I couldn't change the way I move!*" Fendar's damning words echoed in Nagaro's head.

"Well, what if ye can't?" Taru demanded. "He's surely the only one who knows how ye used t' move... *back then*. Now, come on!" He tugged at Nagaro's sleeve.

Nagaro shook him off. Taru was probably right, but he didn't want to be among other people right now. He ran a hand distractedly through his hair, knocking his hood askew and having to pull it back up again as he felt rain on his face. "I just want to get away..." he muttered "...go to my quarters"

"Ye mustn't do that, Nagaro!" Taru insisted. "If ye don't come t' the dining hall, they'll all wonder why."

"You could tell them I'm ill—"

"After a match like *that?* They'd never believe it! Right now, no one thinks there's anything amiss. All they know is ye just bested Kuran's new swordmaster, and they think it's a fine joke on Lord Kuran. Now, come on! Ye'll feel better for a cup o' hot sothiril."

Nagaro still didn't like it, but what Taru said did make sense, and his panic was ebbing in the face of his friends' confidence. So he gave in.

When they entered the dining hall shortly thereafter it was to cheers and shouts of "*Captain Nagaro!*" And, as little as he wanted the attention, Nagaro did find it reassuring to hear the name he'd chosen for himself being uttered on every side.

The three friends got plates of food and made for their usual seats at one end of the dining hall, a long room full of rows of heavy tables with a rough-hewn timber ceiling and smoky oil lamps.

Hot sothiril did in fact help, and Nagaro found that he'd recovered enough to actually have an appetite. Throughout the meal, he was interrupted at intervals by men coming over to shake his hand and speak to him, and it got easier each time.

Towards the end of the meal, he looked up to find there was a tall, broad-shouldered young Leithian, with handsome features and a blond mustache, standing over him. The man stuck out his hand. "Captain Nagaro! Well met. I'm Vell Sobring, and I have to say that was a first-rate trick—disarming the new swordmaster. Absolutely brilliant!"

Nagaro took the hand of Lord Bron's son, managing to murmur something suitably polite. He couldn't recall having seen Vell in the Fleet Compound in the days since his arrival and wasn't particularly pleased to be doing so now. The man's father had been one of those charged with keeping Leyel Virden under control, and Nagaro had also known Vell from that time as a brash, lanky youth with a penchant for pranks. The young Leithian had gotten a bit heavier in the course of seven years, though he was still distinctly shy of his father's massive proportions.

Vell released Nagaro's hand, still talking. "—just returned from Sobring Hold—why we haven't met. There were matters to deal with concerning the succession—"

Nagaro belatedly remembered what Lord Kuran had told him the previous spring concerning his one-time keeper, Lord Bron. "I beg your pardon," he interjected. "I've neglected to offer my condolences on the death of your father."

Vell acknowledged this with an inclination of his head. "You're very kind," he said easily. "It was an honorable death—wounds taken on the field of battle. We all should be so fortunate as to die so well, for I'm sure he rides with Kroneg if there's any justice. But, speaking of riding, I'm glad to have shaken the hand of the man they tell me has tamed my father's horse."

"What? You mean Thunder-Heels?" Nagaro was startled by the abrupt change of subject. He'd first encountered Thunder-Heels the previous spring, and had renewed the acquaintance after joining the Fleet, since the steel-gray stallion was stabled in the Fleet Compound. "*Tamed* isn't the right word," he added hastily. "Say rather, *gentled*. And I wouldn't have had to do anything if someone hadn't mistreated the poor beast—something involving a lead rein, I think."

Vell laughed. "That would be my uncle. I could have told him that beating the animal about the head with a riding whip while holding him on a short rein wasn't the way to master the brute. But words are mostly wasted on Uncle Grimbold. I imagine he thought it a good joke to send the animal down here to the Fleet as a 'gift'—a horse for Kuran's stables that no one could ride! But now Kuran has the last laugh, thanks to you. Well done, man." Vell laughed again.

Nagaro managed a pained smile. He found nothing at all humorous about anything that involved abusing an animal. "I must say you don't seem overly fond of your uncle," he said, to turn the subject.

Vell sobered. "Truth to tell, I'm not," he replied. "And it's not because the lordship went to him instead of me. I didn't want it—not *yet*, anyway. It sounds like a great lot of bother, and I'd much rather keep sailing with the Fleet for a while. I just don't think Uncle Grimbold will do Sobring Hold much good as its Lord, that's all."

"Ah, I see." Nagaro considered this. Vell sounded sincere and the Leithian probably *was* too young to find the responsibilities of governing a Hold very attractive. And it was also true that a man who didn't know how to take care of a horse might not take good care of a Hold. It did say something, too, about Vell that he had such a concern for his Hold. Nagaro was trying to think how to gracefully end the conversation when Vell abruptly gave a little start.

"But what's *this*?" the Leithian exclaimed, with the air of someone who has just turned over a stone and found something a bit nasty.

Following the other man's gaze, Nagaro discovered that it was fastened on Pavo. He immediately stiffened. He had seen this kind of reaction to Pavo before, though it had become infrequent since the Fleet men had come to know the young Hashtep. But Vell was only newly returned to the Fleet Compound and had apparently only just noticed Pavo's existence.

"Pavo Maat is my second mate," Nagaro said rather pointedly.

"You've a *Mahuk* for a second mate? *One of the enemy?*"

Pavo had been regarding Vell with narrowed eyes in a stonily impassive countenance. Now he chose to speak. "My people are called *Hashtep*, not Mahuk," he said calmly. "Those one you call 'enemy' are Mautep. You would say 'warlord.' Mautep sometime make Hashtep be slave. That is what happened to me."

Vell gaped. "Kroneg's blood! He speaks our tongue!"

Nagaro smiled the kind of smile he usually reserved for men standing at the other end of his sword. "Pavo Maat is also my *friend*. He and I spent several months chained to the same bench on a Mahuk war galley. He's never been *your* enemy any more than he's been mine."

"Your pardon! Your pardon!" Vell had the grace to be embarrassed. "I had no idea!"

"Obviously." Nagaro gave the other man an outwardly gracious nod. "My *other* friend, here—" he gestured to Taru, who inclined his head, covering a broad grin with his hand, "—is my first mate, Taru Nareyo. He has the good fortune, as you see, to be Turowan. It was Taru and his family who took me in when I was in need—"

He continued to hold the Leithian pinned in conversation until the salt was gently massaged into the wound. Then he let the man go. He felt considerably better after that, feeling he might have helped Vell learn something without being unnecessarily cruel about it.

*

Half an hour later, the three friends left the dining hall, walking across the compound towards Nagaro's quarters through darkness and drizzle.

They'd been disappointed to find that they weren't allowed to all lodge together, despite the shortage of barracks. Taru and Pavo shared a two-room suite in one of several buildings set aside for officers, but Nagaro, as a captain, was housed alone in a three-room suite in a building on what was called "Captain's Row". Nagaro's rooms weren't large, and were furnished very simply, but Taru had still declared the suite "a sight too grand for one man." Since Nagaro clearly had more room than he needed, the three friends had taken to meeting in his quarters when off duty. This behavior occasioned a bit of eye-rolling from some of the high-born officers, but no one had raised any formal objection.

Taru was still savoring Vell's discomfiture as they walked. "Ye surely taught him a thing or two," he said. "And I'll wager it felt good doing it, consid'ring what his father did t' ye!"

Nagaro hunched his shoulders under his cloak. "I don't hold the son responsible for the father's sins, Taru," he said seriously. "But the truth is, Vell had some of his own."

And then, of course, both Taru and Pavo wanted to know what *that* meant, and Nagaro had to explain that as Leyel Virden he had been an easy target and frequent victim of Vell's pranks. Having just finished successfully dealing with the young Leithian, he actually felt up to augmenting his explanation with several painful examples of the younger Vell's tricks before they reached the small porch in front of the door to his quarters.

He stuck his key into the lock and let them all into the front room, crossing quickly to the fireplace where he used a match from the bundle on the mantle to light a candle. The flame revealed a sitting room with unadorned wooden walls, a bare varnished floor, and rustic furnishings upholstered in shades of rust and brown. Nagaro didn't bother making a fire in the fireplace or lighting either of the oil lamps in a room he knew they wouldn't be using. He paused just long enough to draw the curtains across the front window, shutting out the rainy night.

"I do not understand how you can shake his hand and talk so polite to him," Pavo said as he hung up his cloak. "After he have put egg on your chair, and bug in your hair, and have trip you so you fall down and hit your head."

Nagaro sighed as he led the way into the suite's back room, which functioned as a combined kitchen, dining room, and study. There he used the candle to light the large oil lamp that hung from a central ceiling beam. "Vell was being more thoughtless than cruel," he said, moving to the fireplace and crouching down to kindle a fire. "He had no idea what his father was doing... or what I really was... that I could *feel* the laughter..."

The fireplace occupied the wall to the right of the door, and there was a writing desk and chair immediately to the other side of it. The other furnishings consisted of a table with four chairs in the middle of the room, as well as a cupboard and shelves, and a sink and washstand under the back window. The suite's third room, the bedchamber, was reached by a door opposite the fireplace.

Pavo went to draw the curtains across the back window that looked out on a tiny fenced garden. "But when you fall down, you say you have hurt your head very bad," he pointed out, as he returned to take a seat at the table.

Nagaro had just coaxed a flame from the split wood and kindling, and a hint of pine and wood smoke began to scent the room. As he stood up, he fingered the scar on his right temple, just under his hair. "It knocked me unconscious," he said grimly. "I was out for hours. But I only fell because of the... *the drug*... because I couldn't catch myself..." He jerked his hand away from the scar and took a breath to ease a sudden tightness in his chest as he remembered the helpless horror of the that fall. "Vell didn't know... and he stopped his tricks... after that, so I think he felt bad about it."

Taru had picked up a canvas bag from a shelf and now sat down at the table across from Pavo. He began unpacking the bag's contents: a folding game board and a set of carved wooden pieces for playing *kasadrin*, or King's Men. "What was Vell even doing at the palace?" he asked.

Nagaro had managed to steady himself. "Just visiting." He crossed to the writing desk, where he set down the candle before pulling out the padded desk chair. He sat down on it back-to-front, straddling it to face his friends, gripping the chair-back with his hands. "There were always fine folk visiting the palace—for feasts and dinners..." His voice trailed as suppressed memories of the things he'd endured at those feasts and dinners began to edge their way to the surface.

Taru looked up from the game board, watching Nagaro's face. "But that's all in the past," he said quickly. "And those fine folk at the victory feast last spring didn't recognize ye—nor did Vell, for that matter."

Nagaro shivered. "That's true," he conceded. "But people like Vell aren't the ones I need to worry about. It's the ones like Fendar—"

"Who promised not to tell!" Taru interjected. "And he surely doesn't mean ye any harm, even though ye bested him in front o' Kuran."

Nagaro frowned. "No, he doesn't mean me harm, but I'm afraid he'll let something slip! Like calling me 'lad' the way he did today."

Taru frowned. "Then tell him not to," he said. "Honestly, Nagaro, ye worry too much."

Pavo had been arranging the playing pieces for a game, but now he stopped and turned to face Nagaro. "How many people are there like Fendar, who know you from time before?" he asked.

Nagaro drew a breath and took a tally. "Besides Fendar, there was Chula the gardener... Thorlan the stableman... and Hinda the cook—at the house at Averwin. And there was old Luka the medicine woman who used to come every autumn. And three families of house-holders. A dozen people all together... though Bodano's children were very little and probably wouldn't remember me."

Taru paused with a playing piece in his hand. "That's all?"

"Well, yes... I mean, there was the Lady Maramine, too, but she's dead—" A shadow crossed Nagaro's heart. "Luka may be dead, too, by now. She was an old woman when I saw her last."

Pavo was studying Nagaro narrowly. "How many of these people maybe will come to Lankura?" he asked.

Nagaro frowned afresh. "Fendar just did—but he always traveled... The rest of them were all settled, living right around Averwin—wherever it was—"

"Ye don't even know where Averwin *was?*" Taru's disbelief was audible.

Nagaro frowned harder. "Not *exactly*... It was a small country estate... not more than a day's ride from Lankura, I think. But I don't know which direction..."

Taru stared at him. "Ye didn't find out when they brought ye here?"

Nagaro went rigid. "I was in a closed coach," he said stonily. "With the windows covered. And I was... unconscious part of the way—" *He didn't remember the beginning of the journey. He'd been unconscious under heskial...* His knuckles whitened as his fingers tightened on the chair back.

"Never mind," Taru said hastily. "The point is, *those* folk won't be coming *here*. Master Fendar is far an' away the most likely t' turn up, which means the worst has already happened. And he's *not* going to tell, so stop fretting!"

Nagaro made a very conscious effort to relax his grip on the chair. "You're right, Taru."

Pavo gave him a sympathetic look. "Do you want to play King Man? Or watch while Taru and I play it?" he asked."

Nagaro shook his head. "I think I'll read some, first," he said, "to help me relax." He stood up and turned to retrieve a book from the shelf above the desk, then arranged the chair so he wouldn't have his back to his friends while he read, and sat down on it properly.

The book he was reading was titled *Rule of Loros*, and was written by the deceased Pact Signer, Berinar Sundorin. It was a chronicle of the recent history of Edrovir—something that had been missing from the Lady Maramine's library at Averwin. He was nearly at the end and hoped to finish it that evening.

So he turned pages while his friends played King's Men, and for a time the only sounds were the crackling of the fire, the drip of rain from the eaves outside, and the tap of game pieces on the hardened leather board accompanied by an occasional muttered comment from one of the players.

When Nagaro finished the book, he set it down with a sigh. "*Pity the poor orphan child... and weep, weep, O Edrovir*," he murmured.

"What is that, Nagaro?" Pavo asked, pausing in his play.

Nagaro emerged from his reverie. "It's a line of poetry from a poem called *Night Falls*," he explained. "Berinar quotes it in his chronicle to show how deeply some Kelorin folk grieved over the deaths of King Tevren and Queen Lindra. "Night Falls" has a double meaning, too: Two people died—that is, fell—at dusk. And many Kelorin folk thought those deaths marked the beginning of a darker time—a falling of night."

"Pavo nodded his shaggy head. "They are beautiful word," he said.

"I say it's a lot o' rubbish," observed Taru. "It was a terrible thing, o' course, someone murdering the king an' queen. But the world's gone on just the same. The sun still shines."

Pavo shook his head. "You do not have any poetry in your heart, Taru. That is what is wrong with you."

"Poetry is for women!"

Pavo ignored this. He turned back to Nagaro. "Do you know any more of *Night Fall* poem?"

Nagaro shook his head. "There isn't any more of it in the book, and I don't have any books of poetry. I confess that poetry has never really interested me."

"Ye see!" Taru said triumphantly.

Nagaro smiled faintly. "It was a *man* who wrote the poem, Taru."

Again Pavo ignored Taru. "I know you like best to read history, Nagaro," he said. "Because it teach you thing. What do you learn from this book?"

Nagaro grew thoughtful. "I'm surprised that Kelorin folk were so impressed by Tevren being Darion's son. Kelorin tradition says leaders should be chosen for their ability, not their birth, but it's clear that many among the Council of Lords—including most of the Kelorin—cast their *krits* for Tevren because they expected him to be a great king like his father. They couldn't have had much reason to think so besides his birth. He was only twenty-six and hadn't had a chance to do very much in his life."

Pavo frowned. "You do not think son is like father?"

Nagaro frowned in his turn. "A son *may* be like his father—but not necessarily. Taru's father was quite content to be a fisherman and would be astonished to see his son a sea warrior. And Vell Sobring isn't very much like *his* father either..." Nagaro's voice trailed.

Vell's father had been large and florid, and not much given to jests as far as Nagaro could remember. His memory of Bron Sobring consisted mainly of being caught and pinned by the man while a bladder-thorn was stuck into his arm. He shuddered.

In the silence that followed his words, they all heard the sound of three tentative knocks on the front door.

"Who could that be?" Nagaro wondered as he rose and picked up the candle.

Quickly crossing the unlit sitting room, he unbolted the front door and swung it open. A light rain was still falling and the light of a lantern that hung under the eaves a dozen feet to his right made a golden haze of the tiny drops. Its light also illuminated the face of a boy of twelve or thirteen who was standing at Nagaro's doorstep. The lad had flung his hood back, uncovering fair hair. The blue-and-white livery of the palace messenger service wasn't entirely covered by his cloak. He carried a leather pouch slung over his shoulder and clutched an envelope in his hand.

"Are ye Captain Nagaro?" The boy was slightly breathless and his eyes shown in the lantern light.

"Yes."

"I've a message for ye, then, Zirda." Eagerly, the boy held out the envelope. "It's an invitation t' the celebration of the Festival of the Harvest Moon—at the palace," he added helpfully. "She said t' be sure I got your answer, Zirda—My Lady the princess did, I mean."

Nagaro took the envelope and examined it, noting that someone— probably the guard at the gate of the compound—had scrawled his address, "14, Captain's Row", on the folded parchment. He broke the wax seal that held it closed, and scanned the little square of parchment inside. The engraved message was a standard invitation made in the names of the entire royal family. There were handwritten words at the bottom however.

They said: "*I hope you will come—Nevien Harlind.*"

He swallowed. He hadn't expected this. He had managed to have exactly three conversations with the Princess Nevien inside of a week, the previous spring. They had spoken, then, of continuing the beginnings of a friendship, but that was now months ago, and as a mere captain in the Royal Fleet he hadn't thought there would be much opportunity. The festival was just days away and he'd assumed he would be celebrating it in the Fleet dining hall with the other men.

He realized the boy was waiting for an answer. "I suppose there's no reason I can't go..." he said slowly. "Do you wish to wait while I write an answer?"

The boy grinned broadly. "There's no need, Zirda! I can tell My Lady what ye said. I'll be sure to remember!" He touched his forehead in a quick gesture of respect, pulled up his hood, and dashed through the drizzle to the next door, where he pulled the hood off again as he knocked.

Nagaro thought he understood. He pulled his door shut and walked back to the dining room.

"What was that about?" Taru asked without looking up from the game board.

For answer, Nagaro tossed the invitation onto the table, and stood chewing his lip. He had enjoyed talking to the princess. He wouldn't at all mind doing so again, but she would probably be too busy now that he was no longer the "most honored guest"...

Taru puzzled painfully over the letters on the parchment, then looked up frowning. "The princess!" he said with obvious annoyance. "Adding her two rins. Just being *polite* again, is she?"

Nagaro frowned in answering annoyance. "The messenger boy went on to knock on the next door in the row, so I imagine all the captains are getting these."

Pavo, who couldn't read, had been looking from one to the other. "What does writing say?" he asked.

Taru told him, then turned back to Nagaro. "Ye're not going, are ye?"

Nagaro shrugged. "I couldn't think of any reason to say no."

"Why d' ye need a *reason?* Couldn't ye just say it?"

Nagaro frowned. "It would be rude to turn down a royal invitation without a good reason."

"But you will miss feast here with all of sea warrior," Pavo pointed out. "Taru and I will be here, and you will be at palace."

Nagaro sighed. "I know," he said. "And I don't expect I'll enjoy it much. I mean, it won't be like the last time. Now that I'm just one of Lord Kuran's captains I don't expect anyone will pay much attention to me—which is all right—but I don't care for all the fuss and bother. And I don't like being in the Great Hall, either."

Taru's annoyance turned to sympathy at the look on Nagaro's face. "At least they'll have better food," he said. "I'd put up with a peck o' fuss an' bother for another meal from those kitchens!"

Nagaro shrugged as he picked up the invitation. "Well, I said I'd go, so I'm going," he said. "Now let me watch you finish your game."

He pulled out a chair at the table and sat down.

Taru picked up a playing piece and made his move. Pavo frowned long in concentration before making his.

Taru won that game, as he often did, his somewhat devious nature seeming to give him an advantage over both of his friends. Nagaro played the next game against Taru, and was beaten, after which he played against Pavo, and won. So the evening sped.

4: Festival Of The Harvest Moon

On the evening of the Festival of the Harvest Moon, Nagaro presented himself at the royal palace in his full Fleet uniform: pants and tirka of midnight blue over a crisp white shirt and with his usual black boots. He surrendered his sword to the young guard, Delvin, in the entrance hall, since he couldn't claim noble blood, and followed the other guests to the Great Hall. There Queen Semorel, flanked by two of her fluttering laidies, greeted each new arrival at the door. She was regal in silk of autumn gold with her dark hair arranged to perfection.

"Ah, the gallant Captain Nagaro!" The queen extended a hand like pale porcelain. "One of my daughter's special guests, I believe."

Nagaro winced inwardly at the queen's description of him as he took the hand and kissed it lightly. Semorel looked better than she had the previous spring at the time of the Mautep attack on the palace, though the color in her cheeks was clearly tinted powder.

She smiled indulgently as she retrieved her hand. "You do that so *well*, Captain. You're very well brought-up. And you look so dashing in that uniform!"

He felt his face grow hot. "You're very kind, My Lady Queen," he murmured, bowing. There was probably nothing he could do to lose the queen's favor, he reflected, even if he'd wanted to. Tonight he was gallant, well brought-up, and dashing. Last summer he'd been merely gallant after he'd located the missing princess and returned her to her distraught mother. In the process he'd had to kill a Mautep warrior who'd been hiding in one of Nevien's wardrobes.

Nagaro made his escape from the queen and hurried across the hall. The vast, high-ceilinged room was thronged with richly-dressed folk and decked in autumn colors of red, orange, and gold. It was liberally festooned with harvest-related things—garlands of braided straw, strings of apples, and the like—but he'd seen such decorations before. His eyes were on some tables, glimpsed through the crowd, surrounded by figures in dark blue Fleet uniforms. He was thinking of the words *special guest* and daring to hope that he might have a chance to talk to Nevien after all.

He'd been a bit dismayed to discover that his immediate neighbor in Captain's Row had only received an individual invitation because he was engaged to one of the princess's ladies. Most of the other captains would also be in attendance, but only by virtue of a blanket invitation delivered to Lord Kuran that allowed the Lord of the Fleet to bring several dozen guests.

Kuran had merely chuckled upon learning that Nagaro had been singled out. "Well," he had said, "I suppose Nevien couldn't be sure there'd be room on my list after including all the high-born Fleet men."

When Nagaro had then asked why members of the noble houses were given precedence, Kuran had explained the situation. Very few common folk were invited to the palace for the Festival of the Harvest Moon, but every man and woman of noble birth who happened to be in Lankura would expect an invitation and feel slighted if they didn't get one. This caused a difficulty for high-born Fleet men. They normally accepted being given no special favors as sea warriors, and didn't use their titles as such, but being excluded from a feast at the palace was for many of them unthinkable. The blanket invitation got around this by placing the matter at Kuran's discretion—with the understanding that he'd have some explaining to do if he left any high-born Fleet man off his list.

Nagaro had found the arrangement offensive and had said so, to which Kuran had replied with a shrug that the number of spaces on his list was usually generous enough to allow him to include all of his captains and commanders and almost as many commoners as high-born.

The upshot of all of this was that the princess had apparently specifically wanted Nagaro to be there. She was undoubtedly somewhere in the room, too, and would look for him at those distant Fleet tables. The Great Hall was already crowded and filled with a babble of voices, although the guests were still arriving and the feast wouldn't begin for some time. The people were generally milling about or admiring the many "Towers of Plenty" arrayed on tables and stands set about the hall. These last were a traditional feature of the season's festivities, fanciful sculptures—often several feet high—formed of various fruit and vegetable materials.

Nagaro was not interested in the towers, but intent upon threading his way through the crowd as unobtrusively as possible. When someone abruptly stepped directly into his path, he pulled up short to avoid colliding with the man. He'd begun to murmur an apology before he met the man's eyes, but when he did lock gazes, the words froze in his mouth. He was looking into deep-socketed eyes—black, fierce, and cold—flanking a hawk's beak of a nose in a swarthy face. With a cold wash of horror, he realized that he was staring into the face of Dreigen, the King's Lore Master, the chief architect of his ordeal under heskial. His heart all but stopped in his chest.

Dreigen, however, merely raked him with a chilly glance and turned away with a disdainful curl of his lip, to continue his prowling glide across the polished floor.

Nagaro managed to breathe again. His heart, that had seemed to pause, began hammering against his ribs as if trying to escape. A wave swept over him of mingled nausea and relief. As unpleasant as Dreigen's look had been, it clearly had not been the look of a predator rediscovering its prey.

"There you are, Captain! I was afraid you'd decided not to come."

Nagaro instantly recognized the princess's voice and was extremely glad to hear the warmth in it. Feeling sick, and being surrounded by strangers, what he needed at that moment was a friend. He turned to acknowledge Nevien's approach and found that she was already quite close. Her smile at first was all pleasure in seeing him—until she caught his expression and the beaming glow in her emerald eyes was replaced by concern.

Leaning close and lowering her voice, she asked, "What's wrong, Captain? Are you ill?"

"A little," he confessed, considering honesty the wisest course since his distress was apparently so obvious.

"Here," she said, taking him by the arm and drawing him to a seat at the end of a nearby empty table.

He pulled out the chair and gratefully sank onto it. She took the chair opposite, still watching his face. "I could order you a coach," she said solicitously.

He hastily shook his head. "There's no need for that, My Lady. It's already passing." *Like the effect of an old wound. Several dozen of them, actually...* Unconsciously he rubbed the inner surface of his left forearm. He didn't wish to draw attention to himself by leaving before the party even started, and his words were true in any case. His heart rate was returning to normal and the nausea was ebbing. The princess was all kindness and understanding, and he knew he needn't worry about meeting Dreigen again that evening. The Lore Master's usual pattern had always been to come to feasts only long enough to obtain some of the food, if he came at all.

"Something bothered me about the way that man looked at me," he added, since Nevien was still studying him questioningly. "The hawk-faced one... His eyes were so cold." Making the admission to her felt completely natural. In fact, he was finding it just as easy to talk to her as he had the previous spring, as if no time had passed at all.

"Dreigen?" Nevien's concern eased visibly. "Well, you're not alone there. I don't know anyone who likes Dreigen. It's sad, really. Personally I feel sorry for the man."

Nagaro stared at her. "*Sorry* for him?" He couldn't keep the shock out of his voice. "My Lady, why?"

Nevien sighed. Her green eyes clouded. "Because he's incapable of any sort of caring," she said. "I tried talking to him years ago—to draw him out. But there's no warmth in him. I don't believe he can actually feel anything. *For* other people, I mean, or *from* other people. He feels pride, and pleasure in his work, and anger when slighted. But he'll never know what it means even to have a friend. Can you imagine what a poor, sad, empty life that would be?"

Nagaro gazed at the princess in astonishment, trying to imagine what that conversation had been like—between Nevien and Dreigen. And who but Nevien Harlind would try to understand such a man? *Had the conversation come before, or after, or during the period when he'd been Dreigen's puppet?* Hastily he jerked his thoughts out of that noose. "No," he said, in answer to her question. "I don't think I *can* imagine it. But if he can't feel it, he doesn't know what he's missing, surely, does he?"

She frowned. "Well, I suppose not," she said. "But it's still terrible. I wondered how he could have gotten that way—whether it was something inborn, or because of something that happened to him. So I made some inquiries, and the answer could be that it's a little of both." She stopped, biting her lip.

"What do you mean?" Nagaro was curious in spite of himself.

She looked down at her hands. "I never like to think that anyone shouldn't have been born," she said quietly. "But if ever there were such a one, it's Dreigen. At least it would have been better if he'd never been *conceived.*"

Nagaro waited, in silence, for her to continue. Dreigen had liked to talk aloud while waiting for the heskial trance to reach just the right stage... talking to his victim...

The princess seemed to collect herself. She looked up into his eyes. "Dreigen's mother was a farmer's daughter, a young Kelorin woman—a girl really," she said, speaking quickly as if that made it easier. "She lived near the border of Jinara, and one day a... a Jinari man... caught her when she was alone, and carried her across the border. He held her prisoner for months... raped her over and over. Until finally she got big with child and he wearied of her and let her go, and she crawled back to her family in pain and shame." Nevien paused, then added, "So Dreigen's mother never loved him. Who could blame her? And no one else wanted him, knowing how he'd been gotten."

Nagaro was staring without seeing. Dreigen had said he was a fatherless bastard... that his mother had sold him into service to an apothecary when he was a child. Nagaro had wondered about that last part... but only a little. "What happened to the Jinari man?" he asked. "Was he held responsible for the child he'd fathered?"

Nevien frowned. "The folk of his village put him to death for the crime," she said. "But they wouldn't take the child. They said it was their god's will that the girl had gotten pregnant, so she must bear the child and keep it. I must say I don't think much of such a god—or at least of men who put such words into their god's mouth!"

Nagaro shook his head. "How could anyone insist that a woman raise the child of a man who had so abused her?" he wondered, then added, "But this is a holiday celebration. Let's talk about something more pleasant." He cast about and said, "I thought your mother looked much better than when I last saw her."

Nevien appeared glad to turn the subject. "Yes," she said. "Master Ambras, the healer, gave her another dose of his nasty concoction. It always makes her quite ill for several weeks and then she's better for a time." A shadow crossed her face. "Unfortunately, she seems to need the medicine more and more often." She sighed, then managed a smile that was almost convincing, and added. "You look very fine in that uniform."

He shrugged uncomfortably. "I'm grateful to have it to wear on such an occasion," he told her. "I've nothing else suitable, and no desire to buy something I'd have no other use for. I really don't care for satin—"

Nevien smiled archly. "You don't? *Really?*"

Belatedly he realized that she was wearing a white satin gown embroidered in green and gold. He'd been too distracted to notice. "I mean... to *wear*..." he added hastily. "*Myself*, that is."

This time the princess's merry peel of laughter was quite genuine. "I knew what you meant," she said quickly when she saw him stiffen.

He relaxed. The gown was actually quite lovely. And several tresses of Nevien's honey-colored hair had been braided and coiled in a crown held in place by small combs carved from mother-of-pearl. The effect was really stunning and he knew he was remiss for not having complimented her on her appearance. Anything he said now, though, would sound forced. Instead, he spoke the other thought that her attire brought to his mind: "I see you're out of mourning."

"Yes," she said, but a shadow crossed her face. "Only just. I begged for six months instead of the usual three, because I wanted more time before the courtship dance began again. I think my request was granted more out of respect for Elyan's memory than out of concern for me."

"How soon will the courtships begin then?"

She smiled ruefully. "I expect, tonight. I already know who some of the suitors will be."

"Who, My Lady?" He couldn't help asking.

Nevien began to tick off names on her fingers. "Well, there's Lothard Hurn—everyone knows he wants the crown—and Devral Sedras, who will do it to spite Lothard. And young Nile..."

Nagaro frowned. "Isn't Devral one of the Signers of the Pact of Lankura?" he asked. "I thought they weren't allowed to seek the crown."

Nevien's brows came together to make a little line above the bridge of her nose. "He is," she said. "And they aren't. But marrying me doesn't automatically put anyone in line for the crown. I just would never be queen if I married him. But it's all political. Lothard is the son of Reith Hurn, a Pact Signer who was killed in battle several years ago. Lothard thought he should have his father's place as a Signer because he was the new lord of the House of Hurn, and the Leithian Faction agreed, of course. That would have made three Leithian Signers to match the three Kelorin ones. But the Kelorin Faction said Lothard was too young and inexperienced for such serious responsibility since he was not yet twenty-two at the time."

Nagaro nodded. He remembered the death of Reith Hurn. It had happened while he was living with Taru's family in Wotana. Even at the time, he'd thought that having no established way to deal with such deaths was a serious flaw in the Pact. "I remember there was a threat of war," he said. "But before anything could happen, one of the three Kelorin Pact Signers, Berinar Sundorin, 'conveniently' took sick and died."

She shot him a look. "Yes," she said. "And there's many who say it was no accident that it was Berinar. There was no one more opposed to giving Lothard a place among the Signers than he. But his death did at least set things even. There would either have had to be two new Signers—one Leithian and one Kelorin—or else none."

"And they settled on none."

Nevien nodded. She leaned across the table and lowered her voice. "If you want the truth, the two surviving Leithian Signers don't like Lothard any more than the Kelorin ones do. But ever since Lothard was denied a place among the Pact Signers, he's been determined to have the crown instead. So he wants to marry me. And Lord Devral has said he'll wed me himself before he sees that happen."

"And how do *you* feel about it, My Lady?" Nagaro's concern had been mounting the more he heard. "What do *you* think of Lothard Hurn? And isn't Lord Devral rather old?"

Nevien glanced over her shoulder. "Don't repeat this," she said, "but I find Lothard arrogant and offensive. And although Devral is respected for his deeds, he's older than my father. If he hadn't been widowed two years ago, he'd be in no position to come courting."

Nagaro frowned. "What about the other man you mentioned? I didn't catch the name."

"Nile," she said. "Nile Fendred."

Nagaro started. "The son of Kale Fendred?" he asked, somewhat shocked. "He must be very young, and why does *he* want to marry you?"

She shrugged. "I don't know that he does. He's being put forward by the more moderate among the Leithian Faction—those who don't like Lothard. He's young, and as green as a new leaf. And from what I hear, quite harmless. But that's the best that can be said of him."

Nagaro stared across the table at Nevien Harlind. She had spoken quite calmly, almost resignedly. "Is that *all there are*, My Lady?" he asked, unable to keep the dismay from his voice.

She sat, toying with a stray lock of her hair. "Those are the most certain names," she said. "There are a few other rumors, but they're no more than that, and not to be repeated."

Nagaro leaned across the table, holding her eyes. "Who do you favor, My Lady?" he asked.

She didn't flinch under his gaze, but she shrugged dismissively. "Princesses don't fall in love."

Nagaro frowned. "I don't see why not. A princess is a woman, after all."

This time she laughed. "Oh, *well*," she said. "I suppose a princess *might* fall in love, but it wouldn't be wise, so I don't permit myself the luxury."

Nagaro's frown deepened. He didn't think it was as simple as that, but he didn't feel he should contradict her, so he said, "All the same, My Lady, I would think there must be some men you'd rather wed than others. Who would you have, if you could choose?"

"If I could *choose?*" Nevien considered Nagaro closely, as if trying to discover his motive for questioning her so. "*If* I could choose," she said after a moment, "I'd have to give the matter serious thought. But since I can't choose, it really doesn't matter what I think."

The wrongness of this struck Nagaro so forcefully that he quite forgot to address her by her title. "Well it ought to matter!" he declared. "It ought to matter a great deal! Doesn't your father even consult you about it?"

For an instant Nevien only stared at him. Then she drew herself up. "Of course my father consults me, *Captain*," she said stiffly. "How do you suppose I know the names on the list? And if there were two of equal merit, I'm sure he'd ask me which one I preferred!"

Nagaro felt the sting in her tone. "I beg your pardon, My Lady," he said quickly. "It's only that I *thought*, well, if there were someone you favored who hadn't put himself forward, perhaps I might speak to the man..." His voice trailed off, for she was looking at him with the most odd intensity.

Nevien was, in fact, quite astounded. She could read nothing in Nagaro's eyes but earnest concern. It truly seemed that this man was only interested in her happiness and that he meant to do her a service if he could. This was, in her experience, rather novel behavior—at least for a young bachelor. "Your thought is kindly meant, I'm sure, Captain," she said carefully. "But it could never be so simple as that."

Nagaro sighed. "Oh, very probably not," he conceded. "But there might be something that could be done, and I'd like to be your friend if I could."

"Ah! There he is!" It was Kuran's voice, interrupting from fairly close at hand. "And your daughter as well, My Lord."

Nagaro twisted in his chair to see Lord Kuran and King Elgurn approaching, shoulder to shoulder. Knowing what was expected of him, he promptly rose and bowed to Elgurn, murmuring, "My Lord King." Since he knew Nevien was watching, he made it one of his better bows.

"Captain." The king acknowledged him with one word and a nod.

Nagaro couldn't help noticing how Elgurn's glance shifted between him and the princess. The king's pale blue eyes, as usual, revealed little of his thoughts, but the stiffness of his demeanor suggested disapproval. Nagaro felt a surge of anger—that this man who had gone to such cruel lengths to secure the marriage of Leyel Virden to his daughter nearly eight years ago should now take exception to his merely speaking to her. He half expected the king to make some comment, but it was Kuran who spoke.

"Captain," he said, "I've a matter for your attention. If you would join me at our table?"

Nagaro answered, "Of course, My Lord." He bade Nevien farewell with the words, "My Lady Princess," accompanied by a gracious bow. To the king he gave a parting bow that was somewhat less gracious. As he and Kuran moved away, he clearly heard the king say, "Come, Nevien, we mustn't neglect our other guests."

*

Nevien made no response to her father's comment as she rose and took his arm. Elgurn gave her a probing glance. "Why is it," he asked, "that both my wife and my daughter seem to find that man so charming?"

"Charming?" Nevien frowned, thoughtfully. "I wouldn't call him that, exactly, though I suppose there's an element of charm in simple honesty."

The king snorted. "What did he say to you, then, in his *simple honesty?*"

Nevien smiled demurely. "That he wishes to be my friend."

Her father eyed her sharply. "You should be careful of men who say such things, Daughter. Especially men of uncertain birth."

Annoyed now, Nevien frowned. "I think I'm careful enough," she answered. "And I'm sure that he and I both know we can't be more than friends. In fact, I believe he has a lady somewhere since he wears a lady's ring. Really, Father," she added, "There's no need to look so askance. He seems like a man who knows how to be a friend."

"Hmm." Elgurn's response turned thoughtful. "Kuran *did* say that he was the kind of friend he would like to have... Perhaps we *should* cultivate him, just a little..."

*

Nagaro and Kuran seated themselves at one of the Fleet tables, and the older man leaned close to speak confidentially. "I'm sorry to intrude on your holiday," he said in a low voice. "But I want your opinion on a matter I've been discussing with the king and the members of the Council."

"What matter, My Lord?" Nagaro asked, frankly surprised that his opinion should be so valued.

Kuran leaned closer still. "It's been proposed," he said, "that the Royal Fleet make a raid on the capital city of the Mahuk Baar—to answer the recent Mautep attack on Lankura."

Nagaro frowned. "A raid on Sar Tipaal? Emperor Baalkir's capital?"

"Exactly. I believe you've seen the city?"

"I've seen something of the harbor, and the shipyards. And rather a lot of the inside of one of the slave barns."

"Well that's more than I've seen. And it's the shipyard that would be our target. Do you think it's assailable from the harbor?"

Nagaro considered. "If you could get enough ships to the place, it wouldn't be difficult to attack the shipyard. All its physical defenses are on the landward side and the harbor mouth is wide. But I don't like this plan, My Lord."

Kuran crooked an eyebrow. "Why not?"

"Because it punishes the wrong party. It wasn't Baalkir who was responsible for the recent raid on Lankura—nor the one seven years ago, for that matter. Both those attacks were made by Lord Angkat, Baalkir's chief rival."

Kuran looked skeptical. "But surely the more recent attack would have been made on the Emperor's orders."

Nagaro shook his head. "That's not what I heard from the Hashtep slaves we freed this summer, My Lord. Angkat still nurses hopes of displacing Baalkir as Emperor. The first target of his expedition was the gold ports, where he hoped to gain wealth to build up his military strength. Lankura was only attacked when Geldoran foiled the other attempt. And the rumors are that Baalkir wasn't at all pleased about it, except in the sense that Angkat's warriors came home empty-handed and got their noses bloodied into the bargain."

Kuran's brows furrowed. "You're certain of this? You speak their tongue so well?"

Nagaro shrugged diffidently. "I understand more than I speak," he said. "But I keep Pavo at hand as an interpreter when there's something important I wish to understand."

"So you have this information through your Hashtep friend?" Kuran's eyes narrowed.

Nagaro shrugged again. "Some of the finer points I learned from his translation, but I understood enough myself to be confident of the gist of it."

"I see." Kuran frowned. "So your counsel would be what, then? To attack the stronghold of this Lord Angkat instead?"

"It would be more just. Angkat's capital is the port of Ulaad, which is farther south and more difficult to reach. There are shipyards there, as well, but I know nothing more of the place. And there are close to a dozen Mautep warlords, each with a least a few ships at his disposal. So there are a great many little fleets always sailing about."

Kuran grunted. "Is that *all?*" he inquired dryly.

Nagaro earnestly shook his head. "You'd also have to worry about the Emperor's revenge. If you succeeded in burning the shipyard at Sar Tipaal—or any other on the Baar—Baalkir would almost certainly come in force to burn *yours*. And Edrovir has only one shipyard—here at Lankura." Nagaro paused. Kuran was regarding him intently, but with narrowed eyes and a face that betrayed nothing. Nagaro finished with a shrug. "On the whole, I think attacking either port would be rather foolish."

"Indeed?" Kuran's face was still unreadable. "Would you have me say so to Lord Odus Morbern when we discuss his plan in the council?"

Nagaro shifted in his seat but he held the older man's eyes. "My Lord," he said, "you asked my opinion, and it would be the same no matter whose plan it was. But the plan being foolish doesn't mean the one who offered it is a fool. Any man may choose unwisely if he doesn't have all the facts."

Kuran sat regarding him for several long seconds during which Nagaro's gaze didn't falter. Then the older man sighed, bent his head, and rubbed the bridge of his nose. "Well, you've given me fodder for thought," he said. "And I expect you to keep this matter in strictest confidence of course." He raised his eyes again. Looking across the hall, he said suddenly, "But what's this?"

Nagaro turned to follow the older man's gaze.

Two men had stepped out of the crowd, an older one leading, and a younger trailing. As they approached the table where Kuran and Nagaro were seated, Nagaro realized that the older of the two was the same pale-eyed Kelorin who had approached him the last time he'd sat in the Great Hall, a man whose name he couldn't immediately recall. The younger was one of the Fleet's best swordsmen, the young officer named Rastian.

Nagaro's first thought was that the pale-eyed man must have come seeking Kuran, but the man gave the Lord of the Fleet no more than a nod of acknowledgment before turning his attention fully upon Nagaro.

"Zirda," he said, with a perfunctory bow. "May I present my son, Rastian." He gestured to the younger man beside him.

Nagaro blinked. The man's strange pale eyes bored into him, while Rastian gave him what seemed almost an apologetic look and bowed also.

Nagaro rose hastily. "Ah, yes... My Lord," he replied, bowing in his turn, and having enough presence of mind to note that the pale-eyed man wore a sword at his hip. "I'm already acquainted with Rastian—though I didn't realize he was your son." Now that he saw the two men together, the relationship was quite plausible. Though Rastian's eyes weren't as pale as his father's, they were light gray, and there were other similarities in the men's features.

"No matter." The pale-eyed man swept Nagaro's admission aside with a wave of his hand. "But I want you to know that if my son can serve you in any way, you have but to ask."

Nagaro stood, completely at sea, struggling to think what might explain this announcement. All he could imagine was that it somehow had something to do with the sword training. Rastian merely shrugged.

Nagaro cleared his throat. "Well," he ventured, feeling the need to say something, "Certainly Rastian is very skilled with a blade, and he might serve well as an instructor. But I am no longer serving as swordmaster to the Fleet."

"Ah." The pale-eyed man seemed to check himself. His glance flicked quickly from Nagaro to Kuran, who was regarding him quizzically. The pale eyes returned to Nagaro. "I... see," the man said carefully. "Well, doubtless you're glad to be rid of that onerous duty. I commend your good fortune, and may Lokundas send you no ill." Then, turning to Kuran, he added, "Your pardon, My Lord, for interrupting your discourse." And with that, the pale-eyed man gave a quick nod of farewell, turned, and was gone.

Rastian rolled his eyes, offered another shrug and a half-hearted salute, then turned and followed his father.

Kuran coughed. "I didn't know you'd found the task of swordmaster an onerous one," he observed, dryly.

Nagaro wasn't smiling. "Who *is* that man?" he wondered aloud. "This is the second time he's confronted me oddly. The first time I thought he'd mistaken me for someone else, and seen his error, but now I don't know what to think."

Kuran raised an eyebrow. "He is Lord Rastyl Korven."

Nagaro gestured impatiently. "He told me his name the first time, though I confess I'd forgotten it. But a *name* doesn't tell me who a man is! What's his history? What does he do in the world? He seems to think I should know him."

Kuran crooked an eyebrow once more, but then apparently took pity on Nagaro's frustration. "Rastyl Korven," he replied, "is the current Lord of Irvenen Wared, in the far north. It was his mother's Wared, and he was chosen as lord there after the folk were left leaderless. But Rastyl grew up, like his father, in Loros Wared, which no longer exists. It was broken up after the upheaval surrounding the death of King Tevren—who was also the lord of Loros. Rastyl was a very young man at the time. He escaped the general bloodletting by being in Irvenen."

Nagaro still frowned. He knew the general history, and was only mildly interested in this explanation of how Rastyl fit into it. "But what does he want with *me?*" he asked.

Kuran shrugged. "Who can say? Rastyl was always a bit strange, and he's only grown stranger in the years since Tevren's death. The loss hit him hard: Tevren had no closer friend than Rastyl Korven." Kuran sighed. "But there's many who say that Rastyl is seeking support for his man. If he thinks you're a possible recruit, that could lead him to offer you friendship—or service."

"Support for *his man*, My Lord? Do you mean Rastian?"

A bell sounded in the hall at that moment, indicating that dinner would soon be served and Kuran leaned close and lowered his voice as folk began to take their seats. "No," he said. "I mean Darion's grandson, the heir of the House of Loros. There are those who believe that Rastyl has Tevren's son in his keeping, though he's always denied it."

Nagaro lowered his voice as well. "You don't sound as if you believe it, My Lord."

Kuran's shrug was ambivalent. "I asked him about it once, and he denied it to my face. But that would be his best protection, wouldn't it? And Irvenen Wared is wide and wild and sparsely peopled. One could hide a dozen king's heirs in that place." He paused, then added, "But that's enough. Here's Rastian again."

Rastyl's son had indeed returned, this time without his father, and he now seated himself across the table from Nagaro. As he did so, he glanced covertly at Nagaro, and hastily withdrew his gaze when he found Nagaro's eyes on him.

Nagaro would have liked to question the young Kelorin about his father's words, but preferred not to do it publicly. He swept the room with his eyes instead, wondering where Rastyl had gone. He failed to find the pale-eyed lord, but he did catch sight of the princess, and his gaze lingered.

He had found Nevien seated at a table near the head of the hall, near the raised dais. The latter wasn't being used on this occasion. He thought her table was rather oddly arranged, with young women seated all along one side, and young men on the other. The princess was placed at the head of the table across from a petite older Leithian woman with corn-silk hair. One of the young women at the table, a dark-haired Kelorin girl in a gown of dusky rose, was looking in Nagaro's direction, but she dropped her eyes when she felt his gaze.

Nagaro wondered idly who the men and women might be, but he couldn't fathom it, so he went back to scanning for Rastyl. He only succeeded in locating the queen's table where Semorel sat apart with her ladies, and the king's table in front of the empty dais where Elgurn sat, flanked by the four remaining Signers of the Pact. Nagaro recognized them all from years before, including Odus Morbernm who was a man of about fifty, blond, bearded, and impressive for the breadth of his shoulders.

Nagaro's attention was drawn back to his own table when the food began to arrive amid a mouth-watering flood of aromas. The food was brought by an army of liveried serving men and women. It came in great profusion and a multitude of unusual shapes, for the dinner served at the Festival of the Harvest Moon was a feast of fancy. There was bread baked in the shape of pumpkins and squash. There were thin slices of roast meat wrapped around seasoned rice and dressed up to look like fishes. There were fried slices of potato and yam cut into the shapes of animals, and meat-stuffed pastries made up to look like carriages. And so it went, on and on in a similar fashion, each new course a surprise, ending with a desert of mock plums and peaches molded from a paste made of sugared ground almonds and chestnuts. Each had a hazelnut or candied cherry for a "pit".

Nagaro enjoyed it all immensely. The Festival of the Harvest Moon was celebrated very much more modestly on Pakoa, and it had always been his favorite as a boy at Averwin. Hinda the cook had managed every year to produce a few such fanciful creations, though nothing to rival this night's outpouring from the royal kitchens. Fortunately, the conversation at Lord Kuran's table remained safely focused on the food, with everyone making comparisons to culinary wonders from past celebrations. Nagaro was pleased that he could offer a few examples of his own.

He was finding it easier to relax in the Great Hall than he'd expected, probably because this was his favorite festival, but also because the occasion was unsullied by the dark shadow of heskial enslavement. As Leyel Virden, he had missed the Festival of the Harvest Moon entirely, thanks to having tripped over young Vell's deliberately outstretched foot. Dreigen had feared that the length of the affair would exceed the duration of a dose of heskial, and had taken the risk of bringing him out while still in the early "deep trance" state. The Lore Master's strategy had gone awry before his puppet had even reached the Great Hall. Vell had tripped him in a hallway, and being in the deep trance, he hadn't made any reflexive move to catch himself. Instead, he'd fallen at full length like a statue, striking his head on the edge of a low marble table and knocking himself senseless. As little as he'd liked having a cracked skull, he hadn't been sorry to be spared the torment of being on display during the feast. The mishap had kept him out of the public eye for days afterwards, as well, though it had eventually brought more ridicule of its own.

Nagaro's hand unconsciously strayed to the telltale scar above his right temple. When he realized he was fingering the mark under his hair, he hastily lowered his hand and glanced about him. He caught Rastian's eyes on him, but no one else seemed to be looking.

Eventually the meal concluded and folk began to rise and move about the hall once more. Rastian was one of the first to leave the table and Nagaro was glad of it. Rastyl's peculiar utterances had left him feeling ill at ease in the young man's presence.

The musicians, who had played throughout the repast, were granted a respite to have their own dinners. While they were gone, a number of serving-men began moving tables to make more space in the center of the floor for dancing. Nagaro watched this activity with growing unease as he sipped his sothiril. Though he'd missed the Harvest Moon Festival during his earlier ordeal, he'd been forced to dance on numerous other occasions.

Since he'd taken no interest in dancing while living at Averwin, everything he'd known about it he had been taught by the Princess Nevien— and he wasn't sure if he remembered any of it. The subject stirred dark memories, though not because he'd been *bad* at dancing. In fact, the part of his mind that responded to instructions under the influence of heskial— what he called the "puppet part"— had learned the dance steps quickly and executed them with mechanical precision. The wooden perfection of his performances had earned him the mocking title of "dancing doll"— used far too often in his hearing.

Nagaro's brow constricted, as did his stomach as he fought down a knot of bitterness. And just at that moment, he caught sight of the princess bearing down on the table where he and Kuran were now almost the only ones still seated.

Nevien came sailing to a halt and settled into the chair opposite him with a rustle of white satin. Breathless and anxious, she leaned across the table.

"Captain," she said, "do you dance?"

5: Lothard Hurn

Nagaro felt instant panic at Nevien's question. He swallowed, and managed to stammer, "I... ah... no, My Lady." He wasn't sure it wasn't true, and he had no wish to find out. His heart dropped as he read disappointment in her eyes.

In something approaching desperation, she turned to the Lord of the Fleet and said, "Can I at least count on *you*, Kuran? If you see any of the suitors pressing me too unpleasantly, you'll step in and ask for a dance, won't you?"

Kuran returned her a look of sympathy. "I would, gladly, but I can only do so if the need arises very early," he told her with obvious regret. "I have some matters that require my attention, and I can't stay long."

Nagaro felt instantly guilty. Earlier that evening he'd expressed a wish to be Nevien's friend. Now, when she asked for his help, he'd let her down.

Before Nevien even had a chance to respond to Kuran's words, however, their conversation was interrupted by a tall Leithian man who strode to a place beside Nevien's chair. The man looked to be about thirty, and he cut a commanding figure, standing over six feet tall, with a muscular, well-proportioned frame. He was richly attired in charcoal gray silk and burgundy velvet, and the sword at his hip would have proclaimed him a member of the noble class even if his swaggering manner hadn't already suggested a man who was accustomed to assuming his own superiority. Blond and clean-shaven, his square-jawed face was dominated by fierce blue eyes and a mouth that seemed instantly ready to sneer.

"I'll have the first dance, My Lady," he declared, addressing the princess, "Come, now, if you please."

Nagaro was on his feet in an instant, outraged at hearing Nevien addressed in such a way. Kuran must have stood up also, for the older man's restraining hand grasped his shoulder and the words, "*Steady, lad,*" were muttered in his ear.

Nevien had risen in response to the Leithian's words. Her eyes met Nagaro's just for an instant, and she gave the very slightest warning shake of her head. Then she turned to face the Leithian. "My Lord

Lothard," she said coolly. "I will give you the first dance, since you are the first to ask." The smile she gave the man was pretty, perfect, and completely without warmth.

Lothard crooked his arm expectantly, and frowned when Nevien turned back to Kuran and Nagaro without taking it.

"My Lord," she said, and, "Captain," giving each of them a nod. "I see the musicians are returning to their seats, and I fear you must excuse me."

Nagaro had just enough presence of mind to bow, and Kuran did likewise, murmuring, "Until another time, My Lady Princess."

She flashed a wan smile, and only then did she turn again and take the Leithian's arm.

Lothard's gaze had been drawn to Kuran and Nagaro, and now he curled his lip disdainfully. He turned his back on them without so much as a word or nod. Instead, he addressed himself to Nevien as he conducted her away, speaking in voice that was quite loud enough for the other two men to hear.

"The little half-breed bulldog, and the pirate—a half-breed too, by the look of him. *Really*, My Lady. When you're my wife, I shall see that you keep better company."

Nagaro jerked against Kuran's restraining hand. "How *dare* he speak to her so!" he fumed. "Ordering her about, and telling her who her friends should be... And he was surpassingly rude to both of us! Someone should teach that man some manners."

Kuran's fingers tightened on Nagaro's shoulder. "Sit down, man, and cool your temper!" he hissed urgently. When Nagaro remained standing rigidly, looking after Lothard's departing figure, he added, more kindly, "I don't disagree with you, Captain, but by standing so, you only risk letting him see that he has cut you—which is exactly what he meant to do."

Nagaro cast the older man a glance in which anger smoldered, but he grudgingly sank into his seat.

Kuran sat down also. "Captain—" he began, then swept the word aside with a gesture and began again. "Nagaro... *my friend*. I don't wish to see you come to a bad end. Therefore, let me speak plainly. You have the misfortune to have been raised to view the world as one of the noble class, while the uncertainty of your birth—together with your vicissitudes—have placed you outside of it. I can't put it more bluntly than this: As long as you must go without a sword in this hall, you have little choice but to endure whatever may be handed to you by the likes of Lothard Hurn. The man badly needs a lesson in manners, I grant you that, but you're in no position to give him one."

Nagaro returned him a black look. "And what of yourself, My Lord?"

he asked pointedly. "Your sword is at your side at this very moment."

Kuran's black eyes glinted. "I get only indifferent support for my noble status, since I wasn't born to it. And having been born a commoner, I'm well-practiced in bearing offense." He paused and sighed. "Lothard Hurn is the worst kind of high-born Leithian," he continued. "The kind that's as practiced at dealing out offense as I am at bearing it. And unfortunately there isn't any law against treating the princess like a serving woman."

Nagaro's frown continued unrelenting. "I wouldn't treat a serving woman so," he observed coldly.

The Lord of the Fleet smiled fleetingly. "I believe you," he said. "And you're to be commended for it, but unfortunately Lothard Hurn is beyond my reach—quite literally." He extended his arm, which was proportionate to his limited stature, and grimaced at his own joke. "Lothard values skill with a blade above everything. Since he excels in it above all other men, he fancies that he has no equal in anything, and there's no one to convince him otherwise."

"But you're an excellent swordsman, My Lord!" Nagaro protested. "Your arm may not be long, but you have both speed and skill. I've seen you best men in practice who had a considerable advantage in height. Is he really so formidable that you can't teach him anything?"

Kuran heaved a sigh. "I value your praise, the more so because I know it's sincere," he said. "But Lothard *is* truly formidable. He outreaches me in a full lunge by almost a yard, and he's too quick and too skilled to give me any hope of getting inside his guard. He's amazingly fast for a man of his size. He's unquestionably the best swordsman among the men of the noble houses, and widely regarded as the best swordsman in all of Edrovir."

"I see." Nagaro looked down at his clenched hands.

"That's not to say," Kuran ventured cautiously, "that you haven't a fair chance of besting him, Nagaro. I've seen you both fight, and if you were matched against each other, I wouldn't try to guess who'd be the victor."

Nagaro raised his eyes. His expression remained somber. "I see," he said again. He was aware that Kuran had just placed him in contention for the title of best swordsman in the country. He wasn't sure he wanted the distinction, warranted or not. "It's not necessary to begin with the blade," he said. "It's always better to begin with words."

But Kuran swept this impatiently aside. "Lothard isn't impressed by words," he said. "Though he may be annoyed by them. And if you upbraid him too strenuously, you'll find that, as a lord, he can punish you for slander. While you have no such recourse, no matter how badly he insults you."

"But... that's unjust!"

Kuran shrugged. "Of course it is. But it's well-enshrined in custom, if not explicitly set forth in law. And the inequity extends to a challenge to combat. It's unlikely Lothard would ever challenge you, of course. He'd consider it beneath him. But if he did, he'd suffer nothing even if he killed you, while *you* on the other hand would be executed for murder if you challenged him and slew him."

Nagaro scowled. "How would you counsel me, then?"

Kuran held his gaze. "Curb that bold tongue of yours," he said. "Let his insults roll off you like water off a gull's back. And above all, *don't* let him provoke you into a challenge. Even if you bested him fairly in a bout, he'd find a way to make you pay for it. Between his nature and his influence, there's a good chance you wouldn't live very long to savor your victory."

Nagaro sat still, deeply dismayed. In the pause he could hear the musicians tuning their instruments in preparation to accompany the dancing. A glance in the direction of the part of floor that had been cleared for that purpose showed him that couples were beginning to stand ready. "I don't much like what I've just heard," he said, after a moment. "But I see that I'd best pay heed to it."

"Good lad." Kuran flashed a brief, satisfied smile.

Nagaro frowned at the word "lad." It was the second time Kuran had used it, but he decided to let it pass. An older man might call a younger one "lad" as a sign of affection. He was fairly confident of Kuran's kind regard, and the man was marginally old enough to be his father.

Kuran's expression had turned thoughtful. "If we still held the annual sword tourney," he said, "you could have tested your skill against Lothard. Those events allowed commoners to compete with high-born on an equal footing for the sake of entertainment."

"What happened to the tourneys?" Nagaro asked. He knew all about them, having been forced to observe one as Leyel Virden, and had wondered about their disappearance.

Kuran frowned sharply. "The King and Council put a stop to them after Lothard topped the lists two years in a row. The tourneys were for sport, but they drew all our best fighters and ranked them. Folk were beginning to see that, if Lothard were to challenge Elgurn for the crown, he might succeed. The country is much safer with more uncertainty on that score. Men like Lothard and his Brothers of the Blood could clearly see the number and quality of the men Elgurn could draw upon to fight as his champions."

"Still... if someone *could* best Lothard in a tourney... might it take him down a peg?" Nagaro asked, frowning in his turn.

But Kuran immediately shook his head. "I shouldn't have suggested it," he said earnestly. "Besting Lothard in that very public context—with all that's implicitly at stake—would surely put a target on your back. He'd have to be a bit more devious in taking his revenge, perhaps, but that wouldn't stop him."

Nagaro winced and looked at the table. At length he asked, "What exactly are the Brothers of the Blood, anyway?"

Kuran sighed. "They're a troublesome group that's arisen within the Leithian Faction. They're high-born men who believe nobility is only born in the blood—hence their name. They also believe that all the privileges traditionally held by the noble class, long ago when they still lived in Leith, are still theirs by right, here and now in Edrovir."

"So," Nagaro observed darkly, "they believe in the 'right' of high-born Leithian men to insult or abuse anyone of common birth according to their pleasure, and to further show what great men they are, they insult high-born women as well?"

Kuran's gaze hardened. "You've caught the shape of it," he said grimly. Then he pushed back his chair and stood up. "As I told the princess, there are some matters that require my attention. I hope you manage to enjoy the rest of your holiday. And do try to stay out of trouble." He flashed a brief smile as he departed.

Left to himself, Nagaro reflected that his holiday had already been rather spoiled by Lothard Hurn—and by what he'd just been told. The dancing had by this time begun, and many of the guests were gathered around the dance floor. Drawn to it by curiosity in spite of himself, Nagaro took a place among the crowd where he could observe the dancing couples. He quickly found, however, that the sight of Lothard dancing with Nevien turned his stomach. The big Leithian moved with assurance through the figures of the dance known as *The Ivy Vine*, but he also pushed, pulled, and propelled his partner in a way that made it clear that he thought he was the master and the princess was completely at his disposal.

Turning away in disgust, Nagaro nearly collided with a tall Leithian youth. Hastily he said, "I beg your pardon." Then he stopped, staring.

The young man had a loose-limbed frame and gray-green eyes in an honest, open face topped by a tousled profusion of blond curls. Nagaro recognized him by his resemblance to his father even before the young man stuck out his hand and responded by saying, "You're Captain Nagaro, aren't you? I was hoping to meet you. I'm Nile Fendred."

Nagaro recovered himself and took the hand. "I'm pleased to make your acquaintance, Zirda," he said. "And yes, I am Nagaro." To make conversation, he asked, "Did you intend to join the dance, or were you only watching as I was?"

Nile's brow immediately puckered in a frown. "I'm supposed to dance with the princess," he said. "I really should have tried to get the first dance, too, but Lord Lothard puts himself forward so much better than I do. And I don't care to have him think I'm getting in his way."

"Are you courting the princess, then?" Nagaro asked, though he expected he knew the answer.

The youth nodded with little enthusiasm.

Nagaro studied him sympathetically. The young Leithian radiated innocence. "Isn't she just a little... old... for you?" he ventured cautiously.

Nile immediately drew himself up to his full height, which in fact exceeded Nagaro's. "I've just turned twenty-two!" he declared defensively, suggesting that the question had been asked before.

"Ah, I beg your pardon." Nagaro gave the young man a reassuring smile. He knew that Nevien was twenty-four, but still the age difference was less than he'd imagined. He was himself only twenty-five.

Nile, however, promptly sagged again. "The truth is," he confessed, "I'd much rather dance with Alisset Sobring. She's the one over there... in yellow." The youth fondly picked out the object of his affection with his eyes. A sigh escaped him.

Nagaro followed the glance and recognized the young lady in yellow as one of those who'd been at the princess's table. He was fairly sure that Nile hadn't been among the men however. Pretending ignorance, he asked, "Why do you court the princess if you prefer another?"

Nile turned him an earnest glance. "The Elders have said I must, so it's my duty. And I must marry her, too, if the Gods decree that the king chooses me."

"Oh, well, of course." Nagaro had to struggle not to choke on the words. "Well, good luck, then," he added quickly. "I'll leave you to the task."

He shook his head as he moved away. Nile was his father's son, a perfect example of filial obedience and devotion to the Leithian gods. If Kale Fendred weren't a madman, secretly locked away in a tower in this very palace, he would undoubtedly approve completely of his son's attitude. Nagaro tried not to think about Kale. Most people believed him dead, and Nagaro had only discovered the secret by chance the previous spring. The gratitude he'd felt on learning that a man who had shown him kindness was still alive was tempered by the fact that he knew of no way to help him.

Having turned his back on the dancers, Nagaro wondered how long he could bring himself to stay at the festival. He would have liked to enjoy himself but he was distracted by the princess's courtship woes, and meeting Nile Fendred hadn't helped. Nile would have been the most promising of the suitors Nevien had named, but it seemed cruel to hope that the king would choose him, when his heart lay elsewhere.

Nagaro decided to make a round of the hall to view the various displays and then take his leave. There were many prizewinning fruits to be admired, which were of little interest to him, but the Towers of Plenty were really quite remarkable. They weren't so much towers as palatial edifices, with pillars made of pieces of corn stalk and domes of hollowed out squash or pumpkin shells, all exuding a faint vegetable mustiness. They quite put to shame the traditional towers he'd built as a boy out of crisscrossed ears of seed corn.

There was also a new form of art, something he'd never even imagined: elaborate pictures 'painted' with multicolored seeds, bits of leaf, and dried flower petals that must have been carefully hoarded since the spring and summer months. The traditional moon cake, displayed on a table beside the dais, was decorated in this fashion. Baked in the largest of the palace ovens, it was more than two feet in diameter and nearly five inches thick, counting the layer of white icing. It's broad top bore a detailed rendering of the facade of the royal palace with a cloud-fleeced blue sky behind it, all worked in colored vegetable materials. Nagaro stood for a time admiring the moon cake. If he managed to stay long enough, he might sample a piece of it. Cutting the cake would mark the culmination of the night's festivities.

Moving on to the next table, he encountered an even more remarkable sight. There were three life-sized busts, representing the king, queen, and princess. Their features must have been sculpted of almond paste, or something similar, that was smoothly coated with icing and decorated in colors in the same manner as the moon cake. The effect was almost lifelike from a distance. Remarkable though they were, Nagaro found them slightly disturbing. They sat on little pedestals like a row of severed heads. Going closer, he examined some of the finer details of the king's portrait. The circlet crown was made of split straw, pale gold and shiny. The eyes were of sky-blue flower petals. Nagaro shook his head. He was glad not to be a prince if it meant being subjected to such dubious homage.

"What a perfectly dreadful idea," he murmured under his breath.

"Well at least that's one thing we agree upon."

Nagaro started at the words, and turned to find that Elgurn was standing at his elbow. The king wore a rueful smile. His tone had been mild and courteous, and his expression bore every evidence of sincerity. It struck Nagaro that the man was trying to engage him in friendly conversation.

Immediately, the part of him that was still Leyel Virden rose up in outrage. He managed, however, to stifle the urge to make a caustic remark, knowing it would seem undeserved. But if the king wished to make an attempt at open, honest speech, Nagaro could think of matters more important than the culinary portraits on the table. He met the king's glance boldly and said, "I hope there's at least one other thing, My Lord."

"And what might that be?" Elgurn's eyes didn't waver.

"I hope you can tell me that you don't intend to wed your daughter to Lothard Hurn, since she clearly detests the man."

There was a flicker in the cool blue eyes, a slight twitch of the muscles of the king's face, that betrayed some emotion quickly suppressed. When Elgurn spoke, it was in a voice that was ever so slightly less mild. "This is not for the general ear, Captain, but between you and me, I pray every day that nothing may happen to make that necessary."

It was a better answer than Nagaro had expected—though less unequivocal than he would have liked. "I see," he said and looked away, somewhat abashed at having gotten so candid an answer. He hardly knew what else to say. As his eyes swept the crowded hall, he caught a distant flash of white satin. The dance had just finished and the musicians were sitting silent for a space to allow everyone a chance to catch their breath.

It was indeed the princess who had drawn his attention, and the figure beside her in burgundy and charcoal gray was also unmistakable. Nagaro stiffened and his eyes narrowed, for he saw that Lothard was leading Nevien away from the dance floor, moving toward one of several doors along the wall of the Great Hall that led out into the garden. The doors were set in high-arched openings between the tall windows, and they were open despite the crispness of the night to allow some flow of air. As Nagaro watched, the figures of Lothard and Nevien passed out of sight into the shadow of one of the open doorways.

"*Bishka!*" Nagaro swore under his breath. He trusted Lothard Hurn not at all. He turned hurriedly back to the startled Elgurn. "Your pardon, My Lord King," he murmured, with a very perfunctory bow. Not waiting for the king's response, he turned again and strode away across the polished floor, ducking this way and that among the moving guests. He wasn't sure exactly what he meant to do, but he remembered all too clearly the princess's words to Lord Kuran: *If you see any of the suitors pressing me too unpleasantly...* And he knew that Kuran had already gone.

He slowed his steps as he neared the open doorway and glanced about. No one else seemed to be watching, let alone showing any signs of moving to intervene. Either they hadn't noticed where the couple had gone, or else, like young Nile, they were afraid of getting in Lothard's way. Nagaro took a deep breath and stepped abreast of the doorway. He knew there was a kind of terrace outside, enclosed on three sides by wings of the palace, but it turned out that Lothard hadn't gone that far.

Nevien's white gown was a pale glimmer in the dimness of the alcove formed by the portico that framed the doorway.

Hastily Nagaro stepped back out of the line of sight from where Lothard must be standing. As he did so, he distinctly heard the princess say in a distressed whisper, *"No! Please, My Lord, you're hurting me."*

He also heard Lothard's muttered reply: "You only hurt yourself by resisting. Why make such a fuss about a little kiss from your future husband?"

This was more than enough for Nagaro. Moving away from the wall so it wouldn't appear that he'd been listening, he re-approached the doorway more directly. All he could think of as he stepped boldly into the shadowed alcove was what Nevien had said earlier to the Lord of the Fleet. "My Lady Princess," he said, "will you honor me by joining me in the next dance?"

There was a flurry of movement as Nevien started and turned her face towards him, though he couldn't read her expression in the dim light. Lothard was scarcely visible in the shadows but Nagaro saw the man's dark-clad arm hastily withdrawn from around the princess's white satin waist.

The Leithian swore under his breath, but then spoke loudly. "Have you no manners, *pirate*, that you so rudely interrupt your betters?"

Nagaro, recalling Kuran's warning, turned a bland countenance upon the other man. "I beg your pardon, My Lord," he said as innocently as he was able. "I didn't see you there, standing in a dark place and so darkly dressed. I saw the lady, shining in white, and it looked as if she were alone." Under the circumstances, being less than completely honest didn't trouble him.

"Well now that you know differently, perhaps you'll be so good as to leave! We don't need you here to play chaperone." Lothard's tone made his annoyance perfectly plain.

"Of course, My Lord," Nagaro returned smoothly, bowing. "A lady needs no chaperone to defend her from unwelcome advances when she's in the company of a gentleman." He was careful to avoid any hint of irony or emphasis that might have marked the comment as a rebuke. Still, he caught a little inadvertent movement from the princess. He turned to her and bowed. "My Lady," he said, "I hope you'll forgive my interruption."

He stepped back, preparing to take his leave, though with some misgivings. He'd accomplished his immediate objective, but wasn't sure of the long term effectiveness of his strategy.

"Wait, Captain." Nevien spoke for the first time. She turned to Lothard. "I hear the musicians tuning their instruments, My Lord, so we are interrupted in any case. You've had the first dance, and the Captain has asked for the next one most courteously. It seems I should honor his request." With that, she stepped decisively to Nagaro's side and slipped her hand about his arm.

Lothard moved at last out of the shadows. He darted Nagaro a glance like a knife, but then shrugged and smoothed his countenance. "If you *must*," he observed disdainfully. "Since the oaf has caused us to waste all the time in talk." Turning on his heel, he stalked away.

Nevien leaned close to Nagaro's ear. "Thank you for that most timely rescue, Captain," she said in a low tone. "Having been caught once, he may not try it again—at least for a while. But I thought you said you didn't dance."

Nagaro was feeling a rising apprehension. He'd been too concerned with thwarting Lothard to consider the personal consequences, and when the Leithian lord had dismissed him, he'd been prepared to go. The princess's action had placed him in an awkward position. Taking a steadying breath, he started to escort her back towards the dance floor.

"I... ah... had some instruction years ago," he said, since he didn't like to lie. "But I'm afraid I may not remember. I didn't think about really having to *do* it when I spoke."

"Well, I'm sorry to have forced your hand, then" she said, "but I'm afraid you'll have to try your best. You can't take me away from a man like Lothard on the pretext of dancing with me, and then bow out—unless the next dance is one you never learned at all. That, I think, might spare you."

They had reached the edge of the crowd around the dance floor, and Nagaro slowed, hesitating. Just at that moment, the harpist plucked out the notes of a tune to announce the next dance. The flute player echoed the melody.

"There!" said Nevien. "It's to be *Road to Seralind*. Surely you can't say you never learned that one!"

And of course, he couldn't. Not only would it have been a bald-faced lie, it wouldn't even have been credible. *Road to Seralind* was so popular that it was everyone's first dance—as it had been his when the princess had taught him years ago. He'd danced it more than any other. He supposed he should be grateful that this was the dance to test his memory, but his heart quailed. *Why couldn't it have been one she hadn't taught him?*

"Come on." Nevien tugged at his arm as he still hesitated. "They're lining up. Do you at least remember the position?"

Nagaro swallowed hard and licked dry lips. "*Yes...*" He was certain of that much. He forced himself to move forward through the crowd of onlookers and into the circle of couples that was beginning to form. There he took up the familiar position. *Stand on the outside, on her right... left arm around behind her back with the hand on her hip. She places her left hand on top of yours. And when she reaches around your back with her right arm to put her hand on your hip, you cover her right hand with your right.*

He could feel himself sweating, and his heart was beginning to thud. Standing so close beside her, he caught the hint of a scent of violets. She must be wearing perfume, which he didn't recall her doing before. But that small scrap of newness wasn't enough to distract him from feeling her body in the curve of his left arm. *That* sensation was bringing back vividly the lessons she'd given him in her sunlit bedchamber on the third floor. He remembered all too well how he'd let his mind wander, enjoying having his hand on her hip and the touch of her hand on his. He'd left the puppet part of him to learn the dance, knowing that, under the influence of heskial, his body would execute the thing flawlessly no matter what his conscious thoughts were doing.

And now a terrible thought gripped him: *What if only the puppet part of him had learned the dance?* Trying to think of how the steps went, he found his mind a complete blank and his panic spiked.

"*I don't remember the steps!*" he hissed desperately.

The princess quickly whispered into his ear. "It's right, left, right. Side-close, side-close. Then, left, right, left..."

He nodded, steadying a little. That sounded familiar...
But as he calmed, he became more aware of what was going on around him, and now he heard the murmurs of the watching crowd.

"Look! It's Captain Nagaro!"

"The pirate is going to dance!"

And now he remembered what it had been like to *perform* this dance here in the Great Hall under the gaze of all those eyes, and a new fear turned his stomach to ice: *What if remembering the dance meant dancing it the way he'd done it then? What if he became again the dancing doll!* He didn't think he could bear it. A little groan escaped him. "*I can't do this,*" he muttered through clenched teeth.

He felt her searching look, but she spoke reassuringly. "Yes, you can," she said. "If you knew it once, it will come back. You'll see! And I'm right here to prompt you."

She had no time to say more because the musicians began to play. In an agony of suspense, he stood, marking time through the introductory bars. He felt the princess nudge him, signaling him to move... *but the cue was unnecessary.* The moment felt right, and he just stepped forward... *Right, left, right... Side-close, side-close...*

It *did* come back! Perhaps it was the number of times he'd danced it? Once only, in that first rounding of the circle, did he falter slightly and Nevien murmured words of guidance, but after that the whole thing just unwound itself from somewhere inside his head and he followed the unwinding thread.

The couples moved to the music, stepping now forward around the circle, now into the center, now out. He and Nevien were part of the larger whole, as well as a separate unit, linked by their arms around each other's waists.

Nagaro might have begun to enjoy the experience if he hadn't become increasingly aware of the attention he was drawing. The audience seemed to have doubled, and every time he glanced at the throng of finely dressed folk he saw people pointing at him. He saw smiles. He heard laughter. The other dancers were stealing looks at him across the circle.

He felt that he was moving naturally and freely, in compliment to his partner, but he couldn't see himself. Was there something strange or amusing about the way he danced? Were his movements too rigid or too perfect? Desperate not to be the dancing doll, he began to try variations and embellishments that he'd seen others use, but this only seemed to make matters worse. Even Nevien gave him several astonished looks. So he desisted, and tried to shut the reactions of the crowd from his mind as he finished the dance.

He turned Nevien under his arm with a flourish as the last strains of the music died away, then quickly tucked her hand into the crook of his arm. Around them rose a roar of voices, punctuated by laughter. He steeled himself, determined not to see—not to hear.

Nevien leaned close to his ear and said, "Now what were you worried about? You did that... *perfectly.*"

Nagaro made no answer—gave her no glance. He was doing his best not to think about the implications of her little pause, and the word she had chosen. His only thought was to make his escape—but first he had to find Nile. He swept the crowd with his eyes and found the young man, standing quite nearby with his mouth agape. Drawing the princess along beside him, he stepped quickly up to the young Leithian and said, "I believe you wished to have the next dance with this lady?"

Nile had just enough presence of mind to take this very broad hint. Hastily shutting his mouth, he nodded weakly, then swallowed and stammered, "I... ah... yes. My Lady, will you honor me with the next dance?"

A trace of a frown creased Nevien's brow as she glanced at Nagaro, but then she quickly turned back to Nile. "Yes, of course," she told the youth, and favored him with one of her winning smiles, even as she transferred herself to the young man's arm. She turned back to Nagaro. "Thank you again, Captain," she said rather formally.

He bowed to her in response, with equal formality. "You're most welcome, My Lady Princess. And now, please excuse me." He turned to go, but as he moved past Nile's ear he paused just long enough to mutter, *"Lothard was trying to kiss her in the doorway. If you mean to court the lady, I suggest you take better care of her interests."* Then he strode off.

The crowd of onlookers parted to let him pass. He kept his eyes straight ahead but couldn't help hearing some of the comments.

"There he is!"

"The dancing pirate!"

"I never saw anything like it!"

He struck off, straight across the room, making for the table where he had dined. The blood burned in his face. *So now it was "the dancing pirate," was it?*

Arriving at the table, he sank with a groan onto the chair he had vacated earlier. Reaching for a pitcher, he poured himself a glass of cold sothiril, intending to sit and nurse it until the interest of the guests had turned to other things and he could depart unnoticed. As he glanced up, however, he discovered a young woman standing beside him. It was the young Kelorin woman in rose pink whom he'd seen at the princess's table. She must have followed him across the hall, for she seemed a little breathless.

She had a delicate face, large wide-set gray eyes graced by dark lashes, and a narrow pointed chin. Her dark brown hair had been swept up, braided, and coiled in a circle atop her head. The sophistication of the hairstyle might have fooled him, at a distance, into thinking she was older, but seen so close it did nothing to conceal how very young she was. She was watching him with an expression that was both eager and hesitant.

Frowning slightly, Nagaro rose. "My Lady," he said uncertainly. "Is there something you wish of me?"

"I... I'm not a 'lady,' Captain Nagaro," she stammered, blushing. "My father is a merchant. My....my name is Kendira."

Nagaro inclined his head to her and smiled, trying to relieve her shyness. "Well then, Kendira—Zirdyn. What is it you wish?"

"I... I... Captain..." She stopped, then blurted, "Don't you want to dance any more?"

Nagaro's frown returned. "I think not," he said with unintended bitterness. "I've had enough of being laughed at."

Her gray eyes widened. "But they weren't laughing *at* you," she protested. "It's only that no one expected you to be so *good*. They were laughing at how you put all those fine folk to shame. You're very graceful, you know." And she stopped again, turning pink to match her dress.

Nagaro found himself blushing as well. He was *graceful*? Was that something a man was supposed to be? Could he believe her explanation of the laughter he'd heard, or was she only trying to make him feel better? While he was still trying to decide what to do, she spoke again, all in a nervous rush.

"I'd be very glad to dance if you would ask me."

Nagaro shifted uncomfortably. He wanted to find a way to put her off, but he hated to be unkind. "I, ah... I'm sorry, Zirdyn. I was lucky to find that I remembered that one dance," he told her. "I'm afraid there's really no other that I would trust myself to try."

Her face fell, but then she suddenly brightened. "Oh, but come, Zirda," she said eagerly, beckoning. "I'll teach you!"

"*Not here!*" The words sprang from his mouth in his panic, and he saw her flinch and then droop in disappointment. "I mean," he said hastily, "I'd be very glad to have you teach me some dances, Zirdyn, only I'd rather not do it where so many eyes are watching."

"Oh. I see." She cast her eyes down, chewing her lip and frowning, but in a moment she looked up again. "I know," she said, eager once more. "You must come to River House!"

"River House? What's that?" He had been thinking that learning some dances in a normal way would make it easier for him to help the princess, but he was none too sure about this new suggestion.

"It's a villa that Nevien keeps—in the country. We go every few weeks if the weather is fair. All the princess's ladies together... We're each allowed to bring a guest, and I... I haven't had anyone... lately..." Kendira's voice trailed off, and she looked at the floor, embarrassed either by the admission or by her own boldness. "I... I'm sure... if you wanted to come... we could find a place for dancing lessons without anyone watching—except Lady Merriel. She's our chaperone,"she added hastily. She met his gaze again, with pleading eyes.

"Oh." Nagaro relaxed. This sounded harmless. "In that case, I'd be pleased to be your guest." He gave her a little bow. "Now, please go back to the dancing, Zirdyn. I'm sure there must be someone who'd be glad to dance with such a sweet, pretty maid."

Kendira blushed again at the compliment. Then, to his relief, she went, leaving behind a trace of some floral perfume he couldn't identify.

Nagaro sat down. He sipped his sothiril, frowning, wondering what might come of this unexpected development. He could only imagine that Kendira had taken a fancy to him. He had the impression that she wasn't usually so forward, and only a certain strength of feeling would lead a naturally shy creature to be so bold. He found the idea a bit unnerving. The girl's fancy could be based on almost anything: how well he'd danced, his outward appearance, whatever stories she'd heard about him... With greater familiarity, she might well be disappointed.

And what did he think of *her?* His compliment had been sincere:

She seemed sweet, and he found her pretty. And her being a merchant's daughter meant he wasn't barred from courting her. But she seemed so young—a girl not out of her teens. He shook his head and sighed. There was nothing to do but wait and see.

As soon as he dared, after that, he rose to go with only very mild regret about missing the cutting of the moon cake. The uncomfortable experience of the dance still clouded his mood despite what Kendira had told him. He made his escape, passing near the wall and far from the dance floor, purposefully not looking to see whether Lothard was dancing with Nevien again. He found the queen, now seated near the door and looking rather pale, and took his leave of her, murmuring excuses about needing to rise early.

Delvin was alone at his post in the anteroom. He saluted Nagaro and immediately fetched him his sword. "Ye're leaving very early, Captain," he observed as he handed over the weapon.

Nagaro shrugged. "I don't care for dancing," he said as he buckled on the blade. "I hope you at least got some of the food."

Delvin grinned. "Oh yes. One of the cooks is my mother's cousin."

"Good." Nagaro frowned. "Does this posting please you? I wondered whether it was a step up or down, and hoped you weren't being punished for letting the pirates in at the back gate."

Delvin looked a little sheepish. "Well, I did get a bit of a jawing about how to know friend from foe," he admitted. "But I *did* recognize Landros. And he *did* vouch for ye. And it all turned out all right, so they couldn't really be too cross. And this *is* a good posting. All the lads say I'm lucky to have it."

Nagaro smiled. "I'm glad."

A step sounded at the doorway of the antechamber and Nagaro turned to see Rastian entering the room. "Excuse me, Guardsman," he said formally to Delvin. "I would speak to this gentleman."

Rastian gave Nagaro a covert glance, and started to walk quickly past, his eyes straight before him. Nagaro needed only a few strides, however, to fall in beside the other man.

"Good evening, Rastian," he said as casually as he could. "Are you leaving early as well? And without your father?"

Rastian inclined his head slightly without looking at Nagaro. "Captain," he said, by way of acknowledgment. "My father left an hour ago. He has no patience for these affairs."

"Ah." Nagaro digested this. "I can't help wondering," he ventured after a moment, "what sort of service he thinks you might render me."

They had reached the outer doors of the palace. These stood open as long as the revelry continued within, but they were well guarded. Rastian glanced pointedly at the guards, then shot Nagaro a sharp glance and gave a little jerk of his head to signal that he meant to exit before speaking. Nagaro shrugged and passed through the high double doors at the other man's side. Once outside, Rastian descended the steps in the direction of the hitching rails where the guests' horses stood waiting in the care of half a dozen grooms. He came to a halt in the darkness at the foot of the steps, halfway between the lights of the guarded portico and the pool of light from a lamp that illuminataed the waiting grooms. Here, finally, he spoke in a low voice.

"I am sure, Zirda, that he means it to be whatever service you may require."

Nagaro frowned in bafflement. There wasn't enough light where they stood to read the other man's face. "My Lord," he said, using the title since they weren't engaged in Fleet affairs, "I'm only a captain, one of many in the Royal Fleet, while you're a lord's son. So it seems more appropriate that I should ask how I might serve *you*. And I confess that your father's meaning isn't plain to me at all."

Rastian shifted in the darkness, and hesitated a moment before he answered, speaking it seemed with some care. "Captain—and in that uniform you do, in some sense, outrank me—it seems that my father has heard good reports of you. The times are uncertain. Titles are sometimes only words, and men aren't always what they seem. And it's better to have good men at your side than against you. I suppose my father hopes that we may stand together rather than otherwise. So, indeed, do I. And now, Captain, I wish you a very good night."

With that, Rastian made a quick half-bow and started forward again in the direction of the horses.

Nagaro held back, chewing his lip, not nearly as enlightened as he had hoped to be. Rastian had clearly picked the spot to speak because it was out of earshot of both the grooms and the palace guards, as if he'd intended to say something that shouldn't be overheard. But what he'd said all seemed to be riddles. Nagaro could make nothing of it beyond the fact that Rastian and his father seemed to hope he might be an ally. This was consistent with the idea that the father and son were seeking support for Tevren's son, as Kuran had suggested, but Rastian's words had been vague enough for almost any interpretation.

Nagaro shook his head and heaved a sigh.

By this time, Rastian had mounted his horse and was riding away across the courtyard towards the gate in the city wall. Nagaro retrieved Thunder-Heels, mounted, and rode after Rastian's retreating figure at a discrete distance. He was mildly surprised when the other young man turned aside from the main street shortly after passing through the gate. He, himself, continued straight on, bound for the Fleet Compound, rather unsettled in his thoughts.

6: Fleet Matters

"Three hits for Captain Nagaro! Match!"

Nagaro lowered his sword. "Well fought, Rastian," he said, and bowed, but he was frowning as he did so.

Rastian also bowed. "You fought better, Captain."

In the early afternoon light Nagaro could plainly read the young man's features, and he noted that Rastian appeared well satisfied despite having lost the match. He nodded an acknowledgment and turned away.

As he went to retrieve his cloak, Fendar casually intercepted him and addressed him in a confidential tone.

"It seems to me that ye won that bout too easily, Captain."

Nagaro met the man's eyes, and nodded. "He wasn't fighting his best—neither this time, nor the last time I went against him. It seems he's fighting... *cautiously*, at least when he's fighting me."

Fendar scratched his head. "Perhaps your skill has cowed him?"

"Perhaps." Nagaro made a show of shrugging the matter off and left Fendar to his work. He thought it more likely that Rastian's behavior was related to the things Rastyl Korven had said at the Festival of the Harvest Moon, but he wasn't going to share those thoughts with the swordmaster, even though the man was avowed to be his friend and he beleived he could trust him. Fendar had so far kept his promise to keep Nagaro's secret, and he hadn't repeated the gaff of showing too much familiarity. Since Kuran hadn't mentioned it, Nagaro assumed that the Lord of the Fleet either hadn't heard or hadn't thought it important.

Nagaro pulled his cloak about his shoulders. The breeze coming off the sea had a cold edge to it. When he glanced across the practice area, he saw Landros beckoning to him from the sidelines and went to join the older man.

Landros was frowning in annoyance. "Kuran wants to see ye, lad, in his study," the grizzled sea warrior informed him. "And if he means to tell ye what I think he does, ye'll soon be no happier than I am."

"Why? What did he tell you?"

The old sea warrior shook his head. "It's the spring postings. He means to change out half o' my crew and give me Fleet-trained warriors in their place!"

Nagaro frowned slightly. "Well," he said, "I don't think that's actually unreasonable. And at least he doesn't mean to scatter our men across the whole Fleet and give us completely new crews."

"Well, aye, but I'm supposed to pick the men to part with! I don't like having to choose—or having to tell the ones I've chosen that they have to go!"

"I don't blame you, Landros, but I suppose that's a Fleet captain's lot." Nagaro was trying to be philosophical.

"But there's more, and I'm not sure whether it's good or bad." Landros rubbed his chin. "He means to make the *Sea Eagle* Geldoran's flagship."

Nagaro raised an eyebrow. "You have reservations about being a flagship captain under Commander Geldoran?"

Landros frowned afresh. "I don't fancy having him looking over my shoulder every minute!"

"I think you're exaggerating to suggest that he would do that. And haven't you said that you prefer taking orders to giving them?"

Landros gave him a sour look. "Ye've a memory like a pitch pot, Captain. Every little thing sticks in it. And did ye have to go and tell Kuran that I called him an 'old fox'? He's thrown that back at me three times already!"

Nagaro laughed outright. "That's only because he likes hearing it so much! Kuran likes a man who's bold and honest, remember?"

Landros regarded him narrowly. "All right, but can ye honestly say ye wouldn't choke at taking orders on your own ship?"

"I don't think I would," Nagaro told him. "Not from Geldoran. Kuran considers him the best commander in the Fleet and it's not as if he'd be such a fool as to tell you how to sail the ship. You're as good at that as any man alive."

Landros brightened a little. "Ye're right about that," he conceded, with a note of pride. "But I still don't like having to send off half my men."

Nagaro left the old sea warrior still grumbling as he struck off across the compound for the modest building that housed the quarters and offices of the Lord of the Fleet. When he knocked, he heard Kuran's voice from within immediately bidding him enter.

There was a small entry hall inside the front door of the building, with doors leading variously to Kuran's quarters, the clerk's office, and Kuran's study. The door to the study was open and Kuran was sitting behind his desk, which was cluttered with piles of paper.

Kuran's pen was scratching across the sheet directly in front of him as Nagaro entered. The Fleet Lord proceeded to set the sheet on one of the stacks and pick up the next paper. "Another bill of sale," he muttered, scrawling a signature and adding the second paper to another stack.

Finally looking up, he gestured to a chair. "Sit down, Captain," he said. "I've several things to tell you."

"One of them being about the spring postings?"

Kuran grunted. "Did Landros give you the gory details?"

Nagaro nodded. "I expect that you mean to change out half the crew of the *Sword*, also, to be replaced by men with more Fleet experience?"

"That's right. You pick the men to re-post. I'll choose their postings and the men to replace them. I want your list before the first of Idrin."

"Aye, Zirda." Nagaro saluted.

Kuran crooked a brow. "You have no comment?"

Nagaro shrugged. "If I wish to grumble about it, I can commiserate with Landros. It makes sense from your point of view."

"Ah." Kuran nodded with just a flicker of a smile. "I also intend to transfer my flag to the *Sword of Freedom*."

This time Nagaro bridled. It was one thing to tell Landros that he shouldn't mind being a flagship captain to Commander Geldoran. It was another to find himself similarly placed under the Lord of the Fleet. He was remembering how Kuran had once spoken disparagingly of his current flagship captain, Ruald.

"If I understand correctly, My Lord," he said cautiously. "That means I'll still command the ship, while you command me."

Kuran regarded him steadily. "At times I may command you. At other times you'll follow your own command, while I observe."

Nagaro frowned. "*Observe*, My Lord?"

"Of course, Captain," Kuran replied mildly. "If I am to learn how to take ships without sinking them, I must see how you do it. And I do expect this flagship arrangement to be temporary."

"Ah." Nagaro's frown receded. "I'll have to give some thought to the best approach to use with ships of the Royal Fleet."

Kuran smiled tightly. "Yes, you think on it. Perhaps we can discuss that plan, too, before Idrin."

Nagaro inclined his head. "I'll do my best, My Lord. Is that all?"

"Just one more thing. I'd like you to sail one of those ships of yours upriver to the shipyard—so the builders can have a look at her while we're off maneuvers for the winter. We're laying keels for two new warships."

"Very good, My Lord." Nagaro again inclined his head respectfully. "But I think they should look at both the *Sword* and the *Sea Eagle*. The first is from Baalkir's shipyard, the second from Angkat's. There are differences that I believe are of little consequence, since both ships are equally swift. It's the shared features that the builders should emulate.

Kuran nodded gravely. "I've learned to respect your advice," he said. "Let it be so."

Nagaro saluted again and rose to go, but Kuran spoke again as if something had just occurred to him. "I hope the new recruits aren't getting confused," he observed. "This is the third swordmaster they've had since Duleyin, and every master has his own style."

"Actually, I think it's going quite well," Nagaro told him earnestly. "My approach and Master Fendar's aren't very different." His left hand strayed to the pommel of his weapon as he thought of sword practice.

Kuran's gaze was drawn to the hand as the little gold salamander ring on Nagaro's last finger caught the light. The older man's black eyes came quickly back to Nagaro's face. "I'm glad to hear it," he said, then added: "Good enough, Captain. You may go."

After Nagaro had gone, the Lord of the Fleet sat for several seconds, frowning, then began to search through one of the stacks of paper on his desk. Presently he appeared to find what he was seeking, for he grunted in satisfaction. He rang a bell on his desk to summon his clerk. When the man entered from his adjoining office, Kuran placed the paper in front of him. "Estevad, regarding this bill of sale for the lumber we recently received, is the merchant still here awaiting his payment?"

"The merchant's agent is, My Lord," the clerk promptly replied. "The merchant himself dwells in Vered Mahir and doesn't come so far down river."

Kuran frowned again, then shrugged. "The agent can carry a letter, I suppose," he said as if to himself. "I want the merchant's name, please, and the address of his dwelling."

While the clerk went to seek the requested information, a faint smile played across Kuran's face as he fingered the image of a small curling salamander, stamped in red ink, on the upper right-hand corner of the bill of sale.

*

Nagaro spent the rest of the afternoon arranging to move the two ships. He first had to inform Landros of the need to sail the *Sword* and the *Sea Eagle* to the shipyard. Then they both had to confirm the readiness of the two vessels, and choose and inform the men who would be needed to sail them. It would require only a few men on each ship because they would sail in the morning when the incoming tide would flow upriver, and the men could easily return in the ships' longboats.

When these arrangements were finally completed, Nagaro turned his steps towards the dining hall. He intended to announce the transfer of the ships at dinner, making a general announcement of the planned maneuver so the crewmen of the *Sword* and the *Sea Eagle* could retrieve any things left on board that they might need in the next few weeks.

It was still early for dinner, and the dining hall was very nearly deserted when he reached it. As he passed through the little entryway where the cloaks were hung, he noticed Rastian standing at the serving counter, apparently bent on getting a cup of sothiril. The serving man on the other side of the counter seemed to be the only other person nearby, and Nagaro thought he might take the opportunity to speak to Rastian privately regarding the bout they'd fought earlier that day. He still hoped he might shed some more light on whatever "cause" the young man's father was pursuing.

As he was about to step further out into the dining hall, however, Rastian moved aside, revealing a cloaked figure standing behind him. Nagaro hesitated for a moment and was glad he'd done so when the cloaked man turned and revealed himself to be Lord Rastyl. The elder Korven was holding his own steaming cup and appeared to be lost in thought. Nagaro hastily drew back into the entryway, just as he heard the sound of voices from outside and the tread of approaching booted feet.

A dozen Fleet warriors came through the outer door and milled past Nagaro to besiege the lone server, calling for sothiril and stamping their feet to warm them. Nagaro spotted Taru and Pavo among them and quickly joined his friends to stand in line for service. As the three friends made their way to a table with their drinks, Nagaro swept the room with his eyes and saw that Rastian and his father had found a table in a corner. When he located the pair, he found that Rastyl was looking at him. Even at that distance, Nagaro felt the pale stare and hastily looked away.

Taru must have followed Nagaro's gaze. "Who is that man with Rastian?" he asked as he seated himself. "The one that's not in a Fleet uniform. I've heard that lords can make free o' the Fleet Compound and eat at our mess if they choose, but this is the first time I've seen one o' them doing it."

"That's Rastian's father, Rastyl Korven," Nagaro informed him. "He's the lord of Irvenen Wared."

Taru grunted, glancing again at the two men. "Now that ye say it, I see the likeness. And I think I saw the two o' them together in the compound this afternoon."

Nagaro frowned. "They seem to spend quite a lot of time together."

Pavo spoke, addressing Nagaro. "Rastyl is man you say have talk to you twice? Who maybe mistake you for someone else?"

Nagaro's frown deepened. "Yes. He seems to think that I should understand what he's talking about, too, though he never explains it. And the way those pale eyes of his seem to stare makes me itch." He shook his head. "Let's talk about something else."

So they talked about their assignment for the following morning until the food was ready—steaming bowls of mutton stew and baskets of warm bread. After that, Nagaro stood up, pounded on the table with his mug for attention, and made his announcements regarding moving the two ships to the shipyard. Before sitting down again, he glanced over surreptitiously and noticed that Rastyl was no longer sitting with Rastian, who was now alone. He wondered whether the elder Korven had finished his dinner quickly, or whether he preferred to dine elsewhere, perhaps on finer fare. With Rastyl gone, Nagaro could have tried to approach Rastian, but he found he'd lost his enthusiasm for it. It seemed unlikely he would learn anything more than he had at the harvest festival.

The friends didn't linger over the meal, since they meant to enjoy an evening of King's Men in Nagaro's quarters. The wind's chilly fingers tugged at their cloaks as they passed out into the darkened compound and made for the officers quarters. When they turned into Captain's Row, they immediately noticed the figure of what looked like a youth huddled in a cloak, waiting on Nagaro's front doorstep under the light of the oil lamp mounted on the wall.

The lad turned at the sound of their approach and cried out, "There ye are, Captain Nagaro! I've another invitation for ye!"

It was the same young courier in palace livery who had delivered the invitation to the Festival of the Harvest Moon, and he promptly fished an envelope out of the pouch he carried under his cloak.

Nagaro took the envelope, slit it open, and read the handwritten note inside by the light of the lamp. It said:

Captain Nagaro,

You are invited to join me and my ladies for an outing in the country that will take place on the thirtieth of Todrin, providing the weather is fair. We will gather in the yard of the royal stable at an hour after dawn and return before sunset. Please respond so we may know whether to expect the pleasure of your presence. —Nevien Harlind

Nagaro frowned. This must be the outing to River House of which Kendira had spoken. It had come sooner than he'd expected, just days after the harvest festival. The date was at the end of the current eight-day week. While the week's last two days, known as the "week's end," were nominally free for Fleet warriors to pursue their own purposes, officers were sometimes called upon to give service even then.

Nagaro addressed the young messenger. "I'm afraid I'll have to send a reply later," he told the lad. "I'll need to get permission from the Lord of the Fleet."

The boy grinned impishly. "I don't think Lord Kuran'll object t' your going, Zirda, since he usually goes, himself!" With that, the lad bobbed him a bow and was gone, shouting, "Good night to ye, Zirda!" over his shoulder.

Taru immediately tugged the invitation out of Nagaro's hand and proceeded laboriously to read it. "I thought ye said it was a Kelorin girl that asked ye t' this River House place," he said suspiciously.

"It was. But the girl—Kendira—had to ask the princess to invite me. River House is Princess Nevien's villa." Nagaro reclaimed the note and thrust it into his tirka. Then, recalling that he'd seen a light still lit in the window of Kuran's study when they'd passed the parade ground, he added. "I'd like to ask Kuran about this right away, if you'll both excuse me. It shouldn't take long."

Taru scowled. "I still don't understand why ye want to do this," he said. "It's bad enough the whole city knows ye danced with the princess."

Nagaro frowned. "Maybe if I do enough dancing the novelty will wear off," he said. "I'll just be another one of Kuran's officers who happens to know how to dance—instead of the 'dancing pirate', and I may be able to help the princess, sometimes, too."

Taru snorted, but Pavo nodded wisely. "Dancing is useful thing for Nagaro," he said. "I think he should learn how to do it."

Taru gritted his teeth in a gust of wind and growled, "Just give us your key, Nagaro so we can get started without ye."

Nagaro dug the key from his pocket and handed it over. "Go ahead and light the fire," he told them. "I'll be there soon."

He crossed the parade ground quickly to Kuran's quarters, where his knock was answered for the second time that day with a call to enter. He found the Lord of the Fleet still at his desk, bent over his papers. A tray on a side table bore the wreckage of the man's dinner.

Kuran looked up wearily. "If you've come to make a report, Captain," he said, "it could have waited 'til morning."

"I didn't come for that, My Lord," Nagaro replied. "Although we have set up a plan to move the ships early tomorrow." He then proceeded to explain his actual reason for coming.

Kuran listened with a faint smile. "This is an easy request to grant," he said. "I can hardly deny you a pleasure I intend to enjoy myself." He flicked a hand at a small envelope lying to one side among the other papers. "I serve as one of the chaperones. But if you don't mind telling me, to which of Nevien's ladies do you owe the invitation?"

"The one named Kendira."

"Ah. The little mouse." This time Kuran smiled broadly. "That one usually makes herself nearly invisible. You must be discerning indeed to have noticed her."

Nagaro shifted his weight uncomfortably where he stood. "Actually, it seems she must have noticed *me*," he admitted. "She approached me... after I had... ah... done one dance. She's offered to give me lessons."

"*Lessons?*" Now Kuran laughed out loud. "From what I've heard, you don't need lessons! You need something to slow you down so the rest of us aren't left in the dust. 'Do you dance?' said she. 'No,' said he. And here I thought you were a man who couldn't lie!"

Nagaro colored under his kuma stain. "She didn't ask me whether I'd ever done it in my life, My Lord," he said defensively. "The dance was *Road to Seralind*, which is the one I knew best, and I still didn't know if I'd remember how to dance it until I tried!"

Kuran waived his protest aside with a chuckle. "You may by all means join us at River House," he said. "Even if it *is* for dancing lessons."

Nagaro thanked him and hastily made his escape.

7: River House

Nagaro reined Thunder-Heels to a halt and swung to the ground beside one of the hitching rails in the palace stable yard. The big gray tossed his head and snorted steam. There had been no rain for several days and the clear nights had brought frost. Nagaro stroked the stallion's neck, then looped the reins over the rail and stood rubbing his cold-stiffened fingers as he looked about doubtfully. At an hour after dawn, the mass of the adjacent palace loomed cold and intimidating, although the paved yard was awash in the pale light of the newly-risen autumn sun. There were four other horses already tethered at the rail. These, together with the presence of a pair of grooms and a carriage with three of its four horses hitched, indicated that a journey was indeed in the offing. None of the other guests were in sight, however.

A little hesitantly, he approached one of the grooms. "Where is everyone?"

"Ye'll find them upstairs on the third floor where it's warm, Zirda, in the library," the man assured him, bobbing a bow. "One o' the horses had a loose shoe, and it's taking some time to deal with it. Ye can go in by that door." He pointed a short distance along the outer wall of the palace to where a heavy oak door with bronze fittings was set in an arch of stonework. "Just give your name t' the man at the guard post inside and he'll direct ye. But ye'll have to leave your sword here, Zirda. I'll keep an eye on it."

Nagaro thanked the man. He unbuckled his sword belt and hung it on his saddle bow. Approaching the indicated door, he put his hand on the bronze door handle, then hesitated. He was thoroughly familiar with this door and knew exactly what lay beyond it. He had once escaped this way into the palace garden on a wet spring night when the waning of a dose of heskial had briefly allowed him to move of his own volition. The gate leading from the stable yard into the garden was now right beside him. He had run into the garden, looking for a place to die, but had gotten no farther than the harness shed—beside the stable—before the growing agony of heskial withdrawal had brought him down.

The path he was about to take held these and many other unpleasant memories. He would much rather have waited outside in the open air than on the third floor, in company, but he knew that would look odd.

He steeled himself and turned the handle. Inside, he thanked the guard at his post for an excellent, if unnecessary, set of instructions for finding the library, which he had known as a sitting room. He then began mounting what he'd long ago learned to refer to as the "back stair" with a reluctant tread.

In a moment of boldness that morning, he had decided to wear the embroidered shirt that Nevien had given him, reasoning that it was best to wear it when he would be in a smaller company, rather than at some large gathering. He was now regretting the decision as he realized that this small company would include the princess's ladies, some of whom might possibly remember when the princess had made the shirt for Prince Elyan, her third husband. He was wearing a long-sleeved tirka over the shirt, for warmth, but he would likely want to shed the outer garment later, and the embroidered shirt collar already showed at the neck.

These were the thoughts that were troubling him as he turned the corner of the second floor landing. He chanced to glance up as he did so—and stopped in his tracks.

A portrait had been hung on the wall where the final flight of stairs began its ascent. From out of a simple wooden frame, the face of a dark-haired, gray-eyed youth looked down at him with an open, earnest gaze.

"*Vothra!*"

The word came out before he could stop it. He'd all but forgotten about the portrait the Lady Maramine had painted of him years ago. It had been presented to the princess in advance of his arrival so she could see what he looked like. And it had hung on the wall of her bedchamber, mocking him, during the entire time he'd lived in the palace. He hadn't seen the painting in her chamber the previous spring. He'd never expected to see it again. Yet here it was, in this unlikely place, and he was unexpectedly gazing at the image of his seventeen-year-old self.

In spite of himself, he couldn't help examining it more closely. *Had he ever really been that young? ...that innocent?"*

He was so completely lost in examining the image that he failed to notice the approach of a quiet step on the stairs until the familiar voice of the princess spoke quite close to him, making him start.

"Ah, here you are, Captain," she said. "I was just going down to speak to the coachman. I see you've found the portrait of my first husband, Leyel Virden."

Nagaro quickly recovered from his initial shock, but his heart was pounding. He risked a furtive glance at the princess. She was dressed in riding attire and had apparently just descended the last few steps of the stairs from the floor above. *She was only a few feet from him. And from the portrait!*

Hastily he turned back to face the painting, feeling the continued thudding of his heart against his ribs, the prickle of sweat down his sides... He desperately didn't want her to see his face at the same angle as the face in the picture. With such a direct a comparison, she might finally recognize him. *If she hadn't already seen enough...*

He stood, waiting in terror for the telltale gasp or exclamation of dismay. But it didn't come.

Instead, Nevien came up right beside him, and stood there, also gazing up at the painting. She sighed. "It's a striking image," she said conversationally. "As you can see, he was a very handsome young man. This portrait came to me first, and I was quite taken with it. I couldn't wait to meet him."

Nagaro knew he should simply make some harmless answer and go on up the stairs, but he couldn't seem to stop himself. There was a kind of horrible fascination in hearing her talk about him. Something like watching a snake glide across the floor. He heard himself say, "It must have been a terrible disappointment when he finally arrived." He was surprised at how steady his voice sounded.

"Yes, it was." Another sigh, and she continued calmly: "I cried all night. That night and a great many others. But, it wasn't *his* fault. He was... so like a child, in some ways. In other ways, not even that..." Her voice trailed.

He risked a glance at her and saw with a pang that her face was clouded. Then she shook herself, and he looked hastily away again.

"The Lady Maramine—his guardian—painted it," she resumed, still in that conversational tone. "And the Gods know what possessed her to paint him like *that.*"

"What do you mean, My Lady?" He was piqued into speaking again because he'd always been impressed with Maramine's artistic skill. "Isn't it a good likeness?"

"As for the features, the likeness is excellent," she replied. "It's the expression... the look in his eyes... *That* young man," she indicated the painting, "does not look simple minded. Perhaps she saw him that way because she loved him, or perhaps she remembered him as he was before the fever damaged his mind. All I know is, he never gave *me* a look like that."

This made Nagaro think of all the things he hadn't been able to say or do during that time, and he was suddenly bitterly angry. "The 'pretty-faced boy with no more wit than a cabbage'," he said acidly. "That's what they called him. Your father was cruel to bring him to Lankura and trot him about for everyone to gawk at!"

The princess gave him a startled look but at that moment he was too angry to care what she saw in his face.

"Well," she said carefully, after a moment. "Perhaps it *was* a little cruel, but you may be sure my father is very sorry. It was he who told me to hang the portrait here—out of the public eye, but where he still has to look at it. I believe he feels guilty that it ended so badly for that poor boy." She sighed. "Leyel surely didn't deserve to die so young."

Nagaro was in no mood to be impressed by Elgurn's penitence. "If you think death is the worst thing that can happen to a person, you're mistaken," he said, not looking at her. "Leyel Virden would have been better off dead than living like *that*—" He broke off, stifling his bitterness with an effort. Striving for a more neutral tone, he added, "But he's gone now, so it doesn't matter, does it?" He looked her full in the face, then, as if daring her to recognize him, and said, "I was on my way up to find the library."

She seemed relieved to change the subject. "It's the third door on the left in the hall at the top of the stairs. I'm just going to see if the carriage is ready."

The easiness of her tone made it plain she suspected nothing.

Nagaro heaved a huge mental sigh of relief, nodded tightly, bowed, and moved past her to finish climbing the stairs, his heart still thudding.

*

Nevien lingered beside the painting for a moment after Nagaro had gone. She was impressed that the captain could feel so much for someone he'd surely never met. *That he could put himself in another's place—see through another's eyes...* It disturbed her only that he thought the simple-minded youth would have been better off dead... How could that be true of anyone? She gave the portrait a frowning glance and was held for a moment by those earnest, painted eyes... *dark gray with little flecks of blue and green...*

She turned away with a sigh, to continue her way down the stairs. At least she finally knew where she'd seen eyes like Captain Nagaro's. In fact, there was some similarity of features as well. The simple-minded prince and the pirate captain might almost have been brothers. But then, she reflected, any two very handsome young Kelorin men with regular features would necessarily look somewhat alike...

*

Nagaro paused after reaching the safety of the deserted third floor hallway. He stood with his head bowed for some seconds until his heart had slowed to a more normal rhythm. He felt he had just passed his most difficult test—as far as the princess was concerned. If Nevien could see him standing beside his own portrait and fail to know him, it could only mean that the difference in his behavior was so great that it was inconceivable to her that he could have ever been Leyel Virden.

That knowledge brought him relief, of course—and pain. It gratified him that he now had Nevien's respect, but it hurt to know with certainty that Leyel Virden had earned only her pity—and had caused her to suffer. Her words were now etched upon his heart: *I cried all night... That night and a great many others...* Anger stirred again. *None of that should have been allowed to happen...*

With a shuddering breath he thrust aside the anger and the hurt. Raising his head and squaring his shoulders, he walked resolutely along the hallway to the door of the library.

The room, when he entered it, was very much as he remembered. A few of the furnishings had been changed, notably by the addition of a large bookcase, and he also saw that the ceremonial sword and two daggers that had once adorned one of the walls were gone. Considering the murderous use he'd once contemplated for them, he was glad of it.

The other guests present seemed to consist of two young men, one Kelorin and one Leithian, seated at the nearer end of the room. The princess's ladies were clustered at the farther end, accompanied by the diminutive older blond woman whom Nagaro had seen with them before.

This woman immediately rose when he entered and approached him. She bade him welcome, introducing herself as Lady Merriel. Nagaro gave her a bow in return, and the warmest smile he could muster. The lady smiled back, before returning to the window seat.

Nagaro found a chair and sat down. One of the two young men, the Leithian, promptly leaned towards him. Jerking his head at Lady Merriel, he mouthed the word "chaperone." Nagaro responded with a nod of comprehension. The young Leithian made a wry face to signify that the woman's presence was, from his point of view, unwelcome.

"Why did you come then?" Nagaro asked in a low voice. "You must have known there'd be a chaperone."

The young Leithian shrugged. "There isn't any choice, if you want to marry one of *them*." This time he jerked his head in the direction of the young women.

"I see." Nagaro decided not to explain that he'd only come for dancing lessons. In fact he began to wonder, uneasily, if Kendira might assume that he intended something more. Uncomfortably, he glanced at the young woman where she sat among the others. Kendira, it turned out, was at that moment looking at him with a frown. As soon as he glanced her way, however, she dropped her eyes and two spots of pink appeared on her cheeks. Nagaro immediately withdrew his gaze as well. *Why had she been frowning?* Was she having second thoughts about asking him to come?

Nagaro had nothing more to say to the Leithian man. The other guest, the Kelorin, was the Fleet captain whose quarters were next to his and this young man was entirely occupied with making eyes at one of the young women whom Nagaro assumed must be the man's fiancée.

Nagaro gave up on conversation and let his thoughts wander. As it turned out, they didn't have time to wander far before a tall, broad-shouldered Leithian in the white tirka of the Palace Guard put his head in at the door to inform them that all was ready for their departure.

The Leithian guard stood by the door as they all filed past and looked Nagaro up and down in a disconcerting way. Nagaro returned the man a glance, and a nod. He realized that he'd seen the Leithian among the defenders on the city wall during the Mautep attack the previous spring, but whatever the guardsman's thoughts were, the man kept them to himself.

Nagaro moved quickly down the stairs, being careful not to glance at the portrait this time. He was relieved that no one else paid it any attention.

In the stable yard, they found the other guests waiting, including Kuran Kel, astride his horse, and another young Fleet officer whom Nagaro knew only slightly. He returned Kuran's nod of acknowledgment and wasted no time in re-buckling his sword and mounting Thunder-Heels. From his seat astride, he watched as the other members of the party either mounted their horses or climbed into the carriage.

The tall Leithian guard who had brought the news to the library mounted a horse and was joined by three other mounted guards in the same livery. The Leithian maneuvered his horse close to Thunder-Heels and spoke to Nagaro. "You needn't have brought your sword, Zirda," he said. "My men and I are here to provide escort."

Nagaro shrugged. "I'm never really comfortable without it."

The man showed his teeth in a brief smile and said, "Lord Kuran seems to feel the same way."

Nagaro turned to see that Kuran's sword was indeed at his hip.

Most of the princess's ladies, including Kendira, had settled themselves in the carriage. Only the princess and a young woman Nagaro had heard called Lady Rianine were dressed for riding. Both wore Kelorin-style women's riding clothes, consisting of long graceful pantaloons called *shapas*, extending all the way to the ankles, and an upper garment called a *shilka*. The latter was close-fitting in the bodice, belted at the waist, and falling just below the knee. Below the waist it flared like a skirt and was slit, front and back, to allow the wearer to mount a horse and sit astride.

Nagaro had been too distracted to notice the details earlier, but he now noted that Nevien's shilka and shapas were dove gray with a little embroidery in black and rose at the neck and hem. She wore a rose-pink blouse under her shilka. Nagaro thought the entire effect very becoming. Her mount was a snow white mare, and Nagaro watched admiringly as she swung lightly into the saddle.

They were soon on their way, passing out through the city without drawing much attention owing to the earliness of the hour. Once beyond the city's walls, they moved at a brisk trot, eastward along the High Road. Kuran and the tall Leithian guard led the way with the six younger male guests, including Nagaro, close behind. Next came the carriage, then Nevien and Rianine, with the other three guards bringing up the rear.

Before they had gone very far along the High Road, the party turned onto a much narrower road that branched off to the left and led roughly northward into more hilly country graced by farms and small stands of trees. As the sun angled higher, the air began to warm and a mist of evaporating frost rose like smoke from the fields along either side of the road. Many of the broad-leafed trees were already naked, their delicate traceries of silver branches in striking contrast to the dark hues of the evergreens. Other deciduous trees still wore some of their leaves in a light veil of red or gold.

Here, where the road wasn't as straight or level, the carriage horses slowed to a walk. Some of the young men engaged in conversation as they rode, but Nagaro had no interest in joining them and he soon grew weary of holding back his impatient mount. Pressing forward, he informed Kuran that he meant to give his horse a chance to run. Kuran shrugged agreement, and Nagaro let the big gray have his head.

Thunder-Heels leaped away in a joyous burst of speed. Nagaro guided the stallion along the road for a distance, then turned aside into a fallow field, swinging in a great arc to rejoin the road a bit farther on. Once there, he pulled Thunder-Heels to a halt to wait for the rest of the party.

Thunder-Heels wanted more, however, tossing his head in protest and dancing despite the tight rein. Nagaro leaned forward to stroke the powerful neck and speak to the animal, apologizing for the restraint. He was just straightening when he heard raised voices and the sound of hoofs, and an instant later the princess swept past him on her white mare, the skirts of her shilka flying and her honey-colored hair streaming behind her. Nagaro was so startled that he loosed the reins, and Thunder-Heels, sensing a race, sprang after the mare. At the same time, Nevien twisted about to shout back at him, "Catch me if you can!"

Nagaro needed no more invitation than this. Shouting words of encouragement, he gave the stallion his head and they went flying after the princess. It was a wild and glorious run. The mare had a considerable lead at the outset, but the gray stallion was longer-legged and more powerful, and wasn't long in overtaking her. Nagaro immediately reined in a little so as not to outdistance the princess, and the two horses galloped on, abreast. Leaning low over her horse's neck, Nevien gave Nagaro a laughing look. He returned a feral smile, and so they went until the mare began to flag and Nevien drew her down to a walk.

Nagaro reined in his horse as well. Feeling well-warmed by the exertion, he pulled off his tirka and stowed it in a saddlebag.

"Oh, that was fun!" Nevien's eyes danced. Her cheeks were pink with excitement and the cold air. "I'd no idea you were such a good rider, Captain. I thought you were a seaman."

Nagaro laughed. "I learned to ride a horse long before I set eyes on the sea, My Lady, and there's nothing I enjoy more than a good gallop. But I must say I had no idea *you* were such a good rider."

Nevien blushed with pleasure. "I've been riding since I was a girl," she said, "and I love it. But I don't often get a chance to do what I just did. If I'd listened to Merriel and Kuran, I wouldn't have done it today for that matter. They're probably both fit to be tied right now."

Nagaro pulled his horse to a halt and turned the animal about. "I don't see the carriage," he said, "but I see two of the riders."

Nevien had also halted. She shaded her eyes with her hand. "It's Kuran and Brandle," she said with a sigh. "You see? I've gone and divided the escort. I shouldn't have ridden off like that, but seeing you go for a gallop was just such a temptation! We'd best wait here though. They won't worry so much as long as they can see us."

Nagaro frowned. "If it's as serious as that, shouldn't we ride back to meet them?" he asked. "We can let the horses run again on the way."

Nevien laughed. "You're right of course," she said. "Come on!"

So they flew back along the road until they all but collided with Kuran and the big Leithian guard. They pulled up, laughing for sheer pleasure. Kuran gave Nagaro a stern glance, but there was really nothing he could say since Nevien immediately took responsibility for having ridden so far ahead. It wasn't Kuran's place to reprimand the princess, and Nagaro *had* provided at least a one-man escort. The guardsman said nothing and his face betrayed no reaction, though Nagaro felt the man's eyes.

The four of them rode on together at a leisurely walk, enjoying the scenery and allowing the carriage and the rest of the party to gradually catch up. After that, Nagaro rode with Kuran at the front of the little procession, while Nevien dropped back when she heard Lady Merriel call.

The chaperone leaned out of the carriage window and shook a chiding finger at her as she came abreast. "You should know better than to do that, Nevien! Whatever were you thinking?"

Nevien frowned. "It's been a year since we've heard of any trouble on this road, Merriel," she said. "And Captain Nagaro was with me."

Merriel clucked her tongue. "I'm sure he's very brave, but he's only one man. He couldn't do much against a whole band of highwaymen."

Nevien didn't think the matter was worth more than a very small sliver of guilt, so she cast her eyes heavenward and tightened her reins, dropping back to join Rianine and leaving the chaperone to remonstrate with the air.

Rianine immediately steered her horse so close that their stirrups brushed. "That looked like such fun, Nevien," she said conspiratorially. "I wish I could have joined you."

"Why didn't you then?"

Rianine raised a dark eyebrow. "I've always heard that three is one too many."

Nevien shrugged her annoyance. "Don't be silly, Rian. He's only a friend."

"Oh? And will you tell me that isn't Elyan's shirt he's wearing?"

This time Nevien gave the other young woman a sharp glance. "He found it dumped out on the floor after the Mahuk raid last spring, and liked it, so I gave it to him," she said tartly. "He was reluctant to take it too. But I told him no one would notice, so don't you dare say a word!"

"*Me?*" Rianine's expression was all injured innocence. "Perish the thought!"

The two ladies rode on in silence for half a minute, Nevien's brow still knit in a frown. "I think he already has a lady anyway," she said at length. "He wears what looks like a woman's ring on the little finger of his left hand."

"What's he doing here with us, then?"

Nevien shrugged. "He told Kendira she could teach him some dances. That may be all he's expecting."

Rianine put her head on one side. "Well, it's really too bad for poor Kendira if he's already spoken for," she observed. After another little silence, she added, "Did I tell you that I think he's breathtakingly beautiful?"

"Yes. And I'm still trying to decide whether it's an improvement on 'splendidly barbaric', which was your previous assessment."

Rianine laughed merrily. "It's such a pity he's a man. All that beauty wasted!"

Nevien gave the other young woman an exasperated look. "When are you going to tell your parents that you've no intention of marrying, Rian?"

"When life in Lankura bores me," Rianine answered airily. "Which I don't expect will be soon. Lankura has *so* many amusing people to watch. My Wared has nothing but cows and chickens."

*

A little later the party crossed a small river by means of a wooden bridge. On the farther side, Kuran and the tall guard turned left into a narrow road that ran northeast, roughly following the river. From the way the stream flowed, Nagaro presumed it must be one of the many tributaries of the great River Edro. On a whim, he asked the name of the stream, and Kuran told him it was the Tenorin. He frowned at the name. It seemed a little bit familiar. He'd known the river that flowed near Averwin mainly by its Turowan name, the Yuna. He couldn't quite remember the Kelorin name for it, but it might have been Tenorin.

He gazed about then with heightened interest. The rolling hills that surrounded them were not unlike the country around Averwin, and he felt a surge of conflicting emotions at the thought that his boyhood home might lie somewhere along this same river—even somewhere along this very road. *Perhaps he might return to the area alone, or with his friends, to make a thorough search.*

Such thoughts made him restless, and since Thunder-Heels was restless too, Nagaro told Kuran he meant to let the stallion have another run along the road.

"Don't go very far," Kuran advised him. "And turn right around and ride back to us. The last turning isn't far ahead. If we reach it without seeing you, we'll wait for you there."

Nagaro nodded, then shook out his reins and gave the stallion's flanks a squeeze with his calves. The big gray sprang away up the road at a merry gallop. Nagaro bent low over the horse's withers while the world swept past. The frost had burned away and the chill was gone from the air. Much of the rolling countryside was pasture land, with grasses gone to autumn silver and gold, but there were also fields of dark ploughed earth and stands of woodland. The road had curved somewhat away from the river, and it was met from time to time on either side by narrower roads that led to isolated farms or tiny hamlets, some of which could be seen as distant clusters of rooftops.

It was when Nagaro began to notice rocky outcroppings scattered among the fields that he drew on the reins and slowed the stallion to a trot. The rocks were smoothly weathered, black, and splashed with lichen in shades of gold Carol pale green. This land was so very like the country of his childhood that he felt an ache in his heart. *That hill there with the three fingers of rock marching up its side... Or that one with the cleft in its crest... and the way that little bit of woods wrapped itself around it...* Nagaro drew his breath in sharply, and pulled the reins so that Thunder-Heels came to a dancing halt.

There was a little stand of cedar trees, just ahead, on the left-hand side of the road where a smaller road came up a little slope to meet it...

How many times had he ridden up that smaller road and stopped beside those cedar trees to look, but to ride no farther? For surely that smaller road was the road to Averwin. Scarcely breathing, he let out the reins again and let Thunder-Heels carry him the last bit of the way. He drew rein again at the entrance to the small side road and turned about so he could survey the scene as he would have seen it if he'd just come up the road from Averwin.

Yes! There was no doubt in his mind—

"Good mornin' t' ye, Zirda."

Nagaro started, and twisted in the saddle to see who had spoken. The voice, which was that of an old woman, had apparently come from a bent, hooded figure peering at him from the shadow under the cedar trees. He'd seen no one there when he'd ridden up, so she must have emerged from within the grove itself.

Nagaro bowed from the waist where he sat in the saddle. "Good morning, Zirdyn," he said, courteously.

The old woman cocked her head. "Have ye traveled far, young man?"

"I've come from Lankura."

"Ah." A little nod. "And before that?"

Puzzled by her curiosity, Nagaro laughed. "Before that, Zirdyn? A very long way indeed."

"Ah." This time she stepped towards him so that a patch of sunlight fell upon her, and at the same time she threw back her hood. "I knew ye'd come back one day," she said. "And I prayed the Spirits would let me live long enough t' see it. These old eyes see but poorly now, but I know ye by your voice."

Nagaro stared. The old woman's hair was as white as snow. Her eyes were dark, though a little misted by age, and set in a face as wrinkled and brown as an old apple left in the sun. She had changed—aged—but still he knew her.

"Luka!" He was far too astonished to even think of dissembling. "But what are you doing here? Surely you don't still come to Averwin every autumn?"

The ancient Turowan medicine woman smiled up at him serenely. "These days, I'm never far from Averwin, *Captain Nagaro*," she said. "But please, let me touch your hand. I want t' feel that ye're real, and not an old woman's dream."

Nagaro gladly swung down from his horse and held out his hand to her. He also wanted to be sure that she was no figment of his imagination.

"How do you know I'm Captain Nagaro?" he asked.

Luka took his strong, young hand in both of her ancient wrinkled ones. She gave him a little secret smile. "I have eyes and ears in far places," she said archly. "Besides, who *else* would ye be?" She squeezed his hand hard with her fingers as if trying to feel the shape of his bones. Nor did she stop with his hand, but began working her way up his forearm, feeling through his shirt sleeve along the outer side of the arm where the bone lay close under the skin.

He thought he knew what she was doing. "It's farther up, closer to the elbow, if you're looking for the place where I broke my arm when I was a boy."

He'd tried to climb too far out along a limb and had slipped from the tree when the branch bent suddenly. Luka had set the bone. He remembered her feeling for the break, probing with her fingers while he'd wept unashamedly at the pain.

She darted him a glance, then pursed her lips and ran her fingers farther up his arm and smiled when she found the little bump where the bone had knit together. She let the arm go with a sigh, nodding to herself. On an impulse, Nagaro stepped right up to her and folded her in his arms, bending down to gently kiss her forehead. "Luka," he murmured, suddenly overcome with gratitude at finding her alive. She'd already seemed old to him when he'd last seen her, nearly eight years ago. He released her and stepped back once more, abashed by his own forwardness. He'd held her in far too much reverence when he was growing up to have ever taken such a liberty.

Luka, however, merely gave him a beatific smile. "Ye were always a good lad," she said. Then she dug into the pocket of her plain brown skirt. "I have some things for ye."

"What... *things?*" He frowned, puzzled, for he didn't see how she could possibly be carrying something she meant to give to him.

Her hand came out holding two small objects and she reached for his hand again. "This is for remembering," she said, as she placed a folded square of leather into his open palm. It was stitched along the fold and wound about and tied with a bit of faded yellow ribbon. "And this is for long life." The second object was a flat, rounded pebble, about an inch across. It was smooth and silver-gray, and had a symbol inscribed on it. Luka held it for a moment and seemed to study it. "I've kept it a long time," she murmured. "And it's kept me. But 'tis long enough, now, and time t' pass it on." So saying, she pressed the small stone into his hand beside the bit of folded leather.

Something about the way she'd spoken disturbed him—almost as if she were choosing the moment of her death. "No," he said, trying to give the stone back to her. "I want you to keep it, Luka."

But she stepped away from him, raising both hands and shaking her head, "It's passed on," she said. "Ye can't give it back."

It was at that moment, as he stood uncertain, that a shout rang behind him from along the road. Closing his hand on Luka's gifts, he turned quickly and moved to a spot beside his waiting horse where he could get a clear view of the road. The carriage and the rest of princess's party were some distance off, but rapidly approaching.

"They're coming—" he began, and turned back toward the cedar trees, meaning to warn Luka to pretend that they didn't know each other. He stopped and stared. Luka was nowhere to be seen. The old woman had disappeared as completely as if she had never been. He might have believed he'd imagined the encounter if it weren't for the two objects in his hand. Hurriedly he thrust them into his pocket.

He scarcely had time to mount his horse before Nevien and Kuran came cantering up, with the big Leithian guard close behind them.

The princess's golden-brown hair was all a-tumble, and her eyes were dancing. "Now how did you know this was the turning?" she asked.

"*This?*" Nagaro nearly choked and had to cover his mouth and pretend to cough. "This is it? I didn't, of course. I just chanced to stop here."

"Who was that I saw under the trees?" The question came from the guardsman.

Nagaro met the man's questioning eyes. "There was an old woman. She spoke to me, but she's gone now."

The answer was broadly accurate if uninformative. Still, it seemed to satisfy the Leithian, for he nodded. "That'd be the old Turowan witch-woman that lives somewhere about," he observed with a shrug.

Nagaro would have liked to counter this description, based on his knowledge of Luka, but of course he didn't dare. He merely shrugged and said, "She seemed harmless enough."

Nevien turned to include Kuran and the Leithian guard and spoke with breathless enthusiasm. "Come on! Lets race to River House!" She shook her reins and the white mare sprang away. Kuran gave a shout and urged his bay to follow. The Leithian cried a word to his mount as well and sprang after them both in hot pursuit. Nagaro had to pull hard on his reins to prevent Thunder-Heels from joining the chase.

River House.

Averwin...

He knew the whole length of that narrow road, from where he now sat on his horse to where it ended at the last of a half dozen farm houses. There was nothing along that path that anyone might call a country villa, except Averwin. Something might have been built, of course. It had been seven—almost eight—years. But barring that...

"*Oh Vothra...*" He felt a rising swell of hope and fear. What might he find there?

The other riders and the carriage came up along side of him, and he reined Thunder-Heels aside to let them pass. Rianine gave him a probing glance as she rode by, but he scarcely noticed. He was aware of little else but the tide of his emotions, the hammering of his heart. He shook himself back into action just in time to swing his horse in behind the last of the guards. This wasn't how he would have chosen to make his homecoming, but it seemed there was nothing to be done about it.

His heart measured every inch of the road. The closer he came to Averwin, the more he lagged behind the carriage, tightening his reins though Thunder-Heels tossed his head resentfully. *There was the river again, bending back to meet the road. There was the hill, rising to a kind of bluff where the river had cut into it.* He passed the spot where it was just possible to make out his old "stone seat" high on the face of the little cliff that rose above the water. Then the stand of trees that flanked the house cut off the view. And then, of course, there was the house...

And the carriage was turning off onto the short spur that led to the front gate...

The house looked very much as he remembered. There were two stories... a rust-colored tile roof... walls of whitewashed plaster accented with dark stone. A stand of cedar trees flanked it on the one side and a cluster of oaks, nearly leafless with the season, on the other. There were a few changes, too. The old dead oak by the garden wall was gone—probably cut up for firewood—and there were a pair of new buildings of dark stone, long and low, beside the old stable. Nagaro saw the guardsmen making for them and decided they must have been built to serve the princess's guards when they accompanied Nevien and her ladies. One of the guardsmen, who had already dismounted, was leading his horse towards the nearer of the new buildings, indicating that it must be a second stable.

Nagaro saw the young male guests disappearing into the original stable, leading their horses. He dismounted but hung back, waiting, until they emerged again before approaching the building himself, bypassing the ladies who were disembarking from the carriage.

He paused at the stable entrance, allowing his eyes to adjust to the dimness. Then he drank in the familiar sight—the row of stalls, the tack stowed on pegs and racks on the opposite wall—even as he inhaled the blessed aroma of leather, hay, and horse manure. This was *his* stable. In the sacred book of his boyhood memories it was a holy shrine.

Nagaro's eyes stung, and he blinked. Looking about, he saw that the white mare was already there, along with Kuran's bay and the other mounts, all comfortably housed in stalls. He saw no sign of a stableman, which suited him well enough. It meant that he could tend to his own mount and take his time about it, thus delaying the moment when he would have to enter the house that had once been his home and was now filled up with strangers.

"Come, Thunder," he said, taking the gray horse's bridle. "I see a comfortable place for you." He led the stallion into an empty stall, to stand amid fresh straw. There he unbuckled and removed the bridle and the saddle and found places for them with the others. Returning to the stall, he patted the horse's arching neck. "There you are, brother," he murmured. "Now you can rest. And I think I know where to find water and hay and oats in this place."

"Master Leyel?"

Nagaro's heart jolted in his chest and he started violently, twisting about in the stall beside the gray stallion. The speaker wasn't visible from where he stood, but Nagaro could hear the sound of shuffling steps on the worn planks of the floor, drawing nearer. The man's voice spoke again.

"I'd know yer voice anywhere, young master, but I don't see ye..." There was a momentary pause as an aging Turo, graying and a little stooped, moved into view opposite the entrance to the stall where Nagaro stood. The man gaped at him. "*Hamanei mata noa, Master Leyel!*" he exclaimed. "Is that ye standin' there?"

"*Chula!*"

Nagaro crossed the gap between them in three strides and caught the old gardener in an embrace so enthusiastic that the man's breath was audibly squeezed out of him. An instant later he released the old man and stepped back. "But you mustn't use that name, Chula, or let on that you know me," he said, lowering his voice. "I'm Nagaro now. You should call me Captain Nagaro, or just 'Captain' will do."

Chula's jaw dropped, revealing the gap where he was missing a tooth. "*Ye're* Captain Nagaro? *Hakura!*" He shook his head. "I always knowed ye'd make a name fer yerself. 'Course I thought it'd be with the one the lady gave ye." He chuckled, enjoying his own jest as he looked Nagaro up and down. "Oh, but ye've changed, lad! Ye wear that sword like it was made for ye. And just look at yer shoulders! And ye've a beard on ye t' make any Turo proud. But what've ye done t' make yerself so *brown?*"

Nagaro lowered his voice another notch, speaking urgently. "It's kuma stain—part of my disguise, Chula. I can't tell you how good it is to see you again, and I'll try to find another chance to talk to you. But if I take much longer now, I'm afraid someone will come looking for me. I just need to know one thing: Are there any other folk about the place who would know me?"

The old man's face turned somber. "No, Master Ley— I mean, *Capt'n*. They're all gone. 'Cept me. Thorlan's dead—two year. 'Course he'd already gone from *here* afore it all happened. I'm all there is for a stableman now, and not much o' one at that. I don't know where Hinda's got to. There's a new housekeeper an' cook. Decent woman, but not from these parts. An' the householders are all gone too—I don't know where. The king bought 'em out, an' then turned 'round and sold the farms t' strangers..." The old Turo's words ran out and he shook his head morosely.

Nagaro reached out and gave the man's shoulder a squeeze. "Poor old Chula," he said sympathetically. "I'm sorry there's no one else left, but I'm glad you're still here." This won him another gap-toothed smile. "Can you help me get feed and water for my horse?"

Chula sighed. "I'll fetch it if ye put's it in the manger, Zirda. Truth is, horses scares the piss out o' me—great monster beasts!"

*

A few minutes later, Nagaro was mounting the steps to the covered terrace at the rear of the house. The back door that opened onto the terrace was the closest entry when coming from the stable. He paused at the top of the steps to gaze across the terrace and the scene beyond. The terrace was paved with flagstones, its three open sides lightly screened by trellises spaced at intervals. The vines that covered the trellises were already leafless, so he could look out through the tracery of bare stems. Through that tracery, he saw one end of the garden that lay behind the house, surrounded by its low wall, as well as the chicken coop and goat pens. The pasture was there too, with its grass gone to autumn gold, and the shining line of the river beyond that, and the shadowy woods.

The scene had changed little, and it held a trove of memories, achingly bitter-sweet, belonging as they did to a time that was past and could never be reclaimed. He dragged his eyes away from the scene, taking passing note of the three round tables arranged on the terrace, each covered with a crisp white cloth and ringed by rustic wooden chairs, all waiting presumably for the guests to take their lunch.

He drew a breath. It was time to enter the house.

If the sight of the terrace and grounds wrung his heart, the inside of the house would likely be worse. It held not only the memories of a long-lost happier time, but also those of the horrific events that had marked his final days in this place. He wondered warily what he would find changed inside, and what would be the same—and which of the two would be harder to bear.

As it turned out, the little back hall was comfortingly familiar in most respects. *Though there was something missing...* The clean white plaster walls were the same as ever, and one of Maramine's paintings, depicting the house as seen from the pasture, was hanging where it always had. The only obvious physical change was the presence of a small carved table bearing a white porcelain vase with an arrangement of twisted cedar wood and dried rushes. The table and the vase had formerly stood in the upstairs hall. Nagaro liked the new location and he found himself thinking that it was something Maramine might have done. And thinking about *that* made him realize with a pang what it was that he missed: *the nearly omnipresent subtle scent of the Lady's lavender sachet...*

He swallowed, and had just put out his hand to touch the glazed surface of the vase, when he was interrupted by the voice of the princess.

"I was beginning to think you preferred the company of the horses, Captain."

He turned to find that she had stepped out of the dining room into the hall. From her tone, he understood that she was teasing and he gave her his pirate smile. "Perhaps I do, My Lady."

Laughing, she beckoned for him to follow her into the dining room.

Before Nagaro could do so, the tall Leithian guard appeared behind her in the open doorway. "Do you mean to take your sword *everywhere*, Captain?" he inquired.

"Everywhere it's permitted." Nagaro gave him a fractional bow.

The man's teeth flashed briefly. "There's no rule against it here, Zirda."

The dining room was also much as Nagaro remembered it, though the modest dining table had been replaced by one long enough to seat a dozen. There were also new white lace curtains on the two large windows that looked out onto the terrace and into the garden. In all other respects, the furnishings were unchanged: the dark wood chairs with dark blue cushions, the fireplace done in terra cotta tiles, and the Jinari carpet with the stylized floral design in hues of blue, red, brown, and gold that graced the polished wood floor. The room might have felt comfortably familiar if it hadn't been full of the sights and scents of unfamiliar people.

The men were mostly seated around the periphery, while Merriel and the princess's ladies were clustered at the table—except for the eldest, Tulevian, who was standing to one side in deep conversation with her fiancé. Those at the table had a book of poetry open and one of them was reading aloud from it while the others exclaimed over the prettiness of the accompanying illustrations. The poem of the moment was about flowers and gardens and Nagaro recognized the volume as one of the Lady Maramine's.

"Did someone bring a book all the way from Lankura?" he inquired as innocently as he could, seeing an opportunity to escape the unwanted company.

Nevien answered from close behind him. "Oh, no," she said. "That book came from the library."

"There's a library?" Nagaro did his best to sound appropriately surprised. "Where?"

Nevien smiled. "Upstairs—second door on the left. It's rather a fine collection. And take your time, Captain. Lunch won't be for another hour."

So Nagaro escaped the strangers in the dining room to face his memories instead.

8: Lessons And Lilies

Nagaro had to go back out into the hallway to reach the stairs. He shivered involuntarily as he passed the open kitchen door despite the cheerful sounds of clinking dishes and warm smell of fresh bread emanating from it. He'd been intercepted there while trying to escape from the house on that fateful night. His attackers had leaped out of the dark kitchen, knocking him to the floor in the pitch black hallway. *Bron Sobring had pinned him while Dreigen inflicted the first stab of the bladder-thorn. The sadistic Gillard Marchent had lit a candle and watched, holding the light for Dreigen to work by. Even the kind-hearted Kale Fendred had sat on his legs...*

With an effort, Nagaro shook off the suffocating coil of memory. Taking a deep breath, he passed on along the passage and climbed the stairs. He stopped at the top to look into his old room and was surprised to find it quite untouched. It seemed smaller than he remembered, but sunlight was spilling through the familiar window, framed by white curtains, and the plaster walls glowed with reflected light, just as he remembered. One of Maramine's paintings—his favorite with the three horses grazing in the pasture—still hung on the wall. His bed was there too, with the little night stand beside it. The feather mattress was still covered by his old blue and white quilt.

He had awakened there on so many peaceful, happy mornings. But there had also been those final days... lying there, paralyzed by the effects of heskial, until someone—usually Dreigen—had bidden him rise. The table was still there, and the two chairs, where he'd sat across from Dreigen while the Lore Master's pen had scratched a record of his agony and the hourglass had measured out the minutes and seconds of his desperation...

Nagaro shuddered and wrenched himself away, hurrying along the upstairs hall past more of Maramine's paintings. He tried to calm himself even as he shied away from any thought of going to the end of the hall where her bedchamber lay. He couldn't bear to look into the room where he'd been forced to watch her die.

He stopped instead at the library, halfway along the hall, where he paused outside the door and cautiously looked in. Apart from minor changes in the furnishings, the room had been left as he remembered. The bookcases were still in the same positions. At a glance, at least, their contents appeared unchanged. There was still a low table by the window with some comfortable chairs for reading. The chairs had different cushions, but the color scheme was still in green, rust, and wheat-straw gold. The unpleasant memories associated with this room were mild compared with those evoked by his own bedchamber.

Nagaro drew a long sigh, and entered.

The room had served also as Maramine's study, and her old desk had been moved to a different wall. The change drew his attention. He crossed to the desk and touched the smooth wood, running his fingers over the familiar carvings. Moved by memories of the lady seated there, he opened first one and then the other of the two little sliding doors that covered the places where writing materials were kept. To his surprise, he found that there were still pens, ink, and sealing wax on the right-hand side, and paper on the left. The pens and inkwell even looked the same. He picked up a quill and reverently stroked the feather. Replacing it, he slid the little door shut.

He was about to turn away, when a thought struck him. There was another door, a secret door.

The desk had been made to look as if the central panel remained fixed while the two sliding doors moved in front of it when opened, but Nagaro had seen the Lady Maramine open the middle panel once. She hadn't realized he was watching. Being at the time a curious ten-year-old, he'd returned after she'd gone, and found the secret locking mechanism. The papers in the compartment had held no interest for him, however, and he'd never opened it again, content to let the lady keep her grown-up secrets.

On impulse, he bent down to feel for the catch on the undersurface of the desk. His fingers quickly located the slight dimple in the wood that marked the place. He pressed firmly. With a faint click, the top edge of the secret panel tilted forward an inch, and he swung it open the rest of the way to reveal a small trove of papers, some loose, some tied in little bundles. For a long moment he only looked at them. These must be Maramine's private papers, untouched since the time of her death. It was unlikely anyone else knew of their existence and he felt suddenly guilty, as if he were intruding.

But the idea was absurd. The lady was seven years dead. Her spirit had joined with Vothra, and she existed now only as one of Vothra's myriad strands of memory. Her purposes were now Vothra's purposes, and nothing she had left behind would hold any special meaning for the Benevolent Spirit.

Drawing an uneasy breath, Nagaro picked up a thick bundle tied with a single loop of white ribbon. He slipped the topmost letter from under the silken strand. The letter had been folded so that all of the writing was on the inside, and fastened with sealing wax. Although the seal was broken, he could see clearly that the writer had pressed a thumb—a man's thumb by the size of the impression—into the warm wax. Very gently, he unfolded the letter and read the first few lines, written in a fine, strong hand:

My Dearest Maramine,

How is it possible that I can endure these terrible days of waiting? This is cruel indeed, not knowing when or how I may be permitted to see you again...

Nagaro didn't need to read any further. He knew who the ardent young man was who had penned those words even before seeing that the signature at the bottom read *"Beloras."* The Lady Maramine hadn't spoken often of her murdered lover, but Nagaro knew the gist of their tragic tale. Beloras and Maramine had been in love, but she'd been above his station and her father had disapproved. Beloras had ultimately been challenged to combat and slain by Maramine's own brother, Varsyl. The unfortunate affair had led to an estrangement between Maramine and her family, and to her exile to Averwin. Such was the cruel folly that had cut one life short, and blighted another. In all the years that he'd known her, Maramine had worn only widow's gray.

Nagaro sighed, refolded the letter, and slipped it back under the ribbon.

At that moment, approaching footsteps sounded in the hallway—a man's heavy booted tread. Nagaro hastily put the letters back, closed the secret panel, and stepped away from the desk. Moving quickly to the nearest bookcase, he had just enough time to raise his hand as if in the act of taking down a book before the tall Leithian guard strode into the room.

The man halted a few paces from him. "Captain Nagaro," he said. "I was hoping I might find you alone."

Nagaro lowered his hand. "Well, you've done so," he said, regarding the man warily. Being on duty, the big Leithian wore his own sword at his hip, and he stood with a thumb hooked negligently into his sword belt. Nagaro was suddenly aware that a sword fight in this place might not be heard by anyone in the dining room downstairs.

The guardsman was studying him keenly and must have seen that Nagaro had noticed the proximity of his hand to his sword hilt, for he abruptly unhooked his thumb and extended his hand. "Well met, Zirda," he said. "I'm Brandle Furthing, and I've no wish to cross swords with you after seeing you handle a blade last spring during the Mahuk attack."

Nagaro relaxed. He took the man's hand and shook it. "Well met, indeed," he said. The man's hand was as large as the rest of him and his grip was like iron. "I remember you from the fight on the wall," he continued. "You have a formidable sword arm, yourself, and I saw you wounded if I'm not mistaken. I'm glad to see you're fully recovered."

The Leithian searched Nagaro's face. "Your memory serves you well, Captain, and I appreciate the compliment. But it seems my name means nothing to you." There was a quick flash of the man's teeth. "And here I'd begun to think you might be keeping that sword with you on my account."

Nagaro was frankly surprised. "I certainly was not," he said. "I just prefer to wear it, as I've said. But should I know your name?" He frowned. "You are, I suppose, Lord Furthing's son..." Something stirred in his memory. "*Bishka!*" he muttered. "Would you be...?" and his words trailed into embarrassment as he struggled with how to say what was in his mind.

"Simion's lover?" Brandle finished for him, grinning like a wolf. "Would those be the words you're looking for? He's told me a great deal about you."

Nagaro shifted uncomfortably. "So, I guess that Simion came safely home to Lankura," he said. "I'm glad of it. But I was trying to think of something less... *blunt...*"

"I expect that you were." The Leithian's feral smile flashed again. "Personally, I find bluntness suits me. Good Mother Solbrid, when she gave me life, made me crossed. And Great Father Hrathgard when he laid his hand upon me, made me a warrior—so it seems that I can love men or kill them with equal facility. But I don't see why I should apologize for one and not the other, when neither was any of my choosing and men who love women don't feel any need to apologize for it."

Nagaro was nonplused by such straightforwardness. "I didn't mean that I thought it was anything to be ashamed of," he said hastily.

Laughter rumbled in the Leithian's throat. "Nothing to be ashamed of? Yet we must whisper, or use other words, and do our best to hide it from the world."

"Your pardon, Zirda, but I've found that crossed men usually do try to keep it close."

Brandle dismissed Nagaro's words with a shrug. "I hide nothing—not since the incident with Simion that exposed us six years ago. Simion had a huge row with his father over it, and ran away to join the Fleet to prove he was a man. So what had I left to lose that I cared about? My father tried to hush it up and pretend it never happened. I wouldn't let him."

Nagaro attempted to cover his astonishment. From what he'd heard, the incident in question had involved Brandle being cast into the street stark naked. "I don't personally disagree," he said carefully, "about speaking openly. But a great many other men seem to think otherwise."

Brandle laughed again. "My father wouldn't speak to me for nearly a year, my rank was reduced to guardsman, and I was given a *change of posting*. Not that I'm complaining," he added, grinning wickedly. "I'm back up to lieutenant again, and I've been put in command of the Princess's Guard, 'til they find someone *more suitable*—which they won't." He laughed again. "Some say that I got the posting because Lady Merriel is my mother's sister, but the truth is, Commander Harthred—may he ride with Kroneg to the end of the world—was wise enough to see the value of setting men of *my* kind to protect women from men of *yours*."

Nagaro stiffened, but Brandle instantly added, "My Lady Princess assures me you're a gentleman, Captain. What I meant by 'your kind' was men who are straight-sailors rather than crossed. Actually, I want to thank you for looking out for Simion, and for sending him back to me."

Nagaro frowned. "He gave me water when I was out of my head with fever, and he did his part in the fight, too. And I didn't *send* him home. That was his choice."

Brandle gave him a frank, appraising look. "And you showed him kindness. Which is more than many men would do."

Nagaro swallowed. "I should have done more, but... I, ah... didn't wish to encourage him—" He stopped, feeling the blood in his face.

"I know all about that." The Leithian smiled tightly. "And the more I see of you, the more I understand what Simion said about you—which I won't embarrass you by repeating. Let's just say that I'm glad I don't have to regard you as a rival."

Again Nagaro felt himself blushing. "I might say the same," he observed with complete candor. Brandle was half a head taller and two inches broader in the shoulders, and he had the kind of rough-hewn masculine good looks that Nagaro would gladly have exchanged for his own prettiness.

This time Brandle laughed outright. "Thank you for the compliment, Captain, and I must say that I like you as well as any man of your kind I've ever met." He winked slyly. "But if at least one of us doesn't show himself downstairs soon, there might be talk—which would do you a good deal more harm than it would me. I should go do my patrol of the grounds". And with that, the Leithian executed a mock salute, turned, and left the library.

Nagaro breathed a sigh of relief. He waited a little after Brandle had gone before returning to the dining room with a history book in his hand.

When he stepped into the room, he saw that Kendira was seated with one of the other young women on the couch under the window, bent over the book of verse. She looked up as he entered, and their glances met, but she immediately frowned and dropped her eyes. Nagaro pulled his gaze away as well.

The princess and several of the other guests were gathered around the table, playing a game called Oskampo using a set of pictured cards and small wooden counters. Kuran and Merriel were seated in two comfortable chairs near the room's large fireplace, conversing.

Nagaro took a third chair and did his best to appear to be immersed in the book he had chosen, though his thoughts kept jumping from his encounters with Luka and Chula to how close Brandle had come to catching him going through Maramine's papers. He'd managed to read less than two pages by the time a bell rang to announce lunch.

As he had expected, the meal was served at the tables outside on the terrace. Nagaro took a seat to the left of Tulevian who was focused entirely on her captain, seated on her right. The chair on Nagaro's left remained empty until almost everyone was seated, at which point Rianine abruptly dropped into it.

She met his startled glance with a challenging look. "If you were saving this seat for Kendira, you've missed your chance," she observed pointedly. "She's found a place over there."

He followed her gaze and saw Kendira sitting at the table with the princess and Merriel. She was not, at that moment, looking at him.

"Oh," he said. "I'm afraid I hadn't thought about it."

Rianine put her head on one side. "She *was* the one who got you an invitation, wasn't she?"

"I believe so."

"And have you said a single word to her?"

"Well, no..." He hesitated. "She offered to teach me some dances, but I'm not sure she still wants to. All she's done so far is frown at me."

"Well what do you expect?" Rianine was indignant. "If you're already spoken for, the very least you can do is explain yourself!"

He stared, mystified. "*Spoken* for?"

She gave him a probing look. "Well," she said, after a moment. "Either you're very innocent, or you're a complete cad." She sighed. "But really, Captain, you simply *must* speak to Kendira." Abruptly she leaned towards him, bringing her lips close to his ear. "She thinks you're *terribly handsome*, by the way." Straightening, she looked him up and down critically while he sat there in utter dismay, burning with embarrassment. "I don't see it, myself," she said after a moment. "The only thing I find 'terrible' about you is your manners." She gave him one last teasing smile, and was gone in a ripple of laughter.

Somehow Nagaro got through the meal after that. Rianine clearly thought he was acting badly—and it upset him. He could think of only one interpretation of the young woman's words. And while he thought it rather unfair for anyone to assume that he had a romantic interest based on his single brief conversation with Kendira, he was also guiltily aware that he'd been too distracted since arriving at the house to give her any thought. By the time lunch was over, he had formed a resolve.

When the guests rose to leave the terrace, he approached Kendira as she was about to re-enter the house, cleared his throat, and addressed her.

"If you're still willing to teach me some dances, Kendira, I thought now would be a good time. We could use the parlor—" He stopped, biting his tongue. For all he knew, the parlor might have been made over for some other purpose.

Kendira gave him a look like a frightened rabbit, and for an instant he feared he'd said something seriously amiss. But then she rallied and gave him a timid smile. "Why, ah... of course, Captain." Her face went pink as several pairs of eyes turned her way. "We'll need a chaperone," she murmured, casting a pleading glance at Kuran and Merriel, who were following close behind her.

Kuran caught her look and gave her a kindly wink. "Say no more, my dear," he said. "I've an eye to spare and I'm sure My Lady Merriel is quite capable of watching the others."

Merriel gave him a fluttering smile. "Of course I am, Kuran."

Nagaro was relieved. If there had to be a witness to this, he was glad it would be the Lord of the Fleet.

As it turned out, the parlor only had a few new furnishings. The pedestal table Nagaro had been so fond of playing under when he was a boy was still there, but he and Kuran quickly moved it to make a clear space in the center of the floor. Then Kuran found himself a comfortable seat on a couch and sat down.

Kendira nervously began the lesson with a circle dance that was called *Tatapan*. Since Nagaro had never been taught this one before, he let himself be quite natural about the learning process. Kendira first walked him through the steps, which he mastered quickly. She gave him an encouraging look. "You're very good at this," she told him.

Nagaro shrugged. "It helps that you laid it out so plainly."

Kendira smiled nervously at his praise. Then she demonstrated the dance for him, singing a set of cues for the steps in time to the dance's melody as she went.

Nagaro watched with interest. "Who taught you to do that?"

"No one taught me," she said. "It's the way I used to remember the steps when I was a girl."

"Well, I think it's very clever," he told her, which earned him another blushing smile. "Sing it again for me."

She shook her head. "You should sing it for yourself."

Nagaro gave her a rueful glance. "If I try that, you'll either cover your ears or laugh at me. I can't sing a note."

At this, Kuran spoke up. "No more can I, so *I* certainly won't laugh. Don't worry about the tune; just try to get the rhythm right."

So Nagaro tried, and Kendira laughed a little, but not too unkindly. And so it went. After *Tatapan*, Kendira went on to *The Ivy Vine*, then to the *Balandir*, and finally *Tavinskala*, progressing from circle dances to couple dances as she became more comfortable with holding his hand or having him put his arm around her waist.

After a time, Nevien tiptoed in and sat down next to Kuran. After watching with him for a while, she leaned over to whisper, "Can one say a man is graceful?"

He raised an eyebrow. "Well I wouldn't say it to his face, but I do know what you mean. It's the same when he handles a sword. Watching Nagaro fight is like watching a dance."

Nevien winced. "Oh," she said, "a deadly dance. What a frightening thought." She turned back to watch the two at their practice. "But this isn't frightening at all, is it," she said after a moment. He handles her so... *delicately*."

"Mmm." Kuran grunted his agreement. "What's more remarkable is the *amount* he has learned. Four dances in an hour and a half! Though he did say he'd been taught two of them years ago."

Nagaro and Kendira paused, and Nagaro called out to Kuran and Nevien to join them. "We're just going to practice the *Balandir* again," he explained. "And it will work much better with two couples."

Kuran immediately rose, laughing. He bowed to the princess, gave her his arm, and they all went through the dance with the two women humming the tune. After that, they practiced *Tavinskala*, a complicated dance that involved changing partners at the end of each repetition of the pattern. After Kuran and Nagaro had handed Nevien and Kendira back and forth several times, the two couples spun to a stop, laughing.

Kuran made a great show of puffing and panting. "Is that enough for one day's work?"

Kendira nodded. "It's more than enough." She glanced shyly at Nagaro. "Do you think you can remember all that, Captain?"

"I think so," Nagaro replied earnestly. "And thank you. You're a very good teacher."

Kendira turned bright pink and looked at the floor. "I scarcely did anything," she murmured. "You learn everything so quickly!"

Nevien turned to Kuran. "If we're finished here, My Lord, I mean to go for a ride around the grounds."

Kuran made her a bow and offered her his arm as he straightened. "Very good, My Lady."

Nagaro gave Kendira his arm as well. As they followed Kuran and the princess from the room, he turned to her on an impulse and asked, "Do you like to ride, Kendira?"

Her fingers jerked on his arm. "Oh no! I... I'm sorry, Captain. I don't know how."

He was frankly surprised. He'd imagined that she simply preferred the carriage—or that she had wished to wear a gown for the dancing lessons. "Oh," he said. "Well, perhaps I can teach you, then, to repay you for the dancing lessons."

This time she blanched and nearly let go of his arm altogether. "Oh no, please!" she cried, turning frightened eyes to him. "I'm terrified of horses!"

Nagaro did his best to conceal his disappointment at this revelation. "That's all right," he said. "I'll find some other way to repay you. At the very least I'll give you the first dance I know the next time I'm invited to a feast at the palace."

They had reached the dining room. Kendira thanked him and fled, to join two of the other young women who were chatting at the table. It appeared the other guests had gone outside. Nagaro sighed. He wasn't sure whether Rianine would think that he'd redeemed himself, and she wasn't there to ask.

In any case, he wanted to find Chula again.

He slipped quietly out by the back door. From the terrace he could hear voices, male and female, from the direction of the pasture where the goat pen and the henhouse lay, but he made for the garden. There his steps slowed as the familiarity of the place smote him. The vegetable patch was nearly all bare earth at this season, but the trees and shrubs in the flower garden were merely dormant, some still bearing leaves. They hadn't changed much in seven years. *Chula must have kept them so...*

He followed a curving path past a pair of cedars to where a little stream ran along the back edge of the garden on its way to the river. A large chestnut tree grew between the path and the water, overarching both. Only a few amber leaves still clung to its branches, and the pale autumn sunlight falling through the tracery cast a network of shadow on the stones of the path.

Nearby there was a stone bench in a little patch of dry grass near two beds that had apparently been planted with lilies. Chula was there, down on his knees with a trowel, carefully digging up the withered plants, stacking the stalks in one neat pile, the bulbs in another.

Chula looked up at the sound of Nagaro's footsteps. "Time t' be layin' these in for the winter." He patted the bulbs with a calloused hand.

Nagaro stopped beside him. "You never had lilies here before," he said. "Though it seems a good place for them."

Chula's expression instantly turned somber. "They're for her," he said, pointing a gnarled finger to where a gravestone lay half-hidden among the drooping lily plants.

Nagaro read the name chiseled there: *Maramine Virden*. "So they buried her here," he murmured. "I never knew..."

"Didn't ye?" Chula blinked up at him. "I warn't here when it all happened, but I thought ye were..."

Nagaro froze. "I... *was*..." Horror settled on him like a pall, dimming the sun. He sank onto the cold stone bench. "They killed her, Chula—" he began, and stopped. Chula was gaping at him, and he realized that he had to be careful what he said. Too much knowledge might endanger the old man. "It wasn't a fever of the brain as they said," he began. "It was Dreigen's doing—mostly. The king knew... but I don't think he meant it to end that way. It was a kind of *accident*."

That was being much too kind. Elgurn had ended Maramine's life—smothering her with a bed pillow to shorten the agony of fatal heskial withdrawal. It had been an act—he now realized—more of mercy than of murder. *But it was still Elgurn who had let Dreigen go ahead with his abominable plan in the first place—drugging Maramine to secure her 'cooperation', and trying to get his, through her. Though of course the Lore Master hadn't told Elgurn the whole truth about the properties of heskial...*

He saw that Chula was nodding with an expression of relief, and decided that he'd said enough to satisfy the old gardener. "I'm glad they laid her here," he added.

"Aye, she would ha' liked it."

"And I'm glad you've been here to tend the place, Chula... and to plant lilies. She always loved lilies."

"Aye, that she did..."

There was a pause, that lengthened, until Chula broke it. He was looking at the grave marker. "I expect there's one for ye somewhere in the palace garden," he said quietly. "I heard there was a funeral an' all... But they never said they'd found ye dead, so I always *hoped* ye was alive somewhere..." He glanced searchingly at Nagaro. "What 'd they do t' ye, lad?"

Nagaro looked away. Of course the man must wonder. He should try to explain. "It was... *a drug*..." He faltered. "But.. I'd... rather not talk about it."

Chula got to his feet with surprising nimbleness, considering his years, and came to sit down on the bench beside Nagaro. "That's all right, Mas—ah... Capt'n. What matters is, ye got away. Ye're alive. An' ye're here now."

There was another pause—a longer one this time—while Nagaro collected himself. At length he spoke, asking a question that had troubled him since their earlier conversation. "How is it that you are here, Chula? When everyone else is gone?"

The old Turo chuckled. "Oh, well, I *belongs* wi' the place, don't I? Been here since afore yer Lady Maramine ever came. Those seventeen years she was here was good years. She was a good mistress, was Lady Maramine. Always let me do anything I wanted wi' the garden." The old man sighed wistfully. "I warn't here when she died, 'cause I was with me old mother that was dying, herself." The old man sighed.

"I did hear about that, Chula. I'm sorry."

The gardener gave him a clear-eyed look. "She'd had a good life, an' it was her time," he said. "And I'll see her in Hanuroa. But there was the dyin', an' the buryin', and I had t' help my sister put the house t' rights. It was months afore I come back here, and found the place empty. I took odd jobs 'round about, t' keep food on the plate. And I did a bit o' tidying here in the garden—'cause I couldn't bear t' see it all go to weeds. I'd no reason t' doubt what they said about how the Lady died. An' I found her grave here, so I knew she was really gone. I heard tales about ye from Lankura, too, but I couldn't hardly believe 'em."

Here Chula cocked his head at Nagaro, as if hoping for some further enlightenment, but Nagaro avoided the old Turo's eyes.

The gardener shrugged again and continued. "It went on like that for a time, an' then, one spring day—there *she* was. The Lady Princess— wi' that Lady Merriel, an' four o' them soldiers in uniform. That's the first I knew the place belonged t' the king. She found me here, workin' in the garden. 'What are ye doin' here?' she asks. So I says t' her—just like I said to ye—'I *belongs* wi' the place.' 'Who's payin' ye?' she asks, 'for doin' all this work?' 'Nobody but the trees an' flowers,' I says t' her. So she hired me back, on the spot, she did!"

"And she's never asked you anything about... about... Leyel?"

Chula blinked at him. "She did, once. Right at the beginning. But I told her I was just the gard'ner, ye see. Said I didn't talk much t' the great folk. Didn't like t' *lie* to her, Zirda, but I didn't want t' be run off the place like the householders. She never asked again." He sighed. "She's a fine lady, the princess is—an' a good mistress too. She leaves the garden t' me, just like yer Lady Maramine used t' do."

Nagaro nodded. "She's also kept the house very much as Maramine kept it, and I'm glad. I... wondered, though, what she's done with... the Lady's room..." He paused, hopefully.

"Oh, she's changed it all." Chula waved a hand. "Said it was too gloomy. She's made it her room whenever she stays th' night."

Nagaro frowned at the thought that Nevien was sleeping in the room where Maramine had died. But it was better than leaving the room the way it had been... Maramine *had* decorated it rather somberly. It had suited her to be somber. He forced a smile. "It's good that someone is using it."

Chula gave him a brave smile. "'Course it is."

Nagaro looked at the ground. "I'm sorry I didn't come sooner, Chula—to see if I could find you, I mean—and any of the others. But I couldn't remember anything at first—after... *the drug*... Not for a whole year. And then the Mahuk sea raiders took me for a slave and held me for a year and a half. And since I've been free... well... I never actually knew where Averwin *was*. And for a long time I didn't even think it would be safe for me in Lankura."

Chula shook his head in amazement. "Ye really were a slave, then?"

"Yes."

"And ye really fought yer way free, an' stole a Mahuk ship like the tales say? And ye've been sailin' around, takin' more o' their ships, and settin' slaves free, an' all?"

Nagaro smiled weakly. "The tales make it all sound too grand, I'm sure. And I had a lot of help from good friends and comrades. But, yes, I've done all that."

Chula gave a low whistle. "*Hakura!* But ye don't seem very *different*, for all that."

Nagaro gave him a disbelieving look. "Surely I must have changed. I was scarcely a man when you last saw me, Chula."

"Oh, aye. Ye *looks* different." Chula regarded him sagely. "But ye don't *feel* different, if ye know what I mean."

Nagaro didn't, in fact, know what Chula meant. He certainly felt different to himself. Rather than let the pause lengthen again, he said, "I met Luka under the cedars at the crossroads. She talked as if she lives somewhere close by."

Chula nodded. "She lives in a house, now that she's got too old t' be traveling about—down in th' hollow, t' other side o' the road. I sees her from time t' time. I let her know she was welcome on the place any time the great folk weren't about, but she's shy o' me. Hasn't said more 'n two dozen words t' me in four years."

Nagaro wasn't sure he should tell the old gardener that Luka had probably said more than that to him in four minutes. Instead he dug in his pocket. "She gave me these." He cupped the two objects in his palm.

Chula reached out and turned the little stone over so the symbol on it showed. "*Hamanei*," he murmured. "A life stone! Is *that* why she's lived so long?" Abruptly his hand jerked away. "But she's passed it on to ye—"

Nagaro shifted in his seat on the bench. "I tried to give it back. She scared me a little, saying she'd lived long enough and didn't need it any more."

Chula blinked at him. "Oh, but ye can't give it back," he said, shaking his head. "An' I can't see why ye'd want to. That stone 'll keep ye safe, it will—long as ye carries it. There's powerful magic in them special stones. An' don't worry about old Luka. She prob'ly won't live more'n a year now that she's passed it on, but that's how she wants it, see? That's why she give it up."

Nagaro laughed shortly. "I've come so close to dying so many times, Chula, you have no idea. And I'm still here—without any stone in my pocket. If Lokundas sends me my death tomorrow, I'll be dead, stone or no stone." He stopped, seeing the old Turo's reproachful look. "Don't worry," he added seriously. "I'll keep it, Chula, for Luka's sake—and for yours. But if I have to believe in it to make it work, it's wasted on me."

He put the stone back in his pocket, keeping the bit of folded leather in his hand. "What do you make of this?"

Chula eyed the folded leather. "Ye can shave me with a hatchet," he said. "I've no idea. Why don't ye open it?"

Frowning, Nagaro untied the bit of ribbon and carefully parted the un-sewn edges of the leather. It opened like a book, to reveal a small sprig of dried plant inside, pressed flat. "It must be one of Luka's herbs," he said. "Do you know what it is, Chula?"

The old Turo peered at the specimen, but then shook his head. "It's nothin' I ever grew in me own garden. An' I've never seen it in any other."

"She said it was for remembering," Nagaro mused. The plant was very delicate-looking, with feathery leaves dried to a pale green, and tiny flowers that were cream-colored and brown-edged like old paper. "It's a good choice, I guess. Herbs always make me think of Luka." He closed the folded leather, retied the ribbon, and slipped the thing back into his pocket with the polished stone. "I wish I had something from *you*, Chula, for remembrance."

Chula smiled his gap-toothed smile. "That'd have t' be a *live* plant, wouldn't it?"

"*Yes*—" Nagaro suddenly straightened. "Why not a lily, Chula! I'll wager I could grow one in the little garden plot behind my quarters in Lankura!"

Chula chuckled. "Well, ye're in luck then lad—*Capt'n*. I'll put some o' these bulbs in a sack an' leave it for ye in the stable where the saddles is hangin' so ye're sure not t' miss it. They'll travel a sight better 'n a lily plant ever would. Jus' keep 'em somewhere cool, an' dry, an' dark 'til it's time t' plant 'em."

Nagaro pressed Chula for instructions. Then he rose to go, fearing that someone would notice how long he'd talked with the gardener. He checked the angle of the sun as he left the garden and decided there was still time for a ride along the river. He particularly wanted to visit his old stone seat.

9: Confidences

Nagaro took the road that wound along the river at an easy canter, looking eagerly ahead through the trees for the first glimpse of the wooden bridge that spanned the stream where the cliff rose on the farther bank. The princess's horse hadn't been in the stable. He assumed she was still out riding, but he hoped to avoid crossing her path since Averwin's woods and grounds were fairly large. Much as he enjoyed Nevien's company, he was looking forward to privately savoring some his boyhood haunts. He wanted to tie his horse to a low-hanging branch, cross the river, and mount the steep narrow path that led to the little ledge where he'd sat so many times, looking out over the trees to the pasture and the house beyond.

When at last the bridge came into view, however, he drew rein in dismay. There were two horses, a white and a sorrel with their riders astride, under the oak that sheltered the nearer end of the bridge. He recognized the riders as the princess and Brandle, and it was too late to turn aside because they'd already seen him. In fact, Nevien was standing in her stirrups, beckoning to him.

Nagaro brought Thunder-Heels to a halt under the big oak, hoping to say a few polite words and excuse himself to strike off in a different direction. There were other places to visit, after all, besides the stone seat. His hope was dashed, however, as soon as Nevien spoke.

"Well met, Captain," she said. "Will you ride with me?"

He smiled as warmly as he could, and said, "Of course, My Lady." He found it impossible to simply say no.

"There, Lieutenant, you see?" She turned back to the big Leithian. "My friend Captain Nagaro will escort me, so you can go back to your patrol."

The muscles of Brandle's face didn't so much as twitch, though his gaze went from the princess to Nagaro and back again. "Very good, My Lady," he said, in a tone that betrayed absolutely nothing. He turned to Nagaro, inclined his head slightly, and said, "Captain." Then he turned his horse towards the house and set off along the path at an easy jog.

Nagaro spoke his thought aloud in his astonishment: "He'll leave us alone together, just like that?"

Nevien arched a delicate eyebrow. "What, you can't be trusted?"

Nagaro didn't flinch. "Of course I can," he said matter-of-factly. "But everyone seems so concerned with appearances."

She gave him an impish smile. "Lieutenant Brandle and I have an understanding. He lets me do what I wish, and I take responsibility for the consequences. I expect he'll stay within call, but won't disturb us. And these woods are really quite safe. We have foresters patrolling all the borders. They're armed with bows, and they carry horns that they can sound if they see anything alarming."

"Oh. That seems reasonable." Nagaro wondered why reasonableness seemed so rare.

Nevien laughed merrily at his seriousness. "Come on," she said, lifting her reins. "I'll show you some of my favorite places."

She led him on along the road beside the river, pausing now and again to enjoy the beauty of a deep green pool, or the reflections of the overarching trees on the surface of a still stretch of water. Nevien didn't speak a great deal as they rode, and Nagaro had long moments to savor his memories. The result was that he soon forgot his annoyance and began to enjoy her quiet company. It was remarkable how many of her favorite places were his as well.

After a time, the princess turned aside onto a narrower trail that followed a tributary stream deeper into the woods, and they passed through filtered sunlight under oak and ash that had already lost most of their leaves, and through a small meadow with grass of pale autumn gold. Beyond the meadow, the horses' hooves splashed through a ford where the path crossed the stream. Then the way climbed through more woods, where evergreens outnumbered broadleaf trees and the way grew darker under their shadow, until the two riders reached a dense grove of tall cedar and spruce where the princess drew rein.

Nagaro drew up beside her and sat in his saddle, inhaling the cedar-scented air as he let the peace of that pillared woodland hall wash over him. He knew the place well. He'd often gone there on hot summer afternoons because it was always cool under the trees where the sunlight never penetrated. Today, however, it was almost chill.

Beside him, the princess shivered. "I usually like it here," she said, "But it's a little too cold today."

Nagaro nodded his agreement, but he was looking at a scattering of bright flecks of sunlight showing through the trees a little way ahead. He urged Thunder-Heels in that direction. "Come this way," he said.

"Where are you going?"

Nagaro didn't answer, but beckoned for her to follow. He wanted to show her a place he knew, but dared not say so. The tree limbs grew low ahead of him, so he dismounted and led the big gray forward, pushing cedar boughs aside to emerge into a little sunlit glade, ringed by evergreen trees. A tiny rivulet flowed through it, feeding a small clear pool. The grass still had some life in it here and was silver-green. Someone had long ago placed two rustic cedar-wood benches just at the forest's edge on either side, east and west, so that one of them caught the sun, and the other shade, at any time of day.

The princess had followed him, leading her mare. "Oh Sweet Lady!" she exclaimed as she looked about her. "I've never been here before! Whatever made you think to push through the branches like that?"

Nagaro shrugged. "I saw the light shining through them and wanted to see what was here," he said. It was an accurate description of how he'd first found the glade, though it was at least fifteen years out of date.

"It's *lovely*—and it's so much warmer here than under the trees!"

Smiling, Nagaro circled the pool, moving towards the sunlit bench. Once there, he slipped the stallion's bit and released the bridle, setting the big gray free to crop the grass. He sat down on the weathered wood. "It seems like a good place to rest before riding back."

Nevien turned the white mare loose to graze beside the gray and joined Nagaro on the bench, sitting at a discreet distance from him. "Who could have built these benches?" she wondered aloud.

Nagaro shrugged. "If you don't know, My Lady, it must have been some previous owner. They've obviously been here a long time. They're so weathered." In fact, the benches had already been silver with age when he'd first discovered them.

A long moment passed as they admired the place—the sun-warmed grass, the still pool, and the encircling curtain of branches. The only sounds were the faint trickle of the tiny brook, the soft rustle of leaves stirred by the breeze, and the chirping of birds concealed among the trees. The air smelled of clean earth, grass, and cedar.

At length, the princess spoke. "So, Captain, what do you think of River House?"

The sun was warm on Nagaro's shoulders and he was feeling very much at peace. "I like it very much, My Lady. It's a pretty place." He paused, then couldn't resist asking, "How did you come by it? It's rather far out of the way. This isn't part of Harlind Hold, is it?"

Nevien shook her head. "No. My young husband, Leyel, lived here with the Lady Maramine Virden. Father bought it from the Virden family after the lady died. I suppose he must have liked it, though he never comes here. *I* didn't come until after Leyel had... disappeared..."

She faltered and he looked at her, surprised. She was gazing straight before her, looking troubled. After a moment, she seemed to collect herself and continued. "I know he must have died, but they never found his body. We held a funeral, but it never felt... *finished*... somehow.

I came here hoping it would help."

She paused again and Nagaro sat studying her profile. The warm glow he'd been feeling had died at the first mention of his former name. Still, he felt touched by her words. She'd never really known him, of course, but he was glad to think she'd felt a little kindness towards the apparently simple-minded youth who had brought her so much pain.

"Did it help?" he asked.

Her frown deepened, and now she turned towards him, her wide green eyes thoughtful. "In a way," she said. "I'm not sure what I expected. What *happened* was that I fell in love with the place—both the house and the grounds. I've kept them as much as possible the way they were. I liked it that way, but it's also a kind of memorial... to both of them. And of course I've also put the place to use, bringing people here to enjoy a day in the country. I like to think that both Maramine and Leyel would have liked that."

It was Nagaro who looked away this time, unable to bear her earnest gaze. He swallowed past a tightness in his throat. "I'm sure they would have, My Lady," he said with feeling, and then sat silent, trying to think of how to change the subject. Fortunately Nevien did it for him.

"I hope you'll forgive my curiosity, Captain" she said. "But I can't help wondering about the ring you wear. It looks like a woman's ring—the sort of thing a man would wear as a love token."

She was looking at him sideways, as if fishing for information, and Nagaro was glad to put less pleasant thoughts aside. He shook his head and laughed. "This ring has nothing to do with me, My Lady. Most likely it *was* a love token, exchanged between two people I never met, who are both long dead. I was charged with returning it to their kin, but I don't know where to find them and I wear it in hopes that someone may recognize it."

Nevien raised an eyebrow. "Who on earth gave you such a charge?"

Nagaro's teeth flashed in his best pirate smile. "A young Mautep sea warrior named Roheed jir-Akaan, the nephew of the Emperor of the Mahuk Baar." He laughed at the look she gave him. "I swear it in Vothra's name."

"But why would he give it to *you?*"

"It's a long story, My Lady. To make it short, the lady who wore that ring was taken captive by Roheed's father and given the task of raising Roheed when his own mother died. She did so, faithfully, until her death. The story was well known in Sar Tipaal. When I and my comrades won our freedom, we spared Roheed and some of his men, and he gave me the ring to return to the family of the woman who had raised him, whom he remembered kindly."

Nevien shook her head. "That's a marvelous story, Captain. Though it's strange to think of such behavior in one of those sea raiders."

Nagaro's expression grew sober. "Some of them are better and some worse, like folk everywhere, My Lady. The Mautep practice honor among themselves. They just don't extend it to others."

"Oh." She absorbed this. Then abruptly she laughed. "I thought the ring must belong to your daughter's mother. You told me once that you'd lost her, remember? And when I mentioned to Rianine this morning that you wore a woman's ring, she immediately imagined you were playing caddish games with Kendira—"

"Is *that* what Rianine was on about?" Nagaro was so startled that he forgot his manners.

Amusement briefly sparkled in the princess's eyes before she read the hurt in his. "Did she tease you about it? I'm sorry, Captain. She shouldn't have taken the liberty, although it might have been a fair judgement of some other man. You see, Kendira asked me to invite you, and you accepted. That would usually mean that she was interested in you, and you in her. The purpose of my having ladies is nominally to give me company, but everyone knows they're looking for husbands."

Nagaro winced. "I confess I was beginning to wonder about that."

Nevien smiled sympathetically. "Well, don't worry. There's no real harm done if you didn't mean it that way. It's not as if anyone *told* you. I can explain to Kendira that you are still looking for your daughter's mother."

But Nagaro shook his head. "My daughter's mother is a Turowan woman named Jila," he said. "And there was never any love between us—although I'd like to find her for my daughter's sake—" He stopped, because Nevien was looking rather shocked. And then he suddenly found himself telling her the whole story of his fall.

Somehow he felt that he needed to explain this to her, who had been his wife: how it was that he had lain with another woman. Of course he made no mention of the part his imperfect memory of the last night in the palace had played in the whole affair. Fortunately, there was no need to mention the wine the princess had given him that night. His fear of being thought a crossed man was sufficient to explain his motive for the ill-fated experiment that had led to the conception of his daughter Narei.

The princess listened with keen attention, asking gentle questions that gradually drew out the details of Taru's plotting, Jila's manipulation, and his own mistakes.

"It was nearly a year later that she came to me with the baby," he explained finally. "It turned out that she'd only lain with me to get a child. She was a sea-captain's mistress, and she'd hoped to convince him that the child was his so he would marry her and take her away from the island. When the captain would have none it, she came to me."

"And you didn't marry her either?"

He shook his head. "I was too angry, and I knew it would end badly. I acknowledged the child, and I gave Jila money for the baby and for herself—so she could leave the island as she wished." He paused, staring across the glade. "I told her I never wanted to set eyes on her again, and she made it clear, in a letter she wrote to her sister, that she means to see that I don't." He stopped speaking, and lowered his eyes.

Nevien sat very quietly for several seconds before asking earnestly, "How old were you when you lay with her?"

He looked up, frowning. "Twenty."

"So young?" She sounded surprised. "And you'd only just escaped from slavery, and this was your first experience with a woman?"

Nagaro shifted position uncomfortably on the bench. "Well... my first experience of *that* kind, certainly." His mind shied away from the memory of lying woodenly on a bed while the sixteen-year-old Nevien wept beside him.

Nevien shook her head at him, frowning also. "I don't know why you berate yourself so about this, Captain," she said. "You were an innocent youth, and this brazen creature took advantage you. Any decent woman would have seen you taken safely home to your own bed, instead of taking you to *hers* She shamelessly seduced you!"

Nagaro frowned harder. "She didn't have to try very hard."

"Of course not! You were drunk!"

"Which was *my* fault, My Lady."

She stared at him. "*Your* fault, Captain—" Abruptly she stopped and shook her head. "This doesn't feel right—calling you 'Captain' all the time. "I'm going to call you Nagaro, if you don't mind, and you can call me Nevien—when no one is listening."

Nagaro was caught off guard by this sudden change of subject. "All right," he said, with some misgivings. "We can do that—"

"Good!" She nodded decisively and plunged back into her argument. "Now, about it being your fault, Nagaro—" She began to tick things off on her fingers. "Your conniving friend, Taru, *knew* you had no experience with wine because you'd always kept the Vothrin ban. He didn't tell you that wine is *stronger* than ale. And he left you *alone* with a bottle of Southern Borlundian—which is very strong wine indeed. So of course you quite naturally got into trouble because you had no idea what you were doing!"

Nagaro shook his head. "I knew I was breaking the ban... Nevien—"

"Oh, you impossible man!" she cried in exasperation. "Vothra would never condemn you for that!"

Nagaro blinked "You know Vothrin teaching? I thought you followed the Leithian gods."

Nevien drew herself up. "I do, but I've had instruction in both."

"But... you drink wine..."

"My parents decided it was better that I have experience with it, rather than not. You have to learn how to drink wine safely, Nagaro. And if you don't want to get into trouble while you're learning, you need guidance—from someone you can *trust*. Not like that friend of yours. *I* had guidance. *Lots* of it." Her brow furrowed. "People take very good care of princesses."

Nagaro still wasn't prepared to relinquish the blame. He cleared his throat. "The Writings warn about getting into trouble with wine. So I should have known better than to break the ban."

She threw up her hands. "But you didn't know how *much* trouble you could get into—or how easily. And at least you didn't get drunk on purpose, like I did—" She stopped abruptly, as if she'd said more than she intended.

He stared at her in dismay. "You made yourself drunk on *purpose*, Nevien? *Why?*"

She studied her hands. "Does it matter?"

"I think so. My friend Pavo did that once because he thought he'd lost his true love and he was trying to numb the pain. If it was something like *that*, well... anyone can make a mistake..."

"Well, I've never lost a true love," she said in a small, tight voice, "But I got myself drunk on purpose. Three times."

He started to reach for her hand and thought better of it. "Do you want to talk about it? You must have had a reason."

She made a small, nervous gesture, and her fingers strayed as if unconsciously to the thin scar on her cheek. "I... thought it might make some things more bearable—"

He stiffened. "*Gillard!* He hurt you, didn't he?"

She started so sharply that he knew he had struck the mark even before she met his eyes. "Yes," she said quietly. Then she shook back her hair defiantly. "And I *will* tell you! Because you're my friend, and I want to tell *someone*."

She paused for a moment to collect her thoughts, then began to talk, sitting with her gaze on her hands where they lay clasped in her lap. "It's a strange thing... but I think Gillard *enjoyed* hurting people," she began. "At first he... curbed... the inclination when he was with me. But after we were married... more and more... he showed his true nature. He would hold me so tightly that it hurt. He'd grab my hair and hold it so I couldn't resist him. And he liked to... play with a knife... to see how close he could come to cutting me." She shuddered. "I grew more and more afraid to be alone with him. I never knew what he'd do next." She glanced at Nagaro as if doubtful he would believe her.

Nagaro dared not tell her, of course, that he knew first-hand what kind of a man Gillard Marchent had been. Instead he said, "And you thought that if you were drunk, you wouldn't feel things as much?"

She nodded. "It *worked*, too, after a fashion. So I did it three times... and I might have kept on doing it, if... things hadn't happened, that put an end to it."

Nagaro frowned. "Why didn't you tell your parents what he was doing?"

She darted him a look. "I just couldn't! I mean... I never tell Mother things like that. Anything ugly always upsets her so much. So Father and I just don't tell her. And my father... well, I knew he'd been under terrible pressure to wed me to Gillard. He'd managed not to believe the things people said about Gill. He'd *told* me they weren't true! I didn't want to have to tell him he was wrong—that he'd made a bad choice for me. And then there was what Gill said."

She shut her mouth, dropping her eyes.

"What Gill said...?" he prompted.

She drew a long breath. "He... he had some kind of hold over my father—something he knew about, something Father had done. Even before we were married, Father hinted to me about it. I think it was part of why he had to wed me to Gillard. And Gill told me he would tell the whole world about it if I said anything to spoil his 'fun'. He said it would bring my father down."

"But he never told you what it was?" Nagaro was thinking of how the Lady Maramine had died, and the fact that Gillard Marchent had witnessed it.

Nevien shook her head. "No. He just hinted broadly. And threatened. I couldn't be sure that it was as bad as he made out, but I was afraid to take the chance." She gave a bitter little laugh. "So I drank too much wine instead. I wasn't very clever about it either. I just drank a lot at dinner and of course people noticed. My ladies made excuses for me. People do that when you're a princess. It might have gone on much longer, but the third time, my mother noticed and everything blew up in my face."

Nevien brought her feet up onto the bench and hugged her shapa-clad knees. "Mother confronted me. And—being drunk—I said things I never would have said otherwise. So of course, she went to Father. And *Father* confronted Gill." Nevien shivered. "I've never seen my father so angry in my life! Mother hustled me off to bed so I missed seeing most of the storm, but I could hear Father and Gill shouting at each other—right through the walls."

Nevien swallowed, then went on. "The next morning Father came to me and told me that he'd sent Gill home to Marchent Hold for the time being. He looked very grim. He said there'd likely be a price to pay before the end, but if it came to that, he meant to pay it. But the war was on with Jinara, and he had to go. So he rode off with his soldiers, saying he'd deal with everything when he returned." Nevien sat for a moment, gazing at the grazing horses, hugging her knees so tightly that her knuckles showed white. "But of course," she said finally, "by the time Father returned, Gill was dead."

Nagaro sat silent for a long moment. He'd heard the tale of these events before, though not, of course, from the princess's perspective. He found the new insight darkly disturbing. When Nevien didn't immediately continue, he said, "Gillard came back to the palace the next day though, didn't he? To fetch you away with him. And you refused to go."

She gave him a quick, startled look. "Did the story get out then?"

He nodded. "I heard it from a fisherman in Harmoth harbor, a month or two after it happened. Apparently, some of the palace servants heard or saw things. But all the sympathy was on your side. No one liked Gill very much."

Nevien made a rueful face. "I know," she said. "But the way he died was so *horrible*." She shuddered. "I suppose you know that he went mad and jumped from a balcony? And it might not have happened at all if he'd just stayed away as Father told him."

Nagaro felt a chill. He swallowed, and tried to sound casual when he said, "I thought the madness sounded like Dreigen's work. I wondered if the king might have ordered—"

"*No!*"

Nevien had swung around to face him, her eyes blazing. "My Father has *never* ordered anyone murdered. And he never would!"

Nagaro drew away from her. Her anger cut him. "He needn't have *ordered* it, exactly. Dreigen could have just *thought* he wanted it done..."

Still she shook her head at him, though her eyes blazed less fiercely. "I don't know if Dreigen did it or not, but if he did, it would have been because he hated Gill in his own right. Gill used to insult him openly! And when Father returned and found what had happened, he was terribly upset. He felt quite horrible about it!" She caught herself, then added in a small voice, "So did I."

Nagaro decided to drop the subject of Dreigen. The Lore Master might very well have acted on his own, as she suggested. It rang true based on what he personally knew of the man, and of Gill's treatment of Dreigen. He would have liked to ask why the king continued to keep a murderous man like Dreigen under his roof, but decided to leave the question for another time and focus on Nevien's last three words.

"You told me I shouldn't feel guilty, Nevien," he said. "And I'm going to tell you the same. You're not the one who set those events in motion.

Gillard made his own kettle of soup, and you couldn't have predicted what would happen."

She gave him an anguished look. "Nagaro, I prayed to Lady Lissafel *every day* that something would happen to make Gill stop!"

Nagaro frowned. He didn't believe that prayers were answered. And yet, he had once prayed that Gill's mistreatment of the princess would come to her father's attention. Clearly it had. He held her eyes. "Nevien," he said. "Edrovir was surely full of folk who were praying for that very same thing."

"What do you mean? How could that be?"

He sighed. "You have a great many friends that you've never met, Nevien. Many of them have never even set eyes on you. Taru's mother was one, though she was slain before any of this happened. And there's an innkeeper's wife I know in Pakoa Town. Of course, *she* would have prayed to Hakura Kili or to the World Spirits. But still I think that if your maiden goddess truly hears prayers, she must have been quite deafened by the din. And if she *was* steering events, whose prayer, exactly, do you think she intended to answer?"

She stared at him. "Do you really think there are so many people who care about me as much as *that?*

He nodded emphatically. "Oh, yes. And I *really* don't think that what happened was your fault."

"Well, I suppose not *entirely*," she conceded. "But I was part of it. And getting myself drunk was a stupid thing to do."

Nagaro gave her a crooked smile. "How old were *you?*"

"Twenty." She smiled fleetingly in return.

"You see? You were as young as I was, and you were in a much worse situation. No real harm would have come to me if I'd just done nothing at all. What did it matter what other men thought of me? But Gill was actually hurting you. Sometimes a bad situation doesn't have any good solution."

Nevien sighed. "I suppose you're right. And thank you for listening. I do feel better for having talked about it." Abruptly she shivered a little and glanced at the sky. The sun was moving westward and the shadow of the trees had crept out almost to the end of the bench where she sat. The afternoon warmth was ebbing from the air. "It's getting late," she said. "We should go."

Nagaro stood up. "Yes. We've stayed longer than I intended."

The horses were grazing together beside the pool, having followed the sun. Thunder-Heels had left off cropping the grass and was at that moment nibbling on the white mare's mane.

"They make a pretty pair, don't they?" Nevien said, rising. "Your Thunder, and my Snow."

"Snow? Is that her name? Nagaro crossed the little clearing to take Thunder-Heels by the bridle.

"Snowdrift, really." Nevien had followed him. "I call her Snow, for short."

"Well, Thunder is short for Thunder-Heels, and he is being a gentleman now because she's not in her season. But I think he quite fancies her, so we'll have to be careful. Unless, of course, you'd like a little 'Snowstorm' to raise..."

Nevien laughed. "That would be a good name, wouldn't it? For a colt, maybe. What else might we have... Wind-Foot? Rain-Puddle?"

Nagaro laughed with her.

Together they led the horses back through the screen of tree branches, mounted, and made their way back to the river by a more direct path. Nagaro knew the way but he let the princess lead until they were on the road where they could ride abreast. Once there, she turned to him with her brow puckered in a frown.

"If you were only twenty when you fathered Narei, and she was four last spring, then you can't be more than twenty-five or twenty-six."

"Ye-es..." Nagaro felt a vague misgiving.

"I thought you were older. I would have guessed thirty, at least."

"It's the beard," he told her, and mentally kicked himself for giving her the means to calculate his age.

Her frown turned thoughtful. "It's more than that," she said. "It's all the things you've done in your life. Twenty-six years don't seem enough."

He shot her a look. "A lot of things have happened to you too."

"That's true. Three times married at twenty-four. Three husbands dead." She drew a sigh.

A frown gathered on Nagaro's brow. He rode on, not looking at her. "You should never have had to go through all that."

Nevien managed a laugh. "Oh, well," she said lightly. "It's the lot of a princess."

He didn't answer, but rode on, submerged in dark memories. He could never let her know the unwilling part he'd played in her dark life history.

Nevien glanced at Nagaro sideways, watching his face in profile, surprised at the severity of his expression. She supposed he must be one of those people he had spoken of, who'd been her friend from a distance. It would explain why he'd taken such an immediate interest in her. She smiled faintly at the thought. Now that they *had* met, he was proving to be a very good friend indeed. She hadn't previously told that story—at least not so thoroughly—to anyone. She remembered Rianine's teasing about three being one too many, and sighed. She'd felt twinges of regret before when she'd encountered a man she found attractive but who had no chance of ever being on the very short list of her suitors. She knew she would have to be content with seeing Nagaro happily paired with some other woman.

They had reached the path that ran beside the river. "Do you want to see more of Kendira?" she asked. "Since you're not courting anyone?"

Nagaro frowned afresh, remembering that Kendira couldn't ride and didn't wish to learn. *If only she were more like Nevien...* but... he had told Sindar, the disappointed former slave whom he'd left behind on Pakoa, that he should try to develop an interest in Gedras's daughter Lissel because *she* was interested in *him*. Wasn't that as good a place to start as any? If Kendira was interested in him, shouldn't he at least give her a chance?

"I suppose I could try to see whether I'd like to court her," he said.

Nevien smiled. "If you want to do that, I'll invite you again the next time we come to River House. And I'll also give you a place at the 'match table' whenever there's a gathering at the palace."

"The *match table?*"

This time the princess laughed at the alarm in his voice. "That's what I call the table where I sit with my ladies—with the women on one side of it and the men they're paired up with for the evening on the other. It doesn't mean anyone assumes there's necessarily going to be a *match*."

"Oh." He felt sheepish. "That would be all right, I guess."

They rode on, past the bridge and the oak tree and the stone seat on the other side of the river. It was just beyond that point that Brandle appeared again, riding out from among the trees beside the road as if he'd been there all along. He saluted the princess, stone-faced, and gave Nagaro a nod, then fell in behind them. Nevien promptly suggested that they hurry their pace, and all three riders covered the last stretch of the path at a canter.

They found the carriage horses already harnessed and waiting. The other horses had been saddled, as well, and the guards were standing about.

Kuran was holding his horse by the bridle. "Here you are at last," he observed dryly, as the three truants drew rein in the stable yard. "I was beginning to think about sending a search party." The frown he gave them belied the laughter in his eyes.

One of the guardsmen went into the house to call out the rest of the party, and Nagaro quickly dismounted and went into the stable to retrieve his saddlebags. He found a dusty sack beside them, tied with string. A quick look inside confirmed that it contained a half dozen lily bulbs. He took both the saddlebags and the sack back to the waiting Thunder-Heels. There he secured the saddlebags and had just decided to take his tirka out and wear it, to make room for the sack, when he heard a crunch of hooves on gravel and a small cough behind him. He turned around with the tirka over one arm, and the sack in his hand, to find Rianine looking down from astride her horse.

"I saw you in the garden with the gardener, Captain," she said in a tone that sounded quite casual. "Whatever did you and he find to talk about for so long?"

Nagaro answered her with barely a second's hesitation, since the answer was in his hand. "Lilies," he said. "I've often thought I'd like to grow some, and he was kind enough to give me some bulbs. Would you like to see?" He unwound the string and held the bag open to display the six smooth brown lumps inside.

She leaned over to take a look. "How lovely," she said, with every appearance of sincerity.

After retying the string, he glanced up at her again and spoke on an impulse. "I couldn't help wondering what the rest of you were doing for so long over by the goat pens."

Rianine smirked. "Well, we *did* look at the goats," she said. "But the chicken coop was the main attraction."

The *chicken coop?* Nagaro couldn't conceal his surprise. He had thought chickens were funny when he was a small child, but had since come to the conclusion that they were rather stupid, noisy birds.

"Some of the young women wanted to look for chicks. The rest of us went because we were bored with Oskampo."

Nagaro gave her a look of mild surprise. "There might be a few eggs, but they wouldn't see chicks at *this* season," he said.

"I know, and I told them so." She gave him a penetrating look. "But they wouldn't listen—"

At this point, their conversation was interrupted by a shout from the coachman and the carriage started forward with a lurch. Nagaro gave Rianine a quick nod as she turned her horse to follow the carriage. Then he stuffed the sack of bulbs into the empty saddlebag, hastily donned the tirka, and swung into the saddle.

*

The ride back to Lankura was uneventful. By the time they reached the stable yard, the afternoon light was deepening towards dusk and the air had turned cold. Nagaro dismounted to better express formal thanks to his hostess, and to thank a blushing Kendira again for the dancing lessons. After that, the group quickly dispersed, it being late and everyone being tired. The women rapidly disappeared into the palace, and Nagaro was just about to mount his horse again for the ride back to the Fleet Compound when Brandle suddenly appeared at his elbow.

"Captain," the Leithian said in a low tone, though there was no one within earshot. "I must say I find you a most extraordinary gentleman—

to have sat beside her for an hour and never so much as touched the lady."

"*What?*" Nagaro exclaimed in shocked surprise. "Did you watch us the whole time?"

Brandle's teeth flashed in the light from one of the stable yard lanterns. "No," he observed calmly. "But I now know as much as if I *had*."

Nagaro stared at him. Then his face darkened. "That was a very unnecessary trick, Zirda!"

Brandle's smile widened slightly. "Apparently," he said. "But relax, Captain. I'm the princess's bodyguard, not her chaperone. I just like to know which way the wind is blowing. I truly don't wish to offend you."

At this Nagaro actually laughed. "In that case I'll resolve not to be offended, since I've no wish to quarrel with you either. In fact," he added, "I want to ask you a favor." He'd been thinking earlier about the ring on his finger, and Brandle's appearance had just reminded him of Simion.

Brandle raised an eyebrow. "What would that be?"

"I'd like to talk with Simion privately if you can arrange it. There's something I think he could help me with."

Brandle stiffened a little, and his stance became noticeably more guarded. "I hope you don't mind my asking what sort of *something* you wish to discuss," he said levelly.

The Leithian's reaction reminded Nagaro of nothing so much as that of a jealous husband. "I'm trying to find the family of the owner of this ring," he said, raising his hand. "It might be a merchant family, and I expect Simion would know all of the local ones."

Brandle relaxed. "Well, that's harmless," he said, then leaned down to peer at the ring. "Rather an unusual design, isn't it. And Simion would know if anyone would." The Leithian's eyes glinted in the lantern light as he straightened. "My father keeps offices in a building on Broad Street, to look after his affairs in Lankura. Simion works there. When next I see him, I'll see what can be arranged, and I'll send you word when I have something to tell you." There was another flash of teeth. "The princess's favorite runner happens to be one of my nephews."

Nagaro thanked Brandle and they parted, the Leithian disappearing into the palace and Nagaro mounting Thunder-Heels for the ride through the dusk-dimmed streets.

10: A Summons

"**S**o this River House place is *Averwin?*"

It was Taru who asked the question. He and Pavo had joined Nagaro for breakfast in Nagaro's quarters. They'd brought a tureen of fried potatoes and sausages from the dining hall, to which Nagaro had added a bag of currant buns and a pot of fresh-brewed sothiril. Taru and Pavo had used their week's end to ride to Wotana to visit Gama, Taru's grandmother, and had begun with their own tale of being caught in the first winter snow on their return journey, before Nagaro had revealed his news about River House.

"Yes." Nagaro took a swallow of sothiril. "But apparently it now belongs to the Crown. Elgurn bought it from Maramine's family. He got rid of all the old householders and brought in new ones. Chula the gardener is the only one left. I met Luka, too, the old medicine woman who set my broken arm."

Taru frowned. "Why hasn't the king gotten rid o' Chula?"

"I doubt Elgurn knows he's there. Nevien said her father never visits the place." Nagaro's face darkened. "I can guess why. He wouldn't want to be reminded of what happened there—of what he did—" He stopped, cutting off the thought, then added, "It's Nevien's place now. And she's mostly kept it as it was." He stopped again, not wanting to talk about *why* the princess had done that.

Pavo put down his fork, and asked, "Did it make you more happy, or more sad, to see your house again?"

Nagaro sighed. "It was hard thinking about what happened there... at the end. And sad seeing Maramine's grave. But it was good to see Luka and Chula. Chula was always more like an uncle to me than a servant. And I enjoyed riding through the woods and along the river with Nevien... seeing all the old places."

Taru frowned harder. "But what about the other girl?" he asked suspiciously. "The Kelorin one. Did she give you your dancing lessons? Wasn't *that* what ye went for?"

Nagaro felt mildly annoyed. "We did that right after lunch. She taught me four dances—though I'd been taught two of them before—"

"*Well?*" Taru demanded. "What d' ye think of her?"

"Kendira?" Nagaro yanked his thoughts away from rising memories of being instructed by the princess, and shrugged. "She's nice enough. But rather shy."

Since they had all finished with the plates, he stood up and began to collect the dishes.

"Did ye *talk* t' her?"

"A little, about dancing mostly, during the lesson." Nagaro started for the wash basin with the plates and forks in hand. "I also asked her about riding, but it turns out she's afraid of horses."

"Oh." Taru took a bite of bun, chewed, and swallowed. "A woman doesn't have t' ride," he offered philosophically.

Nagaro sighed. "No," he conceded. He lowered the dishes into the basin and poured in some of the water he had pumped earlier. "But you should have seen the princess, Taru. *She* rides like the wind!"

This time Taru gave him a sharp look. "Which one did ye spend more time with? Kendira—or the princess?"

Nagaro shrugged, his eyes on the dishes that he'd started washing. "I'm not sure. I took quite a long ride with the princess, and we sat and talked. But Nevien and I were already friends and I'd only just met Kendira. And Nevien will send me more invitations so I can get to know Kendira better."

Pavo rose from his seat and picked up the empty tureen. "Let me help you with dish, Nagaro," he offered.

Taru was still eyeing Nagaro askance, though the look was wasted since Nagaro's back was turned. "Well," he observed between bites of scone. "If ye and the princess are *just friends*, as ye say, I guess ye won't mind telling me what ye talked about."

Nagaro put a washed plate into the rinse basin so that Pavo could dry it. He turned around to give Taru a frowning look. "I talked about what happened with Jila. But I don't think I should tell you what *she* talked about. She meant it to be in confidence, and I'd be a pretty poor friend if I didn't keep it that way."

Taru's hand stopped, holding the last bite of scone. "I don't believe this, Nagaro. Ye've known me *years* longer than her, and ye won't tell me what she said?"

Nagaro turned back to the wash basin. "No, I won't, Taru," he said firmly. "And if you told me something in confidence, I'd wouldn't tell *her*, either."

Several seconds ticked by while Nagaro washed the forks and Pavo stood with the dish towel in hand, his glance shifting warily between his two friends.

Taru studied the last bite of scone in his hand as if it were an object of great fascination. "I don't think that a man and a woman can be just friends," he said at last.

"I don't see why not." Nagaro handed the forks to Pavo, and started on the tureen. "Nevien and Kuran are just friends."

"That's different! Kuran's old enough to be her father!"

"Tulara and I were friends for years, and never anything more."

Taru sagged. He couldn't argue about Tulara. Angrily he stuffed the bite of scone into his mouth. "I just hope ye know what ye're doing," he muttered around the mouthful.

"Of course I do." Nagaro passed the washed tureen to Pavo and dried his hands before returning to his seat at the table. "Now, I want you to tell me what you think of these things that Luka gave me." He pulled the two gifts from his pocket and laid them on the table.

Taru's gaze went immediately to the small smooth stone and he reached out to touch it. "This is a sacred spirit stone," he said in an awed voice. "A life stone. This Luka must be very wise, I'm sure—being so old—but it's odd that she gave ye this stone, Nagaro, instead o' passing it on to a younger medicine woman. Ye're not even a Turo!"

Nagaro's brow furrowed. "I was going to keep it for Luka's sake, and also because Chula wanted me to. But if you don't think it's right, Taru, I'll give it to you—"

"*No ye won't!*" Taru jerked his hand away from the stone as if he'd burnt his fingers. "She gave it to ye, Nagaro—so ye'll live a long life! Ye have t' keep it!"

Nagaro scowled. "First Chula, and now you," he muttered. "No one was worried about how long I was going to live before yesterday. Now you act as if I'm going to die the instant I part with the thing."

Taru shot him a worried look. "Maybe there's some danger coming your way... something Luka can see..."

"More than all that I've faced already?" Nagaro was skeptical. " I could have been killed a dozen times, and I didn't have any stone in my pocket."

Pavo had dried the tureen and returned to the table to finish his sothiril. He'd been listening quietly, as was his way, but now he lowered his cup and said, "Sheptuum always have protect you, Nagaro. You do not need little stone."

Taru was instantly offended. "Ye believe in your spirit-ways, Pavo, and I'll believe in mine!"

Nagaro sighed. He didn't believe in Sheptuum or in the power of the life-stone—which he nevertheless picked up and returned to his pocket. "If you've no objection, either of you," he said, "I think I'll go on doing my best to look after myself." Then he changed the subject. "Do either of you know the plant that's in that little leather book?"

As it turned out, they didn't. Pavo only knew cooking herbs, and declared that the little dried sprig wasn't one he was familiar with.

Taru's botanical knowledge was even more limited than Pavo's. "It doesn't look like much, does it?" he observed. "It's hardly got any leaves t' begin with, and those flowers are so small they couldn't ha' looked like much even before they got squashed flat and dried up like that."

Pavo stood up and began collecting the remaining dishes. "I will wash all of our cup," he said. "And sothiril pot too."

Taru rose and picked up the dish towel. "It's my turn to dry."

Nagaro heaved another sigh as he put the little folded book back into his pocket. "How is Gama?" he asked.

"Well enough," Taru answered absently as he waited for Pavo to hand him a washed cup.

Pavo twisted around at the wash basin to give Nagaro a meaningful look over his shoulder. "I do not think Taru have hardly look at Gama," he observed. "He only have eye for very pretty girl in house on other side of street. Girl named Jitali."

"Hamani's *little sister?*" Nagaro directed a shocked look at his other friend's back. "Is this true, Taru? She's rather young for you, isn't she?"

Taru shrugged without turning around. "I don't know what ye're on about," he said testily. "She just turned sixteen and is quite grown up."

Pavo laughed. "Oh yes, she is all grow up now! She is great beauty, with very nice shape. Next time we go to Wotana, I think we will see many young man stand in line at her door. Only Taru will be there first, because already he have talked to her father!"

Taru stopped drying and turned indignantly to Pavo. "What makes ye think I did that?"

"Because I have see you talking!"

"Well how do you know we were talking about Jitali?"

Pavo shook the dish rag at him. "You have not said more than six word ever before to that man. What else are you go to talk about?"

Taru scowled and turned his attention to vigorously washing the sothiril pot. "Well it's my affair and not yours!"

Nagaro shook his head. "Of course it's your affair, Taru. And if you don't want to talk about it, you don't have to. But I think it's a shame for poor Hamani. She's a very kind, sensible, young woman, and hardly anyone notices her because she's so plain. She's twenty-three and has never had a single suitor that I know of. And now I imagine no one's going to notice her at all, because of her sister."

Taru sniffed disdainfully as he picked up the basin of wash water. "If ye think so much of Hamani, why don't ye go court her yourself, Nagaro?"

Nagaro laughed. "Maybe I should," he said. "But I can't do it right now. Not when I've just arranged to spend more time getting to know

Kendira." He sobered and stood up. "Could you two please finish with the dishes and lock up for me? I was supposed to see Kuran about the men's postings first thing this morning, and I don't want to keep him waiting."

He barely waited for his friends' assurances before heading for the door.

*

Kuran addressed him pointedly as soon as Nagaro settled into a chair.

"I see you've chosen to keep both your first and second mates."

Nagaro shifted uneasily. He'd expected that there might be trouble about this. "Yes, My Lord," he said carefully. "Since you said you'd be sailing with us to observe how we do things, I thought it best to keep my team of officers so you would see a fair demonstration."

Kuran considered him narrowly. "There is some degree of merit to that argument—"

"And you've already posted me a third mate."

"Yes. Young Peldred—as keen as he is green, that one. But third mates are nothing more than officers in training. When I asked you to divide your crew, I meant you to divide the officers as well as the men."

Nagaro returned him an innocent look. "Then you should have said so, My Lord."

Kuran sighed. "I may let you have your way at the outset—on the basis of your reasoning. But tell me, Captain, if you had to let one of the two men go, which would it be?"

Nagaro paused only fractionally. He had thought about this more than a little. "Taru," he said.

Kuran raised an eyebrow. "You made that choice easily enough. What's your reasoning?"

Nagaro's frown deepened. "My *choice* is to keep them both, as I've said. But I choose most especially to keep Pavo with me because I know *I* won't mistake him for an enemy."

Kuran frowned. "He'll be wearing a Fleet uniform."

Nagaro sighed. "In a melee, someone might see the face and not the uniform. But that's not what I meant."

"Ah. You're thinking of your promise."

Nagaro inclined his head.

"I had the impression that Pavo has been well accepted."

Nagaro made a wry face. "He's well accepted as my second mate, My Lord, giving orders to *my* crewmen. But there are some who'd be unhappy with him as *their* second mate. Some of the men might take exception to taking orders from a Turo as well, for that matter, but I think the difficulty would be less severe for Taru than for Pavo."

"Mmm." Kuran nodded. "I'm inclined to agree with your assessment." He made a notation on the list Nagaro had prepared, which lay before him on his desk. "I see you also want to keep Tredhold."

"Yes, My Lord." Nagaro kept his face and voice carefully neutral. Tred knew things about him that it was good for a healer to know, and had always kept his secrets.

Kuran appeared to consider. "You'll need a ship's doctor, of course, and Tredhold was a Fleet man before he came to you. He's a good man at building bridges too—a good choice."

Another mark was added to the list and Nagaro relaxed. He wasn't going to have to fight to keep Tred.

"And now, Captain, I'd like your impression of each of these men you're proposing to let go. What of this first one, Olendar?"

"I don't think you'll have any complaint with him, My Lord. He lacks imagination, but his swordsmanship is excellent and he's steady as a rock in a real fight."

"Good enough." Kuran made another note on the list. "And Tonada?"

"His swordsmanship is solid, and he's very dependable. Anything you tell him to do will be done properly."

And so it went.

Finally the Lord of the Fleet put his fully annotated list aside. "That's done. Are you off to sword practice now?"

"Yes, My Lord." Nagaro rose to go, but Kuran raised a hand to stay him.

"I almost forgot, Captain. I want you to accompany me to the palace this evening when I attend the King's Council."

Nagaro stared. "May I ask why, My Lord?"

Kuran bent over the papers on his desk. "You're summoned because some of the Pact Signers wish to ask you some questions."

"Oh." Nagaro thought he understood. "Is it about the undertaking you spoke of at the Festival of the Harvest Moon?"

Kuran's face remained carefully neutral, but he made a small, stiff inclination of his head. "Be ready to leave at a half hour after dinner. And this is not a matter for other ears, Captain. Do you understand?"

"Aye, Zirda!" Nagaro saluted crisply before turning on his heel.

Outside, he made for the building that housed the room used for sword practice whenever the weather turned inclement. He frowned as he navigated the mingled snow and mud of the parade ground. Did he dare to hope this summons meant that the Council was considering a more reasonable course of action?

11: The King's Council

When he and Kuran arrived at the palace that evening, they were admitted and proceeded immediately to the Audience Chamber, finding it rather dimly lit with only half its elegant bronze lamps alight. The simple grandeur of the room had been fully restored since the previous spring's Mautep attack. The great oak doors at the entrance had been replaced, the tapestries were rehung on the walls, and every trace of soot and debris had been removed. Nagaro would have been awed by the place if he hadn't seen it under other circumstances. Still, he looked around with interest as he trod the marble floor at Kuran's side.

Some of the tapestries were hard to make out in the gloom, but he saw one depicting a weary-looking group of men, women, and children fleeing out of Arlinas across the rugged Goreitha Mountains. Another showed an encampment in a lush green valley beside a river, representing the founding of the settlement that had become the city of Vered Mahir. A Turowan chieftain stood in the center of a third, joining the hands of a young Turowan woman and a Kelorin man beside a small boat drawn up on the sand. The wide green sea formed a backdrop for the scene, and Nagaro knew that the young couple must be Princess Minowei and the young Lord Nevrath, the parents of Edrovir's first king, Darion the Great. These tapestries were among those closer to the hall's entrance. Farther on, there were battle scenes, and one that showed Darion meeting with his Council of Lords. At the far end of the hall, behind the high seats on the dais, were a pair of tapestries depicting the signing of the Pact of Lankura and the crowning of King Elgurn.

Kuran was making for one of the side rooms near the far end of the Audience Chamber. Light flooded from the room's open door, which was flanked by a pair of guards. The members of the King's Council must have just finished dining, for several servants were just exiting the room bearing trays piled with dishes and the remains of a rather sumptuous repast. Kuran pulled up short to allow the kitchen staff to pass.

Nagaro decided to take advantage of his last opportunity to speak privately to the Lord of the Fleet. "My Lord," he ventured, moving close to Kuran's ear, "May I ask what you've already told these men regarding what I said to you?"

Kuran cast him an apologetic glance. "I'm sorry," he said. "But it's best that I tell you as little as possible since the Council won't expect me to have told you anything at all. Just answer their questions straight, and keep everything you hear in strictest confidence. And keep your boldness in check too. These men aren't accustomed to being spoken to the way you speak to me."

Nagaro eyed the older man uneasily. "I'll try, My Lord." The way he spoke to Kuran seemed to him the best way to speak to anyone about a serious matter, and he wasn't sure how he could answer straight while being less bold.

A moment later, he was entering the council room in Kuran's wake. The chamber had a high ceiling, and a row of high windows in the wall opposite the door that would provide ample light by day. Since it was currently night outside, the illumination was instead being supplied by oil lamps set in the four corners of the room. Though lofty, the room was not otherwise large, and was dominated by a massive round table at which were seated King Elgurn and the four remaining Signers of the Pact of Lankura.

The king sat opposite the door, with the other two Leithian lords—Odus and Pendrik—on the right, and the two Kelorin lords—Devral and Anduar—on the left. Elgurn wore black and charcoal gray with gold embroidery. He looked both tense and tired. The plain gold circlet of his crown contrasted with hair that had once been golden but was now mostly silver. The red-gold of his impeccably trimmed beard was similarly shading towards gray.

Nagaro had no difficulty identifying each of the other four men. Pendrik Glenmark and Anduar Tyronin were the two he'd met at the feast the previous spring. He'd been introduced to all four men, however, years ago as Leyel Virden. Fortunately, there was no sign that any of them recognized him from that time. In fact, they were staring at him with varying degrees of interest and annoyance.

The annoyance radiated chiefly from Odus Morbern, seated at the king's left hand. A broad-shouldered, compact man, he was wearing an elaborate deep-green velvet tirka with a band of matching satin across the chest embroidered with leaf patterns in rust and gold, all of this over an elegant white silk shirt. He had a sun-bronzed face, and his hair and close-cropped beard were more bronze than gold. The hair was graying only at the temples, and the beard a little at the sides. His fierce blue-green eyes drilled into Nagaro disapprovingly.

Although Nagaro felt Odus's gaze, his attention was drawn more immediately to Devral Sedras, on Elgurn's other hand, because Nevien had mentioned him as a potential suitor. Devral appeared obviously older than the king, with grizzled hair that had once been black, a pronounced beak of a nose, and an ugly scar from a wound that had narrowly missed his right eye. He sat slightly stooped and Nagaro remembered that, even seven years ago, Devral had walked with a limp, the legacy of an old battle wound. In contrast to Odus's finery, the old Kelorin's dress reflected a warrior's practicality. His tirka was of unadorned leather, though the quality of it was unmistakable. His shirt was unbleached linen, though well-tailored.

None of the five men seated at the table had risen when Kuran and Nagaro entered, and Elgurn simply said, "Ah, Lord Kuran... and Captain Nagaro. Please be seated, gentlemen." His tone reflected neutral courtesy.

There were two unoccupied chairs on the near side of the table. Kuran drew out the one on the left and motioned for Nagaro to take the other. Seven sets of porcelain cups and saucers were distributed about the table, and there were a pair of matching teapots.

Lord Anduar lounged in his chair. The pale, middle-aged Kelorin was ascetic and clean-shaven, steel-eyed, with formerly coal-black hair now liberally shot with gray. He was somberly dressed in a pale gray shirt and dark blue tirka with minimal decoration worked in black and silver thread. As Kuran and Nagaro seated themselves, he gestured languidly to the nearer teapot. "There's hot sothiril to warm you, gentlemen," he observed. "Please help yourselves."

"A pity it's been decreed that we have no wine at these meetings." This comment came from Lord Pendrik. Large and ruddy, the middle-aged Leithian's massive presence was amplified by a wine-red tirka and a shirt of amber satin, in spite of which he appeared distinctly less *comfortable* than the last time Nagaro had encountered him. "If we had wine, we could offer them some of that as well."

"I do not drink wine, My Lord." Nagaro spoke reflexively.

Pendrik gave him a pitying glance, but Nagaro thought he caught a hint of approval in Anduar's eyes.

Kuran reached for the pot of sothiril and poured for both of them. Nagaro murmured his thanks, and reached for his cup. The night outside had been cold and the hot drink was welcome.

Lord Odus had been drumming his fingers on the table, but he now stopped abruptly and straightened. "Remind me, My Lords, exactly why we must have this... *pirate*... among us?"

Nagaro froze with his cup halfway to his lips. Beside him, Kuran made a small movement of his hand to indicate that Nagaro should hold his peace.

Anduar turned a mild gaze upon his fellow Pact Signer. "Have you forgotten that we agreed we wished to question him?"

"*You* agreed. You and Devral. Pendrik and I didn't care to."

"What I *said*," Pendrik rumbled, idly turning his cup on its saucer by pushing the handle around with his forefinger, "was that I didn't see the need, but I had no objection."

"I thought that it was a good idea, and I said so," Devral interjected gruffly. He paused to cough heavily into his fist. "And my Lord Elgurn agreed as well, as I recall."

Elgurn cleared his throat. "Since my lords were divided," he said with evident care, "I felt the need to speak."

"And to take the Kelorin side—as usual." Lord Odus's tone was just short of accusing.

At this point, Nagaro set his cup down on its saucer with a sharp clink and stood up. The sound and the unexpected movement drew every eye. Kuran was mouthing something at him, but he ignored it. "My Lords," he said in the most level voice he could muster, acknowledging them with a small bow, "Perhaps I should wait outside while you resolve the question of whether you wish to have me here."

There was silence for the space of several heartbeats during which Nagaro was aware of Pendrik and Devral staring at him in surprise and Odus scowling. Anduar's expression betrayed nothing, and Elgurn was watching the other men. It was Lord Anduar who broke the silence.

"Do sit down, Captain." The Kelorin lord's tone was indistinguishable from the one he had used when offering them sothiril. "The matter has already been decided." Anduar turned back to the other members of the Council. "Three of us wished to question Captain Nagaro, and three is sufficient. That is the rule, is it not?"

The question elicited three nods from around the table, and a disgusted acquiescent shrug from Lord Odus.

Nagaro sank back into his seat and covered his tension by picking up his cup and finally taking a swallow. The sothiril was Erantil Crimson. Apparently, the king brought out his best for the Signers of the Pact. Kuran gave Nagaro a quick, tight smile that seemed to indicate that he hadn't blundered too badly.

Anduar watched silently until Nagaro had put the cup down. Then he cleared his throat and said, "Perhaps, Captain, you could begin by telling us what you know about the various ports and shipyards of the Mahuk Baar. I understand there is a new capital since the crowning of this new emperor?"

Nagaro was relieved to be allowed to do what he had come for. The king and the other Pact Signers appeared at least prepared to listen, so he addressed Anduar's question. "That's correct, My Lord. Whenever a new warlord becomes emperor, that man's home port becomes the capital of the entire country. Baalkir jir-Akaan is emperor now, so the capital is Sar Tipaal."

"And how many other... ah... *potential capitals*... are there?" Anduar continued the questioning.

Nagaro frowned. "I'm not sure how to answer that, My Lord. There are at least eleven warlords, all making their homes in port cities. Any of them could theoretically become emperor, but only four or five were strong enough to be serious contenders during the last conflict."

"And do all eleven of these warlords have shipyards? Or only the strongest?"

"They all have shipyards, My Lord. The stronger ones have *larger* shipyards. That's part of what makes them stronger."

"Ah." Anduar nodded. "Do all of these shipyards contribute, then, to the fleet of the emperor? Or does each warlord possess his own fleet?"

"*Really* now, Anduar!" Lord Odus exclaimed. "What does any of this matter? If we're sure the capital is now Sar Tipaal—and no longer Puul Chak—that's all we need to know. And Kuran was able to tell us *that*."

Anduar returned Odus a cool stare. "I believe one can never know too much about one's enemies," he observed calmly.

"I agree." Devral had been leaning forward in his seat, listening with keen interest to Nagaro's responses. "It surely can't harm us to know how the Mahuk conduct their affairs."

Odus waved a hand in the air. "I might agree as well if I had reason to *believe* this man's information."

Nagaro stiffened. Kuran placed a restraining hand on his arm and spoke for the first time. "I assure you, My Lord Odus, that Captain Nagaro is a man of the highest integrity. I've had occasion to verify a number of things he's told me—some of them seemingly quite improbable—and have yet to find an instance where he hasn't spoken the truth."

"He may be *honest*," Pendrik drawled, leaning back in his chair and stifling a yawn with the back of his hand. "But how can we be sure he knows what he's talking about?"

Kuran's warning fingers dug into Nagaro's arm as the Lord of the Fleet spoke for a second time on his behalf. "The captain has lived among our enemies, My Lord Pendrik, having been a galley slave for a time. And since winning his freedom, he's spent several years sailing in and out of Mahuk waters, observing their activities and obtaining further information from the slaves he has freed from their war galleys. This history gives him a knowledge of Mahuk ways that extends beyond that of anyone else at this table—myself included."

"These are the man's credentials?" Odus's scorn rang in every word. "That he's been a *slave?* And a *pirate?*"

"He is now wearing the uniform of an officer of the Royal Fleet," Devral pointed out. Once more he coughed, covering his mouth with his fist.

"For how long? A few weeks?"

"Nearly three months, My Lord," Kuran offered.

Odus dismissed this with a gesture. "I'll be more impressed when he's served in some successful action. And do you really expect us to accept whatever the man says because he talks to *slaves?* What do slaves know of their masters affairs?"

Nagaro's irritation had been steadily growing and at this point he could keep silent no longer. "Slaves have ears and eyes, My Lord," he said, keeping his voice carefully level. "And men who think themselves superior to other men have a habit of speaking in front of them as if they were not there."

There was dead silence in the room while Lord Odus's startled annoyance deepened into an angry frown. A slow smile spread across Devral's scarred countenance while Pendrik appeared to be trying to work out whether he should be annoyed or not. Watching Elgurn's face across the table, Nagaro saw something he couldn't quite identify flicker in the king's pale blue eyes.

Again it was Anduar who spoke first. "Do they indeed, Captain?" he said mildly. "An ungracious habit. Perhaps such men should consider that it might work to their detriment."

Though Anduar hadn't so much as glanced at Odus, the younger Leithian lord plainly felt the barb. "Why should this *pirate* be allowed to speak so boldly?" he angrily demanded.

Devral spoke quickly on a conciliatory note. "Surely Captain Nagaro has proven himself by his service to this city. And we've heard much regarding his exploits—"

"*Exploits!*" Odus exploded, turning upon the scarred Kelorin. "I don't care about his supposed exploits! What of his parentage?"

"I don't see that it matters."

"How can it *not* matter? How can we be sure of the man's integrity without knowing the quality of his family?"

Devral's color was rising. "Surely you must concede that deeds are of *some* importance—"

Nagaro sat, stonily contemplating his cup as the barrage continued back and forth across the table. The argument was between a Leithian and a Kelorin Signer, and Elgurn was, as usual, a silent observer. Beyond noting those facts, he was only half listening. He didn't like the way they were treating him, and he was beginning to fear that he would not be allowed to say the things these men needed to hear.

He realized vaguely Kuran was speaking again, explaining that his parentage was unknown. Then suddenly, Pendrik was leaning across the table towards him, his ruddy face registering simple curiosity. "What exactly does Kuran mean by *unknown*, Captain?" the Leithian inquired in a stage whisper that was quite loud enough for everyone to hear. "You surely don't mean to say that you don't know, *yourself?*"

Nagaro frowned in the sudden silence that followed, feeling every man's eyes on him once more. Since he'd actually been addressed, he supposed he must reply. "I was told I was a foundling, My Lord Pendrik," he explained rather coolly. "That's all I know."

"So you only know what you were *told?*" Lord Odus's tone was pointedly derisive.

Nagaro turned to the bearded Leithian, his slender black brows coming together in a sharp line. "I don't see how anyone can know more about his own birth than what he's been told, My Lord," he said seriously. "You, I assume, were told you were a lord's son. *I* was told I was a foundling."

At this, Lord Odus gave him a look of such umbrage that Nagaro really feared he had said something seriously amiss.

Kuran's eyes were locked on Odus. He gave the Leithian a small, decisive shake of the head.

Abruptly, Pendrik slapped the table. "Oh, ha-ha! That's *good!* He's got you, Odus. No man remembers his own birth!"

Odus forced a smile. "Yes," he said rather stiffly. "A good joke. Ha-ha."

There was some more polite, awkward laugher around the table, but it died quickly. Anduar had not joined in, having instead lowered his gaze and picked up his teacup. Appearing presently to stare at nothing in particular, he took a sip and said quite casually, "What else have you to offer us, Captain?"

Nagaro had sought refuge in his own cup of sothiril, which he now put down, aware of the watchful silence of the other men. "I could be more certain, My Lord," he said cautiously, "if I knew what plans you were considering."

There followed a number of small, furtive movements around the table. Anduar's eyes darted to Nagaro over the lip of his teacup, then shifted to Kuran. The latter's face was a picture of innocence, though he kicked Nagaro sharply under the table.

Anduar seemed to banish an incipient frown as his gaze came back to Nagaro. "What we're planning need not concern you, Captain," he said blandly. "I asked you whether the Mahuk emperor commands a single combined fleet, or whether each warlord has his own."

Nagaro inclined his head to Anduar. Apparently, the man wasn't going to tell him anything, but he wasn't going to let his disappointment show. "It's a little complicated, My Lord," he explained, matching the Pact Signer's tone. "The warlords each have their own men and ships, but they all owe allegiance to the emperor. The emperor is therefore empowered to command every ship on the Baar—at least in principle."

"In *principle?*" Nagaro now had Anduar's full attention. The steely glance impaled him. Indeed he had the full attention of everyone at the table, although Odus still wore a frown.

Nagaro fingered the handle of his teacup. "It's not unlike our own situation. Here, all the lords owe allegiance to the king, in principle, and yet—"

Kuran coughed, and Nagaro felt another blow to his boot.

Lord Anduar smiled a smile that failed to include his eyes. "We were discussing the Mahuk Baar," he observed in the mildest of tones.

Nagaro inclined his head and continued. "The level of control that the emperor has over his warlords depends on his strength of arms and his skill as a leader. The old emperor's hold was weak at the end of his reign. Each of the warlords went his own way and we didn't have to deal with a single will or a united force. Baalkir is much stronger, but is still consolidating his power. His recent rivals are still exerting some independence."

"Might that be a weakness we could use against the emperor?" It was Devral who asked the question.

Nagaro turned to the scarred Kelorin. "I suppose it might, My Lord. But I see no advantage in undermining Baalkir's power."

"You don't see any *advantage* in weakening an enemy?" Pendrik was plainly incredulous.

Nagaro shook his head. "My Lord Pendrik, there is no advantage in weakening the one man who can hold the warlords of the Mahuk Baar in check. You may consider Emperor Baalkir our enemy, but I doubt that Baalkir sees Edrovir that way."

Pendrik stared, dumbfounded.

Odus, however, found his tongue. "Have you taken leave of your senses? Saying the Mahuk Emperor isn't our enemy!"

Anduar drew every eye by pointedly clearing his throat. "Perhaps, Captain, you would care to explain?" he said cooly."

Nagaro drew a breath and let it out. *Could he make them understand?* He began carefully. "Before a Mautep considers another man his enemy, he must first find the other man a worthy adversary. From the point of view of Baalkir, or any of his warlords, Edrovir simply doesn't qualify."

He did not expect this pronouncement to sit well with the Pact Signers, nor did it. Angry voices burst from both sides of the table. Anduar silenced them with an upraised hand. There was steel in the Kelorin's gaze when it returned to Nagaro. "And the reason for this?" he asked. There was steel behind the words, as well.

Nagaro withstood both the look and the words with equanimity. He ticked points off on his fingers. "First, our entire fleet amounts to what two of the stronger warlords could amass if they put their ships together; so they think us weak. Second, they don't ascribe honor to any but their own people; so they assume we have none. And third, they were sailing this coast before the nation of Edrovir even existed—before the Cataclysm of Fire and Water. So to them we're an upstart nation. They may know we have a king, but I doubt they'd be curious to learn his name. They enter our waters and take gold and slaves at will, not out of enmity, but because they *can*. Our attempts to stop them make us an annoyance—not an enemy." Nagaro stopped speaking and looked around to meet glowering frowns and outraged stares.

"*Preposterous!*" Pendrik's huge fist smote the table.

Devral growled, "That's insufferable!"

Elgurn leaned forward across the table. "Kuran, is there any truth to this?"

Kuran shifted in his seat, looking uncomfortable. "My Lord King," he said. "I have brought you the best source of information that I have. Captain Nagaro is an accurate observer and a shrewd judge of what he sees. Much of what he's just said rings true from my own experience. For the rest, I have no reason to doubt him."

"I see." The king sank back into his chair, his blue eyes brooding.

"*Kroneg's Blood!*" Lord Odus spoke with considerable heat, "It's clear we need to teach these arrogant sons-of-dogs a lesson!"

Pendrik and Devral echoed Lord Odus's sentiment, crying, "Hear, hear!" and "I should say so!"

Nagaro pinched the bridge of his nose. This was not the reaction he had hoped for. "With respect to you, My Lords," he said quickly. "I would counsel against an attack on one of their ports, if that's what you have in mind." He was glad he was wearing strong boots since the kick Kuran gave him would otherwise surely have bruised his ankle.

A barrage of looks like barbed arrows sped his way.

Anduar gave Kuran a very pointed glance. Kuran once again managed a look of injured innocence.

Anduar cleared his throat. "Captain," he said quietly, "I hope you can explain that remark."

Once more Nagaro met the steely gaze. "What do you do, My Lord, if you find a swarm of hornets making a nest in your garden?"

Something flickered in the cool gray eyes. "I smoke them out," he observed. "Pull down the nest. Burn it. Destroy them completely."

Nagaro nodded. "Exactly, My Lord. That would be the Emperor's response."

"You don't think it practical, then, to teach them a lesson?" Elgurn inquired sharply, even as he and Anduar exchanged glances.

Nagaro sighed and addressed himself to the king. "If we attack

Emperor Baalkir, My Lord, you may be sure he'll learn *something* from it. He might learn that we have more teeth than he thought, but in that case, he would simply send a larger force against us. We might even find that we had *become* an enemy of the Mahuk Baar—and *that* would surely not work to our advantage."

Pendrik thumped the table again. "But we've already successfully beaten off two of their attacks!"

"Those attacks were not ordered by the Emperor, My Lord," Nagaro countered. "Not by Baalkir, nor by his predecessor. Both were the work of men wearing brown and gold—the colors of Lord Angkat, Baalkir's strongest rival. They may not even have involved all the ships or men that Angkat could muster. It would be unwise to—"

"*Captain!*" Anduar interrupted him sharply, then continued more coolly. "If you please, Zirda, I would like to hear your solution. Speaking theoretically, what would *you* do if you had the governance of Edrovir? If you can imagine such a thing."

Nagaro frowned. "I can imagine it, My Lord ," he said earnestly. "But I hadn't thought about it." He paused to collect his thoughts, then spoke slowly, measuring his words. "We should continue to defend our seas and our people as best we can against all attacks. That is our right, and ought to be respected by any who understand honor. But at the same time, I would seek to meet with Emperor Baalkir—to treat with him. To try to persuade him that we're an honorable and worthy people—"

"—so he'll see fit to hold his warlords in check?" Anduar arched a brow.

"Yes, that's—"

Vehement protests from the other members of the Council cut him off, and Anduar had to hold up a hand for silence. "Patience, My Lords," he said, without taking his eyes from Nagaro. "I shall be finished with him momentarily. "So, Captain," he continued. "Do you believe you could obtain such a meeting? And would Baalkir pay any heed to what you had to say? On the face of it, neither seems probable."

Nagaro ran a hand through his hair. "I expect it doesn't, My Lord," he confessed. "The more so because it's Baalkir's brand that I bear, and he's set a price on my head. But you said this is theoretical. I've never met Baalkir jir-Akaan face to face. I don't know what manner of man he is. I *have* met his nephew, Roheed, however. *He* at least is a man who can be reasoned with. A man of integrity. So I hold out hope for the uncle."

"You have spoken with the *nephew* of the Emperor of the Mahuk Baar?" Anduar leaned back in his chair, outwardly neutral though his skepticism was audible.

"Yes, My Lord. Though Baalkir wasn't emperor at the time."

"A pity it wasn't the man's son," Devral interjected.

Nagaro shook his head. "Baalkir has no sons. Roheed is the only male heir of the House of jir-Akaan. He now sails with his uncle."

Anduar raised a hand to massage his temples. "When did you speak with this nephew, Captain?"

"While I was a slave, My Lord."

"While you were a *slave*?" Anduar was staring hard at him.

"Yes, My Lord."

"How did this occur?"

Nagaro drew a breath. "Roheed began his military career on the oar deck of the ship where I was chained. During the plague, the ship's captain forbad his crew to come amongst us to give us water. Something had to be done or we would have perished in a matter of days."

Anduar's stare continued. He spoke slowly, as if feeling his way. "So you spoke to the nephew... regarding water?"

"Yes, My Lord. I pointed out that Lord Baalkir might not be pleased to lose so many slaves when a little water could have saved them. There were a few... other... instances when I spoke to Roheed as well. And when we took the ship, we spared Roheed and the surviving men who stood with him."

For several long seconds, Anduar held Nagaro's eyes, probing, as if seeking some sign of falsehood. Nagaro didn't flinch. At last the Kelorin lord withdrew his gaze. "I see," he said. "Thank you, Captain. This has been most enlightening." He turned to the other men who encircled the table. "My Lords, have you any other questions for Captain Nagaro?"

There had been muttering among the other lords while Nagaro and Anduar had been speaking, and Odus immediately raised his voice. "This man's suggestion is the counsel of cowardice," he said flatly, "— to leave the enemy's attack unanswered! But what else can we expect from a pirate? One who only attacks when he's sure of victory? This man knows nothing of valor or glory!"

Nagaro had been watching Anduar, trying to read the man's eyes— where he caught what looked like a flash of annoyance—even as he felt the sting of Odus's words. At the same time he felt Kuran's hand on his arm and heard the Lord of the Fleet mutter, "*Let it go.*"

But it was too *wrong* to be let go.

He turned to face Lord Odus. "I've sworn an oath of service to the Fleet, and to uphold the interests of the people of Edrovir, My Lord," he said, speaking into the silence that had followed Odus's outburst. "I don't fear to die, but I can't help anyone if I'm slain. Therefore I prefer not to pursue vengeance that's only likely to beget more vengeance. And valor and glory are of no use to anyone if they are dead or in chains!"

Nagaro heard Pendrik, who was nearest, gasp, and the sound was echoed elsewhere around the table. Everyone was staring at him, and he feared he had gone too far. Angering these men would do his cause more harm than good.

Before anyone else could speak, however, Elgurn said, "Thank you for being so candid, Captain." His face was stiff. "Your further presence is not required. You have leave to go. My Lord Kuran, I think you had best remain."

Nagaro stood up, relieved. "Thank you, My Lord King," he murmured with sincerity as he gave Elgurn one of his better bows.

Anduar and Devral had their heads together, muttering, and he was struck by the look on Odus's face. The Leithian lord had gone pale.

Kuran was frowning, but he gave Nagaro a quick nod and managed a small, tight smile.

Nagaro made a second more general bow to the Pact Signers before making his exit. He was glad to get away, but he'd barely passed into the dimly lit Audience Chamber when he felt a hand on his shoulder, restraining him. Turning, he was surprised to find that the hand belonged to Lord Anduar. The Kelorin lord had followed him out. "My Lord?" he said uncertainly, supposing the man had come to chastize him for his boldness.

Anduar spoke in a low voice that was meant for Nagaro's ears alone, though his tone was conversational. "As a matter of curiosity, Captain, what would you think of an attack on this rival of Baalkir's? Lord Angkat, was it?"

Nagaro was surprised, but he had a ready answer. "I believe an attack on Angkat, if it were successful, would benefit both Baalkir and Edrovir," he said seriously. "Even an unsuccessful attack would show Baalkir that we know who harmed us. But Angkat's port of Ulaad lies farther south, deeper into the Baar. The risks of striking at either port would be very great. The entire Baar is patrolled by multiple fleets, because there are multiple warlords. If you go with many ships, you increase your chance of being discovered before reaching your goal. If you take fewer ships, for stealth, you decrease your chance of success when you get there."

"I see. Thank you." Anduar actually smiled, fleetingly. "If you wish to wait for Kuran, I suggest you do so in the entry hall where you left your sword—not here. But you needn't wait. We may continue for some time. Good night, Captain."

Nagaro murmured his thanks, and bowed again to Anduar, before striking off across the hall. His boots rang on the polished stone floor and the sound echoed in the lofty space. His mind was in a whirl, and he did not look back. Therefore he didn't see that Anduar stood for a long moment looking after him.

*

It was more than an hour later when Kuran made his appearance in the entry hall. He found Nagaro there, pacing the floor.

"I hope they didn't take you to task for my missteps, My Lord," Nagaro observed anxiously as he fell in beside the Lord of the Fleet.

Kuran glanced at him keenly. "Not too much," he said. "I told them to put it all down to a combination of impetuous youth, ignorance—and an occasional lucky guess."

"Oh. Good." Nagaro sighed with relief and refrained from further speech while they collected their cloaks, gloves, and Nagaro's sword from Delvin. The young guardsman stifled a yawn as he bade them good night.

"I'm afraid I'm not very good at curbing my tongue," Nagaro said apologetically as they moved towards the front doors. "And I'm even more afraid that some of those men will disregard my words simply because it was I who said them."

Kuran laughed shortly. "Don't fret so much, Captain," he said. "They're likely to believe what they wish to believe in any case."

"That's not very reassuring—" Nagaro began, then stopped as they passed through the great double doors, with the guards on either side within earshot.

Outside in the portico, with the doors closed behind them, they paused to pull their cloaks closer against the cold night air. Nagaro was grateful that at least the wind had ceased. "What did they decide?" he asked. "Or can't you tell me?"

Kuran started down the steps, shaking his head. "I shouldn't tell you," he said. "But as it happens, they've decided nothing. The matter was put off until another time."

"They decided *nothing?*" Nagaro was astounded. "What did they talk about for an hour then?"

Kuran stopped, this time at the bottom of the steps, at the edge of the stable yard. He turned to study Nagaro by the light of a lantern that hung from a post. He seemed to be trying to make up his mind about something. At last he said, "For the most part, they talked about *you*, Captain. You seem to have made an impression. In fact, you have a positive talent for doing so."

Nagaro stared in dismay. "About *me*, My Lord? For an *hour?*" This couldn't be good. "*Keshaal!*" he muttered, stepping into the stable yard, out of the pool of lantern light. "What was it?" he added bitterly. "My insolence? Or my doubtful trustworthiness? Or weren't they finished with my unknown parentage?"

Kuran had moved after him, but stopped again before answering. "Actually it was mostly about that last little speech of yours—the bit about vengeance begetting vengeance, and valor and glory being of no use to dead men. Some of them seemed to think you were deliberately paraphrasing Darion."

The light was behind Kuran, and Nagaro couldn't see the older man's face well enough to read it. He frowned. "I was only saying what seemed right to me."

"Yes, of course." Kuran sounded relieved. "But apparently King Darion said something very similar once. It was an incident to which *they* were among the few witnesses and none of them could remember it ever having been written down. And Darion would have died before you were born."

Nagaro shrugged impatiently. "I suppose I got it from the Vothrin Writings. And Darion probably got it from the same source."

Kuran nodded. "That makes sense to me. But it seems that Darion said it to Harl Sobring, after Harl had said something very like what Odus said about you. Darion wanted to make peace with Jinara and Hran. Harl challenged him over it, and they fought a match that ended with Darion having to kill Harl because the man fought dishonorably. I witnessed that match, by the way," he added. "It was fought here in this plaza, and I was one of a crowd of young lads, come to try for places in the Fleet. Darion was *magnificent...*"

Kuran paused, caught in the coil of memory, then shook his head to recapture the thread of his thought. "Being cast in the role of Harl Sobring gave Odus a bad turn. The more so when he learned that you're an exceptional swordsman."

Nagaro laughed. "This is foolishness, My Lord," he said lightly. "I know that part of the story. Berinar describes the match in his *Rule of Loros*, and it's not a very close parallel. I am not the king, and Odus didn't challenge me. I don't imagine he will, either, since I am so far beneath him."

Kuran looked grim. "You may be sure he won't—not *now*. But he very nearly *did* earlier this evening when you said you assumed he'd been told he was a lord's son. You see—" Kuran lowered his voice "—Odus was born rather too soon after his mother's marriage, and there was talk about her and a handsome stable boy, although the family has always maintained there's no truth to the rumor. Odus imagined you were trying to insult him, and he actually considered challenging you to a match to force an apology. I was sure you hadn't known, and I told him so after you'd gone. I also told him it would have been only the difference in your stations that would have forced an apology and nothing to do with skill, since you could surely have beaten him handily."

Nagaro looked at the ground. After a moment, he said, "If what I saw tonight is an illustration of what men of noble blood are like, I'm just as glad not to be one."

The Lord of the Fleet laughed. "You didn't think much of the King's Council?"

Nagaro frowned. "I wonder why it's called the *King's* Council, since Elgurn seems almost afraid to speak in front of the others. And I don't think much of the wisdom of the councilors, either—except perhaps for Lord Anduar. He at least seemed to listen—and to think. Although he speaks so little that it's hard to know what he's *really* thinking."

Kuran whistled. "Nagaro, you are remarkably astute. The six Pact Signers were the greatest of the lords in strength of arms, not necessarily in wisdom. Anduar is easily the sharpest knife of the lot, and he does indeed play a close game. And as for Elgurn, well, the king knows that the Pact Signers gave him the crown and can as easily take it away again. But I've probably said enough," he added. "Let's call for our horses. My fingers are freezing in spite of these gloves."

12: Winter Turnings

Nagaro was not invited back to the Council Chamber in the weeks that followed. While he was grateful for this, he was not grateful for the fact that Kuran offered him no news of the Council's deliberations. He was intensely curious to know what the Pact Signers would decide. Since it did him no good to fret about it, however, he tried to focus on other things—such as sword practice and training exercises. Most of his evenings were filled with reading or playing King's Men with Taru and Pavo. At week's end, he and his friends often went riding along the road beside the river, or through the streets of Lankura. And of course there were the occasional invitations from the princess.

As it turned out, there was only one more outing to River House before the weather became too cold and the roads impassable. The last expedition provided another welcome opportunity for Nagaro to ride with the princess, and talk to her—as well as adequate time to learn every dance Kendira could teach him. With the worsening of the weather, the outings were replaced by evening dinner parties at the palace. These modest affairs were arranged for the entertainment of the palace residents and visiting guests, and Nagaro soon found his command of the social graces being regularly tested at the "match table". To his relief, he found he was adequately prepared, owing to the combination of Kendira's dance instruction and the broader tutelage he'd received years before from the Lady Maramine.

It was at one of these parties that he was first approached by Lord Devral to dance with Nevien in the lame lord's stead as part of the established courtship ritual. Devral's limp made him a poor dance partner, which placed him at a disadvantage in the competition for the princess's hand. Nagaro agreed to the request and Devral pressed him into frequent service that winter, taking shameless advantage of the fact that being a member of the King's Council often kept the old lord in Lankura when his rivals were not.

Nagaro was all too happy to indulge the older man. Dancing with the princess was always pleasant, and talking with her in any setting even more so. He would have been quite satisfied with the winter's activities if he hadn't found that he was growing weary of Kendira and was at a loss to know what to do about it. He felt he was in her debt, and he also didn't wish to lose his entry ticket to the palace. When he tried bringing the matter up with Taru and Pavo, he found his friends of no help. Taru didn't like to see Nagaro mingling so much with "highborn folk". He worried that Nagaro was too interested in the princess, and was suspicious of his friend's desire to cease pursuing Kendira. Pavo, on the other hand, thought it quite natural for Nagaro to associate with the nobility—seeing Nagaro as one of them—but the Hashtep fisherman's son didn't understand why Nagaro couldn't simply tell Kendira that she wasn't right for him and pursue someone else.

Then, a week before the beginning of Idrin and the turning of the year, Nagaro returned to his quarters from a dinner party to find a note from Brandle pushed under his door. It contained directions to the building on Broad Street where Simion was employed, and set a time for Nagaro to meet with the young Kelorin clerk.

*

On the apointed evening, Nagaro set out on foot with the hood of his cloak pulled up to ward off a cold drizzle. He was grateful this time for the inclement weather since the hood helped conceal his face from passers-by. Indeed, he drew few glances as he traversed the city's streets, following Brandle's directions. Before long, he was turning off of Broad Street into an alley that ran between two imposing stone edifices. Another turn took him into the back street behind the building that was his destination. There, an archway opened in the wall on his right, just as Brandle had described. He turned into it, pausing for his eyes to adjust to the dimness.

He was in a short entryway, leading to a covered walkway that ran cloister-like around the four sides of a cobbled courtyard. Brandle's note had been apologetic about sending him to the servant's entrance, but Nagaro didn't mind since it meant he was unlikely to encounter anyone of consequence. As it turned out, there were only a few folk present, mostly in the livery of the House of Furthing, and apparently going about their business.

Nagaro did not immediately see Simion. The afternoon was so dim and gloomy that an old man was already lighting the lamps set at intervals along the wall of the cloister walk, using a lighted punk on the end of a stick. Nagaro was considering asking the man for directions to the clerk's room when he heard Simion's voice breathlessly whisper, *"I'm over here."*

Nagaro turned to scan for the young Kelorin. He spotted the youth's the slender figure and recognized him elfin face with its luminous deep blue eyes watching from the shadow of one of the pillars supporting the roof of the cloister walk.

"Well met, Simion," he said as he approached the young man.

"Well met... Zirda." Simion gave him a small bow. "Please follow me."

Simion led the way along one side of the cloister-walk to a doorway and up a flight of stairs to another covered walkway. The young man continued along this second-floor walkway, past several doors, before stopping in front of one. Unlocking the door, he held it open and gestured for Nagaro to enter.

The small room was furnished with several bookcases full of books and ledgers, a pair of chairs, and a long table against the far wall. A large desk stood where the light from the single window fell upon it. An oil lamp on the desk was already lit to supplement the feeble daylight.

Nagaro removed his damp cloak and hung it on a waiting hook while Simion closed the door firmly behind them. When Nagaro turned, he found the young man regarding him with such frank admiration that it made him blush.

"You haven't changed, Nagaro."

Simion was one of a very small number of people who knew Nagaro's former name, and Nagaro was uncomfortable under his gaze. Trying to shed the awkwardness, he said, "*You* have, Simion. Whatever life you have found here in Lankura, it must agree with you. You look... happier."

Simion laughed. "*That* wouldn't be difficult." He pulled his eyes away. "Please sit down," he added, indicating one of the two chairs. He himself took the desk chair and turned it around before sitting down so he could face Nagaro.

"I suppose it wouldn't." Nagaro sat down gratefully. "I take it your parents were glad of your return?"

Simion leaned back in his seat. "Yes, and we are fully reconciled. My mother would have welcomed me regardless, and my father was so overjoyed to find I wasn't dead, that nothing else mattered."

"And you're working for Brandle's father?"

Simion smiled wryly. "Bookkeeping and record-keeping—useful work that I can easily do. And I live in this building. I have a chamber upstairs."

"Does Madred Furthing know... about you and Brandle?"

"Oh yes." Simion smiled again, without pleasure. "It seems Lord Madred has come to realize that nothing will change Brandle, so he's decided to make the best of it. If Brandle is bound to consort with someone, let it be someone *known*—and well kept. It's so much tidier that way. The man says I'm 'very nearly a woman,' so that makes Brandle 'very nearly a man.'"

Nagaro winced. "That... doesn't sound very good."

Simion shrugged. "I have my living, and Brandle comes to see me whenever he can." He paused, then said with an eager catch in his voice, "If only Tevren's son would come, he'd surely make things better for people like us."

Nagaro frowned at this reference to a cause he had so far associated with Rastyl Korven. "Well... *maybe*," he said cautiously. "Though I don't know how one person could change so many minds."

Simion collected himself. "It's just a dream I have," he said quickly, then turned the subject. "Brandle said that you're courting one of the princess's ladies... named Kendira."

Nagaro looked away. "I've been trying to decide whether to court her..." he began, and then his frustration got the better of him and he met Simion's eyes again. "Actually, I don't think I do want to. I've yet to find anything on which we share an interest. All she wants to do is dance—so I must dance with her. Or else she insists I dance with women who are visiting the palace. She acts as if it's a great privilege that she's sharing with less fortunate souls."

Simion's dark blue eyes sparkled with merriment. "Well you *are* rather famous," he pointed out. "It's probably a bit of a thrill for them—dancing with Captain Nagaro—

"But I feel like a trained pony!" Nagaro jerked impatiently in his chair. "I don't even *like* dancing very much."

"I've heard you're very good at it—" Simion began, before he saw the storm gathering and quickly added, "But if you really don't like it, why don't you just break things off with this girl?"

Nagaro sagged. "I can't figure out *how*. She taught me all the dances, and I'm grateful to her for that. I feel I owe her something in return... but..."

Simion was instantly all sympathy. He leaned forward, dark eyes aglow. "It sounds to me as though you've already given her quite a lot in return," he said seriously, "by dancing with her all this time and letting her show you off. If you just thanked her, and told her all that dancing isn't for you and said you don't want to do it anymore, I can't see that she'd really have much to complain about if you just walked away."

Nagaro frowned. "But I don't want to just walk away—" he began, and stopped. "I've been enjoying some of the... other company," he said carefully. "Kendira may not make good conversation, but there are others who do, and the Fleet Compound doesn't offer anything comparable. But the only reason I'm being invited to the palace is because I told the princess I wanted to get to know Kendira."

"I see." Simion's expression turned thoughtful. After a moment, he said, "I think you should give Kendira a gift—to thank her. Something nice, so you can bid her farewell with a clear conscience. Then, once that's done, perhaps you could tell the princess you want to try to get to know someone else."

Nagaro considered this. "A gift..." he murmured. "That's a good idea... Thank you, Simion." *Perhaps Nevien could suggest someone else he might try...*

Simion became suddenly businesslike. "Brandle said you wanted me to look at a ring. Is it the one Roheed gave to you?"

Nagaro was relieved to get to the subject of his visit. "Yes. Emril's ring. I wondered whether it might belong to any of the merchant families that you know." He slipped the ring from his finger and held it out. "I already showed it to Mendorel in Kel Tierna, but he didn't recognize it."

Simion took the ring and moved his chair closer to the desk so he could examine it by the light of the oil lamp, turning it in his fingers and frowning in concentration. "A salamander... biting its tail..." he murmured, "...with green eyes..." He looked up. "I'm afraid it doesn't match the marks of any of the merchants based here in Lankura."

Nagaro sighed. "And with Mendorel having ruled out the ones in Kel Tierna, that leaves Galenor to the north, and Harmoth to the south..."

"It also leaves the towns up-river, and other places inland," Simion put in, handing the ring back to Nagaro. "I'll keep my eyes open. And if I turn up a likely merchant house, I'll get an address so you can write to them."

Nagaro slid the ring back onto his finger. "Thank you, Simion. I'd be very glad if you'd do that."

There seemed to be nothing more to add, so Nagaro retrieved his cloak and departed.

*

Outside, the rain had turned into very fine, light snow that dusted window ledges and the tops of walls but failed to accumulate on the wet, slushy pavement. The sun had nearly set, leaving only a lingering glow in the low-hanging clouds to the west.

Nagaro walked quickly though the dimming streets, his thoughts skipping lightly over the hope that Simion might be able to successfully trace the origin of the salamander ring. The problem of disengaging from Kendira weighed much more heavily on his mind, and he liked Simion's suggestion. He'd begun to worry that he was using Kendira as an opportunitiy to talk to Nevien. Giving the young woman a gift should indeed ease his conscience.

He shook his head with a faint smile. Talking to Simion always made him nervous, but paradoxically, it seemed to elicit confidences. Perhaps it was because he and Simion both had vulnerabilities, and knew it— and they both wanted nothing more than each other's happiness.

Nagaro came to a stop at the corner where Brass Bell Lane opened off of River Street, suddenly remembering that he'd meant to visit a bookseller's shop on the short cull-de-sac. He turned under the archway bearing the street's namesake: a bell gone green with age, cracked and missing its clapper. The book shop was on the right, halfway to the end of the lane.

He'd discovered it soon after his arrival in Lankura and had bought several books there already. Today he was looking for something for Pavo, whose illiteracy had come to Kuran's attention. The Lord of the Fleet had declared that the deficiency must be rectified, and Nagaro had begun teaching his friend his letters. This, in turn, had produced a need for something to use for reading practice.

Entering the shop, Nagaro found he was the only customer. He took his time browsing among the collection of children's primers, choosing one with particularly fine drawings. He brought it to the shopkeeper's counter.

"Will there be anything else, Zirda?" the man asked as he drew out a piece of oiled cloth to wrap the book in to protect it from the weather.

Nagaro started to shake his head, but then remembered Simion's suggestion. "Do you have any books of poetry?" he asked, poetry being something that Kendira had often prattled on about.

The bookseller beamed. "Certainly, Zirda. Right over here."

As it turned out, there were two whole shelves of poetry books, and Nagaro had no idea how to choose one. Some of the books were prettier on the outside than others, but he didn't want to choose based on appearance. He realized, to his chagrin, that he had no idea what Kendira would actually *like*—or what she might already *have*.

He asked the shopkeeper for help, but the man clearly didn't want the responsibility of choosing for him, and resorted to touting the merits of half a dozen different books, beginning each pitch with, "Or perhaps the young lady would like this one—"

In the end, Nagaro paid the proprietor for the picture book and left the shop without a gift for Kendira. He told the bookseller he would think about the options, but he actually felt quite discouraged. He knew he could think for a month and it wouldn't help.

Outside the bookshop, the little street's single lantern had been lit, although the street was quite deserted. The lamplight glistened on new snow and wet paving stones, gilding the tiny motes of snowflakes in the air. Across the street, it fell on the shabby front of an old apothecary shop with a weathered sign that was badly in need of paint. The windows were dark and the door boarded up. Nagaro frowned. Brass Bell Lane didn't get much traffic, and it occurred to him to worry that the bookseller might suffer the same fate as the apothecary. He thought he really should try to give the bookshop more custom, which only increased his regret at not being able to choose a poetry book.

*

At home that evening, Nagaro and his friends sat sharing hot sothiril in the warmth of Nagaro's kitchen as the snow continued to fall outside and the wind scurried about the eaves. Pavo gazed in frank admiration at the first illustration in the picture book, depicting a fisherman in his boat casting his net. "This is just same way we do it in Mahuk Baar!" he exclaimed.

Taru rolled his eyes. "It's a picture-book. For *little children*."

Pavo shook his head at Taru. "I do not care," he replied calmly. He turned to Nagaro. "Thank you very much. Having picture means I will not mind so much making my head hurt from remembering all those little letter!"

Taru pushed one of the carved playing pieces across the playing board with his finger. "Since we're not playing, Nagaro," he said, "could ye at least tell us what ye learned from Simion."

Pavo raised his eyes from the picture book. "Yes, Nagaro. I want to know that too."

Nagaro sighed and reported what Simion had told him regarding the ring, there being nothing else from the conversation that he cared to share.

Taru frowned. "If Emril's people were merchants, why was she out on the sea with nothing in the ship, and her husband and all those other men carrying swords?" he wanted to know.

"I have no idea." Nagaro shrugged. "But if the family were merchants, and Simion found out the family name, he could get an address so I could write to them."

Taru looked startled. "Ye'd write a *letter* about that?"

Pavo nodded sagely. "You see! It is good thing to know how to write. And with my new book, I will learn very quickly."

This got another eye-roll from Taru.

Since they could shed no further light on the puzzle of the ring, they played King's Men until they were yawning. When Pavo and Taru donned their cloaks to go out into the night, the wind had died but the snowflakes were still falling.

*

In the days that followed, Nagaro racked his brain, trying to recall anything Kendira had ever said concerning her preferences in poetry, only to be forced to admit that he'd never really paid any attention to anything she'd said on the subject. He then tried to think what other gift he might give her, and he finally resorted to asking Pavo what kinds of gifts he'd given to his wife, Tenepti. Pavo's list included such things as a comb and hairbrush, a vase for flowers, and a necklace made of shells. The last item seemed the most promising.

Not mere shells for Kendira, of course. The daughter of a wealthy merchant couldn't be expected to be impressed with seashells. No, it should be some more signifiicant item of jewelry. With the last palace dinner party before Idrin fast approaching, Nagaro fished out his cash box and emptied it onto his bed. There wasn't much left by that time of the jewelry that had come to him as part of his "captain's share" from his pirate days, but he found a pretty thing that he thought would do.

At the dinner party, he had to wait until the very end of the evening for an opportunity to present the gift without an unwanted audience. When he pulled it out of his pocket and laid on the table in front of Kendira, he stumbled some over his planned explanation, trying not to be too blunt. Kendira seemed rather stunned—quite tongue-tied, in fact—and he wasn't sure when he left her that she'd actually understood everything he had said. He told himself he could straighten out any confusion at the mid-winter festival, after Idrin, when he could also speak to Nevien about the prospect of changing his pairing at the match table.

He might have worried more about the matter, but other things intervened. The seven Dark Days of Idrin always brought a lull in social activities because they were considered unlucky, and the month lived up to its reputation that year by bringing a sharp turn of bitter cold weather with heavy snow and ice storms that damaged many roofs in the city of Lankura. When Kuran called for volunteers from among the Fleet men to help some of the city's poorer residents with repairs, Nagaro was one of those who answered. Charity work came naturally to him, and since he didn't believe the Idrin superstitions, he had no fear of climbing around on icy rooftops during the Dark Days. The work dragged on, as such things do, into the first days of Genorel when most of the people of Edrovir were making preparations for the festival that marked the coming of the new year.

13: Feast Of A Thousand Lights

The long-awaited mid-winter Feast of a Thousand Lights was one of the four great festivals that punctuated the seasons of Edrovir's calendar. Marking as it did the "turning" of the year, it was celebrated on the third of Genorel when the ill-omened seven days of Idrin had sped and the winter solstice—the fourth of Idrin—was already five days past. The palace staff had been busy during those five days—cleaning, polishing, and decorating—and the Great Hall was resplendent by the time the guests began to arrive.

Those who were not too jaded gasped at what they beheld. The walls of the huge, shadowed room shimmered with gold cloth hangings, festooned with garlands of dark evergreen, intertwined with snow-white ribbons. The air was scented by the centerpieces that graced each table, woven out of cedar boughs and decorated with cinnamon-colored cedar cones and bunches of golden sothiril berries. Massive logs burned brightly in the two great fireplaces that stood at either end of the room's exterior wall, flanking the darkened windows. And of course, the lights were everywhere, each one the flame of a small votive candle protected by a crystal sconce set in a gilded base. A row of these lights marched down the center of every table. More were placed on ornately carved stands set at intervals along the walls or around the open space in the center of the floor where the dancing would take place. Still more graced the royal dais. The oil lamps along the walls all had their wicks turned down to show off the candles to better advantage. On this night, at least one candle was burning in every house, great and small, all across the land of Edrovir, giving the festival its name. But in the Great Hall that evening, it seemed that a thousand lights burned under a single roof.

The princess's ladies were gathering at the match table, waiting for the young men to arrive. Brendet was conversing with Clarimel at one end of the board, while Rianine and Alisset were engaged in a separate conversation near the other. Kendira sat silently at the far end, her pretty face wearing a slight frown as her hand kept straying to a necklace of silver-gray pearls encircling her throat.

"The red and purple that we had last year was *much* more colorful, "Clarimel said critically.

Brendet primped her hair. "Well, personally, I've never cared for red and purple together," she said. "The gold and white go better with the evergreen. And you *must* have evergreen..."

Rianine leaned closer to Alisset and lowered her voice. "Then I told Clarimel that if she wished to borrow anything else from me, she must first return my silver comb that she's had for over a month."

"What did she say?" Alisset was breathless.

"She had the nerve to say that she'd misplaced it! And I *know* she covets it too much to be so careless. So now she's not speaking to me because I wouldn't lend her my pearl earrings."

"Oh my!" Alisset put a hand to her mouth to hide her glee.

Rianine turned to Kendira. "Speaking of pearls, my dear," she said pointedly, "I've heard that handling them too much spoils their luster."

Kendira guiltily dropped her hand. "Do you think it's true, Rian?"

Rianine laughed merrily. "I have no idea," she replied. "Pearls are scarcely to be found in Irvenen. But it quite spoils the effect of wearing any jewelry if you keep acting as if you know it's there." She gave Kendira a closer and more sympathetic look. "I suppose that ill-schooled pirate still hasn't spoken to your father?"

"No-o..." Kendira dropped her eyes. "I'm beginning to think he never meant to."

"Oh now, really!" Alisset exclaimed, her blue eyes wide in her round face. "He really *must*. I mean, after all, a whole pearl necklace!"

Kendira twisted her fingers together. "Sometimes I've thought he was courting me without asking Father, and sometimes I think he hasn't asked Father because he's never meant to court me! And then, all of a sudden, he gave me this necklace!"

"Maybe he's just a bit nervous about talking to your father." Alisset offered kindly.

"That's possible," Rianine put in. "Men are really terrible cowards. So you're wearing his present to prod him, is that it?" She arched a questioning brow. "It isn't very subtle, but sometimes one has to hit them over the head. Captain Nagaro probably knows more about sailing ships—or even feeding chickens—than he does about what a woman expects of him. Have you found out yet who his 'Lady Guardian' was, by the way?"

"No. He... he just won't talk about it. I've told him *everything* about my family, too, but he only talks about his friends—or about being a *slave*." She shuddered. "Which is quite dreadful!"

Rianine's eyes narrowed. "Personally," she said, "I don't think the Lady Guardian ever existed. I think he's just a farm boy turned pirate who is putting on airs. If wearing that necklace doesn't work, I might speak to him myself."

"Speak to whom?"

Nevien had come up behind them and she now settled into the last chair at Kendira's end of the table.

"Why Captain Nagaro, of course." Rianine responded with obvious relish. "I know he's one of your favorites, Nevien, but someone really *must* tell him how to behave."

Nevien frowned. "Then maybe I should do it."

"Oh no, you'll be much too lenient with him."

"I'll be diplomatic," Nevien observed coolly. "Which you would not, Rian. And you're a fine one to tell other folk how to behave!"

"*Shhh!*" Alisset put a finger to her lips. "Here comes Rese—and Vanhold!"

Two young Leithian men promptly approached the table, bowing and murmuring courtesies before taking their appointed seats—Rese across from Alisset, and Vanhold opposite Clarimel. There followed an exchange of banal pleasantries during which the Lady Merriel arrived and took her seat across from Nevien.

When the conversation settled, Nevien turned to Kendira. "Would you like me to speak to the captain about his intentions?"

Kendira nodded. "Would you please, Nevien? I really don't know why he gave me the necklace! I mean, he's polite, and he always dances with me—or with any lady I tell him to, because *all* the ladies want to dance with him and it would be rude not to let them—" Kendira had started to nibble a nail but caught herself and shoved her hand into her lap. "But he hardly ever says anything to me, and when he does, half of it doesn't make sense. And he always seems glad to talk to *you*—" Kendira turned pink and looked at the table.

Nevien bit her lip. It was quite true that Nagaro was always glad to talk to her, and he seemed to have no shortage of things to say when he did. "He's been very good to dance with me in Lord Devral's stead," she said, rather unnecessarily. "And I will see what I can do."

"Oh, thank you, Nevien." Kendira was twisting her fingers again.

At this point Merriel leaned close. "What exactly did he say to you, dear, when he gave you the necklace?"

"Well first he... he said he was grateful for the dancing lessons." Kendira's brow constricted as she wracked her memory for the details. "And... and... that he wanted to give me something *pretty*. And then he pulled the necklace out of his pocket, and I don't know what he said after that because I was too flustered."

Merriel glanced at Nevien. "Do you suppose he just meant it as a thank you gift?" she asked. "*A pearl necklace?*"

Nevien sighed. "It's possible. It's not that he doesn't know the value of things. He just doesn't seem to particularly care."

They were interrupted by the arrival of two more young men who sat down opposite Rianine and Brendet, leaving only the seat across from Kendira unoccupied.

Clarimel spoke up loudly from her end of the table. "Your captain is late again, Kendira. What do you suppose it is this time? Some pitiful request from a thief pretending to be a beggar?

Kendira's cheeks turned pink again. She seemed to have no ready answer.

The young man facing Rianine, an eager-looking young Kelorin with a narrow, shaven chin and carefully combed dark hair said, "Oh come now, Clarimel. It's well known that Captain Nagaro is careful with his charity."

Clarimel sniffed. "*Well*," she began, "one hears it repeated that—"

A peremptory cough and a sharp look from Lady Merriel ended the exchange just as the bell sounded, calling all the diners to table.

It was only then that Nagaro finally made his appearance, in his captain's uniform, threading his way among the tables. He paused when he reached the match table long enough to give a general bow to the ladies before pulling out the one remaining chair and sitting down.

"I'm sorry that I'm so late," he said seriously, addressing Kendira. "I belatedly discovered a matter that it took me some time to deal with."

Kendira managed a wan smile. Beside her, Rianine's expression turned predatory. "I am curious, Captain," she said, "to know what you found it so necessary to do at midwinter festival time."

He turned her a polite glance. "Mending a roof."

"Really?" Brendet sounded simply curious. "I would have thought the Fleet had... *people*... to do that sort of thing."

Nagaro gave the Leithian maid a disapproving look. "They do," he said, "But the old woman whose roof it was had no one. She'd told me her neighbor would do the mending. But when I went to see if it was done, I found that the neighbor was sick in bed and the slates were still lying where the delivery man had left them."

Clarimel spoke up languidly from her place farther along the table. "Surely you could have found some *other* time for this?"

Nagaro turned to regard her rather coldly. "I don't believe you would have thought so if it had been snowing into *your* bedchamber, My Lady," he said, reaching for the nearest of several porcelain teapots and prepareing to pour himself a cup of sothiril.

In the dimly lit hall, the glazed ceramic winked in the light of the candles arrayed along the table, drawing eyes to the motion of his hand. Alisset suddenly emitted a squeak. "Oh, *mercy!*" she cried. "His hand is bleeding!"

There was an immediate stir along the table as all the men leaned forward for a better look while the women—most of them—drew back in alarm.

Nagaro glanced at his right hand, apparently unperturbed by an irregular two-inch red line running along the outer edge of it. "Actually," he said, "it stopped bleeding an hour ago."

"But to come to the table *without covering it?*" Clarimel delicately held up a hand between her eyes and the offending sight, although she was seated so far along the table that she could hardly have made out any details.

Rianine had leaned forward with the men. "Is it a sword wound?" she inquired, with most unladylike interest. On the other side of the table, her carefully groomed young man gaped at her.

"No," the Leithian named Rese responded, leaning in for a better view. "A sword cut would have cleaner edges—"

"*Mercy!*" "*The Lady protect us!*" The cries of Alisset and Brendet were uttered very nearly simultaneously.

Kendira sat rigid, eyes averted.

At this point, Lady Merriel, who had at least retained her composure, addressed Nagaro. "Captain," she said pointedly, "you really should have that hurt properly tended."

Nagaro was frankly surprised by everyone's reaction. He'd finished pouring, and as he set the teapot down, he turned to Merriel. "It's only a scratch, My Lady," he said. "I've washed it, and it will be quite all right without any covering. If I had stopped to get it bandaged I would have been later still."

Nevien spoke for the first time. "My mother's physician, Master Ambras, is here tonight, Captain." She gave him a meaningful glance. "If you'll accompany me, I'm sure he can tend to it."

Nagaro read her eyes and closed his mouth on the reply he'd been about to make. Instead he said, "Perhaps that would be a good idea." Rising, he came quickly around the end of the table and offered his left arm to the princess, who had also risen. As they moved away from the table, he heard Clarimel say quite pointedly, "Really! How uncouth!"

Nagaro sighed. "I suppose that I must be," he murmured to Nevien, "since it never occurred to me that anyone would be bothered by it."

The princess gave him a quick, sharp glance. "It *is* a scratch," she said. "Alisset is overly squeamish, and Clarimel is intent upon proving you a barbarian by any means. But it would be wiser not to come to the table with any unbandaged cut, even if it's only a pinprick."

"I see." He nodded ruefully. "I'm afraid you'll have to lead, My Lady, since I don't know where we're going."

"This way." Nevien guided him past tables of seated guests, their faces lit by flickering candles. "I can see that Master Ambras is sitting where I placed him."

"I hope that he's only here for the festivities and not for anything concerning your mother's health."

A frown immediately creased the princess's brow. "Unfortunately, it's both. We would have invited him in any case, but Mother has also been feeling very poorly. Father gave Ambras a chamber here in the palace three days ago so he'd be close in case he's needed."

Nagaro had just time to say how sorry he was to hear this before they reached the place where the healer was seated. Nevien spoke quickly into the man's ear. The spare, graying Kelorin immediately rose, smiling and saying he was pleased to be of service as he led them away towards the end of the hall opposite the dais, and through a door into a corridor.

The healer's chamber turned out to be one among those usually assigned to the palace guard, located close to the foot of the palace's back stair that led up to the royal apartments. The room was divided by a screen into a sleeping portion and a somewhat larger half that had been fitted out as a combined office and dispensary. Ambras quickly fetched a basin of clean water and insisted upon washing the hand despite Nagaro's protest that he'd already done so—and had once trained as a healer, besides.

"I must make it appear I'm worth my price," was the healer's jesting response.

Nagaro laughed. "Then before you do so, perhaps you should make certain I can pay it."

Ambras bowed to him with mock gravity. "For the great Captain Nagaro, there will be no charge."

Nevien had seated herself on a stool. "How did you come to injure yourself, Captain?" she inquired.

"It was while mending the roof," Nagaro informed her. "The slates were so slick with ice that I slipped, and I just caught myself with my fingers. I must have cut myself on the edge of a broken slate, though my hands were so cold that I didn't feel it until later."

Nevien winced at this description. "Dare I ask how high the roof was?"

"It was a second-floor roof, My Lady—but there was a balcony," he added hastily, seeing her expression, "that would have stopped my fall."

Master Ambras dried the small wound, rubbed a little salve into it, and bandaged Nagaro's hand with two turns of clean linen. "There!" he said, as he tied the knot. "That should more than suffice. The cut was already well past bleeding, just as you said."

Nagaro thanked him, and all three started back in the direction of the Great Hall. As they neared the doorway at the end of the corridor, however, Nevien drew Nagaro to halt, allowing Ambras to go on ahead of them.

"My Lady?" he asked uncertainly.

She turned her green eyes to search his face. "Captain," she said, "I must ask whether you intend to court Kendira,"

He looked down. "I don't think so," he said. "I tried to tell her that— when I gave her the necklace. I may have been too subtle."

Nevien sighed. "It seems she hardly even heard what you said. A pearl necklace is rather... *extravagant*... for a parting gift."

Nagaro winced. "I wanted to give her something pretty—because she was so good about teaching me all those dances. I didn't mean her to... to think that it meant something else..."

Nevien frowned. "A gift is only a gift, no matter what its value, and you're in no way obligated by it. *Most* men, though, wouldn't have given anything that valuable without expecting something they valued greatly in return."

"*Bishka*." Nagaro ran a hand through his hair. "I was going to give her a poetry book, but there were too many, and I didn't know how to choose! I was fairly sure she'd like the necklace. It was something left among a little trove of pirate plunder, so it cost me nothing, and I told Kendira that when I gave it to her." He sighed. "I can't exactly take it back now, can I?"

Nevien could only shake her head.

"Ahem!"

They both started at the carefully cleared throat, and turned to look back along the hall towards the source of the sound. A door had opened, and Brandle Furthing stood in it, his stature and bearing unmistakable even with the light behind him.

"Is anything amiss, My Lady?" the guardsman calmly inquired.

"No, Lieutenant," the princess assured him. "You are not witnessing anything untoward. The captain and I will return to the Great Hall very shortly."

"Very good, My Lady." Brandle bowed and withdrew.

Nevien turned back to Nagaro and picked up the thread of their interruped conversation. "I will explain to Kendira about the necklace. You shouldn't have to repeat yourself just because she was too flustered to hear you and too meek to say so. But," she added, "If you haven't any intention of courting her, you must tell her so."

Nagaro shifted his weight from one foot to the other. "I feel badly about that. I mean, she's gentle and kind, but she seems to attach a great deal of importance to dancing while I really don't care to spend a whole evening at it."

Neviens glanced quickly about, and stepped closer. "Nagaro," she said earnestly, "you two clearly are not well suited to each other. You're both good people, but it takes more than that to make a happy marriage, and there's no reason you shouldn't hope for one—" She broke off as a shadow passed behind her eyes.

Nagaro understood. "I don't see why anyone shouldn't expect to have a happy marriage, My Lady. Including you."

She gave him a brittle smile. "*That*, I'm afraid, would require the intervention of the Gods."

"There are still no other suitors?"

She sighed. "Well, it seems that Lord Ferenan will join the ranks. He's politically neutral because he had a Kelorin father and a Leithian mother. He was recently widowed, and I expect he'll ask me to dance tonight—and at least he's younger than Devral." Nevien grimaced, then waved the matter aside. "We should return to the feast."

As it happened, the path they took back across the Great Hall led past the table where Lothard Hurn was seated. The tall, broad-shouldered Leithian must have been watching the princess's movements, for he immediately rose and deliberately stepped in front of them, addressing Nevien with a haughty curl of his lip.

"If you must be conducted somewhere, My Lady, you should find a better escort—one who doesn't take so long about it. My sword is ready to defend your honor if this pirate tries anything improper." The words were spoken as if Nagaro were either absent or incapable of hearing.

Nevien's hand on Nagaro's arm gave him a warning squeeze. "I was delayed by speaking with one of my guards, My Lord Lothard," she said curtly. "And I need no defense in the company of a gentleman. Besides, you would do yourself no credit by drawing your sword here, since the Captain doesn't carry one."

Lothard's mouth twitched at the rebuke. His eyes narrowed.

Not liking to be ignored, Nagaro raised his bandaged right hand. "I required a healer's services," he said easily. "My Lady Princess was kind enough to have Master Ambras tend to it."

Lothard deigned to glance at the hand, but when he spoke he still addressed himself contemptuously to the princess. "Did the pirate cut himself on a butter knife?"

Nagaro's teeth flashed in a sudden smile, even as he felt Nevien's fingers dig into his arm again. Before the princess could answer, he said in a deceptively casual tone, "That would be nearly as difficult as to cut oneself on My Lord's wit."

He heard Nevien's intake of breath.

Lothard goggled at him for an instant, but then laughed derisively. "What an ignorant fool you are, pirate!" he declared. "My wit couldn't cut anyone!"

Nagaro made the man a formal bow. "You're right, of course, My Lord," he said smoothly as he straightened.

Nevien squeezed his arm a third time. "We should return to our table, Captain," she said in a voice that was neutral in inflection. "Please excuse us, My Lord," she added, inclining her head slightly to Lothard.

The big Leithian stepped aside, still smirking at what he supposed was Nagaro's discomfiture.

They were nearly half way to the match table before Nevien spoke again, low and close to Nagaro's ear. "Captain," she murmured, "you just managed to get away with insulting Lothard to his face, but you'd best not make a habit of it. He can make serious trouble for you if he figures out what you're doing."

Nagaro sighed. "You're right," he said. "At first I was merely trying to maneuver him into speaking to me directly, but then he gave me an opportunity I couldn't resist. But you should be careful, too, My Lady. You rebuked him openly, and he *did* mark it."

Nevien's expression turned somber. "I couldn't bear his rudeness to you. And Lothard can't make any trouble for me as long as he still hopes to wed me."

Their arrival at the match table precluded further discussion.

*

The lavish repast was finished, and the dancing was well underway. The musicians drew out the last few notes of the *Balandir* to a quavering crescendo. As the dancers spun to a halt, Nagaro turned Kendira under his arm with a flourish and made her a low, sweeping bow. Straightening, he gave her the best smile he could manage. She stood there, radiant with exertion, her eyes alight. Her dark hair was braided and wound around her head like a crown and the pearls glowed softly at her throat, a stunning contrast to the deep blue satin of her gown. He suppressed a small sigh. If the fairness of her face or form could ever have moved him, surely it would have been at such a moment—and just as surely he was unmoved.

It had been a relief to admit this to the princess, but how could he speak to Kendira about it tonight? The feast had offered no reasonable opportunity. And when the musicians had taken seats and begun tuning their instruments at the conclusion of the banquet, he'd seen the familiar longing in her eyes and had dutifully risen and offered her his arm as he'd been doing for the past two months. That had been two dances ago, but what else could he do?

Kendira took his arm, turning her fine-featured face up to look at him. "And now you must dance with Tira Milandra," she said, a little breathlessly.

"I must?" He did his best not to make it sound like a complaint.

"Oh yes! I told you—remember? She's only here in Lankura until the end of the week. And I've told her how *very* kind you are."

"Ah." Again he forced a smile. "Well then, point out the lady."

Kendira turned around slowly, sweeping the dim, cavernous room with her eyes, searching the gowned figures in the softened lamplight. "Over there," she murmured presently. "The woman with brown hair all piled up on her head, in the pale pink satin gown."

"Ah yes, I see her." Nagaro made Kendira another bow, to which he added formal thanks for the last dance, before relinquishing her to the surrounding ranks of the temporarily un-partnered. Then he started across the dance floor in the direction of the figure in pink. He hadn't gone far, however, before realizing that his path was converging with that of the Pact Signer, Lord Devral, who had the princess on his arm.

Devral hailed him in a clarion voice. "My good Captain! Stay!"

The aging lord was advancing at a game pace despite his bad leg. He was beaming jovially—or trying to. The scar that marred his face tended to make the expression resemble a leer. Nevien, at the old warrior's side, was moving with the best grace she could manage under the circumstances, her expression studiously neutral.

Nagaro mentally set the matter of the pink-gowned lady, Milandra, temporarily aside, as he executed his very best bow. "My Lord Devral, how may I serve you?"

"As if you couldn't guess, my lad." Devral gave him a very broad wink, then had to pause to cough. When he had his breath again, he continued in a more subdued voice. "I trust I can prevail upon you to escort My Lady Nevien in the next dance on my behalf? The old wound is rather stiff tonight." He tapped his thigh.

Nagaro winced at the older man's familiarity, though the request was of course no surprise. He met Nevien's eyes, just long enough to read her delighted acquiescence, before saying, "I'd be glad to, My Lord."

Nevien's responding smile was carefully demure.

"Ah, excellent!" Devral proceeded to transfer Nevien to Nagaro's arm. "And I'll be watching, Captain, to see that you do me credit— though I'm sure you will. It's an admirable solution," he added with another wink. "Your legs do the work, while my eyes admire the view." The Pact Signer's laughter was interrupted by another brief bout of coughing.

The musicians were by this time playing the opening bars of the next dance. Nagaro gave Devral a final bow and hastily conducted the princess to a position in a circle that was forming for *The Ivy Vine.*

Nevien leaned her head close to his as they stood waiting for the bars that would begin the dance. "I wish he wouldn't treat you like a lackey, Captain," she said, "though I'm glad to have you as a partner."

Nagaro simply nodded. "Have you seen Lord Ferenan?"

She shook her head. "Not yet."

The musicians launched into the tune, and the dance began.

*

They bowed to one another other, linked by their fingertips, as the last notes died away. Nevien straightened, laughing.

Nagaro couldn't help but admire her, although this evening she seemed to have tried to down-play her charms. Her golden-brown hair was swept up very simply on either side of her head, held in place by her two ivory combs, and she was wearing the same dark green gown he remembered from the day he'd found her atop the bed canopy, with no other jewelry than a slender gold chain about her neck. The gown was the color of evergreen—perfect for the season—but the dark color made her figure easy to lose in the half-light, amidst all the evergreen decorations. Her sea-green eyes could suffer no detraction, however, and just now they sparkled like a pair of emeralds.

She stepped close to him, still smiling. "Nagaro, that was wonderful!"

He held a warning finger to his lips. "To which of your suitors shall I deliver you, My Lady?"

The emerald sparkle died. "I've been around the floor with all three of them, once—counting you for Lord Devral—and Lothard was the first. That would make it his turn again, unless we can find Ferenan. But the truth is, I'd far rather sit down and rest."

"Well then, let's see if we can sneak off." Nagaro gave her his arm and began to move as unobtrusively as possible towards the edge of the dance floor closest to the match table. Within a few steps, he frowned, however. "Here comes Lothard."

The Leithian was in fact bound in their direction, and since he was clad in scarlet and black, there was no mistaking him even in the dim light.

"And *there* is Ferenan!" Nevien gestured in a different direction. "And he's looking right at me."

Nagaro promptly changed course, away from Lothard's path and in the direction the princess had just indicated. Lord Ferenan wasn't difficult to pick out: He had light brown hair, a coloring that was rather unique to those of mixed Kelorin and Leithian blood. He was dressed in caramel-brown. Once they drew near enough, Nagaro could see that he was somewhat less than fifty, with a clean-shaven face set in a somber expression.

Ferenan slowed his steps as they approached. "My Lady Princess," he said, bowing to Nevien. "And Captain Nagaro, I believe." The last was accompanied by an inclination of the head.

"My Lord Ferenan." Nagaro gave the man one of his better bows. "I'm pleased to make your acquaintance."

Nevien offered a gentle smile. "I hoped we might see you here at last, My Lord, returned to society after your grief. I hope the season may warm your heart."

Lord Ferenan's answering smile was fleeting. "You're very kind as always, My Lady. And it would be a balm to my heart indeed if you would join me in the next dance."

"Of course I will."

To Nagaro's ear, Ferenan's tone had contained more resignation than enthusiasm, but the man's respect seemed genuine and Nagaro understood his part. He allowed Nevien to transfer herself from his arm to that of the older man, but before she had even completed the action, cries of alarm arose in the hall.

"*The queen!*"

"*Oh Gods! Where is Master Ambras?*"

Nevien instantly turned towards the dais, her hand reaching for Nagaro's arm. "*My mother!*" she cried. "What has happened?"

14: Warnings

Ferenan stepped immediately aside. "Pray don't stay on my account, My Lady," he murmured urgently. "Go quickly!"

Nevien turned a beseeching glance upon Nagaro, and the grip of her fingers tightened on his forearm. "Please come with me!" she begged.

Nagaro nodded, and they struck off across the floor together, he making long strides to keep up with the princess, who was very nearly running. They found a path between the tables and approached a dense knot of people clustered at the edge of the dais.

The little crowd parted for Nevien with murmurs of, "The princess!" and, "Let the princess through!"

Nagaro would have extricated himself at this point, but Nevien still clung to his arm and he was drawn to the edge of the platform. Queen Semorel lay at the verge of the dais. Her gown was a deep rose red that made her face look deathly pale by comparison in the glow of a nearby lamp. Elgurn stood beside his wife, his face etched with worry, his hands helplessly clenched. Master Ambras was already there, bending over his patient.

Nevien pushed immediately to the healer's side, finally releasing Nagaro's arm in her haste to comfort her mother.

Nagaro stepped back, moving out of the press. He stood uncertainly at the crowd's edge, filled with dread and counting the seconds, until a murmur of relief moved through the group of onlookers.

The bodies parted then and Lady Merriel appeared before him. "It's all right, Captain," she told him. "The queen fainted, that's all, and she has already come to herself. Nevien and I will take her to her chamber. We'd be grateful," she added with a weak smile, "if you'd reassure the musicians that all is well."

Nagaro bowed. "I will, My Lady. And thank you."

He moved quickly back through the candle-lit hall, but before he had reached the dance floor, the strains of music rising over the babble of voices told him that he wasn't needed to bring the news. Since it was too late to join the dance, he sought a place to sit. The match table held little attraction without the princess, so he chose the Fleet table where Lord Kuran normally presided.

Kuran wasn't there, and the table was nearly empty, so he chose a seat at random. A glance at the dance floor revealed that both Kendira's midnight blue and Milandra's pale pink were among the rotating figures. He sighed and sat staring somberly at the row of little candles decorating the table. *Lives were rather like candles. The wax was the flesh, the flame the spirit... and the flame of Queen Semorel's candle had begun to flicker...*

"Captain Nagaro? Might we speak with you?"

Nagaro looked up to find three men standing on the farther side of the table. All were Kelorin, and they were of varying ages. The youngest, in his forties, was tall and thin with an eager face, dark brown hair, and a well-trimmed beard. The oldest was gray and gaunt, but unbowed, with melancholy eyes. The last of the three was heavy-framed and moderately tall, his black hair sprinkled finely with gray, his fierce gray eyes entirely in keeping with his sharply chiseled features.

Nagaro didn't recognize any of them, which was not particularly strange. His own distinctive appearance rendered him easily identified by people he didn't know. His quick eye took in the swords that hung at the men's sides. "Certainly you may, My Lords," he said, rising, though he had little desire at that moment for the company of strangers. He added, "I fear you must introduce yourselves, however."

The tall thin man, who was apparently the one who had addressed him, extended his hand. "I am Therin Oranil," he said simply. "And my friends are the lords Soren Tuveilas," he indicated the gray-haired man, "and Rathdar Sundorin."

Nagaro bowed to each man in turn, giving extra attention to Lord Rathdar, who he knew was the lord of Sundorin Wared and heir of the deceased Pact Signer Berinar Sundorin.

Rathdar returned him a keen glance and a wry smile. "Well met, Captain," he said, "I am told that you've walked the streets of my city a score of times. I find it amusing that I must come to Lankura to meet you face to face."

Nagaro deepened his bow. "I trust that you haven't found anything amiss in the way I've conducted myself in Kel Tierna , My Lord."

"Hardly. It seems I hear nothing but good spoken of Captain Nagaro on every side."

"Indeed, Captain," the gray-haired Lord Soren put in. "Your wide popularity among the ordinary folk of Edrovir is quite remarkable. It is on that account, in particular, that we've sought you out."

Nagaro gave the aging lord a questioning look.

Soren gestured for him to be seated. "Sit, Captain, and be at ease."

All four men then sat down, Nagaro on one side of the table, the three lords on the other, with the little row of candles in between lighting their faces with a flickering glow.

Therin cleared his throat. "You are Kelorin, Captain, are you not?"

Nagaro frowned slightly. "Opinions differ on the subject. Since you see me, you may judge as well as any."

Soren made haste to speak before Therin could respond to this. "The exact proportion doesn't matter, Captain. As long as you were raised to Kelorin ways."

"I was raised by a Kelorin lady," Nagaro conceded cautiously, "and according to the teachings of Vothra."

"Yes, exactly." Soren appeared satisfied. "But the point is, if there should be a conflict between Kelorin and Leithians, you would naturally take the Kelorin side."

Nagaro returned the old man's gaze with an open countenance. "Since Vothra teaches us that conflict should be avoided," he said, "I would seek a resolution."

Soren frowned, and the younger lord, Therin, burst in. "But surely, Captain, you'd stand with us, to keep our Kelorin ways?"

Nagaro eyed the man sharply. "We may have different ideas of what it means to keep Kelorin ways, My Lord. I, at least, would mean *Vothrin* ways."

"Then you would surely have to fight to uphold the Path of Vothra!" exclaimed Rathdar. "I know you to be a warrior."

Nagaro gave the black-haired man a cool stare. "I'm a warrior when need compels me, My Lord. But I follow the Path whenever I serve any just cause, whether with my sword or otherwise."

"Ah! My Lords Soren, Therin, and Rathdar—and Captain Nagaro, as well. May I join your company?"

Nagaro turned in surprise to find Lord Anduar standing at his left hand. From the way the other three men started, it was clear that they had been equally unaware of the Pact Signer's approach.

"Of course you may join us, Anduar." The words were spoken by Soren, though not, it seemed, with great enthusiasm.

"Yes. Do join us, My Lord." Nagaro spoke with genuine relief.

Anduar took a seat beside Nagaro, across from Rathdar. The Pact Signer lounged in his chair. "So," he said, "if we are discussing how best to keep the ways of our people, I would invoke the principle—set forth in the Writings—that it is more noble to end a conflict than to begin one. And I might add that when men agree on most points, they should not quarrel about the few points on which they differ."

Rathdar sat silent and subdued at this, and Therin chewed his lip. Soren, however, the only one of the three who was plainly older than Anduar, appeared unimpressed.

"What else may we expect from a Signer of the Pact?" he asked sourly. "We all know how *you* ended the conflict, years ago—in a way that gave power to you and a handful of others, while wresting it from a much larger number."

Nagaro heard Therin suck in his breath, and he turned quickly to see Anduar's reaction to Soren's pointed criticism.

Anduar had not altered his slouch, but there was now a tightness to his jaw and a new glint in his eye that was more than the reflection of the candle flames. "If you had any idea how narrowly bloodshed was averted," he said coldly, "or how that peace was secured, you wouldn't speak so. But how could any of you know? None of you were there." His gaze swept the three men who faced him and returned to Soren. "And what should we expect from one who still looks for the coming of the heir of Darion?"

Soren stiffened, and his answer rang more hot than cold. "He may yet come! Even now there are rumors from Irvenen Wared. They say that Rastyl has gone home to look into them. And what words will the scion of the House of Loros have for *you*, Anduar, when he comes?"

The dangerous light had died in Anduar's eyes, and the Pact Signer dismissed Soren's words with a flick of his hand.

"There's nothing I have done that I'm ashamed to answer for," he said. "And every year or two there are *rumors*. Who truly knows where Rastyl goes or why? It's been twenty-five years, Soren. You and I have grown old—and these other two gentlemen have passed from youth to maturity—waiting for Darion's grandson. Most likely he died within days of his birth and is buried at Loros Hall, as it's keeper, Lord Endemar, has always said. But have you anything else to say to my trusted counselor?" He indicated Nagaro with a slight motion of his head. "Or have I your leave to take counsel from him of my own?"

Therin and Rathdar exchanged startled glances, but Soren didn't take his eyes from Anduar's face. "What more *could* we say, since you're determined to stifle our conversation?" He pushed back his chair and stood up stifly. His two companions immediately followed his example. Turning to Nagaro, Soren inclined his head with a forced smile, and said, "Perhaps another time, Captain?"

Nagaro hastily rose and bowed. "At your pleasure, My Lord," he said, using a courteous but neutral tone. He re-seated himself as the three men moved away.

Anduar's eyes briefly followed the retreating figures, then turned to Nagaro. "So, the Kelorin Faction has at last decided to have a look at you," he said almost idly.

Nagaro frowned, glad to at least be told the men's affiliation. He hadn't much liked their questions, though now he was uneasy at being left alone with the Pact Signer. Still, perhaps he could learn something. "There must be others in the Kelorin Faction," he ventured. "Have those three been chosen to represent the entire group?"

Anduar gave a short, dry laugh. "They represent its heart, hand, and soul," he said. "Not its head, I fear. I don't believe there's anyone who qualifies for the last position. And they're all self-appointed. Who will you have here next, I wonder? Rastyl Korven?"

"What, again?" Nagaro looked about in dismay.

Anduar's eyes narrowed slightly. "Rastyl has spoken to you?"

Nagaro attempted not to frown. "He has, yes, more than once."

"Ah."

The last remains of the repast had been cleared away, and the servants had re-supplied the table with mulled wine in crystal decanters and silver goblets, as well as fresh pots of hot sothiril and porcelain cups and saucers. Lord Anduar now reached for a steaming pot and filled two cups with sothiril, one for himself and one for Nagaro. Raising his own cup, he spoke over it. "May I ask what Rastyl had to say?"

"I might tell you if I thought I understood it," Nagaro replied. "He wasn't very plain."

"Ah. Yes." Anduar appeared to relax. "The unfortunate man's mind has suffered some, I'm afraid. He isn't what he once was." The Kelorin Lord took a long sip of sothiril, as if savoring it.

Nagaro also drank some of his sothiril, thinking hard. Anduar had briefly seemed concerned, and he wondered why. When the Kelorin lord didn't immediately break his silence, Nagaro decided to pursue his own curiosity. "You don't seem to have come to seek my counsel, My Lord, despite what you said to those men. And 'trusted counselor' seems to me an overstatement. I'm left to wonder whether it was said more for their benefit or for mine."

Again, there was a flicker of something that was not candle light in the other man's steel-gray eyes. Anduar had been holding his cup in both hands, toying with it. Now he carefully set it down on its saucer with the faintest clink and brought his eyes back to focus on Nagaro. "Perhaps you'll explain what you mean by *benefit*," he said in the mildest tone imaginable.

Nagaro did not flinch under the cool stare. "I mean, simply, did you say it to flatter me? Or to persuade the other three that I'm already committed to your cause—whatever it may be—rather than to theirs?"

This utterance quite unexpectedly earned Nagaro the very slightest suggestion of a smile, which fled almost before it could be recognized. Anduar reached for his cup again. "When you've learned to find the right answers, Captain," he said quietly, "as well as to ask the right questions, you'll be ready to sit in my place."

"I haven't got the slightest desire to sit in your place, My Lord, particularly if it means having to listen to men argue all night about whether a man is fit to give them counsel, rather than listening to what he has to say. But I think I've found an answer to the question that was behind my question."

Once more the steely eyes flickered. The Kelorin lord stroked the rim of his china cup. "How so?" he inquired. His tone suggested nothing more than mild curiosity.

Nagaro met the other man's bland look with a hard stare. "Had I *truly* been a trusted counselor, My Lord, I think I would have deserved a straightforward answer."

"Ah." Anduar briefly inclined his head as if in concession, and his eyes grew serious. "I regret, Captain, that you seem to trust me less than I trust you."

"If that is so, My Lord, you have it in your hands to remedy the matter."

Anduar sighed. He took a long swallow of his sothiril and set the cup down heedlessly this time, so that it rattled on its saucer. "My good Captain," he said, with every appearance of earnestness. "If you observe carefully, you will find that I never bestow false flattery—especially not on men that I value. It's a poor way to win a man's favor. I may at times use irony, but I think you have the wit to discern the difference. I *have* taken counsel from you in the past, and I *do* consider you trustworthy."

"And that," said an ironic voice from across the table, "is as much explanation of himself as I've ever heard Lord Anduar give to anyone. I regret, Captain, that I wasn't here to see how you managed to drag it out of him."

Nagaro turned quickly to confirm that he had recognized the voice of Lord Kuran. Turning back to Anduar, he caught a glimpse of a smile crossing the Pact Signer's face—a smile quite impossible to interpret.

"He did it by being bold enough to demand it," Anduar observed mildly. "Will you sit with us, My Lord?"

Kuran smiled wryly. "This *is* my table," he said, and sat down facing the Pact Signer.

Anduar turned back to Nagaro. "Perhaps I should proceed to what brought me here in the first place, Captain," he said. "I confess it was more to give counsel than to ask it."

Nagaro regarded the man warily. He was not at all certain of his apparent victory. "I'm listening, My Lord."

The cool gray eyes considered him. "I wonder why you allow Lord Devral to use you as his proxy on the dance floor."

Nagaro shrugged. "Why shouldn't I oblige him, when the labor is not unpleasant?"

The other man's glance didn't waver. "Some might suppose you had other motives."

"What other motives could a man in my position possibly have, My Lord?"

"Ah. Yes..." Anduar frowned very slightly. His eyes sought Kuran's with a look that seemed to say, *you explain it to him.*

Kuran was already frowning. "I have meant to speak to you about this myself, Nagaro," he said. "It's good that you are seen to be courting Kendira, since it offers you some protection from jealousy. And the pearl necklace was a most fortuitous move, but you should speak to her father soon."

Nagaro shifted in his seat. "I'm not at all sure that I want to," he said uncomfortably. "And what do you mean by *jealousy?*"

"He's referring to Lothard." Anduar had leaned forward in his seat a little and lowered his voice.

Kuran coughed. "As I've implied before, there's reason to believe that Lothard has, in the past, proven dangerous to those he saw as rivals."

Nagaro laughed outright. "Lothard treats me as if I were either deaf or invisible," he said. "And since I'm not actually courting the princess, why should he consider me a rival?"

"Not for the princess's hand," Anduar put in dryly. "But simply as a man. And he wouldn't wish to show it."

Nagaro was frankly mystified. "Lothard stands over me by inches," he pointed out. "He's accounted handsome, he's distinguished himself in the border wars, and I've heard him described as Edrovir's greatest swordsman. Why would he be jealous of *me?*"

Anduar and Kuran exchanged glances.

It was Kuran who answered. "Lothard isn't well-liked. He has few genuine friends even among the nobility, beyond the more extreme members of the Leithian Faction. And he lacks any kind of popularity with the common folk."

Nagaro's mystification was scarcely diminished. "But I'm not one of the nobility!" he protested. "And I can't believe that Lothard cares what the common people think."

Anduar seemed suddenly to have taken a great interest in his cup of sothiril.

Kuran sighed. "Whether or not you understand the reason," he said, "you would be wise to be careful of Lothard. And if you continue to stand in for Lord Devral, I'd advise you to at least *appear* to cultivate Kendira. You need only maintain the pretense for a few more weeks, until Fleet maneuvers begin to take up your time."

Nagaro sat for a moment, silently frowning. Anduar seemed to be studying him while trying to appear not to. "Very well," he said soberly. "I will take heed of this advice as best I can." He sighed. "And if I'm to please Kendira," he added, "I've already been too long away from the dance floor. If you will excuse me, My Lords..." He pushed back his chair and rose, giving each of the other two men a bow. After receiving their acknowledgment, he took his leave.

Anduar's cool gaze followed Nagaro's departing figure. "Is the man really as innocent as he appears?" he asked presently.

Kuran sighed. "I believe so, My Lord. But he's no fool for all that."

"I have seen that he is not." Anduar leaned forward and lowered his voice. "Take good care of that one, Kuran."

The Pact Signer didn't stay to wait for a reply. Rising, he turned and disappeared into the gloom of the hall, bent on some purpose known only to himself.

*

Nagaro's feet slowed as he approached the circle of moving dancers. The Great Hall's oil lamps had been turned down yet a little more while he'd been talking with Anduar and Kuran, to further enhance the effect of the candles as the night progressed. He peered through the gloom, searching for Kendira. Her choice of dark blue now made her nearly invisible. His thoughts were running in circles. Nevien had also warned him about Lothard, so he supposed he should be careful of the man, but he didn't like the idea of deceiving Kendira about his intentions—not when he'd just agreed with the princess that he should tell Kendira the truth.

The dance presently wound to a close, and he had just managed to catch sight of a gown of royal blue, when a woman's figure moved in front of him, blocking his view. The image of towering brown hair and pink satin penetrated his distraction, reminding him that he had promised Kendira he would dance with this young woman. With a sigh, he gave her what he hoped wasn't too forced a smile and said, "Will you honor me, Zirdyn, by joining me in the next dance?"

The words of Milandra's reply were lost in the breathless flutter of her excitement. As she moved to take the arm he offered, the dance floor was again revealed to his view. Kendira was there, on the arm of a tall, broad-shouldered Leithian. The Kelorin maid cowered away from her escort, and the man held his hand on top of hers as if to prevent her escape. As Nagaro watched, the man turned in his direction and the haughty gaze of Lord Lothard met his own. Their eyes locked only for an instant before the Leithian turned away again, but in that instant, Nagaro saw the man's lip curl in a smirk of satisfaction.

Somehow Nagaro got through the dance that followed. It was a couple dance called *Analul* that was slow enough to allow speech between partners. Some part of Nagaro's mind managed to make polite and innocuous responses to Milandra's continuous prattle, though he could not afterwards have given any account of the conversation. His thoughts were racing madly while at the same time he was trying to avoid even the slightest suggestion of interest in Lothard and Kendira.

Even if he had not just been warned of the Leithian's potential jealousy, Lothard's motivation for dancing with Kendira would have been suspect. The arrogant young lord chose only high-born Leithian women when he danced with anyone other than the princess. He could not possibly be genuinely interested in a Kelorin merchant's daughter. Nagaro had never felt the least bit possessive about Kendira. As far as he was concerned, she might dance with whomever she pleased. What concerned him now, to the point of distraction, was that she plainly was *not* pleased to be dancing with Lothard—and he knew it was his own association with her that had placed her in that position.

The dance seemed to take an age, but at last it concluded, leaving Nagaro still obliged to engage in parting pleasantries with Milandra, who alternately blushed and gushed. When he did finally manage to extricate himself and searched the dance floor with his eyes, he spotted Kendira standing alone, a little beyond the edge of the area set aside for dancing, chewing the knuckle of one hand while the other was tensely clutched to her breast.

He immediately cut across the floor to where she stood, moving as quickly as he could without appearing to be in a hurry.

"I'm sorry that I've been so long in returning to you," he said when he reached her. "I was interrupted first by Lord Devral's request, and then by the queen's fainting. And then I danced with Tira Milandra, as you wished."

Kendira had taken her hand from her mouth when he approached, though her other hand remained at her breast. She seemed not to have heard him, for she made no response to his words, but said, "Captain, I... I must speak to you." She reached out to catch his arm.

"All right," he said uneasily, allowing her to draw him away to a more deserted spot near one of the great fireplaces.

"Did... did you see me dancing with Lord Lothard?" She asked anxiously.

"I, ah... did notice, yes. I hope he didn't offend you. He can be rude at times."

Kendira dropped her eyes. The firelight played on her well-formed features. "He... he wanted me to say that he was the best of the men I'd danced with tonight, but I wouldn't—because it was *you!* Only I was so afraid of making him angry that I... I said I couldn't choose!" She looked up at him, seemingly in anguish.

Nagaro was immensely relieved. "It's quite all right. I don't really care that much about dancing." And he saw instantly that this had been the wrong thing to say.

She frowned up at him. "But... if you don't care about dancing, why did you have me teach you?"

"I... thought it might be a useful thing to know..." He floundered, wincing at her scandalized look.

"*Useful!*" she cried, with surprising heat. "Is *that* all? Was it just *useful* sitting with me at the match table, and... and... everything?" Her fingers strayed to the pearls at her throat. "Is it just because my father is rich?"

"Of course not!" he said quickly. "You're sweet, and very pretty, and I was trying to see if I wished to court you—" He broke off, uncertain how to proceed. It seemed he should tell her the truth, but he'd just been warned to maintain a pretense of interest in her.

"Oh, *Captain*..." She blushed and once again dropped her eyes, clearly mistaking his meaning. Then she raised her chin and said with unaccustomed boldness, "Why won't you tell me your real name? The one your Lady Guardian gave you—"

"*I've told you I don't wish to!*" The words burst out before he could stop them, and now he fought to tamp down rising anger.

"I wouldn't tell anyone," she pleaded. "I'd keep it a secret. I've told you everything about *my* family—"

Nagaro's anger notched higher. "I have told you about my daughter Narei." he said, trying to keep his anger from tightening his voice. "I have no other blood relations!" When he had tried to tell her about Taru, Pavo, and the other friends he'd made while a slave—who were like family to him—she hadn't wished to hear it. Yet now, after not allowing him to say what he'd wanted to say, she was upset because he wouldn't tell her the one secret he wished to keep!

Kendira seemed not to have heard his words. She was twisting her fingers together distractedly. Perhaps she failed to read his expression accurately in the flickering light for she abruptly blurted, "Lothard says there probably never *was* a Lady Guardian! Or if there was, she wasn't a lady. But if *that's* your secret, I'd still keep it. He said if you cared for me at all, you'd tell me!"

And Nagaro's anger flared like a flame. "Is *that* what Lothard was doing?" he cried. "Insinuating that I'm a liar? Saying my Lady Guardian was no lady, when she was of better quality than he'll ever be? *And you thought it might be true?*"

She shrank away from him, but he plunged on. "You needn't worry about keeping my secrets, Kendira, because I'm not going to tell you any! I don't wish to court you! And I'm sorry if I mislead you into thinking otherwise. *Now good night!*"

He spun away from her and strode off across the polished floor, rage throbbing through him. Behind him, he heard Kendira burst into tears, but he drove on, skirting the dance floor and making for the main door of the Great Hall, bent on escape.

Within a dozen strides, however, his steps began to slow as his seething outrage began to contend with the guilty sense that he had just behaved very badly—that he'd hurt Kendira more than was necessary, certainly more than he'd intended... His steps faltered. *He should go back. But what on earth could he possibly say?* He couldn't un-speak the words. They'd been true, though spoken unkindly, and he wasn't calm enough to trust himself to do better.

As he neared the door of the hall, he heard a rustle of skirts beside him. For a shocked instant, he thought Kendira had followed him, until the woman spoke at his elbow and he recognized Nevien's voice instead.

"You're not leaving so early, are you, Captain?"

He shot her a wordless glance as he kept walking. "Where is your escort?" he muttered.

"Merriel is within call, but not within earshot. Nagaro, I just saw something that didn't look good at all." She caught his arm. "Will you come sit with me?"

He could easily have shaken her off. He wasn't at all sure he was ready to talk, but he allowed her to steer him to a nearby table. One of the candles at the end of it had burned out and he sat there, where the light was dimmer, hoping she couldn't read his black look.

The princess sat down beside him rather than across the table. He didn't look at her, fixing his gaze instead on his clasped hands, resting on the tabletop where he tried not to clench them. He could feel her eyes.

After several long seconds, she spoke in a measured voice. "You don't have to talk about it if you don't want to, but I've found it usually helps. Kendira was... rather upset..."

For several seconds more, he struggled with his ebbing anger and rising guilt. Then at last he drew a deep breath. "I shouted at her," he confessed in a low voice. "She said things I didn't like... I lost my temper..."

Nevien's movement betrayed her dismay. "Nagaro, what on earth did she say?"

He raised a hand to massage his brow. "It wasn't her... not really— not mostly..." He did his best, then, to reconstruct the conversation. "I'm not sure exactly why I'm so angry," he finished. "I should be used to Lothard insulting me—since he's done it when I'm standing right in front of him. Maybe he struck at something that really matters to me this time. Or maybe it's just that he didn't say it to my face—that he said it to *her*. It didn't help, though, that she thought the part about my Lady Guardian might be true."

There was a little silence after he had stopped speaking. Then the princess said, "It's pretty obvious that Lothard was trying to make trouble between you."

"Trouble between Kendira and me?" He turned to stare at her. It was too dark to read her expression, but he saw her nod.

"I think he hoped to spoil what he fancied was your plan to marry a rich merchant's daughter," she said. "That's what *his* plan would have been, if he were in your position. He doesn't understand that you were never interested in Kendira's money. And he certainly didn't know that you'd already decided you weren't going to court her."

Nagaro sat silently for a long moment. "I thought he was just being rude out of spite," he murmured. "Would he really go out of his way to hurt my prospects as he saw them, and use Kendira in that way?"

Again she nodded. "You've annoyed him, though he'd never admit it. He wouldn't hurt you openly, but he *would* try to do it behind your back."

"*Bishka...*" Nagaro sank his head in his hands. "It worked, didn't it?" Abruptly his head came up and he turned to stare at Nevien. "Kuran and Anduar both just warned me about Lothard too. Kuran said I should keep up a pretense of being interested in Kendira if I meant to go on dancing with you in Devral's place. And now I've gone and made an end of it! I couldn't possibly pretend to patch things up with her after what I said tonight—not and break it off again later!"

Nevien sighed. "Kuran has a point," she said. "You are being a dear friend to me, Nagaro, and I hate seeing you and Kendira hurt because of it." She paused, and her hand found his and gave it a quick squeeze before she withdrew her fingers. After a moment, she said, "But I think it will be all right. If Lothard thinks he's succeeded in spoiling your plans, he won't feel the need to try anything else. When he sees that you're not sitting at the match table any more, or dancing with Kendira, he'll draw the obvious conclusion—and of course, the tale of your quarrel will spread quickly among my ladies."

Nagaro winced. "I should apologize to Kendira," he said. "I should tell her that I lost my temper because of what Lothard said and that it had nothing to do with my decision not to court her."

Nevien sighed. "Ordinarily, I would say you should. But since we're trying to maintain the fiction that this was a serious quarrel, I think you'd better let me do it."

"You do?"

Nevien nodded decisively. "Trust me, Nagaro. Kendira will get over this. She's pretty and sweet, and there will be other young men. Tonight, I think you should just slip away."

"Well, all right..." That at least was easy. Nagaro stood up, feeling guiltily relieved of an uncomfortable burden.

Nevien also rose, but then hesitated. "Unfortunately, Devral won't be pleased to lose his proxy," she said, and there was regret in her voice that Nagaro suspected was not on Devral's account.

"Could you... perhaps... find me another pairing?" he suggested. "Just not right away?"

He couldn't read her face, but he heard relief when she said, "Yes, I'll see what I can do, though it probably won't be before spring." She moved then, suddenly, glancing across the Hall. "And now I see Ferenan, and I'm sure he's looking for me. Good night, Captain."

*

Outside the palace, the snow had stopped falling and the clouds had parted. Even the wind had died away. Candles burned in every window along the streets of Lankura, their tiny golden lights answered from above by the diamond glitter of the stars. So men celebrated that night of a thousand lights with their fleeting offerings of hope for the year to come. And the heavens answered with thousands upon thousands of enduring sparks of fire.

Thunder-Heels' hooves crunched softly on a dusting of new-fallen snow as Nagaro rode alone through the silent streets. He was glad that he had let Nevien cajole him into talking about what had happened. She would explain things to Kendira in the kindest way and smooth things over. He felt some regret for the end of a thing that he'd begun with a modest hope, but he was more relieved than disappointed. And he saw now that Lothard had been right about one thing: If he had truly cared for Kendira, he would have been willing to tell her his secrets. He couldn't imagine being married to a woman who didn't know everything about him. The fact that he found it impossible to lay his past open to Kendira was a clear sign that she wasn't right for him.

Nagaro heaved a sigh that made a little cloud of silver mist in the air. Somewhere... *somewhere*... there had to be a woman that he could tell these things to. A woman who would understand—a woman he could tell his secrets to as easily as he'd just confessed his mistakes to Nevien.

He sighed again. If only he knew where to look...

15: The Honor Of Kiraam Shaku-Tal

It was a bright, blustery day in early Evrel. The wind was gusting across the Lomoan isles, whipping the sea into whitecaps. Overhead, a few shreds of cloud trailed like rags on the breeze. Sheltered in the narrow strait between the massive green bulk of the island of Boka Omei and the little rocky isle of Soku, a war galley lay at anchor, her oars poised, half out of their ports. Her bow was pointed across the broad channel of the Inside Passage. She flew the flag of Edrovir—white hawk with wings outstretched on a field of blue—and there were alternating diamonds of black and white along her sides. In nearby Boka Bay, half a mile to the south, five more ships lay waiting. The tips of their masts, also displaying the white and blue hawk banner, just showed above the spit of land that separated the bay from the Soku strait.

Lord Kuran stood on the stern castle of the *Sword of Freedom*, his eyes fixed on a point beyond the bay where the base of Boka Omei's massive headland, called Stone Head, met the gray-green sea. Beside him, Nagaro rested his elbows on the rail to steady the spyglass he held trained on the crest of the grassy ridge connecting Stone Head to the highlands that formed the island's core. Without the glass, it was just possible to make out the figure of a man standing there, atop a vantage point that offered a view of the eastern shore of Boka Omei and the Inside Passage that lay beyond.

"Still no sign from Doren?" Kuran shifted tensely.

"No. Nothing since he signaled that the Mahuk craft were in sight. But it should be soon."

Kuran grunted. "I'm still don't like using you for bait, Nagaro."

Nagaro frowned, without taking his eye from the spyglass. "This ship is the bait, really, since the Mautep know her markings— though they may wonder at the flag she flies. And everyone aboard her will be in equal peril—including you, My Lord."

"I'm not the one with a price on my head."

A slim blond youth stepped up beside them. "I don't like this lying in wait, Captain," he said, speaking boldly, though with a little catch in his voice. "I'm for a good clean fight!"

Nagaro handed the spyglass to Kuran and gave his young third mate a measuring glance. "I expect there *will* be a fight, Peldred," he assured the young Leithian. "And I hope it will be both clean and brief. Our object is to force a surrender."

"I know. But we'll have a chance to kill some of them first, won't we?"

Nagaro sighed. "If we have to. They may kill some of us as well."

Peldred frowned, but he nodded. Turning, he stared in the direction of Stone Head, his hand gripping the hilt of his sword, drawing the thing half an inch from its scabbard and letting it slip back again.

Again Nagaro sighed. Peldred was a newly-commissioned officer who had come in with the spring recruits. Being from a noble family, his rank as a third mate had been assured. He'd proven fair to good with a sword in the practice yard and had shown enthusiasm during drills at sea, but this would be his first encounter with the Mautep. Nagaro had dealt with green recruits before and had found such nervous bravado a common response—a mixture of too much confidence and too little. Only experience could teach this aspiring sea warrior to have faith in his own skill and also respect that of his enemies.

"Ah, the signal!"

Kuran spoke with suppressed excitement. He handed the spyglass back to Nagaro, who quickly confirmed the signal. The local town chief, Doren, atop Stone Head, was waving something white urgently back and forth.

Nagaro immediately went into action. "Raise the anchor!" he cried. "Get some sail on her!"

An answering cry of "Aye Zirda!" came from Pavo, amidships.

Nagaro turned to his third mate, who was frozen with his mouth agape. "Peldred, get to your post!"

The young Leithian snapped him a hasty salute and sprang for the ladder leading to the main deck.

The rattle of the anchor chain was drowned out by the cries of the men who swarmed up the masts to shake out the waiting canvas. A few strides carried Nagaro to the captain's platform. Mounting it, he called into the speaking tube to his first mate, below with the oarsmen. "Ply oars, Taru. Take us ahead, easy." Through the tube, he heard Taru's "Aye, Capt'n!" followed by the repetition of his order, and presently, the slow rhythmic beat of the drum, marking time for the rowers.

With a creaking sigh, the *Sword of Freedom* eased forward under power of her oars, gathering way. Moments later, she moved gracefully out into the channel. The hastily-lowered sails immediately caught the wind with a ripple and a snap, and the *Sword* surged ahead.

"Ship oars, Taru! Steersman, make for the Lapoa passage!"

The ship slowed almost imperceptibly as the oars were drawn in, the sails having caught the full force of the wind. Atop the crow's seat, Kunoa pointed out the heading, and the steersman swung the tiller to align the Sword's bow with the gap between the isles of Tunapa and Lapoa. The blue-green rampart of Tunapa rose out of the sea directly across the channel from their position. Lapoa was a long, ragged purple silhouette a little way to the south. Pavo set his men to adjusting the angle of the sails. The new course would take the vessel obliquely across the width of the Inside Passage on a southeasterly heading. More to the point, it showed the *Sword's* distinctively-marked flank to any ships that might be sailing up the channel from the south.

And three such ships there were—the ones that Doren had been watching for the last half hour. They were beating north along the coast of Boka Omei and just now drawing abreast of Stone Head. Standing on the captain's platform, Nagaro studied the three vessels with his glass. "War galleys under banners of green, gold, and black, just as the fishermen said," he observed. "The colors of the warlord Tuluptak."

"Have they seen us?" Kuran had joined him on the low platform.

"It seems so. They just increased the pace of their oar strokes and have started to turn east to intercept us."

The *Sword* continuied to make rapid headway in the direction of the Lapoa passage as the three ships of the small Mahuk fleet assumed a northeasterly heading that was set to converge with their intended prey. Minutes passed, and the distance between the Mahuk galleys and the *Sword* decreased steadily as all four ships stayed on their courses.

"All according to plan so far." Kuran spoke over a gust of wind. "So we hold course?"

Nagaro nodded, lowering the glass. "Yes. But we have to look as if we're trying to beat them to the passage." He turned to the speaking tube. "Oars out, and *row*, Taru!"

A moment later the oars came out and began to dip and rise as the drum started to throb. The *Sword* surged forward. Shortly thereafter, the three pursuing ships altered course again to a heading still more easterly, steering for a point ahead of their prey, adjusting to the *Sword's* more rapid progress.

"Pavo, give us more sail."

"Aye, Captain!" Pavo shouted from the main deck.

Men scurried up the masts. Kuran turned his gaze towards Boka Bay, shading his eyes with his hand. "Landros should bring those ships out soon," he muttered tensely. "What's he waiting for?"

"For the Mautep to turn enough to put the bay astern of them, so he can approach them from behind. If we increase our speed just enough, we can get them to turn a little more..."

The *Sword of Freedom* was well out into the channel now and still making for the Lapoa Passage. The distance between her and the Mahuk warships was a quarter mile and shrinking. At the *Sword*'s present speed, it was hard to judge whether she would escape her pursuers. As Pavo and his main-deck crew adjusted the sails, however, the *Sword* began to widen the gap. The Mautep captains, seeing the change, altered course a third time, finally putting their sterns towards Boka Bay as they aimed to intercept the *Sword* at a point still farther along her southeasterly course.

"*There!*" Kuran breathed, "Landros is coming out!"

The Lord of the Fleet knew better than to point. The Mautep would be watching their adversaries through their own spyglasses.

Nagaro flicked a glance in the direction of the bay, to see the sails of several ships emerging from the harbor entrance. "Good," he muttered. "Watch for the first sign that the Mautep have seen them."

For some minutes, the ships all continued on their established courses, the *Sword* pacing her pursuers as all five ships under Landros's direction cleared the harbor entrance and headed eastward across the channel, making straight for their quarry, moving single-file so as to hide behind one another. Their crews were rowing hard and the Edroviran ships were visibly gaining on the Mahuk craft.

Nagaro stood tensely at his post, frowning in concentration, judging speeds and distances. As the *Sword* passed the middle of the channel, he addressed the speaking tube. "Slow the pace, Taru, and wobble the oars a bit to look like we're flagging."

"Aye, Capt'n."

Shortly thereafter, the *Sword's* oars began to waver and slow, and the ship lost way. From astern came the Mautep's excited cheer, carried on the wind.

Kuran showed his teeth. "They think that hey have us," he growled. "And they may, indeed, if Landros and the others aren't quick enough."

Nagaro flashed his pirate smile. "We're going to play with them a bit." He put his mouth once more to the speaking tube. "Slow a little more, Taru." To the steersman he called, "Bring her a half point to port, Bouno." He glanced at Kuran. "Let them think we've decided our only hope is to run straight before them."

The captains of the Mahuk craft, apparently feeling sure of a catch and wishing to spare their slaves for the encounter, soon slackened speed in response to the *Sword's* change of course. The *Sword* still fled before them, oars moving raggedly, now clearly being overtaken.

Intent upon their prey, the Mautep had yet to notice that slowing their craft was allowing the five Edroviran warships behind them to gain more quickly, but that situation couldn't last. Before long, one of the Mautep lookouts must have looked over his shoulder, for shouts of alarm suddenly rang on the wind.

Kuran had the spyglass. "They've seen our fleet!" he cried. "They're dashing about their decks like madmen."

It was time stop running.

Nagaro spoke urgently into the speaking tube: "Drag starboard oars! Pull hard on the port!" To the steersman, he cried: "Hard turn to starboard, Bouno! Bring her full about, tight as you can." And to Pavo on the main deck, he shouted: "Reef sails!" They would soon be running into the teeth of the wind.

The *Sword of Freedom* came full about onto a westerly heading, nearly pivoting on the dragged blades of the starboard oars while the port rowers reached and pulled and Pavo's deck crew aloft in the rigging scrambled to furl the sails. When the ship was heading straight for the nearest of the three Mahuk craft, Nagaro called through the speaking tube for moderate forward speed.

"That was a pretty piece of work, Captain. You've trained your new crew well." Kuran spoke at Nagaro's elbow. "Do you think the Mautep might break to south, since north would take them into Farano's Mouth and all those hidden rocks?"

Nagaro shook his head. "Their best course is to head east-southeast and try to get past us into the Lapoa passage."

The *Sword*'s rapid turn-about had brought her to within a hundred yards of the three Mahuk galleys. On their decks, confusion temporarily reigned. One started to veer south, only to be called back by the captains of the other two, as all three debated their course. Wind and momentum still carried them along their easterly heading, though more slowly since they'd put up their oars. If all held steady, they would pass the *Sword of Freedom* a little to starboard.

The five pursuing Edroviran ships had not slackened their pace in the meantime, and they were fanning out to north and south to catch the Mautep like fish in a net. The nearest of the Fleet craft, the *Sea Eagle* under Landros's command, was only a few hundred yards behind her prey and coming on fast.

A shout from one of the Mahuk galleys was heard over the water, and a moment later, the leading ship's oars dipped into the sea as her slaves were set to row again. At the same time, the warship altered course, making straight for the *Sword of Freedom* as her speed increased. The other two Mahuk vessels promptly followed the first one's lead.

"*By the Eyes!*" Kuran swore. "Do they mean to sink us? Our fleet will still catch them even if they succeed."

"It's more likely they hope to frighten us into getting out of their way," Nagaro answered grimly. "The *Sword* lies between them and their escape through the Lapoa passage. Bouno! Take us a quarter point to starboard... *and hold...*" He counted out half a dozen oar strokes. "Now a quarter point to port, then hold steady!"

The course adjustment put the *Sword* onto a collision course with the leading Mahuk craft, with the other two galleys running on parallel courses to the north, but trailing.

Kuran sucked in his breath. "This is a dangerous game, Captain," he said tensely. "Even if you truly meant to ram that ship—"

"We've done this before," Nagaro said soberly. "And if we don't delay at least one of these ships long enough to be caught, our trouble has been for nothing." He'd spoken without taking his eyes off the approaching war galley. He knew what Kuran feared: When two war ships met head on, there was a good chance both would go to the bottom when their iron-clad rams simultaneously bit timber. Even if the rams both missed, one or both hulls might crack if the two ships struck too directly and too hard. He measured the distance between the two craft with his eyes, judging the speed of the approach, his hands gripping the rail.

Seventy yards... and closing.

"The wind is dropping," Kuran observed. "That's a bit of luck."

Nagaro had felt it as well. He nodded, his eyes still on the Mahuk ship. Less wind meant less force driving the oncoming vessel. It also meant safer maneuvering in close quarters. "Pavo," he cried, "ready the speaking trumpet! Taru, quicken the pace a little."

"Ready Zirda!" Pavo sprang up the ladder onto the forecastle deck with the trumpet in his hand.

Taru's affirmation came through the speaking tube, and the rhythm of the drum increased perceptibly.

Sixty yards...

The Mautep captain must have also been aware of the risk, but he kept his heading, doubtless hoping his adversary would be the first to blink. Nagaro marked time.

Fifty yards...

Beyond the three Mahuk craft, the *Sea Eagle* was now less than two hundred yards from her prey. The other four Fleet ships flanked the *Eagle* in pairs, to starboard and port.

Nagaro spoke to Kuran, at his side. "My Lord, stand ready with your men at the port rail. I want a strong guard on our open side."

Kuran smiled ironically, and snapped a salute. "Aye, Zirda! You're the captain." Leaning over the stern castle rail, he called down orders to the half dozen men under his direct command who were waiting on the main deck just below. Then he made for the ladder.

Forty yards...

Still the Mahuk ship came on, her ram aimed directly at the *Sword*'s bow. Nagaro frowned. *Her captain had courage, but it was time to begin the dance.* Nagaro raised his voice to call to the steersman. "A quarter point to port, Bouno—" He waited through six surging oar strokes, then called "—and a quarter point back to starboard." The jog to port brought the *Sword* back to a parallel course, a little to the south of her previous one, thus revealing Nagaro's intent, not to ram, but rather to board the other vessel from her starboard side, the obvious choice with the other two Mahuk galleys to port.

Thirty yards...

The Mautep captain obviously had no wish to be boarded with five enemy ships bearing down on his stern, but turning north would expose his starboard side to the *Sword's* ram. He took the only remaining course of action, making a shallow turn to the south, toward the *Sword*, meaning to ram her if she continued on her present course. The movement, being made by slave oarsmen, was noticeably more clumsy than the *Sword's* had been. At the same time Mautep crewmen were sent up the masts to furl the sails. Canvas on the yards was a liability in close quarters if there was any wind.

Nagaro observed these developments from the *Sword's* stern castle. His eyes narrowed. "A quarter point to port, Bouno! Taru, all speed!" The *Sword* veered again, then surged ahead. A dozen strokes of the oars carried her forward, clear of the Mahuk ship's ramming course. "Slacken speed! And a quarter point back to starboard!"

Twenty yards...

The most recent jog had put the *Sword of Freedom* once more on a boarding course, parallel to that of her quarry and slightly farther to port, but with the two ships only half as far apart.

The Mautep captain's response was to begin to turn again clumsily onto a new ramming course, but before the maneuver was more than barely begun, Nagaro snatched up a speaking trumpet that hung from the rail, raised it to his mouth, and shouted, "*Slaves! Ship oars for Captain Nagaro!*"

Pavo, on the deck of the forecastle, took this as his cue and repeated the cry in Droviri and in Hashti: "*Shaku! Ship oar for Kiraam Shaku-Tal! Ship oar for Thief of Slave!*"

They were shouting into the wind, but it had slackened and the two ships were close together. Nagaro watched tensely, silently praying that the slaves had heard.

And the Mahuk ship's oars began to waver and be withdrawn as Nagaro's prayer was answered and the slaves ignored their masters' orders. The vessel immediately began to lose way, and Nagaro easily repeated his jog to port a third time before shipping oars as the two ships closed, bringing the *Sword* neatly in along the Mautep's starboard side without breaking a single oar. His deck crew needed no order to tell them what to do. Half a dozen men were ready at the starboard rail with grapples. The rest stood behind them, ready to seize any fending pikes their adversaries might bring to bear. Kuran and his six men were arrayed along the port rail, their swords ready.

Nagaro checked the course of the other two Mahuk craft. Both were passing to northward, still on course for the Lapoa passage. He cupped his hands and shouted to the lookout in the crow's seat. "Watch those two ships, Kunoa! Shout if they turn back! And keep an eye on Landros's fleet!"

"Aye Capt'n!"

Satisfied, Nagaro vaulted over the stern castle rail, landing on the main deck and striding to his place among his men just as the grapples snaked out to snag the Mahuk warship's rail.

The struggle that ensued was fierce. The Mautep were desperate not to be boarded, and plied their fending pikes with such energy that for a short time they had the upper hand against the *Sword*'s main deck crew. When the rest of the *Sword's* crew came swarming up the ladders from the oar deck, however, the tide turned. Fending pikes were flung clattering on the deck. Wood ground against wood as the grappling ropes were drawn tight and lashed in place, binding the two ships together. Steel flashed on both sides of the opposing rails as swords were drawn. The Mautep backed away from the railing, expecting the worst.

Nagaro was in the thick of things, moving wherever he was needed. When the swords came out, he had his own in his hand in an instant. In the next instant, he heard Kunoa's cry from the mast head.

"The Mahuk ships are comin' about! They're coming back t' fight!"

The lookout of the embattled Mahuk craft must have also seen his compatriots' change of course, for a shout went up in Hashti followed by a cheer from the Mautep crew, mingled with curses from the officers. The ambivalence of the sea raiders was understandable. Even with all three Mahuk ships together, the Mautep would be outnumbered two to one as soon as Landros's fleet joined the fray. They had no hope of winning, and past experience with Kuran's sea warriors led them to expect only death. The choice of the other two Mautep captains was thus an act of honorable but futile suicide.

Nagaro swept the sea with his eyes. The two ships that were lashed together had turned under the influence of their momentum and now lay athwart their original course with the *Sword* on the southwest and the Mahuk craft on the northeast. Nagaro could look past Kuran's guard and see Landros's five Edroviran ships less than a hundred yards away and already turning, some north, some south, to encircle the grappled pair. The other two Mahuk craft were out of sight from where he stood, hidden by the enemy ship that lay between, but they must be close.

Turning back, he scanned the ranks of the sea raiders and identified the other ship's captain by the gold on his tunic, a dozen feet aft along the railing. A stocky man, broad shouldered, in his thirties, he was in the act of rallying the Mautep around him. Nagaro had barely time to call his own front-line men to his side and begin to move aft, before the Mautep captain came over the rail with a dozen of his best warriors flanking him. The man laid furiously about him with his sword, and the crew of the *Sword of Freedom* fell back before the onslaught. Two of them staggered, wounded. One of them fell.

"Where is man who calls himself Thief of Slave?" The Mautep captain bellowed in Hashti.

Nagaro immediately raised his voice to answer in the same tongue. *"I am here, Captain!"*

At this, the Mautep captain cried, "Whoever you are, Droviri, you will die!" and he turned his full wrath upon Nagaro.

Nagaro waded in, taking the full brunt of the man's fury with his sword. The two blades rang and rang again as Nagaro parried stroke after stroke.

To either side, the *Sword's* crewmen were engaging the Mautep who had come over the rail. Taru, Pavo, and Tredhold were keeping the sea raiders busy on Nagaro's flanks. Peldred was getting his first real taste of battle. Yet many of the men on both sides had a sliver of their attention on the two leaders, knowing the outcome of the entire conflict could hinge on how their captains fared.

A gap opened briefly to Nagaro's right and Kuran leaped in to fill it. "Thought you could use some help," he gasped as he parried a thrust from a Mautep sea warrior who had also tried to take advantage of the opening.

The Mautep captain, thinking his opponent distracted, redoubled his attack. If this was to be his last battle, he was determined to make it count. He had assumed that the infamous name of Kiraam Shaku-Tal had been used to trick his slaves into disobedience, and he was furious at the deception. Now, however, his wrath began to give way to doubt, for try as he might, he couldn't get past this man's guard. Furthermore, although the Droviri captain wore the uniform of Edrovir, he resembled the description of Kiraam Shaku-Tal, and the sword he wielded was Mautep-made.

For his part, Nagaro had every respect for his present adversary. The Mautep captain was highly skilled and was fighting courageously. He knew the man expected to die, but he hoped to show the Mautep a different way. *If he could just—*

He saw his opportunity and took it, twisting the Mautep captain's sword from his grasp so that it fell clattering to the deck. In the next instant, Nagaro's voice rang over the melee, speaking in Hashti.

"Man of Mahuk Baar, surrender and you will not be harmed!"

The Mautep captain stood empty-handed, his chest heaving. There were two thoughts in his mind: first, that he was outmatched by the man in front of him, and second, that the man could have easily slain him if he'd wished.

The clash of swords faltered all along the line, many of the Mautep being unnerved by the disarming of their leader. Their captain raised his voice to shout to the lookout atop his mainmast, something in Hashti that Nagaro didn't understand. The lookout answered with something equally incomprehensible.

Kunoa immediately gave a shout of his own from the *Sword's* crow's seat. "The Mahuk ships were trying to get 'round us, Capt'n—one on each side—but Landros's ships are closing with 'em. They're going t' board!"

Pavo spoke from his place along the line. "Mautep lookout have just told his captain same thing."

The Mautep captain stood rigidly erect while one might count to three, his struggle visible in his eyes. Then he apparently made a decision, for he raised his hand. Signaling his men to lower their weapons, he said to Nagaro, "We will talk."

These words Nagaro understood. He cried, "parley!" in the Common Speech, making a sign to his own men to lower their swords.

All fighting ceased.

The signal had no sooner been given than Peldred pounced on the sword that had been struck from the Mautep captain's hand. Picking it up, the third mate raised it aloft triumphantly.

Nagaro extended his left hand. "Give it to me, Peldred."

Reluctantly the Leithian youth handed over the prize, then stood gaping as Nagaro promptly offered the weapon back to its owner with a small bow. At his side, Kuran's intake of breath was audible.

Dazedly, the defeated captain reached out and took his sword by the proffered hilt, but before his hand had even returned the blade to his side, one of the other Mautep standing beside the captain lunged at Nagaro, crying in Hashti, *"Die, Shaku-Raal!"*

Quicker than thought, Nagaro whipped his sword around to parry the attacker's blade and then pierce the man's heart, in one continuous motion. The slain Mautep toppled to the deck, and Nagaro withdrew his sword from the man's chest, his lips moving with the murmured words of the executioner's prayer. Raising his eyes, he met the other captain's stunned gaze. "Do you surrender?" he asked calmly in Hashti, "Or must more man die?"

The Mautep captain quickly regained his composure. Like all of his people, he was black-haired and tawny-skinned, and when he chose, his narrow black eyes betrayed nothing. His face now became a mask, though his knuckles showed white on the handgrip of his sword. He asked, "You are truly Kiraam Shaku-Tal?"

Nagaro conceded the fact with a bow. He'd become resigned to the title bestowed upon him by Lord Baalkir's nephew. He didn't like the name, but understood that the Mautep expressed a certain respect when they called him "Thief of Slaves." As always, what he said was, "I am Captain Nagaro."

The Mautep bowed stiffly in his turn. "I am Captain Keertak jir-Bantao," he said without noticeable inflection.

Pavo Maat had moved to a place just behind Nagaro and Kuran, and he spoke now in the Common Speech. "This man is oldest son of Lord Tuluptak."

Captain Keertak flicked the very briefest of glances at Pavo. Nagaro thought he caught a hint of comprehension in that glance, as if the man had recognized the sound of his father's name. He decided on a show of openness. Speaking in Hashti, he said, "My friend says you are first son of Lord Tuluptak."

"That is so." There had been a flicker of surprise in the man's eyes at the use of the word "friend," and there was noticeable pride behind his acknowledgment. "You say we will not be harmed, Kiraam Shaku-Tal," the Mautep continued. "In what name do you promise this?"

It was a fair question, and Nagaro answered it. "In name and honor of Edrovir."

Keertak shook his head. "I know nothing of this honor."

Nagaro frowned. Pavo bent and spoke into Kuran's ear, apparently translating. Abruptly, Kuran spoke.

"Tell him he can trust the honor of Kuran Kel, the Lord of the Royal Fleet of Edrovir."

Nagaro gestured for Pavo to translate this, and the massive young Hashtep promptly rendered Kuran's words into Hashti.

The Mautep captain once again shook his head. He made a face and muttered, "*Hatakei-Raal!*" under his breath. Then he added coldly, addressing Nagaro, "I care nothing for honor of this man. But honor of Kiraam Shaku-Tal, I will trust."

Nagaro very deliberately smoothed the frown from is forehead and mustered his knowledge of Hashti. "It is good thing, Captain Keertak," he said carefully, "that My Lord Kuran does not understand Hashti. He holds his honor very high, and his sword is very quick."

There was a flicker in the man's eyes. "He is now your lord?"

Nagaro made a small bow of affirmation. "You see this?" He indicated his uniform with a gesture. "And you see flag, there." He pointed to the blue and white hawk banner. "I have sworn oath to Edrovir. I make no trick."

At this, Keertak turned an appraising gaze upon Kuran, raking the Lord of the Fleet with his eyes—all five and a half feet of him. Kuran returned the stare, sharp-eyed and keenly attentive. His glance had been shifting back and forth between the two captains as they spoke, doubtless reading what he could from their tone and their faces, since Pavo had wisely ceased translating.

Keertak turned back to Nagaro. "You hold honor of this man so high?"

Nagaro nodded. "Yes. I have told him that Mautep have honor. This he did not understand before. Now he asks your surrender instead of killing all your man."

Captain Keertak stood still for a long moment while the brisk Evrel breeze strummed the rigging. The only other sounds were the wash of the sea against the ship's hull and the creak of her timbers. Beyond the heads of the waiting Mautep warriors, and beyond their ship, Nagaro could see three mainmasts, one flying a green banner, the other two with banners of blue. Behind him, in plain view of the Captain Keertak and his crew, four more ships rode the swells—one with a green banner, three with blue. Men lined their rails, and here and there a spyglass was trained upon the scene unfolding on the deck of the *Sword of Freedom*.

Captain Keertak again made a decision. He turned to Kuran and executed a stiffly formal bow before addressing himself to Nagaro. "Tell your lord I hold his honor equal to honor of Kiraam Shaku-Tal," he said, speaking with dignity. "Tell him that I, Keertak jir-Bantao, make surrender of this ship, and these two other ship, and of all my man, on his promise and promise of Kiraam Shaku-Tal that all these man shall not be harmed. I swear to keep this surrender on my honor and in name of Great God Sheptuum."

*

Two hours later, all nine ships—six Edroviran, and three Mahuk— lay safely anchored in Boka Bay to the wonderment of the local populace. The anchorage offered a convenient place to tend the wounded, make a preliminary search of the captured Mahuk craft, and give attention to the slaves who had just been freed.

Seated in the great cabin of the *Pride of Lankura*, Kuran finished pouring himself a glass of sothiril. "When you handed the man back his sword, I thought I was going to have to keep him from killing you."

Nagaro took a long swallow from his own glass. "It was a gesture of respect," he explained. "And I was ready if he had tried to kill me. One of the others did, as it turned out."

Kuran eyed him. "Yes. You dropped him before I could move."

Nagaro sighed. His eyes momentarily focused far away. "It was the right time to make a point," he said quietly. "Vothra forgive me. I'm better at making the decision than living with it. The point is made, and a man is dead. With luck, his death may help prevent the deaths of others. And altogether, it went better than I expected."

Kuran studied Nagaro for a moment, then shook his head. "That's all you can say? When we've captured three war galleys, a hundred sea warriors, and the son of a warlord—all without losing a single one of our men?"

Nagaro took another swallow of his sothiril and met Kuran's gaze. "Two of my crew will have to end their service as a result of the wounds taken, My Lord," he observed. "But the casualties could easily have been higher. And I'd have been glad to have taken a single ship. Finding they were commanded by Lord Tuluptak's son was a pure gift of Lokundas."

Kuran laughed shortly. Then he sobered. He swirled his sothiril and took a luxurious swig. "You explained to this lord's son—this Keertak—that we mean to take him and his ships to Lankura so that he may stand before the king. What did he make of it, do you think?"

"He seemed not happy about it, but I think, resigned."

"Can we trust him? And even if we can trust *him*, what if any of the other rascals try to make a break once we're in the Great Channel?"

Nagaro sighed. "I'm sure Keertak is asking himself similar questions about *you* and the other Fleet officers—not to mention about the King of Edrovir. Winning trust requires risking trust. Neither your reputation, nor that of Edrovir, was enough for him. It was only after I explained that *I* considered you an honorable man that he agreed to place himself in our hands. So his surrender rests on his belief in the honor of Kiraam Shaku-Tal. I hope I haven't misled him."

Kuran's brow darkened. "You know I'll do everything I can to—"

"It's not you that I'm worried about, My Lord," Nagaro put in hastily. "It's the King and his Council. Elgurn may have agreed in principle to what we proposed, but I'm not sure what he or any of the Signers will do when actually faced with what we bring them." He drained his glass and rose. "The sooner we sail, the better. I'd prefer to be safely in Lankura harbor before nightfall."

Kuran grunted agreement. He finished his own sothiril and stood up. Pausing as he started for the door, he asked, "What does *Hatakei-Raal* mean? And I want an accurate translation. Keertak said it, and I know it applies to me."

Nagaro met the older man's gaze. "It means 'running dog.'" He saw Kuran's look, and quickly added, "The ones who don't like *me* call me *Shaku-Raal*, meaning 'slave dog,' which is even more insulting. The man who went for me called me that."

Kuran's eyes narrowed. "But you killed *him*," he observed dryly.

"But not for that. I don't really care what they call me. I killed him because he tried to kill me after his captain had called for a parley. And I told Keertak he was lucky you didn't understand Hashti."

"Ha!" Kuran grinned wickedly. "I see I shall have to learn it—that and some other things."

16: The Honor Of Edrovir

King Elgurn sat in his high-backed chair on the Audience Chamber's raised dais, the pale golden circlet gleaming on his brow. He wore purple and black, trimmed in white and gold, more color than was usual for him. Perhaps it was for the benefit of the three Mautep captains who stood before him. Whatever the case, he looked every inch a king, down to the rings on his fingers and the commanding gaze of his pale blue eyes.

"My Lord Kuran," he said acerbically, "you've captured three ships and over a hundred Mahuk sea warriors, including the son of a warlord, and your recommendation is that these men should be turned *loose? With* their ships?"

Kuran, standing at attention before his king, didn't flinch.

Beside and a little bit behind the Lord of the Fleet, Nagaro drew a worried breath. Pavo stood with him, ready to translate. Several paces behind Kuran, Keertak and the other two Mautep captains waited to learn their fate. The three captains were unbound but were escorted by a dozen Fleet warriors.

It was morning of the day following the capture of the Mahuk ships, and despite the earliness of the hour, a number of men were watching the proceedings from one of the room's two side galleries. Nagaro had noted that two of the Pact Signers, Anduar and Odus, were among them.

Kuran cleared his throat. "Not simply *turned loose*, My Lord King," he said calmly. "They would give up their slaves—we discussed this, as you may recall. We would also seize any monies or valuable cargo, and we would obtain oaths of honor from the three captains that they will never again venture into Edroviran waters for the purpose of robbing us, or taking our people for slaves, or otherwise working ill against us. After all of this, they and their ships would be escorted south, to a point beyond the boundary of our waters."

Kuran ceased speaking and there was a low murmur among the spectators in the gallery.

A frown creased the king's brow. "You would rely on their oaths?"

Nagaro took a step forward. "My Lord King, may I speak?"

Elgurn's expression did not change as he transferred his gaze to

Nagaro, unless it darkened fractionally as he gestured acquiescence. "It seems I can scarcely prevent you," he said dryly.

Nagaro bowed, suppressing his annoyance. "Thank you, My Lord King," he said evenly. "I have spoken already regarding Mautep honor. Any man may break an oath, but if any of *these* men does so, he will be foresworn, and we'll be justified in slaying him if he again falls into our hands. I might add that it's the respect these men have for the honor of myself and of Kuran Kel that brings them here alive to stand before you."

The king cast a shrewd glance at the impassive faces of the three Mautep. "You don't suppose it was a desire to *live?*"

"Well, of course, My Lord," Nagaro replied. "Given a choice between honorable death and honorable life, they chose life. But Captain Keertak led a boarding party onto my deck with five Fleet galleys bearing down on him. He clearly expected to die. And the other two captains entered the fight—against two-to-one odds—when they could have fled. These were acts of courage—and of honor."

"I see." Elgurn clipped the words. "Thank you, Captain." He turned back to Kuran. "There may be reason to believe they are honorable men, My Lord Kuran, but I don't see why we shouldn't hold them for ransom."

Kuran shifted his feet. "With respect, My Lord," he replied, "that would seem to be excessively... *provocative*... since it appears they hadn't been in Edroviran waters long enough to actually *do* anything. Their only provable offenses, on this voyage, are entering our waters without our leave and carrying slaves, many of whom are Edroviran citizens."

"What of past deeds? What of intentions?"

"My Lord, why don't you ask them?" Nagaro put in. "My second mate, Pavo Maat, is here to translate your words, and theirs."

Elgurn leaned forward and his lips curled in a smile. "I believe I will, Captain." He turned his attention to Pavo. "You, there, second mate, ask the Mautep commander what their purpose was in sailing into our territorial waters, and how they come to be holding Edroviran citizens as slaves."

Nagaro gave Pavo the barest nod and the young Hashtep turned to Captain Keertak, making a rapid translation of the king's question.

Keertak regarded Pavo with disdain equal to Elgurn's. Nevertheless, he answered in his own tongue.

Pavo turned back to Elgurn. "My Lord King, he says that this is first voyage for him and for all his man into territory of Edrovir. He says some other man of Lord Tuluptak have taken Droviri slave that are in his three ship, and Lord Tuluptak have given those slave to him. He says also that he and all his man came here by order of Lord Tuluptak to take Droviri gold."

Elgurn scowled, his gaze flicking to Nagaro, then moving to Kuran.

"What he says is rather predictable. And he takes very little blame onto himself and his men."

Kuran coughed. "Yes, My Lord. You see the difficulty—"

"A difficulty, certainly—if we *believe* the man."

Nagaro spoke quickly. "Whether we believe him or not, My Lord, we cannot prove he is lying, and what he says is consistent with what I know of Mautep ways. Therefore I suggest we punish him only for what we are sure of. To do otherwise would not speak well of *our* honor."

There was rustling and some muttered talk among the watchers in the gallery at this, and Nagaro's quick glance caught Anduar speaking to Odus. Anduar's expression was neutral. Odus was frowning.

The king had glanced at the gallery as well, and he now smoothed his own countenance. "There is some merit in what you say, Captain." He coughed into his fist, then turned once more to Pavo. "Tell Captain Keertak that we are greatly displeased that men of the Mahuk Baar come to take our gold. Since his men seem not to have taken any *yet*, however, they shall be released, provided they accept this ban: They are not to enter again willfully into Edroviran waters—which means passing north of the southernmost tip of the Island of Pakoa. This they must swear to by their most sacred oath, and the penalty for violation of their oaths shall be death."

There was a pause while Pavo translated this. Keertak received the information without any change of expression, nor did he seem to feel any need to confer with his fellow officers. Instead, he simply bowed, albeit rather stiffly, to Elgurn, and spoke a few words.

Pavo relayed them. "My Lord King, he says he and his two captain accept these term, and they are ready to swear."

There followed the ritual of oath-taking. The three men swore, each upon his honor and in the name of Sheptuum, with Pavo translating for the benefit of those who didn't speak Hashti. Nagaro further confirmed the content of the oaths based on his own knowledge of that tongue.

When this was finished, Kuran cleared his throat. "And now the slaves, My Lord?"

"Yes, of course." The king turned his baleful blue gaze upon the Mautep commander. "We are not finished," he said with evident relish. "We are even more displeased about the taking of our people than we are about the taking of our gold. Since we now know the great number of these captives, and the magnitude of their suffering"—here Elgurn inclined his head stiffly to Nagaro—"we are resolved that this shall stop! Therefore, we declare that all of the slaves you hold captive shall be set free. And to recompense them for what they have suffered, we shall take anything of value from your ships that can be sold. The monies will be used to provide for the immediate needs of these men as they return to lives of freedom."

This speech, also, Pavo translated, with pauses to inquire of Nagaro the exact meanings of several words. As the young Hashtep spoke, the faces of the three Mautep began at last to show signs that they didn't much like what they were hearing. Elgurn was watching those faces and clearly enjoying their discomfort.

When Pavo finished, Captain Keertak instantly burst forth with a sheer torrent of angry Hashti, to which Pavo listened impassively before turning back to the king. "Lord King," he said, "Captain Keertak asks how he and his man are to sail quickly out of Edroviran water without any slave to row ship, since wind may not be favorable."

Elgurn smiled a chilly smile. "You may tell Captain Keertak that he has sea warriors enough to row, and this is not, therefore, our concern. Besides which, My Lord Kuran and Captain Nagaro are prepared to take as long as necessary to escort their ships from our waters."

Kuran and Nagaro bowed their acquiescence.

Pavo's translation of the king's speech did nothing to improve the mood of the three Mautep. More rapid Hashti followed, which Pavo promptly rendered into Common Speech. "My Lord, Captain Keertak says that it is justice for you to take Droviri slave because you are king of Droviri, but he says Hashtep slave are man of Mahuk Baar and belong to Lord Tuluptak and to Emperor."

The king frowned at Kuran. "I was afraid that it would come to this. How can we tell them what they're to do with their own people?"

Kuran cleared his throat, but Nagaro was quicker. "My Lord King, may I speak to him?" He'd been listening with growing concern. Kuran had tried to explain to the king the rationale for freeing Hashep slaves, but Elgurn lacked Nagaro's personal experience.

Elgurn shot him a look, but shrugged. "Proceed," he said with an air of resignation.

Nagaro drew a quick breath and began, using the Common Speech because he didn't have all the words in Hashti. "Captain Keertak, you must understand that our law says it is wrong for any man to own another man. Therefore, there can be no slaves in Edrovir, neither on our lands, nor on our seas. We cannot tell you what to do with your people in your own country, but if you bring slaves into *our* country, they will become free men. Being free, they may choose for themselves what they will do. If any of them choose to row your ships as free men, or to go back with you to the Mahuk Baar to become slaves again, we will not stop them."

There was a ripple of voices in the gallery and some suppressed laughter. Kuran's teeth gleamed in a brief, hard smile, and Elgurn's face twitched as he suppressed one of his own. Nagaro's expression remained deadly earnest while Pavo rendered his translation.

Keertak was frowning darkly when he made answer, and Nagaro understood the words well enough to wince even before Pavo put them into Common Speech.

"Captain Keertak says he understand. But he says Hashtep slave have done crime and you do wrong to end their punishment."

This brought more murmurs, and Elgurn's brows knit. "What about this, Captain?" he demanded sharply.

Nagaro held up a hand and addressed Keertak. "Are any of them guilty of murder?"

The Mautep's reply to Pavo's rendition of the question was brief and emphatic.

"He says no. Slave are thief. In Mahuk Baar, punishment for killing man is death."

Nagaro nodded. "And a quick death, I believe, by hanging?"

Pavo didn't bother to translate. "Yes," he said. "That is true."

Nagaro nodded once more, and his eyes were hard. "Then, if the punishment for killing a man is a quick death by hanging, ask him why it is that the punishment for stealing two rabbits, or a loaf of bread, is to spend the rest of the man's life in chains, doing hard labor, being beaten with a whip, and living in the filth of his own body until he is smashed by a broken oar, carried to the bottom of the sea with a sinking ship, or thrown overboard, still breathing, with a bag of rocks tied to his feet?"

The shocked expression on Elgurn's face spoke volumes, and it was mirrored on the faces of the watchers in the gallery.

As Captain Keertak listened to Pavo's translation, his face became a frozen mask. His response was simple, and Nagaro understood it.

"Always it has been this way. Slave are only Hashtep."

Pavo's translation was met by shocked silence.

Nagaro's eyes smoldered, but his voice was level as he addressed Captain Keertak directly in Hashti, drawing whispered exclamations from the onlookers at hearing him use the tongue of the Mahuk Baar.

"You have seen my second mate, Pavo Maat, who is Hashtep." He indicated Pavo with a gesture. "You have seen how he sets sail to wind. You have seen him fight. He has followed me in honor for five year. Now he follows flag of Edrovir. He could have given same service to Baalkir jir-Akaan, but Baalkir have thrown him away for taking two rabbit— because he is 'only Hashtep'—while Mautep take our gold and have no punishment at all! I say Emperor have lost very good man. I say justice is not justice if it is not same for all man. And justice is not justice if punishment is so much worse than crime."

Keertak's face was like stone. "Always it has been this way," he repeated, but to Nagaro it seemed there was just the hint of discomfort under his flat assertion, as if he were being made to see, for the first time, how his people appeared in the eyes of others.

Pavo's translation of Nagaro's speech brought a general murmur of approval from the hall.

"Well said, Captain!" Elgurn leaned forward in his chair. "It's quite obvious that the claim of punishment for a crime is only an excuse to enslave these poor wretches." He held up his hand to Pavo as a signal that there should be no translation of the words he'd just spoken, then addressed himself formally to the Mautep commander.

"Captain Keertak, I do not accept your complaint. By our standard of justice, any man who has labored at an oar all the way from the Mahuk Baar to the waters of Edrovir has already more than paid for such crimes as petty theft. As we have said, we cannot prevent you from doing as you please in your own country, but if you bring slaves such as these into ours, we will set them free. I hope you will carry my words to Emperor Baalkir."

Once Pavo had made his translation, Keertak responded with a stiff bow, and a frozen-faced rejoinder to the effect that he would convey what he had heard to the Emperor of the Mahuk Baar.

That might have been the end of the audience, but Elgurn raised the subject of the Mautep sea warriors who had been captured during the assault on Lankura the previous spring. He was determined to ransom the six captives for gold, as Nagaro had suggested, and he wished to know whether Captain Keertak would consent to carry one of the six men back to the emperor, together with the ransom demand.

Keertak's response, once Pavo had made all of this clear to him, was short and delivered with some force. Pavo promptly rendered it into the Common Speech. "Captain Keertak says that these man who attack this city are man of Lord Angkat. Emperor did not send them to do this, and he does not think Emperor will pay ransom for these man."

Nagaro glanced at the lords Odus and Anduar in the gallery, and he was gratified to see Odus frown at this confirmation of what he had told the King's Council, while a fleeting smile crossed Anduar's face. Glancing back at the king, however, he found that Elgurn was scowling.

"What is this?" Elgurn demanded hotly. "Will the Emperor not take responsibility for the actions of his warlords?"

Nagaro spoke quickly without asking permission. "I think perhaps the Emperor may take responsibility for seeing that Lord Angkat pays the ransom. And I think that the amount might be set equal to the sum of Edroviran gold that was paid in ransom to Angkat's men after they raided the palace eight years ago."

Elgurn's scowl lifted as he listened, and his eyes narrowed shrewdly. "*Yes...*" he said with measured care. "I like this. Translate your captain's words, Pavo Maat."

Pavo nodded, and there was a gleam in his dark eyes. His translation brought a smile to the face of Captain Keertak that would have made any pirate proud. The Mautep sobered quickly, however, and his answer was spoken with perfect deadpan. Pavo's relish in repeating it in Droviri was nevertheless obvious.

"My Lord King, he says he thinks that amount of ransom is fair for Angkat to pay, and he thinks Emperor will make sure Angkat pay it."

There remained then only a few details to be sorted out. King Elgurn put a round figure to the ransom, and it was agreed that whichever of Angkat's men was chosen to return to the Mahuk Baar would carry the details of the ransom demand. It was also agreed that the response—presumably with the ransom—would be brought before the end of the summer, in a single ship that would fly a white flag and anchor off the east coast of Pakoa Island to await an escort.

The audience being finally at an end, the three captive Mautep were marched out of the hall. Nagaro, Pavo, and Kuran bowed to the king and began to follow, but Elgurn called the Lord of the Fleet back just as they reached the door, saying, "My Lord Kuran, will you please attend us?"

Nagaro had been feeling buoyant, but he now cast a glance over his shoulder to see that "us" apparently consisted of Elgurn, Odus, and Anduar. The last two lords had descended from the gallery to stand with the king beside the dais. He saw the three men put their heads together after glancing in his direction. He gave Kuran a questioning look. The older man made only the minutest shake of his head before turning and striding away to answer his lord's summons.

Nagaro hastily followed Pavo through the door into the Compass Room, a new worry wriggling in his stomach. The knot of apprehension he had carried into the Audience Chamber had been loosened, but it now began to retie itself as he, Pavo, and the three Mautep prisoners with their Fleet guards passed out of the palace into the stable yard.

He stood in the yard beside his horse's head, waiting for Kuran, with Pavo a few feet away and the three prisoners and their guard a little more distant. He had gotten everything from the audience that he'd hoped for, but he feared he'd been too outspoken. Too much boldness might undermine his purposes if it set the council members against him. *And if they decided to make a raid on Sar Tipaal, it could ruin everything...*

Presently, a movement near the door that opened from the side of the palace into the stable yard caught Nagaro's eye and he was surprised to see Lord Anduar emerge with a pair of saddle bags over his shoulder.

The Kelorin lord's steely gaze met Nagaro's across the intervening distance and he approached at a leasurely pace. "Ah, Captain," he said easily. "You and that sword of yours must have a formidable reputation among these Mautep if a man like Keertak surrenders as soon as he's convinced of your identity. Or did Kuran exaggerate?"

Nagaro frowned. "Keertak was avoiding death, My Lord. I used my reputation to persuade him to trust Kuran's honor."

"And what happens if you lose your reputation, Captain? If any part of the bargain we have just made today isn't kept?" Anduar's expression was opaque.

Nagaro's frown deepened. "Then I could lose the ability to make such bargains—something that has taken me years to acquire."

"Yet you risk your honor in the hands of others?" The tone was mild, though the sharp gray eyes watched him keenly.

Nagaro spread his hands. "There is sometimes nothing to be gained without risk."

"True." Anduar withdrew his gaze and turned it upon the three Mautep captains where they stood a short distance away, surrounded by their guards. Keertak appeared to be guardedly studying his two captors as if their conversation were of some interest, though he surely couldn't understand the words.

"I find you have a peculiar capacity for trust, Captain." The steel-gray eyes came back to Nagaro. "Considering it's being applied in part to men at whose hands you have suffered so much."

Nagaro returned the measuring glance. "The Writings say: *Speak to a man's better nature, and that nature will likely answer*. But surely you know that, My Lord."

Anduar very slightly raised one eyebrow. "I confess I have not made such a detailed study of the Writings. Does Vothra explain the reasoning behind that precept?"

Nagaro's brow furrowed. "That's in the Second Book of Vothra—the *Book of Questions*, My Lord." He quoted the words from memory: "Most men believe themselves to be good. And of those who don't believe it, more than half wish it were true. Most of the rest have never thought about it, but may do so if given the opportunity."

There was a pause while Anduar simply stared at him, and Nagaro realized that he'd actually surprised the Pact Signer.

Anduar said a last. "In my experience, men don't always agree upon what it means to be *good*."

"That is true, My Lord. And Vothra says that much of the world's conflict is a result of it."

"So, what's to be done?"

"Ideally, men should talk to one another, and listen. Also, we can show each other what is good by our actions. That's where trust comes in."

"Ah." Anduar considered him. "Perhaps I shall read these passages,

Captain, the better to understand you."

Nagaro frowned. "Surely there are better reasons than that to study the wisdom gleaned from a thousand lives, My Lord."

Anduar laughed, a brief dry chuckle. "Which is also true. But I must get to my horse as I have a distance to ride. Here comes Kuran, in any case, with a face like thunder."

Kuran had indeed just burst from the same door by which Anduar had exited the palace. The Lord of the Fleet strode to where his horse was tethered, scowling darkly, even as the Pact Signer called for the grooms to saddle his mount.

Kuran jerked at the reins so fiercely as he untied his bay that the creature tossed its head in protest. Swinging astride, he shouted an order for the entire party to be off, then wheeled his mount and maneuvered to take a position at the head of the column of Fleet men that hurriedly formed up in response to his command.

Nagaro had sprung lightly to his saddle and urged the gray stallion to a place beside the bay. "My Lord," he said urgently, leaning over so he didn't need to raise his voice. "I hope they didn't take you to task for my boldness."

"No." Kuran shook his head. "They saw how well you handled those negotiations."

This was a relief, but... "You're more vexed than I've ever seen you. What has happened?"

Kuran gave him a quick, stabbing glance with eyes that smoldered. "I've just come within a hair of losing my temper rather badly," he said through his teeth. "And with it, quite possibly, my command. Ask me no more!" Raising a hand, he signaled for the little detachment to move forward.

As they passed from the stable yard into the broad court that lay between the palace and the city gate, Nagaro glanced repeatedly at the older man's profile. By the time they reached the gate, he thought Kuran had calmed a little, and he dared to raise the matter of his fears.

"I thought the audience went well, My Lord," he ventured. "But it could all come to naught if the Council decides to make an attack on Sar Tipaal before the Emperor has a chance to respond to what we've proposed. Have you heard anything more about what they're planning?"

This time Kuran didn't even look at Nagaro, but the muscles of his jaw tightened visibly. "I'm sorry, Captain," he said tightly. "I can tell you nothing."

Nagaro set his eyes straight before him, frowning, as they passed in silence through the tower-flanked gateway that let to the streets of Lankura. As they emerged from the gate, a cheer arose from many throats. Startled, Nagaro swept the scene with his eyes. All along both sides of the street were lines of townspeople.

The cheer became articulate: *"Nagaro! Nagaro!"* The cry rose on either side. And a lesser number of folk were also crying, *"Kuran! Kuran!"*

Nagaro turned to Kuran in dismay. "Where did all these people come from?"

To Nagaro's surprise, he saw Kuran smile as the older man's mood underwent a miraculous transformation. "It was very early when we came this morning," he said, acknowledging the crowd with a nod of his head. "Scarcely anyone was awake. But a few must have seen us, and word has spread. Go on, Captain! They're shouting for you. Give them what they want!"

"I didn't capture those ships all by myself. They're shouting for you as well!"

A shadow crossed Kuran's face, but he shook it off and laughed. "Good enough!" he said, and spurred his horse.

They rode forward then, side by side, with Pavo and the Fleet men and their three charges trooping behind. As the three Mautep passed out of the shelter of the gate and into full view of the crowd, however, the cheering became intermingled with angry shouts and catcalls. Someone threw a stone, and within a few seconds there came a small volley of such objects, aimed at the captive sea warriors. A stone struck Captain Keertak on the chin, breaking the skin so that a trickle of blood ran. Though the Mautep commander flinched involuntarily, the three captives otherwise marched on stoically, their heads held up proudly, faces impassive, narrow black eyes hard.

Nagaro wheeled his horse as soon as he understood what was happening. *"Stop!"* he cried out commandingly. "Good people, stop! You mustn't hurt these men!"

Raising both arms and guiding the gray stallion with his knees, he maneuvered himself between the Mautep and the part of the crowd from which the most accurate missiles had come. His voice rang in the sudden silence. "These men have surrendered honorably, trusting my promise that they won't be harmed. Let's show them how the people of Edrovir treat prisoners of honor!"

There came a murmur from the crowd. Someone called out, "We're sorry, Capt'n! We didn't know!"

And then the chant began to rise again: *"Nagaro! Nagaro! Nagaro!"*

Nagaro waived his arms again for silence. "Good people!" he cried, cupping his hands so his voice would carry. "We're going to release the Edroviran slaves from the oar decks of the Mahuk ships. They'll need clean clothes. If you would do good rather than harm, think if you have anything to spare and bring it to the gatehouse of the Fleet Compound!"

The cheer that followed these words was very nearly deafening.

Nagaro turned his horse about again to face Keertak and his compatriots. He inclined his head to them. "I ask pardon, Captain," he said in Hashti. "At first they did not know of your honorable surrender. Now they do."

Keertak solemnly inclined his head in return.

Nagaro swung his big gray about, and returned to the head of the party. Kuran gave him an appreciative wink as he came abreast, and signaled again for the column to advance. The little cavalcade proceeded briskly along the street to the rhythmic chanting of, "*Nagaro! Nagaro! Nagaro!*"

None of them happened to turn and look behind them, and so they did not see the cloaked horseman who left the shadow of the gate a little behind the last of the Fleet guard, his laden saddlebags behind him. From under the hood that shadowed his face, Anduar's eyes followed the progress of the little procession. With just the slightest nod, he turned his horse and disappeared into a side street.

*

When Kuran's small cavalcade finally reached the broad stretch of cobbled ground beside the wharfs, in front of the gate of the Fleet Compound, the Lord of the Fleet issued orders to the Fleet guard to return the Mautep captives to the ships where they were being held.

Nagaro dismounted, and Pavo joined him. As they approached the gate of the compound, one of the gatehouse guards raised his voice in a hail.

"Captain Nagaro! There's a man here that's been asking after ye." He grimaced as he indicated a figure sitting on the ground by the gatehouse wall, knees drawn up and dark head bowed, a dusty sack at his side. "A strange sort of a man he is, too," the guard added under his breath.

The seated man seemed to have heard the guard's words, for he abruptly raised his head. Then he unfolded himself and stood up with an excited cry.

"Nagaro! You come! Tell man I want be Fleet warrior!"

Nagaro stared in astonishment. "*Sindar?* How did you get here?"

Sindar beamed at him. "I pay money and sail on ship!" he declared proudly. "I learn many word. Now I be Fleet warrior!"

17: Sign Of The Salamander

Nagaro set out plates and cups, sliced bread, cold meat, and a dish of dried apricots on the table in his small kitchen. He checked the color of the sothiril brewing in the pot, then went to the door that opened into the parlor. There he paused to consider the man who lay curled on the hearth rug under a spare blanket.

Nearly a month had passed since Sindar's unexpected appearance at the Fleet Compound. Nagaro had gotten permission for the former slave to stay with him in his quarters temporarily, then had almost immediately been called away to help escort the three Mahuk war galleys out of Edroviran waters. Pavo's Hashti had been required to explain that, no, Sindar could not sail with Nagaro. Nor was it allowed for Nagaro to lend Sindar the key to his quarters, nor to leave the quarters unlocked. So Sindar had slept in a hay loft above the Fleet stable during Nagaro's absence. He was now back to sleeping on Nagaro's hearth rug.

Nagaro shook his head. While it was convenient that his house guest was perfectly willing to sleep in a stable loft or on the floor, it also underscored how woefully out of place Sindar continued to be among civilized folk.

Nagaro cleared his throat. "Come to breakfast, Sindar."

The former slave stirred and sat up. Casting off the wool blanket, he yawned, stretched, and began rummaging in the sack that contained the sum of his belongings.

Nagaro returned to the kitchen and sat down at the table.

Presently, Sindar came padding into the room. "Thank you for food, Nagaro," he said. "Tomorrow I pay."

Nagaro acknowledged this with a nod as he poured sothiril into two cups. Sindar had spent nearly all of his share from the previous summer's piracy to pay for his passage from Pakoa to Lankura—a fact that didn't seem to trouble the former slave in the least. Nagaro had found employment for the young man with the head stableman, and Sindar now cleaned stalls, forked hay, and hauled water—tasks he knew how to do—in exchange for a few rins a week. This income was enough to pay for his daily food, but little else, and Nagaro had been unable to persuade him to accept more than the most limited charity.

Nagaro watched as Sindar hungrily devoured his share of the bread, meat, and fruit, and noisily gulped sothiril, holding the cup with both hands. Nagaro consumed his own food and drink more delicately—and waited with resignation for the question that Sindar had asked every morning since the *Sword* had returned to its Fleet mooring.

At length Sindar put down his cup, wiped his mouth with his hand, and said, as expected, "Today we talk to Lord Kuran? Tell him I ready be Fleet warrior?"

Nagaro was not looking forward to witnessing Sindar's probable disappointment. Although the young man's command of the Common Speech had improved noticeably in the months he had spent on Pakoa, it clearly wasn't going to be good enough to satisfy Kuran. This morning, however, Nagaro had run out of excuses, so he did his best to smile, and said, "I have orders to report to Kuran early." He spoke carefully so he would be understood. "He must have something to tell me. You can come with me and wait outside until we finish our talk. Then you can go in and we will talk to him together."

Sindar followed the words with a frown of concentration. At the end, he nodded eagerly. "Oh yes! That is good!"

Nagaro winced. "I'm not sure what he will say, Sindar. You must not hope for too much."

Sindar only nodded again. "Is good. We talk. He see I want be Fleet warrior very much!"

If only wanting were enough...

*

They made their way between the barracks buildings, past two new ones that were under construction. It was a bright, clear morning, nearly windless, and the scent of fresh wood shavings mingled with the ever-present salt smell of the sea. There were very few men about as they crossed the parade ground, owing to the earliness of the hour, and Nagaro was surprised to see a coach and team of horses drawn up outside the building that housed Kuran's office and quarters.

"Someone is here before us," he murmured, more to himself than to Sindar. "Someone from outside the Fleet."

"We have to wait?" Sindar sounded distressed.

"I don't know. We may have to come back later. Sit down while I see what the clerk can tell me—No, Sindar! *Not on the ground!*"

Sindar had begun to lower himself onto the planks of the wooden porch in front of Kuran's quarters, rather than onto a bench placed there for men to sit on while waiting. The young Kelorin leaped up at Nagaro's exclamation, his face a picture of chagrin.

Nagaro was bitterly reminded of a time while under the influence of heskial when he had sat down on the floor instead of a nearby chair because someone had given him a similarly imprecise directive. His reaction to Sindar's error had perfectly echoed the princess's response to his.

"I am sorry, Sindar," he said hastily. "That was my fault. I forgot that you might not understand what the *bench* is for." He gestured unambiguously at the object. "I shouldn't have shouted. But free men don't sit on the ground when there's a bench or a chair to sit on."

"Oh. Yes. *Bench*." Sindar nodded wisely, his distress abated. He sat down somewhat gingerly on the bench, patting the wooden seat for emphasis and frowning with the effort of adding another new word to his vocabulary.

Nagaro turned to the door and knocked.

The knock was answered by Estevad, the clerk. The dapper little Kelorin had a capacity for deadpan that rivaled the Hashtep. In response to Nagaro's question he blandly replied, "No, Zirda, you needn't go. My Lord Kuran said you were to be sent directly into his study when you arrived."

Nagaro was puzzled by this. He could hear voices coming from the study, and the conversation seemed to be centered around the price of good lumber and the difficulty of obtaining adequate quantities of it. Telling Sindar again to wait, he crossed the entry hall and paused in the study's open doorway.

The conversation of the three men in the room ceased as soon as he appeared, and all eyes immediately converged upon him. Kuran was seated behind his desk, as usual, and two well-dressed older Kelorin men were seated on chairs to one side of the door. The younger was perhaps sixty, a handsome man with hair nearly completely gray, though he sported a neatly-trimmed beard that was still mostly black. He wore expensive-looking matching britches and tirka of deepest green, and sat very erect in his chair. The second man was closer to eighty, white-haired, and slightly stooped. The fine material and impeccable tailoring of his dark gray britches and burgundy-colored tirka marked him also as a man of means. An ivory-handled walking stick leaned against the wall beside him.

"Ah, there you are, Captain. Do sit down." Kuran gestured to the one remaining chair, which faced the visitors.

Nagaro did as instructed, uncomfortable under the eyes of the two men who were studying him with great interest. Both of them almost immediately began to frown.

"Is *this* the man, then, Kuran?" the older one inquired querulously. "Really, I think this is a mistake. I see no family resemblance—"

"Nor do I," the other man put in. "And his complexion is much too dark in any case."

Kuran shot Nagaro an apologetic glance. "His coloring is not... I believe... natural."

"Well perhaps it isn't, but *still!*" The older man brought his hand briefly to his chest.

The casual movement drew Nagaro's attention to a small emblem embroidered in gold on the left breast of the man's tirka. It appeared to be a red-eyed salamander, curled with its tail in its mouth. Nagaro had listened in embarrassed dismay to the discussion of his appearance, but now he thought he understood.

"Gentlemen," he said hurriedly, to forestall further discussion, "I think it may be this ring that has occasioned your interest." He slid the little green-eyed salamander ring from his finger and held it out to the two men. "It has no direct connection with me—other than the fact that I've had it in my keeping for the past five years."

The white-haired man leaned eagerly forward to take the ring, and his hand shook as he fumbled for a reading glass he wore about his neck. The bearded man rose from his seat to look closer.

"Oh, *yes!*" the older man murmured excitedly as he examined the ring with his glass. "This is the very ring that my son had made as a gift for his bride!"

The bearded man nodded. "Yes," he said. "It's my sister's ring. The last time I saw it, it was on her finger—" His voice caught, and he sank back into his chair, putting a hand to his brow, momentarily overcome by emotion.

"I beg your pardon, young man." The older man addressed Nagaro, blinking eyes that were unmistakably moist. "I'm afraid we have been rather rude. You must forgive our fond delusions. I had hoped you might be my grandson, the child of my son, Kendral, and Evran's sister..." He gestured at the other man even as his gaze seemed to focus far away. He was silent for the space of several heartbeats, apparently gathering his thoughts and his strength before continuing.

"They sailed out of Harmoth harbor with a few of my son's comrades from the Fleet. It was twenty-six years ago, and alas, they sailed into an unexpected storm and the ship was never seen again. Where they were sailing *to,* we've never known. But they were sailing away from *me,* it seems—though they needn't have." The old man sighed and shook his hoary head. "I would never have stood in the way of their marriage once I learned of their love. But you see, I'd always hoped that Kendral would marry the daughter of a dear friend of mine. And fool that I was, I told him so—often. And my son was headstrong... high-spirited... so much his own man. He *wouldn't* be a merchant like his father and grandfather. He would be a Fleet warrior instead... and he'd marry the woman he chose—"

"And that woman was my sister," the bearded man, Evran, finished. "She was carrying Kendral's child when they sailed. They'd been married less than a year. We've always assumed they were lost in the storm—all of the men, my sister, and the unborn child she carried. Then Kuran wrote to Burdal of a new man in the fleet—a man close to twenty-six years of age, of unknown parentage, who wore a lady's ring in the shape of a salamander with emerald eyes. What were we to think? We allowed ourselves to hope..."

Kuran coughed awkwardly. He looked more than a little chagrined. "I confess I had hoped, as well," he said. "But it *was* only a hope. I didn't mean you to think it was anything else. But I'm remiss," he added. "I've neglected the introductions. Captain Nagaro, these two gentlemen are Burdal Korinos, of Vered Mahir—" The old man inclined his white head. "And Evran Marvenen, of Harmoth."

The bearded man, Evran, rose and bowed. "Will you tell us, Captain, how the ring came to be in your possession?"

Nagaro drew a long breath. Apparently, Simion had been right to think of looking inland for the ring's origin, but Kuran had beaten him to the prize. He had listened with growing excitement to the men's tale, and he was trying to decide how to explain his convictions concerning Sindar. *It would be cruelly hard if he were mistaken...*

"How I came by it is a long story," he said after a moment. "To be brief, it was entrusted to me by Roheed jir-Akaan, the nephew of the present Emperor of the Mahuk Baar, with the charge that I should return it to its rightful owners."

All three of the other men in the room stared at him in astonishment.

"I'm afraid I haven't done very well with the charge," he continued. "For years, I could learn nothing, and I've had nothing to go on but the ring itself and the name of the woman who wore it."

Burdal was staring at him. "By the nephew of the Emperor of the Mahuk Baar? Return it to its rightful owners?" he murmured in disbelief. "What mystery is this?"

Evran was also plainly intrigued. "What was the woman's name?" he asked eagerly.

"Emril."

Evran frowned at this, and the light died in his eyes. "But that isn't right," he said. "My sister's name was Almerin."

It was Nagaro's turn to frown. "*Almerin... Emril...*" he murmured. "I suppose it might have gotten twisted, but..." He felt his own hope fading, until suddenly the answer struck him. "Wait! Almerin means *emerald*, doesn't it?"

"Well, yes, certainly—"

Nagaro half rose from his chair in his excitement. "She must not have wanted to give her captor her true name! So she gave him its *meaning*, instead—emerald! And emerald got twisted into Emril!" He laughed aloud as he sank back into his chair. "No wonder I've gotten nowhere asking about the name!"

"Her *captor?*" Evran's brow darkened in anger. "Did this nephew of the Mahuk Emperor hold my sister *captive?*"

"Not the nephew, no," Nagaro told him hastily. "Roheed is a man of my years. It was his father, Notep, brother of the Emperor, who was responsible for slaying Emril's husband and carrying her off to Sar Tipaal." He looked from one to the other of his listeners' dismayed faces. "If you will be patient, I'll tell you the story—as I know it."

So he told them the tale that Pavo had told to his fellow slaves, years before, in a slave barn in Sar Tipaal... the tale of how two storm-battered ships had met somewhere off the coast of Jinara—a Mahuk war galley and an Edroviran merchant ship carrying a man and his pregnant wife. The Mautep sea warriors had killed all aboard the Edroviran craft except the pregnant woman. "The story says that the defenders were led by a man who was a skilled swordsman, a man who 'fought like a tiger.' He was the last to fall, and Notep was able to slay him only when he lay helpless from his wounds." Nagaro met Burdal's eyes. "I suppose that describes the death of Kendral Korinos."

Burdal sat very erect in his chair. His eyes were wet but they shown with pride. "Thank you, Zirda," he said huskily. "It was worth the journey just to hear that."

"But what of my sister?" Evran exclaimed. "If she was taken captive, what was her fate? She can't still be *alive?*"

Sadly Nagaro shook his head. "No, she is dead, though she lived for fourteen years in captivity in the Mahuk Baar."

He told them, then, of how Notep had taken the woman he called Emril to his home in Sar Tipaal... how he'd intended to ransom her but had become enamored of her and decided to keep her for himself, even though he already had a wife who was with child. Nagaro described the disapproval this passion had earned the man, endeavoring to explain to Evran and Burdal that the people of the Mahuk Baar had clear ideas of right and wrong. "They do keep slaves," he told them. "And they regard the folk of other lands as uncivilized and unworthy of respect. But they have their god, Sheptuum, whom they fear; and they also have a code of honor and standards of conduct. I don't think there was any law against a man taking a slave woman as a concubine, but it was seen as an offense to Notep's wife, who was of very good family."

Evran scowled darkly. "I suppose I must take your word for that," he said. "But I don't like the idea of my sister being any man's concubine!"

"She was never taken to his bed," Nagaro put in quickly. "She bore her child, a son she named Sindar—"

"So I had a grandson after all!" cried Burdal.

"Ye-es..." Nagaro responded carefully. "The child was born... healthy and strong. And very soon thereafter Notep's wife gave birth to a son as well—Roheed, whom I've mentioned—but she died in the birthing. Notep gave his child to Emril to nurse." Nagaro paused. "Here's where the tale becomes less certain," he continued. "Apparently Notep feared that Emril wouldn't have enough milk for two babies, so the tale says he abandoned Emril's child in the forest, beside a stream—"

"*Vothra!*" "*What villainy!*"

Nagaro nodded grimly at the horror in his listeners' faces. "Yes," he said, "but the story also says that Notep was seized with remorse. He went back to the forest to retrieve the child, but the child was gone, and there were tiger tracks in the earth beside the stream."

Burdal groaned aloud and covered his face with his hands.

Evran sat stiffly, his eyes ablaze. "Oh, this is hard," he said. "My little nephew eaten by a tiger!"

Nagaro met the man's eyes. "The tale does not say there was any blood," he observed carefully, "or other evidence that the tiger actually killed the child—though that was the usual interpretation."

Kuran had started upon hearing the name of Sindar, and looked hard at Nagaro. Now he cleared his throat. "You haven't yet explained how you came by the ring, Captain. Why would Roheed—this son of a Mautep lord—give the ring to *you?*"

So Nagaro had to explain about the blood debt... about the tiger-haunted dreams that had come, first to Notep, and later to Roheed, and what the dream reader at the temple of Sheptuum had told the father and son. He described Emril's captive life, and death, and how Roheed had thought that he, Nagaro, must somehow be Sindar returned from the dead, because he'd been a foundling.

Evran spoke. "You believe, then, that this Notep never defiled my sister, though she lived for years after she was no longer nursing his child?"

Nagaro met the other man's eyes. "I have no reason to doubt it," he said. "She'd been given the protection of Sheptuum—that's what Notep believed—because he'd dishonorably slain her husband and stolen her child. This was his punishment."

Burdal snorted. "It's a pity that the dream reader didn't tell him to return Almerin to her people instead!"

Nagaro nodded. "I agree. But I also believe that Almerin did have a comfortable life for those fourteen years that she lived. And I truly believe there was love between her and Roheed. Certainly he cared for her."

The old man's brow darkened. "How could she have loved the child of that monster?"

Nagaro studied the man somberly "I suppose because she was a good woman," he said. "Roheed was helpless, motherless—a babe who needed her. And he was innocent of his father's crimes. He didn't know her tale until she told it to him on her deathbed."

Evran smiled fleetingly. "That would have been like her, Burdal. Hers was a proud but gentle spirit."

Nagaro turned to the man. "Roheed said two things to me, Tor Evran, when he gave me Emril's ring—using the broken Common Speech he'd learned from her. He said that his father was very sorry—and this may well have been true. And he said that if I found Emril's family, I should say to them, *'Thank you for Emril. Because she was so good to me.'*"

Evran bowed his head. "I wish I could say he was welcome, but I can only think of how much I would rather that she'd come home to us. Still, I suppose it was a worthy sentiment."

Nagaro nodded. "And not unique to Roheed, I think. The tale of the brave Droviri warrior and his beautiful bride has become a part of the story-lore of the Mahuk Baar—a land where such stories are important and their lessons are taken to heart."

Burdal and Evran exchanged looks.

Kuran again cleared his throat. "So Roheed gave the ring to you at the time of your escape? When you spared his life?"

"Yes. Roheed said his father had given it to him after Emril's death."

"I see." Kuran nodded, then pursed his lips and drummed his fingers on the desk top. "And Emril—Almerin—named her child Sindar?"

"Ye-es—"

Kuran's eyes narrowed. "Which—by a remarkable coincidence— just happens to be the name of that strange young man that you have staying in your quarters—the one who speaks the Common Speech so imperfectly..." Kuran let the sentence dangle suggestively.

"*Sindar?*" His two visitors spoke in unison.

Burdal turned to Nagaro. "What is the meaning of this, Captain?"

Nagaro drew a long breath. "The young man in question is called Sindar because I suggested the name to him," he explained. "His history has certain similarities to that of the abandoned babe in the story, so I thought it appropriate."

"What manner of similarities?" Burdal's eyes were alight with avid interest.

Nagaro answered carefully. "He appears to be Kelorin—a man with light skin, gray eyes, and hair nearly as dark as mine—yet he grew up in the Mahuk Baar. When I first encountered him nearly a year ago, he spoke only Hashti, the language of the Baar. It seems he'd been a kind of slave, held captive by the people of a little village not far from Sar Tipaal, but he'd made his escape and walked all the way to Jinara before he was brought to my attention."

"How very extraordinary!"

Both of Kuran's visitors had been listening with rapt attention, and it was Burdal who had spoken.

Nagaro nodded. "Yes, I thought so as well. And what is even more remarkable is that the Hashti name this young man had gone by meant *Thing Found by the Water*, because he'd been found, as a babe, beside a stream in the forest—"

"*Vothra!*" cried Evran. "Surely this must be Almerin's child!"

Burdal shook his head. "No," he said. "It cannot be. You've forgotten about the tiger—"

Evran turned on the older man. "But the Captain said only that the tracks were there, and the child was gone! Someone could have found the babe, and the tiger came afterward!" He turned excitedly to Nagaro. "We must see this young man!"

Burdal nodded gravely. "Yes," he said. "I believe we must."

Nagaro stood up. "As it happens, I left him waiting outside the door, though I didn't know you were here." He turned to Kuran. "Since he's been free, My Lord, Sindar has acquired a single ambition—which is to be a Fleet warrior. I rather doubt you'll think he's ready: His command of the Common Speech is still very limited, though he shows considerable talent for swordsmanship. He's been very eager to speak to you about his hopes. He's extremely single-minded about it—"

"But this is just exactly like my son!" Burdal interjected. "*He* insisted on becoming a Fleet warrior, and there was never a man more certain of his mind."

Nagaro smiled wryly. "And I believe these are natural character traits in Sindar, Tor Burdal. There was nothing in his up-bringing to have engendered them."

Kuran gestured impatiently. "Don't keep us waiting, Captain. Bring the man in."

Nagaro moved towards the door, but paused and turned back to address Burdal and Evran. "I caution you not to expect too much from him, Zirdas. His mastery of our language is limited, as I have said. His manners are... rough. He has had no education at all. And, though he's been told the tale of Emril and the ring, it means nothing to him. He's shown no interest at all in finding his kin."

When he went out, Nagaro found Sindar still waiting on the bench. The young man sprang up eagerly.

"I go in now? Talk to Kuran?"

Nagaro smiled gently. "Perhaps we will talk to Lord Kuran after you meet the two men who are with him. I believe they may be your kin."

"Two man? My...*kin...?*" Sindar stared blankly. "What is *kin?*"

Nagaro sighed. "One may be the father of your father—we say, your *grandfather.* The other may be your *uncle*—the brother of your mother.

"Oh." Sindar frowned. "Do I have to meet kin?"

"I think you should, Sindar. They've come a long way and this is very important to them. And if they *are* your kin, you can't just wave them away. You're part of their families."

Sindar squared his shoulders as if bracing for an ordeal. "All right. I meet kin. Then talk to Kuran."

Knowing he could expect no more from the former slave, Nagaro led the way back into the entry hall and ushered Sindar through the doorway into Kuran's study.

Kuran's two guests turned eager eyes upon the young man as he entered the room.

Immediately Burdal uttered a cry as he rose unsteadily from his chair, the blood draining from his face. He clutched at his chest. *"By the Eyes and Ears..."* he murmured. "This man is so like my Kendral—as last I saw him—it's as if my son had come back to me!"

*

Nearly three hours later, Nagaro was back in Kuran's study, waiting for the Lord of the Fleet to return. He had finally seen Sindar depart with Evran Marvenen, and although the hours just past had been light work physically, he was surprisingly weary.

Burdal's reaction to Sindar's appearance had been quite sufficient to convince everyone of the young man's identity, but when the old man had tried to embrace his grandson, Sindar had reacted with alarm. Then, in their haste to reassure the young man, Burdal and Evran had bombarded Sindar with such a torrent of words that he'd been completely unable to follow any of it. Seeing that he clearly didn't understand them, the two merchants had then given up any effort to communicate with Sindar and had launched into their own discussion of what to do with him. Sindar, meanwhile, seeing that the two older men were no longer speaking to him, had promptly pursued his own agenda by trying to talk to Kuran.

Kuran had, at that point, brought everyone up short by declaring that he would consider Sindar for a place among the new recruits in a year's time—*after* the young man had improved his knowledge of the Common Speech. He had further suggested that learning the language should be accomplished by Sindar spending the year with his newly-discovered relatives—six months with Burdal's folk in Vered Mahir, and six months with Evran's family in Harmoth.

Burdal and Evran had both immediately seen the merit of Kuran's plan—except that Evran had insisted that Sindar must come to Harmoth *first*, since Evran's mother was old and ill, and might miss the chance of meeting her grandson altogether if there were a six-month delay. Burdal had, thankfully, acquiesced, although he'd pointed out that *his* claim was of direct descent—Sindar being entitled to bear the name of Korinos, rather than Marvenen. And at that point, Evran would have dragged a mystified Sindar away with him if Nagaro hadn't insisted that the young man needed to understand what was being proposed—*and consent to it.*

Obtaining that understanding and consent had taxed both Sindar's knowledge of the Common Speech and Nagaro's knowledge of Hashti. Predictably, the young man hadn't liked being told that he must delay entering the Fleet for another year. Nor had he been enthusiastic about spending months with people who were complete strangers to him. Once he'd come to understand, however, that Kuran absolutely would not consider taking him any sooner, he had begun to view the offered arrangement more favorably—until he'd realized that he was to go to Harmoth, a place far away from where he wished to be, in Lankura. At that point, he had again raised vehement objections.

Nagaro had nearly despaired of persuading the former slave, until someone had happened to mention that Sindar would be traveling in the carriage that waited outside. Sindar had never laid eyes on a carriage before his arrival in Lankura, and the prospect of actually riding in one excited his imagination so much that he had dropped his objection to going to Harmoth.

Nagaro massaged his forehead. He wished Kuran would appear.

It had been during the discussion of the carriage ride that Kuran had announced that he needed to inspect the two newly constructed warships, the *Swift* and the *Harbinger.* The Lord of the Fleet had left his guests in his study to finish working out their plans, assuring them of Nagaro's assistance. As he was leaving, however, he had drawn Nagaro aside to say that he had news for Nagaro's ears alone and had told him to report back to the study after dealing with Sindar's affairs.

This was what Nagaro was now trying to do.

He stretched impatiently. It had not been an unreasonable thing to leave him to deal with Sindar and the two visitors since he'd been responsible for bringing them together, but he had found it very trying. Evran had wanted to take Sindar away immediately, but Sindar had looked so alarmed that Nagaro had begged for him to be given time to collect his things and tend to his affairs (although Sindar had very few of either). To his relief, Evran had agreed to wait until after lunch. Burdal had bidden Sindar farewell, reiterating his happy expectation of seeing the young man again in six months, and the two visitors had ridden off in the carriage to take their meal at a local inn.

As soon as the merchants were gone, Nagaro had taken Sindar to the stables, where he had explained the situation to the head stableman and seen that Sindar received his wages. Then he'd found himself again trying to reassure Sindar that the discovery of his kinfolk was in fact a good thing—which he'd done over lunch in the dining hall where Taru and Pavo had attempted to add their own persuasions.

Taru had first heartily congratulated Sindar on his good fortune. "If Evran has his own carriage, he must be rich!" he'd declared. "Ye'll not want for anything, Sindar. Ye'll only have t' ask your Uncle Evran."

Pavo had then spoken to Sindar at some length, both in Hashti and Droviri. This had seemed to go well until he finished with, "I think they will be able to help you very much, Sindar. They will teach you many thing you do not know, and many new word."

At which Sindar had burst out angrily with, "Everyone say help, help, help! Lissel say *she* go to help, but I not *want* help! I want do—" He waved his hands in frustration as his vocabulary failed him. "—thing! Every-thing! *I want do every-thing my-self!*"

Sitting there in Kuran's office, Nagaro heaved a sigh. Sindar had expressed similar annoyance with Gedras's youngest daughter Lissel when Nagaro had asked about her immediately after the young man's arrival. *Poor Lissel...* He'd already written to her, through her father, to tell her that Sindar had come safely to Lankura. Privately, he hoped the young woman's interest might have waned, since the young man was so ungrateful. *Now he supposed he would have to write another letter, explaining about Sindar's newfound kin...*

In the dining hall, he had tried to smooth things over by saying, "Of course you do things yourself, Sindar. You listen, and watch, and ask questions yourself. You have learned many things that way, and you will learn many more if you keep on listening and watching and asking questions. So you need people to listen to, and to watch, and to ask." The tactic had worked well enough that Sindar had been waiting with his bag of belongings in a state of only mild apprehension when Evran and the carriage had arrived.

Nagaro had taken Evran aside and explained that Sindar's desire for independence, and his pride, were asserting themselves with a vengeance. He'd advised Evran to avoid the words 'help' and 'teach.' Then, *finally*, he had watched Sindar climb into the carriage. As the vehicle pulled away, he'd caught one last glimpse of Sindar's face at the window wearing a smile of childlike bliss as the carriage began to pick up speed. He wasn't overly encouraged. The smile would probably only last until the novelty the carriage ride wore off.

Nagaro let out his breath in a long sigh. His right hand strayed to the last finger of his left hand where Emril's ring had been. It was a relief to have finally passed it on. Burdal was keeping it for Sindar. Plainly it belonged to the young man, and just as plainly, he didn't want it—at least not yet. But one day he might wish to wed, and the saga of the emerald-eyed salamander ring would come full circle...

Nagaro's hand shifted to rest over the small, hard lump that was *his* ring where it lay hidden under his shirt, beneath the dark blue uniform tirka. Leaning back, he rested his head against the wall and closed his eyes. There was an unexpected tightness in his throat. He might, one day. give his ring as a love-token—as he imagined that his father must have given it to his mother. But unlike Sindar, he had no inkling of who that father and mother had been. He had worn the salamander ring in plain view in the hope that someone would see it who could uncover its history—and it had worked. Kuran had recognized the sign of the salamander. What if he were to show his own ring to Kuran?

It was a poor gamble, at best. His ring wasn't made of gold or set with precious stones. Its simple bronze design seemed to point to a more humble origin, not a family of wealth or prominence. And he dared not show his ring to Kuran in any case. He couldn't risk the possibility that Kuran might describe it to the king. Elgurn had seen that ring in Leyel's possession more than once during that terrible time...

A memory rose vividly to Nagaro's mind.

He was standing in the dreary little room on the palace's third floor where he'd been made to sleep. He saw the drab gray walls and sparse furnishings clearly in his mind's eye—the narrow bed, the small bed-side table on which his clothes had been laid out every morning, and the washstand with its basin of lukewarm water, sponge, and towel. In his memory he was standing naked, under the power of heskial, while the puppet part of him methodically wetted the sponge and squeezed it and ran it over his skin, starting with his face and working its way down.

Kale Fendred, one of his "keepers", was sitting at the larger table with an open book—monitoring his charge's progress while keeping his eyes averted as much as possible—when Elgurn had suddenly come in. Nagaro remembered hearing the door open and close, and catching the figure of the king with the tail of his eye, since the heskial didn't let him turn his head of his own volition. The king had murmured something in a voice too low for him to catch, but he'd heard Kale's response:

"Yes, he's a well-formed youth. She can have no cause for complaint on that score."

He remembered burning with embarrassment at the words—and at being unable to stop what he was doing, or to cover himself with the towel. His hands had continued mechanically bathing his naked skin, while Elgurn, to his horror, had come to stand in front of him, within arm's reach.

"*That's enough,*" the king had said, then frowned when this had proven ineffective, and tried again. "*Stop what you're doing, Leyel, and stand up straight.*"

At that, he had frozen stiffly upright like a statue, wet and shivering with the sponge dripping in his hand—mortified and furious—while Elgurn's glance had traveled over him. The king had reached out and idly picked up the ring that hung about his neck on its silver chain. The Leithian's pale blue eyes had studied the object for a moment, without expression, before he'd let it fall again. The pale eyes had studied his face, then, searching for something there, it seemed, but finding only the blankness of heskial.

With a grimace, the king had turned to go, pausing at the door only long enough to speak over his shoulder. "*He looks thin to my eye, Kale. See that he eats more.*"

"*Yes, My Lord—*"

"Ah, Captain. You're here." It was Kuran's voice.

Nagaro started violently, his eyes snapping open as he snatched his hand from his chest. He'd been so deeply rapt in the memory that he hadn't heard the tread of Kuran's boots on the floor as the older man entered the room.

"My Lord," Nagaro managed, rising hastily.

Kuran eyed him keenly for a moment before continuing around to the other side of his desk and seating himself. "Sit down, Captain," he said and waited until Nagaro had complied before asking, "Are you all right?"

"Yes, of course. I was just... thinking about something..."

The Lord of the Fleet considered him with some concern. "I am sorry, Captain. I can't regret having seen old Burdal be united with his grandson, but I'd truly hoped that I had found *your* grandfather."

Nagaro sighed. "Thank you, My Lord, for your good intentions. But if you'd asked, I could have told you the ring had nothing to do with me."

"Evidently." Kuran gave him a wry look. "And again, I'm sorry. I'd intended to tell you before they arrived, but the letter they sent must have gone astray. I still haven't received it and their coming this morning took me by surprise."

"How did you make the connection, My Lord? Were you acquainted with Tor Burdal?"

Kuran shook his head. "The Fleet has been buying lumber from the Korinos family since before my time. I simply recognized the salamander sign because of that."

"What about Burdal's son? He was in the Fleet."

Again Kuran shook his head. "Kendral Korinos was a few years my senior, and his career in the Fleet was brief. I would have been a green recruit, fumbling with a sword in the practice yard, the year he and his comrades were lost. The Fleet records don't say much about it either. They didn't die in the line of duty."

"I see." Nagaro bowed his head, briefly massaging his brow.

"This can't have been easy for you," Kuran continued, "watching another man find his family when you know nothing about yours. And I expect you'd be more grateful if you were in his place."

Nagaro raised his eyes. "I'd like to think so, but I don't know. Sindar has been unconnected to anyone most of his life. I don't know whether anyone ever really cared for him, while I was raised by people who loved me. And I had advantages of education and training besides. I'm not sure I'd wish to trade places."

Kuran leaned back in his chair. "I confess, Captain, I'm still surprised that Roheed gave that ring to a Droviri slave. I suspect you impressed the man."

Nagaro sighed. "I spoke with him several times, and we did each other some small services. And, having been raised by a Kelorin woman, Roheed had learned some of our speech and a little of Vothrin teaching. So he understood my words, and was perhaps prepared to favorably consider my meaning. Whatever the reason, he took it into his head that I should not be a slave even before he realized that the blood debt might apply."

"Was the blood debt... useful?"

Nagaro cast the other man a wry glance. "Actually, it complicated things. He kept trying to single me out—and I was determined not to be treated differently from my comrades."

"I see." Kuran's black eyes studied him.

Nagaro sighed wearily. "Now, of course, I could tell Roheed that there is no blood debt—because Sindar is alive."

There followed a little silence during which Kuran picked up the quill pen from his desktop and ran a finger along the feather blade. At length he looked up and met Nagaro's eyes. "I fear I must now turn to the matter I originally summoned you to hear."

Nagaro shifted. "You *fear*, My Lord?"

Kuran resumed his consideration of the quill pen. "You must keep what I'm about to tell you in confidence, for a time. I'll call a meeting of the officers tomorrow evening to give them the full information, and the rest of the men will be told after that, and only what they need to know.

"I understand, My Lord... but... what is this information?"

Kuran chewed his lower lip, still studying the quill. "The King and the Council have decided to mount a full-scale attack on Sar Tipaal, with all the men and ships that can be spared."

Nagaro sucked in a breath. He leaned forward. "*When*, My Lord?"

His voice was taut. Outside the window it was bright afternoon on the parade ground, but he felt a shadow, as if a cloud had occluded the sun. *He had hoped it wouldn't come to this...*

Kuran ran his thumb along the feather blade, his eyes still fixed upon it. "As soon as we can be ready. Their intention is that we should sail within two weeks' time."

"*Two weeks!*" Nagaro reeled backward in his chair. "So soon? We've only just returned from shepherding those three Mahuk ships across our southern border! They *might* have reached Sar Tipaal by now—barely!"

At this, Kuran raised his eyes from the pen. "I know," he said levelly, meeting Nagaro's gaze.

Nagaro's thoughts whirled, and he spoke with increasing agitation. "We have to give the Emperor more time, My Lord! Even if he acts swiftly, it will take days for any ship to sail back to us. Our fleet could be sailing south while his envoy is sailing north! We could pass each other, unseen, and all the good we've wrought by peaceful negotiation will be lost—"

"*I know!*" Kuran's black eyes were like flint, his jaw tight.

"But don't *they* know, My Lord?" Nagaro was on his feet. "The King? The Council? Can't they *see* how foolish—"

"*Captain!*" Kuran's tone was peremptory.

When Nagaro froze, the older man continued more gently. "Please sit down, Nagaro. I anticipated your reaction, knowing the stake you have in this. That's why I've taken the unusual step of telling you now—in private. You're still new to Fleet ways, and I'll overlook your outburst, but you must understand that I simply cannot tolerate such insubordinate speech in any more public a setting."

Nagaro sank back into his chair. He put a hand to his forehead. "I'm sorry," he muttered, trying to think clearly. "And I *do* understand, My Lord. I appreciate your telling me like this... but..." *If only this decision could be changed...* He lowered his hand and sought Kuran's eyes. "This is not a wise choice," he said, keeping his voice steady. "And it's worse, coming now, than when you and I first spoke of it—because we sent that message to Baalkir. It will look as if we're playing tricks. Have you tried to persuade the Council to delay until we have his response?"

Kuran emitted a bark of laughter and tossed the pen onto the desk. "It's only at their whim that I am permitted to attend their meetings! I wasn't there when this decision was made. But Elgurn knows what I think of it. I gave him some choice words earlier, and he made it quite clear he didn't wish to hear any more."

Nagaro remembered Kuran's thunderous look when they'd left the palace after dealing with the captured Mautep. His heart sank. *Had there ever been any intention of bargaining with the Emperor in good faith?* After a moment, he said, "I'm surprised that Anduar couldn't convince them to wait. Was the vote close?"

The quill pen lay where it had fallen. Kuran reached out with his forefinger and turned it in a slow circle like a compass needle, watching it. "Apparently the four in attendance were in agreement. Anduar wasn't there. He's been detained at home for some time by affairs in his Wared."

For a moment Nagaro could only stare in dismay. "How can they permit themselves to *do* that?" he wondered aloud. "To decide a matter of such importance when they're not even all *present?*"

Kuran raised his eyes again. "If four agree, the fifth is unnecessary. His vote wouldn't have changed the outcome."

Nagaro shook his head in exasperation. "But Anduar might have offered some *persuasion—*"

Kuran cut Nagaro off with a chopping gesture. "This is out of my hands," he said sharply. "And yours, Captain. The thing is done. I have my orders."

Nagaro rose again, to stand in front of the desk, breathing slowly to stay calm. "Can you at least tell me their *reasons*, My Lord?"

Kuran grimaced. "They don't think that the Mautep will ever take us seriously if we don't bloody their nose," he said wearily. "That's one reason. The other is politics: They're afraid of losing the support of the moderate members of the Leithian Faction—having already lost the support of the Brothers of the Blood. Vengeance is dear to the Leithian heart. Peace is not. They're afraid to forgo vengeance for last summer's raid on Lankura."

Nagaro considered. "I suppose there might be some truth in the first argument—though we shouldn't assume it. As for the second, these Leithians may regret pursuing their vengeance if the Emperor turns *his* vengeance on us!" He shook his head. "This course is folly!"

Kuran's face went rigid. "I told you there might be orders you didn't like when I offered you the commission, Captain," he said stonily.

Nagaro swallowed. *Had the Council been questioning his loyalty? Was Kuran questioning it now?* "You may be sure that I will follow your orders, My Lord," he said stiffly, but he seemed to read doubt in the older man's eyes.

Once again Kuran picked up the quill, his fingers picking at it blindly while his eyes watched Nagaro's face. "Considering the part you played in our negotiations with the captured Mautep," he said carefully, "I'm afraid there may be serious danger for you in this expedition. I could find a place for the you and the *Sword*, here, guarding Lankura."

"*Stay behind?*" This time Nagaro bridled. "What would I be if I did that? This mission means sailing deep into the Baar! Every man who takes part in it will be in danger. And you were part of those negotiations, too, My Lord."

"Yes, but *you* have a price on your head." Kuran's black eyes held Nagaro's. The quill was in tatters.

"But there's nothing new about that! And... what if there were a call for further negotiations?" Nagaro was thinking aloud, his thoughts leaping ahead. "My Lord, I need to be there! Peaceful coexistence might still be possible, if I could—"

"*Captain!*" Kuran had dropped the bedraggled feather. "You must not undertake anything that would interfere with the purpose of this mission!"

"But... if the mission were plainly failing, My Lord... and I saw a chance—"

"*No,* Captain!" Kuran looked as if he were tasting bile. "I must have your assurance that you will follow orders. I want to hear you swear you will not attempt anything on your own!"

"I've already sworn an oath—"

"To serve the Fleet!" Kuran interrupted sharply. "And to 'uphold the honor, laws, and interests of the people and nation of Edrovir.' But the interpretation of *how* to do that isn't up to you, Captain! Not this time!" Kuran's eyes blazed. His fists were clenched. "I must hear you swear not to act at cross purposes to this mission—*or you will not sail with us!*"

Nagaro stiffened. The words stung. *Kuran surely would not demand such an oath from his other officers!* His eyes flashed. "Then I do so swear! You have my word that I will adhere to your orders—upon my honor and in Vothra's name!"

There followed a silence that stretched, while Kuran's black eyes impaled Nagaro like twin knives and Nagaro returned the look, steel for steel. At last Kuran's fire receded. "Is this your final word, Captain?" he asked, almost sadly. "I could still order the *Sword* to remain here on guard duty, if you will reconsider—"

"I see no reason to reconsider, My Lord," Nagaro told him rather coldly. "I don't see why I shouldn't face this danger with the other men of the Fleet." He was thinking it was conceivable that Kuran's orders might change when confronted with changing circumstances... *He could do nothing if he wasn't there...*

Kuran blew out a sigh. "Very well, then," he said, sounding suddenly weary.

Warm afternoon sunlight was still pouring in through the window, suffusing the room, but Kuran's face looked gray as he reached blindly for the next paper on a stack to his left. He appeared to notice the condition of the quill with some dismay. "You may go, Captain," he said, without looking up. "And remember... don't speak of this to anyone until after I've made my announcement."

Moments later, Nagaro was striding across the parade ground. The flawless spring afternoon was lost on him. He moved under a cloud. *The orders were to mount an attack on Sar Tipaal, and he had just sworn he would adhere to those orders.* And what was worse was that it seemed to him that Kuran had hoped he would refuse to swear. *For some reason, Kuran didn't want him on this mission!* The reluctance might be partly out of concern for his safety, but there was more to it than that. Did the man trust him so little?

Nagaro's frown deepened. Was Kuran uncertain of what he, Nagaro, might do? And was that doubt, perhaps, justified? Could he himself be certain of what he'd do in every possible contingency? He wished he hadn't sworn the oath—or rather, he wished that Kuran hadn't asked it of him. Once it had been asked, how could he not have sworn?

He muttered a curse under his breath as he walked. He *had* sworn, and so he must do his best to keep his word. A second muttered curse followed the first as he realized that he couldn't even unburden himself to Taru and Pavo that evening. Everything must be kept in confidence...

18: The Mission

"That bloody old barnacle! He's changed my posting, bodger him! I won't be with ye on the *Sword*, Nagaro."

The three friends were at their usual table in the Fleet dining hall. It was the morning after the meeting at which Kuran had explained the intended mission to his officers. The midday meal had just concluded, and Kuran had taken advantage of the gathering to make the general announcement to the men that there would be a large military expedition into Mahuk waters. Although the exact objective of the expedition had been revealed to the officers the night before, it was being withheld from the rank and file until the target was actually within view to reduce the possibility that any man captured in Mahuk waters might reveal the plan to their enemies.

The announcement, vague though it was, had caused quite a stir. The Lord of the Fleet had not waited for the commotion to subside, but had departed, leaving Estevad to give the men their duty assignments. The clerk had posted a number of lists on one of the walls, each providing the crew assignments for a named ship. The lists were currently being mobbed by sea warriors, but Estevad had gone around the room and handed each of the officers his orders, folded and sealed, sparing them the indignity of joining the press.

Taru had frowningly read his posting from the paper he had been given and he now brandished the offending object under Nagaro's nose.

Nagaro took it and scanned it, striving for a neutral tone when he replied. "You're to be the first mate on the *Pride of Lankura*—Kuran's flagship. That's a step up, Taru—"

"It bloody well *isn't!* Not for me! Did he shift ye as well, Pavo?"

Pavo had needed Nagaro's help with reading his orders. He shook his head. "No. Still I am posted for second mate on *Sword*."

"That bloody bastard! Why me, then?"

Nagaro winced. "Keep your voice down, Taru, or curb your tongue. It's not a death sentence."

Taru turned on him. "Ye knew about this!" he said, accusingly. "Just like ye knew there was going t' be a mission before the rest of us. And ye didn't tell me!"

Nagaro shook his head. "No, I didn't know about your posting. But it doesn't surprise me. Kuran asked me months ago to tell him how I would split my men. I made it clear that I didn't want to part with either of you. But he asked me who I'd let go if I had to."

"And ye chose *me?*"

"Yes. *Not* because I'd rather be parted from you, Taru, but because I thought you'd fare better under another command than Pavo—because he's Hashtep and some might not trust him. Kuran saw the wisdom of it. He might very well have made the same choice if I'd said nothing."

And there was nothing, really, that Taru could say to this, especially not in Pavo's presence. So he confined himself to shaking his head and muttering, "First mate t' Captain Ruald! I'm not lookin' forward t' this."

Pavo's face was a study in neutrality. Now he broke his silence. "I do not like it either, Taru. I do not want to have strange man for first mate."

Nagaro sighed. "Nor do I. And I wonder who Kuran has assigned to me."

A rather pointed cough sounded behind them, and all three men turned on their stools to find Vell Sobring standing there. The Leithian had approached unnoticed, and Nagaro wondered how much the man had overheard.

Vell cleared his throat again and addressed himself to Nagaro after giving Taru and Pavo the barest of nods. "It seems it's to be *me*, Captain," he said. "I'm posted as first mate on the *Sword of Freedom*.

Pavo eyed the new arrival stonily and Taru managed a fair imitation of the young Hashtep's deadpan. Nagaro, for his part, regarded the tall Leithian in frank astonishment. "*You*, Vell? The rumors I've heard were naming you captain of the *Swift!*"

Vell's blond mustache twitched. "Apparently not," he said stiffly.

Nagaro winced. "Then I'm sorry for your disappointment, Zirda. I'd hoped to congratulate you on a well-deserved promotion. The words you may have overheard just now weren't intended to reflect on you. It's just that any unfamiliar man is unwelcome on such short notice. We'll have little time to train together, and we're likely to see heavy action."

"I quite understand." Vell's tone was conciliatory. "An unfamiliar posting on short notice isn't exactly welcome to *me* either—even under a captain of your talents."

Nagaro shifted uncomfortably. "You give me too much credit."

"I think not." Vell's smile was stiffly polite. "May I join you, Captain?"

Nagaro knew that Vell pssessed a naturally jocular disposition. If the Leithian's conversation now seemed forced, he hoped it was because of the young man's disappointment, rather than any lack of sincerity. "By all means," he said, with what warmth he could muster.

Vell circled the end of the table to take a seat directly opposite

Nagaro. Turning to Taru, he said, "So, I gather that you've drawn my old posting on the *Pride*. You had best go introduce yourself to Captain Ruald."

Taru rose stiffly. "I was just going t' do that," he said, casting Pavo a pointed glance. "Can't be hanging about with the fancy folk, can I?"

Pavo stood up as well. "Excuse me, Zirda," he said with absolutely level inflection. "I have some place to go."

Vell briefly watched the two men's retreating backs as they moved away, shoulder to shoulder. "A bit rude, that Turowan lad," he observed once both were out of earshot. "And the Mahuk is as stiff as a stick—and nearly as silent."

Nagaro's slender black brows drew down sharply. "I don't wish to begin our service together on a bad footing, Vell, so I'll let that go with a warning. I've told you before that those two men are my friends— besides being first-rate officers. Their histories are different from yours or mine. They're fisherman's sons. Taru can be a bit blunt when he's out of temper, but I wouldn't be parting with him if the choice were mine. And as for Pavo—he's *Hashtep*, and don't forget it. The less his folk like a situation, the quieter they get. If you don't think you can treat him with respect, I'll go to Kuran right now and tell him that I won't have you on my ship."

"Whoa now, Captain!" Vell's blond eyebrows shot up. "No need for that! Now that I know how you feel, I'll mind my manners. I've seen how smartly the *Sword* goes on maneuvers. I can tell your crew knows their sea-craft."

Nagaro gave the other man a smile resmbling a flicker of lightening in a thunderhead. "That's better." He picked up his mug of sothiril and drained it, intending to find some graceful way to end the conversation.

Vell was eyeing him warily. "You're rather a flinty fellow, it seems, Captain."

Nagaro shook his head. "Not really. But there are some things I care about."

"Ah." Vell stroked his mustache. "Speaking of caring about things, I have the impression that you don't much care for this mission."

Nagaro frowned. He'd sat silently throughout the officers' meeting the previous evening, not joining in the cheers that had arisen from some quarters. In fact, he had been so quiet that Taru had kept casting him disbelieving looks. The young Turo had pounced on him as soon as they were alone, which was how he'd learned of Nagaro's prior knowledge. It appeared that others had noticed Nagaro's silence as well.

"I have reason not to like it," Nagaro said quietly. "But I intend to do my duty."

"Huh! A good Fleet warrior, eh?" Vell cocked his head. "That's what we all have to be, no matter what our feelings—or our posting. Your two friends will have to learn that too."

Nagaro shrugged. "Of course."

Vell glanced down at the table, then raised eyes that had grown speculative. "I do think that Kuran might have given us our postings last night, don't you? Could have given us some explanation for them, too."

Nagaro shrugged again. "It's possible that he only made some of the decisions this morning."

"Well, perhaps." This time Vell shrugged. "He hasn't given *you* any explanation for my posting, then?"

"No."

"Do you intend to ask for one?"

Nagaro shook his head. "If Kuran wishes me to know, I assume he'll tell me. But I think I can guess the reason."

Vell crooked a blond eyebrow. "Really, Captain? I'd like to hear your thinking."

Nagaro met the other man's questioning look with a level gaze. "I think you're to be my watchdog," he said. "Kuran isn't sure what I might do in some situations, so he wants someone aboard the *Sword* who can take command if I step out of bounds. And you're ready for a captain's posting."

For a moment, Vell could only gape at him, then, "*Kroneg's blood!*" he murmured. "You think *that*, and you calmly sit there and tell me so? Where's your righteous indignation, man? I'd be livid!"

Nagaro sighed. "I'm not pleased. But I have to admit that I'm not sure, myself, what I might do. It would depend on the exact circumstances." He smiled fleetingly. "So I can't very well blame Kuran, can I?"

Vell frowned, then replaced the expression with an awkward smile. "Well, he's written into my orders that I'm to report to him before sailing on the *Sword*, so maybe he'll give me an explanation when I see him."

Nagaro inclined his head. "That seems likely."

Vell abruptly stood up and stuck out his hand. "This has been an enlightening conversation, Captain. I appreciate your forthrightness, and I look forward to serving with you."

Nagaro gratefully rose and took the proffered hand. "And I, with you," he said with as much sincerity as he could manage. Then he went to look at the general postings, since the crowd had largely dispersed, before going to look for his friends.

He had barely stepped out of the dining hall when Taru and Pavo appeared as if from nowhere and fell in beside him. They all struck off together across the compound.

"So ye finally got away from that stuffed peacock?" Taru's temper clearly had not improved.

Nagaro decided to let the words go. He merely nodded. "Did you present yourself to Captain Ruald?"

"I did." Taru's tone became more bitter, if that were possible. "Ye should ha' seen the look he gave me. Ye'd ha' thought he was sucking on lemons! This 'll not be an easy posting."

"It may not be as bad as you think, Taru. Most of the men I picked to let go have been assigned to the *Pride*. You'll be seeing a lot of familiar faces on that oar deck—more than Vell will be seeing on the *Sword*."

Before Taru could growl a reply, Pavo spoke up. "I do not like Vell," he said. "He is rude to Taru and me."

Nagaro sighed. "Unfortunately, Pavo, Vell was brought up by people who think themselves naturally superior—rather like the Mautep—and he says things without thinking them through. But I've given him a few choice words and I think he'll try to treat you decently."

Taru snorted. "I don't know why ye always try to make the best o' things!"

Nagaro came up short in front of the door of his quarters. "Because I'm a captain, Taru. And it's my task to see that the *Sword* sails with a crew that's ready to work together. I'm sorry you won't be on the *Sword* this time—I really am—but I want you to give your best to the crew of the *Pride*. Show them what a first mate from the *Sword* can do."

Taru stuck out his chin. "Oh, I'll show 'em, all right!" he declared. "I know *all* the Fleet commands! But ye just see if that Vell doesn't spoil things for ye. Ye'll be in a tight place, an' ye'll give him one o' *our* oar deck commands—one that Vell doesn't know—and he'll miss it. And when he does, ye'll remember what I said!"

So saying, Taru turned aside and stalked off in the direction of the quarters he shared with Pavo. The young Hashtep gave Nagaro an apologetic shrug and went after his roommate. Nagaro stared after his two friends for a long moment before fishing his key from his pocket. He fervently hoped that Taru would prove to be mistaken.

*

Fourteen days later, a dozen ships of the Royal Fleet set sail on a damp, gray, thoroughly inglorious morning. Departure had been set for an hour after dawn, but the hour was missed due to fog. Nothing could be done until the mist had lifted enough above the surface of the sea to make it safe to leave the shelter of the mouth of the River Edro.

Nagaro stood on the captain's platform at the forward rail of the *Sword's* stern castle, scanning the gloomy scene before him, feeling the slow, rhythmic forward surges that marked the oar strokes. They had no choice but to row since there was no wind, and the Fleet's drummers were marking a pace that could be sustained for some time.

The sea arround the *Sword* was as smooth as if it had been oiled.

The featureless gray layer of cloud that shrouded the sky hung so low it seemed that Kunoa, aloft in the crow's seat, could have touched it if he'd stood on tiptoe. To port, the mainland coast was discernable as a long blue-gray outline, and one of the Lomoan isles was a distant dim silhouette to starboard. Nearer at hand, and all around, were the shapes of ships. The misty air obscured the details of their forms and muted all colors so that the nearest were dark outlines, gray on gray, while the more distant were as pale as ghosts.

A step sounded on the deck, and Nagaro turned to give Pavo a nod as the young Hashtep came to stand beside him at the rail.

"There isn't much for your deck crew to do in this weather, is there, Pavo?"

The second mate shook his great head. "This morning there is not enough wind to fill teacup," he said solemnly. "That is always what Landros have say when weather is like this."

Nagaro smiled faintly. Landros with the *Sea Eagle* and her crew were somewhere out there among those gray shapes, and Geldoran was with them. The *Eagle* was still serving as the commander's flag ship. "Poor old Landros," he murmured. "Our first real action, and he's still sweating under Geldoran's eye." And Taru was out there somewhere, too, on the *Pride of Lankura*, sweating under Kuran and Ruald.

Before Pavo could respond, they heard the sound of booted feet on the ladder. Both friends turned to see Vell's blond head appear as he negotiated the last few steps. Presently, he came jauntily across the deck of the stern castle to take a place at Nagaro's other side.

Nagaro regarded his first mate with mild annoyance. "You've left the oar deck again, Vell?" It wasn't the first time the man had appeared on deck without having voiced his intention via the speaking tube.

The Leithian shrugged. "I sent young Peldred down on my way up. There's nothing for the men to do but keep rowing. Peldred knows how to give an order to ship oars—even as green as he is. And I can get down there quickly enough, I'm sure, if anything else is needed."

Nagaro attempted to un-furrow his brow. Vell was never seriously insubordinate, but his behavior seemed to be unusually casual for a Fleet officer. Ordinarily, Nagaro preferred informality. He suspected he was only annoyed with Vell because he wasn't comfortable with the man—which wasn't a good reason. Vell had come aboard the *Sword* following his interview with Kuran looking uncharacteristically sober. Since the Leithian hadn't said a word about the content of that interview, Nagaro assumed he'd been right in his guesses. If he'd been wrong, Vell would probably have told him so, even if he'd told him nothing else.

"You do have a point," he told Vell, reflecting that Taru might very well have done—and said—the same thing. "But perhaps next time you could tell me first what you mean to do."

Vell seemed not to have heard him. The Leithian was frowning up at the low-hanging ceiling of cloud. "Beastly weather," he observed. "Bad luck to get this on the day we picked to sail, wouldn't you say?"

"Nagaro sighed, and nodded. "It's rather late in the season for a fog like this."

"What do you think, Pavo?" Vell's blue eyes had suddenly come to focus on the young Hashtep. To give him credit, he was at least trying to treat Pavo like a fellow officer, even if his efforts often sounded forced.

Pavo turned his impassive gaze on the Leithian. "I think Sheptuum does not smile on our sailing," he said matter-of-factly.

Vell stiffened. "You think your god is angry because we're going to make an attack on the Mahuk Baar? Do you think Sheptuum protects the Emperor?"

"Sheptuum does not protect anyone, even Emperor, if he do bad thing." Pavo hadn't so much as blinked.

"Like attacking Lankura?" Vell was probing.

Pavo's narrow eyes became, perhaps, just slightly narrower. "It was not Emperor Baalkir who did that. It was Lord Angkat."

Abruptly Vell turned to Nagaro. "So you got that bit from *him*, did you?"

Nagaro frowned. Apparently Kuran had told Vell a few things. "The attackers' uniforms were brown and gold, Vell—Angkat's colors," he said coldly. "It was rather obvious. And Angkat has never been keen on taking orders from Baalkir." He stopped short of saying anything more, aware that he should be trying to diffuse the tension between his two officers, not adding to it. Before he could think of anything else to say, however, Vell spoke again, addressing Pavo in a more challenging tone.

"Aren't you afraid to be sailing with us, then? If you think your god disapproves of our mission?"

Pavo returned him a look that was absolutely opaque. "No, I am not afraid," he said calmly. "I am with Nagaro. Always Sheptuum smile on *him*, because *he* is such good man."

Vell's look of astonishment was comical. His gaze traveled from Pavo to Nagaro, who winced helplessly.

"I go now to check sail." Pavo made his little half bow and exited in the direction of the ladder, to all appearances completely oblivious to the effect of his pronouncement.

As the young Hashtep's head disappeared from view, Vell tugged distractedly at one side of his mustache. He gave Nagaro a quick sideways glance. "Your... *friend*... has an unusual point of view regarding you."

"I know." Nagaro sighed. "And he's so sensible about very nearly everything else, too. But it's no use arguing with him about it. I've tried."

"Well it explains why he doesn't seem to mind being here," Vell muttered under his breath. Then he shook himself. "So," he said with a brittle smile. "What do you think our chances are of making Harmoth before nightfall?"

*

"Tomorrow—as you all know—we will be entering Mahuk waters."

Lord Kuran was addressing his twelve captains in the great cabin of the *Pride of Lankura*. A few were seated on the available chairs, a few more were on the two bunks. The rest were standing. Although the cabin was quite crowded there was no sound but Kuran's voice—unless one counted the little creaking noises a wooden hull always made when afloat.

"Our plan from this point onward is to divide our fleet into four squadrons of three ships each. Each of these squadrons will be under the command of myself or one of the three commanders who are part of this mission. We will advance, one group at a time, at intervals of several hours to be sure the squadrons are well separated, and will proceed south by way of the seaward passage to rendezvous at the anchorage *here* on the south coast of the island of Paktaar." Kuran stabbed his finger at a chart spread out on the table before him. "Once the entire fleet has been reassembled, we will sail east through *this* strait—" again he stabbed a finger "—and continue to our objective, *here*, at Sar Tipaal." Kuran raised his eyes to sweep the room with his hard black gaze. "Are there any questions before I announce the squadron assignments?"

There were a number of questions and even a complaint or two. Nagaro stood silent through it all in his place near the cabin door. All of the concerns being voiced were ones that he and Kuran had already spoken of, and he was content to let Kuran deal with them. He waited only for Kuran to read off the assignments, and left the meeting as soon thereafter as protocol would allow.

He emerged before any of the others from the stern castle into the balmy, salt-scented night that swathed their anchorage off the island of Kurubaba, one of the most southern isles in the territorial waters of Jinara. They were a week out of Lankura, and at least the weather had been good for the last several days. He heard the door open again behind him, turned, and found that Landros had appeared.

"Nagaro, lad, I hoped to catch ye. What do ye make o' this plan?"

Nagaro shrugged. "I think it's as good as any—if we're to reach our objective without raising any alarm."

Landros nodded. "Aye. That's true, mate. I wish I liked the objective better, though, and that's a fact."

Nagaro nodded and sighed. "I know." There was no point in saying more. Voices and footsteps sounded, muffled, through the door behind them. Nagaro stooped to pick up his shielded lantern from the place where he'd left it beside the door. "Goodnight, Landros."

"Goodnight, lad."

Lighting his way with the lantern, Nagaro crossed the deck to one of several rope ladders hanging from the rail. He descended to the waiting longboat in which he'd come and rowed back to the *Sword of Freedom*.

Once aboard his own ship, he immediately called his officers to his the great cabin. They came, Peldred looking curious and eager, Pavo impassive, Vell stifling a yawn. He quickly outlined the plan the Lord of the Fleet had described. "Kuran himself will command the squadron that sails first," he informed them. "The *Sword* will be part of the third squadron, along with the *Dolphin*, and the *Valor*, all under Commander Strad. Geldoran will command the group that brings up the rear."

Peldred's face wore a worried expression. "So there's just three ships together? That doesn't seem very safe."

Nagaro sighed. "It's not meant to be *safe*," he explained patiently. "It's meant not to look threatening when glimpsed at a distance. No one would expect a major attack from only three ships. And since all the groups have the same number, they'll all look the same. Anyone who sees two different squadrons at different times won't realize that they're different. At least we *hope* they won't. For safety we'll be keeping out to sea as much as possible."

"Oh." Peldred looked impressed. "That's clever!"

Vell coughed. "They don't call Kuran the old fox for nothing. Shall we be off to our bunks, then?"

"That is good idea," Pavo observed. "We will have to wake up early."

Nagaro nodded and dismissed them, then sat at the table for a time after they'd gone. It surprised him that Vell hadn't remarked at all on the *Sword*'s assignment—almost as if the man wasn't surprised. *Had Kuran told Vell something in advance that he hadn't told Nagaro?* He tried not to let the thought annoy him. It also seemed odd that Kuran had placed him with the least experienced commander—if he wasn't sure what Nagaro might do. But perhaps Kuran felt that Vell's presence was enough. And perhaps Vell wasn't disturbed simply because Strad was another Leithian. The *Valor*'s captain, Brodig, was Leithian too, for that matter. Nagaro frowned, then reminded himself that the *Dolphin*'s captain was Kelorin. He decided he was worrying too much and stood up to get ready for bed.

*

A day and a half later, Nagaro was frowning darkly as he leaned on the stern rail and watched several of his crewmen working to repair the *Sword's* damaged rudder.

Taru's prediction had proven accurate after all.

The *Sword* lolled at anchor in a nearly land-locked bay encircled by the island of Osfaraad. Late morning sunlight glinted off the placid blue-green water. Behind him, and on either side, the island's low hills rose fair and green. Impressive stands of cedars grew on the lower slopes, and a charming fishing village nestled beside a simple stone quay, to which a score of small fishing boats were moored. It was an idyllic scene, but Nagaro had a tight knot of tension in his stomach.

He turned to glance up at a small figure atop the high shoulder of one of the hills. The channel that formed the entrance to Osfaraad Bay had a sharp bend where the rising buttresses of land that formed it overlapped one another, making it impossible to see the open sea from the quiet anchorage where the *Sword* now lay. The lookout on the hill was placed high enough to get a view over both of the arms of land that flanked the channel.

Turning again, Nagaro squinted upward against the light to check the progress of another group of seamen aboard the only other ship in the bay, the *Valor*. They were rigging a replacement for the top quarter of the mainmast of Commander Strad's flagship. Frowning still harder, he returned his attention to the repairs on his own vessel.

The rudder shaft had been drawn up so that its lower end was clear of the water, and three men, perched on a plank that had been lowered over the rail on ropes, were preparing to remove it from its housing so it could be hoisted to the stern castle deck where two more men waited to receive it. Questions and directives were flying back and forth. A great slab of wood—the newly-fashioned portion of the rudder blade—lay on the deck already, waiting to have holes drilled for pegs to join it to the broken part that was still attached to the shaft.

"How much longer, do you think, Bouno?" Nagaro inquired of one of the men on the plank.

The weathered Turo looked up from his precarious perch. "Maybe an hour, Capt'n—maybe two—but no more 'n that."

"Good. It looks like the men on the *Valor* have nearly finished the splinting, though they still need to get the spar back into place."

"Aye, well, they had the easier task by half. If they hadn't had to go ashore t' cut that piece o' timber, they'd ha' been finished already."

Vell's tall blond figure appeared at the top of the ladder from the main deck. He crossed to where Nagaro stood, taking a place at the rail beside him.

"Going well, is it?"

"As well as can be expected."

Vell studied Nagaro's brooding face. "Listen," he said, "I'm really sorry that I didn't know what to do with that order. What was it again? 'Starboard, stop. Port, full ahead?' Half the men seemed to know what it meant and the other half didn't." Vell's chagrin appeared quite genuine.

Nagaro made an effort to relax his brow. "It wasn't a Fleet order, Vell, so you couldn't have known it." He struggled to keep his expression neutral. Taru would have known. But even Taru might not have been able to execute it in time when half the crew had never heard it before. "We only use short-coded orders like that in a tight spot when there isn't time for the usual kind. I needed something to happen fast and I said it without thinking."

"Oh, well, all right then. It was bloody bad luck, anyway, getting a storm that sudden—with winds that strong—this time of year, wasn't it? At least Captain Brodig got his oars shipped in time."

Nagaro nodded moodily, his gaze tensely sweeping the peaceful scene. Today Lokundas smiled, but the previous afternoon had been a different story... *And today's peace might be interrupted in a different way at any moment...*

The storm had blown up very suddenly indeed, catching the *Sword*, *Valor*, and *Dolphin*, on the seaward side of the islands where there was no shelter. Since the three ships could have been blown onto shore, Commander Strad had ordered them to turn in between two islands, seeking a safe harbor. Whether the wind had been funneled by the space between the islands, or had just increased its intensity by merest chance, wasn't clear. And it didn't matter, really. All Nagaro knew was that they'd suddenly found themselves being lashed and driven by the force of it. To make matters worse, the channel had proven rocky, not easy to negotiate even in fair weather. It hadn't been a time or a place to have canvas spread, and Pavo's crew had luckily gotten the *Sword's* sails furled before the worst gusts struck. The deck crew of the *Dolphin* had done very nearly as well, but there had still been men aloft in the *Valor's* rigging when a screaming blast had struck, with the three ships sailing close together for the sake of communication.

Nagaro had found the *Sword* with a mass of rocks to starboard, the *Dolphin* ahead, and the *Valor* bearing down on her stern, driven by the force of the wind in her half-furled sails. His hastily shouted command had been intended to pivot the *Sword* sharply to port, driving her through the space between the *Dolphin* and still more rocks. It was the only action that could have saved the *Sword* from being struck from behind by the *Valor*. But Vell hadn't understood the order. Nagaro had shouted for his steersman to jump clear, and Captain Brodig on the *Valor* had managed to get his vessel turned enough to spare the *Sword* from her ram. But the action had put the *Valor's* port oars in jeopardy and Brodig had barely gotten them shipped before her port side had collided with the *Sword's* stern, snapping the *Sword's* rudder blade.

Things might not have ended there, either, if the top of the *Valor's* mainmast hadn't chosen that moment to snap under the strain, bringing down her remaining canvas. Four of the flagship's crew had gone down with the mast-top and yardarm, and only three had been pulled from the water. Somehow the three ships had managed to limp into the safe anchorage of Osfaraad Bay, with the *Valor* trailing her main yardarm in the sea and the *Sword* steering by means of her oars.

While Nagaro had been standing lost in this recollection, the men manning the ropes at the stern rail had begun hauling up the rudder shaft. Bouno and the other two men on the plank now scrambled over the rail. Nagaro shook off the memory. "Come on," he said to Vell. "We should give them room to work."

The two officers descended to the main deck, where they met their third mate.

Nagaro immediately addressed the Leithian youth. "Have Pavo and his party returned with the water casks, Peldred?"

"Not yet, Captain."

Vell raised an eyebrow. "You think there's trouble there?"

Nagaro shook his head, glancing towards the shore. "Everything's quiet. I'd just rather have them aboard, that's all." He beckoned to his first and third mates, then, and led the way to the forecastle deck. "I want a better view," he told them. "Of the lookout, and... other things."

As it happened, the forecastle deck was a good place for the three officers to speak privately at that moment, since the crewmen were all elsewhere. Vell followed Nagaro to the rail, Peldred trailing after him.

The older Leithian cleared his throat. "You really do not like this place, do you, Captain?" he said as he came up beside Nagaro. "You're as nervous as a cat with kittens."

Nagaro answered without taking his eyes off of the figure of the lookout on the hill. "I explained my objections to Strad last night. I was overruled."

A frown briefly crossed Vell's features. "You don't think much of the commander's orders, do you?"

Nagaro's head came around at that, and he eyed Vell narrowly. "I haven't entirely agreed with any of the decisions Strad has made since he first decided to make for Osfaraad," he said carefully. "But I've followed orders. If we're lucky, all may be well. If we're not, we may be very neatly trapped here."

Vell spread his hands. "Well, the harbor entrance *is* narrow" he admitted. "And there *is* the town there, as you say. But the shelter's much better here than on the other side of the island, and the townsfolk are all staying inside—afraid of us, I suppose. I haven't seen a single fishing boat go out all morning."

Nagaro's brows drew down darkly. "I've put freed Hashtep slaves ashore on Osfaraad a dozen times, and I have *never* come into this bay. The anchorage on the north side of the island is more open, it's true, but from there you can *see!* And you can *run*—in any direction. Here we're like flies in a bottle! Flies with our wings clipped."

Peldred had come up on Nagaro's other side. Now he blinked. "But, Captain, if the other anchorage is so open, surely it wouldn't be as good for making repairs. The water's so calm in here—"

Nagaro flung a hand skyward. "Does it look like we need a place *this* calm? On a day like *today?*" Seeing Peldred shrink back in dismay, he quickly added in a milder tone, "I'm sorry I snapped, Peldred. I'll admit we would have spent a less comfortable night at the north anchorage— until the wind died—but we could be making our repairs there this morning without any trouble at all. *And*, if the winds had kept blowing all night," he added, seeing Vell open his mouth to raise an objection, "We could still have come around to this bay at first light. There'd be fewer ships abroad on a blustery day, and I'd be far less worried about being in here."

"It's a fair bet no one saw us come in here yester-eve," Vell ventured. "And no reason to think any Mahuk warship will just happen by."

"No, I don't expect we were seen coming in—except by the folk in that village." Nagaro jerked his head shoreward. "But they are quite enough to worry about. And the *Dolphin* sailed out this morning under a clear blue sky." He frowned. The *Dolphin* had been sent to tell Geldoran what had happened. *Sailing alone, and reducing the strength of those left behind, not to mention breaking the pattern of threes...* That was another of Commander Strad's orders that he'd taken exception to.

Vell raised his hands. "The *Dolphin* sailed hours ago! If anyone had seen her, they'd be on us by now. It's obvious she got away clean. That's why Strad has called back his own lookout. And as I've said already, the villagers aren't going anywhere."

"Not that you can *see*," Nagaro observed darkly. "Not with *these* boats. But these houses all have back doors, and these are not the only fishermen on the island, either, or the only boats. There are plenty of little coves and inlets around the shore—" Abruptly he broke off. "Here comes Pavo and his crew with the water casks, and they're rowing fast and hard!"

Vell had already begun to look a bit worried. Now he cast a glance at the longboat that had just been pushed off from the sand beside the quay. The men rowing it did indeed seem to be plying the oars rather vigorously. "They're probably just eager to get back aboard," he said, with what sounded like not quite complete confidence. "The lookout hasn't given any—"

A distant shout interrupted him. The lookout high on the hill was signaling wildly with his arms.

"*Keshaal!*" Nagaro was staring fixedly at the gesticulating figure of Kunoa, the lookout.

"What is it?" Vell also had his eyes on Kunoa. "He's using that pirate code of yours, isn't he? What's he saying?"

"Three ships! To the east and coming this way! And he's coming straight down now, so they must be close." Nagaro's eyes sought Pavo's longboat. It would soon be drawing alongside. Without another word, he sprang for the ladder that led to the main deck.

Vell and Peldred exchanged glances.

"I wish the commander hadn't sent the *Dolphin* away." Peldred was plainly trying not to sound frightened, but his voice quavered. "Three against three would have been even odds."

Vell nodded grimly. "I know," he muttered. "Don't tell Nagaro I said so, but I'd rather have kept the *Dolphin* here as well." He hurried after Nagaro with Peldred on his heels.

19: The Incident At Osfaraad

The first thing Nagaro did was send two men in the second longboat to fetch Kunoa. Then he turned his attention to Pavo's party. Their longboat had pulled alongside the ship in the meantime, and the men aboard her were hefting one of the water casks into the hoist that had been lowered.

"What news, Pavo?"

The second mate looked up at him, the tension plain in his usually impassive face. "Captain, we must go from here now!" he said urgently. "One freed man we have brought to this island have taken risk to talk to me. He says three ship of Emperor Baalkir were seen close by here only two day ago. And he says two boat have gone out from other side of island to look for them this morning, very early."

Nagaro's jaw tightened. "Kunoa has just signaled that he saw three ships coming—signaled and made for the beach." A hurried glance in that direction revealed that the young lookout had reached the sand. The longboat Nagaro had sent was halfway there, with the two oarsmen pulling frantically. Nagaro spun about, looking for his other officers. Vell and Peldred were both standing right behind him. Peldred's eyes were wide with alarm and the older Leithian's face registered dismay as well.

"Vell, get your crew below decks!"

Vell stared at him for a moment as if distracted, then seemed to focus. His jaw worked. "I should stay on deck until the order comes from Commander Strad," he said woodenly.

Nagaro stared in his turn. With difficulty he managed to stfle the urge to say *Bodjer Commander Strad!* Strad *was* technically in command of both ships, and Vell presumably had his orders. So instead he turned to his third mate. "You, then, Peldred," he said. "Get below and man that station!"

The young man actually jumped. He glanced uncertainly at Vell, but apparently got no help from that quarter, for he turned back to Nagaro and blurted, "Aye, Zirda!" then bounded away, without giving any order to the men on deck.

Nagaro rolled his eyes and spun again. Cupping his hands to his mouth, he shouted, "All oarsmen get to your benches!" Amid the trample of feet that followed, Nagaro strode past Vell, moving farther along the rail to give himself a better view of the *Valor*'s deck. He cupped his hands again. "*Commander!*" he bellowed, "*Commander Strad!*" He saw the man, distinguished by his white-blond hair, turn towards him and shade his eyes. "We have to sail, Commander! My lookout saw three Mahuk ships coming. Very close. There's word Baalkir may know we're here!"

On the deck of the *Valor*, Commander Strad cupped his hands in turn. "What word?" The question carried across the glassy water.

"Pavo Maat talked to one of the islanders!"

There was a little pause and then the Commander shouted back, "I want to finish our repairs." Strad turned his back to the *Sword*, and looked up at the top of his mainmast. Some of the *Valor*'s crewmen were in the process of hauling the big yardarm up the mast and into position, where it would then have to be secured.

Nagaro stood with fists clenched. "He doesn't need the bloody spar to make a run out of here," he muttered through his teeth. "There isn't a breath of wind!"

Vell seemed to have been studying him. Now he turned and raised his hands to his mouth to voice a shout of his own. "Commander! If the Hashep is worried, I think we should be too!"

For answer, all he got was, "This won't take long."

Vell gave Nagaro a rueful glance and a shrug. "Thought he might listen to me."

Nagaro snorted in disgust. He turned to see that Pavo's men were just finishing with the last water cask. A glance towards shore told him that the men he'd sent with the second longboat had Kunoa aboard and were rowing back to the ship.

"I'm going to check the rudder," he said tightly to Vell. "When the lookout gets here, send him back to me—and get down to that oar deck!"

He began to move in the direction of the stern castle, but Vell suddenly stepped around him and barred his path. The Leithian's face was contorted. "I'm sorry, Nagaro—" he began. Then he stopped, and his expression changed. He seemed to try again. "Just tell me—are you thinking of sailing without an order from Strad?"

Nagaro's eyes blazed. "I'm going to do my best to get that order!" he snapped. "And no, Vell, I will *not* sail away and leave the *Valor* to defend herself alone—not without a direct order to do so!" He began to move again and this time Vell got out of his way.

Atop the stern castle, he found a knot of men still busy with the new rudder blade. Bouno, the steersman, looked up from the drill he held, and shook his head in response to Nagaro's question.

"Not yet, Capt'n. I've drilled two holes, see—top an' bottom. But there's still these other two."

Nagaro frowned. "We may have to sail any minute, Bouno. What if you put it on right now? With just two pins? Would it stand service for a little while?"

The old Turo squinted thoughtfully. "I suppose she *might* hold, if ye was *gentle* with her," he ventured. "But ye couldn't go putting her *hard over*, mind."

"Then do it, Bouno. We don't have time to wait." Nagaro paused, considering. "Can you rig some lashings around it, too? I don't want to lose that new blade if the pins snap."

Bouno grinned. "Oh, aye, Capt'n. I was going t' do that anyway. To hold her while the pitch set. 'It'll have t' be thin line—"

"Yes, I see that! This is just until we have time to mend it properly."

Nagaro left the steersman and his fellows to the work, and mounted the Captain's platform. He put his mouth to the speaking tube.

"Peldred!"

"Aye, Zirda!" The third mate's voice came hollowly from below.

"Open the oar ports, and put the oars out—just hold them at the balance point."

"Aye, Captain!"

Through the speaking tube, he could hear the order being repeated. Behind him, he heard the solid *thock, thock* of a mallet as the wooden pins were driven home. A glance at the main deck showed him that Pavo and his men were all on board and securing their longboat to the deck. The other longboat, bearing Kunoa, was nearing the *Sword's* side.

Nagaro shifted tensely from foot to foot, and he turned his gaze again to the *Valor* to check on the progress of the other vessel's main yardarm. He felt a brief surge of hope. *The spar was being lowered.* Had Strad perhaps decided not to finish the task after all? *But no...* When he squinted harder, he could see that one of the crewmen had gotten out a chisel and was applying it to the mainmast. There must have been something wrong with the shape of the mast-seating.

"*Bishka!*" Nagaro swore. He glanced over his shoulder. Behind him, two crewmen were readying the mended rudder to be lowered over the stern rail. Bouno and the other two must already be down there, on their plank.

When he turned again, Kunoa was coming over the rail. Vell all but pounced on the young lookout, gesticulating. Nagaro could catch the urgency of the Leithian's voice, but not the words. The agitated tenor of Kunoa's response was similarly evident. Presently the young Turo broke away, making for the mainmast and his appointed post in the crow's seat. It was Vell who turned and made for the stern castle.

Nagaro frowned in annoyance. Could the man never just follow an order?

Vell sprang up the ladder and crossed to the captain's platform in a few long strides. His extreme alarm was apparent both in his haste and his expression. "It's the Emperor!" he exclaimed, running a worried hand through his hair. "The banners are all red and black, and one of the ships is also flying a gold flag with some kind of symbol on it that Kunoa says is Emperor Baalkir's.

Nagaro knew that symbol, just as Kunoa did. It was burned into the skin of his left shoulder. He felt a further tightening of the growing knot in his stomach. "How close are they?" he asked impatiently.

"They could be very close by now. He says they came around the end of the island across the way, rowing fast and making straight for this bay! He let out a yell as soon as he could make out their course and their colors. Ah... here's the spyglass."

Nagaro took the foot-long cylinder distractedly and slung it about his neck. If Baalkir's ships were *that* close, he wasn't likely to need it. He reached for a speaking trumpet that hung from a hook on the railing. Directing it towards the deck of the *Valor*, he shouted, "Commander Strad! Lookout confirms three of Emperor Baalkir's ships, making for this harbor! They could be here any minute!"

He had the satisfaction of seeing a number of the men on the other ship's main deck jump, and begin to move as if in alarm. One of them he thought was Captain Brodig. Commander Strad's tall, blond figure stood conspicuously still in the midst of the commotion, however. Nagaro saw the Commander look up at the top of his own mainmast. The seamen who were busy there had stopped dead upon hearing Nagaro's cry. Now Strad made a motion for them to continue. Then he turned to face the *Sword*. Cupping his hands to his mouth, the Commander shouted back, "We'll sail as soon as we're finished. Make your ship ready, Captain!"

Vell burst out, "*Kroneg's Blood!*" then cast a guilty glance at Nagaro.

Nagaro returned the Leithian a thunderous look. "Do *you* have anything more you can say to him?"

Vell opened his mouth, and shut it again. "No," he muttered. "You couldn't have made it any plainer, and it's not my place to tell him how to run his command."

A tentative cough sounded behind them, and they both turned to find Bouno standing there. "All finished, Capt'n," Bouno reported. "Can't promise she'll hold for long, but we can't do better. Not without a deal more time."

"I know, and I appreciate what your men have done. Now get them all to their posts."

"Aye, Zirda!" Bouno saluted and spun away.

Nagaro turned back to his first mate. "And now, Vell—*if* you don't mind—will you please go down to the oar deck?"

Vell was looking uncomfortable, fingering his mustache. "Nagaro... I don't know how to say this—"

Abruptly Nagaro lost his temper. "I don't care what your orders are, Vell! I'm going to have to move this ship *very* soon—and *very* fast—and if the rudder goes again—*which it probably will*—I'm going to have to steer with the oars! I need someone more experienced than Peldred down there handling the oar deck. Or do you think you can do better up here with Peldred or me down below?"

Vell stood frozen with his fingers still on his mustache. Presently he seemed to become aware of them and self-consciously dropped his hand. "No, Nagaro," he said, as if measuring the words. "I *don't* think that I can do better up here." He sounded almost relieved. "You're the best man to have on the captain's platform right now. Carry on, Zirda!" And with that, he turned and made for the ladder.

Nagaro made an effort to untwist the skein of his anger. He would consider the implications of Vell's behavior later. Although, when he thought about it, he couldn't recall the man having addressed him as "Captain" once since they'd entered Mahuk waters... He pushed the thought aside. If Vell was contemplating taking over command, at least he didn't seem very eager to do it.

There followed a wait that felt interminable, though Nagaro knew it was only his mounting apprehension that made it seem so. Vell's acknowledgment that he had arrived at his post came quickly enough. After that, there was simply nothing to do but watch the painfully faltering efforts of the *Valor*'s crewmen, as they dealt with the seating of the mainmast spar while the moments ticked away. Nagaro paced the captain's platform—three strides right, and three strides back. He tried to visualize the distance between the nearest island and the entrance to Osfaraad Bay... Tried to guess how much time had passed since the three ships had been sighted... How much of that distance they might have already covered...

Below, on the main deck, Pavo was also pacing back and forth. Presently, the Hashtep approached the stern castle. "Captain," he called up to Nagaro, his tone uncharacteristically anxious. "Should I put my man up in rigging, to be ready? It do not look like we will need sail."

"I know, Pavo, but there thight be more wind once we're out of the bay. Send them up, but tell them to be ready to come down and fight."

"Aye, Zirda!" Pavo saluted and strode away to convey the order to his men.

Nagaro resumed pacing. After a few turns, he ordered the anchor weighed. Commander Strad had bidden him make ready to sail, and there certainly wasn't enough wind to worry about drifting.

After a few more turns, he issued orders to Vell, via the speaking tube, for a few subtle motions with the oars.

"What's happening?" Vell's interjected question sounded alarmed.

Nagaro laughed shortly. "*Nothing at all*," he said bitterly, into the speaking tube. "I'm adjusting our heading to align perfectly with the harbor entrance, that's all."

"With the oars?"

"There's no *wind*."

"Ah. Right." There was a pause, and then, "Nagaro? Would you mind keeping me informed of whatever's happening up there? It's bodjering awful just waiting down here where I can't see a bloody thing!"

Nagaro smiled grimly. *This* was something he understood. "I'll do my best, Vell," he replied, with sympathy. "But if things start to happen fast, I can't promise."

Finally, after much too long, the spar was in place atop the mainmast of the *Valor*, and Commander Strad shouted across to make ready to sail. Nagaro muttered under his breath that the *Sword* had been ready for a quarter of an hour. Aloud, he shouted back, "*Aye, Zirda!*"

The commander had his speaking trumpet now, so his words rang out like a bell across the intervening water. "The *Valor* will lead, Captain. You follow!"

Nagaro winced as he shouted a second acknowledgment. Into the speaking tube, he said, "Hold the oars ready, Vell. We wait for the *Valor* to lead."

"*Bloody Hel!*"

Nagaro suspected he hadn't been meant to hear Vell's muttered reaction, so he ignored it. He waited impatiently while Captain Brodig ordered the *Valor's* oar ports opened, the oars extended, and her anchor weighed. At last the *Valor's* oars dipped and she began to move. Nagaro let out a pent-up breath and gave the order to row.

The two ships gathered way, their oars steadily rising and falling. Within the bay, Nagaro kept the *Sword of Freedom* as close behind the *Valor* as he dared, watching tensely for anything unexpected that might require a sudden change of course. As the *Valor* approached the inner mouth of the channel, her captain swung her into a wide turn to port, anticipating the channel's bend. Nagaro issued his own order to his steersman a few moments later. "Full point to port, Bouno—gently!"

"Aye, Capt'n!"

Nagaro tensed as the old Turo put the tiller over. To his relief, the imperfectly repaired rudder held. Putting his mouth to the speaking tube, he explained to Vell. "I'm turning a little tighter than the *Valor*. We'll go into the channel a quarter point off her port stern."

As the *Sword* swept easily through her turn, the channel began to come into Nagaro's view, a relatively narrow stretch of sparkling blue, embraced by the arms of Osfaraad. The arm on the left rose as a rocky bluff, out of deep water, while the one on the right sloped more gently. The water was shallower there, a light turquoise marking the presence of shoals. In that moment, as the channel began to come into his view, Nagaro couldn't help offering up a prayer—to no god in particular—that they would find the passage empty. If they could just get out into open water, they had a chance of outrunning the Emperor's war galleys, even if the three ships were near the harbor entrance.

But Lokundas must have been laughing. Even before Nagaro could see the whole width of the channel, the warning cries rang out aloft simultaneously from both ships' lookouts.

"Ships! Three ships!"

"Mahuk warships! Dead ahead!"

A few seconds later, Nagaro saw the first of them emerge. A sleek war galley, rowing briskly, glided from behind the left-hand bluff. She was no more than fifty yards from the *Valor*. The black and crimson banner atop her mainmast fluttered in the breeze of her own passing. Painted on her prow was a gaping red mouth with cruel white teeth that gave her the look of a hunting shark.

Cries of alarm rose from the men on the deck of the *Valor*, and were echoed by the members of the *Sword's* main deck crew. Pavo shouted an order, and the men aloft began immediately to descend.

The sounds of the shouting must have carried indistinctly to the oar deck below, becasue Vell's voice came urgently through the speaking tube. "What is it, Nagaro?"

"We've met them in the channel! They're nearly on top of us!"

"The Mahuk? All three of them?"

"Yes!" The other two warships had already come into view. The three craft were sailing in close formation with the Emperor's flagship, identified by the golden banner that flew from her mainmast, the last to make its appearance.

"That's not good, is it?" This last was Peldred's distraught question, and surely not addressed to Nagaro, though he heard it plainly through the speaking tube. He heard Vell mutter some response to the youth.

No, it wasn't good. Nagaro's heart was already in his throat. It was too late to escape without a fight... and two ships against three was not good odds—not when you had no advantage over your foe in position, skill, or armament...

"Slacken the pace a little, Vell!" he shouted. "The *Valor* is slowing."

He could see Commander Strad's big, blond figure standing atop the *Valor's* stern castle beside Captain Brodig.

The Commander turned towards the *Sword*, cupped his hands, and shouted: "You go to port! We'll go to starboard. If you get by, don't wait.

Make rendezvous!"

"*Aye, Zirda!*" he bellowed back. "Vell, Strad's splitting us up. Give me all speed. Now! And tell them to lean on those starboard oars—drive us to port!" He glanced over his shoulder. "Bouno, put the tiller over to port as hard as you dare!"

"Aye, Zirda!" "Aye, Capt'n!"

Vell and Bouno acknowledged the orders.

Strad's strategy was an uncertain one at best, although Nagaro at least understood it. They might divide their enemy's efforts by going in different directions, and one might escape. Still, they were nearing the narrowest part of the channel—where it was no more than twenty yards wide. There was little room to maneuver.

As the oar deck crew responded, the *Sword* surged ahead, veering left—but something quickly became evident that Strad probably hadn't foreseen. The three Mahuk craft had been sailing almost in a line when they first appeared, then had begun to fan out across the width of the channel, presumably to better ensnare their prey. Now, however, there came shouts from the warriors on their decks, and all three enemy ships altered course—towards the *Sword*.

The enemy war galleys were less than forty yards from the *Sword's* prow and the distance was closing fast.

"*Keshal!*" Nagaro swore. "They're all coming for *us*, Vell! Letting the *Valor* go. More speed! Bouno, hold the tiller over!"

"*Kroneg's Blood! Why*—" Vell cut off his question to give the order, and Nagaro had no time to spare for an answer, though he thought he knew.

Thirty yards now, and it was plainly no good. The *Sword* couldn't avoid meeting the Mahuk craft by swinging more to port because she would run onto the rocks at the base of the cliff. The *Valor* was sailing wide and clear to starboard, completely ignored, her only concern to avoid the shoals in the shallower water. And the shouts from the Mautep sea warriors were becoming louder and clearer, until Nagaro could at last make out the words:

"*Shaku Raal! Shaku Raal!*"

Nagaro felt a cold hand on his heart as his suspicion was confirmed. "Vell!" he cried. "They want *me!* For the price on my head. The *Sword* was Baalkir's ship!"

I'm going to be the death of us all, he thought. *No! Don't think about that... Just keep trying to get us through this...*

With an effort, he forced himself to focus on the three ships in front of him. The two leading war galleys were maneuvering in an effort to flank the *Sword*. The one to port had moved to try to cut her off, while steering clear of the rocks, there, that edged the channel. The Emperor's flagship had swung a little to starboard of the other two and was lagging slightly, though not enough to be of any help.

"*Nagaro!*" Pavo shouted up to him from the deck below as he waved one of the speaking trumpets. "Let me tell slave to put up oar—to let us pass, in name of Kiraam Shaku-Tal!"

Nagaro's heart leaped briefly, but then he felt a wrench of anguish. "No Pavo!" he cried. "We can't save them, and they would be punished!" *Doubtless brutally*...

There was still one thing he could try.

"Hold the starboard oars in the water for two strokes, Vell!" he shouted. "Bouno, put her hard over to starboard!"

"Aye, Zirda!" The words came in unison from Vell, below, and the steersman, behind him.

The ship shuddered and began to turn hard.

Nagaro held his breath.

But he heard the rudder pins snap and knew he'd lost the gamble even before Bouno cried, "No good, Capt'n! The rudder's gone!"

Nagaro ground his teeth. "Lash the tiller, Bouno. And ready your sword!"

Under the influence of the oars, the *Sword* had swung to starboard, but neither far enough nor fast enough to save her. The Mahuk galleys were only twenty yards away, and the *Sword* rode at an angle across their course. She couldn't hope to get clear of them in time, and if she turned any further at this late juncture, she'd only be in more danger from her enemies' rams. Nagaro didn't imagine that the Mautep meant to sink the *Sword*. They would much rather reclaim her. Indeed, the two flanking ships were already slowing, preparing to grapple and board.

Nor did Nagaro wish to see his ship go down—to end all their lives in the sea instead of with their swords in their hands. Accordingly, he took the only course that remained to him, though he felt a weight in his stomach like a stone.

"Hold the port oars in the water, two strokes, Vell. *Good!*"

The *Sword* swung back to port, her course parallel to those of the two closest Mahuk craft. These now neatly flanked her path to port and starboard, so close together that their sides would nearly brush those of their quarry. The Emperor's flagship, a little farther to starboard, was turning and closing—clearly intending to bring her forces to bear upon the *Sword* as well.

"Steady ahead..."

Nagaro was moving now in a waking nightmare. Moving, because to stop would be to admit that he was as good as dead. *They were all as good as dead*. One ship against three was impossible odds... and the Fleet way was to die fighting... *Don't think about it!*

"Prepare to ship oars on my word!" he shouted.

Through the speaking tube he could hear Vell repeating his orders, but then the Leithian interjected a desperate request for information.

"What's happening, Nagaro?"

Nagaro felt his heart beating in his chest like a hammer of doom. Leadenly, he answered, "We're going to be taken, Vell. The rudder broke. I couldn't save her, but we'll get the chance to fight."

"*Kroneg's Blood!* What about the *Valor*?"

Nagaro risked taking his eyes from the two nearest Mahuk craft to look. "She's well away to starboard. They don't want *her*, Vell."

"She's not turning back?" Vell sounded incredulous.

"No! The order was to make the rendezvous if either ship got clear." His attention was back on the ships in front of him. It was time. "*Ship oars!*"

"*Aye, Zirda!*" Vell knew better than to risk delay when he heard that tone.

The *Sword's* oars were pulled in, just in time to prevent them from being riven to splinters as the two Mahuk craft passed close along each of her flanks.

Nagaro leaned close to the speaking tube and raised his voice so it would carry both above and below:

"*All men on deck! Final defense position! We're about to be boarded from both sides!*"

He waited just long enough to hear Vell's harried acknowledgment, then vaulted over the railing to the main deck below. He landed in a crouch and straightened, just as the grapples began to fly.

The waters of the Osfaraad channel lay incongruously still under the brilliant midday sun as the four ships came together. The Mautep had ceased shouting as they made ready for their attack. In the sudden quiet, half a dozen grappling hooks bit the wood of the *Sword's* port rail with a series of crunching thuds, and a few seconds later, an equal number came pelting down on the starboard side. Nagaro shouted to Pavo's main deck crew, and the deck erupted into action as they engaged in a brief struggle to dislodge hooks and fend off boarders. There weren't nearly enough crewmen for the task, working both sides of the ship at once and with the number of attackers they faced. The only function of resistance was to delay the inevitable long enough for the *Sword's* oarsmen to get on deck and into formation.

In those seconds, the *Sword's* rowers came pouring out of the aft hatch and through the stern castle door to form a defensive arc across the width of the deck from rail to rail with the wall of the stern castle at their back. Nagaro barked an order and Pavo and the other main deck crew fell back to take their places in the double line of men. This was the final defense position, well-practiced by all Fleet warriors—though every man of them hoped he would never have to use it.

Nagaro stood at the front and center of the line, on his guard, his sword ready in his hand. Only once did he check the position of the men. Then he returned his eyes to the scene before him, ready for the foe... Ready to face his end...

And all these men would die with him, because they had taken ship with 'Shaku Raal'...

On his left stood Pavo, as solid as a rock. On his right was Vell, standing pale and grim-faced, with Peldred just beyond him, white-knuckled and wide-eyed with fear. He knew that Tredhold was there too, beside Pavo, and that old Bouno and young Kunoa were at his back.

Sword blades bristled all along the line.

With a chorus of wild exultant cries, the Mautep sea warriors came surging over both rails and charging down the deck.

"Now, by the Mark on Kroneg's brow, we will show them how to fight!" Vell muttered. "We'll send their souls to Hel, and feast together tonight in Seralind!"

Behind him, Kunoa whispered hoarsely, "Soon I will see my father in Hanuroa—"

Nagaro drew a long breath. "Vothra be with me now and guide my spirit," he murmured. "I fear my time has come." *And guide the spirits of these other men...*

"It is not yet, Nagaro." Pavo's voice was strangely calm, even as the Mautep storm was about to break upon them. "You will see. Sheptuum will not let you die for Strad making all those bad order."

Nagaro had time to do no more than frown in response, because the storm of steel was breaking.

"*Death to you, Slave Dog!*" The words, spoken in strident Hashti, sprang from the mouth of the Mautep who led the charge. The man dove at Nagaro with leveled sword. Nagaro's first stroke turned the warrior's blade aside. His second silenced the man's mouth forever. The warrior fell, but another leaped instantly to take his place, screaming, "*Shaku Raal!*" even as he went down, pierced to the heart.

Several more came after that, but they still came one at a time— each trying to be the one to slay Shaku Raal, the one who would claim the price Lord Baalkir had placed on Nagaro's head. And that was their undoing. If they had all come together, it would have been different...

And the rule of the moment was to kill as many as you could, before you died...

The thought appalled Nagaro. He tried to distance his mind from the bloody work his hands were doing. He was dimly aware that there was furious fighting all along the line... that Pavo and Vell were both very busy with their blades.

Eventually his assailants must have realized that attacking one-by-one wasn't working, and three of them came at him at once. Pavo instantly came to his aid, even as Nagaro dispatched the center man before the Mautep could blink. Pavo took on the second the man, and Nagaro closed with the third. His blade rang twice—and the man went down, though not before cutting Nagaro on the left arm. He was bleeding through his shirt sleeve, but he took no notice.

Pavo had killed his man in the meantime, but another one came at Nagaro with a triumphant cry, emboldened by the sight of his enemy's blood. All along the line, men stepped back to watch what they fancied would be Nagaro's end. Cries arose in Hashti on every side.

"Demon swordsman bleeds!"

"Sheptuum favors Fakaar! Fakaar will finish him!"

Unfortunately for Fakaar, Nagaro believed in neither the favor of Sheptuum nor the omen of drawn blood. The warriors who turned to look did so only in time to witness the death of Fakaar.

Nagaro yanked his blade out of the body, and came back on his guard, crouching, looking for the next attack. Instead, he found that all movement had ceased, and all eyes were on him. The bodies of the men he had slain lay strewn before him. The last three piled on top of one another, forming an obstacle that hampered any further assault. In all that melee, he had given not an inch of ground.

Nagaro felt sick. His heart beat like a hammer—not entirely from exertion—and his breath came raggedly. Hasty glances to right and left showed other corpses scattered along the line, some clad in scarlet, others in royal blue. Unconsciously Nagaro took note the latter—five—the *Sword's* fallen. The blade in his hand ran blood.

And this was wrong... that so many should die for the life of one man...

That the crew of the *Sword* would die was certain. This lull couldn't last, and the press of scarlet-clad warriors that filled the deck before him was wide and deep, too many for his eye to number. They'd surely send a dozen against him now, and once he was gone, the Mautep would turn all their attention on the others. The end would not take long.

Unless... There was one thing he still could try.

Nagaro raised his left hand, palm open. In a firm voice, speaking in Hashti, he cried, "Hold! Tell Emperor I want to talk!" He repeated the words in the Common Speech so his own men could understand.

"*Kroneg's Blood, man!*" Vell muttered between his teeth. "What are you doing?"

Nagaro didn't take his eyes from the crowd of waiting Mautep. "My life is surely forfeit, Vell," he murmured. "But perhaps I can bargain for yours."

Nagaro's pronouncement had caused a little stir among the Mautep, lengthening the pause, and now there was a greater stir as the crowd of sea warriors parted and a man stepped through.

He was perhaps fifty years of age. Although not particularly tall, he was impressively broad in the shoulders, and he moved with an unmistakable air of command. His tunic was divided vertically—scarlet on the left, pure gold on the right. He wore both sword and dagger, though both were still sheathed, and he stepped fearlessly forward to stand at the very front of the Mautep line, directly before Nagaro. There he stopped and crossed his arms. The man's face was tawny like all of his people, and broadly handsome, though as expressionless as if carved from stone—except for the black eyes, which blazed with fierce intelligence.

Even before the man spoke, Nagaro hadn't the slightest doubt that he was in the presence of the Mautep Emperor. Beside him, he heard Vell suck in his breath, and Pavo murmured, "*Great Sheptuum!*" in an awed whisper.

"I am Baalkir jir-Akaan, Emperor of all Mahuk Baar. You fight well, Droviri, but if you are man who calls himself Kiraam Shaku-Tal, you will die this day!" The words were addressed to Nagaro, and spoken in Hashti. The voice was deeply resonant, commanding, entirely in keeping with the man's appearance.

Pavo had recovered enough to hastily clear his throat and translate, more for the benefit of Vell and the others than for Nagaro.

Nagaro bowed to the Emperor—from the waist. It seemed wise to show respect. He was in the man's power, and Baalkir was a man who had, by skill of arms and of command, made himself the ruler of a nation. As he straightened, Nagaro spoke, using the Common Speech because he was more sure of it and because he was aware of Vell, standing beside him. "I am Captain Nagaro of the Royal Fleet of Edrovir. Some other men call me Kiraam Shaku-Tal."

Baalkir did not wait for Pavo's translation, but raised his right hand without turning. He beckoned with one quick, commanding gesture to someone behind him and said, "Roheed! Come!"

A second man moved through the ranks of Mautep. This man was much younger—in his mid-twenties—shorter than the Emperor by an inch and much slighter in build. A narrow, neatly-trimmed mustache graced his upper lip. Even had Baalkir not named him, Nagaro would have immediately recognized the Emperor's nephew.

The intervening years had done nothing to alter the young man's features, though he moved now with greater confidence, and there was more gold on the collar of his scarlet tunic. He advanced quickly, as if anxious to comply with the Emperor's request, coming to a precise halt close to his uncle's right hand. He leaned his head close to the Emperor's ear—speaking words too low to reach Nagaro—then straightened and stood to attention, his face as expressionless as a mask.

A spark of hope had kindled in Nagaro's mind at the sight of Roheed, but it quickly died. Though the young man's glance had plainly fallen on him as he approached, Roheed had shown no hint of recognition, let alone of sympathy.

The Emperor's eyes had not moved from Nagaro's face, and now he spoke again in his own tongue. "Speak then, Kiraam, before you die. Speak as you will, in your own tongue. This man understands your word and will make them known to me." He indicated Roheed with a negligent wave of his hand.

Nagaro winced inwardly as Pavo translated for the benefit of Vell and the others. *Kiraam* meant "thief." It was a little better than *shaku,* meaning "slave," for the Mautep had respect for a successful thief. But a thief that was caught would be swiftly punished. The use of the word also underscored Baalkir's perceived grievances against him.

He drew a long breath, and said, "Lord Emperor, we will surrender now if you will swear on your honor and in the name of your god that all of my men will not be slain, and will be honorably ransomed to the King of Edrovir."

Roheed's face acquired a look of concentration. He spoke low and at length into Baalkir's ear. The Emperor's face darkened. "Do you dare to speak of King of Edrovyr and honorable ransom in one breath?" he inquired angrily. "Your king asks ransom for man of Mahuk Baar, who have made attack in *his* water, yet he sends his own warship into *mine* before he hears my answer!"

Nagaro's heart sank as Pavo rendered this into the Common Speech because he had understood enough to get the gist. Baalkir was reasoning exactly as he had feared the man would. As he debated how to reply, he heard Vell beside him make a startled sound when he understood the translation.

"Lord Emperor," Nagaro began after a moment, "sometimes honor needs trust, and trust may need to see many deeds." He was choosing his words carefully, knowing that Roheed's command of the Common Speech was not as good as Pavo's. "Here there are not enough deeds for trust, yet I will trust the honor of Emperor Baalkir without seeing his deeds, because I hear his honor is great." He felt Vell's hand urgently on his arm, but his attention was on Baalkir.

The Emperor's eyes narrowed shrewdly as he listened to Roheed's murmured translation.

"What of you, Kiraam Shaku-Tal? If you surrender and I spare all your man?"

Nagaro's throat felt tight. He said, in Hashti this time, "Do with me what you will."

"So I will have your life, Kiraam? But, already it is in my hand."

Nagaro gestured at the fallen men lying at his feet. In the Common Speech, he said, "How many more do you think we can kill before you kill us all? I offer my life as price for all my men's lives. Do you prefer to buy my life with the blood of many of your men?"

The Emperor frowned when he understood. There was a pause while Baalkir appeared to consider.

Vell took advantage of the pause to murmur urgently, "Nagaro, this is very irregular! Surrender is not the Fleet way. And can we really *trust* this man?"

Nagaro returned him a level glance. "His honor should not let him break the oath I've asked of him, Vell. But if he *is* false, you may suffer dishonor as well as death. Since I am dead in any case, I will leave the choice to you. If you'd rather follow the Fleet way, then take command and I promise to give you the best service of my sword. But if you let *me* choose, I'd rather spend my life trying to save the lives of these men who wouldn't be in this fix if they hadn't shipped with me."

"You really mean that, don't you?" Vell's face was pale. His clouded gaze revealed his conflict. He glanced about at the men, well aware that some of them had overheard the conversation. Several of them looked back. Pavo appeared to be listening closely. Peldred's face was ashen— the youth was barely nineteen. None of the men spoke. Vell swallowed visibly. "We'll do it your way, Nagaro," he said, "Carry on, Zirda."

The Emperor had been in deep conference with his nephew, but now he seemed to have finished. It was Roheed who addressed Nagaro: "Lord Emperor ask you, Kiraam, on what do you swear what you have promise?"

"I swear it on my honor, and in the name of Vothra."

Roheed turned back to the Emperor and there followed a very rapid and extended exchange, in which the Hashti word for honor— *kajadeem*—figured prominently. Nagaro stood frowning. He had no idea what account Roheed had previously given of their final encounter at Jaamra, or what the young officer might be telling his Emperor right now concerning the honor of Kiraam Shaku-Tal. He half expected to be told that his honor wasn't good enough.

The Emperor, however, nodded in apparent satisfaction when at last Roheed stopped speaking. His response was a rapid rumble.

Roheed turned back to Nagaro. "Lord Emperor say, he will take your life if you make surrender. He say he promise to ransom all your man—except he make no promise for Hashtep called Pavo Maat. Pavo Maat must face judgement."

Nagaro stiffened. "Pavo Maat is an officer of the Royal Fleet, and a citizen of Edrovir!"

Roheed shook his head. "Lord Emperor make no promise for Pavo Maat!"

Pavo had moved slightly at the first mention of his name. Now he spoke with flat inflection. "It is all right, Nagaro. If you die, I do not wish to live."

"*Pavo!*" Nagaro was stricken.

The young Hashtep met his gaze, and his narrow dark eyes were very bright. "If I live or if I die, I will trust to Sheptuum," he said simply. "But Sheptuum will not let you die this way. You will see."

Roheed had been translating this exchange, and the Emperor's brow had constricted in apparent puzzlement. Nagaro swallowed past a lump in his throat. He respected his friend's choice, but didn't share his optimism. He took a breath and addressed Baalkir directly.

"Lord Emperor, I will accept these terms if I hear you now swear to them as I have asked."

Roheed's translation drew a nod from Baalkir. The Emperor spoke, then, in ringing tones, and Nagaro didn't need Pavo's rendition to know that the man had given him what he'd asked for.

When he had finished his oath, the Emperor extended his right hand to point at the deck in front of him. "Put your sword there, Kiraam, if you accept."

Nagaro felt the cold hand of death on his shoulder. He bent, wiping his sword blade clean on the nearest scarlet tunic. With a deliberate motion, he sheathed the elegant weapon. Then, stepping around the pile of corpses, he took two strides that brought him to a point a few feet in front of the Emperor. For a moment he met the man's eyes. Then he unbuckled his sword belt, and stooping, he laid the Sword of Shofeer at Baalkir's feet.

As he straightened, a sudden gust of wind sept across the deck, ruffling hair, fluttering tunics, and singing ominously in the rigging.

20: Urchak's Revenge

Landros finished scanning the sea and islands lying ahead of the *Sea Eagle* and lowered the glass. "Nothing to concern us," he reported. "If ye'd like to take another look at that chart, Commander, now 'd be the time."

Beside him, Geldoran nodded. "All right, Captain."

The two men stepped down from the captain's platform and made for the ladder to the main deck, Landros leading the way. The day was fair and the sails fully spread to take advantage of what little breeze there was. The rowers were supplying most of the ship's forward way with light, firm strokes. Landros was halfway down the ladder when, without warning, a powerful blast of wind struck the ship, causing the sails to belly and strain at their lines. The *Sea Eagle* shuddered and heeled so violently that Landros, taken by surprise, was flung from the ladder. His head struck the ship's rail as he fell and he landed sprawling, stunned, on the deck.

Geldoran, at the top of the ladder, was nearly thrown from his feet by the sudden lurch, but he managed to catch hold of the stern castle rail. Seconds after the ship righted itself, he was down the ladder and kneeling at Landros's side as an excited babble of voices broke out all across the main deck. The crewmen were responding to half a dozen mishaps, but Geldoran's call for the ship's doctor to attend the injured captain took precedence.

The doctor, a lanky Keloran named Albured, knelt beside Landros where he had fallen. He looked up after a quick examination. "I only find this mark from where his head hit the rail," he declared, indicating a sharp red welt above Landros's right brow. "One o' ye fetch some water, and I'll see if that brings him around."

The water, when it arrived, was sloshed liberally across the face of the unconscious man. Landros stirred a little, without opening his eyes. "*Bodjerin' bilgewater,*" he mumbled thickly. "*If 'm not dead, 'n nobody else is dead either, what're ye doin' inside my head?*"

The healer looked startled. "I'm not sure I liked the sound of that. Do ye know what he's talking about, Commander?"

Geldoran shook his head, frowning. "It sounded like nonsense to me, Albured. Let's move him to the great cabin." He turned to his second mate. "Tell all of the men to take extra care moving about the ship for at least the next hour—in case we get any more gusts like that."

*

Nagaro was fighting a growing sense of unreality. He had watched while Vell and all the others had laid down their weapons, making the surrender complete. Pavo's hands had been bound behind him, and he'd been taken away to one of the other ships. The young Hashtep had given Nagaro one last brave glance before being led away. The other members of the *Sword's* crew—except for the two remaining officers, Vell and Peldred—had been bound also, but with their hands in front of them, and marched through the door of the stern castle and down into the oar deck below. More than a few of those who had joined the Fleet with Nagaro had given him agonized looks before passing from sight. The face that haunted him the most was Tredhold's. The healer had looked for a moment as if he'd been contemplating some desperate act, but he must have seen the futility of it. He'd gone quietly in the end.

Nagaro still found himself unbound, although he'd been divested of his royal blue uniform tirka by a direct order of the Emperor. The symbolic significance of that was obvious. Being a captain in the Royal Fleet wasn't going to help him. He was now standing in his shirt sleeves, where he'd been placed, directly in front of Baalkir. There were armed Mautep on either side of him and more behind him as well. Roheed and various other men who appeared to be officers stood with the Emperor. Vell and Peldred, both with their hands still free, had been placed some distance to one side, close enough to hear all that passed but not close enough to interfere. A half dozen armed Mautep surrounded the pair, making it clear that no chances were being taken. More Mautep, rank upon rank, stood all around, filling most of the *Sword's* main deck.

Roheed had been speaking at length with the Emperor, but now the conversation ceased and the young Mautep approached Nagaro, coming to a halt in front of him and addressing him.

"This is time for you to hear all your crime." Roheed's face was without expression. His voice was perfectly level. Although he met Nagaro's glance, his eyes were hard and they betrayed nothing. "Also is time for you to say any thing you can say, to make answer. Other two Droviri"—he indicated Vell and Peldred—"are here to see and to hear all that happen." *A little pause.* "Do you understand?"

"Yes, I think so."

Nagaro heard himself as if in a dream. His thoughts seemed to float outside the moment. Apparently what was about to transpire was a kind of trial, or hearing, and the other two officers were witnesses. *At least it appeared that Baalkir meant to keep his word regarding the fate of the other men—otherwise why bother having two of them watch this?* It was something, too, that he'd be allowed to speak, though he doubted that he could say anything that would save his life—not when Baalkir considered his actions to be crimes.

Roheed had returned to his place beside the Emperor, and Nagaro suddenly realized that Baalkir was speaking. He strove to focus on the Emperor's Hashti.

"...already you have said you are man called Kiraam Shaku-Tal. So you are thief. Do you repent of this crime? Or do you try to deny it?"

Nagaro waited through Roheed's translation, partly for the benefit of Vell and Peldred, but also to confirm his guesses at the meaning of the Hashti words he had interpreted as "repent" and "deny." As soon as Roheed finished, he answered.

"For everything that I have done, I have good reason. I am sorry for nothing—except that, with all that I have done, there are still slaves in the Mahuk Baar."

Out of the corner of his eye, he saw Vell flinch at this speech. It had not been, perhaps, the wisest thing to say to the Emperor, but Nagaro doubted it would matter in the end. And if he was to die, he would at least speak his mind.

The Emperor's immediate response to Roheed's translation was a short, mocking laugh. He gestured briefly at the Sword of Shofeer, still lying sheathed at his feet.

"Did you think you could free all slaves? With *this?*"

Nagaro shook his head, without even waiting for Roheed to finish translating. "No, Lord Emperor," he said. "That victory will not be won by one sword, or by many. It will take something stronger than swords."

Roheed's brow darkened as he translated Nagaro's words, and the Emperor also frowned when he understood. Baalkir spoke quickly to the younger man, who turned again to Nagaro.

"Emperor ask, what you think is more strong than sword?"

Nagaro spread his hands. "Words," he said simply, and as he did so, a second gust of wind swept over the channel, rippling the glassy water and pressing the white cotton of Nagaro's shirt against his side.

The wind caused some muttering among the Emperor's men, but Baalkir ignored the second gust as he had ignored the first. The ships had all dropped anchor in the channel and were thus in no danger of being blown against the rocks, so what did a little wind matter? Baalkir regarded Nagaro with narrowed eyes. "Perhaps you are not so much fool," he conceded in his sonorous Hashti, "But you are still thief. You have stolen more than eight hundred slave from lord of Mahuk Baar!"

Nagaro waited as Roheed translated, although he had understood. Vell tried to say something, but was cuffed into silence by one of the men guarding him. The number of freed men sounded roughly correct to Nagaro, counting all the ships he and his men had taken since the battle of Jaamra. Of course, he hadn't personally freed all those men, but that wasn't the point. He returned Baalkir a level stare.

"A man cannot steal from you what you do not own, Lord Emperor."

This bold statement made Vell flinch visibly, and it seemed to cause Roheed some difficulty. The young Mautep officer appeared hesitant, for the first time, in the translation he provided to the Emperor. He gave Nagaro a reproachful look. Nagaro returned an unrepentant gaze.

The Emperor's response was an angry one. Roheed rendered it as, "Emperor say that all lord of Mahuk Baar have swear oath to him. So to steal slave from any lord is same as to steal slave from Emperor."

Nagaro shook his head, perceiving that he'd been misunderstood. He sought to explain.

"The law of my people says that no man may own another man... that it is a crime to make men slaves. I have made men free, and it is right that they should be free."

Roheed's translation this time was even more hesitant and halting than the previous one had been. The Emperor glowered and produced an utterance that Nagaro understood without translation.

"You have made Hashtep slave free too. Not only Droviri!"

Nagaro let Roheed finish his version before calmly nodding. "Yes," he said. "Freedom is right for all men."

The Emperor's black eyes narrowed when he understood. "Hashtep slave are thief! For their crime they belong to me!"

Remembering Vell and Peldred, Nagaro once again waited through Roheed's translation before answering. "To my people, making a man a slave is a much worse crime than stealing a loaf of bread to feed yourself."

Roheed seemed by this time to have gotten himself better in hand. He hesitated only slightly before delivering his stony rendition of this provocative statement.

"*Basirah!*" The Emperor's anger was obvious, and he went on at some length. Roheed apparently decided to summarize, for his version was considerably shorter.

"Lord Emperor say he have heard enough about law of Droviri. Law of Mahuk Baar say you are thief of slave." The young Mautep sounded as if the last three words, "kiraam shaku-tal"—the name he had first bestowed upon Nagaro at the battle of Jaamra—now tasted bitter in his mouth, and he hesitated noticeably before finishing with, "For this you will die."

Nagaro didn't allow himself to flinch at hearing this pronouncement, knowing that the Mautep way was to show no emotion in the face of adversity. Evidently he might say as much as the Emperor would allow, but the outcome of this hearing wasn't really in doubt. Vell seemed to sag where he stood as he understood the uselessness of argument.

"Do you deny that you have stolen Sword of Shofeer?" The Emperor demanded, pointing at the weapon where it lay on the deck.

Following the translation, Nagaro spread his hands. "The warrior who carried that sword fell into the oar deck and broke his neck. The sword fell where I could put my hand on it. I have used it with honor, and surrendered it with honor, and I have fought many men for the right to carry it."

For the third time, a gust of wind swept the deck, and this time it didn't die completely, but continued to blow, though lightly. Again there was a stirring among the onlookers, and again the Emperor paid no heed. Roheed seemed to be having some difficulty with his translation, but at length the Emperor understood. He spoke sternly.

"Only Mautep should carry sword of Mautep! Other man do not have right to fight for this sword."

Nagaro heaved a small sigh. "Men have fought me for it all the same, Lord Emperor," he said. "And I believe all men are born equal under the sun."

"Basirah!" the Emperor declared, again, when he had the translation. The word meant "enough." He swept the matter of the sword aside with a wave of his hand. "You have also stolen gold, and other rich cargo— and you have stolen four ship!"

Again Nagaro sighed. "The gold I took from warships of the Mahuk Baar was stolen from Edrovir, and most of the other cargo was stolen as well—from Edrovir, Jinara, or Hran. These things—and the ships—I have taken to pay for the work I do, which is to make slaves free, because it is a crime against all people for you to keep slaves."

This time, the reproach in Roheed's eyes was unmistakable. He left Baalkir's side, approaching Nagaro, and lowered his voice. "You should not say such thing to Lord Emperor," he admonished.

Nagaro returned the other young man's gaze rather coolly. "If the Emperor is going to kill me for what I have done," he explained, "I think he should know my reasons. If you don't wish to tell him, then I will try."

"No!" Roheed hastily raised a hand. "I tell him." The young Mautep returned quickly to Baalkir's side, and there followed a rapid exchange between the two men, which Nagaro couldn't follow. From the few words he did catch, it seemed that Roheed was trying to explain, not only about the gold and the ships, but also what Nagaro had said about stating his reasons. Roheed must have been somewhat diplomatic, since the Emperor did no more than frown. In the end, however, he once again dismissed everything that had been said with a gesture and the words, "This does not matter." With that, he raised his hand again, beckoning, and said commandingly, "Urchak tok-Faar, come forward!"

The ranks of the Mautep immediately parted to allow the newly-summoned man to step through. Again Nagaro would have known the man at once, even if he had not been named. The former captain of the *Fist of Death* was moderately tall and powerfully built. He was a little gray about the temples now, and it seemed to Nagaro that there was a little less gold on his tunic than there had been at Jaamra. His most distinguishing feature, however, was the black leather eyepatch that covered his left eye. As he stepped through the crowd, the gaze of the man's good eye riveted itself upon Nagaro, burning with such hatred that Nagaro's heart quailed. If Baalkir had listened to *this* man, it did much to explain the Emperor's attitude.

Urchak came to a halt exactly where the Emperor indicated, and stood, continuing to glare at Nagaro.

The Emperor spoke. "Urchak tok-Faar, here is thief that stole your ship at Jaamra. I give him to you. Show me how you punish unrepentant thief and disobedient slave. Please me, and perhaps I will give you back your ship as well."

Nagaro understood enough of this speech, even without Roheed's translation, to make his stomach turn over. He had dared to hope that his execution would at least be mercifully quick, but he doubted Urchak was in a mood for mercy. *Oh, Lokundas,* he thought, *why do you send me such an end?*

Roheed was taking some time with his translation, but Nagaro was only half listening. He was scarcely aware of the murmuring among the assembled Mautep—of Vell's movement, then Peldred's exclamation. It wasn't until a number of the Mautep began to point at the sky above the headland on the other side of the channel that he bothered to turn his head to look.

The wind had been freshening, bringing with it some weather out of the north. Looming beyond the headland could now be seen a billowing mass of cloud, whiter than purest snow above, with a thunderous gray shadow underneath.

*

Albured dabbed carefully at the bruise on Landros's forehead with a dampened rag, then draped the cloth over the edge of the basin set on the floor beside his stool. He bent over the unconscious man lying on the bunk. With cautious fingers he began to probe the wound, feeling the bones beneath the skin.

Landros's head moved from side to side, as if in response. "*Ge' off me...*" he muttered indistinctly. "*Can't listen when ye do that...*"

Abruptly, the ship lurched and tilted under another gust of wind, spilling some of the water from the basin and nearly tipping Albured from his stool. The healer caught at the edge of the bunk for support as the ship righted itself.

Landros's hand moved to grasp the bunk edge at nearly the same time, colliding with Albured's, and his eyes immediately snapped open. "Bodjer! I've lost it!" he exclaimed much more clearly, and sat up. "How do ye expect a man to concentrate on what's being said to him, if ye keep poking at him and knocking him about?"

"Knocking you about?" Albured stared at Landros in astonishment. "That was the wind, Captain. Now please hold still while I examine your head." He reached out again to put his hands on Landros's brow.

Landros brushed the hands away impatiently. He rubbed absently at his forehead. "There's nothing wrong with my head," he said crossly. "Perfectly ordinary little bump, that's all."

"I... I think you ought to lie down, Captain Landros. You've been unconscious, and... and talking to yourself... for the last half an hour."

Landros gave the healer a look of extreme displeasure. "I was not unconscious," he said patiently. "And I wasn't talking to myself, either. I was talking to the Spirit. And I would be still, if ye hadn't kept poking—" He suddenly stopped. "Did ye say *half an hour?*"

"Aye, Captain."

"Bloody Hel!" Landros was on his feet and making for the door. "We have to set course for Osfaraad!"

"Captain, I really think you should lie down!" Albured flung himself after Landros, catching his arm.

Landros shook him off and grabbed for the door handle. "We have to make for Osfaraad, I tell ye! They're going to kill him!" He yanked the door open and plunged through it, almost into the arms of Commander Geldoran who apparently had been about to enter.

"What's this?" Geldoran caught Landros by the shoulders. "What did I hear about Osfaraad? And who are they going to kill?"

"He's out of his head, Commander!" Albured pressed through the doorway, catching at Landros from behind.

"I bloody well am *not!*" Landros protested indignantly. He stopped trying to push his way on along the passage and addressed himself to Geldoran with exaggerated reasonableness. "The *Sword* has been taken at Osfaraad, Commander. Nagaro surrendered to the Emperor—traded his life for the lives of his crew—and the Emperor's going to kill him! If we hurry, there's a chance we can stop them."

Geldoran looked from Landros to Albured, and back again. His hands remained on Landros's shoulders. "Steady now, Landros," he said. "You're not making a lot of sense. What would the *Sword of Freedom* be doing at Osfaraad? That's well off our course."

Landros shifted impatiently. "That storm we had last night caught 'em in a bad place. The *Sword* lost her rudder—and the *Valor* her main spar. They put in at Osfaraad for repairs."

"Well, I suppose they *might* have done that—"

"Not *might* have! They *did*, I tell ye! Strad sent the *Dolphin* off this morning to tell ye about it."

"Landros!" Geldoran looked exasperated. "Nobody here has seen the *Dolphin*. How do you think you know these things?"

"The Spirit told me! I was talking to Vothra, until this meddlesome healer interrupted!"

Geldoran's face froze. Behind Landros, Albured said, "Ah... maybe you *dream*ed about talking to Vothra, Captain..."

This time Landros looked exasperated. "It wasn't a dream! That bump stunned me a little, see, and Vothra caught me just as I was waking up, and held onto me—" He gestured vaguely. "That's how the Spirit explained it." He turned back to Geldoran. "But that's not important, Commander. What matters is, we've got to set a course for Osfaraad to save Nagaro!"

Geldoran looked uncomfortable. "Ah, Landros, the healer, here—"

"*Hel's bilge!*" Landros swore. "Ye don't believe me, neither one o' ye!" He tried to shake Geloran's hands from his shoulders, and succeeded because just at that moment another lurch of the ship threw Geldoran off balance.

Landros managed to stay on his feet, and he dodged past Geldoran, traversing the tilting passage and bursting out of the door at the other end, just as the ship righted itself. Cupping his hands to his mouth, he bellowed, "*All hands set course for Osfaraad!*"

"*Belay that!*" Geldoran thundered, emerging from the door behind him. "Captain Landros, get back to your bunk! That's an order!"

All across the deck, men stared. The closest was the second mate, the sturdy old Turo named Rubo. He cleared his throat and addressed Geldoran. "Ah, Commander, the *Dolphin*'s just come out from between the islands over there." He pointed. "But she's seems t' be all by herself."

For a long moment there was no sound but the slap of waves against the ship's hull.

The *Dolphin* was in fact there, plain for anyone to see, not more than a quarter mile ahead and headed towards them. The *Sea Eagle* was making fair way on a southward heading with a light wind in her sails. The other two ships under Geldoran's command, the *Swift*, and the *Morning Star*, were matching that course off the *Eagle's* starboard beam. The long coast of an island was slipping past to leeward and the sky to the south was still clear and blue, though there were clouds gathering behind them in the north, threatening bad weather to come.

Landros had been staring at the *Dolphin*, his face gone pale under its weathering. Now he squinted at the sun, moving towards its zenith and still clear of the rising cloud-bank. "It's nearly noon," he muttered. "That ship's terribly late in coming. She left Osfaraad at the first hour o' the morning. And they sighted the Emperor's ships two hours later. But Nagaro was still alive when Albured interrupted me..." His voice trailed.

Albured had come up to stand beside Geldoran and was staring at the approaching *Dolphin* in stunned silence.

Geldoran glanced briefly at Albured and wiped his brow with the back of his hand. "Captain Landros," he said quietly. "You may disregard my last order." He turned to the second mate. "I want more speed, Rubo. Pass the order down to the oar deck. I want to see what tale the captain of the *Dolphin* has to tell. And while we're waiting to hear that," he added, addressing Landros. "I think you had better tell me anything else your talkative spirit had to say—about how the *Sword* was taken, and what's happened to the *Valor*..."

*

Nagaro stood numbly while one of the Mautep bound his wrists behind his back. Urchak had ordered it done, though it was the crooked-nosed slavemaster, Baruk, who was doing it. There were a number of men apparently under Urchak's command, and Nagaro had instantly recognized the *Fist of Death's* old slavemaster among them. Both Urchak and Baruk were obviously approaching their appointed task with relish, although at the moment, the one-eyed captain had gone back to the Emperor's flagship to attend to something, leaving Baruk in charge.

Baruk had first removed Nagaro's shirt by the simple expedient of slitting the garment from neck to waist with his knife and ripping off what remained by brute force. The blade of the knife had nicked the skin of Nagaro's belly in the process, and there was a thin trickle of blood running down, soaking into the waistband of his pants. He scarcely felt it. Baruk had then instructed him in broken Droviri to remove his boots. Nagaro had complied without protest, with the result that he now stood barefoot and bare-chested, clad only in his dark blue uniform pants. The significance of this was all too clear. If Urchak's men hadn't bothered to add a leather ankle cuff and iron chain, it was probably because there was no point in wasting the effort on a slave who would soon be dead.

Nagaro shivered in the wind that now blew continuously across the deck of the *Sword of Freedom*, though he wasn't cold. He was thinking about dying—in this time, and this place—wishing he had been given a few more years to pursue the things he'd set in motion... Wondering whether they would continue without him...

Would Kuran go back to sinking Mahuk war galleys? Would both Mautep and Fleet warriors continue fighting to the death, rather than surrender...?

Most of the crowd of Mautep that had filled the *Sword's* main deck had dispersed. Many had gone with the Emperor, back to his flagship. Roheed had been one of those. A few remained, perhaps as future deck crew. And a contingent of eight grim-looking sea warriors continued to stand guard over Vell and Peldred. The latter group was quite close by, since the role of the two Fleet officers was apparently still to witness Nagaro's fate. Vell stood tensely, his eyes alternately glancing at the sky and coming back to rest on Nagaro with an expression that revealed his disapproval of the way another Fleet officer was being treated. Peldred just stared at Nagaro, looking sick.

A small part of Nagaro's mind was aware of them. It was unfortunate that the two men were being made to watch this... *especially Peldred. The third mate was so young... and this wasn't likely to be pretty...*

Nagaro was not afraid of dying, as such, but he felt considerable trepidation regarding the manner of it. He wondered what it would be like to experience the void—the place of darkness, between lives... To become aware of all the past lives his spirit had lived... *To see the life he had just left as only a chapter in a much longer book... with all of his hopes, regrets, and unanswered questions reduced to nothing more than notes scribbled in the margins...*

Baruk had finished tying his wrists and was now waiting for some word or signal, while jerking at the end of the rope and talking to his prisoner tauntingly in Hashti. The word shaku figured frequently in Baruk's monolog, but Nagaro wasn't listening. He was wondering if it would even matter to his spirit, once it was in the void, that he had never known who his parents were. And then he wondered what it would be like to be born again as a tiny helpless babe—knowing nothing of all of this. *At least he'd probably know who his parents were the next time...*

Thinking about babies and parents made him think of Narei, and thinking of her made him think of all the people he would never see again: *Narei, and Animara and her family... Taru and Pavo... Tredhold and Landros... and, yes, Kuran, too. And of course, Nevien...*

Ani's family had flourished before he had come into their lives, and would continue to thrive after he'd gone. He knew that. And Narei would be well cared for. Ani would raise her well, he had no doubt. *But he'd told his daughter he would come back to her, and Lokundas was about to make it a lie... and Narei was too young to understand...* A shadow crossed his heart, but there were things that couldn't be helped.... *best to follow a different thread...*

Kuran, he thought, might regret his loss. And Tredhold and Landros would grieve for a time, but they would still go on with their lives. Taru would miss him, but Taru was not a sentimental man. He would go on. Nagaro felt more regret for Pavo. He could only hope that Pavo's belief in Sheptuum would sustain him through whatever fate awaited him, whether immediate execution, or being chained to an oar...

And Nevien?

Strange as it was, he felt the most regret for leaving the princess. Nevien had so much ahead of her that would be so difficult. There was her mother's worsening illness, possible death... the prospect of another loveless marriage... and of one day becoming queen... He was sorry that he wouldn't be there to offer his support in whatever way he could...

"Move, shaku!"

Baruk gave him a hard shove towards the area of the rail where the *Sword* was lashed to the Mahuk flagship. Nagaro blinked and shivered. Around him, men were stirring and words were being spoken in Hashti. Rapt as he'd been in his own thoughts, he had missed the coming of some messenger or signal. He started forward in the direction he had been pushed. Mautep guards flanked him. Baruk came behind him with more guards.

Vell and Peldred were also being moved by their guards, in the same direction, with the result that Nagaro's path converged with theirs. As both groups reached the ship's rail, there arose some argument among the guards about how to negotiate crossing the rail—perhaps regarding which group was to go first. The question didn't interest Nagaro in the least and his mind began to drift again, back to things he would leave behind... To things he'd never have a chance to say.

Vell, finding that the Mautep were distracted, managed to jostle Nagaro's shoulder, claiming his attention. The Leithian cast his glance briefly to the northern sky, where the mass of clouds was darkening minute by minute. "It isn't Kroneg that's got his hand on you, Nagaro," he said, speaking low. "It must be Father Hrathgard, the Lord of the Wind!"

Under other circumstances Nagaro would probably have protested this invocation of the highest of the Leithian gods, but now it didn't matter. "Will you do something for me, Vell?" he asked.

"If I can—anything..."

"Tell my daughter that I'm sorry I couldn't come back to her. Tell her I didn't want to die."

Vell swallowed visibly. "I will," he said, his voice suddenly husky.

"No talk!" Baruk interrupted any further interchange by yanking Nagaro away from Vell with a violent jerk on the rope he still held.

The Mautep must have resolved their differences because another push now propelled Nagaro towards the railing. Apparently the prisoner was to go first, and the witnesses to follow. Two of Nagaro's guards had already crossed onto the deck of the Emperor's flagship, where they stood flanking the place where they intended him to cross.

Getting over the rail would have been easy with his hands free.

Having them bound behind him made it awkward, but he managed amid some laughter—which he ignored. Baruk sprang over easily after him and gave another pointed jerk on the rope.

Standing there on the deck of Baalkir's ship, Nagaro shook himself out of his thoughts long enough to take note of what confronted him. There were a large number of Mautep on the main deck. Two parallel rows of scarlet-clad sea warriors defined a path, beginning right in front of him and leading away in the direction of the stern castle, where more ranks of Mautep were arrayed as spectators. Nagaro couldn't see from where he stood, but he knew there would be a pair of stanchions used for holding slaves for punishment near the stern castle, probably on the port side, not far from the rail. He understood also why he had been taken off of the *Sword* for his execution. The stanchions had been removed from the deck of the former *Fist of Death* when she'd been re-christened the *Sword of Freedom*.

Nagaro received another ungentle shove from Baruk, and he began to walk—with measured tread—along the path laid out for him.

So many things he wished he had been given a chance to say...

At the end of the path, between the scarlet-clad warriors, he could see the Emperor, seated on a chair with Urchak standing to the right of him. Before he got there, however, he would pass by Roheed. The young Mautep was standing at attention among the line of men on his left, eyes straight before him, not looking at Nagaro.

Wasn't there something he wanted to tell Roheed?

He was almost abreast of Roheed's position when he remembered. He took two more steps, keeping his own eyes fixed straight ahead, then stopped dead. Still without turning his head, he said quickly in the Common Speech, "Roheed, the ring is returned and there is no blood debt. Sindar is alive. He found me—"

He had no chance to say more than that because Baruk swore violently behind him and lashed out with a kick, knocking Nagaro's feet from under him so that he fell to his knees, hard, on the planking. With his hands tied so awkwardly behind him, he barely avoided sprawling on his face.

"No talk, shaku!" Baruk spat the words as he hauled on the length of rope, dragging Nagaro up again.

Nagaro staggered to his feet and resumed his slow walk, trying not to limp, though his knees were badly bruised and he suspected one of them was bleeding. He had no idea what Roheed had thought of his words, or even if the man had understood him. *But at least he'd tried...*

Another dozen steps took him to a clear space before the Emperor's seat, where a backward jerk on the rope brought him to a halt.

The Emperor's expression was, as usual, quite inscrutable. Beside

Baalkir, Urchak was managing to control the muscles of his face, though his single eye burned with fierce exultation. There was a pause while the guards and the men who had flanked the condemned man's path arranged themselves into a semicircle where they could easily observe what was to come. Vell and Peldred were escorted to a place a little distance to the left of the seated Emperor. Roheed took up a position between the Emperor and the two witnesses. He didn't look at Nagaro.

The Emperor immediately began speaking to his nephew in low, rapid Hashti. Baalkir was frowning as he spoke, and he went on at some length. Roheed made a number of responses, and he glanced twice in Nagaro's direction.

Only a part of Nagaro's mind was taking any heed of these events. Mostly his thoughts were elsewhere, but he pulled them back when he realized the Emperor's attention was on him again. Baalkir had finished speaking, and Nagaro found himself looking to Roheed.

The young Mautep spoke. "Emperor ask if there is any thing you want to say to him, Kiraam, before you die."

Nagaro frowned. *He had so many things to say... And one of them was for the Emperor...* "Yes," he said, looking directly into Baalkir's face. "This is important: Free men row better than slaves."

As he spoke, a shifting shadow moved across the deck, darkening the place where he stood and falling also across the Emperor and those who stood with him. Nagaro didn't bother to look up. The cloud bank had doubtless advanced enough to obscure the sun. What did it matter? Clouds wouldn't save him.

There were some murmurs. The name of Sheptuum was heard from more than one mouth, and even Roheed glanced skyward. The Emperor, however, did not appear to be impressed. He spoke to Roheed in a peremptory tone. Roheed listened, made an answer, listened again, then turned to Nagaro.

"What you mean, free man row better?"

Again Nagaro frowned. "Free men row better, because they want the same thing the captain wants," he said simply. "I know. I have seen both. Been both."

For several seconds Roheed only stared at him, then the young Mautep turned to convey Nagaro's meaning to the Emperor. Baalkir's face betrayed no reaction, except that his eyes narrowed slightly. The Mautep ruler turned and said something to Urchak, who scowled briefly before his face resumed its rigid deadpan. The Emperor spoke, then, slowly and distinctly.

"Tell this thief that we have seen six ship of Droviri Fleet sailing in Mahuk water. If he tells me, now, plan of his master Running Dog, I will let him keep his life."

Nagaro understood enough to know what he had been offered, but to him, it was not a choice. He waited for Roheed's rendition, and saw both Vell and Peldred start in alarm. Distressing as it was to know that the Mautep had counted so many of the Fleet ships, Nagaro didn't expect to live long enough for the outcome of their mission to matter to him. He stood stiffly erect under Baalkir's gaze. "Lord Emperor," he said, "I have sworn oaths both to Edrovir and to my commander, Lord Kuran. It would dishonor me to answer you, and I will not."

"So, you will not answer me by choice?" The Emperor's response followed immediately on Roheed's Hashti translation. He did not sound surprised. "Then we will have to make you answer by other way. Urchak tok-Faar, you may now proceed."

Nagaro felt an instant wave of dismay. He had never heard of the Mautep using torture to gain information from their own kind. "Lord Emperor!" he exclaimed in protest, "this goes against honor!"

Roheed hesitated before translating, as if uncomfortable delivering the message. The Emperor merely waved aside the translation when he heard it and spoke angrily in response. Roheed listened, frowning.

"Emperor say Droviri have no honor. Droviri say Mautep should not send ship into their water, but still they send their war ship into water of Mahuk Baar."

Nagaro could offer no defense against this accusation, but he didn't drop his eyes as he answered: "That decision was not mine." More than that, he felt he shouldn't say.

Again the Emperor waved Roheed's translation aside. He turned to Urchak. "I will now see you punish this slave, Captain. If you can get from him what we wish to know, you shall have gold I have offered for his head."

Urchak now stepped boldly forward, smiling wickedly. He began to issue orders and Nagaro found himself forcibly jerked around to face the ship's port side. Baruk pushed him roughly forward, and the spectators parted to reveal the whipping stanchions. They were two heavy posts, bolted firmly to the deck about four feet apart. Each one was as tall as a man, as thick as a man's thigh, and equipped with several iron rings to facilitate the securing of a slave's wrists or arms.

The stanchions were not the only thing revealed when the crowd parted, however, and it was the unexpected object that seized Nagaro's attention like a pair of pincers. A dozen feet away, two men squatted on either side of a large metal brazier set in a tub of sand. The brazier was full of glowing coals, which a man was vigorously fanning with a large leather bellows. The wooden handles of a number of branding irons were plainly visible protruding beyond the brazier's curved black rim.

Nagaro's stomach went to ice. *Vothra, help me,* he thought, though he knew of no way that Vothra could give him aid.

There were more orders coming from Urchak. Nagaro's mind was too frozen to comprehend, until the one-eyed captain pointed to a spot between the brazier and the stanchions, in full view of the Emperor's seat, and said, "Hold him, there!"

Just as Baruk shoved Nagaro into the indicated position, a distant low grumble of thunder was heard over the sound of the wind. Urchak had picked up one of the branding irons. When he heard the thunder, he merely brandished the iron and laughed.

Nagaro expected to be thrust down onto the deck, but instead of that, another large muscular man stepped forward to join Baruk, and each of the two powerful Mautep seized one of his arms, just above the elbow. He was held standing upright in a pair of vise-like grips.

Urchak advanced on him with the iron, drawing a little circle in the air with the glowing tip, teasingly, before Nagaro's eyes. The grinning Mautep did not stop until the red-hot end of the iron was inches from Nagaro's face. Nagaro could feel the heat of it.

"Talk, shaku!" Urchak said, drawing on his limited knowledge of the Common Speech.

Nagaro stood straight and still, refusing to struggle or flinch. He knew what this man wanted and was determined not to give it to him. There was no possibility of placating Urchak, and he could only think of one way to shorten his ordeal. *If he could just make the man angry enough to draw his sword...* He looked the Mautep captain in his single eye and spoke loudly, so that all could hear.

"I remember the man who took your eye, Urchak. Jomo Nareyo was his name. He was only a common fisherman, but he would rather die than be a slave!"

Urchak turned eagerly to call for Roheed. But if the vengeful captain had hoped that Nagaro had decided to divulge the Droviri plan, he was badly disappointed. Roheed stepped forward and rendered a smooth, unhesitating translation, his face impassive and his eyes on Urchak all the while.

Urchak's countenance darkened as he listened, and Roheed had scarcely finished speaking when the one-eyed man moved without any warning. Side-stepping swiftly, the Mautep captain thrust the glowing iron against Nagaro's un-branded right shoulder and held it there until the flesh smoked.

Nagaro had barely time to make his mental preparation. He'd been branded before, and so had some idea of the magnitude of the pain. He clamped his teeth shut and managed not to cry out, but his body jerked and stiffened involuntarily.

There was a cry when the iron struck, but it came from other lips.

It sounded like Peldred's voice, but Nagaro had no attention to spare for the young Leithian. The burn was a searing scream of agony that continued undiminished after the iron was withdrawn. He was aware of Urchak, leering gleefully. The man gave a short barking laugh of satisfaction, then gestured at the stanchions with the hand that held the iron.

"Tie him!"

Nagaro was dragged stumbling to the stanchions, where his wrists were untied from behind his back and his arms stretched wide and bound one to each of the posts. The movement of his right shoulder cruelly exacerbated the pain of the burn, and he again had to clamp his teeth.

Urchak had in the meantime exchanged the branding iron for a braided whip. Planting himself in front of Nagaro, he deftly flicked the lash to raise a long red welt diagonally across Nagaro's chest. The man showed his teeth in a gloating smile, and said in the Common Speech, "You talk now, shaku!"

The sting of the lash was small compared to the pain of the brand, and Nagaro bore it without flinching. Still, the burn was bad enough. He knew his suffering would be audible in his voice, but he didn't care. Unclamping his teeth, he drew a gasping breath and said, "I should have killed you at Jaamra instead of throwing you into the sea. It would have been justice. But I don't kill a man who can't defend himself."

Let Roheed translate that...

Roheed had been there at Jaamra, and also there when Nagaro and Taru had been captured. But there was no telling what report he had made of those events. Roheed was standing beyond Urchak, between the Mautep captain and the Emperor. At that distance, Nagaro couldn't make out his expression. The young man's voice, when he offered his Hashti rendition of Nagaro's words, was firm and level. As nearly as Nagaro could tell, the translation was accurate.

Urchak's anger was plain in his face upon hearing it. Once again the Mautep lashed out with the whip, catching Nagaro on the side of the head. Nagaro's hair and beard fortunately prevented the leather from cutting him, though it stung. He stood erect between the stanchions and returned the one-eyed captain's glare with a level gaze. Somehow, through his pain, he managed a rather stiff version of his pirate smile.

Urchak uttered an oath and sent the lash snaking out to cut a second welt across Nagaro's chest. But in the next instant the Mautep mastered himself. The glare of his eye grew coldly malicious. He stalked around the stanchions until he stood behind Nagaro and began methodically to apply the whip to Nagaro's naked back.

Nagaro had felt the lash many times before, and he initially bore it well. The first strokes served as distractions from the greater pain of his burned shoulder, but this effect did not last long. All too soon, the blows of the whip became a new agony to rival the first. His back was on fire—each stroke a red-hot knife cut. His mind found words from the Book of Vothra:

All pain ends, if only in death. And death is not an end, but the path to a new beginning. All pain ends... if only in death...

He didn't count the blows. There might have been ten or even more before Urchak paused the first time to say, "Tell plan, slave!" Reverting to his native tongue.

"*Nan!*" Nagaro answered through his teeth, meaning "no" in the same language.

The rain of blows resumed, with a faster tempo, betraying Urchak's mounting frustration. This was not the quick end that Nagaro had hoped for, but he remembered the man he'd once seen beaten to death on the oar deck of the *Fist of Death*. There had been a certain terrible nobility in the Hranji's silent endurance of stroke after stroke of the mad slave driver's whip. He hoped he might do half as well as that proud, brave, black-skinned man.

He had to try, knowing the Mautep respected stoicism. He planted his feet firmly apart, held his arms stiff and straight, and clamped his teeth together with all his might.

Again and again, the razor-tongued lash licked his back.

All pain ends... only in death... a new beginning... pain ends... in death... new beginning...

By the second time Urchak paused, Nagaro had begun to doubt his ability to endure without at least crying out.

"Tell plan!"

"*Nan!*" Somehow he managed to get the word out through his teeth.

So the whipping resumed. Perhaps it was faster still, but it didn't matter anymore.

Nagaro felt each stroke as a physical blow, but not the pain of it as a separate thing. Pain was everywhere... building towards impossibility...

...pain ends... death... beginning... ...pain... ...death... ...beginning...

He didn't seem to be inside himself anymore. There was a red tide rising... obscuring his sight...

"*Tell plan!*"

He moved his mouth... forced air from his lungs, past his teeth...

"*Nan!*"

*

Landros stood on the captain's platform, gripping the rail, his gaze fixed straight ahead, his face rigid. The wind, which had grown blustery, lifted his graying hair. For the third time, Geldoran, beside him, glanced

　　　　　　Carol Louise Wilde

at the captain, studying his expression in profile.

"You do understand the reason for my decision? Why we have to continue south?"

"Oh, aye." Landros' voice was tight and flat. "If we were t' meet the bloody Emperor *now*, and get into a fight, it could put the whole mission in danger. Can't take the chance for the sake of one ship—or one man. More 'n likely he's dead already, anyway..."

The captain of the *Dolphin* had confirmed much of Landros's story, even to the presence of three Mahuk warships in the vicinity, with the Emperor's flagship among them. It had been the need to avoid those warships, by lying in hiding and taking a longer way around, that had delayed the *Dolphin's* coming.

Geldoran glanced briefly at the *Dolphin*. The ship was now sailing beside them on a parallel course and all four ships were running under the gray shadow of storm clouds that were chasing them out of the north. On their left, they were approaching the gap between the two islands from which the *Dolphin* had emerged. Geldoran returned to studying the man beside him, his brow furrowed in concern. "I'm sorry, Landros," he said gravely. "I truly am. He was a very good man. Exceptional, I should say. It's a great loss to the Fleet."

"Aye, well, if *I* were to choose between him and Strad, right now..." Landros was suddenly bitter. "Which man t' throw away—"

Geldoran quickly cut him off. "Strad will face a reckoning. I know for a fact that Kuran advised him to heed Nagaro's counsel, especially in these waters. For some reason, it seems he chose to do the opposite. I'd like to know why."

There was a sudden flash, followed by a resounding thunderclap. Landros blinked and rubbed his head. "Didn't like that," he muttered. "Makes the stars dance, it does—" He broke off, staring. "*By the Eyes*—" he whispered in an awestruck voice.

"What is it?" Geldoran sounded worried.

Landros didn't answer. He blinked hard, still rubbing his head. He blinked again, then held his eyes shut for several seconds, and opened them. "The sign..." he said, gesturing at the empty air in front of him. "Ye don't see it, do ye?"

"No... ah... Landros, I think maybe you should lie down—"

"*Oh, bodjer!*" Landros had closed his eyes again. He stood for several seconds, as if listening to some inner voice. Then his eyes snapped open. "Steersman!" he cried. "Put her over hard to port! Rubo, set sails for an easterly heading! We're going into the channel—"

"Captain—" Geldoran seized his shoulder.

"He's *still alive!* This very *minute*, he's still alive! With a favorable wind like this, we're not much more than an hour from Osfaraad by the shortest course. I *can't* just sail away and leave him! I have to try!" Landros was pleading.

Geldoran considered him, frowning hard. "Did Vothra tell you to do this?" he asked guardedly.

Instantly Landros shook his head. "The Spirit doesn't tell a man what t' *do*, Commander," he said reproachfully. "Ye surely know that. But Nagaro's mind is like a window into the world to Vothra, ye see, and I don't think Vothra wants t' lose that window."

Geldoran's frown deepened. Conflict clouded his gray eyes. "You know what I'd rather do, Landros, but—" He cast about, checking the configuration of his little fleet.

The *Sea Eagle* was already executing the turn Landros had ordered. The *Dolphin* was turning, too—wider and farther to starboard. Both of the other two ships, to stern, were beginning to alter course, following the flagship's lead.

Geldoran gnawed his lip. He hadn't told the other captains about Landros's apparent communications with the Benevolent Spirit. It was too strange, and too complicated to be shouted across from ship to ship. And men who weren't Vothrin might well not believe a word of it. "Hang it on Talebra's horn," he muttered, after a moment. He reached for the speaking trumpet that was strapped to the rail in front of the captain's platform. Raising it and directing it at the *Dolphin*, he shouted, "*We're taking a diversion through the isles—to see if we can find the Sword and the Valor!*" He turned to face aft to give the same message to the other two ships.

*

Death... beginning... beginning...

Nagaro was adrift in an all-encompassing miasma of scarlet pain. He heard only a strange singing in his ears—saw only the red mist...

Spirit that calls itself Nagaro!

The words cut urgently across his mind.

"Wha—?" He moved his lips. "Vothra? ...is it time...?"

Not yet, brave spirit. Can you stand up?

In his mind, he frowned. Wasn't he already standing? He forced himself to take a mental inventory, and discovered the pressure of what had to be hard planks against his knees. His arms were being pulled up at an angle, not straight out. He tried making the suggestion to his legs that they raise him, but nothing happened. "*Can't...*" he murmured.

You must! They are waiting for a miracle.

He tried to laugh. He suspected none but the Spirit could hear him. "*Vothra,*" he tried to say, "*please... you must give me strength...*" He had no idea whether he'd spoken aloud.

There was a little pause, and then the words of the Spirit intruded themselves again into his mind.

The one you call Landros is coming. He is between the isles, an hour away.

Weakly he shook his head. *"Too far... too late..."*

There was another pause, then: *I will put my hand between you and the pain... but I cannot do it for long. Be ready.*

Nagaro gasped. The pain had abruptly relented. He was still aware of it, but it had become remote. He was aware of wind, now, whistling and tugging at him—of voices, though they made such a tangle that he couldn't find the meaning in them. The red mist was receding from his eyes. Shapes were swimming into focus.

Stand up, Nagaro! The voice in his head was unusually commanding.

Obediently, he struggled to move his legs and get his feet under him, but his feet slipped on the planking. He opened his eyes and looked down, and saw that the deck was running crimson. His feet were sliding in a slick of his own blood. He should have been appalled, but the horror seemed remote. With a final effort, he straightened his legs, pulling with his bound arms at the same time, until he stood upright, swaying.

His action coincided with several cries, which were followed by an abrupt cessation of the general babble. He was concentrating his full attention on not losing consciousness, however, and had none to spare for guessing the reason for the sudden silence. Standing up had made him terribly dizzy.

His head had just cleared enough to begin to focus his eyes again when there came a brilliant flash of light that dazzled him, immediately followed by a loud *crack* and a thunderous rolling boom that reverberated between the sides of the narrow channel.

As the echos died away, there were more cries raised in Hashti. Nagaro couldn't focus his mind enough to understand them, though he thought he heard the name of Sheptuum. There came a pattering hiss all around him, then, accompanied by the delicious sensation of something cool gently sprinkled onto his skin...

Rain... of course... Some part of his brain found the answer, and immediately set it aside. Rain wouldn't save him. Frowning with the effort of concentration, he remembered that the only hope to end his suffering was to make the short-tempered Urchak angry enough to draw the sword he wore at his hip and use it. He forced open eyes that had somehow closed again, and struggled to focus his remaining strength on the power of sight, even as the red mist began once more to swirl around the edges of his vision.

Fortunately, Urchak was there—right in front of him, only a few feet away, the bloody whip coiled in his left hand while he brandished a red-hot branding iron in his right. There were other men out there as well. One of them, hovering behind Urchak, Nagaro's mind distantly identified as Roheed. The Emperor... Vell... and Peldred... didn't matter.

Urchak was advancing, the iron extended, its bright end circling. The hated design of Baalkir's brand was a glowing scarlet flower floating before Nagaro's eyes.

"*Tell plan now, slave!*" The Hashti words were spat at him in a voice edged with something that might have been desperation.

Nagaro answered with Hashti words of his own. They were words he had imagined saying, long ago, but had never thought he'd have the chance to say. Somehow, his failing mind found them now, and he mustered the last of his strength to fling them at Urchak in a voice that rang firm and clear.

"*Man without honor! Killer of woman!*"

Urchak's comprehension was instantaneous. The man's maimed face contorted hideously with rage. With a furious bellow, he lunged, thrusting the incandescent iron against Nagaro's chest, striking him just below the meeting of the collarbones.

This time, the sizzling, smoking pain was beyond any possibility of endurance. Nagaro screamed. The scarlet mist rose like a tide to drown in, then darkened and faded to an empty, silent black.

21: Baalkir's Justice

There was pain... pain that was by now like a part of him... that might almost have been his entire world. Pain meant he was alive...

Still alive.

Which could only mean that his gambit with Urchak had failed. The Emperor wasn't satisfied that he had suffered enough. There would be more punishment, then, before death came...

Best not to think about that... Best to lie still in the darkness behind his eyelids. Grateful that right now, for this moment, he didn't have to move...

*

Eventually, other things began seeping in. There was the metallic smell of *blood*... a sensation of *planking* against his left cheek... He was lying face down. His head was turned to the right, his left cheek pressed against the hard wood.

There was also an *absence* of things... like *wind*... and *rain*... It was quiet... there were just the familiar little creaking noises. And he could feel *an undulation*... the subtle rising and falling of being in something afloat. *So he was still on a ship...*

Curiosity stirred a little in the haze.

Gathering his strength, Nagaro risked opening his eyes—to find the foggy dimness of an interior space seen through faltering consciousness. He strove for better focus, and the image that resolved itself—about four feet from his face—was of varnished boards, a familiar wooden bunk with a name scratched in the wood. It was a Kelorin girl's name—one he remembered belonging to some crewman's sweetheart. For several seconds he could only stare at it. Then shock propelled him past the pain and into full awareness.

He was in the crew cabin of the *Sword of Freedom*.

In the light of this astonishing discovery, he began an effort to assess his situation in more detail. He was lying face down, yes. His arms were unbound. They lay at his sides. He unwisely moved them in an attempt to raise himself—and sucked breath at the immediate escalation of pain, even as blackness welled inside his head. He had to wait a dozen heartbeats for it to clear. He tried again, then, much more cautiously, and this time groaned aloud before giving up the attempt.

"Nagaro? Are you awake? Can you hear me?"

The voice was Vell's, and it had come from behind him—or rather from behind his head, since he still lay with his head turned to the right. He drew a painful breath and managed to say, "*Yes...*" The word came out husky-sounding, but at least his voice worked. He shut his eyes against the pain, and managed to raise just his head—without moving his arms. He turned his head and lowered it again, his right cheek now resting on the cabin floor.

Vell hadn't sounded very comfortable, and when Nagaro opened his eyes again, he saw why. The Leithian was lying on his side, facing Nagaro, in a position that made it plain that he was hogtied. He'd been stripped of his tirka and his shirt, and his right shoulder—which was uppermost—bore the fresh crimson mark of a branding iron. Nagaro felt a surge of outrage at the sight of the burned skin. *He'd tried to negotiate an honorable surrender. This was not honorable treatment!*

"They... *branded*... you, Vell..?" Speaking wasn't easy, but at least it was a distraction from how much everything hurt.

Vell looked pale. "On both sides," he gasped. "The one I'm lying on hurts like Hel's fire! They wanted the plan. Branded Peldred too—one side. Didn't tell 'em anything, did we, Peldred?"

There was a small unhappy sound from beyond where Vell lay, and Nagaro made out the top of a second blond head, just visible past Vell's.

Nagaro groaned. "*Oh, Vothra,*" he murmured. "I'm *sorry*. Never... thought... they'd do this..." He stopped. In his mind, he could hear the Emperor explaining why he thought Droviri had no honor. He felt sick. *Sick and angry*. There might indeed be dishonor behind their presence in Mahuk waters, but neither he nor his officers had chosen that course. After a moment, another unpleasant thought nudged its way through the morass of physical and mental anguish. "Is *that* why... I'm not dead?" he asked hoarsely. "They still want... the plan?"

There was a pause, and Vell said, "Not *exactly*. It, ah, seems you've been pardoned."

"*What...?*"

Nagaro's mind reeled with the impact of a new idea—that he might actually survive this ordeal. But in the next instant, he remembered the Hranji who had been beaten so badly... still alive when the whipping ended, yet dying of his wounds. This "pardon" might be nothing more than a final irony. "*How?*" he croaked. "What... *happened?*"

Vell groaned as he shifted position. "It was that reedy little fellow... with the mustache," he said, his voice sounding strained. "Eyepatch drew his sword when you went down... the second time. Looked like he meant to finish you. But Little Mustache drew *his* sword and turned

Eyepatch's blade. Then he started jabbering. And the Emperor asked a lot of questions. Went on for a while. Then Little Mustache tells us... the Emperor says... you're a brave man—man of honor, and all that. That you're not a slave. And no one's to hunt you anymore."

Nagaro shut his eyes. "Oh Roheed," he murmured. "Why'd you wait so long?"

"You know that man?" Vell inquired dubiously.

Nagaro drew a shuddering breath. "Knew him... when I was a slave. He seemed decent... mostly." That was as much explanation as he could manage. After mustering his strength through several more heartbeats, he asked, "What'll... happen next?"

"I've no idea." Vell moved uncomfortably again and grunted in pain. "Fainted when the iron hit me the second time. Woke up here... like this. You were here... so was Peldred. Peldred says he fainted and woke up here too." Vell jerked ineffectively at his bindings. "Your hands are free, Nagaro. Can you untie your feet?"

Nagaro frowned. He'd put himself in the Emperor's hands, saying "Do what you will." So, if he now tried to *escape*... He frowned harder. He hadn't bargained on any of them being tortured. And if he was *pardoned*, did that cancel the other terms of his surrender?

He tried to move his legs and discovered that his feet were indeed bound. "I'll try..." he murmured.

He attempted to roll onto his left side—where the shoulder wasn't freshly branded—thinking he could then draw up his knees and reach his feet. He failed completely. His agony spiked so cruelly that his head began to swim, and he fell back, gasping.

"Try again!" Vell urged. "I'm sure you can do it. You stood up... when we all thought you were done for!"

Nagaro was trying to steady himself, breathing slowly. "Vothra... helped me," he said through clenched teeth. "...took the pain..."

He did try again, though, and this time managed to roll onto his side. But his back screamed agony. Blackness rose, and he slid sideways into the waiting darkness...

*

When next he became aware of anything, it was the improbable sensation of someone gently smearing something oily-feeling onto the burned skin of his right shoulder. It stung horribly at first, then gradually began to ease...

"*Roheed...?*" he mumbled vaguely, eyes still closed.

"It is me, Nagaro. This is chutapak for your burn."

Nagaro's eyes snapped open at the sound of the familiar voice, though at first they refused to focus on its owner. "Pavo!" he exclaimed weakly. "You're alive!" Relief flooded through him.

"Oh yes." Pavo was squatting on his heels beside him, bending over him. Beyond the young Hashtep's massive figure, he could make out Peldred, sitting, leaning against one of the bunks with his head down and his eyes squeezed shut. Nagaro felt an instant surge of pity for the young Leithian, but Pavo was speaking to him again.

"They did not hurt me," his friend was saying, "But, oh how much they have hurt you, Nagaro!" Pavo's anguish was audible. The young Hashtep had finished with the brand on Nagaro's shoulder and began applying ointment to the one on his chest.

Nagaro groaned unashamedly at the fresh agony that resulted, and closed his eyes again. Flinching involuntarily away from the pressure of Pavo's fingers, he nearly rolled onto his back. Another pair of hands fortunately prevented it.

"Steady there!" Vell's voice unexpectedly spoke from behind him, explaining the other pair of hands. "Your back's a bloody mess, Nagaro. The burn'll be better in a minute. That ointment works wonders!"

Nagaro was well aware of the properties of chutapak. He clamped his teeth and waited while the searing pain at the base of his throat gradually receded to a dull ache. Unfortunately, this only made him more aware of how much his back stung and throbbed. "What's... happened..?" he murmured when he could speak.

"Pavo came in a minute ago and cut all of the ropes," Vell informed him. "Brought the ointment too. He says that the Mautep have all gone—sailed away. Says the Emperor's given you back everything—your sword, ship, and crew—"

"*What?*" Nagaro could scarcely believe he had heard right. "*Why?*"

"So that you can sail back to Edrovir," Pavo offered. "I think you have impress Emperor very much!"

Nagaro managed a small bitter laugh and spoke through his teeth. "It could've come... a little sooner..."

"Oh, no," Pavo responded calmly. "It could not be soon. It need a lot to impress Emperor!"

"I expect that the storm helped," Vell put in, and his voice had more than a trace of awe in it. "Uncanny the way it blew up so suddenly. And right when you stood up, it started to rain. Hrathgard's Tears, we call it—the rain that washes away the blood of the fallen. Then, when the Emperor pardoned you, it all blew over, and the sun came through the clouds like a sword!"

Nagaro groaned. "It was just... a thunderstorm, Vell... A small one..." He tried to twist around to look at his first mate, but the effort made him gasp as it twisted the skin of his lacerated back.

"It sound like frown of Sheptuum." Pavo was speaking to Vell.

Nagaro hadn't the strength to argue with Pavo. He shut his eyes and tried to breathe slowly.

"And they didn't torture you at all?" Vell was still speaking to Pavo. "Didn't try to get Kuran's plan from you?"

"They ask me," Pavo said matter-of-factly. "First they say they will kill me if I do not tell. But I say it is better they kill me, if they are going to kill Nagaro. So they tie me to chair and leave me with two man for guard. Then Emperor come, and he say it is good I am so loyal, but I should be loyal to *him*. Not to Droviri captain who is thief and enemy of Mahuk Baar. He say he will make me Mautep. Give me land and ship and many man to follow me, if I swear to be loyal to him."

"The Emperor said he'd make you a *Mautep?*" Vell's incredulity was obvious. "Isn't that like... taking a commoner and making him a lord? He can't have meant it! If he really said it—"

"I do not tell lie!" Pavo was suddenly very stiff.

"Sorry, mate," Vell said hastily. "But, I mean, you didn't *believe* him, did you?"

"It is not good to say that you do not believe Emperor," Pavo chided. "He is honorable man. I tell him I do not want to be Mautep. I tell him that I have swear oath to Captain Nagaro, and oath to Edrovir, and I will not break oath that I have swear."

"Huh!" Vell scoffed. "What did he think of *that?*"

"Emperor say Kiraam Shaku-Tal will soon be dead. But I tell him that Sheptuun have always protect Nagaro, and Sheptuum will be very angry if Emperor kill him!"

Vell whistled. "Kroneg's Blood, you've got nerve! What did he say?"

"He said he will test two man today, Kiraam Shaku-Tal and Urchak tok-Faar, and he will see which is better man. Then he go out. When he come back, he say he have decided to spare my captain, so I know Nagaro have won. He say I have chosen worthy captain—that I may keep my life as long as I keep my oath. He say he will give back everything to Nagaro. Then Emperor go out, and Roheed come in. He bring chutapak, and my sword—and he put them on floor where I can put my hand on them if I make my chair fall. He say I must wait until everyone have gone. Then I make myself free and go to make everyone else free too, and we must all go back to Edrovir."

The two men had been speaking back and forth over Nagaro as he lay on the floor. Now, however, Vell suddenly put his hand on Nagaro's arm. "What shall we do, Captain?" he asked. "Little Mustache says we're to go back to Edrovir, but our orders are to make for the rendezvous at Paktaar."

Nagaro had been following the conversation with an effort as he drifted, close to the edge of the sea of unconsciousness. Now he frowned. "It's... your command... Vell..."

"*What?* No, Nagaro! I won't take it from you. Not *now*."

Nagaro shook his head weakly. "I... can't stand up... Can't move... without fainting. I can't captain a ship."

"But the *Sword* is *your* ship!"

"Then see that you give her... back to me... in one piece! If Urchak... hasn't killed me." In his mind he could see the Hranji lying on the bloody planking with his back a mass of gore. He could hear Tredhold saying the man needed doctoring. He focused on Pavo's worried face and asked, "Where's Tred?"

Pavo answered. "They have told me that all of other man are on oar deck, tied to bench."

Vell had moved around to where he could see Nagaro's face. "You're not going to die, Captain," he said, as if the very idea were absurd. "And if you're going to faint, you can at least give me an order first."

Nagaro shut his eyes. "All right," he mumbled. "I order you... to take... command..."

"That's not fair—" Vell began.

"*Then... go... get... Tred—*" In his frustration, Nagaro tried to sit up, but the effort was too much. The black sea rose to claim him.

*

Some time later, he became aware that there was something cool being repeatedly pressed against his back, working its way from one side to the other, across his shoulder blades. Cool though it was, it still hurt cruelly. He groaned, and the dabbing pressure immediately stopped.

"Nagaro, I'm sorry. I know this must hurt, but I have to clean it up enough to see what I'm working with."

For the second time, Nagaro felt a great surge of relief. The voice belonged to Tredhold.

The dabbing began again, punctuated intermittently by the little soft splashing sounds of a cloth being dipped into a basin of water. He risked opening his eyes and determined that he was lying face down on his own bunk in the *Sword's* great cabin. Tredhold was sitting on a stool beside him. He got a glimpse of the healer's face, wearing an expression of grim intensity. Hastily, he closed his eyes again, and endured the continued sponging until there came another pause, when he asked, "How bad... is it, Tred?"

"Bad enough." The words were spoken very soberly, but then, as if in haste to soften them, Tredhold added, "But not as bad as I thought. There's more skin left than it looked like at first."

"Oh..." Nagaro suspected that the last words had been intended to be more reassuring than he found them. Shortly thereafter he faded out again.

*

When next he came to wakefulness, his back felt different—not better, exactly, just different. He was vaguely aware that there was now a bandage on his left arm. He'd forgotten there was a sword cut there. There was also a murmur of voices in the room, which he struggled to resolve.

"...I've put a medicinal plaster on it—as ye can see. I can't do more for him." *That was Tred speaking.* "I'm relying on the natural strength he has to see him through, but it'll take time, and it won't be easy. Thank the gods Vell has decided to make for Pakoa—"

Nagaro opened his eyes, blearily frowning. "Shouldn't do that," he said, as distinctly as he could. "Not for... one man. Should make for... th' rendezvous..."

Tred's voice had stopped, and a face suddenly appeared in Nagaro's field of view, as one of the room's occupants came to crouch beside his bunk. It was a weathered Kelorin face, topped by grizzled black hair. "Easy lad," said a familiar voice. "Ye gave command o' the ship to Vell, and it was the right thing to do. Now let him do the task. The *Sword's* had her fight—taken casualties. Ye're fairly out o' this."

"Landros!" Nagaro managed to give him a weak smile. "So you got here... after all. Vothra said you were... an hour away." Then he frowned again, wondering how Vothra had known that.

"Aye, well, if that's when I think it was, it's more 'n two hours ago now," Landros told him. "We had to go 'round the other side o' the island, and send scouts up onto the hill to see how things lay. Make sure the Mautep weren't still about."

Nagaro blinked. "You knew... about them?"

"Vothra told me," Landros said, looking distinctly smug. "Oh, aye," he added in response to Nagaro's stunned look, "I've been talking to the Spirit. It wasn't near as bad as I thought it'd be. Jolly good mates we are now, Vothra 'n me. I have to say, though, I can see why the Spirit's taken such a shine to ye, lad. Vothra's a regular conversationalist."

Nagaro had been staring in astonishment. Now he tried to laugh, but it made the pain in his back flare so much that he nearly fainted again. "You'll have to... tell me about it... later," he gasped.

Geldoran's voice said, "Let me speak to him."

"Aye, Zirda." Landros moved aside to make way for the commander, who crouched by the side of the bunk in the other man's place.

"I understand the Emperor tortured you for information, Captain."

"Yes..." Nagaro frowned. "I misjudged. Never thought... he'd do that. They hurt Peldred... and Vell..."

"But you didn't tell them anything?"

Nagaro tried to shake his head, but it was too hard, the way he was lying. "I didn't," he managed. "Vell said... the same. But I was unconscious.

Didn't see..." He drew a gasping breath. "They've counted six ships."

"So Vell told me." Geldoran frowned. "There's no help for that. They cleared out of here in a hurry by the look of it too. They may have seen my four ships coming. Do you know where the *Valor's* gone? We've seen no sign of her."

"To the rendezvous. Strad said don't wait... if we got by. I think... he—" Nagaro had to stop. The effort of speaking was making him light-headed. "I'm sorry..." He shut his eyes.

"It's all right, Captain. Don't tire yourself." He felt Geldoran's hand on his arm. "They've finished mending the rudder, and the *Sword* is ready to sail. Vell's orders are to take the *Sword* to Pakoa and wait there for the Fleet. *Your* orders, Nagaro, are to heal. I'm putting you in Tredhold's hands. You do as he says. Do you understand?"

Nagaro did his best to nod his head as it lay on the bunk mattress. "Aye, Zirda."

He was vaguely aware of Landros and Geldoran going out.

*

It was some indefinite time later. Pain made him hazy, but he was aware that Tredhold was sitting beside him again on his little stool.

"I want ye to drink this." Tred held out a cup.

Reflexive suspicion reared its head. "What is it?"

Tred smiled wanly. "*Dedrel*, to make ye sleep. Ye remember dedrel. We used it on Pakoa. If ye sleep, ye won't feel the pain."

"Oh. All right." *Dedrel seemed safe...*

Drinking while lying face down was impossible. Tredhold had to bring Pavo in to help raise him a little. While waiting for the drug to take effect, Nagaro ate some biscuit and let Pavo lift him again so he could drink some water. Soon, however, he was drifting into a fog of drugged sleep.

*

It was so dark... and the ship was moving strangely... turning...and turning... It shouldn't be doing that...

"Vothra... where are you?"

"Nagaro?"

"Vothra...?" Nagaro frowned. *Was he dead?* "It's so cold... an' I can't find th' door..."

There were sounds as of someone moving about in the dark. A light flared, then, and Tredhold's face appeared, floating vaguely before him. A lantern swung oddly in the man's hand, it's light blurring in his vision.

"It's all right, Nagaro. I'm here."

Nagaro frowned, shivering. "Where's... Vothra?" he asked vaguely.

An awkward pause followed. "Ah, not here, I'm afraid. Ye'll have to make do with me."

Was Tred trying to make a joke? Nagaro shuddered as a powerful chill shook him. "Won' do," he mumbled. "Need Vothra... if I'm going t' die..."

"Ye're *not* going to die!" The lantern receded, and a hand was placed on Nagaro's forehead. "*Kroneg's Blood!* Ye're burning up!"

"No... I'm *cold*..." Nagaro shivered again.

"I'm sorry, Nagaro. I have to take a look at your back. This is going to hurt."

The pain had been there all along, a constant part of him, but when Tredhold peeled off the dressing, it increased so sharply that he hadn't the will or strength to keep from crying out. At the same time, he twisted in a spasm of agony—which only made the pain spike more sharply. He shut his eyes, gasping... trying to lie still...

"*Pavo!*" Tredhold shouted. "Pavo! Come here! I need you!"

There were sounds... boots in the passage, then in the room... and Pavo's voice saying, "What is wrong, Tred?"

"There's some suppuration." Tred sounded distraught. "I *knew* I should have used salt, but I thought it'd be too painful. Now I'm going to have to open these up, and use it. Hold him while I get what I need."

Nagaro felt two strong hands grasp his upper arms on either side, holding him against the mattress. The sudden pain had receded, and the shock of it seemed oddly to have left his head a little clearer. "What're you doing, Tred?" he asked, with a clarity that surprised him. He could hear the healer moving about, but when he risked opening his eyes, he could only see Pavo bending over him.

"I'm going to give ye opa, Nagaro." Tredhold's voice was now steady. "There's something I have to do, and this'll help ye get through it. Just close your eyes."

Nagaro obeyed, but a moment later his eyes snapped open again as he felt his right forearm being turned palm-side up and the sensation of fingers probing along it in a way that ignited powerful memories. "*No!*" he cried, desperately trying to move his arm. "*Not the thorn!*"

"I'm sorry, Nagaro. It's the best way. *Hold him, Pavo!*"

The prick of the bladder-thorn was so tiny that he wouldn't have felt it at all if the fear hadn't sharpened his awareness...

*

He'd stopped struggling some time ago—stopped fighting what was happening. He was drifting... floating... swimming face down through crystal-clear water that it seemed impossible to drown in. Perhaps he was breathing water... like a fish... He laughed, amused at the thought of being a fish. He moved his arms... trying to swim...

"Watch him, Pavo! Don't let him fall off the bed!"

The voice seemed to come from far away. He felt himself restrained again, but he didn't really care. "I'll flip my tail, an' swim away from you..." he said aloud.

"Is he all right?" That was Pavo.

"Yes. He's in an opa dream, that's all. We can begin now. Hand me the knife and the bowl of salt..."

"What for, Tred?" Nagaro asked, dreamily. "Are you going t' eat me for dinner?" He laughed, giddily. Something was happening... but that couldn't be his back that was being cut into... That pain surely belonged to someone else... He heard someone gagging, and the hands that had been holding him faltered and let go. And then Tred was saying, "I know it smells bad, Pavo. Go get some air... Come back when ye can..."

A moment later, Tred's voice spoke very close to his ear. "Think of something that makes ye happy, Nagaro. What's the happiest thing ye can think of?"

And he was walking through sun-dappled forest shade... emerging into a meadow, impossibly green, stirred by a breeze that carried the scent of roses. He turned, and Nevien was walking beside him... He reached for her hand, and she let him take it. They walked... talking, and not talking... through sunlit fields... and into a garden with deep pink roses and snow-white farusia...

Somewhere, at a great distance, someone was doing truly terrible things to someone's back—things that hurt horribly. But it didn't seem to have anything to do with him.

Some time later he was with Nevien in her bedchamber... lying on the bed. Only now she was weeping... and he couldn't seem to move... and someone was feeling along his arm again to place the needle of a bladder-thorn...

There was more. It got worse...

*

"Oh, Vothra! It *hurts*—"

"Are ye awake, Nagaro? Can ye tell me where ye are?

"*Where...?*" Nagaro didn't know what to make of the question. He opened his eyes and found that it was daylight. "I'm *here*. On the *Sword*," he murmured. "But I don't know... where the *Sword* is. Feels like we're moving... so we can't be at Pakoa..."

Tredhold moved into his field of view. "We're somewhere off the coast of Jinara. The wind's been against us, so we've been tacking and rowing. Do ye think ye can eat something?"

"*No!* Tred, I'm sick!" His stomach felt awful.

"Mmm. Well, I did have to give ye rather a lot of opa before the end. Ye were very ill, Nagaro. Ye look much better now." The healer bent to touch Nagaro's forehead. "The fever's gone."

"Fever...?" Nagaro frowned, trying to remember. Things seemed to have gotten very jumbled after Geldoran and Landros had left. There was something in there about opa... and some extraordinary dreams... but he couldn't quite figure it all out. And he was so stiff from lying on his face... He tried to move, and groaned aloud. "Oh, Tred, it hurts so *much!*"

"I'm not surprised."

Nagaro frowned up at the healer. Tredhold's manner seemed oddly cautious. Unusually distant.

"Is... something wrong, Tred?"

"No, no. Nothing." The little sandy-haired Leithian abruptly smiled, though it looked a bit forced.

Nagaro drew breath for the effort of further speech, and asked, "What happened? Last night... or whenever that was?"

Tredhold smiled again, a little less stiffly, and squatted beside the bunk, bringing his face down close to Nagaro's. "Your back had begun to abscess in several places," he said seriously. "I had to open the wounds that were festering and wash them clean. Then I had to put some salt on them—and everywhere else, to be sure the suppuration didn't spread. It was rather nasty." He paused. "I'm afraid I'm going to have to uncover your back again in a little while to put on more salt. I won't have to cut anything, though, unless there's some new suppuration—so it shouldn't be as bad. I'll give ye a good stiff dose of dedrel before I begin. With any luck, ye'll sleep through the worst of it."

"Dedrel?" Nagaro hurt so badly already that he wondered whether dedrel would be enough. "Why not opa? It was... like the pain was... far away."

Abruptly Tredhold stood up and moved away so Nagaro couldn't see him well without awkwardly twisting his head. The healer began doing something with some things on the table. After a little pause, he said, "Ye shouldn't have opa, Nagaro. I won't give it to ye again."

"Why?" Nagaro wondered aloud. "I had... amazing dreams. I don't remember much..." He frowned, breathing and concentrating. "In one... I was riding a horse... a horse that could gallop on clouds."

Tredhold continued with whatever he was doing at the table. "Oh, yes," he said quietly. "Opa does give men dreams. Usually very pleasant dreams—and quite harmless. *But*, if a man has any really bad memories, and the opa starts to work on *those*..." He glanced at Nagaro, and quickly looked away again. "Things can get ugly," he finished.

Nagaro lay, with his head twisted around, staring at what he could see of the healer. Tredhold's back was half turned to him. He could make out part of the Leithian's profile, but not the man's expression. "What do you mean, Tred...? he began huskily, and stopped, because a sudden image had emerged out of the jumble in his head. "*Oh, no!*" he murmured in alarm. "Did I attack Vell?"

Vell had looked really frightened as he'd backed away...

"Ye tried to." Utensils clinked together in Tredhold's hands. "Pavo stopped ye."

"*Oh, Vothra!*" Nagaro closed his eyes, suddenly overwhelmed by the combination of unrelenting pain and this new calamity. "I... I must have... thought he was someone else—" He stopped again, realizing, too late, where that thought led. Vell was Leithian. *It was the hair, the blond hair... and Tred was Leithian too! No wonder Tred seemed wary.*

"Well, aye," Tredhold was saying. "Vell thought ye took him for Strad. He seems to think it only natural ye'd be angry with *that* gentleman."

"Strad?" It took several seconds for Nagaro to make the connection. "I... I, yes. I was." *But he knew it wasn't right...*

Tredhold was still moving things about on the table. "There's one other thing," he said, after a pause that ran just a little too long. "Besides causing dreams, opa can, well... loosen a man's tongue. It's worse than strong wine, that way."

Nagaro had been lying still, with his eyes closed and his mind in a dizzy, dismal whirl. When Tredhold's new words penetrated, he felt a shock of pure, cold terror. "*No!*" He wrenched his eyes open and twisted painfully around to stare, aghast, at the healer. "Tred! *What did I say?*"

Tredhold didn't turn his head, although his hands stopped moving. After three long seconds, his hands began to move again, and he said lightly, "I couldn't make head nor tail of most of it, Nagaro. And even if I *had*, I'd keep it in confidence. But if a man's got secrets, he should stay away from opa. I've said I won't give it to ye again, and if any other healer talks about giving ye opa, I'd advise ye to refuse it. Ye can say it made ye violent. There'd be truth in that."

Nagaro relaxed, with a groan, and closed his eyes again. "Yes... of course..." he murmured. "Thank you, Tred."

A little while after that, he managed to drink some broth, and eat a little porridge. Later, when Tredhold brought him the cup of dedrel, he was glad to take it. The salt-burn came through the dedrel in the end, but by that time, Tredhold was nearly finished and he managed to get through it.

22: A Traitor Among Us

Nagaro spent most of the days that followed face down on his bunk. Tred kept his back covered with plasters that were not bound on with bandages because they had to be changed so often, and the best thing he could do was sleep. In fact, he spent a large part of the voyage to Pakoa in drugged slumber.

When he was awake, he had to try to sit up during the brief times when the plasters were off so he could eat and drink, and to relieve the stiffness brought on by prolonged immobility. The pain from his back lessened gradually as the days passed, though he continued to be very weak and was dizzy whenever he tried to move. He talked some to Tred, and to Pavo when he came. And he tried not to worry about the mission—about Taru... Landros... all those other men. Tredhold was adamant that he shouldn't trouble his mind because his body needed to heal, and the mission was out of his hands in any case.

When at last they heard the three short, low notes from Pakoa's southern lookout horn, he was sitting on the edge of his bunk with Pavo's hand steadying him. Pavo had brought him a bowl of honeyed porridge and a cup of warm sothiril for his midday meal, and Nagaro was waiting for his head to stop spinning so he could eat.

"Finally," he said fervently. "I can get out of this cabin and into my own house."

At the table, Tred's chair scraped as he turned. "Ye'll do nothing o' the kind, Nagaro," he said firmly. "Ye're not nearly strong enough to walk that far."

Nagaro gestured with his spoon. "I could ride a horse—"

"I'm *not* having ye on a horse!"

There came a sharp knock at the door, and it was Tredhold who said, "Come in."

Nagaro sighed. It hardly seemed to be his cabin anymore.

The door opened and Vell began to enter. He stopped dead when he saw Nagaro sitting on the bunk, and said, "Oh." His shocked apprehension was almost comical.

It was the first time that Nagaro had seen the Leithian since the unfortunate episode involving the opa. He grimaced. "I'm really sorry,

Vell," he said quickly. "I don't know what mad idea was in my head that night, but I'm quite sure it had nothing to do with you."

"Oh. Good." Vell sounded a little sheepish. He came the rest of the way into the great cabin, closed the door behind him with elaborate care, and turned to face Nagaro. "And *I'm* sorry, too, Nagaro," he said. "I had no idea how badly hurt you were—or I never would have argued with you about the command instead of fetching the healer. When Tredhold came and said you'd seen a man die from a whipping like that, I felt *awful!*"

Nagaro managed a wan smile. "It's all right, Vell. Just forget it."

Vell looked relieved. He glanced at Tredhold, and back at Nagaro. "I came to tell you that we should be anchoring in Pakoa Harbor in half an hour. I'm giving the men permission to go ashore and take lodgings at the inn, or in the barracks, for as long as we're here. Or to stay with their families." He looked at Tredhold. "I think your wife is here?"

Tred nodded.

"My wife is here also," Pavo observed, and Vell looked startled, as if surprised at the idea that Pavo had a wife.

Nagaro cleared his throat. "Two of the men who we lost at Osfaraad came from Pakoa," he said somberly. "Atao and Vindel. You should try to contact their families now, rather than have them find out when the official notice comes from Lankura."

Vell stared at him. "Right. I'll, ah, see to it," he said.

After Vell had gone, Nagaro turned back to his porridge and sothiril. "So," he said, "if the crewmen all go ashore, I guess I'll be the only one left on the ship."

Tredhold looked up from the book he had open on the table. "No, ye won't," he said flatly. "I'll stay with ye."

Pavo immediately nodded. "I will stay also."

Nagaro looked from one to the other. "This is not right," he said seriously. "Tred, you haven't seen Ilsafeth or your children since last Sedrin. And you, Pavo, haven't seen Tenepti either, not to mention your new baby. Neither of those two dear women would ever forgive me if I kept you both here playing nursemaid."

"Pavo and I will spell each other so that we can visit our wives," Tred informed him. "I don't want to move ye, and ye should *not* be left unattended—especially at night."

"Tred, I sleep like a *stone* with the dedrel."

"Ye *think* ye do—" Tredhold caught himself. Then, in answer to Nagaro's dismayed expression, he added, "When it begins to wear off, ye get restless. I've had ye try to get up out o' that bed more than once, though I wouldn't expect ye to remember. I can't have ye blundering about in the dark in your sleep with no one here."

Nagaro looked down, studying the bare planking between his feet.

Tredhold had been living in the great cabin since they'd left Osfaraad—sleeping in the second bunk. Nagaro had wondered why, since it seemed the crisis was past. Now he understood. "I'm sorry, Tred," he said. "It seems I'm being a great deal of trouble for you... and for everyone..." He glanced at Pavo.

Tredhold swept the words aside with an impatient gesture. "This is a healer's work, Nagaro, as ye should know, since ye once tried to learn the trade."

"And you have save us all with what you did at Osfaraad," Pavo put in.

Nagaro frowned. "I think you saved yourself at Osfaraad, Pavo. It seems to me that I put the entire mission at risk—"

"That's enough of that!" Tred cut him off. "The best way to heal the body is not to fret the mind, remember? Ye have your orders, Nagaro. Now I need ye to lie down again so I can replace the plasters."

Nagaro groaned. He handed the empty bowl and the spoon to Pavo to take back to the galley and lay down on the bunk for what seemed like the hundredth time. He'd been finding it harder in the last few days not to "fret" about the mission, or about what had happened at Osfaraad. As Tredhold began applying fresh compresses to his back, he asked, "How does it look, Tred?"

Tredhold grunted. "It *looks* like Hel raked ye over and then some bodjering great beastie chewed on what was left. But if ye were to ask me how it's *doing*, I'd say it's healing well. Ye're a wonder for healing, Nagaro. It's just that it takes a long time to grow so much new skin."

"Then it's not... fit to be seen?"

"Not by anyone ye don't want to scare half to death. Why?"

Nagaro winced at a stab of pain. Changing the plasters always hurt. "Ani will want to come," he said between his teeth. "She'll want to bring Narei—and the other children. If you turn them away so as not to scare them, it'll only make them worry more. And I don't like to think what they'd make of seeing me flat on my face."

The healer's hands had stopped moving. "Ye know, ye're right," he said. "Bodjer it!" He began working on the compresses again. After a moment he said, "If ye could hold yourself up on your hands and knees, with your back level—so I could get a bandage all the way around your chest—I think I could bind the plasters tight enough to keep them from falling off, without it being so tight ye couldn't breathe."

"Could you do that now, Tred?"

"*Now?*"

"Please, Tred?" Nagaro pleaded. "I want to get some air! And see Pakoa Bay. I haven't seen the sun in days! I thought I'd never see it again with these eyes."

Tredhold muttered something about it being too soon, but in the end, he relented, saying, "I suppose it's a good idea to try it out ahead o' time—to see how it goes before we have women and children coming to look at ye."

It was more than an hour later, and the *Sword* was securely moored at the wharf, before Nagaro finally made his way, barefoot and leaning on Pavo, down the corridor and out through the stern castle door onto the main deck. Tredhold followed nervously, keeping an eye on the bandages. The mid-afternoon sun dazzled Nagaro's eyes, and he sank painfully onto the barrel that had been placed beside the door as a seat for him.

"Maybe you were right about it being too soon, Tred," he gasped, shutting his eyes and clutching at Pavo's arm. "It hurts... and my head's going 'round—"

He was interrupted by a cheer, and cries of, "*Look! The Capt'n's come out!*" Startled, he reopened his eyes. There were crewmen on the deck, making the *Sword* ship-shape before going ashore. He saw hands raised to him in greeting and enthusiastic smiles. He raised his own hand to acknowledged them, and his voice as well. "Thank you all!" His throat felt tight. "They're a good crew," he murmured to no one in particular.

Vell was on the deck, and he bade the men return to their tasks, but without any real disapproval. Then he sauntered over to where Nagaro sat, with Pavo and Tred standing protectively on each side. "It's good to see you out and about, Captain," he said. "Here's the *Sword*, safe and sound. Are you ready to take her back?"

"Not yet!" Tredhold put in sharply before Nagaro could respond.

Nagaro gave Vell a rueful look. "The *Sword* isn't going anywhere, for a few days at least. And as you can see, neither am I."

At that moment, the door opened beside them, and young Peldred emerged with his seaman's bag on his shoulder. He started to walk past them, eyes straight ahead, expression fixed.

Vell frowned. "Here now, Peldred," he said sharply, "Aren't you going to pay your respects?"

Peldred halted and turned, stiffly. "Good day to you all," he said woodenly. Then to Nagaro, he added, "It's good to see you looking better, Zirda."

Nagaro nodded, but the youth's manner smote him. "I've wanted to talk to you, Peldred," he said seriously. "I'm sorry the Emperor made you watch that—and about your being branded. I'm afraid this has been a very hard first mission for you."

Peldred's stiffness didn't ease. His eyes turned sullen with anger. "A warrior should be able to bear anything!"

Nagaro thought he saw the root of the young man's trouble. "There's no one who can bear *anything*, Peldred," he said earnestly. "Warrior or no, we all have limits. If you weaken or fall, you just have to get up again and go on as best you can."

"That's easy for you to say!" Peldred blurted. "You stood up! You taunted that monster..." His voice caught. His knuckles were white where he clutched his bag.

Nagaro sighed. "Standing up wasn't my idea. Vothra more or less ordered me to—*and* took the pain away, which was the only thing that made it possible. And I was taunting Urchak because I hoped he'd put an end to it by killing me quickly."

Peldred was staring at him, and there had been startled intakes of breath from the other three men. Then Peldred dropped his eyes, his jaw working silently. No one else spoke.

Nagaro drew a long breath. "The Vothrin Writings say that we all have different strengths and weaknesses... That we shouldn't judge a man by what he can or cannot do."

Peldred did not raise his eyes. "Thank you for trying, Zirda," he mumbled. Then he turned and fled. His retreating footsteps clattered on the gangplank.

There was a moment's silence. Tredhold broke it. "There's wisdom in your Writings, Nagaro."

Nagaro shook his head. "It wasn't enough, Tred—or else it wasn't on the mark. That young man's trouble has not been answered."

Vell tugged at his mustache. "I don't know what ails the lad," he said with an air of frustration. "He's been like that ever since Osfaraad."

"Has he?" Tredhold sounded concerned. "I should have noticed. Though I've scarcely been out o' the great cabin. I'll have to try and talk to him in private."

"Yes, Tredhold, you do that." Vell sounded glad to turn the puzzle over to the healer. Then he gave Nagaro a half-jesting salute and went off about his business.

Nagaro sat for half an hour more after that, talking with Tred and Pavo—gratefully breathing the air that wafted across the harbor from the verdant hills, carrying mingled scents of land and sea. The sun was warm on his skin, gently touching the places where his recent burns were healing with the aid of chutapak. From his seat on the barrel, he could see the wharf, the Bay Tree Inn, and the town. Familiar shops and dwellings, fashioned half of field stone and half of timber, straggled up the slopes that rose from the edge of the bay. He could just make out the bend in the Hill Road and the modest house that he and Taru shared.

Looking at that house, he grew quiet, thinking of Taru and of the ill-considered assault upon Sar Tipaal. He felt afresh all of his misgivings about the mission. This was the first time that he or Taru had ever gone into serious danger without the other.

*

Nagaro lay face down on his bunk once more, only half listening as Tredhold explained in detail to Pavo how to change the plasters on his back. He had eaten some stew for dinner—a little early. Tred had seemed reluctant to go before he'd eaten. The two men had drawn sticks to see which would stay the night with Nagaro and which would spend it with his family. Pavo had drawn the short stick, and Tred was plainly eager to be off. At last the healer seemed satisfied that Pavo could perform the delicate task, and moved to the table to prepare the cup of dedrel. When he pressed Pavo to give it to Nagaro immediately, however, Pavo spoke in protest.

"Still it is early, Tred. Maybe I can talk to Nagaro some before he go to sleep."

For once, Tredhold seemed not to remember his concerns about fretting the mind. "All right," he said briskly. "But just until the stars come out." Then he picked up his seaman's bag, containing the few things he needed for one night's stay, and took his leave.

Nagaro managed to laugh. "Good for you, Pavo. You've gotten rid of the old hen. But now that the hen's away, how can the chicks play?" He gestured awkwardly, indicating the way he was lying on the bunk.

Pavo pulled up Tredhold's stool and sat down at Nagaro's side. He frowned. "I do not think we can play. But I want to ask you something. Is it true, what you said to Peldred? About how Vothra have told you to stand up?"

"Yes, it's true. Why?"

Pavo sat silent for a moment. "And is it true also what Vell have said before, about storm?" he asked at last.

Nagaro sighed. "There were some gusts of wind... clouds that blew up over the headland... a little lightning. I remember rain—but I don't know what happened after I fainted the second time."

"Do you think Vothra have make storm?"

Nagaro twisted his neck to see Pavo more clearly. "Vothra can't do that, Pavo," he said. "Vothra is only a spirit—not a god."

Pavo considered him with his narrow, dark eyes. "Are you sure it was Vothra that tell you to stand up?"

"Yes, I am."

"But you have told me, Vothra does not tell man what to do."

Nagaro frowned. "Vothra usually doesn't, because Vothra *chooses* not to. Usually the Spirit just gives advice."

"This was advice? To stand up?"

"In the end, it was more like an order," Nagaro admitted. "But it *had* to be, Pavo. I was past thinking... past choosing..." Nagaro was frowning deeply now—trying to remember exactly what the Spirit had said to him. "Vothra said they were waiting for a miracle," he murmured.

"Yes!" Pavo spoke decisively. "Sheptuum have send you storm—at Osfaraad, and at Jaamra, before that. Sheptuum always send you miracle. Vothra must be servant of Sheptuum who is trying to make miracle be little bit better!"

Nagaro shut his eyes. "If Vothra serves Sheptuum, Pavo, no one has told Vothra about it," he said wearily. "And there's nothing you can do to convince me that weather is anything but weather." He yawned. "Kelorin folk may say that weather is sent by Lokundas, but we don't really believe that Lokundas does anything specifically to help or harm any single person." He opened his eyes again, then, worried about how Pavo might react to such words.

Pavo had risen and gone to the table. "You are tired, Nagaro," he said calmly. "Here is medicine that Tred have made for you." He came back with the cup and set it on the floor near Nagaro's head. "I will take off old plaster now. Then you can turn little bit so you can drink it."

Nagaro twisted his head to look at the great cabin's window and saw that it was already getting dark outside. The stars must already be visible. "It's not 'medicine,' he grumbled, closing his eyes again as Pavo began to work on his back. "It's a cup of bloody oblivion." But he drank it all the same when Pavo handed it to him. Lying there, beginning to feel it, he said thickly, "It wasn' the storm that saved me anyway... it was Roheed."

Pavo's voice came to him as he was beginning to drift. "Yes. Roheed have paid his blood debt." And a moment later, more softly, as if from farther away, *"Blood dept has now been paid to Sheptuum..."*

Nagaro wanted to say that there *was* no blood debt—that he'd told Roheed as much—but his mind was sinking into gray fog, and his tongue wouldn't do his bidding.

*

"Can I feel your bandage now, Papa?" Narei gazed up at him with eyes that had every appearance of seriousness.

"If you're careful, little one. It's still very sore."

The little girl stepped around the barrel and reached up to pat at Nagaro's bandaged side. Tredhold hovered nervously, but Ani shook her head at the healer. She knew this was a game.

"It doesn't *feel* sore, Papa!" Narei looked up at him, and now she was laughing.

Nagaro laughed with her. "Of course not, silly! It's my *back* that's sore, not my side."

"Uncle Nagaro! Watch this!" Pilo interrupted, and Nagaro hastily transferred his attention to his two young nephews, who were squaring off on the deck in front of him with stick swords in their hands.

"I'm watching."

Tavo and Pilo promptly went at each other enthusiastically, their sticks making loud cracks when they came together.

Beside him, Nagaro heard sixteen-year-old Bahiri give a derisive snort. He risked taking his eyes from the two boys long enough to give his niece a quick glance and a wink. Bahiri was growing very gracefully towards womanhood, he thought. "Have you got a sweetheart, Bahiri?" he asked as he turned his eyes back to the stick battle.

"Huh!" Bahiri was indignant. "The boys my age are all so silly—or just plain awful!"

Nagaro considered this. "Yes, I remember being silly, and awful. Did I ever tell you about the time I found a pile of fish bones by the river? I brought them home and tried to build fishes out of them on the floor in the back hall."

"*That* wouldn't be so bad—"

At that moment, Pilo made a sudden lunge. Twisting with his stick, he sent Tavo's clattering across the deck to lie a few feet from Nagaro's barrel. "There! I did it!" He exclaimed triumphantly. "Did ye see that, Uncle Nagaro?"

"Yes, Pilo. That was really quite good." Nagaro noted that Tavo was grinning. The older boy had given his brother an opening, but even so...

"I bet I can do it too!" Narei scampered out to snatch up the fallen stick. Turning on Pilo, she went after her cousin with such ferocious concentration, that the boy began to back away.

"Hey!" Pilo cried. "I can't fight a little girl! Make her stop!" He was parrying desperately in self defense.

Nagaro was watching intently. "Steady, Pilo," he said. "Forget that she's a little girl, and don't let her beat you! Narei, turn your body more to the side—the way I showed you."

Narei immediately made the suggested correction. She was darting back and forth, and Pilo looked as if he had his hands full, even though he was six years older and a foot taller than his little cousin.

"Nagaro!" Ani exclaimed. "Ye shouldn't encourage her."

"Why not? Because she's a girl? Just look at her, Ani! I believe she's going to be better than either of the boys."

Narei must have hit Pilo's hand just then, because he gave a sudden yelp and dropped his stick. Narei immediately dropped hers as well. "Oh, poor Pilo!" she cried, running to him. "Did I hurt you?"

Ani immediately went to them, but it soon was apparent that Pilo was not seriously injured. "Ye *know* it's not fair to do that," he was saying to Narei. "A *real* sword has a metal part t' guard my hand."

Standing beside Nagaro, Tred said, "If ye ever had any fear that she wasn't yours, Nagaro, ye can put it to rest. It seems your daughter has inherited her father's gift." Then he raised his voice to say, "Time to go, I'm afraid. The sun's getting low and Nagaro needs his rest."

There followed protests, and then farewells with careful hugs—and handshakes for the two boys, who thought they were too old for hugging.

As Nagaro was watching Animara and Bahiri shepherding the three younger ones down the gangplank, there came a long, low blast of the great south horn. It was followed by a second, and then a third. Nagaro and Tredhold both stiffened at the first note. As the last died away, they relaxed, but only fractionally, and looked at one another.

"So soon?" Nagaro asked. "I thought they would have been farther behind us." He made no move to leave his barrel.

"We had to fight a north wind nearly all the way," Tredhold observed. "But the wind's been out o' the west these last few days. They'd have made a faster passage." He put a hand under Nagaro's elbow to help him up. "Now come inside."

"Can't I stay out here, Tred? To see them come in?"

Tredhold shook his head. "The sun's already setting. If it gets too dark before they make the harbor mouth, they'll have to wait 'til morning anyway. Besides, I have to take care of your back. Now, *come on!*"

Nagaro stood up and allowed himself to be escorted back to the great cabin. When Tred began almost immediately to mix his nightly dose of dedrel, however, he balked again.

"Must I, Tred? If any word comes tonight—about the mission—I want to hear it." His anxiety had been rising ever since hearing the horn.

"If there's no news, ye'll lie awake and fret."

"But if there *is* news—"

"Time enough to get it in the morning, then." Tredhold held out the cup.

Nagaro frowned darkly at it. "What if I just don't drink it, Tred?" he demanded. "What's the worst that could happen?"

Tredhold frowned in his turn. "Ye could move wrong in the night... tear that new skin... open those wounds again. The healing would have to start all over, and it won't heal as prettily the second time."

"Maybe I don't care if it's pretty." Nagaro gestured angrily—and winced.

"It's not appearances I'm worried about, Nagaro," Tredhold told him sternly. "If it heals badly, so the scars are tight, it'll give ye pain every time ye move, even after it's healed. Do ye want that?"

And of course he didn't want that. So he gave in and took the cup. He drank the liquid in one angry gulp, handed the cup back roughly, and lay down, turning his face to the wall.

*

Someone was shaking him. Nagaro stirred, groaned, and struggled groggily to open his eyes. Even when he got them open, they didn't seem to focus properly. "*Bishka...*" he mumbled, and his tongue felt as if it were still asleep.

"There ye are, at last." He was aware of Tredhold standing over him.

"Le' me sleep..." His eyes closed.

Tredhold's hands shook him again. "I'm sorry, Nagaro. I gave ye a stronger dose than usual—because ye were getting wrought up and I wanted t' be sure ye'd rest all night."

"Wha—?" He opened his eyes again and twisted his neck, striving to focus on the window. Blearily he saw that sunlight was streaming in. From the angle of it, it must be nearly midmorning. "How'd it get... s' late?" he mumbled.

"I may have overdone it a bit with the dedrel." Tredhold sounded genuinely apologetic. "And I didn't count on Kuran sending a messenger over at first light to tell me he'd be coming here before noon to talk to ye. So here it is, well past breakfast, and I've been trying to wake ye for the past hour. Can ye sit up?"

"*Bloody hel!*" Nagaro flung a borrowed expletive at the Leithian. He could tell that the healer had already taken the night plasters off of his back. He must have slept right through it—and he still felt half asleep! He groaned. He supposed the man had meant well, but... "You'll have t' help me..."

Tredhold quickly helped him to sit up. "Can ye eat something?" the healer asked, holding his shoulders.

"Not yet... head's spinning..." He squeezed his eyes tight shut and opened them again. "They all came in... las' night?"

"Aye. The bay is full o' ships." Tredhold read his anxious look. "The *Pride of Lankura's* out there. And the *Sea Eagle*."

"Wha' about the *Valor?*" Tredhold had let go of him, and Nagaro clutched dizzily at the edge of the bunk. His tongue still felt slow.

"I can't see the *Valor* from the window," the healer said as he went to the table. He came back with a plate of pancakes and a fork in his hands. "I'm afraid your breakfast has gone cold, but it will be no less nourishing."

Nagaro stared queasily at the food. "Pu' it down, there." He pointed to a spot beside him on the bed. "Is there any soth'ril?"

"Aye. Of course."

Tredhold brought him a cup of the amber liquid, and he was glad to find that it was still warm. He sat sipping it while his head gradually cleared. The clearer it became, the more troubling were his thoughts. "Did the messenger give any account of the mission?" he asked, finding that the words came easier.

Tredhold shook his head, frowning. "I tried asking, but he wouldn't say."

"That's odd, isn't it?" Nagaro tried to reach for the plate, and froze in the midst of the movement, sucking air through his teeth.

Tredhold hastily moved to hand him the plate. The Leithian's frown deepened. "He said he had orders."

Nagaro balanced the plate on his knees while studying the healer. "What do you think is wrong, Tred?"

The Leithian shook his head. "Nothing—I hope. But I wonder why he would have such orders. And I've only counted six ships out there..." Tredhold shook off his frown. "Like as not, Kuran just sent some o' the ships on ahead and the rest are following."

Nagaro had taken a bite of cold pancake. He chewed and swallowed. "Yes. Like as not," he murmured. He took another bite of his breakfast. He knew it was important to eat, but he had no appetite, and his heart misgave him.

Tredhold had gone to the table and begun to busy himself with the things he needed for a fresh set of plasters. "Try to eat as quickly as ye can," he said with forced lightness. "Kuran might come at any time, and I'd far rather ye were bandaged and able to sit up when he does."

As it turned out, they had just enough time for Tredhold to put fresh plasters on Nagaro's back and bind them in place, and for Nagaro put a shirt on over the bandages. Nagaro begged for the shirt, and Tredhold grudgingly agreed. Nagaro wished he had his boots, too, but they'd been lost at Osfaraad.

It was Kunoa who knocked on the cabin door with word that Lord Kuran was approaching with a small party. Nagaro begged to meet the Lord of the Fleet outside on the deck, so Tredhold helped him to his place on the barrel beside the stern castle door.

He had barely settled himself when he looked up and felt a wave of relief at seeing Taru coming across the deck. The young Turo must have come with Kuran. The Lord of the Fleet was near the ship's rail with several other Fleet men, talking to some of the *Sword*'s crew, but Nagaro's attention was on Taru.

The young Turo wore his left arm in a sling and a worried expression on his face, and Nagaro's joy at seeing his friend alive was immediately tempered by concern. "Taru! What happened to your arm?"

Taru glanced distractedly at the sling. "I, ah, took a sword-cut. I wanted Tred t' look at it. I trust him better."

"I'm sure that the ship's doctor on the *Pride* is perfectly competent," Tredhold said quickly.

Taru scarcely seemed to hear Tred. He wasn't looking at the healer.

"Have ye still got that stone in your pocket, Nagaro?" he asked urgently.

Nagaro put his hand on his pocket. "Yes—"

"*Don't lose it!*" Taru hissed. "Nagaro, ye have to—"

"Hold that thought, Zirda!" Kuran had stepped up. His glance was as hard as flint and his tone peremptory. "Remember your orders!"

The three other Fleet warriors who had come with Kuran stopped a few paces behind the Lord of the Fleet and stood stonily at attention. Nagaro recognized them from the Fleet Compound, but didn't know any of them well.

Taru shut his mouth and stood biting his lip.

Kuran inclined his head briefly to Tredhold and to Nagaro. "Good morning, Zirda, Captain. Well, go on then, Taru. Have that arm looked at. Tredhold, will you see to it?"

Tredhold appeared about to speak, but something in Kuran's face seemed to make him think better of it. He shrugged and moved to open the stern castle door, gesturing for Taru to follow him. Taru gave Nagaro one strange, desperate look, and followed the healer.

As soon as the door had closed, Kuran addressed Nagaro. "I'm glad to see you're up from your bed, Captain." The words were accompanied by a smile, but the face around that smile lost none of its grimness.

Nagaro had been sitting still on his barrel, observing everything with growing dread. He didn't mince words when he spoke. "It's plain that something's wrong, My Lord. Did the mission go badly?"

Kuran regarded him, and the lines of the older man's face shifted subtly, revealing pain, mingled with anger. "Yes," he said bitterly. "Very badly. We lost five ships and eighty-four men—including seven ship's officers, and Commander Strad."

To Nagaro, it seemed that the sun had grown suddenly dark. "*Oh Vothra!*" he murmured, shutting his eyes and clutching at the edges of the barrel. The sheer magnitude of the loss struck him like a physical blow.

A hand gripped his arm, steadying him. Startled, his eyes flicked open again and he was staring into Kuran's worried face, right in front of his.

"Steady, lad," the older man muttered, low, under his breath, before stepping back to arm's length.

Nagaro found his voice again. "*How—?*" he asked huskily. "*What happened?*"

Kuran's expression turned grim once more. "They were waiting for us at the Strait of Paktaar—hiding on either side of the channel. When we came through to make our run at Sar Tipaal, they fell on us from both sides in overwhelming numbers. I counted more than twenty ships— the Emperor's among them."

"*The Emperor!*" Nagaro stared. "How could he have gotten there with all those ships... unless... he knew—" Nagaro stopped, his heart suddenly ice.

"He knew." Kuran's eyes were hard, his voice flat. "Even before he spoke to me, it was in my heart that he must have known where we'd be."

"He... *spoke* to you?" Nagaro seemed to hear his own heart pounding in his ears.

"Through an interpreter—a smallish fellow with a thin mustache..."

"*Roheed...*"

Kuran gave him a quick, sharp glance. "Mmm. I thought it might be. As I said, they attacked from both sides, and they did us a lot of damage in a very short time. The Emperor's flagship came straight for mine, flanked by two galleys, and they boarded us. When the Emperor stood before me, he called a halt to the fighting." Kuran paused, biting his lip, but after a moment he continued. "I thought he meant to demand our surrender. They could have finished us—to the last man. But instead, the Emperor just told us to go home. He told us our plan to attack Sar Tipaal had been revealed to him—that instead of the King of Edrovir teaching him a lesson, he had taught us one: Not to come again into his waters. He said that next time he wouldn't be so merciful."

Again Kuran paused.

"But *how* was the plan revealed—?" Nagaro's voice was scarcely above a whisper. He dreaded the answer.

Kuran fixed him with a glance like a knife. "The Emperor specifically wanted us to know that it was from someone on *this ship*—the ship of Kiraam Shaku-Tal. He said we have a traitor among us."

"*Vothra, no!*" Nagaro could hear, in his mind, Peldred's words: *A warrior should be able to bear anything...* He remembered the set of the young Leithian's face... the look in his eyes. How he'd nearly run from the deck of the *Sword* with the words, *Thank you for trying, Zirda.*

The world turned gray.

For the second time, Kuran gripped his arm. "Do you wish to make a statement, Captain?"

"A... statement?" Nagaro stared dully, not comprehending. If what he feared were true, what must Peldred's anguish be...

Kuran was speaking to him, more gently now. "There'll be an inquiry into everything that happened at Osfaraad, Captain. I'd have asked for one in any case, even without this matter of treason—and that's what the charge will be. Do you have anything to say to me? And remember, Zirda, that anything you say I may repeat as part of my own testimony."

Nagaro felt as if he were going to be ill. "My Lord..." he said brokenly, "I... told them nothing... but Peldred—"

Kuran cut him off. "Peldred, Vell, and Pavo have all professed their innocence. Unless you *know* otherwise, these men are no longer your concern." Kuran was studying him closely. "*Do* you know otherwise?"

Nagaro stared in confusion. He had been witness to nothing of the other two men's torment or Pavo's interrogation. *And Peldred had claimed innocence!* How could he accuse the young man? Yet, who else could it have been? "No, I... I don't, My Lord..." he stammered.

"Then I'm presented with four men who possessed the knowledge, all of whom say they parted with none of it." Kuran spoke tersely. "I have no choice but to place all four under arrest. Should I widen the net any further?"

"*What?*" Nagaro's thoughts were still reeling.

"Were there any others on the ship who knew the plan? I know you prefer your men to know what they're about. Did you tell anyone? Tredhold, perhaps?"

"*No!*" Nagaro was affronted. "Your orders were very clear, My Lord. And I gave you my oath! This was *my* error... I never imagined they would torture us for information!" He was speaking with increasing agitation, and he now stood up, rising unsteadily from his seat. He was thinking about Pavo as well as Peldred, and the direction of his thoughts alarmed him. The tale Pavo had told would sound preposterous to men who didn't know Pavo and who didn't believe in the honor of the Mautep, or understand the beliefs of the Mahuk Baar.

He swayed on his feet.

Kuran made a movement towards him, looking worried, and said, "You shouldn't try to stand, Captain. Let me call the healer—"

Nagaro shook his head, which unfortunately brought on a wave of dizziness. "No!" he said. "I'm all right. I want to talk to Pavo!"

It might have been the residual effects of the dedrel, or perhaps it was simply how weak he was. Whatever the case, he felt suddenly very unsteady and groped for the barrel. His hand missed it, and he started to fall, catching the barrel awkwardly with his arm and coming down on one knee on the deck beside it. The action pulled at his healing skin under the bandages. Pain ripped across his back like a knife slash, making him gasp. He clung to the barrel as a gray tide rose, threatening to overwhelm him.

Kuran had sprung towards him with an exclamation when he fell, and now put an arm across his back, under Nagaro's arm, intending to raise him to his feet. The pressure of that arm, however, made Nagaro cry out again in agony. Realizing his mistake, Kuran immediately let go with an oath, then gripped Nagaro's upper arm again to prevent him from toppling to the deck. "*Healer!*" he shouted. "*Tredhold! Come quick!*"

Nagaro was vaguely aware of hearing shouts... of running feet... of more voices—though he couldn't seem to see. Taru, somewhere, was saying his name over and over. He heard Tred's voice demanding, "*What have ye done, My Lord?*" and Kuran saying, "*He fell, so I put my arm on his back without thinking... I'm sorry—*"

His back was stinging... throbbing... burning... he felt someone's hands gently probing... Probing until they touched a certain spot, and he winced violently. His faintness was ebbing a little, but the pain in his back seemed to intensify in proportion.

There were more words, again, that he wasn't listening to, then Kuran's voice saying, "You two! Come lift him! Carefully! Take his arms..."

He felt himself being lifted to his feet, by his arms this time. *This is ridiculous*, he thought, *I'm not dying...* "Jus' a little faint..." he mumbled as he felt his feet under him. He was being supported by two men, one on either side. He made an effort to open his eyes—though he couldn't recall having closed them—and managed to focus on Kuran who was standing directly in front of him.

His mind still clung to the thought that had remained unfinished at the beginning of this mishap, and he sought to finish it, speaking with difficulty through the pain and dizziness. "My Lord... I mus' talk to Pavo. He'll go on about Sheptuum... They won't understand—"

"It's all right, Captain. Don't try to talk." Kuran sounded as if he were uncertain of the state of Nagaro's mind. The Lord of the Fleet turned to the healer. "He should be in bed, Tredhold."

"He should be *now*, My Lord. I want to look at that back! I'm afraid he's bleeding again."

Nagaro was shaking his head, making the world spin again. "No," he said, "...'s not all right... I should've thought... Should've *seen*... I need to talk t' Pavo!"

Kuran was saying something—giving orders. *Not listening to him.* Nagaro tried to twist around. "Tred? Did you talk to Peldred? I set him up t' fall, Tred... I didn't mean to..."

But Tredhold was saying, "Ye never should have sent me away, My Lord. That sword cut didn't need my attention—" *Not listening to him either.* Nagaro tried to pull free of the men holding him, but it *hurt*, and he lacked the strength. And a moment later he was being half-carried through the door into the stern castle. Behind him he heard Kuran say, "No, Taru, you stay here! Help stand guard. Don't let anyone in!"

Taru's protest was cut off by the closing of the stern castle door, and Nagaro was being quickly conveyed along the passage, with Tred and Kuran still talking.

"What did ye say to him, My Lord? To put him in such a state?"

"He's under arrest! By the law, he has to know it, Tredhold. He has to know *why*—"

"It could've waited—"

In the great cabin, Nagaro was maneuvered to a seat on the edge of his bunk. Tredhold went immediately to the table, and started going through his little bottles while Kuran dismissed the two Fleet warriors, bidding them stand outside and guard the door.

Tredhold turned. "Get that shirt off, Nagaro!"

"*No*—" Nagaro tried to stand up. "I have to... talk t' them, Tred—"

Kuran promptly grabbed Nagaro's shoulders and pushed him back down onto the bunk. With one hand, the older man began to work on the buttons of Nagaro's shirt. Embarrassed at having the Lord of the Fleet trying to undress him, and wishing to show he wasn't helpless, Nagaro gave up his other efforts long enough unbutton the shirt himself and painfully shrug his way out of it. The sharp stinging worsened with the motion, and the burning ache increased. He no sooner had the shirt off than he addressed Kuran.

"My Lord, please! I *have* t' talk to Peldred an' Pavo—"

Kuran answered, still holding his shoulder while gazing earnestly down at him and speaking deliberately. "It's out of the question, Nagaro. There can't be any communication between the prisoners before the tribunal. They must be held separately. You'll be confined to this cabin for the voyage to Lankura. Surely you understand the need for this."

Nagaro stared, his mind foggy with pain and weakness. "Tred," he said pleadingly, turning to the other man. "*You* can talk t' them—"

But Kuran interrupted him. "Tredhold is charged with your care, Captain. He will be *here*. With *you*."

The healer had approached, meanwhile, and was standing in front of him, holding out the all too familiar cup. "Here, Nagaro. I want ye to drink this."

"*No!*" Nagaro shook his head emphatically, blinking as stars danced in his vision. "Tred, I don't want it! *I need to think!*"

"What ye need is to *not* think!" Tred extended the cup towards him. "Now, drink it!"

Nagaro tried to push the cup away with his hand.

"Captain!" Kuran spoke commandingly. "You are under the healer's orders—and mine! You will do as he bids!

Still Nagaro made no move to take the cup. He sat numbly. "*This is all wrong...*" he mumbled.

Tredhold drew breath. "Nagaro," he said quietly. "I can call for the guards to come in and have them hold ye... and do it the other way."

"*No! Don't...*" Nagaro shot the healer a resentful look, knowing he was beaten. He couldn't fight both Tred and the Lord of the Fleet. Mechanically he took the cup and drained it quickly, only belatedly noticing that the contents had a slightly different taste. "What is it?" he asked, suspiciously. "...not dedrel?"

"There's dedrel in it. It's something to calm ye down. Ye'll sleep, and I'll have a look at that back. Now please lie down."

They had to help him lie down on the bunk because he was very sore and his arms began to shake uncontrollably as soon as he tried to support his weight. Tredhold sat down on the stool beside him, slitting the bandages from neck to waist with a knife, and began to remove the underlying plasters.

Lying there while Tredhold worked on his back, Nagaro's thoughts spun wildly, wondering how he could possibly undo some of the harm his actions had caused. *Something... something, surely, must be done. But he couldn't think...*

The other two men were talking, though he only half listened.

"Where's Vell to be held, My Lord? Not here on the Sword, surely."

"No. Geldoran has him on the Sea Eagle..."

And now Nagaro's thoughts were beginning to slow as a profound lethargy crept over him... At first he tried to fight it, but it wasn't a thing that could be fought. The two men's voices continued, seeming to grow fainter, and he had to concentrate to understand their meaning.

"Who'll captain of the Sword, then?"

"Brodig—since the Valor was lost at Paktaar."

"That's good—but this isn't. See, the wounds have opened here... and here... This will set him back, My Lord. He needs to lie very still..."

He was drifting... inexorably descending into thick, gray fog. The last thing he heard was Kuran's voice.

"I want him kept in that bed, Tredhold—until we reach Lankura. Do whatever you have to..."

23: Prisoner Of The Crown

He came to awareness behind closed eyelids. His head ached dully. There was a vague sense that he had just emerged from a tunnel full of shadow-images. Those imges consisted of sitting on his bunk or his bed, eating and drinking whatever Tred gave him—over and over—for an indefinite period of time. With his eyes still closed, he frowned.

How much time?

He was lying face down, of course. But he could tell that he wasn't bandaged. There was no pressure of plasters on his back. And his back finally didn't hurt. How long had the pain been gone? Would it return if he tried to move? He decided to risk opening his eyes.

His limited field of vision encompassed a stretch of polished stone floor and parts of two adjoining walls, paneled in dark wood. The head of the pallet bed on which he lay abutted one of the walls. The other wall contained a door, which was ajar. Through the opening, he saw a sliver of a hallway and part of a man's back, clad in the white uniform tirka of the Palace Guard. The only furniture he could see, besides part of his narrow bed, was a chair, placed near the bed as if for the use of whoever was tending him. The quality of the light suggested daylight, entering by a window. The room smelled of Tredhold's medicinal concoctions. It was very quiet.

He tried calling for Tred, and his voice came out hoarse and husky, as if from disuse. Notably, no one answered.

Had Tredhold left him alone?

Again he frowned. He had the distinct feeling that he'd been in the room for some time. He closed his eyes to concentrate. *If he was right, there should be another bed—one with a feather mattress—and a table and two more chairs.* He opened his eyes, twisted to look past his bare feet, and saw the expected table and chairs in the middle of the floor, and the end of the other bed against the far wall, confirming his familiarity with the room. Yet he had no memory of how he'd gotten there. The last thing he remembered with any clarity was being in the great cabin of the *Sword of Freedom*, lying on his bunk. Tred had given him a cup of something to drink and had made him lie down. Between that memory and the present there was nothing but that gray tunnel full of shadows.

The length of that tunnel, he realized, must correspond to several days. Probably less than a week, but long enough to have sailed from Pakoa to Lankura, because he was obviously in the palace at Lankura—on the ground floor, since the flooring was stone rather than wood. And the presence of a guard at his door made sense if he was a prisoner of the Crown. Kuran had said he was under arrest.

This left the problem of the nature of the tunnel. He remembered having fallen. *He'd hurt himself... rather stupidly...* Had he been ill with a fever again? The trouble with that idea was that the shadow-images weren't like any fever-dreams he'd ever had. Fever-dreams were bizarre and distorted, while the tunnel-images were monotonously ordinary—just Tredhold telling him what to do. And he would not have minded *that*, except that he couldn't remember saying anything, or having any thoughts, or any feelings about any of it. He frowned harder as memories stirred of his experiences under heskial... *Sitting, staring dumbly like a wooden puppet... obediently drinking whatever was in the cup as often as it was given to him—*

Abruptly there were sounds from the hallway—voices.

"My Lady Princess, I'm sorry. You cannot pass."

"I know that, Sargent. But even if he's too ill for visitors, surely he can receive a gift. This basket of fruit—"

Nagaro was out of the bed and on his feet in an instant at the first sound of Nevien's voice. "*My Lady!*" he croaked. "*I'm all right... I—*" That was as far as he got. That, and two steps towards the door, before pain struck him like a blinding stab between the eyes and a wave of dizziness crashed over him. Somehow, he managed to find the bedside chair and collapsed onto it as points of light swarmed around him. He clutched his throbbing head.

The voices came to him as if from far away.

"*Captain?*"

"*My Lady, you can't go in!*"

There were footsteps, as of someone running, and then Tredhold's voice, sounding breathless. "My Lady Princess... we are very honored, of course, but he can see no one."

"But I heard him say he was all right—"

"He spoke?"

Nagaro's faintness was receding, and he distinctly heard surprise in the healer's voice. He released his head. He wanted to get up and go to the door so Nevien could *see* that he was all right, but he was barefoot and shirtless. And he was afraid he might fall if he tried—which would hardly be reassuring to her. He heard very clearly Nevien's response to Tredhold's startled question.

"Yes, he spoke!"

"Well... he, ah, has been steadily improving..." Tredhold sounded flustered. "I must go in, now, and tend to him. Thank you for the fruit, My Lady. It's a very kind thought, and will do him good. A very good day to ye, Zirdyn."

Tredhold came in then, moving urgently, carrying a basket and a seaman's bag awkwardly in his arms. He came to a dead stop, staring at the empty bed, then saw Nagaro sitting on the chair. "Now what can have happened to get ye out o' bed—?" he began.

Nagaro met the healer's eyes, frowning. "Has she gone, Tred?"

"Oh Gods!" Tredhold turned pale. "Ye've come right out of it!"

"Out of *what*, Tred?" he asked. And then, when the healer did not immediately answer, his frown darkened and his anger flared. "*What have you been doing to me?*"

Tredhold looked acutely uncomfortable. "I... I'm sorry, Nagaro. I had orders—No, *don't* try t' get up! Stay where ye are!"

The healer distractedly deposited the basket and the seaman's bag on the table, then hurried to the narrow bed Nagaro had just risen from. He squatted beside it, searching the floor around and under the bed and bedside table.

From where he sat, Nagaro could see what looked like a little puddle there—a stain on the floor, still damp in the middle. Tredhold wiped a finger across the puddle and held the finger to his nose. *"Oh bodjer!"* he muttered. He straightened his legs and then sat down heavily on the edge of the bed, putting a hand over his eyes.

Nagaro was searching among the shadow-images. "I knocked the cup over..." he murmured, "...and it rolled..." But he'd made no effort to pick it up, or to tell Tred what had happened. And it hadn't been an act of rebellion. *There simply had been no impulse to pick the thing up... no words in his mind to be spoken...*

Tredhold took his hand from his eyes. "I can see what must have happened," he said numbly. "Last night, I thought ye'd dropped the cup *after* drinking what was in it..."

Nagaro's brows came sharply together. "What *was* in it, Tred?"

Tredhold looked uneasy. "Ah... a mixture of several things," he said cautiously. "There's no reason ye need to know exactly."

"Not just dedrel, then?"

"Ah... *no-o*... Tred was eyeing him warily. "Dedrel is a *soporific*—it makes a man sleep. The effect of this other is more... ah... *hypnotic.*"

"*Hypnotic?* What does *that* mean?"

The healer stood up. He moved away a little, not meeting Nagaro's eyes. "It... puts a man into a trance—not quite sleeping or waking. He'll follow simple instructions, but won't know what's happening—won't remember. I'm surprised ye know what happened to the cup..." Tredhold glanced at him, then, and saw the storm clouds gathering. *"I'm sorry, Nagaro!"* he said in an agonized voice.

"So I was *a puppet?*" Nagaro had not moved from where he sat, but he spoke with suppressed fury.

"Nagaro, no! It wasn't like that! It was so ye could *heal—*"

But Nagaro was not listening. "You *bastard*, Tred!" he said through his teeth. "How *dare* you do that to me!"

It had been very much like being under the influence of heskial. That was the thought that made him scowl like thunder. Not quite like heskial, though... With heskial, he had known *exactly* what he was being made to do—every single minute. But this was too close... *too close...* He clutched the chair, his knuckles whitening.

"I'm *really* sorry, Nagaro!" Tredhold was speaking again. "I had to keep ye *still*—keep ye in *bed*—to make sure ye didn't hurt yourself again. Ye needed to *not* think... *not* worry. And I couldn't think of any other way to do it! If I'd just put ye to sleep for days, ye wouldn't have been able to eat, and ye *needed* to eat. And I had to make sure ye didn't talk... in case someone *heard*..." Tredhold faltered, and ceased his explanation. His eyes were riveted on Nagaro's face, pleading.

"How many people have seen me... like that?" Nagaro's voice shook.

"No one! No one but me, I *swear* it! I've put everyone off by saying ye were too ill to be disturbed. I made sure ye were unconscious when they brought ye in here."

Nagaro put his head down, closed his eyes as a wave of pure relief washed over him, sweeping away the anger. A sigh like a sob escaped him. The world hadn't seen him acting like Leyel Virden. That was what mattered. Tred had seen, of course, but he could trust Tred...

At least he had thought he could. Outrage welled again. He raised his head and impaled the healer with a frowning gaze. "Blast you, Tred! You had no right to do that without asking me! I would have lain still if you'd told me—"

Tredhold took a step back, shaking his head. "Ye were blaming yourself, Nagaro—saying things that could be misconstrued. Ye weren't listening to me, or to Kuran!"

"Because you weren't listening to me!" Nagaro's anger shook him. He started to stand, but the way his head felt made him think better of it, and he sank back onto the chair. "Don't *ever* do that to me again, Tred!" he rasped. "*I won't have it!* I won't drink it—not if I know what it is! And *don't* try to trick me!"

Tredhold had backed up another step. He looked pale, shaken, and he spoke fervently. "I pray I never need to even consider it!" He mopped his brow with his hand. "But once I'd started, it was hard to stop, ye see. Because I *knew* ye'd be angry. Which ye plainly are. I've been dreading having to explain it to ye. I hope I haven't lost your trust altogether."

Nagaro glared at the other man for several long seconds before he drew a shuddering breath. He let it out slowly, striving to master himself. Lost somewhere between anger and tears, he put his head down into his hands. Tred sounded completely sincere, and very distraught—*and that hurt*. What use was anger now, after all? The thing was done. It was over. The man had been trying to heal him the best way he knew how.

"I'm trying not to be angry, Tred," he said huskily when he was able. "I don't like being angry. It... *scares* me."

"Aye. It scares me too."

Nagaro raised his head and found that Tredhold was watching him warily.

"I *was* going to stop it soon," the healer said apologetically. "I *swear* I was. I was going to taper it off so it wouldn't be such a shock, starting tomorrow. I just needed to be sure your back was healed enough that ye couldn't hurt it again by moving wrong or falling."

"And *is* it?" Nagaro demanded.

"Aye... I think so. Only just."

"*Good!*" Nagaro stood up, though cautiously this time. His head still throbbed. Standing up this time made that pain a little worse, but he felt only moderately dizzy. *"Don't touch me!"* he added fiercely, as Tredhold started towards him. The healer froze immediately and stayed out of the way as Nagaro transferred himself back to the bed and sat down on the edge of it.

Sitting there, trying not to look at Tred, Nagaro's eyes strayed to the table—to Nevien's gift, the basket of fruit. With a pang, he realized he had forgotten all about it. Tredhold must have followed his gaze, for the healer went to the table and reached for the basket.

"Could you... bring it to me?" Nagaro hesitated after his outburst to ask the healer for anything.

"Just let me have a look at it first," Tredhold muttered. "I'm the old hen, remember?" He had lifted the white cloth that covered the basket's contents. It appeared to be a handkerchief with some embroidery on it. The healer began to go through the contents, and Nagaro caught glimpses of strawberries, apricots, plums, and even oranges that must have come from far away in the south. Abruptly, Tredhold paused holding an object that seemed to have come from the bottom of the basket. It was a folded piece of paper.

"A note?" Nagaro asked eagerly. "Give it to me, Tred!"

But the healer stood still, frowning.

"Tred? It *is* for me, isn't it?"

"I don't know..." Tredhold turned the paper over slowly in his hands. "It's... sealed. Not addressed on the outside." He continued to frown and didn't look at Nagaro.

"Well, open it, then, and look. Go on!"

Tredhold hesitated, but then broke the seal and opened the paper. He'd scarcely begun to scan the writing inside, however, when he pulled his eyes away. "*Oh bodjer...*" he muttered. "I shouldn't be reading this." He crossed quickly to the bed and thrust the paper into Nagaro's waiting hands. "Here!"

Nagaro frowned in his turn as he smoothed the paper and read silently to himself:

Dear Captain Nagaro,

I have been so worried since I heard about what happened. And being told day after day that no one can see you because you are too ill is very hard. I have offered prayers to the Blessed Mother for your recovery every day at the Temple of Solbrid. It seemed there was nothing more I could do, but then I remembered what my mother has always told me—that there is virtue in fruits that can be restorative to the sick and wounded. So I thought to bring you fruit. I hope the healer will give it to you, and that you are strong enough to eat it. Please know that you are ever in my thoughts, and I wish that you may soon be well.

Nevien Harlind

Nagaro's frown had been deepening as he read, and now he flung the paper down on the bed. "Now see what you've done, Tred! With all your telling everyone that I'm so ill! You've made her worry more! About *me*—when she has so many troubles of her own already!"

Tredhold was watching him with a frozen face. "Nagaro," he said softly, "my *wife* writes me letters like that."

"Well I hope so! Since she cares about you—"

"*Nagaro!*" The healer interrupted, sounding a little strangled. "Are... are ye... ...ye and her...?"

Nagaro stared at him. "Are we *what*, Tred? We are friends—very good friends. Is that what you mean?"

Studying Nagaro's face, Tredhold seemed suddenly embarrassed. "Ah. Yes. Right," he said. "Of course." He gave his attention back to the contents of the basket, though he'd been through them already. Presently, he carried the basket to the bed. "Eat some of the strawberries," he said, not meeting Nagaro's eyes. "They'll spoil the soonest. Not too many! Your stomach's not used to this sort o' thing."

Tredhold watched as Nagaro picked up a handful of the berries and began to eat them. Then he rose and returned the basket to the table "I'm sorry if I caused the princess to worry unnecessarily," he went on. "I didn't know what... good friends... ye were. Though I suppose I should've guessed. She's come so often to ask after ye—not every day, but a dozen times at least..."

"A *dozen times?*" Nagaro had stopped with a strawberry halfway to his mouth. "But *not* every day? Tred, *how long have I been here?*"

Tredhold cast him an uneasy glance as he picked up the seaman's bag from where it lay beside the basket. "Almost three weeks."

"*Three weeks!*" Nagaro was stunned. *He had been a puppet for three weeks—longer, since it had started on Pakoa.* The horror of the thought was displaced an instant later, however, by concern for the princess. "Poor Nevien," he murmured. But then yet another thought intruded. "Tred!" he exclaimed in dismay. "What about the inquiry? Have I missed the tribunal?"

Tredhold had cautiously approached the bed. He stood, holding the seaman's bag. "It started three days ago."

"Only three days? What took them so long?"

Tredhold shrugged. "The king had to name a High Judge, and three Judges-Major, and there was a lot of politics in that. And they had to send word to all the families of the men that were lost, and give time for all o' them to send witnesses to watch the tribunal. Altogether, I'm surprised they opened it as soon as they did. But then, emotions are running high. Everyone wants to punish someone for all those deaths."

Nagaro's fears all came back in a rush. "But I have to give testimony, Tred! And if it started three days ago—"

"Steady, Nagaro! They haven't called ye yet. I've asked for a day's warning on when they mean to call ye."

This was scarcely any less alarming. "But I'm not ready, Tred! My head hurts just sitting here. And I get faint whenever I stand up! What's *wrong* with me, if my back has healed? Is it that cursed concoction of yours?"

Tredhold winced, but he shook his head. "The headache probably is," he said apologetically. "That should ease in a few hours. But as for the rest of it, ye're just very weak, Nagaro. Ye lost a lot o' blood to begin with, and since then the healing's taken all of your strength. And in spite of all I could do, ye've not been eating as well as I'd like. I *do* mean to see that ye're ready. That's why I brought your things." He dropped the seaman's bag onto the bed beside Nagaro. "Go on, open it."

Still frowning, Nagaro pulled open the bag's drawstring. From the contents it was obvious that Tredhold had been into his sea chest aboard the *Sword of Freedom.* There were three clean shirts, two pairs of pants, and undergarments, as well as other personal items such as scissors and comb. Near the bottom, his hand touched something smooth and hard, and he pulled out a small clay jar of kuma stain. His stomach turned upside-down looking at it, as he noticed for the first time the paleness of the skin of his forearm. "*Bishka!*" he murmured. *It must be six weeks since the last time he had applied the ointment. The stain on his skin had faded almost completely!*

"I thought ye'd be wanting that. I expect I'll have to help ye with it, though."

Nagaro swallowed. He was thinking of how he'd nearly gone to the door to let Nevien see him. "Tred... I... *Thank you...*" He gazed up at the earnest blue eyes looking down at him. "You're a true friend, Tred. And all those things I said before, I want to take them back—"

Tredhold shook his head. "Forget it, Nagaro. I don't blame ye for being angry. Ye've been through far too much."

*

Tredhold did help him with the kuma stain—and with trimming his hair and beard with the scissors. The healer also arranged for a tub to be brought into the room so Nagaro could take a proper bath.

It was while Nagaro was undressing for the bath that he missed something.

"*My ring!*" He cried before he stopped to think. "Tred, where is it?"

Tredhold looked up, frowning, from where he was seated at the table. "That little gold one? I thought I heard that ye gave it away."

"No! *My* ring!" At that moment he didn't care that it had always been a secret. *He could not have lost it!* "It was on a cord—tied around my waist."

"Oh, *that.*" Tredhold dug in his pocket and immediately produced the heavy bronze ring, together with its leather cord. "I'm sorry. I should have put it in the seaman's bag with your other things, but I took it for safekeeping so long ago that I forgot. I'm afraid I've been moving it from pocket to pocket for days without thinking. Let me put it in the bag for ye." He rose.

Nagaro felt weak with relief at sight of his treasure. "No, Tred," he said as he lowered himself gingerly into the tub of water. "Put it with the clothes I've laid out. I always wear it—around my neck... or my waist."

The healer did as he was asked, but he gave Nagaro a puzzled glance. "Do ye? I wonder that I'd never seen it before."

Nagaro frowned. "I... keep it hidden... It... could connect me to my past."

"Ah." Tred nodded wisely. "Ye'll want it around your waist then for now." He squatted beside the tub and began carefully washing Nagaro's back with a soft cloth. "They'll want to see your back—your chest, your shoulder. The evidence of what ye went through."

"But... if my back has healed?"

"Don't worry." Tredhold grimly dismissed the concern. "It still looks quite *impressive*. It'll come to look better in time, but that will take months, and we'll be long done with the tribunal by then."

*

"Tell me about the tribunal, Tred. Where are they holding it? Who are the judges?"

For several days they had avoided talking about the trial, as if by mutual consent, but Nagaro's concern had grown apace as he gathered strength. He now sat cross-legged on his narrow bed with a tray balanced across his knees. He had devoured an orange and two apricots and was now diligently applying himself to a plateful of stew. Tredhold had told him it was important to eat well—especially plenty of red meat—to get his strength back, and Nagaro was taking the recommendation very seriously. Filora, the Mistress of the Royal Kitchens, remembered him well from the attack on Lankura and was providing him the most tasty fare she could within the limits of what was considered appropriate for a prisoner of the Crown.

Treadhold, who was seated at the table, looked up from the letter he was writing. He appeared to consider for a moment, then seemed to make a decision. "It's being held in the Audience Hall. Lord Madred is the High Judge—the man who will direct the proceeding and render the verdict—"

"Madred Furthing?" Nagaro knew of the man as Simion's employer and the father of Brandle Furthing, and the details from that context did not paint a very positive picture. "He's one of the Leithian Faction! Why *him?*"

Tredhold looked a little surprised. "By tradition, the High Judge is supposed to be someone who will care about the outcome," he explained. "So he'll be sure that justice is done with no waste of time. Lord Madred qualifies on that score because half a dozen men from Furthing Hold were among those killed at Paktaar. And since two o' the accused are high-born Leithians, they wanted a High Judge who was one too—to be sure that Vell and Peldred get a fair trial. It was a touchy point because the charges were put forward by Kuran and Geldoran, who are both Kelorin—more or less."

"What about seeing that Pavo gets a fair trial?"

Tredhold sat up a little straighter. "Lord Madred has a reputation for being a fair-minded man," he said a little stiffly.

Nagaro frowned. He tended to forget that Tredhold was a Leithian, despite the evidence right before his eyes. "What about the other three judges?" he asked hurriedly.

"The Judges-Major?" The healer nodded and ticked them off on his fingers. "They're the lords Odus, Soren, and Anduar."

Nagaro continued to frown. He chewed and swallowed. "So," he said, "all together that would be two Leithians and two Kelorin, with one each from the Leithian Faction and the Kelorin Faction, and the other two being Pact Signers."

This time, Tredhold looked more than a little surprised. "Ye've been taking lessons in politics?"

Nagaro grimaced. "*Not* because I enjoy it. I don't like Odus being one of them, either."

"Why?"

Nagaro shot the healer a look. "Because the mission was his idea." He looked down at his plate, glad that he had nearly finished the stew since he suddenly wasn't hungry. He put the tray aside and sat staring at his hands. "He also knows I didn't think much of the idea. I as much as predicted it would be a disaster. And now it has been, because *I* decided to surrender—"

"Stop right there!" Tredhold put his pen down on the table. "I won't have ye saying that what happened was your fault!"

Nagaro scowled. "It wasn't *all* my fault, But you saw the look on Peldred's face, Tred. You heard what he said. I had thought he was being hard on himself for fainting after being branded only once. But now I wonder if he even *did* faint. The Mautep made him watch what they did to me, and to Vell. And he's so young! When they came at him with the second hot iron—after he knew how much it would hurt—would it be any wonder if he broke down?"

Tredhold cast a furtive glance in the direction of the door, which was closed, and made a motion for Nagaro to lower his voice. "I think ye're right, Nagaro. I've talked to all four accused men since Osfaraad, and Peldred's the only one who seems to have something on his conscience. I got a chance to talk to him on Pakoa—after ye spoke to him—but he wouldn't tell me what was troubling him. I thought I'd just let him be for a time, but I never got another chance!"

Nagaro shook his head. "This is all wrong, Tred. This isn't a matter of treason. It's about one young man, who weakened—under torture— and hasn't found the courage to admit it to the world."

Tredhold sighed. "Unfortunately it becomes treason—technically, at least—exactly because he didn't admit it. He should have told Vell— or Geldoran—right from the start, there at Osfaraad. Word could have been sent to the other ships, to call off the mission."

Nagaro sighed in his turn. "I don't think Vell made it easy for him to admit it, Tred. Vell's a decent fellow when he understands things, but he's not very perceptive, and he has about as much sensitivity as a brick. So now Peldred's caught himself. The more times you tell a lie, the harder it gets to tell the truth, and putting him on trial is only going to make it worse! I wish Kuran hadn't been in such a hurry to arrest everyone."

"There are *laws*, Nagaro. He hadn't any choice."

"I suppose not."

There was a short silence, and then Tredhold said, "Try to finish that stew. Mistress Filora cooked it for ye herself."

Nagaro picked up the fork, stabbed a piece of meat, stuck it into his mouth, and chewed without enthusiasm.

Tredhold picked up the pen, and then put it down again. "Kuran's a better friend to ye than ye know, Nagaro. Taru told me a few things while we were alone in the cabin. He wasn't supposed to, of course. He swore me to secrecy. But I think Kuran knew he'd talk, and that's why he brought him along—that, and so ye could see that he'd survived the battle. That sword cut was perfectly well-tended."

"So, what did Taru tell you?" Nagaro's hand hovered, poised with another fork-full of stew.

Tredhold motioned for Nagaro to continue eating, and said, "Kuran was furious when the *Valor* arrived at Paktaar without the *Sword* and he found out why. He took Strad into the *Pride*'s great cabin, and there were heated words. When they came out, Strad looked like a man with a sword hanging over his head, and Kuran was wearing a scowl like thunder. Then, when Geldoran arrived half a day later with the news that the *Sword* was back in our hands with most of her crew alive, the first words out of Kuran's mouth were, *What of Nagaro?*"

Nagaro swallowed the last bite of stew. "That *is* gratifying, Tred, but it happened before he learned that the plan had been betrayed."

Tredhold gave him a stern look. "He has been *extremely* concerned about the state of your health."

Nagaro's eyes flashed. "He wanted me kept in bed! 'Do whatever you have to.' Wasn't that what he said?"

"It was for your own good! And don't go blaming Kuran for what *I* decided t' do!"

Nagaro deliberately unfurrowed his brow. "I'm sorry, Tred. I know I shouldn't blame him and I've been trying not to blame you, either. Did Taru say anything else?"

Tredhold appeared mollified. "This is *really* not to be repeated, mind ye, but there was something Captain Brodig said after being fished out o' the water when the *Valor* went down. It was after they knew they'd lost Strad. Brodig said that Strad had seemed to have two sets of orders at Osfaraad—*conflicting sets of orders*—and Brodig thought he'd chosen to follow the worst o' them. Kuran told Brodig to save it for the tribunal."

Nagaro frowned. "Did he say where the orders came from?"

"Taru said he thought Brodig didn't know. But I ran into Landros when I went to get your things, and *he* told me that Geldoran told *him* that Strad had orders from Kuran to heed your counsel in Mahuk waters. So that'd likely be one set of orders, and the others were *conflicting*."

Nagaro's slim, black brows drew sharply together. "If Strad had taken my council, it's unlikely the Emperor would have caught us."

"That's right. I've been trying to tell ye it wasn't your fault. It was that bloody fool, Strad—or whoever told him not t' trust your advice."

Nagaro's brows did not relax. "I still did what I did, Tred, and the outcome would have been different if I'd done otherwise. Strad is dead, so he can't speak—and whoever gave those other orders won't want it known. Not after what happened."

Tredhold urgently shook his head. "Ye've nothing to worry about, Nagaro. They'd never convict ye o' treason after ye nearly got yourself killed keeping your mouth shut."

Nagaro shook his head at the healer. "I'm not worried about *me*, Tred. Not as long as Vell and Peldred give honest accounts of what I did. I'm worried about Peldred and Pavo—Peldred, if he confesses, and Pavo if Peldred *doesn't* confess. Do you think any of the judges will believe a word of Pavo's story?"

A shadow crossed Tredhold's face. "There is that," he said. "That, and... ah... the fact that Strad is one of those dead men who came from Furthing Hold. He was from Lord Madred's House."

They sat still for a long moment, looking at each other.

Nagaro swallowed. "What's happened in the first three days of the tribunal?"

Tredhold shifted his position in his chair and scratched nervously behind his ear. "I only know what I heard at the *Golden Tankard*. That's a tavern in High Street where I stopped while I was out getting your things. It's a good a place for news. There's some folk staying there who've come to witness the tribunal."

Nagaro gestured impatiently. "So what did you hear?"

Tredhold looked even more uncomfortable. "*Well...* it's just this, ye see. I'm not supposed to tell ye."

Nagaro frowned darkly. "You just told me all those things you heard from Taru."

"That was only against Kuran's orders. *This* is against the law of the Tribunal. Prisoners aren't supposed to be told any o' the details of the testimony."

"*Bishka!*" Nagaro angrily swung his legs over the side of the bed and stood up shakily. His impulse had been to pace the floor, but he felt too unsteady for that, so he went to the table where Tredhold was sitting and sat down in the second chair.

The healer watched him warily. "I'm sorry—" he began.

Nagaro waved the words aside. "If you're not supposed to tell me, then you shouldn't, Tred." He sat frowning while Tredhold toyed with the quill pen. "But look here, Tred," he said after a moment. "Can you tell me who's been called to give testimony—just not what they said?"

"I suppose I could do that." Tredhold relaxed visibly, settling back in his chair. "They spent the first day hearing from Kuran and Geldoran in a session that wasn't even open to view for the dead men's families. I suppose it was about why Kuran and Geldoran wanted an inquiry. The second day they led off with the official testimony from those same two. That *was* open to the families, and the folk at the *Golden Tankard* seemed to think the judges questions had been set in advance, and the answers were what they expected to hear."

"Did Geldoran make any mention of Landros saying he'd talked to Vothra?"

Tredhold looked startled. "I think that would be in the nature o' detail," he said. "But there wasn't any mention of it at the *Tankard*."

Nagaro nodded. "Good." He was happier having Vothra left out of it. "What else can you tell me?"

"Well..." Tredhold scratched his ear. "Pretty much all the rest of the time has been given over to Vell's testimony. That's all been open, and there's been a *lot* o' questions from the judges. Nobody seemed to think that any of it was rehearsed, either."

"A whole day and a half? Poor Vell!"

Tredhold rubbed his chin. "Ye needn't feel so sorry for him. It seems they're calling him *Captain* Vell."

Nagaro shrugged easily. "He was captain of the *Sword* for a time, and if they want to make that rank permanent, I'll not begrudge it to him as long as I get the *Sword* back in the end. *And* as long as he gives his testimony straight."

Tredhold frowned and seemed to be considering. Presently he said, "By all accounts, Vell has been doing right by ye, Nagaro. He hasn't changed the story he's been telling ever since Osfaraad."

Nagaro gave him a grateful glance, then hastily put a finger to his lips. "No details, remember?"

*

"Now just put yer right foot *there* on th' leather, Zirda, and stand on it... That's right..."

Tredhold had arranged for a shoemaker to come to Nagaro's prison-room to measure him for a new pair of boots, since Baruk had flung his old ones into the sea. The shoemaker was a short, plump Turowan with hair cut in the Kelorin fashion and a round, clean-shaven face. He hummed to himself as he painstakingly drew around Nagaro's right foot with a stick of oiled chalk. He then pulled a tape out of his pocket and measured the distance over the top of the foot just at the ball, and again at the instep, marking the positions and noting the numbers on the leather.

"And now the height up to the knee... right, Zirda?" The shoemaker twisted his neck to grin up at Nagaro from where he knelt on the floor. "I've seen ye ride by in the street, and I know what kind o' boots ye favor." He took the measurement, and also the circumference of the thickest part of Nagaro's calf, making more notes on his piece of sole leather. "This is a day t' remember," he pattered on. "Something to tell my grandchildren, Zirda. The day I measured Captain Nagaro. The day I made boots for th' Hero of Osfaraad!"

"The *what?*" Nagaro was so taken aback that he moved his foot while the shoemaker was taking a measurement.

The shoemaker clucked, but then gave him another cheerful grin. "It's what they're callin' ye all over town, Zirda. All th' plain folk like me, anyway... I don't know what the lords is sayin.' Now, if ye'd be so good as t' stand still..."

Nagaro stood still, frowning. "I'm not a hero," he said grimly. "The real battle was at Paktaar. "Eighty-four men died there. *That's* where you should be looking for heros!"

"Ah, right ye are, Captain," the shoemaker said, with the air of one who has heard exactly what he expected to and hasn't had his mind changed in the least.

Nagaro frowned down at the top of the man's head. "I mean it," he said earnestly. "I don't want anyone calling me 'Hero of Osfaraad!' You can tell that to anyone you hear repeating it!"

"Ye may be sure I will, Zirda." This time the shoemaker didn't even look up. "If ye'll just put yer other foot on the leather, Captain."

The man traced around Nagaro's left foot as he had the right and repeated the other measurements on the left leg before rising to go. He turned to Tredhold. "I'll not forget this, Zirda," he said seriously. "The honor ye've done me... I swear by the Spirits ye'll not be sorry!"

"I expect not to be," the healer observed briskly as he ushered the man out the door. "As long as ye deliver the finished boots by week's end."

"As good as done, Zirda!" Standing in the hallway, the shoemaker bobbed a little half bow, then winked and lowered his voice. "He's the best sort o' hero, ain't he, Zirda? The sort what says he ain't one!"

Nagaro was sitting on the bed, frowning, when Tredhold closed the door and turned around. "They're not *really* calling me that all over Lankura, are they, Tred?" he asked in exasperation.

The healer returned him a sympathetic look. "I think it's probably an exaggeration," he said. "But it's not the first time I've heard it."

"I thought no one was supposed to talk about it!"

Tredhold sighed. "I'm afraid neither Vell nor Pavo were shy about telling their tales on Pakoa before Kuran arrived with the Fleet. It was all over the island, and ye know how fishermen are. The tale probably got to Lankura before ye did." The healer paused, then added, "It's another reason ye needn't worry about the judges convicting ye of anything, Nagaro. The people wouldn't stand for it There's more than a few are tired o' losing sons or husbands or fathers because some high-born captain fought to the last man."

*

"Why haven't they called me?"

Nagaro was pacing the floor. He was wearing clean pants and shirt and his new boots, and displaying considerable vigor. All that healthy fruit, and eating meat three times a day, had begun to make a difference.

Tredhold looked up from his writing. He had been working on the same letter to his wife for three days, and it was getting rather long. His expression was unusually serious. "Ye should sit down for a while, Nagaro. Ye're wearing a track in the floor."

"Is that the old hen talking?"

Tredhold sighed. "No, just your friend, Nagaro. Ye know I haven't objected to your pacing these past two days—now that ye're strong enough to keep your feet. It's good exercise. It's just that ye're getting yourself wrought up, and ye know that does no good."

Nagaro cast him a scorching glance. "I can't *bear* just sitting here! I want to know what's happening! You have to find another excuse to go out and get some news."

Tredhold sighed. "I've been trying to think of one that would pass with the guards. But ye know I'm not allowed to tell ye much anyway."

Nagaro stamped to the table and dropped into the chair opposite the healer. "They've finished with Vell. They've questioned Brodig. From what you *did* tell me, it seems they barely asked Peldred any questions at all—just let him go. They must be on to Pavo by now! What's *taking* so long? And why haven't they called *me?*"

Facing him across the table, Tredhold frowned, but then managed a shrug and said, "I expect they're giving ye as long as possible to recover from your wounds."

*

Tredhold shouldered his way past the guard at the door with barely an acknowledgment. Crossing the room in a few strides, he dumped a crudely wrapped bundle onto the table in front of Nagaro. "There," he said. "There's your set o' King's Men," and he passed around the table, making for the place where he kept his own seaman's bag at the foot of the room's other bed.

Nagaro pounced on the package, pulling off the cloth that covered it. He stared, frowning, at the board and the wooden playing pieces that spilled out onto the table. "This isn't Taru's set," he said in confusion. "Didn't you manage to talk to him?"

"Ah, no—" Tredhold sounded distracted. He had pulled his pen, ink, and paper out of his bag and was staring at them. "I... never got to the Fleet Compound. I bought that set to satisfy the guards—since it's what I said I was going out for."

"Is something wrong, Tred? You haven't gotten any bad news from home, have you?"

Tredhold glanced up, and away again, too quickly. "No," he said hastily. "Nothing like that. Ye'll not have much use for the game, though, Nagaro. They've finally called ye. Ye're to appear tomorrow, at the third hour o' the morning."

Nagaro froze with one of the wooden pieces in his hand. "Well it's about time—" He stopped. "Now what is *wrong*, Tred? You've heard something from the tribunal, haven't you? Is it something you can't tell me?"

The healer had moved to the table as if to sit. He was still holding the writing materials. "I don't know, Nagaro," he began without meeting Nagaro's eyes. "I don't really know any details, but—"

"Well if you don't know any *details*, then you can tell me what you *do* know, can't you? At least tell me why you've gotten out your pen and paper!"

Tred sat down heavily, setting the writing implements on the table. He raised his eyes. "I was thinking of writing a letter to the judges," he said grimly. "Something in the line of a testament to Pavo's character. Though I don't suppose it'd do much good."

"Pavo's character!" Nagaro was becoming alarmed. "Tred, what's *happened?*"

"I'm not even sure." The healer ran a hand through his sandy hair. "And I *am* pretty sure they wouldn't want me to tell ye what I heard. But the truth is, it's got me so shaken that I really have to talk to *somebody*, and ye're the only one I've got!"

Nagaro leaned across the table. "Tred," he said seriously. "If it's that suspicion is falling on Pavo, it's no more than I expected. You don't have to tell me *why*—"

"I don't even know why!" Tredhold gestured in the air. "All I know is that I went into the *Golden Tankard* and the whole place was buzzing about 'seeing the traitor hanged.' 'What traitor?' I asked one of them. And he said, 'Why, that piece o' Mahuk garbage of course!'"

"*Keshaal!*" Nagaro's alarm was warring with rising anger. "None of those folk know Pavo at all! If they did, they wouldn't say such a thing!"

Tredhold gave him an agonized look. "I talked to some others—out in the street—and it was the same everywhere! Nagaro, I... I keep thinking... he couldn't have *confessed* to it, could he?"

Nagaro's brows came together in an immediate frown. "Of course not! Pavo wouldn't confess to anything he didn't do, and if he *had* done it, he'd surely have told us."

Tredhold bent his head, closing his eyes and pinching the bridge of his nose with his fingers. "I want to believe ye're right," he said. "But they all sounded so *sure.*"

Nagaro sighed. "He won't have confessed to it," he said quietly. "But you know how Pavo is, Tred. If he thinks he's being treated unfairly he'll just close up tighter than a clam. And men are apt to construe silence as guilt."

The healer's head came up. "Yes! That'll be it! He's gone silent. If only there were someone to explain it to the judges!"

They stared at each other.

"There's us," Nagaro said decisively. "Are you going to write that letter?" He gestured at the writing material.

Tredhold sighed. "I should try. But it may not do much good—coming from me. I'm just a ship's doctor."

"You're *the* ship's doctor, Tred. The one who was *there*... the one who knows Pavo. And you watch all the members of the crew, don't you? You have to measure the character of a man to judge whether he has some trouble of mind, and how serious it is. Your judgement ought to be worth *something.*"

Tredhold sighed. "It ought to be," he said. "But I'm not sure it *will* be." He pulled the paper towards him and picked up the pen. "Why don't ye set up the game board, while I'm about it."

"I will." Nagaro gave him a nod of encouragement. "And don't worry, Tred. I'll be at the tribunal tomorrow to explain Pavo's ways, and attest to his good character. They should listen to *me.*" He gave his attention to setting up the game pieces.

Knowing that his long wait was finally over made a tremendous difference to his mood. He thought most of the judges would listen to him. It was true that it had been Odus's plan, and the man might try to blame him for it having gone awry, but Anduar had always seemed to stand up to Odus. And Soren—being one of the Kelorin Faction—probably wouldn't favor the Leithian Pact Signer. There was Madred, too, of course, but Tred had said that the High Judge had a reputation for fairness. *It should be all right,* Nagaro told himself. As long as the judges gave him a chance to speak for Pavo's character—which by tradition they had to do.

"After all," he said, half to himself, "they always turn to the ship's captain for an accounting of the character of the members of the crew, don't they?"

Nagaro had his eyes on the board and the game pieces as he asked the question, and therefore he didn't see the shadow that passed across the healer's tense face.

"Ah... yes... I believe so," the Leithian murmured as he hurriedly unstoppered the ink bottle, dipped the quill, and began to write.

24: Testimony

The four guards who came to escort Nagaro to the tribunal were all extremely polite and seemed more than a little in awe of him—which made him more than a little uncomfortable.

Their leader, a young Kelorin, actually bowed and said, "Will ye be so good as to come with us, Zirda? Your physician may come as well, if he's needed."

Tredhold immediately insisted that he was indeed needed. Nagaro might have argued the point, but he was too glad of the healer's company. The guards escorted them down the hallway and around a corner, then along another corridor. Nagaro had just concluded that the guards' intention was to enter the Audience Chamber by its small rear door, when they turned another corner and encountered another company of guards escorting a prisoner in the opposite direction.

"Pavo!" Nagaro uttered his friend's name out of sheer joy and relief.

The lead guardsman immediately made a disapproving gesture, indicating that Nagaro shouldn't speak to the other man.

Pavo's head swung around at the sound of Nagaro's voice. "Nagaro!" he said, raising his hands in acknowledgment and revealing that they were bound together in front of him.

"Silence!" The leader of Pavo's escort barked the word and gave his charge a rough push that had little effect on the massive Hashtep.

Pavo turned hastily away, though not before giving Nagaro a quick glance that was much more desperate than the one he'd given him on the deck of the *Sword of Freedom* when the Emperor's warriors had led him away.

Nagaro stopped dead, his heart in his throat. He stood watching with rising anger as the other troop of guards turned and disappeared with their prisoner through a low-arched doorway. *"Why is he bound?"* he demanded of the young guard beside him as soon as the other group was out of sight.

"Well, ah... he's a prisoner—"

Nagaro instantly presented his crossed wrists to the young Kelorin, his eyes blazing. "In *that* case, you seem to have forgotten something!"

The guardsman gaped at him. "But I... I don't need that with *you,*

Zirda!" he stammered. "I know *ye* won't try to escape—"

"No more would *he!*" Nagaro gestured after the other guards.

"But he's a *Mahuk!* And everyone's *saying*—"

Nagaro cut the man off, his voice taut with controlled anger. "He was born of the Hashtep people, in the Mahuk Baar, yes. But he is now a citizen of Edrovir—and a sworn officer of the Royal Fleet. And any man who's been saying that Pavo Maat is anything but a man of honor is simply wrong!"

The unfortunate guard could find nothing to say to this, and the other three guards were equally dumbstruck when Nagaro raked them with his eyes.

Nor was Nagaro finished.

"And why are they taking him to the *dungeon?* That doorway leads nowhere else!" Nagaro's eyes bored into the lead gurad.

"Ah... Nagaro..." It was Tredhold who spoke, much to the guard's obvious relief. "That's where they've been holding him."

Nagaro turned on the healer. "Pavo's been in a *prison cell?* While I've been housed in one of the guest chambers?"

Tredhold stood his ground. "They'd have had ye in the dungeon, too, Nagaro," he said calmly. "But I wouldn't stand for it. Not considering the condition ye were in when ye came here."

"Oh." Nagaro dropped his belligerence, only to pick it up again an instant later as another thought struck him. "What about Vell? And Peldred?"

Tredhold looked uncomfortable. He coughed and turned back to the guardsman.

The young Kelorin licked his lips and swallowed visibly. "They, ah... They've been in rooms like yours, Zirda. Because they're high born—" He retreated a step before Nagaro's thunderous look. "It's the *law!*" he protested. "No son of a noble house is to be kept in the dungeon while there's been no crime proven against him."

"*This isn't right!*" Nagaro was vibrating with outrage, perilously close to losing hold of his remaining self-restraint.

Tredhold placed a calming hand on his arm. "There's nothing this man could have done about it, Nagaro! Come on, now. The judges are waiting for us."

Nagaro gave the healer a seering glance. "He could stop thinking that it's *appropriate*," he muttered darkly. Turning back to the guardsman, he said rather stiffly, "Lead on, Zirda."

The man quickly conducted them the rest of the way down the hall to the Audience Chamber's rear door. The other three guards stepped along smartly, their eyes carefully directed straight ahead.

The door through which they were ushered entered the Audience

Chamber near the dais. It was on the side opposite the row of doors that led to the Council Chamber and the other rooms where the king and his guests had taken refuge a year ago during the Mahuk attack.

Once inside the chamber, Nagaro and Tredhold were turned over to the custody of more guards, one of whom announced their arrival to the four judges seated at a long table in front of the dais. There were three other tables there as well, forming the other sides of a rectangle and each equipped with several chairs. A clerk with pen and paper sat at the farthest side-table, ready to record the proceedings. The queen's physician, Master Ambras, was seated at the nearest table.

Nagaro briefly swept the rest of the room with his eyes, noting with some surprise that the side galleries were empty except for three seats in the gallery on the opposite side of the room. As he advanced into the hall, he saw that the three men seated there were King Elgurn and the Lords Pendrik and Devral. He had just time to wonder where all the relatives of the fallen were before his attention was drawn to the judges, one of whom was speaking.

"The prisoner is to stand *here*, before us. The healer may sit *there*, at the end of that table." The words were spoken with formal gravity, the voice was even, resonant, and austere.

Nagaro hadn't heard that voice before, and he saw that it belonged to the only one of the four judges whom he had never met—presumably Lord Madred, the High Judge of the Tribunal. The judges' chairs stood in a row behind the long table at the foot of the dais, with Lord Madred seated just to the left of center. He was a man in the prime of middle life—tall, fit, and broad in the shoulders, with piercing blue eyes in a handsomely chiseled face. His impeccably trimmed hair was silvered bronze. Every inch of the man's physical form and every nuance of his demeanor matched his imposing voice.

Lord Anduar had the seat next to Lord Madred, just to the right of center. Soren and Odus flanked them—Soren beside Anduar and Odus beside Madred.

Anduar lounged negligently in his chair as was his habit, but his steel-gray eyes followed Nagaro with keen attention. Nagaro returned the look briefly before glancing at the remaining two judges. Lord Soren was also watching him avidly, his interest revealed not only in his eyes but also in the tension of his mien and the way he leaned forward in his seat. Nagaro remembered how this man and two other members of the Kelorin Faction had approached him, trying to win him to their cause. Nagaro had done his best to put them off even before Anduar had done so more pointedly. The enthusiastic gleam in Soren's eyes suggested the rejection had not been taken much to heart. The fourth judge, Lord Odus, just as obviously harbored the opposite bias. The Leithian Pact-

Signer was sitting upright in his seat, staring at Nagaro with undiguised distaste.

Tredhold took his seat as directed at the table that faced the judges' table, about a dozen feet from it, while Nagaro moved as instructed into the center of the rectangle which the four tables defined. He made a formal bow to the judges, saying, "My Lords" as he straightened.

Lord Madred acknowledged the bow with a slight inclination of his head. "We will not keep you standing long, Zirda," he said mildly, "out of consideration for your convalescence. However, we must first request that you remove your shirt and turn around so that Master Ambras may examine the condition of your back. Master Ambras, if you will be so good..."

Nagaro had been prepared for this, and he wasted no time about unbuttoning and removing his shirt. At the same time, Master Ambras rose from his seat at the side table and approached. As he did so, his eyes met Tredhold's in a significant exchange of glances, accompanied by barely perceptible nods as the two healers acknowledged one another.

As Nagaro turned his back to the dais, he heard indrawn breaths and a murmured exclamation. He smiled grimly to himself. Apparently Tredhold had been right about the condition of his back still being quite impressive.

Ambras gave Nagaro a benign smile and proceeded to examine him with meticulous care, not only the skin of his back but also the healing scars of the two new brands on his shoulder and chest. At length, the healer turned to face the judges, cleared his throat, and gave his report.

"The marks are entirely consistent with what has been described in the other witnesses' testimony, My Lords," he observed. "This man has recently been branded twice with a hot iron, and beaten very severely with a leather lash. He's fortunate to have had excellent care. Without it, he would most probably not have survived the beating."

"Very good, Master Ambras. You may return to your seat."

As Ambras moved away, Nagaro heard a small, distinctly female cry from the general direction of the room's rear entrance, behind him. Startled, he looked over his shoulder and saw to his utter dismay that Princess Nevien had entered the hall. A slim figure in a dark blue gown, she stood just inside the rear door, staring directly at his back—and looking horrified.

"*Bishka!*" Nagaro hastily re-donned his shirt, and faced the judges once more as he did up the bottons while determinedly not looking in the princess's direction.

Lord Madred spoke. "Your pardon, My Lady Princess. Had I known you were at all likely to enter this room, I would have taken steps to spare you this shocking sight."

"I was only startled, My Lord." From the steadiness of her voice, it was apparent that Nevien had recovered her composure. "I have seen healing wounds before. I'm here because I have something urgent to tell my father."

"Very good, My Lady. Pray proceed." Madred turned back to Nagaro. "Please be seated at the table, Zirda—*there,* in the center."

Nagaro circled the indicated table and sat down next to Tredhold while Nevien crossed the room without looking at him. She mounted into the gallery and went to the chair where Elgurn was seated. The king leaned forward and listened, frowning, as his daughter spoke to him in a low voice, after which he stood up, looking very grave, and addressed the judges.

"My Lords, I regret that I must absent myself. The queen is unwell, as you know, and she has been asking for me. I have need of Master Ambras as well. I believe you're finished with him?"

Though the king's voice was steady, Nagaro thought his face looked strained and his announcement occasioned frowns and an exchange of muttered speech among the four judges. Presently, Lord Madred turned to Elgurn and said, "My Lord King, the queen's health is of grave concern to us all. However, it has been pointed out to me that this tribunal requires a royal presence, and your departure will delay our proceedings."

Elgurn gestured distractedly. "My daughter will remain here in my place, My Lord. She has been very close in my councils of late. I trust her fully to observe this tribunal and make an accurate report to me of whatever takes place."

There was more muttered talk among the judges before Madred spoke again. "This will be acceptable, My Lord, although it is somewhat irregular. Today's proceedings are, after all, more or less a formality."

Nagaro frowned. *How could the questioning of the ship's captain in such a case be a mere formality?* He cast Tredhold a questioning look, but the healer sat stone-faced, not meeting his eyes.

The king had descended from the gallery and now strode across the room looking neither to left nor right. Master Ambras hurried after his lord, and both men exited through the hall's rear door. The princess took her father's former seat between Pendrik and Devral.

What followed immediately was in fact very much a formality. Nagaro's full name was requested, for the purpose of the record, which he stated as Nagaro Nareyo. He was then asked what oath he was prepared to offer to attest to the truth of all that he was going to say before the Tribunal. To the latter question he replied, "I swear to speak the truth upon my honor and in Vothra's name."

Lord Madred nodded his acceptance of this oath, then cleared his throat to gain the full attention of all who were present. "And now, Tor

Nagaro," he said with formal stiffness, "we will proceed directly to the questioning." At this point, Odus leaned over and whispered something into the other Leithian's ear. Something flickered across Madred's face, and he added with a scarcely perceptible pause, "The Tribunal wishes to remind you, Zirda, that you are to confine yourself at all times to answering what you have been asked, without elaboration, question, or argument. Is that clear?"

Nagaro met the man's intense blue gaze, and said calmly, "No, My Lord, it is not."

"How do you mean, *no?*" It was Odus who spoke. "What is this new impudence?"

Nagaro turned to the blond-bearded Pact-Signer. "If the meaning of a question isn't clear to me, My Lord Odus, I think I should be permitted to try to make it clear. And if what I am asked misses the heart of the matter, or if a simple answer is misleading without further explanation, I believe I should say so."

Odus's brow had darkened, and he turned angrily to Madred. "You see what we must endure from this man, My Lord?"

Lord Madred was frowning also, though less darkly. "You may ask for clarification, Zirda," he informed Nagaro sternly. "But you are not to attempt to interrogate the judges, or dispute the established facts."

Lord Anduar abruptly cleared his throat. Without changing his languid posture, he said, "Your expressed concerns aren't unreasonable, Tor Nagaro, but you must understand that the Tribunal has already heard a great deal of testimony on this matter. You shouldn't assume that we are ignorant. We will be asking you only what is needed, and it isn't necessary that you understand our reasons for what we ask." He smiled a small, mirthless smile. "I am sure we can expect your full cooperation."

Nagaro returned the man's steely stare with some misgivings. "I think you know that I prefer to understand things, My Lord," he said evenly. "I will try to curb my natural inclination."

Anduar smiled again, faintly. "I suppose that will have to do."

"Very good, then, gentlemen. Let us proceed." Lord Madred was peremptory. He shifted some papers on the table in front of him. "I am going to read aloud an account of the events surrounding the surrender of the ship *Sword of Freedom* to our enemy, the Emperor of the Mahuk Baar. Tor Nagaro, we require that you listen carefully to this account and not interrupt my reading of it."

Nagaro acknowledged this instruction with a nod of his head, and Lord Madred raised one of the papers and began to read.

"In the late afternoon of the twenty-third day of Medrin, of this year, three warships of the Royal Fleet of Edrovir, namely the *Valor*, the

Dolphin, and the *Sword of Freedom*, were passing southward along the seaward coast of the Mahuk island of Saat, when they encountered bad weather, causing them to alter course to pass between the islands of Saat and Hatsetep in order to shelter in the lee of one of those isles. During that passage a strong blast of wind caused a collision between the *Valor* and the *Sword of Freedom* resulting in loss of the *Valor's* main mast spar and damage to the *Sword of Freedom's* rudder. This accident occasioned the decision to put in at the island of Osfaraad for repairs, since that island offered a well-sheltered and well-concealed harbor suitable for this purpose."

Nagaro shifted in his seat and frowned. Tredhold hastily touched his arm, muttering, "Don't interrupt," under his breath.

Lord Madred gave both men a disapproving glance, and continued reading.

"When the three ships arrived in that harbor it was nearly dark, and the storm had only moderately abated, so the repairs were delayed until the following morning."

Nagaro risked a glance in the direction of the gallery and saw that the princess's attention was fixed on the High Judge. Presumably she hadn't heard the tale before and it clearly held her interest. The two Pact Signers seated with her, however, were both watching *him*, and he hastily looked away again, deciding it was best not to look at the gallery.

Madred in the meantime was continuing:

"In the morning, the twenty-fourth day of Medrin, the one sound ship, the *Dolphin*, was dispatched to make report to another squadron of the fleet regarding the reason for the delay of the *Valor* and the *Sword of Freedom*. Lookouts were posted, and foraging parties were sent ashore to secure fresh water and timber for repair of the damaged ships. Before the repairs were complete, however, one of the lookouts warned of the approach of several Mahuk warships. Departure was delayed just long enough to complete repair of the *Valor's* main spar, which was quickly done."

Here again, Nagaro stirred and frowned, but he didn't speak. The High Judge cast him a quick glance and continued.

"The time was not sufficient, however, to properly complete repair of the *Sword of Freedom's* rudder, and the ship set sail with her rudder poorly mended. In passing out of the harbor, the two ships encountered three Mahuk warships entering it, one being the flagship of the Emperor of the Mahuk Baar. At this juncture, the *Valor* and the *Sword of Freedom* divided their courses, one going to starboard and the other to port, in the hope that at least one ship would make good its escape. The stratagem was successful in that the *Valor* did indeed escape capture. The *Sword of Freedom* was taken, however, owing in part to the incomplete repair of her rudder, which broke again during the maneuvers. The *Sword of Freedom* was beset on both sides and boarded by the crews of all three Mahuk warships. Her officers and crew at first resorted to final defense position and a short battle ensued in which five members of the crew of the *Sword of Freedom* were slain and at least a dozen of the enemy sea warriors were killed. This battle came to an end, however, when one of the ship's officers called a halt to the fighting and offered surrender to the Emperor of the Mahuk Baar, which offer the Emperor accepted."

Lord Madred ceased speaking and raised his eyes to fix his gaze on Nagaro. "Our first question is simply this, Zirda: Do you agree that the account I have just read is accurate in its description of these events?"

Nagaro's brows knit together in a sharp, black line. He found the phrase *"one of the of the ship's officers"* unsettling. He wondered why the High Judge hadn't named him. Tredhold had said that the judges had been calling Vell "Captain," and he realized that none of them had applied that title to *him*. Regardless, he didn't much like the question. "Speaking *very broadly*," he said carefully, "there is nothing untrue in that account, My Lord, though there are a number of things left out that would alter the picture if they were included."

Lord Madred turned to address the clerk, whose pen had been waggling furiously as he wrote. "Let it be noted," he said blandly, "that Tor Nagaro has affirmed the accuracy of the written account. The rest of his statement need not stand."

Nagaro started to open his mouth to protest. Two things, however, forestalled him. The first was Tredhold's warning hand on his arm, and the second was Lord Anduar, who pointedly added, "Except for the words, *speaking broadly*."

Nagaro scowled. "*Very* broadly," he muttered under his breath.

The faintest frown flickered across Lord Madred's countenance, but he seemed prepared to accept Anduar's amendment, for he gave the clerk a small, curt nod. He then coughed lightly, and addressed himself once more to Nagaro. "The judges of the Tribunal will now each have the opportunity to ask you a question or two, Zirda. We don't wish to tire you, so we will be brief, as I'm sure you will wish to be brief also." He shuffled the papers before him on the table. "I will begin by asking you to explain the reason for your unprecedented action of offering surrender to the Emperor of the Mahuk Baar."

Nagaro relaxed. At last he was going to be allowed to explain some of what had happened. "My Lord," he said, meeting Madred's questioning blue stare. "It was apparent even before we closed with them that the Mautep's overriding purpose in attacking the *Sword* was to capture or kill *me*—so much so that they completely ignored the *Valor*. I thought it was unjust that the other members of my crew should die because they had shipped with me."

"So you traded your life for theirs?" It was Soren, speaking for the first time, his approval of the asserted action obvious in every line of his face and nuance of his voice.

Nagaro frowned. "Not *exactly*, My Lord. I expected to die in any case. The terms I offered the Emperor were that we would lay down our arms and he might do as he wished with me. In exchange, the rest of my crew would be spared and honorably ransomed. It was therefore the lives of whatever number of the Emperor's men we might have slain that were set against the lives of our men."

Odus was glowering at him. "Is it true, Zirda, that you haven't any stomach for killing?"

Before Nagaro could respond, Soren jumped in. "Eight of the Mahuk fell to his sword, Odus! We know he's not afraid to kill—"

"Gentlemen!" Lord Madred rapped loudly on the table, sweeping them all with a stern look. When he had silence, he addressed the clerk. "Please note my question in the record, and Tor Nagaro's answer," he said rather stiffly. "Note also Lord Soren's inquiry regarding the terms of surrender and Tor Nagaro's explanation of them. We were going to ask for the terms in any case. Strike the rest." He turned to Lord Odus. "My Lord, do you have a more pertinent question for the prisoner?"

Odus looked not the least bit chastened.. His eyes narrowed. "I have, My Lord." He fixed his gaze upon Nagaro. "We are told, Zirda, that you stated *twice*—once to Geldoran and once to Kuran—that you had made an error in judgement. This is a serious and telling admission." Here he paused for effect, seeming to enjoy himself. "Tell us, if you please, the nature of your error."

Nagaro gave an inward sigh. *Trust Odus to bring it up...* Though from the way Madred was looking at him, he suspected the High Judge would have asked the question himself. Soren, on the other hand, was scowling. Anduar was inscrutable as always.

Odus's stare seemed to dare Nagaro to answer. He met it with a level glance and spoke in a firm voice. "I did not foresee the possibility that the Emperor would use torture in an effort to get information from us concerning our mission."

Odus's eyes narrowed further and he smiled rather unpleasantly. "If you *had* foreseen that possibility, Zirda, what would you have done?"

This was something Nagaro had thought about a great deal. "I would have made it a condition of the surrender, My Lord, that there would be no such effort."

To Nagaro's surprise, this answer elicited a whole flurry of startled reactions, including murmurs from the direction of the gallery. Odus stared at him in disbelief, Madred frowned, and Soren looked confused.

Even Anduar, usually so self-possessed, betrayed his surprise by sitting up in his chair.

Odus leaned over and whispered something to Lord Madred. The High Judge made some murmured response, then turned and spoke to Anduar in a low voice. Odus and Soren both leaned in to hear, and a whispered exchange among the four men then followed at some length. When it ceased, they all turned their eyes back to Nagaro.

Odus spoke, his gaze hard, his tone faintly derisive. "Do you actually believe that putting a ban on torture into your terms would have solved the problem?"

Nagaro answered carefully. "It would have avoided having our plans revealed, if that's what you mean. Whether or not it saved our lives would have depended on whether the Emperor accepted the surrender under that condition."

This answer caused more surprised murmurs from the gallery.

Lord Madred spoke, his voice impeccably neutral. "I assume, Zirda, that you mean that you would have fought to the death if the Emperor had failed to accepted your surrender?"

Nagaro turned back to face him. "Yes, My Lord. We were already in position and had begun our final defense before I thought of the possibility of surrender."

Odus gave Nagaro a withering look. "You think there's a chance the Emperor would have *accepted* this condition?"

Nagaro shrugged. "It is possible, My Lord. He was very keen on punishing me. He said that six of our ships had already been sighted, too, so he might not have felt he really needed to get information from us—"

Odus didn't let him finish. "You would have *trusted* him to keep his word?"

"If he had sworn it on his honor and in the name of Sheptuum, his god," Nagaro answered levelly, "then yes."

The room was very quiet when Nagaro ceased speaking. Significant glances were exchanged among the four judges.

It was Anduar who broke the silence. "So, Zirda," he said calmly. "You believe the Emperor of the Mahuk Baar to be a man of honor?"

Nagaro met the Kelorin Pact Signer's steel-gray eyes. "I found him so, My Lord. If I can believe what Vell told me, the Emperor gave me back my life, my sword, my ship, and my crew because I'd shown honor and courage. A man doesn't do that if he doesn't respect such things."

This time it was Soren whose outrage overflowed. "But the man used *torture!*" the aging Kelorin cried, rising from his seat.

"Yes," Odus put in dryly. "Answer *that*, Tor Nagaro!"

Nagaro had thought about this as well. "I was initially offended by his threat to torture me," he said earnestly, "since I had sworn on my honor. And I protested as much. The justification he gave me was that it wasn't honorable for us to have brought our warships into his waters after requesting that *he* not send his warships into *ours*. I suppose he extended the same logic to his interrogation of the other officers. And he didn't kill Vell or Peldred, or any of the others for that matter, so he did keep his word as he had sworn."

Odus pounced. "You *condone* this?"

Nagaro shook his head. "No, My Lord. *I* would have returned him honor, even for dishonor. But I think I understand him. We had every appearance of being hostile invaders within his domain—a domain he is bound to protect, just as we protect ours. In fact we *were* hostile invaders and our actions were not consistent with the last communication that had been conveyed to him."

Odus scowled darkly at this. Lord Madred, however, cleared his throat sharply before the other Leithian could make any retort, and said, "This is all of no consequence, since the torture proved ineffective."

Nagaro stiffened. " My Lord? Why do you say it was ineffective?"

Madred's blue eyes came instantly to bear upon him. "You speak out of turn, Zirda," he said coldly. "You are not to ask questions."

Nagaro shut his mouth, but his eyes smoldered. He was getting a bad feeling. If the judges thought the torture had been ineffective, it could only mean that they suspected Pavo, the one man who hadn't been tortured. Beside him, Tredhold was shaking his head.

Lord Madred swept his gaze to left and right. "Gentlemen, have you any other questions on the matter of the surrender?"

Soren spoke up. "I have one, My Lord."

Madred looked as if he hadn't expected this and was not much pleased by it. "Proceed," he said with stiff formality.

Soren turned to Nagaro. "You said you thought the Emperor would accept your terms because he was very eager to punish you. In fact, we've been told that he had set a price on your head. Tell us, Zirda, the amount of that price."

Nagaro blinked. "The *amount?*" He couldn't see how this mattered, except perhaps to support his reasoning, since Soren seemed to want to take his side. "I believe it stood most recently at fifty Mahuk gold pieces," he said. "Roughly fifty dokans."

There were low murmurs from the gallery, though Nagaro didn't look in that direction. Soren, predictably, smiled, while the two Leithian judges both frowned—Odus darkly, Madred fleetingly.

Lord Anduar gestured languidly. "If I may pursue this, My Lord Madred?"

The High Judge looked resigned. "Proceed, Lord Anduar."

Anduar appeared briefly to study the ceiling. "So. Fifty dokans. Fifty thousand rins." His gaze came back to fix itself upon Nagaro. "An impressive sum, Zirda. You must have displeased the man mightily. Yet he let you go."

Nagaro's face clouded. "He saw me punished first, My Lord. And the punishment was not light."

"Yes. So we've seen." The Kelorin Pact Signer nodded thoughtfully.

"The man he tasked with punishing me was the captain of the first ship that I and my men took, as slaves, My Lord," Nagaro added. "Pavo said the Emperor was testing us—Captain Urchak, and me—"

"—to see who was the better man." Anduar finished the sentence. "Yes, we've heard that tale. And from the outcome, I suppose you'd have us conclude that you won that contest of quality?"

Nagaro frowned, uncomfortable as always with self-praise. "I don't know that I *won* anything, My Lord," he said carefully. "But I do seem to have favorably impressed Emperor Baalkir."

At this, Lord Anduar smiled sardonically. "Well, that would be one interpretation," he said. Then he turned to Lord Madred. "I am finished, My Lord."

The High Judge gave his fellow judge a formal nod. "In that case," he said with what sounded like relief, "We should be finished questioning this prisoner on the issue of the surrender, unless there is something else?"

Lord Soren coughed. "There is one more thing, My Lord."

Madred sighed faintly. "Proceed."

Soren promptly addressed himself to Nagaro with an ingratiating smile. "Vell has said you appeared to taunt the man who beat you, in his own language. Will you please tell us, Zirda, what you said to him?"

Nagaro shifted in his chair. "I called him a man without honor, killer of a woman. I hoped it would provoke him into killing me and ending my suffering."

There were some murmurs from the gallery in response to Nagaro's words. He thought he heard Nevien's voice among them and risked a furtive glance in her direction—enough to see that she and the two Pact Signers seated with her looked rather shocked.

When his eyes returned to the judges' table he saw that Soren did not look at all deflated. "This still required great courage," the aging Kelorin pointed out.

Lord Anduar stirred. "So, you *insulted* the man?"

Nagaro frowned. "What I said was quite true, My Lord. He did kill a woman—which violates the Mautep concept of honor. I saw him do it."

"I see." Anduar appeared to file away this tidbit.

Lord Madred had been making notes on his paper. He looked up as the silence lengthened. "I will assume we are finished with the matter of the surrender, since we have already departed from it," he said dryly. "The Tribunal will therefore continue with the matter of treason, which has been charged in this case." He fastened his piercing blue eyes on Nagaro. "We won't keep you much longer, Zirda, since your testimony can contribute little to this issue."

Nagaro's stomach tightened. It seemed that the judges had already made up their minds and he had seen evidence of the nature of their conclusions. His concerns about what had been left out of the account of the incident at Osfaraad now paled compared to the fear he felt for Pavo. He cast a distraught glance at Tredhold, who looked equally unhappy.

The High Judge noticed none of this because he was running his finger down a sheet of paper as if reviewing a series of points. By the time he looked up, Nagaro had managed to un-furrow his brow. Madred cleared his throat. "We can move through these questions rather quickly, I think, Zirda. I will read them. The first is but a formality: Do you repeat for the record of the Tribunal your profession of innocence with regard to the treasonable offence of giving secret information to an enemy of Edrovir?"

"I'll repeat it as often as asked," Nagaro replied coolly. "I told the Mautep nothing of our mission or our plans." He noted that he was not being read an "official" account this time. He hoped it meant the judges hadn't written one.

Madred frowned over his paper. "A simple 'yes' would have sufficed, Zirda," he said tartly. "We have the testimony of two other witnesses to the effect that you did not." He advanced his finger a little down the page. "Do you also attest to having heard the other three ship's officers profess their innocence in this same regard. If you please, Zirda, answer yes, or no."

Nagaro's eyes met the man's blandly questioning stare. "No," he said after a moment's consideration.

There were instant exclamations from several quarters.

"No?" Madred's voice contained just a hint of annoyance. "Explain, Zirda."

Nagaro resisted allowing any satisfaction to show in his face. "I did not hear *all three* men profess innocence, My Lord. I heard Pavo Maat state his innocence very clearly. As I recall, however, Vell spoke for both himself and Peldred. He said something like, 'We didn't tell them anything, did we?' and Peldred only made a sound as if he were suffering pain."

Odus leaned forward. "What are you implying?" he demanded.

Nagaro returned the Leithian a level glance. "I only mean that I did not at any time hear Peldred state in words that he was innocent."

Lord Madred waved a dismissive hand. "Very well, then. Let it be so written in the record. Peldred has stated his innocence to others who have been questioned by this Tribunal, making this answer immaterial."

Immaterial! Nagaro felt a flood of dismay.

Madred had glanced down at his paper and now looked back up again. "Tor Nagaro, did you or did you not hear the Hashtep man, Pavo Maat, express disapproval of the objective of the mission?"

This time Nagaro felt a shock of alarm. The judges were seeking a motive for what they assumed was Pavo's betrayal. "I did not," he said flatly.

The High Judge once again looked faintly annoyed. "Are you *sure?*" he asked with a deliberate emphasis on the last word. "Vell has testified that the Hashtep spoke so on the morning of the Fleet's departure from Lankura. If I may shake your memory, Zirda, it was on the stern castle of the *Sword of Freedom* and you were present at the time."

Nagaro's slim black brows came together. "I do recall the occasion, My Lord," he said evenly, "and the conversation. It seemed, from Vell's questions, that he expected Pavo to disapprove of the mission and was trying to get him to say so. What Pavo *said* was that the bad weather was Sheptuum's frown. He also said that Sheptuum would not protect a man who acted badly, even the Emperor, and that it wasn't the Emperor who had attacked Lankura. He did *not* say he disapproved of the mission."

Odus slapped the table. "Don't make games with words, Zirda! He plainly didn't like the mission!"

Nagaro returned him a level stare. "I would say that he meant that *Sheptuum* didn't like the mission, My Lord."

"So he took his own opinions and called them those of his god?"

Nagaro's eyes narrowed. "Pavo Maat has a very strong belief in his god, My Lord. Since I am not a man like you who believes in gods, you would know better than I how likely a man is to put words into his god's mouth." He heard Tredhold, beside him, suck in his breath.

"Gentlemen!" Lord Madred rapped the table. "We are digressing."

Odus glared at this interruption, but held his tongue. Nagaro coolly returned his attention to the High Judge. Lord Madred turned to the clerk. "The record will show that the prisoner has explained his answer by saying that Pavo Maat's words indicated he believed his god objected to the mission. The rest you may strike out."

The clerk nodded obediently, dipped his pen, and crossed out several lines of what he had written. Nagaro breathed a small inward sigh of relief.

"My Lord Madred... if I may pursue this?" Anduar still lounged in his chair, though his attention was sharply on Nagaro.

"Of course, My Lord Anduar." Madred was stiffly courteous.

Anduar cleared his throat. "Tor Nagaro, I would like you to give us your *opinion*." His words were spoken blandly, but his steely glance was sharp as a knife. "Do you *think* Pavo Maat approved of the mission?"

Nagaro hesitated, wishing Anduar had not asked the question. An honest answer was likely to undo the small victory he'd just gained. *Yet he had sworn to tell the truth...*

"No, My Lord, I don't think he did, but I—"

"That is enough answer, Zirda." Anduar cut him off. "You needn't elaborate. Can you now tell us what you believe was the *reason* for his disapproval?"

Nagaro winced, but he thought he saw how he still might make his point. "I believe his reason was likely the same as mine, My Lord."

This answer caused a flicker of a frown to cross Anduar's face. He seemed to hesitate fractionally before asking the next obvious question. "And that reason was?"

"That in attacking Emperor Baalkir's capital, Sar Tipaal, we were attacking the wrong target. It wasn't the Emperor who struck at Lankura, but one of his unruly warlords—Angkat—"

Lord Odus cut sharply across his words. "My Lord Madred, this is irrelevant!"

"On the contrary." The gentility of Anduar's tone in speaking to his fellow Pact Signer belied the chilly steel of his glance. "If we are to have Tor Nagaro's answer to My Lord Madred's question recorded, I believe we should have his full explanation."

Madred's glance had moved sharply from one fellow judge to the other. His face seemed frozen in neutrality. He cleared his throat and said, with formal gravity, "The record shall stand as written."

If Anduar felt he had scored a victory, his face didn't show it. Odus was plainly struggling not to glower. Madred spared no glance for either one of them as he returned to his paper. "Tor Nagaro," he continued as if he hadn't been interrupted, "the man Pavo Maat appears to be extremely loyal to you. Would you agree?"

"He is a very good friend to me, My Lord." Nagaro wasn't sure of the purpose of the question, but it provided an opportunity to speak well of Pavo's character. "We have known each other for seven years and have come to trust each other and hold each other in high regard."

Madred's pale brows came together and he turned to the clerk. "Let the record show that the answer was affirmative to the question of extreme loyalty." He referred to his paper again and then turned back to Nagaro, who was frowning at having his answer composed for him. Madred cleared his throat once more. "Vell has told us that Pavo Maat was heard to say that you were not going to die. Do you confirm this testimony?"

Nagaro's frown deepened. He thought he saw where this might lead. "My Lord, if I might explain—"

"We do not require an explanation, Zirda." Lord Madred's words were clipped. "If you would please simply answer yes or no."

Nagaro shifted in his seat. Madreds's brilliant blue gaze impaled him. The light of triumph shown in Odus's eyes. "My Lord Madred," he said carefully, "I cannot fairly answer your question if I'm not permitted to explain."

This time Lord Madred regarded him with very obvious annoyance. Anduar leaned over to speak into the High Judge's ear, however, and Madred coughed as if to cover the interruption before saying, "Very well then, Zirda. You may explain, but be brief."

Nagaro inclined his head in acknowledgment of the concession. "What I recall, My Lord, is that Pavo voiced the opinion that Sheptuum would not allow me to die."

Lord Madred frowned. "His *opinion*, you say?"

Nagaro gave him a look of innocence. "It could hardly be anything but an opinion, My Lord, unless you suppose that Sheptuum exists and speaks to Pavo. Or that Pavo has the power of prophesy."

There was a moment's silence as Lord Madred's expression passed from surprise to anger. Anduar, however, leaned towards the High Judge once more, speaking low. This time, the other two judges bent close to listen, and there followed a long exchange in which all four men became involved.

Nagaro spoke to Tredhold from the corner of his mouth, not taking his eyes from the judges. "I don't like these secret discussions, Tred."

"Nor do I." Tredhold barely breathed his response.

"As if they're deciding what questions to allow, and what answers they're looking for—"

He had no time to say more because the judges' conference had ended and all four men were facing him again. Nagaro was surprised when it was Anduar who cleared his throat and asked. "If you please, Zirda, tell us your *understanding* of how you came to be delivered from your ordeal. We realize that you were unconscious, and did not witness it."

This seemed to be possibly an encouraging development. Nagaro inclined his head. "I believe that the man who had beaten and branded me, Captain Urchak, would have killed me in anger after my accusation, but I was saved by the intervention of Roheed jir-Akaan, the Emperor's nephew, who struck Urchak's sword aside—"

Soren interrupted him. "We were told it was the interpreter."

Nagaro transferred his attention. "Yes, My Lord Soren. Roheed was serving as interpreter."

"How does this Emperor's nephew come to know our speech?" demanded Lord Odus. "And how would *you* know—" He was interrupted by a very pointed clearing of the throat.

All attention returned to Anduar, who had produced the sound and who proceeded to say, "My Lord Madred, might I continue?"

Madred responded with gravity. "By all means, My Lord."

Anduar's cool gray glance promptly returned to Nagaro. "So, Zirda, you believe that the Emperor's nephew interceded on your behalf?"

Nagaro nodded. "Vell said that Roheed spoke to the Emperor at some length, though of course Vell couldn't understand the words— until in the end, Roheed translated the Emperor's decision."

"Which was to spare you for the sake of your honor and courage?"

Nagaro shifted in his seat. "That's what Vell told me."

"Ah." Anduar considered him. "Do you imagine, then, that this man, Roheed, did all of this of his own inclination?"

Nagaro frowned. He was worried about the judges' interest in this line of questioning. That they *were* interested was apparent from the expressions on all four faces. Even Anduar was leaning forward in his seat. Nagaro looked the Kelorin Pact Signer straight in the eyes and said, "I have reason to believe so, yes."

"What reason?"

Nagaro hesitated. "Several things may have contributed—"

"One of them being that you had previously spared the man's life?" Anduar's expression was completely unreadable, and the faces of the other three men suggested that what Anduar had just said came as no surprise to them, although only Anduar and Odus had been present when Nagaro had related the incident to the King's Council.

"Yes, My Lord, that is one. Also, he knew I spoke the truth about Urchak. He was witness to the killing of the woman."

"Ah." Anduar raised one eyebrow a fraction. The other three judges all betrayed surprise and there were murmurs from the gallery.

"Was there anything else?" Anduar's eyebrow had resumed its former position.

Nagaro moved uncomfortably. "Well, we had spoken to one another on several occasions, and had come to respect one another... And then there was the storm," he added almost as an afterthought.

"Ah, *respect*. And a *storm*. Doubtless you mean the little squall of rain. You think that impressed him?"

"It impressed Vell. And the people of the Mahuk Baar also believe that their god controls the weather."

"I see." Anduar cleared his throat. His gray eyes continued their penetrating study of Nagaro's face. "The man Pavo Maat gave a different reason. He described something called a *blood debt*. You have not mentioned it. Why is that?"

Nagaro started in spite of himself. *He should have known that Pavo would do that...* "My Lord," he answered cautiously, "I've never believed in the blood debt, though Pavo told us the story—"

"Ah. It's a *story*." Anduar's tone suggested that a suspicion had just been confirmed.

Odus and Madred exchanged knowing glances.

Nagaro spoke quickly before anyone could tell him not to. "That story, and the *actual events* behind it, are known to everyone in Sar Tipaal, and taken quite seriously there, My Lord."

Lord Madred immediately rapped loudly on the table. "Be silent, Zirda. You were not asked—" he began, only to stop in mid-sentence at a sign from Anduar. Odus had also moved as if to protest, but apparently decided to hold his peace.

Anduar was the picture of benign reasonableness. "If you please, My Lord Madred, I would like to hear why this witness discounts the significance of something he claims is widely believed," and he gestured for Nagaro to proceed.

"My Lord," Nagaro began earnestly. "Roheed could have intervened on my behalf at any time based on the blood dept, yet he waited to step in until *after* I accused Urchak—when it was very nearly too late. Roheed knew my accusation was accurate, as I've said. And he surely could see that it spoke to Urchak's honor—which the Emperor was testing. But Urchak having killed a woman had nothing to do with the blood debt."

Anduar had listened with a hint of guardedness, but he now lolled back languidly in his seat. "Thank you for that intriguing theory, Zirda," he said easily. "Is it your understanding, then, that both Pavo Maat and Roheed believe in the reality of this blood debt, though you do not?"

"Yes, My Lord."

Anduar's steely gaze remained on Nagaro. "Since you knew that the Emperor's nephew had such a belief, I wonder why you didn't try to use your influence over this man to save yourself."

Nagaro lifted his chin. "Because it would have been wrong to use his belief in that way."

This simple statement evoked a small tempest of exclamations from both the judges' table and the gallery. Nagaro heard *"By the Eyes!"* and *"Kroneg's Blood!"*

"What manner of man *does* this?" Soren demanded in querulous astonishment.

Odus protested, "My Lord Madred, this is irrelevant! It should be stricken—" only to have Anduar cut across him with, "On the contrary, My Lord, it shows the extremity of—" at which point both men appeared to catch themselves and lowered their voices. Madred sat listening intently, and presently Soren joined the discussion.

Nagaro muttered under his breath, "I suppose that made me look a bloody fool."

Tredhold shook his head. "Not *exactly*."

The judges must have resolved their issues, for Lord Madred abruptly rapped on the table for silence, then cleared his throat and said in a tone of neutral formality, "The record shall stand as written."

Lord Anduar returned to his usual languid posture and resumed his inscrutable expression. Soren looked smug. Odus looked sour.

Madred briefly shuffled his papers, then cleared his throat. "That concludes the questioning of this prisoner." The Leithian's blue eyes came to focus on Nagaro. "We thank you for your cooperation, Zirda. The guards will now return you to your chamber to await the verdict of this Tribunal."

"Is that *all?*" Nagaro spoke aloud in his astonishment. "My Lord," he added hastily, thinking the man had merely forgotten, "Aren't you going to question me concerning the character of the other three men, who were under my command?"

One could have heard a piece of paper fall.

Tredhold stirred, and murmured a worried, "*Nagaro...*"

Lord Madred sat frozen for a moment with his papers in his hands. Then a frown began to darken his brow. He turned to the clerk whose pen was still moving. "Strike that out," he commanded. "And there will be no need for any further record." Then, turning back to Nagaro, he said sternly, "You are not to interrogate this Tribunal, Zirda. We have already questioned the ship's captain, Vell Sobring, regarding the character of his officers—including you."

Nagaro frowned in his turn. "But he only took command after it was all over—"

"*Ha!*" Lord Odus gleefully slapped the table. "He doesn't know! My Lord Madred, you must enlighten him!"

Nagaro felt Tredhold's hand on his arm. He was aware that Soren appeared distressed, and Anduar was leaning forward in his seat.

Madred set down his papers, looking very stern. "You appear to be laboring under a misapprehension, Tor Nagaro," he said in a deliberately measured voice. "You were not the captain of the *Sword of Freedom* at any time during the mission to Sar Tipaal. The captain was in fact Vell Sobring. He had orders from the King and the Council to that effect, though it was considered expedient that neither you nor the rest of the crew should be told unless he deemed it necessary."

Nagaro felt as if he'd been struck in the face. *Not the captain of the Sword? Not the captain of his own ship?* He felt Tredhold's fingers tighten on his arm—heard the healer murmur, "I'm *sorry*, Nagaro!" He saw the gloating gleam in Odus's eyes.

Not the captain of the Sword...

Nagaro struggled with rising outrage. Judging by Odus's expression, the Leithian Pact Signer was hoping for an explosion. *Which meant this was a good time to hold his temper.* He'd been the one making decisions and giving orders, after all, even if Vell had only been letting him do it. Was this so different from what he'd imagined—that Vell had orders to assume command if he thought it necessary? The only important difference was that he had no traditional right to speak for Pavo. *That was where his concern should lie at this moment. If he could only persuade them to let him speak anyway...*

Avoiding Odus's eyes, he steadily met Lord Madred's. "Regardless of who was officially the captain, My Lord," he said levelly, "I think you should hear what I can tell you about Pavo Maat. Vell may know Peldred as well as I, but he is barely acquainted with Pavo, and I don't believe he understands the man well at all."

Odus's disappointment was plain, though he mastered it. Nor was the Leithian Pact Signer the only one who had apparently anticipated a stronger reaction. There were murmurs from the gallery, and even Anduar's eloquent eyebrow was fleetingly raised.

Madred's glance didn't waver. "We have found Vell's understanding sufficient to explain the actions of Pavo Maat," he said stiffly. "We require nothing more from you, Zirda. The guards will show you out."

Nagaro's stomach turned over. He could guess what "understanding" Vell had reached. "My Lord," he said quickly, "Won't you at least tell me what explanation Vell has proposed? I could then, perhaps, point out any ways in which he might have erred, based on my greater knowledge of the man."

Madred waved this impatiently aside. "There is no need, Zirda."

"How can you know that, My Lord," Nagaro protested, "when you haven't heard what I have to say?"

"*What impudence!*" Odus exploded before the High Judge could speak. "My Lord, I protest this outrageous conduct! This man clearly wishes us to sit here and listen to him praise and defend his traitorous comrade. It's *insufferable!* Isn't it enough that his folly placed the traitor right into the Emperor's hands? Costing us five ships and eighty-four men!"

Lord Anduar made an impatient gesture. "*Really*, Odus," he said, contriving to sound almost bored. "We've been through all that. It was Vell's decision to allow the surrender—which in fact *saved* one ship and thirty-nine men. The attack on Sar Tipaal, had it taken place, could easily have cost us the difference, with further losses occurring during an exit from the Baar under pursuit and potential attack. The most serious avoidable cost of the whole affair has been a blow to our pride—"

"—*Isn't that enough?*"

"And if our ships had reached Sar Tipaal with a traitor aboard—"

"My Lords!" Madred rapped vigorously on the table.

The two Pact Signers subsided, Anduar with aplomb, Odus with a scowl.

Nagaro had sat numbly through the exchange, a horrible sick feeling growing within him. His worst fear had been confirmed: *These men had already decided that Pavo was the traitor.* Odus had said as much, and Anduar's arguments were all aimed at minimizing the consequences of the surrender—of *his* action—not exonerating the young Hashtep.

None of the judges were looking at him at that moment, their attention being all on one another. Nagaro made one more desperate attempt, speaking boldly into the momentary silence that followed the High Judge's reproof of his fellows.

"My Lord Madred, please! As you wish to see justice done, grant me just a few minutes to speak regarding what I know of the nature and character of Pavo Maat!"

The High Judge fixed him with his piercing blue eyes and said very sternly, "I must advise you, Zirda, that you do yourself no service by pursuing this."

"I am not concerned with serving myself," Nagaro informed him indignantly. "I'm concerned with the truth!"

"*Nagaro!*" Tredhold hissed urgently, his fingers gripping Nagaro's arm.

"*The truth?*" Odus roared, leaping to his feet.

Nagaro was on his feet in the next instant, having shaken off the healer's restraining hand. "Yes, My Lord! *The truth!* Isn't that what this Tribunal is supposed to be about?"

"*Enough!*" Lord Madred had risen as well, and he towered in his place, grim and commanding. "Your testimony is finished, Tor Nagaro! If you won't see fit to be escorted out, I shall have you forcibly removed!"

Nagaro met the man's gaze without flinching, storm-gray eyes against that stare of blazing blue. "Very well, My Lord," he said, in a voice that was taut but level. "In that case I am finished with this Tribunal, since it doesn't appear to be interested in seeing justice done." He swept the astonished judges coldly with his eyes. "Good day, My Lords."

So saying, he shoved his chair aside, turned, and made for the door by which he had entered, ignoring the gasps and cries that arose behind him—ignoring Tredhold's unsuccessful effort to again catch hold of his arm. As he approached the two guards who flanked the door—both of whom were standing frozen in attitudes of stunned dismay—he gestured to them peremptorily. "You had best attend me, gentlemen," he said through his teeth, "if you don't wish to be found derelict in your duty."

The two men jumped to obey him as if they'd been goaded with red-hot pokers

25: Verdict

Nagaro strode through the halls, trailing the guards in his wake, stormed into the room where he'd been confined, and slammed the door behind him. He stood there, fists clenched, breathing hard—and suddenly realized that he'd lost Tredhold.

He was immediately seized with a fear that the judges would take out their anger on the poor healer for his own ill-considered outburst. He began to pace the floor. *Should he go back to the Audience Chamber? Try to apologize?* He didn't feel the least bit repentant, and wouldn't have even considered the gesture if he hadn't been so worried about the sandy-haired Leithian. Unfortunately, he wasn't at all sure that the guard at his door would actually permit it.

Before he could make up his mind whether to try, he heard Tred's voice outside speaking to the guard, and a moment later, the healer came in, looking very grim.

Nagaro spoke immediately. "Tred! I hope you didn't suffer because of what *I* did."

"No," Tredhold reassured him. "I stayed to give Lord Madred the letter I'd written. And it took me some time to get his attention. I caught quite an earful of their argument without them even noticing."

Nagaro's relief lasted only for an instant, because a second guilty thought came into his head as soon as the first one went out of it. "What about Pavo?" he asked anxiously. "Do you think I've hurt *his* chances?"

Tredhold shook his head. He crossed to the table and dropped onto one of the chairs with an air of defeat. "Nagaro," he said wretchedly, "I don't think anyone could say anything to make Pavo's situation any worse. The judges are all completely convinced that he betrayed the mission. The only argument is about *why*. Odus thinks it's enough that Pavo's a Hashtep. He thinks it was a mistake to have ever let him into the Fleet, let alone trusting him with the mission plan. And he thinks it was *really* a mistake to have put him into the Emperor's hands by surrendering. And on the *other* side there's Soren—and Anduar, too— who are saying that Pavo traded the mission plan for your life and your pardon. They seem to think that Roheed had advance instructions to step in at the last minute the way he did. It sounded as if Lord Madred was coming around to that side—once Anduar got him to put aside his anger over your lack of respect."

Nagaro had followed Tredhold to the table, and he now sank into a chair. The healer's words struck him hard. "They think Pavo would break an oath, taken in Sheptuum's name, to save *me?*"

Tredhold gave him a sick look. "They're not the least bit impressed with anything to do with Sheptuum."

Nagaro gazed at the healer in agony. "If only they'd let me *speak!*"

But Tredhold's shoulders sagged even further. "It wouldn't have mattered if they had! They think ye have a blind spot for Pavo—whether it's stubbornness, or poor judgement, or just blind loyalty to your friend. They'd never believe anything ye said about him that didn't square with their own notions."

Nagaro lowered his head into his hands. "*Oh, Tred—*"

He had never felt so helpless. This was so wrong. And he wanted *so* much to put it right. And Tred was saying that the only tool he had—the persuasiveness of his words—would avail him nothing! "Why did you bother giving Madred your letter?" he asked bitterly.

Tredhold gave a helpless shrug. "It was all I *had*. And maybe—*just maybe*—it'll carry a little weight. I was a Fleet man for years before I met ye, Nagaro. And my record was clean, too. I never did anything that wasn't straight down the line... no insubordination... no disrespect for authority. And," he added, "there's one thing I am that ye're not, and never will be."

"What's that?"

Bitterness rang in Tredhold's voice when he answered. "A *Leithian.*"

*

"They can't *possibly* execute him! They just *can't!*"

Nagaro was pacing the floor again. Tredhold looked up glumly from the latest letter he was writing to Ilsafeth. He didn't even try to answer, having given up on that several hours before. Everything had already been said, and re-said, until there was nothing left to add. It was close to noon on the day following Nagaro's appearance at the Tribunal. Neither man had slept well. Both were tense and irritable from waiting and worrying.

"They haven't got any *proof*—not any *real* proof, anyway. It's all guesswork! They surely can't execute a man based on *guesswork—*"

The sound of voices outside the door interrupted Nagaro's tirade and brought his pacing to a halt.

Tredhold froze with his pen poised above the paper.

"Aye, My Lord. Yes, of course. Yes, the healer is with him. Just a minute while I knock for ye, Zirda." The guard was being rigidly formal, as if speaking to someone very important. The voice of whoever he was speaking to was very low, almost inaudible. There was no possibility of making out the words.

Nagaro moved to the table and sat down, just as a crisp knock sounded on the door. Looking across the table, he nodded to Tredhold.

The healer went to the door and opened it. "Ah, My Lord Anduar," he said, just as stiffly as the guard, though his surprise at the identity of their visitor came through the stiffness. "To what do we owe this honor?" He stepped aside, ushering the Pact Signer into the room.

"I have come to bring you the verdict of the Tribunal." Anduar gave Tredhold the barest nod as he moved past him. "Good morning, Zirda," he added, absolutely unruffled. "And good morning to you also, Captain." This last was addressed to Nagaro.

Nagaro did not rise. He gave the steel-eyed Kelorin the barest of nods. "My Lord," he said in a voice that carried a distinct chill.

Anduar advanced until he was a few feet from the table and stood, regarding Nagaro with his usual penetrating gaze. Nagaro returned the look in kind. Tredhold had followed Anduar back to the table, and now he went to stand behind the chair he had been occupying a moment before. There he stopped, hovering, looking back and forth between the two men as if wondering whether he might need to intercede.

Anduar addressed himself once more to Nagaro, with the same imperturbable delivery. "It pleases me, Captain, to be the first to address you by that title since your rank has been restored."

Nagaro stared at him coldly. "My rank is of very little importance when a man's life may be at stake."

There was perhaps the slightest flicker of a frown. "Whether you consider it important or not, Captain, there was rather a long discussion about it. There were some who wanted to see you stripped down to seaman and reprimanded for having offered surrender to the Emperor, and others who wished to give you a commendation for outstanding courage and integrity under the most extreme conditions. In the end, it was decided to do both. Therefore your rank was, in effect, taken away and immediately restored again."

Nagaro moved impatiently. "That seems rather a waste of time," he observed with obvious annoyance. "Am I correct, My Lord, in surmising that the judges have decided to find Pavo guilty of treason?"

There was another slight flicker of a frown. "Yes, you are correct. That is the other part of the verdict that I have come to report." This pronouncement was delivered with perfect deadpan.

"And what is to be his fate? If the Tribunal has its way?"

Lord Anduar's glance did not waver. Neither did his voice. "Our judgement is that he should die by hanging," he said coolly, "at the end of the week. Trust me, Captain. This is for the best—"

"It most certainly is *not!*" Nagaro had straightened in his chair, his eyes flashing daggers.

"*Nagaro!*" Tredhold exclaimed, shocked. The other two men both ignored him.

Nagaro wasn't finished. "To *think* an innocent man guilty is merely a mistake, My Lord," he said. "To *execute* him for your mistake is a crime!"

Anduar regarded him calmly and a little sadly. "I am sure you are sincere in your opinion, Captain. And given that, I'd think the worse of you if you didn't defend the man. It's an unfortunate fact, however, that even the best of us are often blind to the faults of our friends. In time I am sure you'll come to understand that it was necessary for Pavo Maat to die. Those who are clamoring for blood will thus be satisfied."

Nagaro felt as if walls were closing in around him. He struggled to remain at least outwardly as controlled as the Pact Signer as he continued to meet the man's eyes. "I can understand how Vell could come to the wrong conclusion," he said evenly, "given what he heard and saw, and how little he knows of Pavo. But I expected better from the Tribunal. I hoped at least *some* of the judges would be more concerned with uncovering the truth than with grasping at a convenient explanation that happened to suit their interests. I thought *you* at least—"

"*Captain!*" This time the frown was more than a flicker. "You should not speak so of *interests*. It happens that I—and also Lord Soren—have been at some pains to insure that this incident doesn't adversely affect your career or damage your reputation."

At this, Nagaro stood up. The scrape of the chair legs on the stone floor sounded loud in the quiet room, and Tredhold edged warily around the table towards him. Nagaro took no notice. "My Lord," he said coldly, "if you did that at the expense of justice or the honor of Edrovir, do not expect me to be grateful!"

Tredhold gasped.

The Pack Signer regarded Nagaro for several long seconds before he smiled a small, satisfied smile. "Well spoken, Captain! You continue to exceed every expectation. But you need not fear for Edrovir—whatever you may believe." So saying, Lord Anduar turned on his heel. He paused at the door and turned back long enough to say, "You are now free to go, Captain—and you also, healer. The guard has orders to show you out, and you will find horses from the royal stable at your disposal. Good day, gentlemen."

The silence that followed Anduar's departure hung heavy with anger and hurt.

After several heartbeats, Tredhold sank into a chair. "Well," he said dismally, "My letter didn't do much good, did it?"

"No." Nagaro gave him a distracted look. Scowling, he punched at the air. "*Blast that man, Tred!* He's so damnably cold-blooded! Did you hear him during the Tribunal? Doing sums with men's lives? What must I say to him to make an impression?"

Tredhold gave him a rueful look. "Oh, ye've made an *impression*—"

"I mean about Pavo's innocence! If Anduar thinks so highly of me that he's at such pains to protect my reputation, why does he dismiss my judgement?" Nagaro gave his chair such a vicious kick that it nearly fell over. He began to pace the floor.

"He thinks ye're just *wrong*," Tredhold said bleakly. That ye can't see Pavo clearly... Ye heard what he said: 'Even the best of us—'"

"There must be *something* I can do!" Nagaro paused in his pacing, his brows knit sharply above eyes that blazed.

Tredhold heaved a sigh. "I don't see anything, Nagaro. We'd best pack up our bags. He said they'd provide horses." The healer stood up. "We can be at the Fleet Compound in an hour." He began to gather up his writing materials.

Nagaro made no answer. He resumed pacing. His expression had only become more intense and furious. Abruptly he stopped in his tracks. "I have to find the king!" he said. He turned and started for the door.

Tredhold came after him with a cry of alarm. "Wait, Nagaro!" He came up short when Nagaro rounded on him with a questioning frown.

"What, Tred?"

The healer licked his lips, embarrassed. "Why the king?" he asked. "What do ye mean to *do?*"

Nagaro stared at him. "Talk to him, Tred. What do you think?

Tredhold's face registered relief, but then he asked, "What good will *that* do? *He* didn't make the judgement."

Nagaro ran a hand through his hair. "The Tribunal functions in his service, doesn't it? Maybe he can change the sentence."

"But ye'll never be allowed—"

"Not if I don't try!" Nagaro turned again and flung open the door. "Guard!" he cried. "Where can I find King Elgurn?"

The guard happened to be the same young Kelorin who had led his escort to the Tribunal. "Z-Zirda? I mean, *Captain*..." he stammered. "Ye can't just see the king—"

"Lord Anduar said I was free to go, didn't he?"

"Free? Aye, Captain. Free to leave the palace. I suppose ye could ask for an audience... The king might see ye in a week or two."

"Not in a week! I need to see him now!"

"But *Captain*—!" The poor guardsman looked completely flustered. Fortunately for him, he was interrupted by a woman's voice, calm but preemptive.

"Guardsman? Captain? What's all this?"

"My Lady?"

The two men spoke in unison. Neither had noticed the princess's approach. The guard then began to sputter.

Nagaro recovered his equilibrium more quickly. "My Lady Princess," he said urgently, "I must speak with your father without delay!"

Nevien read the look in his eyes. She chewed her lip for a moment, then said, "Very well, Captain," much to the obvious astonishment of the guard. "I'll take you to him. It's quite all right, Guardsman," she added. "You needn't accompany us. This man is trustworthy, and I will take full responsibility. Perhaps you could show the healer the way to the stable?"

Tredhold had quietly come up behind Nagaro while the princess was speaking. He made a small bow to her. "Thank you, My Lady." He turned to Nagaro. "I'll... ah... just pack your bag for ye, shall I?" he added awkwardly. "And take it back to the Fleet Compound? It'll save ye the trouble o' coming back here on your way out."

Nagaro gave the healer a curt nod. "Thank you, Tred."

Nevien promptly began to move away down the corridor, beckoning for Nagaro to walk beside her and leaving the guardsman to stare after them for a moment, before shrugging and giving his attention to Tred.

The princess did not make any move to take Nagaro's arm, so he took his cue from her and didn't offer it. As they rounded the first corner into another corridor, she moved briefly closer to him and whispered, "That's good. Keep a little distance. This *is* rather irregular, but if we go boldly and openly as if nothing were amiss, I don't think anyone will stop us." Then she stepped away from him again and continued walking with quick, confident steps.

They passed only one guard, and a pair of servants, before reaching the palace's central hallway. The guard stood rigidly to attention in his little niche. Nagaro thought he saw curiosity in the eyes of one of the servants, but the other's expression remained studiously disinterested as he passed them. They went a short distance along the central hallway, then made some turns. They passed another guard whom the princess acknowledged with a nod, before she halted at the smaller, less public, doorway of the Great Hall. This she opened, and briefly surveyed the room that lay beyond.

The noontide meal was finished and the servants must have cleared whatever tables had been used. Nevien nodded in satisfaction and stepped into the room, ushering Nagaro after her. Once they were inside the huge shadowed chamber she slowed a little, glancing all around to make doubly sure that no one was present before addressing him again in a low voice, even as she kept walking across the polished floor.

"Why do you want to speak to my father? Has it to do with the Tribunal?"

"Yes." He also kept his voice low.

"I didn't think they treated you very well," she said, glancing briefly at him and looking away again. "It made me quite angry. And of course it's very sad that your friend has to die for what he did."

Nagaro came to a dead stop, frowning darkly.

She stopped also, turning, and started at his expression. Her eyes searched his. "What is it, Nagaro?"

"It's much worse than that," he told her severely. "If I can't prevent it, Pavo is going to die for something he *didn't* do."

"*Oh my!* You're sure he's innocent?"

"If Pavo denied it while speaking under an oath sworn to his god, then he didn't do it."

For a moment Nevien studied his face. Then she nodded decisively, her green eyes clouded. "Then of course we must do something," she murmured, as she began once more to lead him briskly along the length of the room.

Nagaro realized that she was making for the small door that gave entry to the part of the palace where the guards were housed. It also gave access to what the royal family called the "back stair", and to the side exit into the stable yard. After they exited the Great Hall, it quickly became apparent that Nevien was making for the stairs. As she set her foot on the first step, Nagaro hesitated, knowing that the stairway led to the royal chambers located on the third floor.

The princess, however, beckoned him on. They were fortunately quite alone, and this apparently emboldened her to risk further speech with him. "As you say, Captain, it is urgent," she said, keeping her voice low. "You must speak to my father, and right now I know he's on the third floor. There's...ah... something he attends to at this time of day." She gave him a quick, awkward glance. "You may have to wait a few minutes for him to finish, but it shouldn't be long."

They were mounting the stairs and had just reached the second floor landing, when they heard the sound of a door being flung open somewhere above them, followed by heavy booted steps coming very rapidly down the stairs. Nagaro paused in alarm, but it turned out to be Brandle who suddenly rounded the corner from the upper flight. The lieutenant took in the princess and Nagaro at a glance. If it surprised him to see them together, he gave no sign. In fact, he appeared quite distracted.

"It's the queen," he gasped as he reached the landing where they stood. "She's fallen—not getting up! I'm going for Master Ambras!" And with that, he plunged past them, taking the stairs two at a time.

Nevien turned pale and put a hand to her breast. "*Sweet Lady!*" she murmured. "I don't like this!" She turned to Nagaro. "You had best wait here, Captain," she said urgently, "while I see what's happened. I'll come back as soon as I can."

She was off then, running up the stairs.

Nagaro stared after her as she disappeared around the turn of the landing. He heard her receding footsteps, and then, a few seconds latter, the sound of the door on the third floor landing above him slamming shut most un-decorously. The sounds of Brandle's progress had also died away, and it was very quiet there on the second floor landing.

Nagaro stood for a moment under the steady gray gaze of his own portrait, hanging on the wall. He glanced furtively at the picture—and hastily away again. The painted gaze reminded him of a time before anything had gone wrong in his life. He realized that it could be risky for him to be there—standing beside his own image—when Brandle came back up with Ambras. They might well be too distracted to make the comparison between him and the portrait, but he decided it would be better to wait on the third floor landing. It was very nearly the same place, after all, and Nevien wouldn't have to come as far to find him.

Somewhat hesitantly, he climbed the last flight of the stairs and stopped on the landing at the top, outside of the door leading to the hallway that accessed the royal apartments. He had scarcely come to a halt, however, when he heard a sound that made his heart go cold.

It was a woman's scream, coming from the other side of the door—at some distance and a little attenuated by the thickness of the wood, but still sharp and shrill.

Without an instant's hesitation, Nagaro seized the door handle, flung the door wide, and burst into the corridor beyond. It didn't matter that he'd been told to wait, or whose scream it might have been. He only knew that there was a woman in fear or in pain, and he meant to see if he could do anything about it.

There was no one immediately on the other side of the door, but the scream had seemed to come from farther away. He could see several figures farther down the corridor, close to the intersection of hallways that formed a large landing around the top of the main central stair, marked by its encircling balustrade.

The closest figures were two women, huddled against the left-hand wall. One of them was lying on the floor and he presumed that this was the queen. He took in dark hair and a dark rose-pink dress he thought he recognized. The other woman, kneeling beside the first with her hands clutched to her mouth, must be the Lady Merriel. No one else among the palace women was so small in stature and so very flaxen-haired.

Nagaro's glance did not linger on the two women, however, but followed the direction of Merriel's horrified gaze to where two more figures, twenty feet beyond her, were locked together in the middle of the hallway. One of them was Nevien, on her knees. The other was a man—tall, thin, dressed in clothes that had seen better days, and crowned by a wild mass of graying red hair. The man must have caught Nevien from behind, for her back was towards him—*and he had his hands about her throat.* Her own hands desperately clutched at the man's wrists, but even as Nagaro watched, they lost their grip as she sagged in her captor's clutches.

In the next instant, Nagaro was running. As he approached Merriel and the stricken queen, his mind leaped to a likely guess, and he shouted at the man.

"No, Kale! Don't hurt her!"

The red-haired man jerked as if startled—and released his grip. Nevien's body slid to the floor, sprawling at the man's feet. The scarecrow figure turned to face Nagaro.

The sight of the madman's ravaged countenance brought Nagaro sliding to a stop in shock a few yards from the man and opposite where Merriel still knelt beside the fallen queen. He was already shaking and out of breath from his sprint down the hall, acutely aware of his weakened state, but also stunned by the change that time had wrought upon Kale Fendred.

The Kale that he remembered had been a gentle man with serious gray-green eyes, meticulously shaven chin, and curly red hair that was often disheveled from the man's habit of running his hands through it. Now, however, the man's eyes stared wildly with the fierce intensity of madness from a gaunt face that was nearly lost between the shaggy thatch of graying curls above and the overgrowth of tangled beard below. The red-rimmed eyes seemed to look right through Nagaro, not seeing him, as the man raised his hands and spoke, chanting a dirge:

"Slay them! Slay them! Slay them all!
Hear the words and heed the warning!
All their plumes and banners fall,
Carrion crows will feast come morning..."

Nagaro felt a rising horror, even though he knew the words were likely part of some Leithian war ballad. On the day he had returned to Lankura, Nevien had told him that the man now often spoke in verse. In fact, everything the mad Kale said seemed to be quotations from books he'd read. Kale had been an avid reader.

Nagaro remembered other things Nevien had said about Kale: He had escaped from his chamber several times, and each time had attacked someone. *And the man had apparently strangled his wife...*

Nevien! She couldn't be dead—

His agonized gaze flicked to the princess where she lay, and back again. He ached to see her show some sign of life, but feared to take his eyes from the madman. The wild-eyed Leithian radiated danger.

Furtive though Nagaro's glance had been, it drew Kale's attention back to his victim. He began to turn and to stoop, arms reaching, fingers clutching...

Nagaro risked another glance and this time he saw Nevien stir!

His heart leaped into his throat at the sight and he willed himself not to look at her again. He had to draw Kale's attention. "*No Kale!*" he cried, desperately edging nearer. "You're finished there—Come to *me!*"

It worked: Kale straightened and swivelled, the focus of his mad gaze coming back to Nagaro.

Unfortunately, at that moment, Lady Merrial screamed—the same sound that had first alerted Nagaro—and Kale immediately swung in *her* direction. He began to advance, now in a ceremonial march, towards Merriel and Queen Semorel, crooning tenderly as he moved:

"*Here lie the pretty ones, side by side.*

Seralind shall sing their praises..."

Nagaro instantly moved sideways to place himself between Kale and the two women—and further from Nevien. He was still more than a dozen feet from Kale and was reluctant to close with the deranged man. He was unsure of the man's strength—and of his own. He had no wish to hurt Kale or to be hurt by him. *If he could just distract the man long enough for Brandle to return with Master Ambras, surely three of them together could overpower one madman...*

"Listen to me, Kale!" he said urgently. "You don't really want to hurt anyone..."

Kale's wild eyes returned to him and locked onto him with such unnatural intensity that Nagaro had to resist the impulse to back away. Instead he shifted to his right, and Kale turned, tracking him.

"*Mercy...*" the man muttered into his beard. "*Mercy on the poor old man...*"

Nagaro managed to give a quick nod to the cowering Merriel—one he hoped was reassuring. Then he had his eyes back on Kale. And at that moment, he caught another movement, near the main stairs.

On a surge of hope, he risked a glance, and he saw—not Brandle or Ambras coming up—but Elgurn and another man in the livery of the palace guard. They had clearly just emerged from the corridor leading to the north tower where Kale was normally imprisoned. Nagaro's brief glimpse told him that the guard was injured—leaning on the king, one leg dangling—and that Elgurn was also hurt, blood trickling from a gash over his left temple.

When he turned back, Nagaro found that Kale had begun to follow his gaze, and he immediately sought to regain the madman's attention. "Here, Kale!" he cried. "This way!" And he began to back slowly away from the red-haired Leithian, moving back up the hall, in the direction from which he'd originally come.

As he had hoped, Kale stalked after him. From the corner of his eye, Nagaro saw Elgurn dart along the wall behind Kale and slip through the doorway of his own bedchamber. Nagaro frowned. *What was the king doing? Where was the wounded guard?*

Kale didn't let him pursue these thoughts however. The deranged Leithian was only a dozen feet away, still coming, and now the madman raised his arm and leveled a boney finger straight at Nagaro. Kale's eyes burned with an unnatural light as he spoke in a voice that was hoarse and ominous.

"Pity the poor orphan child...
Dead is the father... dead the mother..."

Bishka! Nagaro's stomach turned over. The words struck too close to what Kale must once have believed about Leyel Virden. *Had the man recognized him?* Was there some preternatural power in his madness that allowed him to see what others could not?

Kale, however, seemed unaware of Nagaro's reaction. He ceased pointing and instead raised his hands as if in supplication. Casting his eyes upward as if addressing the Leithian gods, he declaimed:

"Pity the poor orphan child that cries in the night, alone.
Dead is the father. Dead the mother, lying in blood.
Gone are they both, beyond hope or recall.
Pity the poor orphan child, and weep, weep, oh Edrovir!"

Even before Kale finished speaking, Nagaro felt relief flood through him as he recognized the words of the poem *Night Falls*, lamenting the deaths of King Tevren and Queen Lindra. Perhaps Kale's tortured brain *had* sensed something familiar—Nagaro's voice, perhaps—and so had dredged up this literary reference to a parentless child, but that was all. And anyone listening would think it nonsense.

With Kale distracted, Nagaro risked glancing at Nevien and saw that she had changed position. He caught a glimpse of her eyes, wide with fear, looking at him, before his own eyes were drawn by the movement of the king emerging from his bedchamber with an object held aloft.

"Look what I have, Kale," Elgurn called coaxingly. "A new book for you!" He waved the small volume enticingly.

Kale turned like a puppet on a string at the sound of Elgurn's voice, and he immediately began to pad away in the king's direction, hands outstretched as a thirsty man might reach for a flask of water.

"Yes, yes... that's right, Kale... here it is..." Elgurn spoke gently as he backed away towards the north corridor, watching Kale, leading him away from where Nevien lay by dangling the book as if he were luring a dog with a bone.

"*Mercy on the poor old man,*" murmured Kale, as he raptly followed the book. "*His hair is white as snow...*"

As Kale began to move away from him, Nagaro edged back towards the princess. When Elgurn saw this, his pale blue eyes locked briefly with Nagaro's and he spoke directly to him in a tone and cadence that were indistinguishable from those he was using with Kale. "Take care of her," he said, before his eyes flicked back to his demented friend. "That's right, Kale. This way... Come get the book..."

It was at this moment that Brandle and Master Ambras finally burst from the top of the main stairway, emerging on the farther side where there was an opening in the balustrade.

Elgurn had nearly maneuvered Kale into the entrance of the north corridor by this time, and he saw the two men immediately. "Lieutenant, to me," he said, again interjecting the words into the patter meant fo Kale. "Ambras, see to the queen. And to this man." He made a gesture with his head to indicate the injured guard, whom Nagaro could now see was sitting on the floor, leaning against the balustrade's north side.

Ambras stooped over the guard for a moment before hastily darting across to where the queen lay with Merriel still crouched beside her.

Brandle followed Elgurn and Kale as he was bidden, though he glanced first at the fallen guard. He followed the king and the madman down the north corridor with evident trepidation.

Nagaro knelt beside Nevien. "Are you all right?" he asked. "Can you sit up?"

She nodded. "I... think so..." Her voice sounded weak and hoarse, as if her throat were bruised, and Nagaro winced to hear it. She managed to sit up by herself, but her hand went to her neck, where the dark imprints of Kale's fingers were already beginning to show. "Help me get up," she said, a little less feebly. "I want to... go to the sitting room—"

Nagaro helped her stand—half lifting her.

Once on her feet, she clung to his shoulder because she had begun to shake. "Oh dear..." she murmured. "Nagaro, I—"

"Here." He put his arm around her waist and began to walk her carefully towards the nearby sitting room that had once been Leyel Virden's small, stark bed chamber. As they passed the place where Master Ambras and the Lady Merrial were busy with the queen, he noted that Semorel now seemed to be conscious. Nevien saw it too and relief suffused her face.

The little sitting room was empty, and the room's green-and-blue peacefulness struck Nagaro again as they entered. He helped the princess to a seat on the small couch against one wall, sitting down beside her. She was still trembling visibly.

"Dear Nagaro," she said breathlessly. "Will you hold me, please? I don't know what's the matter with me. I can't seem to stop shaking."

"You've had a bad shock, that's all." He put a comforting arm around her shoulders and she leaned gratefully against his side. "It's a natural reaction," he added. "It will soon pass."

"I was so *frightened!*"

"So was I," he confessed. "For a moment I thought he'd killed you."

She shook her head. "I was afraid he was going to kill *you!* You'd been so badly hurt, and were so long recovering, and he's much stronger than he looks. I was on my way to tell Father about my mother—and that you wished to speak to him—when I turned into the north corridor and I walked straight into Kale! It was such a shock that I... I tried to run away—which is always a mistake with Kale. It... *draws*... him. So of course he came after me—"

He gave her shoulders a little squeeze. "It's over now."

"*Yes...*" She leaned her head against his shoulder for a long moment before she spoke again. "I've wanted to tell you, Nagaro, that I'm so very glad the Mahuk emperor didn't kill you! And I'm sorry he hurt you like that—after I'd encouraged you to join the Fleet..."

Nagaro shook his head. "You mustn't think that way, Nevien. I could have been taken at any time, whether I was in the Fleet or not."

She turned her face up to him, her sea-green eyes very serious. "Maybe," she said. "But I wanted to tell you that anyway. And I'm sorry I didn't go back again after leaving the fruit. I meant to."

"It's all right," he told her quickly. "The fruit was very good, and I assumed you had heard I was better. And, besides, you have so many things to worry about."

She frowned. "It's silly, I know, but when Kale was choking me and I thought I might die, all I could think of was that I hadn't told you those things."

"That's not silly," he said. "When I thought *I* was going to die, one of the things that bothered me was that I wouldn't be here to be a friend to you when you needed one."

She looked at him with eyes suddenly misty. "You're a dear man, Nagaro, and a dear, dear friend."

Steps sounded in the hallway, and the king suddenly appeared in the open doorway. His face was drawn and pale and there was still blood on his temple. His ice-blue eyes took in the room's two occupants in an instant, and he fastened a frowning gaze upon Nagaro.

"What do you think you're doing, Captain?" he demanded.

Nagaro returned him a look that contained no hint of either guilt or apology, and his arm remained around the princess's shoulders. "Taking care of your daughter, My Lord," he said calmly. "As you bade me."

"Really now, Father!" Nevien was frankly disapproving. She also remained as she was, resting against Nagaro's side. "I needed comfort, and I asked him, and he's been very kind. I was shaking from the shock of Kale's attack, and I'm feeling much better now."

The king's frown eased only fractionally. "He shall not leave without swearing an oath not to reveal what he's seen today!"

"*Father!*" Nevien sat up straight, then put her hand to her throat, wincing.

Nagaro reluctantly removed his encircling arm from her shoulders. It had felt so comfortable having her sheltered in the curve of it...

When the princess spoke again, she did so forcefully, though less loudly so as not to strain her bruised throat. "Hasn't the Captain already shown that he would give his life to protect Edrovir's secrets?" she asked rather pointedly. "And as it happens, he's known about Kale since the last Mautep attack. He found Kale's room while looking for me, and he's obviously kept it in confidence. And before you start in about what he was doing on this floor in the first place, *I* brought him up here. He wanted to speak to you. I told him to wait on the stairs while I went to see about Mother, but I'm very glad he didn't stay there because if he hadn't come when he did, I think Kale would have killed me!"

Elgurn turned white. He seemed almost to shrink as he passed a hand over his eyes. "*Merciful Solbrid, forgive me!*" he murmured. Then he met Nagaro's gaze. "I beg your pardon, Captain. It seems you've done us a service, and I am grateful. Do you still wish to speak to me?"

Nagaro's rising indignation was replaced by surprise at receiving first an apology and then gratitude from the king. He felt a pang of guilt as he realized that the encounter with Kale had displaced Pavo's plight from his mind. He hesitated a little. "You are very welcome, My Lord," he said carefully. "And this may not be the best time—after what just happened—but I do have an urgent need to speak to you concerning the verdict of the Tribunal."

"Ah. The Tribunal." Elgurn sounded grim. He stepped back into the hall and raised his voice, calling, "Merriel, will you come here, please? You must attend Nevien."

He listened briefly to some reply, then moved back into the room and addressed his daughter. "Merriel will come in a moment, and I want you to go with her. Then I'll hear what the Captain has to say."

"What happened in the tower, Father?" she asked him. "Kale hasn't ever attacked you before."

A shadow crossed the king's face. "He broke the wash basin over my head as I stepped through the door... knocked me unconscious for a short time. I don't believe he knew who he was hitting. And it seems he pushed the guard down the stairs. Ambras says the man's leg is broken."

"You're hurt, as well, Father. You must have the healer tend to that cut."

The king brushed at his temple, as if he'd forgotten the wound. His hand came away with a smear of blood. "It isn't serious," he told her reassuringly. "Ambras can see to it when he's finished with everyone else. I'll speak to the captain while I wait my turn."

At this point, Lady Merriel appeared at the doorway, looking pale but otherwise in command of herself. Elgurn immediately turned to her. "Take Nevien to her chamber, Merriel, and stay with her."

"Yes, My Lord." Merriel curtseyed before advancing into the room. "Come, dear child," she said to Nevien. "You've had a most terrible shock. I can get you a cool cloth for your neck." She turned to Nagaro. "You were quite wonderful, Captain—the way you led him away from us. Thank you so much!"

Nagaro felt himself blushing. "All I did was distract him, My Lady," he murmured, as he hastily stood up and helped Nevien to rise before handing her off to the diminutive Leithian woman. Nevien shot him a parting glance of encouragement over her shoulder as the two women went out the door together.

As soon as they were gone, Elgurn motioned for Nagaro to sit down once more. He then waited in the doorway with an ear cocked until he was satisfied that the women were out of earshot before seating himself in a chair, opposite Nagaro. "Now, Captain," he said gravely. "Let's have your complaint."

Nagaro drew breath. "It's simply this, My Lord: I don't believe Pavo Maat is guilty of treason."

The king sighed wearily and rubbed his beard. He looked harried. "All four judges are convinced otherwise, Captain."

"The judges don't know Pavo as I do, My Lord! I've never known him to speak falsely, and I can't imagine that he would lie after swearing in the name of his god to tell the truth. Nor did he have any friend among the judges. I have it from Anduar's own mouth that he and Lord Soren were protecting *me*, while Odus and Lord Madred, I imagine, were protecting Peldred and Vell. It was very convenient for these four men to have a prisoner in whom none of them had any interest—"

"Captain!" Elgurn held up a warning hand. "You tread on dangerous ground—although your argument might have merit. If the evidence against Pavo Maat were less compelling—"

"*Evidence?*" Nagaro jerked in his seat. "There isn't anything but inference and speculation! You have neither his confession, nor the word of any witness who actually heard him say anything."

The king regarded him sourly. "One can't always expect to have such certainty, Captain," he said. "Yet circumstances can be such as to give one confidence. This man, Pavo Maat, had expressed displeasure at the mission's objective."

Nagaro gestured in frustration. "That doesn't make him a traitor, My Lord. I felt the same way, yet I was prepared to do my duty and not divulge the plans when pressed."

Still Elgurn regarded him coolly. "You are, perhaps, somewhat... exceptional."

"Well if I am, so is Pavo!"

Elgurn sighed. "His loyalty to *you* may well be exceptional, Captain, but we can't have men in the Fleet service who put their loyalty to their captain—or to a friend—above their loyalty to Edrovir."

"You don't know that he did that, My Lord! It's only a supposition, and I am telling you that it doesn't fit the man. Pavo swore his oath to Edrovir in the name of Sheptuum—his god—and he wouldn't break it! He wouldn't have seen any *need* to break it—just to save me—because he trusted Sheptuum to do that. He believes Sheptuum *did* do it—the storm, Roheed being there, the blood debt—all of that he sees as the work of Sheptuum!"

Elgurn sighed. "All right, Captain," he said wearily. "Suppose for a moment that you're right. There's still the fact that *someone* betrayed our plans. If it wasn't your friend, then *who was it?*"

This brought Nagaro up short. "My Lord," he said cautiously. "I didn't see what happened to any of the others. I don't want to accuse anyone based on *my* suppositions."

But the king emphatically shook his head. "No, Captain! You cannot take away the most likely explanation and offer nothing in its place. I don't suppose, for example, that you mean to tell me that *you* did it, and induced Vell and Peldred to lie about it."

"How could I possibly have persuaded them to do that?"

"I can't imagine," the king conceded mildly. "Which is a very good argument against that particular theory. But you see, Captain, this is what a judge must do—imagine all possible theories, and weigh their plausibility. You're an intelligent man. Come, then. Perform the exercise."

Nagaro frowned, suppressing his resentment of the king's didactic tone. He thought he knew very well what a judge ought to do, and he also thought it obvious that the judges of the Tribunal hadn't done it. Still, the king had surely seen a great many more tribunals than *he* had, and at least Elgurn was listening. "Very well," he said with the best grace he could, "I'll try—if you're prepared to consider it, as you say, an exercise." He sat in silent thought for a moment, then began to speak.

"If you consider the possibility that one or more witnesses may *lie*..." he began, "then it's possible to suppose that Vell might be guilty and that Peldred is lying to protect him. I know too little of Peldred to know whether he might do that, but I think I can dismiss this theory based on what I know of Vell."

"How so?" The pale blue eyes were watching him shrewdly now.

"Vell had a secret he was keeping from me throughout the mission—that he, not I, was captain of the *Sword*. Now that I know this, I can see clearly that he gave many signs that he was concealing something and was uncomfortable about it. Yet, if it was *he* who betrayed us, he gave no sign at all. And I don't think he could have concealed it so completely, since it would surely have made him very uncomfortable."

Elgurn stroked his chin. "That is well-reasoned. Continue."

Nagaro's frown returned. "I know very little about Peldred," he said carefully. "I don't know how well he might bear pain, how easily he might lie, or how well he might practice deception. Like Pavo, he has no witness to the truth of his claim of innocence. That fact alone should place him under suspicion equally with Pavo."

Here Elgurn raised an eyebrow. "Go on."

Nagaro drew in a long breath. "There is, however, one reason to suspect Peldred, and it is this: He was obviously troubled after what happened at Osfaraad, while both Vell and Pavo seemed easy in their minds. I, Vell, and Tredhold all saw Peldred's trouble clearly after we got to Pakoa. Vell had noticed it earlier, and he told us that Peldred had been like that ever since Osfaraad."

"A troubled mind doesn't necessarily prove guilt," Elgurn observed pointedly.

"No, it need not," Nagaro conceded. "And since I did not yet know that there had been a betrayal, I thought only that Peldred felt ashamed because he had fainted sooner than Vell or I—after being branded only once."

"Which is likely."

"Perhaps. As I've said, I thought so at the time. So I tried to explain to Peldred that I don't judge men that way—that there's a limit to any man's strength, and it shouldn't be a cause of pride or shame that one is stronger or weaker than another."

"Mmm." Elgurn was frowning slightly. "What was his response?"

"It didn't seem to lessen his distress. 'Thank you for trying,' he said, and he left us, almost running. It was then that Vell made the remark about 'since Osfaraad.' He said that he didn't know what ailed the man. Tredhold tried talking to Peldred again before we left Pakoa, but Peldred wouldn't say what troubled him."

Nagaro ceased speaking, and Elgurn sat still, frowning, for a long moment, staring straight before him. Presently the king stirred and his eyes came back to Nagaro. "This is your alternative then? Peldred?"

Nagaro hesitated, but there wasn't any help for it. "Yes," he said, "I believe he is by far the most likely."

"You're aware that he comes from a very good family—a high noble House—the House of Gilforn? He's been schooled all his life in the ways of honor."

Nagaro inclined his head. "I don't doubt that Peldred knows what he *should* have done, My Lord. But what he *saw*—what they made him watch—may have worked powerfully on his mind. He felt the hot iron once—and I can tell you that it is extremely painful. He's very young, it was his first mission, and Vell may have made it harder for him in the beginning by assuming that he didn't tell. To confess *now* would disappoint his family—"

"It would do far more than that, Captain," Elgurn cut in grimly. "*If* he committed the crime and confessed to it, he would bring shame to his entire family—not just himself. That's how Leithians of noble blood see such things. On the other hand, if he did it and *does not confess*, his spirit will writhe in Hel for eternity, but his family will be spared the shame of having the world know that it spawned a betrayer and a coward."

Nagaro shut his eyes and bowed his head at this. *"Oh, Vothra!"* he murmured. "It's worse even than I thought."

"Yes. I wanted you to understand the full implications of what you have suggested."

Nagaro's head came up. He met the king's pale gaze with a piercing look of his own. "It is still wrong to sacrifice an innocent man, My Lord, whatever the consequences to the House of Gilforn."

Elgurn's eyes grew hard. "I agree with you—in principle. But I'm not convinced that Pavo Maat is innocent. Oh, you've raised doubts in my mind," he added hastily, seeing Nagaro's scowl. "Which is more than I expected. But to be quite honest, Pavo Maat didn't do himself very good service during the Tribunal. He told the judges he was offered his life for the information, and refused. He said he warned the Emperor not to kill you—that the Emperor offered him noble rank if he would swear himself to the service of the Mahuk Baar, which he refused. He put forward all of this apparent self-aggrandizement, and then, when pressed on any of it, he refused to speak further—either to take any of it back, or to offer anything further in his own defense—"

"My Lord," Nagaro broke in. "None of this surprises me. From what I know of Mautep ways, they value honor and loyalty more than they value a man's bloodline. And it's also the way of the people of the Mahuk Baar to become silent in the face of unjust treatment. I believe Pavo was telling the truth, and he found he wasn't being *believed*. The judges were questioning his honesty under a sworn oath to his god. What else could he do but refuse to speak any further to such men?"

Elgurn regarded him skeptically. "I see you have devised answers to everything," he said dryly." You might be right, Captain, but it's also very easy to deceive oneself when it comes to one's friends." His eyes clouded and his voice took on a bitter edge. "See how I deluded myself into thinking that Kale was improved enough that he didn't need to be chained to the wall? And see what very nearly came of it?"

"My Lord, that's different. Kale is mad. He's unpredictable—"

The king's countenance contorted in pain. "I will carry this burden until the day I die," he said bitterly "—if Kale doesn't die first. And if I die before him, my daughter will carry the burden. It's the will of the gods." Elgurn sat silent for a moment, looking inward, then gave a little shudder and once more impaled Nagaro with his eyes.

"Have you considered, Captain, that Pavo Maat may have decided he was doing the work of his god? If he believed, as you say, that his god would save you, might he not have seen himself as the instrument of that salvation? What if he believed that his god wanted him to save you by betraying the purpose of the mission to the emperor? It was a purpose he thought was dishonorable, after all."

Nagaro felt a cold constriction around his heart. *A purpose of which Sheptuum did not approve...* "I... hadn't thought of that," he admitted. "But if he *had* betrayed the mission for what he thought was a good cause, he would have said so. He would have confessed it and accepted the consequences."

"Are you quite *sure?*" The pale blue gaze was relentless. "Perhaps he believes it isn't right that he should die at our hands for serving his god. Can you say you're *certain* this isn't so?"

"No..." Nagaro felt sick. "Of course I can't say I'm *certain*. But I don't believe it! I don't believe he would lie when he had sworn in Sheptuum's name to tell the truth. And I can't bear to see him die for this—with no confession... no witnesses..."

Elgurn was studying him. "If your friend were to confess, would you then believe it and accept the sentence?"

"I'd *have* to—if he confessed to it in Sheptuum's name. It wouldn't be right for him to have risked so many other men's lives to save mine."

"And would he confess to *you*, do you think?" The king's pale blue eyes had turned shrewd.

Nagaro frowned. "If Pavo had anything to confess, My Lord," he said carefully, "I believe he would tell *me*, if he would tell anyone."

"Ah. Very good." The king stood up—with a little wince, and put a hand to his head. "I'll send you to speak with him."

"To speak with Pavo?" Nagaro hastily stood up as well. His heart gave a little leap, though it was followed by a terrible pang. "You'll let me go down into the dungeon... to his cell?"

Elgurn shook his head. "He is no longer in the palace dungeon, Captain. They transferred him to the prison barge this morning. It's anchored in the River Edro. According to law, the feet of a convicted traitor must not be allowed to sully the soil of Edrovir while awaiting execution. But you must give me your word that you will do your best to obtain his confession, Captain. I won't send you otherwise. And if you succeed, I expect you to be satisfied as to the justice of this, and that all doubts have been put to rest."

Nagaro frowned. "I give you my word that I will do my very best to satisfy myself as to his guilt or innocence, My Lord," he said earnestly. "I swear it in Vothra's name, since I very much wish to know the truth. But what if I return even more convinced of his innocence? Will you change the sentence?"

Elgurn looked pained. "I am afraid the only thing that could do that would be a confession from someone else," he said uncomfortably. "The judges have spoken. But if Peldred were to come forward and contradict the testimony he gave before the Tribunal, the judges would have to reconsider the case."

Nagaro's frown deepened. "Perhaps I'll speak to Peldred as well."

"You are, of course, free to do so," Elgurn responded stiffly. "But come, Captain. Let us go down to my study, and I'll write out the order for you to speak to the prisoner."

The king led the way into the corridor, which was now empty, and made briskly for the main stairs with Nagaro in his wake. He didn't get far, however, before Master Ambras emerged from the queen's chamber and intercepted him.

"The queen is resting comfortably," he said, responding to a terse question from Elgurn. "But may I ask, My Lord, where you are going?"

"To my study, healer. If you'll be so good as to let me pass."

Master Ambras looked acutely uncomfortable. "I don't recommend that, My Lord. Not so soon after taking a blow to the head that rendered you unconscious. The exertion could cause you to faint. I would like to examine the wound, now, and clean it."

"Oh very well!" Elgurn flung up his hands in annoyance. "I have writing materials in my chamber. I suppose you can work there, Ambras? Yes? Then come, Captain."

A few minutes later Nagaro was standing beside the ornate writing desk in the king's bedchamber while Master Ambras dabbed at Elgurn's temple with a moistened cloth and the king simultaneously penned an order stating that Captain Nagaro was to be conveyed to the prison barge and allowed to have speech with the condemned man, by order of the Crown, etc... When the order was complete, the king applied sealing wax to the paper and pressed his official sign into the hot wax with the bronze seal he wore as a pendant about his neck.

And shortly thereafter, Nagaro had the precious order safely tucked into his shirt and was descending the back stair, quite unnecessarily escorted by Brandle. The big Leithian kept looking sideways at him. Finally the man ventured: "I don't envy you having stood face to face with old Kale. That man gives me chills."

Nagaro laughed shortly. "I don't envy you having to deal with your father on a regular basis. The way he doesn't let a man speak his mind makes my head hurt."

"My father? Oh, of course, you saw him at the Tribunal. He's a stiff old stick, but he does usually come around to seeing reason in the end. You just have to keep on at him."

Nagaro made no answer. He wasn't at all sure he would have any opportunity to "keep on at" Lord Madred.

Brandle left him at the familiar side door that exited to the stable yard. Outside, it was an excruciatingly bright, warm, cheerful summer afternoon, the kind meant for strolls in the garden or picnics in the country. The sky was a perfect crystalline sapphire, and a balmy air from the sea brought a hint of salt mingled with the scent of roses from the garden. It might as well have been a cold day in Vedorel for all that it raised Nagaro's spirits. He grimly called for a horse, mounted it stiffly when the groom brought it, and rode out through the palace gate into the city of Lankura.

The street was thronged with people going about their business, and he had not ridden far before someone recognized him and people began to press close about him, jostling his horse and cheering. Even as preoccupied as he was, he made out the word "hero" among the shouted acclamations.

"I'm not a hero!" he tried to tell them. "Let me pass!"

Hands were extended to him.

"The Spirits bless ye, Capt'n!"

"Vothra keep ye!"

"The Gods protect ye!"

He couldn't smile, but still he took the hands of as many as he could reach, humbly thanking them. Their kind words moved him, though they couldn't dissolve the knot of fear that bound his heart—*fear for Pavo.*

Eventually, he reached the Fleet Compound, where he finally left the adoring crowd behind him with a sigh of relief as he rode under the high arch and onto the parade ground.

"Nagaro! Ye're finally here!"

Taru appeared so suddenly from one side that Nagaro's horse shied violently, giving him a sharp twinge in his back. He quickly mastered the animal and dismounted gingerly, then took his friend's outstretched hand. "Taru! I've missed seeing you—"

"It's been *awful*, Nagaro!" Taru interrupted him, gripping Nagaro's arm as if he never meant to let go. The young Turo's face was drawn, anguish audible in his voice. "All that time! Not knowing what they were going t' do to ye! And now it seems they're going t' kill poor *Pavo!* Everyone's saying he must have betrayed the mission—and he surely never would've... and... and... *What are we going t' do?*"

26: Something I Must Do

Kuran surveyed the written order and looked up with an arched eyebrow. "Well, Captain," he said, "you must have risen in the king's good graces."

Nagaro scowled. "He hopes I can coax a confession from Pavo to satisfy myself—and to spare him from having to consider the doubts that I've raised."

Kuran frowned. "You don't think Pavo will confess?"

"I don't give it more than one chance in a hundred that he did this crime."

"Yet you mean to go?"

"I want to see him... to talk to him. I had hoped I'd be able to give him some encouragement, but... I have already tried to talk to Peldred several times, and the man all but runs away from me!"

Kuran considered the severe black line of Nagaro's knit brows and his burning gaze. "Small wonder," he murmured. "If you showed him *that* face!"

"I didn't!" Nagaro's frown was replaced by a look of pure anguish. "I approached him with the gentlest manner I possibly could. I think he's afraid of what I'll say to him."

"Mmm." Kuran reached across his desk for pen and ink. "I am rather inclined to agree with Tredhold's assessment. Peldred seems to me like a man with a guilty conscience. I'll add my signature to this, Captain, though with the king's name and seal, it's hardly necessary. Take it to the bailiff and he'll see that you're rowed over to the barge."

"Thank you, My Lord." Nagaro reclaimed the signed paper and turned to go.

"Nagaro—"

The unexpected use of his first name brought Nagaro to a stop at the door. "Zirda?"

"I want you to know that I posted you under Strad because I thought my least experienced commander would benefit from your council. For the space of three hours I thought that decision had cost you your life. I'm glad it turned out otherwise."

Nagaro stood still in the doorway, considering Kuran's clouded countenance. "Thank you, My Lord," he said with feeling. "I didn't *mean* to do anything to jeopardize the—"

Kuran stopped him with a raised hand. "No, Captain, this is on me. I should never have taken either you or the *Sword* into Mahuk waters, regardless of what you were prepared to swear to. It begged for trouble of *some* kind—though I never imagined the thing that actually occurred. There's little use in being older and wiser if one lets youth and pride prevail."

Nagaro dipped his head. "Not pride, My Lord. I hoped your orders might change... in the field..."

"That also had occurred to me." Kuran's glance was not unkind.

Nagaro swallowed. "The judges said that I wasn't the captain of the *Sword*. That it was Vell."

Kuran raised an eyebrow. "I wouldn't have put it so—and I didn't when I spoke to Vell. His orders came through me, but not from me, and there were two of them. The first was to take command if he thought it necessary to prevent you from interfering with the mission. The *other* was to bring you safely back if at all possible—saving only if it conflicted with the mission's purpose."

Nagaro frowned. "The first one sounds like Odus... the second one like... Anduar..." He deduced the accuracy of his guesses from the shock on Kuran's face. He made a low bow. "Thank you for your candor, My Lord."

Kuran recovered quickly. "There is one thing that has been troubling me ever since Paktaar," he said gravely. "It is this: Why did the Emperor tell me there was a traitor on the *Sword*, but not who that traitor was? I keep wondering... Is it possible that this is a... test?"

This time it was Nagaro who stared in shock. *His fear for Pavo had been narrowing his vision*. "It's more than possible, My Lord," he said with sudden clarity. "There is more at stake here than one man's life!"

*

The longboat, with two Fleet men at the oars, cut an angled path across the Edro's broad channel from the Fleet's quay to the prison barge. The latter was anchored near the center of the channel and a distance downstream, but the rowers were having to work hard because the river mouth was tidal and the tide had just turned from ebb to flow.

Seated in the boat, watching as the barge drew nearer, Nagaro reflected somberly that he had sailed past it in the *Sword* a dozen times without knowing what it was. He'd never bothered to ask. Now that he knew, he wished he didn't.

The two Fleet oarsmen were not inclined to conversation, which suited Nagaro's mood. Both of them surely knew that Pavo was one of Nagaro's officers, and now they probably thought he was guilty. Yet they had drilled with the young Hashtep on the parade ground, taken meals under the same roof with the him, crossed swords with him at practice... Their respect for Nagaro still showed in the way they addressed him, but their averted eyes made it clear they were not comfortable with their present duty.

In fact, scarcely anyone Nagaro had encountered in the day and a half since his return to the Fleet Compound had been willing to talk to him about Pavo. Taru said that the ones who had sailed on the *Sword* and had known Pavo well still favored innocence, but outside of that group, the scales tipped towards guilt. Nagaro's brows knit. Before the ill-fated mission, the Fleet warriors had mostly accepted Pavo, even respected him. *How quickly some of those men had turned...*

"Hoy there! State your business!"

The longboat was nearing its destination, and a guard at the railing that encircled barge had just hailed them.

One of the oarsmen answered the hail. "Someone t' speak with the prisoner. King's orders, signed by Lord Kuran!"

"It's Captain Nagaro... *by the Eyes!*"

The longboat scraped the side of the barge at a gap in the railing where a short wooden ladder hung over the side. The guard threw a rope to the man in the longboat's bow. The boat was soon made fast, and Nagaro ascended the ladder to the barge's deck.

The floating prison was called a barge for want of a better name. It was, in fact, no more than a rectangular platform with a stout wooden box-like building in the middle of it. The railing that ran around the edge of the platform had several interruptions for docking, and it was separated from the central building by six feet of open deck on all sides.

The building turned out to contain a cabin of sorts at one end, which housed the three guards when they weren't patrolling the narrow strip of deck. The small group of cells was accessible only by passing through this cabin.

The warden of the prison barge met Nagaro in the cabin, where he had a desk next to his bed. A gray-bearded Leithian with one sightless eye, he applied the gaze of the other to Nagaro's written order.

"Oy! I'd like t' have seen how ye got this!" the man rumbled, with a leer.

Nagaro was not inclined to enlighten him. Instead, he explained what Elgurn had instructed him to do.

"A confession, hey? Good luck t' ye, Captain! The man's not said a word since they brought him here."

The warden stepped out from behind his desk, fishing for his ring of keys. He crossed the cabin to a doorway, passing the third guard, who must have been on the night shift and was snoring in his bunk. Nagaro followed the warden through the doorway into a passage that was lit by a row of porthole-like windows, and along it to the last door in the row of cells.

"He's chained up so's he can't get within five feet o' the door," the warden informed him as he turned the key in the lock. "Which is a good thing t' know if he makes a move at ye, since I'll be locking ye in. Ye'll have an hour, but if ye're finished sooner—or if ye need anything—just give a shout. Oh, and ye'll have t' leave your sword outside, Zirda. Can't risk having *him* get hold of it, can we?"

Nagaro frowned, but unbuckled the sword belt and leaned the sheathed blade against the wooden wall beside the cell door. A moment later, he stepped through into the cell and heard the door close behind him, followed by the click of the lock.

The cell smelled like a slave barn. It was illuminated only by what light entered through a small grated window in the door and through a row of even smaller, un-grated, openings high up on the farther wall, just under the roof. The latter were presumably to provide ventilation rather than light.

Nagaro stood just inside the door as his eyes adjusted to the gloom. The cell was about three times as deep as it was wide and unfurnished except for a narrow shelf across the farther end that apparently served as a bed. Under the bed, an un-emptied chamber pot was contributing to the general atmosphere. There was a man's form lying on the shelf, bent a little because the bed was only about six feet long. The figure had yet to move or make a sound.

Nagaro cleared his throat. "Pavo?"

"*Nagaro?*"

The mingling of joy and hope in Pavo's voice tore at Nagaro's heart. He heard the rattle of chain as the young Hashtep got up from the bed and came towards him across the floor. In the dim light, he could just make out the details of his friend's massive form and could see that Pavo's wrists were both manacled, the iron bracelets linked by six inches of strong chain. Another chain, about a dozen feet long, was attached to the right-hand manacle and ran to a heavy iron ring securely bolted to the wall above the middle of the bed.

Pavo's eager strides quickly brought him to the end of the second chain, and its tightening brought him up short with a jerk. "Nagaro?" he said again, this time sounding more puzzled than hopeful. "What you are doing here?"

Nagaro crossed the remaining distance between them and threw his arms around his friend. He'd never done such a thing before, but at that moment nothing else seemed adequate to express what he felt. "I'm sorry, Pavo," he said, holding his grip for a long second before stepping back to hold the other man's shoulders at arms length. "I wanted to bring you some cause for hope, but I have found none—at least not yet. The truth is, I was sent to see if you would give me a confession."

"*Confession?*" Pavo sounded disbelieving and aggrieved. "How can I make confession? I did not do anything wrong!"

"Pavo, I am only asking because I swore to the king that I would. Otherwise I wouldn't have been allowed to see you. Is there anything at *all* that you have to tell me, other than what you've said before?"

"No, Nagaro! Already I have told it all to you. I swear it by Sheptuum! I have told it all to judge too. They have ask me to swear, and so I swear, but still they do not believe me! How can those judge all be such bad man, Nagaro?"

Nagaro let go of his friend's shoulders. He rubbed his forehead. "Pavo, could we sit down?"

"Oh yes, Nagaro. We can sit."

So they sat, side by side on the hard, narrow bed. Pavo sat with his hands in his lap, the chain dangling. Nagaro gripped the edge of the shelf on either side of his legs. "Pavo," he said uncomfortably. "There are a few more things I have to ask. I have to make absolutely sure that no one can say I didn't try hard enough. Do you understand?"

"Yes, I understand, Nagaro."

"Good." Nagaro paused, then said, "Tell me why you were so sure I wasn't going to die that day."

The chain clinked as Pavo raised his hands to his face to brush his shaggy hair out of his eyes. He seemed to hesitate, but then he said, "It is because story was not finished."

"What story do you mean, Pavo?" Nagaro was studying his friend's shadowy profile, but the light wasn't good enough to read his expression.

Another hesitation. "It started being story of Roheed—story I have told to you long ago in Sar Tipaal—but you have been part of it too. Sheptuum would not let you die before end of story."

Nagaro bowed his head and raised a hand to massage his temples. *Pavo was gifted with far too much imagination.* "Pavo," he said after a moment, "is the story over *now?* Now that Roheed has paid his blood debt by saving my life?"

This time the answer was even longer in coming. "I am not so sure," Pavo said at last. "Now I think maybe it is really *your* story—and Roheed is only part of it. Maybe his part is finished, but I think your story is still going on."

Nagaro drew an uneasy breath. He liked this interpretation even less than the other. "Are *you* part of the story, Pavo?"

"I suppose... maybe... very little part..." Nagaro could see that Pavo was staring at the floor. After a moment the young Hashtep added,

"Maybe now my part is finished."

Nagaro swallowed. "What *was* your part, then, Pavo? What did you do? Did you help Sheptuum?"

Pavo turned towards him, then. Nagaro could see the shine of his friend's dark eyes. "Of course I help Sheptuum. But I do not think you believe in Sheptuum, Nagaro."

"What I believe doesn't matter. I need to know what *you* believe."

"Oh."

"*How* did you help Sheptuum, Pavo?"

This time the answer came immediately. "I have told Emperor how Sheptuum have always protect you—because you have so much honor. I have told him he will be very sorry if he kill you, because Sheptuum surely will not like for you to die. I have told him that I think Sheptuum have more thing for you to do before you die."

Nagaro sat there, very still, feeling acutely uncomfortable. *And the Emperor had let him go... given back his ship, his crew, his sword...* "I see," he said swallowing. "Is that *everything*, now, that you told him, Pavo?"

"Oh yes, Nagaro. I swear it by Sheptuum, and by my honor."

Nagaro looked at the floor, frowning. However little he liked Pavo's view of things, it might have had some bearing on the Emperor's actions. But he had been sent to learn whether Pavo had somehow betrayed the mission. He cast about. "Is it possible you could have given them some clue by accident, Pavo? So that they might have guessed—about the mission?"

"Oh no, Nagaro. I do not think so. They ask me about mission very first thing, so I know what they are thinking. So I be very careful."

"You... ah... didn't happen to mention that it wasn't an *honorable* mission? Or that Sheptuum wouldn't *like* the mission?"

"No! I do not say anything about mission, Nagaro, because I have swear oath in name of Sheptuum!"

Now it was Nagaro who hesitated, shifting position on the hard boards of the bed. "And it didn't occur to you," he said carefully, "to think that maybe Sheptuum might have *wanted* you to betray the mission? Because it was a *bad* mission?"

But Pavo shook his great head emphatically. "No! I have already swear on Sheptuum name, Nagaro! Sheptuum will *never* want me to break my oath! Honor does not come from dishonor. Truth does not come from lie. And Sheptuum can do anything he want to, about bad mission. Sheptuum does not need me to do it!"

Nagaro shut his eyes, offering up a silent apology to this deity in whom he did not believe. "And if you *had* done such a thing, Pavo," he said quietly. "For such a reason—or for any other reason—you wouldn't keep it from me, would you? You wouldn't go to your death letting me think you were innocent when you were not—"

"*No! Never!* On my honor! Never, on name of Sheptuum! Nagaro, how can you think this?"

Nagaro opened his eyes again, but he couldn't look at his friend. "It was the king who thought of it Pavo, and he doesn't know you. But once he'd said it, I had to ask. I wasn't *sure*, and I'm sorry. I don't understand Sheptuum as well as you do... what Sheptuum might tell a man to do..." He felt he was making excuses.

"Of course you do not know." Pavo sounded relieved. "And you do not want to have to say to king that you did not ask me."

"That's right. But I'm still sorry, Pavo."

They sat, then, and the seconds ticked by as the silence lengthened. Nagaro wanted to say so many things. He didn't know where to begin. Finally Pavo spoke.

"I do not want to die this way."

Nagaro's anger rose. "You shouldn't have to, Pavo. It isn't right! Peldred didn't have any witnesses either, and they believed *him!*"

"Why they do not believe *me*, Nagaro?" Pavo asked brokenly. "Is it because I swear by Sheptuum instead of other god? What is use of asking me to *swear* if they do not *believe* me?"

Nagaro heaved a sigh. "It's partly that Sheptuum isn't their god," he said bitterly. "But the rest of it is because Vell and Peldred are born of noble Edroviran houses, while you're a common Hashtep, born in the Mahuk Baar. They don't know you, and they don't know your people. It's easier to believe someone has no honor, or is just a bad person, if you don't know him..."

He stopped dead as his own words came back to him across the days. "Oh Pavo," he groaned. "I promised you I wouldn't let them harm you because you were Hashtep! And now I don't see how I can keep my word!"

"Nagaro... do not worry! I know you have tried..."

"And I'll keep *on* trying, Pavo, I swear I will! It's just that... they don't listen to me. The judges hardly let me speak at the Tribunal. I don't want you to keep hoping. It's better that you prepare your mind to die than to think I'm going to save you."

"This I am trying to do... to make my mind ready, Nagaro. But... sometime... I think Sheptuum is angry with me..."

"Angry? *Why?*" Nagaro turned to his friend in dismay.

Pavo had his head down, staring at the floor. "Maybe I have wanted too much to be in your story, Nagaro. I am not important—just very small man. Maybe Sheptuum is angry because I make myself too proud... just because you have call me friend—"

"Pavo, you *are* my friend! And you are just as important as I am!

Maybe it's a mistake to think *either* of us is important, but Sheptuum surely isn't angry with you for anything you've done!"

Pavo's head came up. "But you do not believe in Sheptuum."

"That doesn't matter! *You* do. If you've done everything the way you know Sheptuum says is right, you can't possibly be wrong just because of who you *are!* You mustn't start doubting yourself now, Pavo!"

Nagaro caught the glint of Pavo's eyes in the half light as his friend seemed to study him.

After a long moment the young Hashtep said simply, "Thank you, Nagaro," and looked away. After another moment he said. "Maybe this is my part of story. That you believe me when no one else do, even though I die. And one day, when everyone know that I did not do this bad thing, they will know that you were right. Then they will believe you when you tell them other important thing."

Nagaro sat silent. He couldn't think of anything to say.

Finally Pavo said, "Will you tell Tenepti I am sorry I could only be her husband for so little time? That I am glad for time we had?"

Nagaro's throat tightened. "Of course I'll tell her."

"And when my son have enough year to understand, you will tell him about me? About what have happened?"

"Yes, Pavo. You know I will. No one on Pakoa will ever believe you were a traitor."

*

"Ye should have just taken your sword and told that warden t' give ye the key, Nagaro! Ye and Pavo could ha' fought your way out o' there!"

Nagaro frowned. "There were four other men within call, Taru—all of them armed," he said wearily. "And I wouldn't really have wanted to harm any of them. Besides, how far could Pavo and I have gotten in a longboat?"

The two friends were sharing their frustrations over a pot of sothiril in the sanctuary of the kitchen-dining room in Nagaro's quarters.

Taru glowered into his cup, knowing Nagaro was right. "What d' ye mean to do now?" he demanded.

Nagaro sighed. He ticked off options on his fingers. "I can try to talk to Elgurn again. I can try to talk to Madred. I can keep on trying to find a way to get Peldred to talk to me..."

"Do ye have any hope that any o' that'll *work?*"

"Not much." Nagaro toyed gloomily with the handle of his cup. "But I have to try anyway."

The silence lengthened. Taru finished his sothiril and set his cup down with an angry clunk. "Some o' the men have had enough of the Fleet," he said darkly. "Some o' the ones from the islands—Turo, mostly. They're talking about quitting and going home."

Nagaro shot him a questioning look. "Kunoa's not the only one, then? He's told me that ever since Osfaraad, he's been thinking that his poor mother has borne enough sorrow already."

Taru nodded. "There are maybe a half a dozen. This thing that's happened t' Pavo is the fish that sank the boat for 'em."

Nagaro gulped the last of his own sothiril and stood up, frowning. "It shouldn't have come to this." He picked up the pot in one hand and his cup in the other, and started for the wash basin. "Come on, Taru, it's time we were at practice."

*

Elgurn looked up from the papers littering his desk with the air of one who has already confronted more than enough crises for one day.

"State your business, Captain," he snapped. "And be quick about it."

Nagaro decided to forgo the luxury of letting himself take offence at the king's tone. The guard who had ushered him into Elgurn's study had hinted broadly that his master was badly out of temper. "I've been to see Pavo Maat, My Lord. I've questioned him very thoroughly, and he maintains his innocence. He says Sheptuum would never want him to violate any oath sworn in his name."

The pale blue eyes regarded him balefully for the space of three seconds before returning to the paper the king held in his hands. "That," Elgurn observed flatly, "is unfortunate."

"My Lord, I believe he's telling the truth."

The king didn't look up from his paper, though it was apparent that his eyes had become fixed and ceased to scan the text. "*That* is even more unfortunate."

Nagaro found himself remembering all the reasons he'd ever had to dislike this man. "It will be far more than merely *unfortunate*," he said coldly, "if an innocent man is executed in the name of Edroviran justice."

Elgurn cast him a look of annoyance. "He's only one man."

"Do you think that he isn't important, then, My Lord? There *were* witnesses to what happened at Osfaraad. The Emperor of the Mahuk Baar was there. He knows the truth. And he's surely watching to see whether Edrovir will hang an innocent man and let a guilty one go free."

This time Elgurn's face froze, and something passed briefly behind the pale blue eyes that told Nagaro that this was a new thought, and one that gave him pause. "Have you spoken with Peldred Gilforn?" the king asked sharply. "Does he also maintain his innocence?"

"I haven't succeeded in that, My Lord. He plainly doesn't wish to speak to me."

"You've been harsh with him in the past, perhaps?"

"Never, My Lord."

"Then it seems you will have to try harder—if you're so convinced."

"My Lord, I try every day, but he avoids me! And time is running out. The execution is now only three days away!"

The king gestured dismissively. "I don't know what you expect me to do about it—"

"Delay the execution! Give me more time!" In his exasperation, Nagaro cut the king off, then bit his lip as he saw the blood start to rise in the other man's face.

Elgurn, however, seemed almost immediately to master himself. "I am truly sorry, Captain," he said with exaggerated patience. "But even to do *that*, I would need to offer Lord Madred some *reason*—something more substantial than your conviction. You must understand that, to many people, your conviction appears suspect. The plain truth is that you have nothing of substance to contribute to the case."

"But My Lord, you're the *King!* Surely the King of Edrovir can delay an execution without asking the judge's permission!"

Elgurn's face grew hard. "How long do you think I would keep my crown if I did that? With two Pact Signers among the judges?"

Nagaro had been barely holding himself in check, and now his anger blazed. He stepped into that white-hot flame and spoke scathingly from the center of it.

"Do you love power so much?"

And Elgurn was on his feet, his face livid, the chair teetering behind him. "*How dare you!*" His voice was pitched surprisingly low, but it shook with anger. Sapphire daggers leaped from his eyes. "You have no idea how weary I am of this!" He slapped at the crown that encircled his brow. "No *idea* what it's cost me over the years! What it may cost me yet! I could lose it tomorrow, and not regret it—save for what it would do to Edrovir. You have seen, among the Tribunal's judges, a sampling of the men who aspire to power in this land. You've seen the motley assortment who court my daughter. If I go down, who will rise up in my place? And how will war be prevented?"

Nagaro had stood still before this onslaught, shaken in spite of himself by the passion of it. More than that, these were sentiments he could appreciate. He swallowed. "My Lord," he said. "I do humbly beg your pardon. I spoke out of frustration—without considering my words."

A moment more the king stood, drawn to his full height, eyes blazing. Then the ice-blue fires dimmed. Stiffly and with dignity Elgurn resumed his seat. He ran a hand through his graying hair, and suddenly he looked old—older than his years and very weary. "And you do not wish your friend to die," he said almost gently. "This I understand. You have still two full days, and a part of this one. Do what you can, Captain. And if you can coax or cajole a confession from young Peldred in that time, I promise you that Pavo Maat shall have a stay of execution."

With that, and a brief gesture of dismissal, the king returned his attention to the papers on his desk.

*

"He's there! With those two stuck-up Leithians."

"Are there enough seats for us near them?" Nagaro shifted uneasily from one foot to the other. This was Taru's plan, and he wasn't entirely comfortable with it—although with only one full day left now before Pavo's execution he was desperate enough to try almost anything. They were standing at one of the doorways leading into the Fleet dining hall. Taru had just drawn back out of view of the gathering diners. Nagaro was standing just behind him with Tredhold and Landros.

"Yes, there's enough seats. If ye don't wait all night about it." Taru looked past Nagaro. "Ye know what t' do Landros? Tred?"

"Aye!" Landros rumbled. "Just give me the heading, matey."

Tredhold merely nodded, his expression sober.

Taru grinned wickedly. "Last table on this side o' the hall, on the right, near the end."

The two older men moved past into the hall. The room was already growing dimmer with the approach of night. Lamps were lit along the walls, playing on the stones of the supporting buttresses and beginning to cast shadows among the hewn timbers that supported the roof. There was a growing murmur of voices as Fleet warriors straggled in, collected plates of food from the counter at the end of the room adjacent to the kitchen, and found seats on stools at the room's many long tables.

Nagaro hung back beside Taru in the shadows of the small entry hall, waiting. Taru put his head around the corner. "They're getting their plates," he reported. "And now they're coming back to th' table. There! They've sat down. Come on!"

Nagaro hastily stepped out abreast of his friend. "We should look like we're talking about something," he said in as easy a tone as he could manage. "Something harmless." He was being careful to avoid looking around the room, looking only at Taru or at the counter where the food was dispensed. The hope was that Peldred wouldn't flee if Nagaro didn't seem to be pursuing him.

"Ye lost the game last night because ye weren't paying attention to my archer."

"What?" Nagaro was caught off guard.

"My *archer*. The one that was moving up on your king's left flank." Taru gave him a broad wink.

"Oh. Right." Nagaro had scarcely paid any attention to the game of King's Men the night before. All he'd been able to think about was Pavo. He struggled to recall any detail and failed. "You, ah, distracted me with your horsemen."

"My horsemen weren't doing *anything*, Nagaro. It was my archer and my minister..."

Somehow they got their plates and cups and re-crossed the hall to approach the chosen table. Nagaro risked a glance just long enough to see that Peldred and the two Leithians were seated on the nearer side, while Tred and Landros had taken seats on the farther side, a few stools down. Landros hailed them, beckoning. Taru gave the grizzled Kelorin a wave of acknowledgment and steered for the two stools opposite the two veteran Fleet warriors, talking about King's Men all the while without missing a step.

"Hoy there, Nagaro! I hear ye've been to see Pavo. How's the poor lad holding up?"

Nagaro breathed a sigh of relief as he sank onto his stool and set down his plate and cup. He had exhausted everything he could think of about the board game. Fortunately Landros was wasting no time in turning the conversation to the condemned man. Nagaro thought he caught movement out of the corner of his eye from the place to his left, beyond Taru, where the three Leithians sat. He willed himself not to look.

"As well as can be expected. You know he has courage. But it's hard to face dying for a crime he didn't commit." This time Nagaro was sure he caught a movement to his left.

"So he maintained his innocence, then?" The question came from Tredhold.

"Yes, and I had to ask him a lot of questions, too, since the king sent me to see if he would confess. It hurt him to hear such things from me—and it hurt me to ask them. He swears he's told nothing but the truth, and told all of it." Nagaro hoped this didn't sound rehearsed.

"Well, I'd expect nothing less of him." Tred was playing his part.

Landros thumped the table. "If ever a man was born honest, it's Pavo! Did he have anything else to say?"

"He gave me words for his wife... Asked me to explain things to his little son—when he's grown—"

Nagaro was forcing himself to keep his eyes firmly on Tred and on Landros, but at this juncture he distinctly heard a stifled exclamation from somewhere to his left, and muttered voices.

"Ah, yes. Pavo's wife, Tenepti. Lovely lass," Landros was saying. "I remember their wedding like it was yesterday—"

"Well it wasn't much more 'n a year ago," Taru chimed in. "And his son was born just this spring. It's a shame to think of that poor babe growing up without a father. But o' course we'll tell him all about Pavo, won't we? And it won't just be us. Everyone on Pakoa knows Pavo. He's a kind o' hero there—"

There was a stifled cry followed by the clatter of a stool on the flagstone floor.

Startled in spite of himself, Nagaro turned to his left just in time to see the two Leithians who'd been sitting with Peldred rising from their seats. One of the men gave Nagaro a black look before they both hurried after Peldred's rapidly disappearing figure. The food on Peldred's plate was conspicuously only half eaten, and some of the other nearby diners were looking at the empty seats, or glancing after their three recent occupants, and whispering to one another.

"Ha! It worked!" Taru slapped the table, grinning. "That'll put hot coals under his conscience!"

Nagaro wasn't smiling. "I've told you I don't think his conscience is the problem," he said quietly. He felt as if he'd just twisted a knife in an open wound, and he didn't like the feeling.

"Well, maybe it isn't," Taru conceded. "But, *hamanei!* Anyone can see he's guilty as sin. Those two friends o' his can't help but have noticed. I'll wager they're asking him some hard questions right now."

Tredhold had been sitting somberly, but now he spoke. "I think they already knew, Taru."

"Already knew? What d' ye mean?"

The healer grimaced. "I was watching them—as much as I dared. Peldred was squirming, and kept starting to say things, and the other two were telling him to sit still and keep quiet."

Landros coughed. "Now that ye've mentioned it, Tred, those two Leithians are a sight older than Peldred. They could be other men from his Hold, keeping an eye on him."

Nagaro frowned. "Well," he said, "We've made sure Peldred knows some things about Pavo that should make it harder for him to let Pavo die. All we can do is hope that some good comes of it."

"Right." Taru looked grim. "We should keep to the plan. Landros, Nagaro, and I will sit here and finish our dinners, and then go to our quarters, while Tred keeps an eye on our rabbit."

Tredhold nodded as he hastily cleaned his plate and stood up. "I'll do my best to be available in case Peldred shows signs of wanting to talk to someone who isn't from Gilforn Hold."

*

Nagaro spent a restless night, rising and dressing before dawn. Shortly thereafter, he heard Taru's knock at the back door. He'd only just let Taru in and closed the door, when Tredhold's knock followed.

"What did ye get from him, Tred?" Taru asked eagerly as soon as the healer joined them in Nagaro's dining room-study.

Tredhold dropped heavily onto one of the chairs. *"Nothing!"* He sounded tired and disgusted. "I kept watch on his quarters 'til well after midnight, and there was one o' those men sitting at the window, *waiting*, the whole time. I thought I'd try to catch Peldred in the morning instead, so I went to my quarters. I tried to sleep for a few hours, but I was too worried. So I went back to Peldred's about an hour before dawn, and the other man was *still there*. I swear he must have been there all night! I feel like my head's full o' fog for want of sleep, and I never even *saw* Peldred!"

"Is Landros watching now?"

Tredhold gave Taru a harassed look, then stifled a yawn. "Yes," he mumbled. "The gods know what'll happen if *he* tries to talk to Peldred— but I'm nearly asleep on my feet."

Nagaro saw Taru's expression and gestured his friend to silence before he could make another complaint. "It's all right, Tred. You go to bed, and try not to worry. Taru and I will check on Landros. And I'll make some excuse for you at sword practice. There won't be many men there, anyway, since Geldoran sailed with his fleet this morning." He stood up. "Come on, Taru. Let's not waste any more time."

Taru and Tredhold both rose. Tredhold covered another yawn. "Go 'round the end o' the last building before his. Don't come at the door straight on."

"We know what to do, Tred," Taru told him confidently.

They parted from Tredhold at the end of the long building that housed the captain's quarters. Being a very junior officer, Peldred was housed in a building at the other end of the next row of barracks. The two friends approached it cautiously, turning between that building and the next as Tred had suggested, and edging their way around the end of it. Fortunately it was still very early, and there weren't many men about to observe their behavior and think it odd.

Taru was taking the lead. "I don't see Landros anywhere," he said tensely, drawing back from the corner of the building. "Did he give up and leave?"

"More likely Peldred left, and Landros followed." Nagaro tried to stand easily, as if he and Taru had merely paused in conversation.

Taru relaxed visibly. "Aye, o' course ye're right," he said brightly. "I'll just go have a look, shall I?" He set off around the end of the building without waiting for any response.

"Taru, wait!" Nagaro started to go after him, but thought better of it, realizing that Taru must have some idea of what he was doing. The young Turo was moving toward the door of Peldred's quarters with an easy swinging stride, whistling as he went. Nagaro leaned against the end of the building, trying to look as if it were the most natural thing in the world.

Taru mounted the steps to Peldred's little front stoop and knocked.

He waited nonchalantly, knocked again, then turned and came back to where Nagaro was waiting. "No answer," he announced, in a low voice, "and no window-watcher. I'm sure they've gone, but there's no way o' knowing where."

Nagaro considered. "They might have just gone to breakfast," he pointed out. "They would, under normal circumstances."

"The circumstances aren't exactly normal," Taru observed. "But it's a good place t' start."

As they set off for the dining hall, curiosity prompted Nagaro to ask, "What would you have said to anyone who answered the door?"

Taru grinned wickedly. "That I hoped Peldred was feeling better, on account o' him seeming ill at dinner last night."

Nagaro shook his head at his friend, and said, "You really have no compunction whatsoever, do you?"

"Ah... what's compunction?"

Nagaro's explanation was preempted by a shout from the general direction of Kuran's quarters that made them both turn.

"Hoy! Taru! Nagaro!"

Landros was striding towards them. The expression on his face spoke of anger, frustration—and despair. Nagaro hurried to intercept the veteran sea warrior's course, with Taru right behind him. Landros waited only until he was close enough to be heard without shouting.

"He's shipped out!"

"*What?*" Nagaro and Taru spoke in perfect unison.

"Peldred's gone and shipped out! He sailed this morning—on one o' Geldoran's ships!"

"But—*how?*" Taru was beyond incredulous. "How'd he get out of his quarters without Tred seeing him?

Landros had come to a stop in front of them, scowling darkly. "I'll wager the little rotter was never in there! He must have been aboard ship—with the other men—since last night. Waiting for the tide."

"But... the man at th' window—"

Landros laughed harshly. "I'll wager *he* was there to turn aside any questions—in case anyone came asking after Peldred."

Nagaro had stood still while the other two men talked. His heart felt like lead. "But when did he get the order?" he wondered aloud. "Peldred was *my* third mate. I've heard nothing about a change of posting—" He stopped, his brow darkening. *He had thought that Kuran was convinced of Pavo's innocence... Peldred's guilt...*

Landros shook his grizzled head. "Peldred just approached one o' Geldoran's captains about it, and the captain cleared it with Geldoran."

Taru's jaw dropped. "Can Geldoran *do* something like that? Without telling Nagaro?"

Landros shrugged his shoulders. "Aye. He can. Ye don't *need* a third mate to sail a ship, after all. A third mate's just a spare officer—barely more 'n ballast. He can finish his training anywhere. Geldoran probably figured it was a chance for Peldred to put this nasty business of Osfaraad behind him. Probably thought he was doing the lad a favor by not making him face Nagaro—"

"*Bloody bodjering Hel!*"

Nagaro's simmering anger had finally boiled over. The other two men turned, stunned by the uncharacteristic outburst.

"*How could Kuran allow this?*" Nagaro was being carried by pure fury. "I thought he believed me about Peldred! Why didn't he *tell* me?"

Landros looked uncomfortable. "Ah... Kuran only saw the papers this morning, Nagaro—*after* the ships sailed. And he didn't seem very pleased about it, either."

Nagaro lowered his head. That spared Kuran from his wrath, but it didn't make things any better! He had spoken freely to Kuran about his suspicions, but he'd never thought to mention anything to Geldoran. *And now this—*

"*By the Eyes of Vothra's Mind!*" Nagaro spun on his heel, striking off across the parade ground in the direction of the main gate.

"Nagaro! *Wait!* Where are ye going?" The other two men hurried after him, Taru with his shorter strides having to run to catch up. "Are ye going back t' the king?" he panted.

Nagaro didn't slacken his ground-eating pace. "No! Elgurn won't do anything against the Tribunal's verdict without a confession. I'm going to see Madred Furthing!"

Landros tried to grab his arm. "What about sword practice?"

Nagaro dodged out of the older man's grasp. "*Bodjer sword practice!* You can tell Master Fendar I'm trying to save an innocent man's life! And Tred was trying to help!"

*

"You shouldn't be hanging around at the back entrance, Nagaro. You're an officer of the Royal Fleet!" Simion spoke low and urgently, being careful to stay in the shadow of the covered walkway surrounding the courtyard of the building on Broad Street. He reached out to catch at Nagaro's arm, to keep him also in the shadows.

"I tried the front door!" Nagaro spoke through his teeth. "I was denied admittance! They told me Madred isn't seeing anyone today."

"Well, it's true! He's riding out within the hour for Furthing Hold. It's all these rumors about the return of Darion's heir. There have been skirmishes around the border between Irvenen Wared and Furthing Hold. Madred's decided he needs to be there and—"

Simion stopped abruptly because Nagaro had emitted a groan.

"Simion, this is *terrible!* He will be gone for *days*—and Pavo's to be hanged tomorrow morning! I have to see Madred *right now!*"

"I'm sorry, Nagaro!" Simion's face registered sincere regret. "It *is* terrible. And the Leithian faction doesn't care, of course. That's why we need the heir of Loros to—"

"—to do what?" Nagaro demanded. "Start a *war?* With the people of Edrovir fighting each other? Can't you think of any way I can get in to see Lord Madred?"

Simion looked hurt and flustered. "I haven't any influence, Nagaro! Madred barely tolerates my presence, and he doesn't like being reminded of it. Any association with *me* will do you more harm than—"

Simion was interrupted by the sudden sound of horses hooves on the cobblestones of the courtyard and of men's raised voices.

Nagaro turned, startled. There must have been a stable behind the side of the courtyard to his right. A number of horses and riders were issuing from one of its archways, accompanied by a handful of grooms. A moment later, there was another commotion surrounding an archway in the middle of the walkway directly opposite, and Lord Madred emerged into the sunlight that angled down from several floors above.

"*By the Eyes...*" Nagaro murmured under his breath. He clearly had no time to lose. A groom was moving purposefully in Madred's direction, leading an impressive and rather skittish white charger with an empty saddle. Lord Madred was exchanging words with an obsequious-looking Leithian with pomaded hair and an oiled mustache. It was apparent that Madred might finish the conversation at any moment and mount the horse that the groom held ready for him.

Nagaro strode out into the courtyard on a course to intercept the groom and charger. Simion gave an inarticulate cry of dismay and took one step after him before thinking better of it and withdrawing into his hiding place.

"My Lord, if you would just give me your written approval—" the oily, mustached man was saying.

"Well, I shan't." Madred spoke shortly. "I don't think I do approve, Minister Torlung. The whole business smacks of lawlessness and deceit, and I see no honor in it."

"But Lord Grimbold is expecting—"

"Grimbold Sobring should learn not to expect things from me before I have fully considered them. He may *expect* all he likes in this case, but if he means to *proceed* with what he proposes, it will be without the involvement of the House of Furthing. That is my answer, and you may convey it to him."

The mustached man—Minister Torlung—didn't look at all pleased, although he bowed and said, "As you wish, My Lord," before backing away and turning to reenter the building.

The groom was startled when Nagaro suddenly appeared at the white horse's head and began to stroke the creature's neck and speak soothing words. When the horse calmed visibly, however, the man's concern eased and he offered no objection as Nagaro remained standing, with a hand on the horse's bridle, where any intended rider would have to pass him in order to mount.

Lord Madred's reaction was predictably rather different from the groom's. "Captain Nagaro!" he exclaimed when he became aware of the intruder. "Who has let you enter my house unannounced?"

"I am not *in* your house, My Lord, but in your yard," Nagaro replied gravely. "Which can be freely entered by the open gateway over there. I would have come by the front door, but I was turned away. I need to speak with you concerning a matter of justice and a man's life."

Lord Madred, who had planted himself directly in front of Nagaro, listened coldly to this speech. "You make rather too free, Zirda," he said stiffly. "And I imagine the man in question is the convicted traitor, Pavo Maat."

Nagaro decided this was no time to take offense, or to beat about the bush. He made a small bow and said, "My Lord, I have reasons to believe that it was not Pavo Maat, but Peldred Gilforn, who betrayed our plan to the Emperor. I urge you to delay the execution until the matter can be fully investigated."

Madred's iciness showed no sign of thawing. "That is a very serious accusation, Captain," he said. "And I have an urgent need to be elsewhere. Still, I suppose it will do no harm to hear these *reasons* of which you speak—provided you're quick about it."

"Thank you, My Lord." Nagaro offered another bow and sketched a picture of his interview with Pavo, and of Peldred's suspicious behavior.

"This is *all?*" Madred was unimpressed.

"My Lord, the king is concerned enough about it to have encouraged me to seek a confession from Peldred, and to say that he would stay the execution if I could obtain one."

Madred snorted. "No less would I. But I assume you haven't gotten a confession, since you didn't begin with it."

"My Lord, I haven't managed to get a single *interview* with Peldred in all the days since the Tribunal. He has avoided me, and now it seems there may have been a conspiracy on the part of men from Gilforn Hold to prevent me—or anyone else—from speaking with him. Such was their success that Peldred shipped out with Commander Geldoran this very morning—making it now impossible for anyone to speak to him before tomorrow's execution!"

"I see," Lord Madred observed sourly. "Hence you now come to me with your vague suspicions and your request for a stay—but *without* a confession. Your loyalty to your friend is admirable, Captain, but you should not allow it to blind you to the truth. Now stand aside."

This was too much for Nagaro. "Perhaps *you* should not let loyalty to your race and to your class blind you to the possibility of injustice, My Lord," he said coldly, not budging from where he stood.

Lord Madred drew himself up, scowling. "You presume too much, Zirda! And I hardly think you would go to such lengths if the positions of Peldred and Pavo Maat were reversed."

This time Nagaro drew *himself* up, and his eyes flashed. "If you knew me at all, My Lord, you would not say that." He bit his tongue then, as he saw the blood rising in the Leithian's handsome face. He drew a quick breath and continued more evenly. "I have no wish to see Peldred hang in Pavo's place, My Lord. If I'm right, he's more to be pitied than condemned. I've no wish to see anyone hang for this."

Madred returned him a stare like a steel blade. "Then you are alone in all of Lankura, Captain—and I have wasted enough time on this! Take your hand from my horse and stand aside, or I will have you forcibly removed from these premises!"

"My Lord... *Please!* I beg you to reconsider!"

"Enough! Stand aside!"

Lord Madred's blue eyes blazed, and the man raised an imperious hand to signal to his waiting men-at-arms. Nagaro heard the ominous jingle of harness and the sharp ring of horses's hooves on the stones behind him as the riders began to move forward. Numbly he dropped his hand from the white horse's bridle.

He took two steps to one side as Madred strode past him.

He stood, then, staring straight before him as if blind to what was passing, as the Leithian lord mounted his white horse and rode out of the courtyard at the head of the company of horsemen.

As the clatter of hooves died away, Nagaro shook himself and began to move. He turned, walking woodenly across the cobblestones, making for the archway into the street. Simion called after him, but the words did not penetrate. He strode on, moving as fast as he could, oblivious to all around him, out through the dark tunnel of the arch.

He had lost... lost Pavo... And it was worse than terrible. It was unthinkable...

He took no heed of where he was or of the other folk passing in the street. Most were, thankfully, intent on their own business. Those who happened to glance into his face got quickly out of his way. He might have gone on indefinitely like this, but the furious pace he had set for himself could not be sustained in his weakened condition. In the end, the need to catch his breath caused him to slow his steps and finally to pause on a street corner.

It was a late summer's morning, fair and warm. Sunlight poured down between the buildings like golden water washing over the paving stones. Overhead the sky was a brilliant blue, marred only by a few long streamers of cloud carried on an air out of the west. Nagaro took notice of these things as if from a great distance.

How could the day be fair? How dared the sun to shine?

He felt very nearly as disconnected from the world as when he had trodden the deck of the Emperor's ship, going—as he'd believed—to his own death. *How could he possibly face Tenepti with this news? It was hard enough when a man had been slain... fallen in battle. Giving the news to those who would mourn was always hard. But this... this, that need not have happened... that shouldn't have happened. That should have been prevented...*

At length, he started forward again, because moving was better than standing still. But he was walking almost blindly. How could he rise in the morning, knowing what it would bring? And every other morning thereafter? How could he go on about his business... about his life... knowing what had happened to Pavo? How could he continue to serve Edrovir when Pavo's life had been wrongfully taken in the name of the Edroviran justice?

Somehow he covered the remainder of the distance to the Fleet compound, now going at a more deliberate pace. His mind kept running through things, dwelling on his last meeting with Pavo on the prison barge. Somewhere between entering Market Street and reaching the Fleet Compound's front gate, a resolve formed in his mind.

Upon entering the compound he made for his quarters rather than for the dining hall, although it was by that time nearly noon and he had missed breakfast. Turning down the path that led to his front door, he nearly collided with Taru, coming apparently from the practice field.

"Nagaro! There ye are!" Taru's voice was eager with a hope that also shown in his eyes. The light quickly faded when he saw the expression on his friend's face. "Nagaro? What's happened?"

"I had no luck with Madred. He won't do anything, and he's left for Furthing Hold."

"But... what will ye do then? Go to the king again?" Taru sounded desperate.

Nagaro shook his head as he dug in his pocket for the key and opened his front door. "It's no use, Taru. My appeals have all failed. More words will not serve us."

"Ye're *giving up?*"

Nagaro had stepped across the doorsill, but he turned back, his jaw rigid, his eyes blazing under his slender black brows. "No," he said quietly. "But it's time to try a different way."

The light re-dawned in Taru's eyes. "Ye've got a plan," he said. "What is it?"

Nagaro glanced past Taru, and up and down the path between the buildings. "I'm still working on the details, but I have a task for you."

"Anything!"

"Good. I want you to find each of the men who have decided to quit the Fleet. Ask them if they're willing to take some risk for Pavo's sake. If they are, bid them come here after dinner tonight. Tell them to come to the back door, separately, and none of you must let anyone else know what you're about."

"What about Tredhold? And Landros?"

Nagaro shook his head. "I don't want them involved. They shouldn't risk their careers over this."

Taru frowned a little, but nodded. "It's as good as done, Capt'n!" He saluted and was gone.

Nagaro stood still, looking after his friend for several long seconds, frowning. As he moved at last to close the door he was brought up short by a hail.

"Captain Nagaro!"

He turned to see one of the blue-and-white clad messenger boys from the palace approaching, hurried and breathless.

"I didn't find ye in when I came by before, Zirda, but here ye are!" The boy dug into his pouch and held out an envelope.

Dumbly, Nagaro took it. The writing, as he'd expected, was Nevien's. It was addressed simply, *Captain Nagaro*. He opened it quickly and read one of the familiar invitations to join the princess's party on an outing to River House in a few days' time. At the bottom she had added in a less formal hand: *No matter what happens, we can talk.* It was signed *Nevien Harlind.*

He stood holding the bit of parchment, feeling a surge of gratitude towards the woman who had believed him about Pavo's innocence, who had done her best to help, and who now so clearly wished to do whatever she could to ease his pain. He swallowed. "Wait here a moment," he told the messenger, "while I write an answer."

He found his pen, as well as ink and paper in his desk. Dipping the pen, he paused, then wrote in fine, quick strokes: *Thank you for your kindness, My Lady. I regret I will be unable to attend. There is something I must do.* He signed it *Nagaro Nareyo,* blew on the note, folded it, and returned it to the errand boy. The lad took it with a bow and a grin and dashed away.

Nagaro remained standing for some time on the doorstep after the liveried figure had disappeared around the corner of the next building.

Withdrawing into his quarters at last, he closed the door and realized that the invitation was still in his hand. He reread the princess's words with a sigh, then refolded it and thrust it into his tirka.

27: The Dawn Comes

Tredhold sat in his quarters, his head down, his hands clasped before him. He had heard the measured beat of the drum moving through the compound, marking the passage of the troop of guards who had gone to escort the condemned man from the prison barge to the gallows that had been erected at one edge of the parade ground. He felt every bit as bad as on those occasions when he'd lost a patient to death in spite of all his skill. In fact, this was worse. This death wasn't the result of wounds that were too severe, or a disease that was just too strong. This death was the result of cowardice... stupidity... prejudice...

Ever since yesterday afternoon when he had learned that Nagaro had been unsuccessful in his last appeal, Tred had felt a weight growing on his heart. Unable to sleep, he'd risen before dawn and dressed. He'd eaten nothing, having no appetite, but sat at the empty table... waiting. He hadn't troubled to open the window curtains to look out, though he knew he would soon hear the drum returning. There would be a general muster, then, to witness the hanging, but he didn't intend to go. He would plead illness...

If only there had been something he could have done that would have made a difference...

The growing disturbance in the compound wasn't what he was listening for, and he didn't immediately mark it. It was only when the tramp of feet and mutter of voices approached his quarters that he lifted his head. Booted feet came right up onto his small porch, and knuckles rapped on his door. *Had he somehow missed the muster...?*

Tredhold got numbly to his feet and went to answer the knock. He opened the door half a foot, meaning to tell whoever was there that he was ill and wished to be left alone— but he found himself confronted by half a dozen armed Fleet warriors.

"What's this—?" he began.

The man who was in charge—a big, broad-shouldered Leithian— gave him a stern look and cleared his throat.

"Tredhold Ferth, ye're to come with us. Lord Kuran wants ye in his office immediately."

"But... *why?*" Tredhold looked questioningly from the leader to the other men beyond him.

A number of the others shuffled their feet uncomfortably, but the leader gave him another stern look. "If ye don't know already, ye'll soon find out. Now come along. Ye don't want t' keep Lord Kuran waiting."

Tredhold shrugged, and went.

The morning had not dawned fair. A wind out of the west blew in gusts, whipping up dust on the parade ground. Long streamers of cloud like the forerunners of a storm were moving across the sky. Tredhold glanced once in the direction of the gallows as he was conducted at a rapid pace, and was surprised to see no crowd around it, although there were several organized groups of men moving among the barracks. Other men stood about in small knots, watching and talking among themselves.

Kuran was in his office, standing behind a desk strewn with the usual papers. He was looking very grave. Landros was there as well, also standing, facing the Lord of the Fleet. The grizzled old sea warrior wore an expression that was both puzzled and oddly expectant.

Tredhold came to a halt beside his old comrade. He looked from one man to the other. "What's this about, My Lord?" he ventured, when no one spoke.

Kuran cleared his throat. "Tredhold Ferth," he said soberly, "You submitted a letter to the Tribunal, containing a defense of Pavo Maat's character and expressing the opinion that he was innocent."

Tred squared his shoulders and lifted his chin. "Aye, Zirda. I did."

Kuran turned to Landros. "And you, Landros Torenin, have also been heard to express that opinion."

Landros returned his commander a feral smile. "I expect I have, My Lord," he drawled. "And I'll repeat it. Pavo's as innocent as a newborn babe, and the guilty man's gone and shipped out with Geldoran—the milk-livered little coward—"

Kuran raised a warning hand. "An affirmative would have sufficed," he said sharply.

Landros stuck out his chin defiantly. "Not hardly!" he retorted. "And anything I may have *said* is no cause to be marching me over here, quick-step, like an ill-behaved schoolboy—"

"Landros!" Tredhold gave the other man a shocked look before turning back to Kuran. "Why are we both here, My Lord? Has something happened?"

Kuran regarded them for several long seconds, frowning. Finally he crossed his arms. "The prisoner is gone," he said. "The guards were found bound and gagged but otherwise unharmed. They were apparently taken so much by surprise that they couldn't give any satisfactory account of what happened. The *Sword of Freedom* is gone as well. So, it appears, are both her captain and former first mate." Kuran ceased speaking and stood expectantly, his gaze flicking from one to the other of the two men who stood before him.

For several seconds Tredhold could do nothing but stare. Then he felt behind him for a chair and sank down onto it. "The Gods be praised..." he murmured faintly.

Landros had been similarly struck dumb, but now he slapped his thigh. *"By the Eyes!"* he chortled. "A jailbreak! It's brilliant!"

Kuran heaved a sigh and sat down heavily in his own chair. He briefly massaged his temples before leaning back. "Did either one of you have any foreknowledge of this?" he demanded. "Tredhold?"

Tred shook his head. "None, My Lord."

"Landros?"

The old warrior snorted. "If I had, do ye think I'd still be here?"

Kuran returned him a dark look, then sighed again. "No, I suppose not."

Tredhold drew a long breath. "I wish I *had* known about it. It would have spared me the worst night I've ever spent."

"Maybe so," Landros put in. "But ye see why he didn't tell us, don't ye, Tred? Ye've got a wife and children to think of. And I've only got a few years more to put in to earn my pension. That's the captain for ye. Always mindful of others."

Kuran was watching them both. "It can't have been only the two of them," he observed mildly. "They must have recruited a few others—to sail the ship."

"Oh, aye," Landros conceded without hesitation. "That'd be likely. Three men *could* sail a ship in a pinch, mind ye, and Pavo's a master-hand with the sails. But they'd have a rough time in rough weather, and we've got some serious weather blowing our way—or I'm a landsman."

"Where do you suppose they'd go?"

Landros gave a low chuckle. "Now, now, Zirda," he chided. "Ye can guess at that as well as I."

Tredhold had been sitting quietly. "What troubles *me*," he said, "is that it's not like Nagaro to do something like this without offering some explanation. Didn't he leave anything? A note... a letter...?"

Kuran grunted. "I thought the same—and I searched his quarters myself. He seems to have taken a few changes of clothes—and his cash box was empty—but he left nothing in the way of a message."

At this point, the inner door of the office opened abruptly, and the clerk, Estevad, appeared in the doorway. The look on his face strongly suggested that he'd been listening. He coughed politely. "Ah, begging your pardon, Zirda," he said, addressing Kuran. "But there's that packet—"

Kuran sat up. "Packet? What packet?"

"The, ah, one on your desk, Zirda." The clerk pointed to a small flat package tied with a string. "I found it at the door when I unlocked it this morning."

"Well, why didn't you say so!"

Estevad coughed again. "I... ah... *did* mention it, My Lord. You were a trifle preoccupied."

"Well, all right, perhaps I was." Kuran rubbed at his chin distractedly. "Thank you, Estevad. You may return to your duties." He barely waited for the door to close behind the clerk before breaking the string on the packet with a jerk of his hand and stripping off the wrapping. Under it was a folded and sealed piece of paper with *Kuran Kel* written on it in a familiar bold hand. Kuran broke the seal and unfolded what was obviously a letter. A second folded sheet of paper dropped onto the desk top, having been inside the first. Kuran let it lie while he scanned the first, frowning. Presently he cleared his throat and read aloud:

My Lord Kuran,

By the time you read this, we will either be safely away or we will have been taken in the attempt. In either event, there is no need for me to describe our undertaking, since it will already be known to you. It is my intention to take Pavo Maat to a place of safety, under my protection, and to keep him in my custody and under my close observation until such time as the matter of his guilt or innocence can be demonstrated by more substantial evidence than opinions and guesswork.

Understand that I would not do this if there were any other recourse. Nor would I willfully so defy Edroviran law were there anything less than a man's life at stake. But a man's life cannot be restored to him if it is later found to have been taken in error. My Fleet service oath binds me to uphold the honor, laws, and interests of the people and nation of Edrovir. I believe that such honor and interests would be poorly served by the execution of an innocent man, and the enforcement of Edroviran laws within her waters would similarly be poorly served by demonstrating a lack of honor in the eyes of our adversaries.

I know Pavo Maat well enough to be convinced of his innocence by all that he has told me. If he should, however, prove himself false to his oath or his sworn testimony by word or deed, I will not rest until I have returned him to Lankura to face justice. This I swear upon my honor and in Vothra's name. In anticipation of the resolution of this matter, I do not resign my commission, but mean to continue my service to Edrovir as best I am able.

Kuran coughed. "It's signed, *Nagaro Nareyo,* and underneath that signature, has been added in another hand the words, *'I, Taru Nareyo, agree with everything that is written here.'* " He lowered the paper, still frowning, and muttered, "I knew the wording of that oath was too broad."

Tredhold shifted in his chair. "What's the other paper, My Lord?"

Kuran reached for it. He scanned it quickly and laid it down without bothering to read it aloud. "It's a letter of request to leave the Fleet service, written on behalf of six named seamen," he said. "Obviously Nagaro wrote it, but each of the six has set his mark to it. And it has also been approved—quite properly, it appears—by the signatures of Captain Nagaro and Taru Nareyo, first mate. That's two officers—all that's required to make it binding. And of course it's dated yesterday—"

"—so those six wouldn't have been Fleet warriors anymore by the time the *Sword* sailed," Landros finished with obvious relish. "Because Nagaro wouldn't have sailed until the tide turned to ebb this morning, not having enough men to row her properly. Which means the six o' them would have been spared any punishment if ye'd happened to catch them—brilliant, again!"

Kuran gave the old sea warrior a long-suffering glance. "Oh, yes," he growled. "It's very clever. Nagaro can claim that those six are civilians whose services were commandeered for a military purpose under his command, and all responsibility therefore falls on him." He sighed and picked up the first paper again, staring at it without appearing to actually see it. "Well," he murmured after a moment, "This is both better and worse than I expected."

"How do you mean, My Lord?" Tredhold asked.

Kuran sighed. "He hasn't given up on the service of Edrovir. He hopes to return. But he makes his situation more difficult by not resigning his commission, since it makes him both a fugitive *and* a renegade Fleet officer." Kuran shook his head soberly. "I was afraid I would lose him over this. If Pavo had died this morning, I fully expected to have Nagaro in here in the afternoon telling me he meant to quit the service. And if *he* quit, I more than half expected most of those who joined with him to follow. This—" he tapped the second paper "—is much better than I could have hoped for on that score—only six men... seven, counting Taru." He glanced up sharply. "Do I have your word—both of you—that you're staying?"

Landros gave a shrug and a nod. "It's plain he meant me to stay, so I'll stay. But if ye get orders to go out and hunt him down, I'll want no part of it."

Tred nodded decisively. "Nor I, My Lord. But, yes, I'll stay. You have my word."

"And you'll try to persuade the rest of Nagaro's former followers to stay as well?"

The two men exchanged glances, then nodded.

Kuran looked from one to the other as if gauging their sincerity. "All right, then. Good enough. I've no cause to detain either of you, and you have leave to go about your duties. But if you take my advice, you'll keep your heads down. There's some folk that were hoping to see a hanging this morning."

He sighed heavily as the two men closed the door behind them. "And there might *be* one, too, when I give the king this news," he muttered under his breath. "Except it'll be my neck in the noose!"

Once outside, the two old friends struck off across the compound. Presently Landros turned to Tredhold. "Ye're awfully quiet, Tred," he said. "What are ye thinking?"

Tredhold gave his friend a somber glance. "I was thinking about how it was only an hour ago that I was sitting in my quarters, wishing there was something I could have done. And there *was*, of course, but it took Nagaro to think of it—and actually *do* it."

Landros's face clouded. "Aye," he said. "It took a cleverer, bolder man than me. That's why Nagaro will always be the captain."

*

Nevien stood with Merriel on the third floor balcony, looking south. She shivered and pulled her cloak closer about her shoulders. The wind was freshening, gusting out of the west. It had a colder edge than was common for the season, and it smelled of rain. This morning she was glad of the fine silk scarf wrapped about her neck. It's real purpose was to hide the bruises that hadn't yet faded, but it also softened the bite of the wind. In her other hand she clutched the folded note that had been delivered to her the day before.

"I'll have to take Kuran to task when next I see him," she said with a severity that was only half jest. "Imagine giving him some work to do on an Eighth day—and so soon after... well... after what's about to happen."

Merriel gave the princess a sympathetic glance. "I quite agree." A particularly strong gust swept along the length of the balcony. "We should go inside, My Lady."

"Not yet. I want to see if I can catch a glimpse of Nagaro's friend when they lead him out. I have a prayer for the keeping of his spirit that I mean to say, and I think it will take hold more strongly if I have him in my sight when I say it." She let go of her cloak long enough to thrust the note into the bodice of her gown. She didn't want to risk losing it.

Merriel was watching the activity on the distant prison barge, near the middle of the river and a bit upstream, about a hundred yards distant. "There seems to be quite a lot of milling about," she remarked, shading her eyes with her hand as she studied the distant figures. "I should think they'd just bring him out and put him in one of the boats, and that would be that. Do you know what he looks like?"

"He is quite a big man. Dark-haired—and of course he will be in chains. I met him once, Merriel, and I remember he was very polite—a sort of gentle giant. This is all really quite awful—" Nevien broke off, frowning at what she was seeing. "Why have they got so many boats? It's well past time, and where on earth is Pavo? *Now* look! Some of the boats are fanning out and making for the south bank—and there are two warships coming down the river! If I didn't know better, I'd think they'd lost him and were trying to figure out where he'd got to—"

Abruptly she stopped dead as the words of the note seemed to parade before her eyes. *There is something I must do.* Her hand went to her breast where she could feel the folded paper under the fabric of her gown. *"Oh, Nagaro..."* she murmured, too low for Merriel to hear above the whistling of the wind. *"What have you done?"*

"Ah! There you are, Nevien." Rianine had stuck her head out of one of the doors behind their backs. "Your father has sent for you. He wants you downstairs in the Council Chamber."

*

Nevien paused to catch her breath and smooth out her hair before opening the Council Chamber door. Distracted as she was, she had given only the most cursory thought on the way downstairs to what this might be about. Her father had been taking her into his confidence more and more of late, and giving her duties such as taking his place as witness at the Tribunal. Still, he had never brought her into any kind of council meeting before. She could hear the men's muffled voices coming from beyond the door. She took one final steadying breath, opened the door, and slipped into the room.

Her father sat at his place at the table, the members of his Council flanking him on either side. Opposite this group, stood a tall blond man with a mustache, whom she recognized as Vell Sobring. Nevien caught her father's eye as he gestured for her to take a chair that was placed near his right hand, a little back from the edge of the table. She moved quickly around to his side and slid into the seat.

Her father leaned over and whispered, "Watch Vell closely. I want to know what you think of him."

Nevien nodded, and did her best to give her attention to what was being said.

All eyes were presently on Vell, who was standing very stiffly with an expression that said he was not enjoying himself. He seemed scarcely to have noticed her arrival. "I'm... ah... very gratified, My Lords," he was saying, "that you look upon me with such favor, but I could hardly think of challenging my uncle for the lordship of Sobring Hold—"

"Who said anything about challenging?" Lord Pendrik demanded. "We wouldn't expect you to do anything so unfilial."

"Indeed not!" This came from Lord Odus.

Vell looked blank. "Then what..?"

Lord Anduar had been sitting at his ease in his chair, and he now cleared his throat, drawing all eyes. "Your uncle is an intemperate man," he observed smoothly. "And such a man is very likely to bring about his own downfall. When that happens—as it likely will within a year or so—the mantle of lordship will naturally fall upon *you*, Captain. What we are seeking now is some assurance of your loyalty."

Vell looked worried. He fidgeted and pulled at his mustache. "My *loyalty*, My Lord...?" He ventured cautiously.

"To Edrovir, of course."

"To *Edrovir?*" Vell goggled at the Kelorin Pact Signer. "But, My Lord! Of *course* I am loyal to Edrovir! I have sworn it as a Fleet warrior, and I'll swear it again if you ask me."

Anduar gave him a bland smile. "Of course you have— and would," he said coolly. "But can we assume that the oath you have sworn takes precedence over any *other* loyalties? To family? To the elders of your House? To the Leithian Faction...?" He let the words hang in the air.

Vell drew himself up. "I believe I can say so, My Lord."

"You can? Good. See that you do. Clearly, and often." Anduar leaned back in his chair studying Vell, who appeared acutely uncomfortable under the scrutiny. The silence lengthened, and some of the others at the table exchanged glances.

Abruptly Lord Devral leaned forward, and asked, "Have you ever had any dealings with the Brothers of the Blood, Captain Vell?"

Vell choked. "I... I *never*, My Lord! That is," he added hastily, "Not any more than I could *help*. My uncle is, ah—that is, I... well... I'm afraid he's one of them, Zirda. And I have to speak to him from time to time—"

Anduar hadn't moved in his seat, but he now smiled a smile that extended no further than the curve of his lips as his gray eyes bored into Vell "We are well aware of your uncle's affiliation, Captain," he said coolly. "And our investigations have—so far—not connected you with the brotherhood."

Vell had begun by turning pale but now looked distinctly relieved. Before anything more could be said, however, a sharp knock sounded at the chamber door.

All eyes turned to Elgurn. The king, who had thus far sat watchful and silent, now cleared his throat. "Enter!" he said in a commanding voice.

The door immediately opened, and Kuran stepped into the room. He stopped just inside the door and narrowly surveyed the scene. Nevien thought she read tension in both his movement and his stance, though his expression was carefully neutral. "My Lords," he said formally, with a bow.

"Ah. My Lord Kuran." Elgurn addressed his Lord of the Fleet with equal formality. "You are earlier than I expected, and so you find us still in council. I assume you have come to deliverer your report of the execution?"

Kuran's jaw tightened perceptibly. "There has been no execution, My Lord," he said flatly. "Nor will there be. The prisoner has escaped— or rather I should say that he's been taken from his cell."

Nevien was less surprised by this news than by the complete lack of an immediate explosion from her father. Elgurn sat unmoving beside her, staring at Kuran.

Other voices, however, erupted from around the table with Pendrik, Odus, and Devral all contributing to the barrage of questions.

"What? *When?*"

"Escaped by what means?"

"Taken by *whom?*"

Kuran's glance flicked over the speakers. "The *Sword of Freedom* is gone," he said tersely. "And this letter was left at my door some time during the night." He moved with quick steps around the table, reached into his tirka, and cast a piece of paper onto the table in front of Elgurn.

The king turned it to face his eyes and bent over it, while all four Pact Signers started up from their seats and gathered around, trying to read the letter over each other's shoulders.

Vell stood quite forgotten at the other side of the table, worriedly chewing his mustache.

Nevien remained rigid in her chair as Pendrik and Anduar inserted themselves between her and the table. Her hand had strayed once more to her breast to feel the tell-tale stiffness of the paper there.

"*This is an outrage!*" Pendrik slammed a beefy fist onto the table. "Captain Nagaro, again! I might have known it. That man will stick at nothing!"

"And how *dare* he speak of the Tribunal in such terms!" Odus's face had been growing pinker and pinker as he read, and he sputtered as he spoke. "*Opinions and guesswork*, he says! Is there no limit to the man's insolence? The pirate has shown his colors here, I think!"

Elgurn raised his head and met Kuran's eyes. "He means to *keep* his commission? He thinks he can *return* after this?"

Kuran started to reply, but Odus cut him off. "What pure *arrogance!* It's... it's *vile!* As if he'd be allowed to keep his commission!"

"If he returns, it will be to the gallows!" Pendrik slammed the table again.

"He *does* say he will bring the traitor back if he becomes convinced of his guilt," Devral ventured in a milder tone.

"*Dog's dribble!*" Pendrik rounded on the old Kelorin. "You can't take that seriously!"

"You've sent ships after him, I assume?" This last was leveled at the

Lord of the Fleet by Odus.

Kuran returned the Pact Signer a pained look. "I have sent two, My Lord. I could spare no more from our defense. Nor did I wish to hazard more in the face of the storm that's brewing."

"*There's a storm?*" Several pairs of eyes turned avidly to the window, which had begun to show a few streaks of rain.

"Why, that storm may turn the pirate back!" cried Pendrik. "And we may be able to witness his capture from the third floor balcony. Has anyone got a spyglass?"

There followed what amounted to a small stampede as three of the council members rushed to exit the room, the burly Pendrik in the lead, Odus treading on his heels, and Devral stumping lamely at the rear.

In the silence that followed their departure, Lord Anduar cleared his throat. "Well," he said sardonically, "it would seem that our meeting is at an end." He turned to Elgurn. "Shall we allow Captain Vell to return to his affairs?"

The king returned him a distracted look. "Yes. By all means," he said with a vague gesture and a glance in Vell's direction. "You have leave to go, Zirda."

Vell was still gazing at the window. He had a strange look in his eyes. "They won't catch him," he said as if he were speaking to himself. "Not Captain Nagaro when the hand of Hrathgard is on him. This storm—"

"—is convenient to his purpose, and not to ours," Anduar cut in sharply. "I expect that's what you were going to say, Captain?"

Vell turned and blinked. "Yes... yes of course, My Lord." He made a hasty bow, looking sheepish, and quickly exited the chamber.

The door had no sooner closed on the young Leithian, than Elgurn addressed himself to Kuran. "You don't believe your ships will catch him, do you?"

Kuran shook his head. "We judge that the *Sword of Feedom* had at least four hours lead, My Lord, by the timing of the tide. And the storm has worsened greatly in that time. I told the captains to search in the Great Channel and the Lomoan Inside Passage, but they won't get far in this weather. They have orders to seek safe harbor to wait out the storm and then return when it passes if they've had no sight of their quarry. I confess that I sent them largely to be able to say I'd done so."

Elgurn winced, but nodded wearily. "It was well thought of."

Anduar had listened grimly, watching the two men's faces. Now he tapped the letter where it lay on the table and addressed himself to Kuran. "He is entirely sincere in all of this, I suppose?"

"Oh yes, My Lord. You may be sure of it."

A shadow crossed the Pact Signer's face. "It's a pity he has chosen to destroy himself in this way," he said with a shake of his head. "He showed so much promise. And now, My Lords—and My Lady," he added with a slight bow of acknowledgment to Nevien. "I will follow my fellow councilors and take my leave of you—although I intend to make better use of my morning than they will."

He turned to go, then turned back to Elgurn as if an afterthought had struck him. "As for Vell Sobring," he said almost casually. "I believe he will keep to the narrow path—with a little encouragement." With that he stepped out, closing the door behind him.

Kuran looked a question at Elgurn. The king responded with a nod toward one of the empty chairs. Kuran sank into it with a sigh.

Nevien had, during all of this, remained quietly in her chair. She had listened with growing alarm to the Pact Signers' reactions to Nagaro's letter, and had felt great relief in response to Kuran's expressed opinion that the *Sword* had likely gotten safely away. With Anduar gone, she rose and bent over the letter, and she felt a surge of pride as she read the captain's words. They seemed to fairly glow in her heart.

"Well, Daughter, what did *you* think of Vell Sobring? Would you say his answers were sincere?"

With an effort Nevien dragged her thoughts away from the letter and the man who had written it. She straightened and stood, frowning. "Yes, I believe Vell was being sincere," she said. "Anduar was making him nervous—but then Anduar makes *everyone* nervous."

"Mmm... yes... quite true."

Nevien focused fully on her father. He still hadn't left his seat, and his expression at that moment appeared introspective. "Why aren't you angry, Father?" she asked. "About what Captain Nagaro has done, I mean. Is it because you're glad to be rid of him?"

Elgurn glanced quickly at Kuran, then leaned back in his chair and considered her carefully. "No," he said. "I confess that the man's forward ways set my teeth on edge, but I've been in the wrong enough times in my life to recognize the feeling. He has done me a service if he's right about his friend's innocence, especially if the Mahuk emperor is watching what we do—testing Edroviran justice. The execution has been forestalled, and any unfortunate consequences of that will fall on the captain's head, not mine." He pushed his chair back from the table and stood up. "On the whole, I am well satisfied with the man's service— unorthodox though it may be."

Kuran raised a brow. "Were you *hoping* he'd do this, My Lord?"

"*This?*" Elgurn gestured at the letter. "How could I possibly have foreseen that he would do *this?* I *hoped* he would get a confession from Peldred Gilforn. It seems he must have failed."

"Peldred wouldn't talk to him," Kuran put in quickly. "And the young man shipped out for Long Harbor with Geldoran, yesterday at dawn, being as secretive about it as it's possible to be under Fleet regulations."

"I see."

Nevien stirred, remembering something she'd heard. "The captain was still trying to do things through proper channels as late as midday yesterday, Father. Brandle Furthing told me that Nagaro confronted Lord Madred at his house in Broad Street—trying to delay the execution until Peldred could be brought back for questioning. But Madred would hear none of it and has ridden off to Furthing Hold. So the captain really had no choice—"

"There's *always* a choice!" Elgurn spoke sharply. Then he passed a hand over his eyes, and added grimly, "Unfortunately the other option is sometimes unacceptable." He picked up the letter and folded it. "I will keep this, Kuran—for now, at least, since it may have a bearing on what the Council decides to do about this."

Nevien's alarm returned. "They wouldn't *really* hang him, would they?" she blurted. "If they caught him?"

The king had slipped the letter into his tirka and had begun to turn away. "That depends on the charge," he said distractedly. "Treason is generally a capital offense."

"But you know there is no treason in his intent!" Nevien stepped quickly around her father to confront him. Her eyes went pleadingly from his face to Kuran's and back again. "You've read the letter!"

Her father gave her a piercing look. "Yes, Daughter!" he snapped. "And so have the members of my Council!" For a moment his eyes blazed, but then they softened. "I don't wish to see him die, Nevien," he told her gently. "For your sake, if for no other reason. I'll do what I can."

The king moved past her and strode from the room.

Kuran gave a little cough. "My Lady..." he began, as he approached her, extending his arm as if for her to lean upon.

"Oh, Kuran!" She clutched at his sleeve. "He hasn't really destroyed himself, has he? He *will* be able to return—?"

Kuran heaved a sigh. "I don't know," he said soberly. "He has put himself in a very difficult position, Nevien. Everything now depends upon young Peldred—upon the quality of his conscience and of his courage, neither of which have proven impressive so far. Still," he added, feeling her fingers tighten on his forearm, and reading her eyes, "We mustn't forget that Nagaro put his life into the hands of the Emperor of the Mahuk Baar and had it handed back to him. There's no telling how Lokundas may choose to turn the world."

28: Lost And Found

"So let me tell ye how we did it." Taru lowered his voice conspiratorially. "There were just eight of us. And we had t' be secret. So we left two men aboard the *Sword* with orders to wait for a quarter hour and then drift downstream to the prison barge and drop anchor. The rest of us took one o' the longboats and rowed to the barge, goin' real easy... as quiet as we could..."

Taru paused for dramatic affect.

Yuli leaned forward on her stool.

Nagaro rolled his eyes. The three of them were sitting at the table in the kitchen of the Bay Tree Inn. Nagaro and Taru had come for a late lunch—eaten there inconspicuously—before returning to the ship that lay anchored in the little cove near Animara's house instead of in Pakoa Harbor. They were being circumspect in their movements on Pakoa—and everywhere else they had stopped since fleeing from Lankura—not wishing to endanger the folk they dealt with.

The *Sword* had blown into Omei Bay on the wings of the storm that had covered their escape, and had left the following day with double the number of men aboard. They'd taken their time sailing south through the Lomoas, picking up men all along the way. Thanks to Taru and the others, the tale of Pavo's plight and rescue had spread swiftly among the fishermen, and they'd arrived at Pakoa with a full crew of oarsmen. The new men weren't sea warriors yet, but that could be remedied. And while the position of Nagaro and his two friends was nominally rather perilous, he wasn't actually worried about capture. Evading Fleet ships was easy thanks to the fishermen's network, and the *Sword* could over-winter in the secret harbor on Chitaopa. If they didn't have to worry about the need to fight, they could stow supplies on the main deck, and Chitaopa had some forage, besides...

What else was there? Nagaro still had half a plate of rabbit stew in front of him and most of a slab of fresh bread. Nothing remained on Taru's plate but a few smears of gravy.

"It was dark that night." Taru resumed his tale. "The moon wasn't up, and there was a mist on the water. We kept our lantern dark so the guard couldn't see us. *His* lantern reflected off the mist and into his eyes, ye see, but it lit *him* up like a beacon."

"There was only one guard?" Yuli asked breathlessly. "That was lucky!"

"But we *knew* there'd be only one," Taru told her. "On account of Nagaro going there afore-hand t' spy things out—"

"I went to talk to Pavo, not to spy," Nagaro put in, frowning. "But I couldn't help noticing there were only three guards, and that they all slept on the barge—"

"—which meant that there'd be only one o' them awake at a time at night, 'cause it's common t' set three watches," Taru finished smugly. "So Nagaro and I got aboard the barge and grabbed the first man from behind. We tied him up and covered his mouth, 'fore he could shout t' wake the others. An' then we went into the cabin and took the other two in their beds. We left all three o' them trussed like pigs, with rags in their mouths!"

Nagaro poked at his stew. He hadn't liked involving the men who had just left the Fleet service in subduing the guards, but he and Taru alone couldn't have safely dealt with so many—and the new "civilians" had been gleefully willing to help.

"We had some trouble finding the keys." he pointed out.

"Well, aye, that's true," Taru conceded amiably. "Would ye believe it, Yuli? The sergeant kept 'em in his bed with him!" Taru paused to take a swallow of sothiril. "But the *hard* part was gettin' Pavo to come with us!"

Yuli's mouth dropped open. "*What?* Didn't he want to *go?*"

"He didn't seem t' understand at first," Taru said, frowning. "When we unlocked the door, he was on his knees on the floor, muttering to himself—praying to Sheptuum, I suppose. It was like he was already half with the Spirits."

"He'd worked himself into a trance," Nagaro explained in answer to Yuli's puzzled look. "I think he'd been up all night doing it. It was his way of facing the death he thought was coming. We had to make him understand that he wasn't going to die. That we'd come to take him out of there—"

"And when he finally did get *that* through his thick head," Taru interjected, "he somehow got the notion that he'd been pardoned! We had to tell him that he hadn't—that we were breakin' him out o' jail. And *then*—when he understood *that*—he told us he didn't want us to ruin our Fleet careers for his sake!"

"*Hamanei mata noa!*" Yuli shook her head. "What'd ye do?"

Taru drained his cup and wiped his mouth with the back of his hand. "Oh *well,*" he said with airy nonchalance. "Nagaro just explained to him that we couldn't go on workin' for the Fleet if they went and killed him. And so, once we had Pavo free, we all got back in the longboat and rowed over t' the *Sword* that was waitin' for us. And we slipped down the river on the ebb tide, slick as a fish!"

Taru sat there or a moment, basking in Yuli's delighted amazement, before pushing his chair back and standing up. "But I have t' go get Pavo an' take him back to the ship. I figure it's been an hour since I left him with Tenepti and that baby o' his."

Nagaro stifled a smile. "Yes, you do that," he said with mock severity. Pavo was taking his parole very seriously. The young Hashtep had been disarmingly hesitant about asking for an hour alone with his wife and child.

"This is goodbye, Yuli." Taru said as he stepped around the table and made for the door that led to the common room. "We may not be back for a while."

"Goodbye then, Taru, and look after yourself!" Yuli called after him. "And kiss the baby for me."

Taru threw her a grimace of disgust over his shoulder before he disappeared through the doorway.

Yuli laughed merrily. "That Taru!" she said, shaking her head. "Such a saucy rogue. Did he tell the story right?"

Nagaro shrugged. "Mostly. Though it wasn't what *I* said to Pavo that got him moving. It was Taru threatening to punch him. Pavo was still trying to argue with me, and Taru just said, 'Now see here! We're your friends. And if ye don't have the decency t' let us rescue ye, I swear I'll knock ye down and *drag* ye out o' here!' It was something to see, Yuli. Taru planting himself in front of Pavo and shaking his fist in his face... And Pavo—who's a foot taller and weighs half again as much—just put his head down and said, 'All right, Taru, I will come,' as meek as milk!"

Yuli gaped at him in astonishment. "Do ye swear that's the truth, Tor Nagaro?"

"On my honor."

She burst out laughing again. "Oh me!" she cried, wiping her eyes. "What a picture! Now tell me again just what Taru said, so I can get it right when I tell the tale."

He did so, although he also warned her to be careful who she told the tale to.

Yuli got up then and went back to washing dishes, murmuring Taru's little speech over to herself and chuckling.

Nagaro tried to give his attention to his lunch. He ate three more fork-fulls of stew and two bites of bread, but his hands soon came to a halt as he sat staring, lost in thought.

It was baffling. Doubt and uncertainty were usually the only things that caused him this kind of lingering unease. Yet he had no doubt at all that rescuing Pavo had been the right thing to do. When the *Sword* had met the *North Wind* and the *Tiger* off of Moluaro, Timegar and Moraga had whole-heartedly agreed with him.

Nagaro frowned. He had gone to see Dakuro, the Town Chief, early that morning, slipping in through the back door of the man's smithy.

"Captain!" the man had exclaimed. "How do ye come to be here? I didn't see your ship."

"That doesn't matter," Nagaro had told him. "We don't mean to stay long." And he'd given Dakuro a brief history of events in Lankura.

"Well," Dakuro had replied gravely when Nagaro had finished, "*Officially* I know nothing, if ye take my meaning. And in the future, ye'd best come and go without telling me. The less I know, the better, 'til this blows by."

Nagaro had left the smithy, worried that he might have put Dakuro in the position of having to lie to protect them both—although he hadn't asked the man to do it.

He frowned and toyed with his fork. The conversation with Dakuro had unsettled him, but his unease had begun long before that. *There had to be something else...*

He had thought that coming to Pakoa would ease his spirit. This had been his home. He should find comfort here. The first thing he'd done had been to go to the house on the Hill Road, just after dawn, to see Farusia. The bay mare had whinnied when she'd seen him coming, and he'd ridden her over the ridge and down to the beach for a gallop on the sand. But the familiar joy that had flowed through him while the gallop lasted had quickly faded as soon as he'd drawn rein.

He'd let the mare walk near the surf line, to breathe and cool her sweat-streaked flanks in the brisk wind that blew from the sea. He had gazed across the Great Channel, sparkling in the morning light, to the low undulating shapes of the mainland hills, blue-violet with distance under an azure sky decorated with snowy wisps of cloud. The scene had been very fair, but he'd found himself thinking that viewing it alone was an empty pleasure—an odd thought since he had never needed his friends' company before to make such a ride complete. Sitting astride Farusia while she shook her mane and pawed the foam, he'd thought of Nevien, laughing on her snow-white mare.

Nagaro absently reached into his tirka and drew out the folded note he had received from Nevien on his last full day in Lankura. He'd kept it with him, though he wasn't sure why, instead of stowing it at the bottom of his seaman's bag with the rest of his meager correspondence. He unfolded the note and read:

No matter what happens, we can talk.

Nevien had generally supported his convictions and sympathized with his uncertainties. Whenever he'd explained things to her, she had understood. If he could talk to her now, she might be able to help him discover the root of his trouble. And if not, it would still be a comfort just to sit with her.

He remembered the last time he'd sat beside her, on the little couch in the blue-and-green room that had once been his prison. How she'd leaned against him, nestling in the curve of his encircling arm... *how she had turned her face up to his and looked into his eyes...*

His left arm moved unconsciously, seeking for Nevien at his side. Suddenly aware of the movement, he came out of his reverie with a self-conscious jerk, to find that Yuli had stopped washing dishes and was watching him. She gave him an oddly knowing look.

"What's that paper, now, Tor Nagaro?" she asked.

"Just an invitation." He hastily folded Nevien's note and slipped it back into his tirka. "To an event I wasn't able to attend."

"Oh." Yuli sounded as if she'd expected something else. When he said nothing more, she abruptly abandoned her dish towel and came to sit on a stool directly across from him.

"Taru told me ye'd been courting a lady," she ventured.

Nagaro frowned. Taru had arrived at the inn somewhat before him, and of course he *would* mention that.

"He was talking about Kendira. And she's a merchant's daughter, not a lady. I was trying to get to know her to see if I wanted to court her. But I decided I didn't, and that was the end of it."

"Oh," Yuli said again, and it was her turn to frown. "Are ye *sure?*"

"Of course I'm sure." Nagaro picked up his fork and held it, poised above his plate. "All she wanted to do was dance."

Yuli gave him a leading look. "I've heard ye're a very good dancer, Tor Nagaro."

The fork remained poised. "There's a difference between being good at a thing and liking to do it," he informed her. "Kendira liked dancing *a lot*. I didn't." He remembered the fork and took another mouthful of what was by now rather cold stew. After chewing and swallowing, he added, "Besides that, she couldn't ride and didn't want to learn."

Yuli brushed at a stray strand of her hair. "Are ye sure ye're telling me the truth, now, Tor Nagaro?" she asked archly. "When a man sits, and stares, and picks at my stew, it's usually on account of a woman."

Nagaro deliberately put down the fork and picked up his cup of sothiril. "I haven't thought about Kendira in months," he said flatly. He could feel Yuli searching his face, but he knew she would read nothing there but the honesty of his answer. He took a swallow of sothiril, also cold, and when he put the cup down, Yuli was looking rather chagrined.

"I could have sworn ye were thinking about a woman," she said, frowning. "Just before I first spoke t' ye."

Nagaro shrugged. "I was," he confessed. "But she's just a friend. And besides that, she *is* a lady—a very high-born lady—whom I'd never be allowed to court even if I wanted to."

Yuli's eyes immediately narrowed. "Tor Nagaro," she said, wagging a finger at him, "don't I remember ye sittin' here, in this very kitchen—on that very stool—and telling Pavo that he should run away with Tenepti if her father wouldn't let them wed?"

"That's completely different." Nagaro spoke without thinking. "A man can't run away with a princess—"

"A *princess?*" Yuli stared at him. Then her eyes widened and she slapped the table. "*The* princess! Ye're in love with Princess Nevien!" And then her glee changed to horror as she realized the implications of what she'd just said and her hand flew to her mouth. "Oh, ye poor man!"

Nagaro was on his feet, his stool toppling to the floor. "*I never said I was in love with her!*"

Yuli cowered. "No, o'course ye didn't! Sit down, Tor Nagaro. Please! Just finish your stew—"

"I don't want it! I'm not hungry!"

Nearly choking, he spun away from Yuli and stormed out of the kitchen. He crossed the common room—which was fortunately empty— in a few furious strides. Thrusting the doors open, he plunged out into the shadow of the great bay tree, and from there into the sun-washed street beyond, moving blindly.

He and Nevien were friends! Just friends!

The idea that he might be in love with her was absurd. He had *excruciating* memories of the fumbling efforts at love-making that the puppet part of him had made under the influence of heskial... memories that still made him cringe after all the years that had passed between...

He could still feel the way she'd gone stiff under his hands—had shrunk away from him... until inevitably she had said some words that had stopped him: "—No, please don't—" had been enough. Time and again it had ended that way—ended with him lying woodenly beside her while she'd wept into her pillow...

With a monumental effort he wrenched his mind away from the abyss.

How could love possibly coexist with memories like those? And if he were in love, he'd know it, surely, wouldn't he? He'd always imagined he would *know*... that he would *feel something*...

And then his feet came stumbling to a stop as he realized that he *had* been feeling something—for days—or rather the *lack* of something, like an empty place inside of him. And all his vague feelings of disquiet came instantly into focus around that perception of emptiness.

Again with an effort, he collected himself and walked on along the street, though he scarcely knew where he was going. His mind was in a turmoil. Now that he *thought* about it, Nevien had been very often in his mind. Even in his dreams... There wasn't a day that he hadn't thought of her—

But being in love should be pleasant... shouldn't it? It wasn't supposed to hurt!

His feet had carried him some distance along Front Street, and he was passing the house of Gedras the merchant. He was too distracted to notice, and was therefore taken completely by surprise when the merchant suddenly appeared from out of a narrow alley that ran along one side of the house.

"Captain Nagaro!" Gedras spoke low and urgently. "I heard you were in town, and I hoped I'd see you. Come this way, quickly." He caught Nagaro's arm, drawing him into the alley.

Nagaro was too startled to resist, or even to ask an intelligent question. The alley gave access to Gedras's house by a side entrance, and he soon found himself in a narrow back hallway.

Gedras peered at him by the light of an oil lamp. "Please excuse my ungraciousness," he said as he let go of Nagaro's arm and adjusted his spectacles. "But I know you're in trouble—or soon will be—and a man of my... ah... standing in the world... must be careful of appearances. Still, I do mean to give you what help I can."

Nagaro managed to collect his wits. "I quite understand," he said. "And it's good of you to think of me—"

"I expect you'll be needing funds—to provision your ship."

"We have provisions," Nagaro informed him. "Each man who came aboard brought something with him."

Gedras looked nonplused. "Well, I suppose if you mean to depend on *charity*..."

"It wasn't so much charity as a kind of contribution. It was Taru's idea. It's yielded a rather mixed assortment of rations, but it will keep us for some weeks."

"Ah!" Gedras pounced. "And after that?"

"*Well—*"

"There! You see? And you'll be needing more than victuals." The merchant produced a pair of leather money bags, one brown, the other black, from somewhere about his person and thrust them into Nagaro's hands. "Therefore, you will need these. The first," here he indicated the brown bag, "is from the sale of goods left in my keeping when you went to Lankura. And you may consider the second an advance—"

"But Gedras—" Nagaro looked at the bags, and back at the merchant. The bags were both quite heavy. "I can't just take these. Anything that was left when we went to Lankura was for the support of Timegar's and

Moraga's ships. And as for an *advance*... well... an advance on *what?*"

"You'll be... ah... *pirating*... again, won't you?" Gedras asked delicately.

"We might *try*." Nagaro gestured vaguely with a bag of money. "It won't be the same as before, since I don't mean to sail into the Baar after Mahuk warships. And we have only one ship, because I can't ask Timegar or Moraga to risk joining us."

"You can't, eh?" Gedras raised an eyebrow. "The next time you cross paths with them, I suggest you show them the money and ask them what should be done with it."

"Well... yes... I could do that."

"Good! That's done then."

"But the *advance*, Gedras!" He shook the black bag. "This is *your* money, isn't it?"

"If you don't like calling it an advance, call it a *contribution*." The merchant stuck out his impeccably shaven chin, and his eyes glinted behind his spectacles.

Nagaro stared at him helplessly. "But I—" He gave up in the face of the merchant's obvious determination. "—Gedras, thank you."

The other man bowed. "You'd best slip out by the way you came in. Turn right, up the alley, and left at the first turning. You'll come out on Upper Mill Road."

"I know." Nagaro bent, managing to conceal the two bags under his tirka. When he straightened, Gedras had disappeared. He turned to locate the door, his head still reeling from the merchant's generosity, and discovered that he wasn't alone in the hallway.

A woman stood in the shadows.

He had no idea where she had come from or how long she'd been there. As he turned to face her, she stepped boldly up to him and he saw that it was the merchant's youngest daughter, Lissel.

"Please, Captain," she said softly, her voice catching with emotion. "I know this isn't very proper, but I have to talk to you. I *must* know what news there is of Sindar. Is he still in Lankura?"

"*Bishka!*" Nagaro slapped his hand to his forehead. "I was going to write you again, Lissel, and I forgot! Sindar is with his kinfolk. He's either in Harmoth with his mother's people, or else he's already gone to Vered Mahir, to his father's family—which is named Korinos. That was the plan." He hastily sketched the story of how Sindar's kinsmen had found the young man. She hung on every word. It hurt him to see it, and he could only think how much better off she would be if she could forget the former slave.

Thinking that he might dampen her affection, he said, "I'm very sorry, Lissel, but Sindar is determined to be a Fleet warrior, and nothing else seems to matter to him. I wish I could say he'd spoken kindly of you, or that he meant to return to Pakoa, but either one would be a lie. He's being terribly ungrateful and behaving rather foolishly—"

She held up a hand to stop him. "I know it seems so," she said, and her eyes glistened with tears. "But it's only because he's been so alone all his life, and there's so much he doesn't understand." She raised her chin, then, looking straight into Nagaro's eyes. "I drove him away," she said, her voice unexpectedly steady, "by constantly telling him how much he needed help. It hurt his pride. So he ran away to prove that he didn't need any help. I'm glad he's found his family, and that at least he's with people who want to look after him. But if *they* try to help him as I did, I'm afraid they'll drive him away too." She sighed. "If you see him again, tell him I'm sorry... and that I'm still waiting for him..."

Nagaro didn't know what to say. He could only promise to pass her message on if the opportunity arose, and murmur words of sympathy before making his escape.

He hurried along Upper Mill Road. There were people passing in the street. Some nodded or spoke to him, and he managed a smile and a nod of acknowledgment. Turning a corner, he almost walked into Tira Zomora on her piebald pony. He halted with a gasp, looking up into the sharp black eyes of Pakoa's medicine woman.

She minced no words.

"Ye did well by saving an innocent man, Captain," she said. "But ye carry danger on your back. Ye can't stay here."

"I know," he said. "And I won't."

"Good." She gave him something like a bow, sitting on her curious sidesaddle. Then she clucked to the pony and rode on without another word.

Nagaro shook himself. For once it seemed that he and Zomora were in complete agreement. *He supposed it had to happen sometime.* But he needed to get away from people so that he could think. He ducked into an alley and made for the path that led over the ridge and down into Ani's little valley where his crewmen were to rendezvous by nightfall. Once on the familiar path that climbed the ridge, his feet found their own way, and he thought as he walked.

He couldn't get the image of Lissel's face out of his mind. The young woman's devotion to Sindar impressed him even as her suffering tore at his heart. He felt enormous sympathy for her—and he also saw the answer to his earlier question: *Love thwarted and denied obviously could hurt.*

He could also see that it would be a complete disaster for him to love Nevien the way Lissel loved Sindar. His situation would, if anything, be worse. Lissel could still hope that Sindar might realize what a precious thing he'd thrown away. While *he* had no hope of ever gaining Nevien—

even if he could somehow return to Lankura. She was a princess. He was a commoner without a family or even a Wared lord to speak for him. Even worse, his experience with Kendira had taught him that he couldn't wed a woman if he couldn't tell her his secret. And Nevien was the last woman in the world that he could ever tell. He couldn't bear to think about the look he'd see on her face if she knew.

His feet faltered, and he groaned aloud as he tried to understand how this thing had happened... tried to imagine what this love consisted of. Nevien was beautiful in his eyes, but so were other women. She was good, and kind, but those traits were not so hard to come by. She was intelligent, and perceptive, too—which was rarer—and she could ride as well as he did. But what made her special, he realized, had more to do with how easy it was to talk to her... the way they understood each other... the fact that she'd been through hard things too... that she wasn't just some wide-eyed innocent. *The world had wounded her and she had survived—even grown stronger. The world expected so much of her, and she took those expectations seriously and strove to meet them. Yet she still could laugh—*

By the time he reached the place where the path crested the ridge-top, it occurred to him that part of the attraction might be the fact that they had been touched by the same evil, long ago, and been marked by it—the very thing he'd thought would make falling in love with her impossible...

And Taru had warned him—

He stopped where the path divided and stood gasping. The climb had winded him, but it was more than that. He tried to focus on the view before him. The near side of the ravine lay warm in the afternoon sun, with terraces of kuma bushes and the little stand of trees at the bottom. The far side was cool with afternoon shade. The roof of the stone house at the foot of the farther slope was kissed by sunlight, its walls submerged in shadow.

The *Sword of Freedom* was still safely moored where he had left her. The sleek war galley was drawn right in between the narrow sides of the cove, where the ravine met the sea, there, away to his left. Anchors, fore and aft, made sure she wouldn't drift against the rocks or into shallow water. Long strips of canvas, painted to match the hull's dark wood, were draped along her sides, concealing the distinctive black-and-white markings that were known from the Faranos to the Mahuk Baar.

He drew a shuddering breath and shivered, though it wasn't cold. He felt alone—in need of help—and not yet ready to talk to the other members of his crew. He could make out a few of them on the *Sword's* deck. One of the longboats lay drawn up on the shingle of the narrow beach. It was still early: He had perhaps an hour before most of the men who'd gone ashore would begin to return. That was good.

He searched the sides of the ravine with his eyes and spotted Sudano at work among the kuma bushes, off to the right where the stream cut across the terraces. The three older children, Bahiri, Tavo, and Pilo, were there too, working beside their father. He didn't see Ani or Narei. Most likely they were at the house. That also was good. Narei would be a welcome distraction, and Ani was always good company when he was troubled. Nagaro turned onto the path that zig-zagged down into the bottom of the ravine. He went quickly, so that Sudano and the children wouldn't notice him, until he got under the trees at the bottom of the slope.

As he emerged from under the big cedars close to the house, he heard Narei calling him from the direction of the beach. Following the sound of her voice, he saw her small head poking up above the gunnel of the longboat.

She put up her hand and beckoned to him. "Here I am, Papa!" she cried. "Will you come sail with me?"

He managed to laugh as he turned aside to approach the beached boat. "Of course I'll sail with you, Little One. Where are we going?"

"Out to that big rock, there, Papa. Where all the seagulls make houses." She turned and pointed. "You row the boat!"

He looked at the rock in question. It lay rather far out in the cove, a little past where the *Sword* was anchored. Sea birds circled it and lit upon it, and the sea-surge was breaking white against it. "Oh no, Narei," he said quickly "That would be much too dangerous."

Narei pouted. "But I want to see the nests!"

He shook his head at her. "I'm afraid not, Ginger Pie. See how the waves are smashing themselves against it? They would smash the boat too."

"Oh." Her slender brows constricted in disappointment, but, as usual, she accepted her father's judgement. "All right, Papa. Then you have to come with me and see the crab king!"

"The crab king?" he asked, bewildered.

"Don't you remember, Papa? I told you last night!"

"Oh. Yes," he murmured, chagrined. He'd come ashore the previous evening to visit Ani's family. Narei had been overjoyed to see him and had prattled on about a lot of things while he'd been thinking about how charmed Nevien would have been with her if they could have met. He thrust the memory aside and gave his daughter a quick smile. "Show me your crab king, Ginger Pie."

Narei leaped out of the longboat and ran off along the curve of the pebble beach to where the shingle ended among a jumble of rocks and tidal pools at the western side of the ravine. Nagaro hurried after her.

Narei scrambled nimbly over the rocks and stopped by the side of a deep pool that was, at that hour, almost completely cut off from the sea. Only the largest of the incoming waves spilled foaming water into it— water that ran back again more slowly as the wave receded.

"There he is, Papa. Look!" Narei had crouched beside the pool and was beckoning eagerly. "He's come out of his house so you can see him!"

Nagaro knelt beside Narei on the rock and peered into the pool. Down at the very bottom, he could make out the shape of a great green crab, it's carapace at least six inches across. "Yes, I see him, Narei. He's a very big crab indeed."

"That's because he's the king! And *I* found him, Papa. Tavo and Pilo didn't believe me—"

She went on, and he tried to listen to the story of how she'd brought her brothers back to the pool, over and over, before they had seen the crab too. "Tavo stays he isn't the crab king, because crabs don't have kings. But they must, Papa, mustn't they? And 'Hiri says maybe it's the crab *queen*, but the crab queen lives in *that* pool over there with all the little crab princes and princesses—"

He nodded and offered encouragement, and they watched as the huge crab crawled slowly across the pebbled bottom of the pool.

Abruptly Narei turned her face up to look at him. "Papa," she asked, her wide brown eyes earnestly questioning, "when you take me with you to Lankura, will I see the king and the queen and the princess?"

He felt an almost physical pang. "I... won't be going back to Lankura very soon," he said carefully. "Remember? I told *you* that last night."

"I know," she said. "But when you *do* go—and you take me—will I get to see the princess? I want to see her *especially*, because she's your favorite person!"

He winced. *What must he have said last night that his five-year-old daughter had read him like a book?* "Someday I hope I'll be able to take you, and you can watch them all go by on parade," he said. "The king, the queen, and the princess too." He stood up. "But right now I need to talk to your Aunt Ani."

"All right." Narei nodded brightly, this time having failed to read the shadow in her father's eyes. "But Auntie Ani says I can't play on the rocks by myself, so I'll have to go back to the boat."

They parted on the pebble strand, and he went to the house. Once there, there was nothing to do but open the door and go in.

Animara was in the main room, kneading bread on a board laid on the table. She looked up when he entered and gave him a welcoming smile. "Ye can just leave th' door open, Nagaro, if ye like," she told him.

Nagaro considered the suggestion and rejected it. Any number of people might come at any time—members of his crew, or of Ani's family.

If they had to open the door, it would give him a little warning. So he closed the door and went to sit at the table. Ani's attention was on her work, and the room was rather dim. The two windows were open, but the house lay mostly in shadow. Nagaro sat watching her for a time as she alternately folded and punched the dough. She had her sleeves rolled up, and her strong brown arms were dusted with flour to the elbows.

The silence lay quite easily between them, their relationship being such that neither one felt awkward at the lack of speech. At length Ani straightened and brushed at her forehead with the back of her hand. "Would ye like some cold sothiril? There's some in the pot there." She gestured towards the fireplace, where the pot hung on a hook above the ashes of the morning's fire. "Ye'll have to get a cup and pour it yourself, though. I'm all flour."

"I don't mind." He got up, found a cup on a shelf, and helped himself to the sothiril. Coming back to the table, he sat down and set the cup down, cupping his hands around it.

Animara settled the kneaded dough into a large earthenware bowl, which she covered with a towel and set aside on the smaller table under the window for the dough to rise. Dusting off her hands, she went and wiped them on a second towel, then fetched another cup and went to serve herself from the pot above the hearth.

"Ani..." He spoke to her back. "You and Sudano love each other, don't you?"

"I'd say that we do." She answered matter-of-factly. She hung up the kettle again and turned back towards the table.

"How was it at the beginning?" He tried to speak as if the question weren't important. "Did you—fall in love?"

She gave a low, throaty laugh. "Did we fall in love? I can't speak for *him*, but I know *I* did. Heels over head!"

He picked up his cup of sothiril and took a swallow to cover his rising agitation, then set it down because he felt a little unsteady and he didn't want to risk spilling it. "How did you know?" he asked.

"Oh, well now." She sat down, elbows on the table, her cup in her hands as she stared past it into memory. "That was a long time ago, but I'll never forget. It was just after Mama died, and Sudano just came t' the door one day askin' to help wi' the kuma harvest. He was so shy and awkward. He said his mother had sent him—that he was her youngest, and one more pair o' hands than she needed. There were some other lads that came too, but he came first, and stayed longest, and he never tried t' pinch me like some o' the others."

She paused and took a sip of sothril. "It didn't happen right away, or all at once, but somehow it came t' be that I was lookin' for him every day, and if he didn't come it felt like there was a shadow on the sun. One time, his mother sent him up-island t' lend a hand to some of his other kin—and he hadn't told me. He was gone for three days, and I got afraid he might never come back." She turned her wide dark eyes upon Nagaro and gave him a self-mocking smile. "I tell ye, I thought I'd go mad for the lack o' that lad. I couldn't eat... I couldn't sleep—"

Abruptly she stopped, reading his face.

He held her eyes.

"There is someone, Nagaro, isn't there?" she said softly. "And ye left her in Lankura, I'm thinking."

His eyes were still on hers. "Yes."

She leaned towards him. "Who is she?"

He swallowed, and this time he dropped his eyes. "Nevien Harlind," he said in a voice scarcely above a whisper.

"*Nevien Harlind!*"

He heard the soft clunk of her cup as she set in on the table.

"Ye don't mean..." she murmured. "Not... *the princess—?*"

He nodded, unable to look at her.

There was a pause, then, "Oh Nagaro, I'm sorry! Ye can't have her, can ye? And she'll be married to someone else afore the winter's out..." Her voice trailed to silence. After a moment, when he didn't speak, she said, "Did ye... do any more 'n look at her across the room?"

He swallowed. "I sat and talked with her, Ani. Traded confidences. Went riding with her. Danced with her..."

"All o' *that?*" Animara couldn't hide her astonishment.

He fingered the edge of his cup. "We were trying to just be friends. But I... guess I lost my way..."

"That's an easy way t' lose," she said gently. "And not know it, 'til ye get there."

She reached out with her warm, calloused hands to grasp his. He looked up into dark eyes full of sympathy.

"Do people ever... fall *out* of love?" he asked.

"It's been known to happen." She gave his hands a squeeze and released them. "And the surest way to shed one love is t' find another, they say." She leaned back and picked up her own cup. "There was a lad I that had my heart set on before Sudano—while Mama was still alive. He was older—and I don't think he ever even knew I was sweet on him. He only had eyes for another girl, ye see, and when he married her, I was heartbroken for almost a year." Ani sighed, and took a sip from her cup. "But then Mama died, an' Sudano came, an' one day I woke up and realized I hadn't thought about that other lad in weeks! So there's hope."

"So all I have to do is find *another woman?*" He took a hasty gulp of his sothiril to hide his dismay. "I've never had much luck with that *before—*"

"Ye have the rest o' your life to do it in," she pointed out.

"That's... *true*..."

"An' the worst thing ye can do is to *look*," she told him. "Just keep yourself busy, and ye never know what the Spirits 'll bring. And if it turns out that this is just something ye have to bear, well, ye have family and friends t' help ye bear it. Folk always say it's not such a bad world as long as there are good people in it."

She smiled at him, and he managed to smile back. He didn't believe in the Turowan World Spirits, but family *was* good. And friends. And there were a great many good people in the world, too. People like Ani, and Yuli, Dakuro, and Gedras. And the future was an unwritten book. Lokundas was full of surprises...

He took a long breath. "You mustn't tell anyone, Ani. It's—"

"Dangerous for ye?" She nodded. "I can believe that. And I wouldn't, anyway."

He felt the blood in his face. "Yuli figured it out before I did. I owe her an apology. I snapped at her—"

Ani brushed this aside. "Yuli 'll live," she said. "And she's got more sense 'n to spread it around. But I'll speak to her, just to be sure."

"Thank you, Ani... For everything..."

He took a longer drink of sothiril. The room was warm and smelled comfortingly of yeast. He could hear men's voices outside now, coming nearer, but he felt steadied, as if he'd found an anchor... or a path...

Not looking for a woman should be easy, at least. And he could certainly do his best to keep occupied, now that he knew what the trouble was. There would be many busy days ahead—doing important things... like making sure the Fleet ships didn't find the *Sword*... keeping Pavo safe... freeing slaves, if the Emperor's ships strayed into Edroviran waters... getting ready to winter on Chitaopa... These were the tasks that Lokundas had set before him. And they tasks he knew how to do.

***

Glossary

Albured (AHL-bur-ehd): A Kelorin healer. Ship's doctor on the *Sea Eagle*.

Alisset (A-lihs-seht): Alisset Sobring. A young Leithian woman. One of the princess's ladies. Daughter of Bron Sobring, sister of Vell.

Almerin (AHL-mer-ihn): True name of Emril. A Kelorin woman. Sister of Evran Marvenen and wife of Kendral Korinos. Mother of Sindar.

Ambras (AHM-brahs): Master Ambras, a Kelorin healer, personal physician to Queen Semorel.

Anduar Tyronin (AHN-doo-ar teer-O-nihn): A Kelorin lord. One of the Signers of the Pact of Lankura and a member of the King's Council.

Angkat (AHNG-kaht): A powerful Mautep warlord whose men have twice attacked Lankura.

Animara (ah-nih-MAR-ah): A Turowan woman, called Ani for short. Sister of Jila and Narei's aunt. Wife of Sudano and mother of Bahiri, Tavo, and Pilo.

Averwin (AV-er-wihn): A small country estate. Nagaro's boyhood home.

Baalkir jir-Akaan (BAHL-keer jeer-ah-KAHN): Emperor Baalkir. A powerful Mautep warlord who has become Emperor of the Mahuk Baar.

Bahiri (bah-HEER-ee): A young Turowan girl. Daughter and oldest child of Animara. Cousin to Nagaro's daughter Narei and therefore Nagaro's niece.

Baruk (bahr-OOK): Mautep slave master, formerly of the *Fist of Death* under Captain Urchak.

basirah (bah-SEER-ah): Hashti for "enough".

Beloras (BEHL-or-ahs): A Kelorin man, Maramine's murdered love.

Berinar Sundorin (BEHR-ih-nar SUHN-dor-ihn): A Kelorin lord. One of the Signers of the Pact of Lankura. Father of Rathdar. Author of *Rule of*

Loros. Died under mysterious circumstances.

bishka (BIHSH-kah): A relatively mild but expressive expletive in the Hashti language.

Bodano (bo-DAH-no): A Turowan man who was one of the householders on the country estate of Averwin. He taught Leyel how to hunt with a bow and set snares.

bodjer (BAH-jer): An expletive. Derived from a Leithian expression that was originally much cruder. It means roughly to "do an injury to'" as commonly used in the Common Speech.

Boka Omei (BO-kah O-may): Northernmost major island of the Lomoa chain.

Bouno (bo-OO-no): A Turowan man. A freed slave, formerly a merchant seaman. A follower of Captain Nagaro and now steersman on the *Sword of Freedom.*

Brandle Furthing (BRAND-l FUR-dhing): A young Leithian, Lieutenant (commander) of the Princess's Guard. Son of Lord Madred Furthing. ("dh" denotes the voiced "th" sound in "this").

Brendet (brehn-DEHT): A high-born young Leithian woman. One of the princess's ladies.

Brodig Fane (BRO-dihg fayn): A Leithian man. A officer in the Royal Fleet of Edrovir. Captain of the *Valor.*

Bron Sobring (brahn SO-bring): A Leithian lord and former lord of Sobring Hold. One of Leyel Virden's 'keepers'. Father of Vell and Alisset. Killed in the border war.

Burdal Korinos (BUR-dahl KOR-ih-nos): An elderly Kelorin merchant from Vered Mahir. Patriarch of the Korinos family. Father of Kendral,

Chitaopa (chih-TAOW-pah): A small uninhabited island off the coast of Jinara.

Chula (CHOO-lah): An elderly Turowan man who was gardener at Averwin. He taught Leyel how to plant things and make things out of sticks and string.

chutapak (CHOO-tah-pahk): A Hashti salve used for burns, to hasten healing.

Clarimel (CLAR-ih-mehl): A young high-born Leithian woman. One of the princess's ladies.

Dakuro (dah-KOOR-o): A Turowan man. Town Chief, head of the Pakoa

Town Council, and principal authority on the island. Also a blacksmith.

Darion (DEHR-ee-ahn): King Darion, called 'Darion the Great'. Lord of the House of Loros and first king of Edrovir. Son of Nevrath and Minowei. Father of Tevren.

dedrel (DEH-drehl): A soporific drug used as a general anesthetic.

Delvin (DEHL-vihn): A Kelorin youth. A member of the Palace Guard, well known to Landros, whom Nagaro met during the second Mautep attack.

Devral Sedras (DEHV-rahl SEHD-rahs): An aging Kelorin Lord. One of the Signers of the Pact of Lankura and a member of the King's Council.

dokan (do-KAHN): A gold coin of Edrovir. There are ten trokins to the dokan, and one hundred rins to the trokin.

Doren (DOR-ehn): A Kelorin, Town Chief of the town of Boka Bay on Boka Omei island.

Dreigen (DREHY-gehn): the king's Lore Master. An expert on poisons.

Droviri (dro-VEER-ee): Name used by the inhabitants of Jinara and the Mahuk Baar for the Edroviran language (the Common Speech), or the people of Edrovir. Also an adjective meaning "pertaining to Edrovir".

Duleyin (doo-LAY-ihn): Seventh month of the Edroviran calendar, equvalent to July.

Edro (EHD-ro): River Edro. Largest river in Edrovir, flowing roughly from northeast to southwest and emptying into the sea at Lankura.

Edrovir (EHD-ro-veer): A country inhabited by the Kelorin, Leithians, and Turowans, stretching from the Gorietha mountains in the east to the western sea, and from the Kor Vaskol mountains in the north to its borders with Hraan and with Jinara in the south.

Elgurn Harlind (EHL-gurn HAR-lihnd): King Elgurn. A Leithian lord whom the Pact Signers chose to be the third king of Edrovir.

Elyan (EHL-ee-ahn): Prince Elyan. A Kelorin lord, third husband of the Princess Nevien. Killed while defending Lankura during the second Mautep attack.

Emril (EHM-rihl): A Kelorin woman. Slave of Notep jir-Akaan who cared for his son Roheed. Mother of Sindar. Died in captivity in the Mahuk Baar.

Endemar (EHN-deh-mar): Lord Endemar. A Kelorin lord of a minor House, to whose territory was added the tract encompassing Loros Hall, ancestral seat of the House of Loros, untenanted since the slaying of

King Tevren.

Erantil (EHR-ahn-tihl) Erantil Crimson: A rare and costly variety of sothiril, of bright red color and superior flavor and fragrance.

Estevad (EHS-teh-vahd): A Kelorin man. Clerk to Kuran Kel, the Lord of the Fleet.

Evran Marvenen (EHV-rahn mar-VEHN-ehn): A Kelorin merchant from Harmoth. Brother of Almerin.

Evrel (EHV-rehl): Fourth month of the Edroviran calendar, equivalent to April.

Faranos (FAH-rah-nos): Either of two island chains off the northern and central coast of Edrovir. The Inner Faranos are the more northerly. The Outer Faranos partially overlap the Inner Faranos, lying farther off shore and extending farther south.

Farano's Mouth: Strait separating the southern end of the Outer Faranos from the Lomoas.

Farusia (fah-ROO-see-ah): The name of Nagaro's bay mare, kept on Pakoa. Also a plant bearing large white trumpet-shaped flower, or the flower itself.

Fendar (FIHN-dar): An older Kelorin man. A swordmaster who was Leyel Virden's instructor.

Ferenan (FEHR-eh-nahn): A widowed lord who is of mixed Kelorin and Leithian blood. One of Princess Nevien's suitors.

Filora (fih-LOR-ah): A Kelorin woman, Mistress of the Royal Kitchens in the palace of Lankura.

Furthing Hold (FER-dhing hold). A lord's territory, governed by Lord Madred Furthing. ("dh" denotes the "th" sound in the word "this")

Galenor (GAL-eh-nor): A coastal city north of Lankura. Also the name of the Wared it is in.

Gama (GAH-ma): An old Turowan woman. Taru's grandmother. (The word *gama* means "grandmother" in the Turowan tongue.)

Gedras (GUEHD-rahs): A Kelorin merchant on Pakoa Island. Father of Lissel. (The "g" is hard as in "get". In fact, "g" is always hard in the names used in this chronicle.)

Geldoran Finrad (GUEHL-dor-ahn FIHN-rahd): A Kelorin commander in the Royal Fleet, second in command to Kuran Kel.

Genorel (GUEHN-or-ehl): The first month of the Edroviran calendar, equivalent to January.

Gillard Marchent (GUIL-ard MAR-chent): A Leithian lord. The second husband of Princess Nevien. Also called 'Gill'. One of Leyel Virden's 'keepers.' He "went mad" and leapt from a balcony.

Great Channel: Channel separating the various island chains from the mainland of Edrovir. It is generally broader than any of the north-south channels separating the various islands and island chains from one another, hence the name.

Grimbold Sobring (GRIHM-bold SO-brihng): A Leithian lord. Brother, and successor of Bron Sobring as lord of Sobring Hold. Uncle of Vell and Alisset.

Hakura Kili (hah-KOOR-ah KEE-lee): Guiding Spirit of the Turo, by whom they tend to swear. The exclamation "Hakura!" expresses awe or excitement.

Hamanei mata noa (hah-MAH-nay MAH-tah NO-ah): A frequently used Turowan exclamation. It literally means 'Spirits protect us.' Also shortened to just "Hamanei!" It expresses alarm.

Hamani (hah-MAH-nee): A young Turowan woman who lives across the road from Taru's grandmother in Wotana. Her name means "spirit". Older sister of Jitali.

Hanuroa (HAH-noo-RO-ah): Turowan name for the afterlife. Equivalent to heaven.

Harl Sobring: (harl SO-brihng): A Leithian lord, father of Bron Sobring. Killed by Darion when he acted dishonorably during a challenge sword fight.

Harmoth (HAR-mahth): Southern-most major port city in Edrovir.

Harthred (HARTH-rehd): A Leithian commander of the Palace Guard killed in the second attack on Lankura by sea raiders from the Mahuk Baar.

Hashtep (HAHSH-tehp): The common folk of the Mahuk Baar. Also the general word for their race, which includes the Mautep or warlord class.

Hashti (HAHSH-tee): Language of the people of the Mahuk Baar (Both Hashtep and Mautep).

Hatakei Raal (hah-TAH-kay rahl): Mautep name for Kuran Kel, the Lord of the Fleet of Edrovir. (Literally "running dog" in Hashti).

Hel (hehl): In Leithian belief, a place of punishment for the spirits of those who have transgressed in life.

heskial (hehs-kee-AHL): A drug that enslaves the will while leaving a person fully conscious. Derived from the heskia vine, it is presumed to possess "spirit magic".

Hinda: (HIHN-dah): A Kelorin woman who was cook and housekeeper at Averwin.

Hranji (HRAHN-jee): An inhabitant of Hran. Also used as the plural, or the people.

Hrathgard (HRAHTH-gard): Patriarchal god of the Leithians, King of the Heavens and Lord of the Wind. He is the patron of kings and rulers.

Idrin (IHD-rihn): Seven-day-long thirteenth month of the Edroviran calendar, surrounding the winter solstice and marking the 'turning of the year'. Commonly considered unlucky.

Ilsafeth (IHL-sah-fehth): A Leithian woman. Wife of the healer Tredhold.

Inside Passage: Irregular north-south path running down the middle between the islands of the Lomoa chain.

Irvenen Wared (ir-VEHN-ehn WAH-rehd): A lord's territory governed by Lord Rastyl Korven, lying in the extreme north of Edrovir.

Jaamra (JAHM-rah): Strait of Jaamra. A passage between two islands on the Mahuk Baar. Site of a sea battle between two rival Mautep warlords, Baalkir and Angkat, during which Nagaro led his fellow slaves to seize the *Fist of Death* and make their escape.

Jila (JEE-lah): A beautiful and notorious Turowan woman. Animara's sister. Mother of Narei.

Jinara (jih-NAH-rah): A coastal country lying between Edrovir and the Mahuk Baar, involved in a long-running border dispute with Edrovir.

Jinari (jih-NAH-ree): Edrovirin name for the inhabitants of Jinara. Also their language and an adjective meaning "pertaining to Jinara".

Jitali (jee-TAH-lee): A young Turowan woman living in Wotana. Younger, prettier sister of Hamani.

kajadeem (kah-jah-DEEM): Hashti word for 'honor'.

Kale Fendred (kayl FEHN-drehd): A high-born Leithian, friend of King Elgurn. One of Leyel Virden's 'keepers' who is now insane. Father of Nile.

Keertak jir-Bantao (KEER-tahk jeer bahn-TAU): A Mautep warrior and captain. Eldest son of the warlord Tuluptak jir-Bantao.

Kel Tierna (kel tee-EHR-nah): Port city on the southern coast of Edrovir, south of Lankura and north of Harmoth.

Kelorin (KEL-or-in): A fair-skinned, dark-haired people originally from the isles of Kelor in the far western sea. Also their language, or an adjective meaning "pertaining to Kelor or the Kelorin people".

Kendira (kehn-DEER-ah): A young Kelorin woman. One of the Princess's ladies.

Kendral Korinos (KEHN-drahl KOR-ih-nos): A young Kelorin man. Son of Burdal Korinos. Husband of Almerin and father of Sindar. Killed by Notep jir-Akaan and his warriors.

keshaal (keh-SHAHL): An expletive in Hashti, fairly strong.

kasadrin (KAHS-ah-drihn): Also called "King's Men". A Kelorin board game similar to chess.

Kiraam Shaku-Tal (KEER-ahm SHAH-koo-TAHL): A name bestowed on Nagaro by Roheed. In Hashti it means "one who takes slaves." Generally rendered in the Common Speech as "Thief of Slaves."

krit (kriht): Plural: "krits". Leithian word for a carved stick used to cast a vote in a council. Originally it referred to a type of dagger for which the carved stick was later substituted. The carving identified the owner, who would place (cast) the krit on the table in the appropriate pile to indicate his vote.

Kroneg (KRON-ehg): Leithian god of war. Arbiter of the outcome of armed conflict and ruler of the dark moon, Naru.

kuma (KOO-mah): Kuma stain or ointment. The ointment stains the skin brown and is made from the nuts of the kuma plant. Used by fair-skinned seamen to prevent sunburn.

Kunoa (Koo-NO-ah): A freed former slave and member of Nagaro's crew who joins the Royal Fleet. A young Turowan from Pakoa.

Kuran Kel (KOOR-ahn kehl): Lord of the Royal Fleet of Edrovir. A man of mixed Kelorin and Turowan blood, from a merchant family but elevated by King Elgurn to the status of Lord of the House of Kel. Also Lord of Kel Wared, a territory the king created for him.

Landros Torenin (LAN-dros tor-EHN-ihn): An older Kelorin sea warrior, former officer of the Royal Fleet of Edrovir, then a slave and one of Nagaro's followers who now rejoins the Fleet. Captain of the *Sea Eagle*.

Lankura (LAHN-koor-ah): Capital city of Edrovir, located at the mouth of the River Edro.

Lapoa (lah-PO-ah): A small island near the northern end of the Lomoa chain. 'Lapoa Passage' refers to the strait between Lapoa and an adjacent island and is somewhat contextual since it could be either north or south of Lapoa.

Leithians (LAY-thee-ens): Fair-skinned, light-haired people originally from a land called Leith. "Leithian" denotes either a single individual or is used as an adjective meaning "pertaining to Leithians".

Leyel Virden (LEHY-ehl VER-dehn) Name given to Nagaro by the Lady Maramine Virden, under which he was ridiculed as the "idiot prince" during his marriage to Princess Nevien.

Lindra (LIHN-drah): Queen Lindra. A Kelorin woman, wife of King Tevren. Killed, supposedly accidentally, along with her husband, by Reith Hurn.

Lissel (lih-SEHL): A young Kelorin woman enamored of Sindar. Youngest daughter of the Pakoan merchant Gedras.

Lissafel (LIHS-ah-fehl): "The Lady". Maiden goddess of the Leithians. Ruler of the hearts of men and women, and of the pale moon, Talebra.

Lokundas (lo-KOON-dahs): Called the "Turner of Worlds". The Kelorin personification of fate. One of the old gods of the Cloud Mountain People from before the founding of Kelor.

Lomoas (lo-MO-ahs): A group of islands off the southern coast of Edrovir. The Lomoa islands lie south of the Inner and Outer Faranos, across the gap called Farano's Mouth.

Long Harbor: Most southernly gold port, located at the northern end of Little Farano Island, at the harbor formed by the channel that incompletely separates Big Farano from Little Farano.

Loros Wared (LOR-os WAH-rehd): A former Wared, lying on the northern bank of the River Edro, near its mouth. Founded by Nevrath Loros, father of Darion and grandfather of Tevren, it was cut into pieces after Tevren's death.

Lothard Hurn (LO-thard hurn): A young Leithian lord, son of one of the Signers of the Pact of Lankura (Reith Hurn) and currently lord of Hurn Hold and the House of Hurn. One of the princess's suitors.

Luka (LOO-ka): An old Turowan medicine woman known to Nagaro from his childhood at Averwin.

Madred Furthing (MAH-drehd FUR-dhing): A highly respected Leithian Lord. Father of Brandle, and a leader of the Leithian Faction. ("dh" denotes the "th" sound in the word "this")

Mahuk Baar (MAH-huke BAR): A coastal country, and islands, lying beyond Jinara to the south of Edrovir. Inhabited by the Hashtep people with their Mautep warlords and ruled by an emperor. "Mahuk" is often used for the nationality, as in "Mahuk warships" or "Mahuk waters". It is also used (ignorantly) for the people of the Mahuk Baar.

Maramine Virden (mar-ah-MEEN VER-dehn): A Kelorin lady, former mistress of the estate of Averwin, estranged from her family. Nagaro's lady guardian. Smothered by Elgurn to end her suffering during what would have been fatal heskial withdrawal.

Mautep (MAH-oo-tehp): Ruling warrior class of the Hashtep people of the Mahuk Baar.

Medrin (MEH-drihn): Fifth month of the Edroviran calendar, equivalent to May.

Mendorel (MEHN-dor-ehl): a Kelorin shopkeeper and candle-maker living in Kel Tierna. A freed slave and former follower of Nagaro.

Merriel (MEHR-ee-ehl): Lady Merriel. A noble Leithian woman. One of Queen Semorel's ladies and chaperon to Princess Nevien and her ladies.

Milandra (mihl-AHN-drah): Tira Milandra. A young Kelorin woman who is visiting Lankura at the time of the new year's feast.

Minowei (mih-NO-way): Princess Minowei. A Turowan chief's daughter who married Nevrath, founding the House of Loros. Mother of Darion.

Moluaro (mo-loo-AR-o): The largest island in the southern half of the Lomoas.

Moraga (mor-AH-gah): A Turowan former merchant seaman and freed slave. One of Nagaro's followers. Captain of the *Tiger*.

Nagaro (nah-GAR-o): Captain Nagaro, also known as Nagaro the Pirate, and Kiraam Shaku-Tal (Hashti for "Thief of Slaves").

nan (nahn): Hashti for "no."

Narei (NAR-ay): Young daughter of Nagaro and Jila.

Naru (NAR-oo): The dark moon, smaller of the world's two moons. It travels slightly faster than the bright moon, Talebra, overtaking her at times in what the Leithians consider a portentious conjunction.

Nevien Harlind (NEHV-ee-ehn HAR-lihnd): Princess Nevien, daughter of King Elgurn and Queen Semorel.

Nile Fendred (nile FEHN-drehd): A young high-born Leithian. Son of Kale Fendred. One of the princess's suitors.

Notep (NO-tehp): A Mautep lord of the House of jir-Akaan. Younger brother of the Emperor Baalkir jir-Akaan. Father of Roheed. He kidnapped and enslaved Emril after killing her husband and was later mauled by a tiger in what the Mautep believed was punishment.

Obai (o-BAHY): An island of the Inner Faranos, the closest island to Wotana Bay.

Odus Morbern (O-duhs MOR-burn): A Leithian lord. One of the Signers of the Pact of Lankura and a member of the King's Council.

opa (O-pah): A potent drug used to relieve pain, noted for giving vivid "opa dreams".

Osfaraad (ose-far-AHD): An island belonging to the Mahuk Baar, near the northern border of Mahuk waters. A place where Nagaro's ships had put freed Hashtep slaves ashore.

Oskampo (os-KAHM-po): A table game played with pictured cards and small wooden counters.

Pakoa (pah-KO-ah): An island off the southern coast of Edrovir where Nagaro made his home during his pirate period. Southern-most isle of the Lomoas. Pakoa Town, on Pakoa Harbor, is its only significant town and its capital.

Paktaar (pahk-TAR): An island belonging to the Mahuk Baar close to the port of Sar Tipaal, which is Emperor Baalkir's capital.

Pavo Maat (PAH-vo MAHT): A Hashtep fisherman's son and former slave. Follower and close friend of Nagaro, now his second mate.

Peldred Gilforn (PEHL-drehd Gihl-forn): A young high-born Leithian Fleet officer, assigned to Nagaro's crew as third mate.

Pendrik Glenmark (PEHN-drihk glehn-MARK): A Leithian lord, one of the Signers of the Pack of Lankura and a member of the King's Council.

Pilo (PEE-lo). A young Turowan boy. Younger son of Animara, brother of Bahiri and Tavo. Cousin of Narei and one of Nagaro's nephews.

Puul Chak (pool chahk): A port city in the Mahuk Baar. Former capital under the previous emperor.

Rastian Korven (rahs-tee-AHN KOR-vehn): A young Kelorin officer in the Royal Fleet of Edrovir. Son of Lord Rastyl Korven.

Rastyl Korven (rahs-TEEL KOR-vehn): A Kelorin man with unusually pale gray eyes. Lord of Irvenen Wared. Father of Rastian.

Rathdar Sundorin (RAHTH-dar SUN-dor-ihn): A Kelorin man, son of the deceased Pact Signer Berinar Sundorin. Current lord of the Sundorin Wared in which Kel Tierna is located. One of the leaders of the Kelorin faction.

Reith Hurn (rayth hurn): A Leithian lord. Father of Lothard Hurn. A Signer of the Pact of Lankura and former member of the King's Council. Killed in the border war with Jinara.

Rese (rees): A young high-born Leithian man, suitor of Alisset.

Rianine (REE-ah-neen): A young Kelorin woman, called Rian for short. One of Princess Nevien's ladies and her frequent confidant.

rin (rihn): A small copper coin, the base unit of Edroviran currency. There are one hundred rins in one trokin, and one thousand rins in one dokan.

Roheed jir-Akaan (ro-HEED jeer-ah-KAHN): A young Mautep officer. Son of Notep. Baalkir's nephew. He speaks some Droviri, having been raised by the Kelorin slave woman, Emril. Since his father killed Emril's husband and left her infant son to die, Roheed bears a "blood debt" requiring him to help anyone who was orphaned, which he can only "pay" by saving the life of such a man.

Ruald Grinard (roo-AHLD grihn-ARD): A Leithian officer in the Royal Fleet of Edrovir. Captain of Lord Kuran's flagship, the *Pride of Lankura*.

Rubo Atatya (ROO-bo ah-TAH-yah): An older Turowan man, retired as a sea warrior/cook with the Royal Fleet of Edrovir. One of Nagaro's followers who has now re-joined the Fleet as a first mate under Landros.

Sar Tipaal (sar tih-PAHL): A sea port of the Mahuk Baar that is currently the country's capital under Emperor Baalkir. Site of his famed shipyard.

Sea Passage (or seaward passage): "Taking the sea passage" means sailing north or south on the seaward side of any of the island chains. Not a channel, as such, but a course easily followed by seamen who lack the skill to navigate out of sight of land.

Sedrin (SEH-drihn): Ninth month of the Edroviran calendar, equivalent to September.

Semorel (SEHM-or-ehl): Queen Semorel. A Kelorin woman, wife of King Elgurn and therefore queen of Edrovir.

Seralind (sehr-ah-LIHND): Name for the place of reward after death in

Leithian religious belief. Equivalent to paradise or heaven.

shaku (SHAH-koo): Hashti word for "slave".

Shaku Raal (SHAH-koo RAHL): A derogatory Hashti name for Nagaro. It means "slave dog".

shapas (SHAH-pahs): A Kelorin style women's riding garment consisting of long pantaloons extending all the way to the ankles, worn with an upper garment called a *shilka*.

Sheptuum (shehp-TOOM): God of the Hashtep people, including both the Hashtep and the Mautep classes.

shilka (SHIHL-ka): A Kelorin style women's riding garment consisting of a close-fitting bodice, belted at the waist and falling just below the knee. The garment flares below the waist like a skirt but is divided, front and back, to allow the wearer to mount a horse and sit astride. Typically worn in combination with *shapas*.

Shofeer (sho-FEER): Name of a Mautep family house. Nagaro's sword is referred to as the "Sword of Shofeer" because it belonged to a Mautep warrior of that house who died at the battle of Jaamra.

Simion (SIHM-ee-ahn): A young Kelorin crossed man who is Brandle Furthing's lover. Former Fleet warrior and galley slave who escaped in the slave mutiny led by Nagaro.

Sindar (SIHN-dahr): A young Kelorin man held captive since infancy in the Mahuk Baar who escaped and is under Nagaro's protection.

Soku (SO-koo): A small island adjacent to Boka Bay on the island of Boka Omei, lying on the seaward side of the north end of the Inside Passage.

Solbrid (SOL-brihd): The Leithian mother goddess. Ruler of earth and giver of life.

Soren Tuveilas (SOR-ehn too-VAY-lahs): An elderly high-born Kelorin man. Lord of Tuveilas Wared and one of the leaders of the Kelorin faction.

sothiril (SO-thur-ihl): Kelorin tea-like drink made by steeping the dried berries of the plant of the same name.

Strad Olbern (strahd OL-burn): A high-born Leithian. A newly-elevated commander in the Royal Fleet of Edrovir.

Sudano (soo-DAH-no): A Turowan kuma farmer. Husband of Animara and father of Bahiri, Tavo, and Pilo. Narei's uncle.

Talebra (tah-LEHY-brah): The bright moon. It is the larger of the world's two moons, and moves more slowly.

Taru Nareyo (TAR-roo nar-AY-o): A Turowan fisherman's son. Nagaro's first friend from Wotana Bay who was enslaved with him by the Mautep sea raiders, freed in the slave mutiny, and has been serving as Nagaro's first mate and now holds that rank in the Fleet.

Tavo (TAH-vo): A young Turowan boy. Older son of Animara and brother to Bahiri and Pilo. Cousin to Nagaro's daughter Narei and therefore one of Nagaro's nephews.

Tenepti (tehn-EHP-tee): A young Hashtep woman of the island of Pakoa. Wife of Pavo Maat.

Tenorin (TEHN-or-ihn): River Tenorin. One of the lesser tributaries of the River Edro. Called the Yuna River by Turowan folk.

Tevren Loros (TEHV-rehn LOR-os): King Tevren. The young second king of Edrovir, killed by Reith Hurn in an event that sparked a civil war. Son of Darion the Great, he was mostly Kelorin but carried Turowan blood from his grandmother, Minowei.

Therin Oranil (Thehr-ihn OR-ahn-ihl): A Kelorin man. Lord of Oranil Wared and a leader of the Kelorin faction.

Thorlan (THOR-lahn): A Kelorin man who was the stableman at the country estate of Averwin. He taught Leyel how to ride and shoot a bow.

Timegar (TIH-may-gar): A Kelorin man from Pakoa. A former Fleet warrior, retired, who joined Nagaro's followers and became captain of the pirate ship *North Wind*.

Tira (TEER-rah): Respectful from of address for a woman, roughly equivalent to "Mrs.", but with no implied marital status. Always used before a given name.

tirka (TUR-kah): A Kelorin (originally) men's upper outer garment, opening down the front, and cut long enough to cover the hips. Generally worn over a long-sleeved shirt and usually belted.

Todrin (TOE-drihn): Tenth month of the Edroviran calendar, equivalent to October.

Tor (tor): Respectful form of address for a man, roughly equivalent to "Mr." Always used before a given name.

Torlung (TOR-luhng): Minister Torlung. A Leithian of the House of Furthing, Chief Minister to Lord Madred.

Tredhold Ferth (TRED-hold furth): A Leithian healer, called Tred for short. A former Fleet warrior and ship's doctor who was held as galley slave, freed in the slave mutiny led by Nagaro. One of Nagaro's followers who has now rejoined the Fleet. Ship's doctor on the *Sword of Freedom*.

trokin (TRO-kihn): A silver coin worth one hundred rins. There are ten trokins to the dokan.

Tulara (too-LAR-ah): A young Turowan woman, employed at the Bay Tree Inn in Pakoa Town. A previous (unsuccessful) romantic interest for Taru.

Tulevian (too-LEHV-ee-ahn): A young high-born Kelorin woman. One of the princess's ladies.

Tuluptak (TOO-loop-tahk): A powerful Mautep warlord.

Tunapa (too-NAH-pah): A northern Lomoan island on the eastern side of the north end of the Inside Passage.

Turo (TOOR-o): The Turo. Turowan name for their people, also used to refer to a Turowan man. Turowa (toor-O-wah) is the female equivalent.

Turowans (toor-O-ahns): A brown-skinned, dark-haired people native to the coastal region and islands of Edrovir. Called by themselves "the Turo". The word "Turowan" can refer to a single male individual and is also used as an adjective to describe anything relating to the Turo.

Ulaad (oo-LAHD): Port in the Mahuk Baar. Home port of Lord Angkat and site of his shipyard.

Urchak tok-Faar (UR-chahk toke-FAHR): Former captain of the Mautep war galley *Fist of Death*, that was taken in the slave mutany led by Nagaro and re-christened the *Sword of Freedom*.

Vanhold: (VAN-hold): A young Leithian man, suitor of Clarimel.

Varsyl Virden (vahr-SEEL VIR-dehn): A high-born Kelorin man, brother of Maramine.

Vedorel (VEH-dor-ehl): The second month of the Edroviran calendar, equivalent to February.

Vell Sobring (vehl SO-bring): A young Leithian officer in the Royal Fleet of Edrovir. Son of Bron Sobring. Nephew of Grimbold Sobring who is the lord of Sobring Hold since Bron's death in the border war.

Vered Mahir (VEHR-ed mah-HEER): A city on the upper reaches of the river Edro, in the valley just above a great waterfall. The "bitter place" where the brothers Hindrath and Nevrath quarreled resulting in the House of Tyronin being split and the House of Loros formed.

Vothra (VO-thrah): The Benevolent Spirit of the Kelorin, an entity composed of the combined spirits of many individuals all of whom have lived multiple lives. Vothra's wisdom, collectively referred to as the "Path" is recorded in the Vothrin Writings. Vothra has an unusually strong connection to Nagaro's spirit.

Wared (WAH-rehd): Kelorin word for the territory governed by a lord. Equivalent to the Leithian word "Hold".

Wotana (wo-TAH-nah): A small town on the bay of the same name, located on the Edroviran coast about fifteen miles north of Lankura. Taru's home town.

Yuli (YOO-lee): a Turowan woman. Wife of the keeper of the Bay Tree Inn on Pakoa.

Yuna (YOO-na): Yuna River (an old Turowan name). Called the River Tendorin by Kelorin and Leithian folk. A lesser tributary of the River Edro.

Zirda (ZUR-dah): A respectful masculine form of address,]. It is roughly equivalent to "sir" in modern casual usage.

Zirdyn (zur-DEEN): A respectful feminine form of address. It is roughly equivalent to "madame" in modern casual usage.

Zomora (zo-MOR-ah): Tira Zomora. Pakoa's Turowan medicine woman. An unofficial power on that island and throughout the southern Lomoas.

About Carol Louise Wilde

Carol Louise Wilde was born in Southern California. A voracious reader as a child, she often spun stories in her head. While she sometimes dreamed of writing them down some day, she considered the idea impractical. Instead, Carol pursued an interest in biology that led to a career as a research scientist.

It was while in graduate school that Carol first got her hands on a computer with word-processing software. That transformative technology together with some stolen time produced an abortive 300-page fiction manuscript that resides in a box on a shelf somewhere. A spark had been kindled, but the demands of career and motherhood got in the way for more than a decade. Ultimately, Carol left the academic world to try her hand at scientific text editing while taking up fiction writing on the side.

Carol began work on The Nagaro Chronicle – a story that had been growing in her head since her teens – in the spring of 2002 and has not stopped writing since. Currently Carol continues to live in Southern California. She has been married for an amazingly long time to a man she met in high school. She and her husband have two sons.